THE
WESTERN
JUSTICE
TRILOGY

THE
WESTERN
JUSTICE
TRILOGY

GILBERT
MORRIS

SHILOH RUN ▲ PRESS
An Imprint of Barbour Publishing, Inc.

Rosa's Land © 2013 by Gilbert Morris
Sabrina's Man © 2013 by Gilbert Morris
Raina's Choice © 2014 by Gilbert Morris

Print ISBN 978-1-61626-603-5

eBook Editions:
Adobe Digital Edition (.epub) 978-1-63409-288-3
Kindle and MobiPocket Edition (.prc) 978-1-63409-289-0

All scripture quotations are taken from the King James Version of the Bible.

This book is a work of fiction. Names, characters, places, and incidents are either products of the author's imagination or used fictitiously. Any similarity to actual people, organizations, and/or events is purely coincidental.

Cover Photo: Jupiterimages/ GettyImages

Published by Shiloh Run Press, an imprint of Barbour Publishing, Inc., P.O. Box 719, Uhrichsville, Ohio 44683, www.shilohrunpress.com.

Our mission is to publish and distribute inspirational products offering exceptional value and biblical encouragement to the masses.

ecpa Member of the
Evangelical Christian
Publishers Association

Printed in the United States of America.

Contents

Contents

ROSA'S LAND

PART ONE

PART ONE

CHAPTER 1

New York City, 1886

"I wish Faye would hurry up and get home. I'm starved."

Caleb Riordan was a massive individual, large and strongly built, with salt-and-pepper hair and penetrating brown eyes. He had an air of aggression about him, and his enemies had long since learned that he did not know the meaning of the word *quit*. . .or *mercy*. At the age of fifty, Caleb was indeed a successful man by anyone's standards—at least those who counted money, power, and possessions as marks of that quality.

He was seated now in the parlor of his home, and as he pulled a cigar from his inner pocket then lit a match, he looked around the room with a sense of displeasure. The parlor was decorated in cream and a muted tone the color of dry sand, with touches of cool liquid green and one splash of pale coral provided by a single chair. On one wall was a fireplace with a painting of Bosphorus looking down from a palace. Fleets of small boats plied the blue-green waters, and in the distance blurred by the haze of heat loomed a distant scene.

Caleb had always disliked the picture but had said little since his wife loved it.

Eileen Riordan was almost a perfect example of opposites attracting, at least to the eye. Whereas Caleb was massive and aggressive, Eileen, at the age of forty-six, was far more gentle than her husband. She had classic features, a wealth of auburn hair, and light blue eyes. Her skin was fair, and there was a grace in her movements. Next to her husband she looked diminutive, although she was larger than the average woman.

She watched as Caleb puffed on his cigar, sending purple clouds upward toward the ceiling. Caleb knew she yearned to tell him not to smoke in the parlor. She did not speak, however. Instead, her eyes went over to the two large young men seated on the horsehide-covered sofa.

Leo, their oldest son, was strongly built. He had Caleb's size and strength, his brown hair and eyes, and some of the same aggressive qualities. Maxwell, at the age of twenty-seven, looked much like Leo. As a matter of fact, they were often taken for twins. They had the same sturdy frame, height, and coloring. Father and sons together made a picture of power that, at times, overwhelmed those they met.

"You know, Dad, I think pulling this deal with Herron was a smart move."

Caleb nodded at Leo, and a look of satisfaction scored his features. He looked at the cigar, knocked the ashes off, and then said, "He's probably sorry he ever got involved with the Riordans."

Maxwell leaned back, locked his large hands behind his head, and studied his father. "We gave him quite a going over. I think he'll go down."

The three men continued to talk about the business deal.

Eileen finally interrupted, saying, "Is this Edward Herron you're talking about?"

"Yes, it is, Eileen," Caleb said. A smile curled his lips at the intense pleasure he felt. "We had a real struggle, but in the end the three of us managed to put him down."

"What do you mean, dear, you 'put him down'?"

"Why, I mean we put him out of business. We've been trying to buy his foundry, and he wouldn't sell, so we had to put pressure on him."

Eileen was silent for a moment then asked, "What kind of pressure?"

"Oh, you wouldn't be interested, dear. Nothing personal. Just a matter of business. We did some manipulating and some maneuvering, and poor Herron got into a spot where he didn't have any choice but to sell his business to us."

"And at a cheap price, too." Leo smiled. "It was a steal."

Eileen considered the three men and finally asked, "What's going to happen to him?"

"Oh, don't worry about it, Eileen. He'll be all right."

"No, I want to know. I like his wife very much, and they have three young children."

"Well, he's pretty well broke now. He had to pay off the mortgage on the factory. But don't worry. If he can't find anything else, I'll put him to work at some kind of minor job at the foundry. He knows the business. We can get him cheap."

The three glanced at each other, and finally Leo said, "Mother, you must understand. The business world isn't like your life. You've got a nice, easy way here with everything you want. But out there in the real world that Dad and Max and I have to live in, it's a matter of survival."

The brothers began trying to persuade Eileen that their dealings with Edward Herron were not immoral, but Caleb saw that she was displeased. For a moment longer, Caleb sat silent, but his mind was racing. Finally he said, "I don't want to bring it up again, but this is the sort of thing that I hate to see Faye unable to face."

"We settled that when he was one year old, Caleb."

Indeed, there had been almost a warlike attitude over their youngest son. Caleb was accustomed to his wife agreeing to anything he said, but when their third son was born, Eileen showed a streak of steel in her backbone. She had come to him and said, "Caleb, you are raising Leo and Max to be hard men. I think that's a mistake. I think a man needs some gentleness."

"There's no place for gentleness in the world," Caleb had answered.

"Well, there's going to be gentleness in Lafayette."

"Lafayette! What a ridiculous name for a boy!"

"One of my ancestors served with Marquis de Lafayette in the Revolutionary War, and my father had his name."

"Well, you should have named him *Tom* or *James* or something sensible, but in any case I disagree with you."

"You may disagree all you please, Caleb," Eileen had said firmly, and her gaze had not wavered. "But this son is going to be mine. I'll make all the decisions about his school, his clothes. I'll raise him to be a gentleman. You got our two other sons, and you've made them hard, callous men."

Caleb Riordan had stared at his wife. "You think I'm callous?"

"Of course I do! If you listen to what people said about you, you would know that."

The argument had gone on for some time, but in the end Eileen had insisted on her way. Since that time she had thrown herself into making a different kind of man out of her son Faye, as she called him. She had chosen different friends for him, and she had talked to him from the time he could understand about the necessity for a man to be honest and gentle and not be cruel to anybody.

Caleb was thinking about that, and he wanted to plunge into the argument again, but he had learned that on this one item his wife was not to be reckoned with.

Leo said, "Mother, you're making a weakling out of him! And all this painting of pictures—what good does that do?"

"He's going to be a great painter. He has real talent."

"How many pictures has he sold?" Max asked sardonically. "Not even one."

"He's learning, and his teachers all say he's going to produce great work."

They kept trying to pressure Eileen, until finally Caleb saw that his wife was upset. Despite his rough ways with others, he had a soft and gentle spot for this woman. On this one thing she had displeased him, but otherwise she had been a good wife. He rose from his chair, went over, and pulled her to her feet. He hugged her and said, "We won't argue about this anymore."

"Thank you, Caleb." Eileen looked up at him and touched his cheek, then she turned and left the room.

"You'll never win that argument, Dad," Leo shook his head.

"No, I never will, but I've got two out of three sons that'll make their ways in the world. You two will have to help me with your brother because Faye will never make it. You boys watch out and take care of him."

"Well, I wish he'd hurry up and get home. I'm starved," Max said. He stretched hugely then leaned back into the sofa and closed his eyes.

The afternoon sun was fading, but Faye wanted to catch exactly that light in the painting. He had set up his easel with a canvas before him and the paints on the collapsible stool. The scene he was painting was difficult, for the vista in New York at this particular spot stretched out in a way that was hard to catch.

"My, that is pretty! I don't see how you do it."

Faye came to himself and, holding the brush poised over the canvas, turned to see that a very pretty young woman with blond hair and large blue eyes was smiling at him. "Thank you, miss. I hope to catch some of the beauty of that scene."

The young woman said again, "I don't see how you do it. Look how you've mixed all those colors together!"

"Well, I don't do it too well yet."

"Yes, I think you do. How long have you been painting?"

"All my life, it seems."

"My, ain't that a treat!"

Faye glanced over and caught a glimpse of the Riordans' driver, Pat Ryan, a hundred feet away. He was talking to a woman and waving his big hamlike hands in the air as he described something. Quickly Faye turned and said, "Well, I've got to catch this light if you don't mind."

"You mind if I watch?"

"Not at all."

Faye continued to paint the delicate leaves that clung to the trees. They kept just the right shades of green, and the young woman kept up a running commentary.

Suddenly he heard another voice and looked up to see a large, husky man wearing a derby hat. His face was blunt, and he had small eyes. When he grinned, gold flashed on two teeth in his mouth. His clothes didn't seem to fit him, for his arms filled the fabric of the shirt he wore, threatening to tear it. "Well, ain't that a pretty little picture now."

Faye said politely, "Thank you. It's not finished yet."

"That's right sweet, ain't it, girlie?"

"I think it's very nice."

"Well, you don't need to fool around with this sissy painter. Come on with me. We'll have a good time."

"Turn me loose!"

Faye twisted his head and saw that the big man had the woman by her arm and was dragging her along. "Don't do that!" he said quickly. He put down his brush and palette and moved toward the two.

"What are you going to do, beat me up?" The big man grinned.

"Go back to your painting, sonny." The big man was squeezing the girl's arm tightly enough to make her cry out.

Faye reached out and pulled at the man's arm. "Don't do that, please. You're hurting her."

"You're going to stop me?"

Faye could not answer. The man was six inches taller than he was and muscular. Muscles from hard work and hands that showed hard usage. The bully was grinning at him, and he could only say, "I'm asking you to let the young woman go, or I'll have to—"

"You'll have to what? Call for a policeman? There ain't none here." Suddenly he threw his meaty hand out and caught Faye in the chest and knocked him backward.

Faye caught his balance, but the big man had released the girl and came at him. Faye took a blow directly to his face and felt the blood suddenly run down his cheek. More blows rained upon him. He could not catch his balance, and finally he fell.

The young woman cried out, "Please, don't!"

The man raised his foot to kick Faye and said, "Don't worry. He needs a lesson."

There was a sound of footsteps just as the man delivered a kick into Faye's unprotected side.

The big man turned to find someone as large as himself coming at him. He got his hands up, but he could not ward off the tremendous blow that caught him in the mouth. He again threw his fists up and tried to defend himself. "Hey, cut it ou...," he tried to yell, but once again a blow struck his mouth. Then suddenly he was struck in the throat. He began to gag. Without warning, Pat Ryan kicked in the side of his knee, and the bully fell to the ground. Pat then delivered a tremendous kick that drove the man's breath out.

"You'll kill him!" the young woman cried.

"Ah, he's too mean to die." Pat Ryan knelt down beside Faye. "You all right, sir?"

Faye could only manage a moan in response.

Ryan picked Faye up as easily as if he were a child and made his way to the carriage.

The young woman followed and said, "Is he going to be all right?"

"I hope so, ma'am." He placed Faye in the backseat, shut the door, and then moved back to retrieve Faye's painting and his easel. He returned and leaped to the driver's seat saying, "Get up! Get up!"

The carriage rocked back and forth as it bounced over the gravel, but Faye Riordan was in too much pain to mind.

❧

The Riordan family had finally sat at the dining table to eat, for Caleb had said, "Well, I'm hungry. Faye can eat when he gets here."

Before anything could be served, Charles Evans, the butler, came running in. He was a tall man, very thin and balding. Now his eyes were open wide. "Sir, it's Mr. Faye. He's hurt!"

The whole family pushed away from the table.

As they got to the front door, the driver was bringing Faye in.

"What happened?" Eileen cried out.

"He got beat up."

"Quick, put him in his bed. Charles, you get Dr. Baxter quick as you can. He's just the second street down."

"Yes, madam. I'll do it right away."

"This way, Pat."

Ryan carried Faye to his room and placed him on his bed.

Eileen was trembling, for Faye's face was battered and he was bleeding freely from a cut on his eyebrow. She took her handkerchief and covered the wound.

"He looks terrible!" Max exclaimed.

"What happened, Ryan?" Caleb demanded.

"Well, sir, he was painting, and I was just wandering around, but I turned and saw this big guy was pounding Mr. Faye and starting to kick him."

"You shouldn't have let him do that."

"I'm sorry, sir. I was too far away. But when I did get to him, I fixed him good." He grinned broadly and nodded. "I busted his front teeth out, I hit him in the throat so he couldn't talk, and then I kicked his legs out from under him and gave him a couple kicks in the side. He was out, whimpering like a baby, when I left."

"I wish you had killed him," Caleb said.

"Well, sir, I couldn't do that. They put a fellow in jail for that, but he won't be fighting much anytime in the future."

"You did a good job." Caleb reached in his pocket and pulled out a roll of bills. He peeled off three or four of them and said, "Here, take this."

"Oh, you don't have to do that, sir."

"No, I want you to have it. Go ahead. If I find this fellow, I'll break his neck!"

"All of you wait outside," Eileen said. "Faye doesn't need any more trouble."

The three men left reluctantly.

Within ten minutes, Dr. Lucas Baxter entered Faye's room. He was a slender man of fifty with black hair and dark eyes. "What's happened?" he demanded.

"Faye was beaten," Eileen said. "He's in pretty bad shape."

"Let me see." Baxter removed the bloody handkerchief and said, "I'll have to put some stitches here, and he'll have a little scar." He touched Faye, who groaned in response. "Must have hurt his ribs."

"Our driver said the man kicked him."

"Well, if those ribs are broken, it's going to take awhile to heal. But maybe they're just cracked."

He tried to get Faye to swallow something from a brown bottle and waited for a minute. When he saw that Faye was out, he began sewing the wound up. He worked rapidly. "Who did this, Mrs. Riordan?"

"Some man in the park."

"Well, if your husband catches him, he'll kill him."

"No, I don't want that. My husband has made the other boys into what he respects, strong men but hard."

"Well, Faye's not like that."

"No, he's not. I spent my life making a gentle man out of him. He's going to be a fine painter."

❧

Caleb was waiting with Leo and Max when the doctor came from attending Faye. "How is he, Dr. Baxter?"

"He'll be all right. I think his ribs are cracked, so he'll be moving slowly."

"Thank you, doctor. Charles will show you out." After the doctor left, Caleb turned to his two older sons and said, "Didn't I tell you? He's just a baby! He's got to have somebody to take care of him."

"We can't be with him all the time," Leo said. "You better pay Ryan more money and have him never get far away from him."

"It's a shame a man twenty years old can't take care of himself any better. . .especially *my* son."

⁂

Pat Ryan was eating a piece of pie that he had begged from Kate Evans, the cook. She was the wife of Charles, the butler, and was the best cook Ryan had ever known.

Doris Stevens, a very attractive maid, was sitting on a chair beside May Satterfield, the other maid. Both were listening to his story.

He had told them about the fight three days ago with the man who was beating Faye Riordan and ended by saying, "It's a good thing I was there. I think that bruiser might have killed Mr. Faye."

"Did you hurt him?" Doris asked.

"I put his lights out. When I left, he wasn't talking much. He had lost some teeth, and I cracked him right in the throat and kicked him in the side."

"Oh, Mr. Faye's such a fine-looking young man," Doris said. "Really handsome."

"You been flirting with him, Doris?"

"You bet. I plan to get him to marry me. Then I'll be your boss, both of you."

"He don't pay any attention to women," May said.

"He's a man, ain't he? I'll catch him off guard. Maybe I'll be lucky enough to get caught. He'll have to marry me then, and I'll be a Riordan. I'll be your boss."

"Nah, that won't happen. Mr. Faye, he wouldn't take advantage of a maid," Pat said, shaking his head.

"No, but I might take advantage of him." She laughed and winked merrily. "In fact, I'll bet he could use some refreshment right about now."

Pat shook his head at May as he returned to his pie.

Faye was sitting at the piano running his fingers over the keys. He turned, holding his side and wincing at the pain from his cracked ribs, when someone entered the room.

It was Doris bringing him a glass of iced tea.

Faye simply said, "Thank you, Doris. You take care of me too well."

"Well, you need someone to take care of you." She reached out and put her hand on his face. "The swelling has all gone down, and you've almost lost that awful-looking black eye you had." She left her hand on his face and said, "I'm so sorry. I wish I could take some of the hurt."

She then leaned against him, pressing her figure against his shoulders. "You need a friend. A lady friend."

At that instant his mother walked in. She took one look and said, "Doris, I think you're wanted in the kitchen."

Eileen waited until Doris left and then came over and looked down at Faye. "How do you feel, son?"

"Oh, I'll live."

She sighed. "You do realize Doris was flirting with you just now."

"Oh no. She just brought me some tea."

Eileen shook her head sadly. "You don't know women."

"I guess not, but she's a nice girl."

"No, she's a flirt. You be careful."

"Well, if you say so, Mother."

"How's the painting going?"

"I haven't felt much like painting. One good thing—I didn't hurt my hands."

"You're going to be a great artist, son."

Faye put his hands out and ran them across the keyboard softly and gently. "I'm letting Dad down, Mother. He and my brothers think I'm a failure…and I guess I am. Any one of them could have taken care of himself. I'm just a failure."

"You're *not* a failure! Your father and your brothers have strong muscles, but they don't have any sensitivity or gentleness."

"Well, I wish I could be an artist *and* a tough man."

"Forget being tough. There's a new teacher in town named John Arlington. He's been studying in Europe."

"I've heard of him."

"Well, I've asked him to come and look at your work, and he's agreed."

"Oh, that's good, Mother. Thank you very much. I know I need more help."

"Why don't you go lie down awhile? You look tired."

"Maybe I will." He rose, leaned over, and kissed her cheek,

something Leo or Max would never think of doing. "I'll see you at dinner."

Faye went to the second floor and into his room. He liked the room, for the window went from the floor almost to the ceiling, and he could catch the morning light. He had picked his own furniture. The chairs were old, the red and blue turkey coverings were worn to center, but he was happy with it. The pictures on the walls were not expensive, mostly watercolors with a few oils and many sketches.

Faye went at once to his desk and opened it, then pulled out a book and sat down in one of the chairs and began to read. It was a book about the Texas Rangers. He had bought it at a used bookstore and was fascinated by the stories of the terrible battles with the Indians and the outlaws that the Rangers engaged in. He sat there reading for a time then closed the book and sighed, "Well, I'll never be able to do that."

He left his room and found Pat Ryan outside cleaning up the barouche. "Pat," he said, "how'd you learn to fight?"

"Why, Mr. Faye, I always knew how to fight. In my neighborhood, you had to fight."

"You think you could teach me to fight? Could I learn?"

"I don't think you need to. How much you weigh, Mr. Faye?"

"About a hundred and eighty-five pounds, I think."

"A hundred and eighty-five? Well, it don't show. That's big enough, but a man has to be quick." He held up his hand, palm out, and said, "Try to hit my hand. I'll try to make you miss."

To Pat's obvious shock, Faye hit him on the hand before he could even move.

"You are fast!" he said. "Try it again."

Again and again Pat held up his hand but never dodged a blow. He said, "You're the quickest man I ever saw with his fists. Hold your hand up and see if I can hit it."

But the result was the same. Pat was faster than some fighters, but he never could hit Faye's hand.

"Well, you've got quick hands, but there's this, Mr. Faye: In a fight you're going to get hurt. If somebody hits you, you just have to grin and act like it don't hurt. Some men just quit."

"Could you give me lessons on fighting, Pat?"

"No, sir! Why, your good mother would have me out on the street quick as a wink! Fighting is a hard world. You stick with your painting. I'll do your fighting, Mr. Faye."

Faye said, "All right" and left, thinking about how easily he had beaten Pat in the game with the hands. *I bet I could fight if I had some help!*

CHAPTER 2

A feeble light filtered down through the tall windows on the palette that Faye had placed on an easel. Carefully he dabbed his brush on the palette, mixed up two colors that he wanted, and then turned again. He glanced at the display he had, which consisted of a silver pitcher, a plate of purple grapes, and a silvery fish lying on a platter. The platter was on an ivory-colored tablecloth. Carefully he touched the tip of the brush to the canvas and slowly pulled it across the surface. His concentration was intense, but his hand trembled slightly, and he smeared the section of canvas he was working on.

"Blast it!" he shouted. He drew back his arm and threw the brush across the room. It hit the light green wall and left a purplish stain before dropping to the carpet where it left another stain.

For a moment Faye stood there gritting his teeth and staring at the two stains. He was strongly tempted to kick the easel across the room to join the brush and make an even bigger mess. He forced himself to breathe slowly, and gradually the impatience and anger, which were such a rare thing to him, began to fade away. He stared at the canvas for a long moment then picked it up by the edges, walked across the room, and stacked it against several other half-finished paintings of the same still life.

His face was distorted, which was unusual for him. Usually his expression was pleasant, and some insisted that he had a baby face, an epithet that he despised. He always admired his brothers and his father who had stern, tanned features. Indeed his own was as innocent as a cherub. His lips twisted in a disgusted expression. *I might as well give it up! Can't do anything right!*

Taking a deep breath, he shook his head with disgust then wheeled and stomped noisily across the room, threw himself into a horsehide-covered chair, and glared out the window. Raindrops were running down the glass. Ordinarily he would have found this interesting, as he did all aspects of weather, but he was so upset at his own failure that he did not notice.

"What's the matter with me?" he muttered aloud. "I can't even paint a FOR RENT sign and do a decent job of it!" He closed his eyes then leaned back, resting his head on the rough leather. The sound of the rain falling on the roof and on the outside windows made a sibilant whisper that ordinarily would have soothed his nerves, but he could not force himself into a good mood.

He had heard of writers having times when they just couldn't write, and they called those periods "writer's block." Faye had never believed for a moment that such a thing existed. In an argument once with a writer, he had exclaimed, "Writer's block? Nonsense! You never heard of a carpenter having carpenter's block, did you? Of course you haven't! When a carpenter has a job to do, he just *does* it! And you never heard of dishwasher's block, have you? If a woman has dishes to wash, she just plunges in and washes the blamed things!"

With an abrupt motion, Faye rose and walked to the window. For a moment he stood watching the raindrops run down. He was fascinated by unusual things, and he watched as two drops that were at least a foot apart at the top of the window began their journey downward. They darted to the right and to the left, and then suddenly both of them moved toward each other. They joined and made one drop. For a moment Faye forgot his agitation and thought, *Just like a marriage. These two drops went hither and yon. Finally they found each other and came together. Now that's the kind of romance I'd like to have!*

A lightning bolt scraped its way across the darkness of a cloud and reached down and touched earth. He waited and counted the seconds, for he had heard you could tell how far away the bolt hit by counting the seconds between a flash of lightning and the resulting thunder. He counted, "One, two, three," and then he heard the rumbling. *A little closer than a mile away.*

He leaned forward, put his head against the glass, and closed his eyes. *Maybe there is such a thing as painter's block.* The thought disturbed him, for he had always been able to do any task he put his mind to as far as painting or other intellectual subjects were concerned. Even as a small boy he had been able to stick with the books that his mother provided, even when they were difficult. He had begun with crayons and graduated to charcoal and then finally paints and oils. His willingness to stick with a job, he understood, was due to his mother's careful teaching, for she had lovingly and patiently curbed his natural instinct to quit when a thing got difficult.

A sudden blinding bolt of lightning startled him, and he opened his eyes and watched as an ominous black cloud blotted out most of the sky. The woods that stretched out to the west of the house were suddenly lost in a deluge. The rain fell in fat drops making slanting lines. His painter's eye noted that, and he resolved that the next time he painted a scene having rain he would be sure that the drops were slanted, not straight down. Usually he rather liked storms, finding them a dynamic setting, but as another fork of crooked lightning clawed the earth, he suddenly realized that he was late for his lesson with John Arlington.

"What am I thinking about?" he muttered. Whirling, he grabbed his raincoat, jammed on a wide-brimmed hat, and left his room at a run. He slammed the outside door and dashed into the carriage house where he found Pat sitting down and eating a sandwich. "Pat, I've got to get to the ferry!" he exclaimed.

"Why, Mr. Faye," Ryan protested, "you can't go out in this weather. You'll drown."

"No, I must go. I'm late for a lesson. Now get the carriage ready and take me to Port Jefferson."

The burly Irishman started to protest, but seeing the stubborn expression on Faye's lips, he shrugged, saying, "All right, sir. . .but it ain't a good idea."

The Riordan estate was located in the eastern part of Long Island. It was a wooded section where rich people built their mansions tucked away in deep woods. It was not too far from downtown New York City to make the journey daily, but the setting bore the illusion of deep woods such as was found in the secluded parts of upper New York State.

By the time Ryan had pulled the carriage to an abrupt halt at the wharf where the ferry that carried passengers across Long Island Sound was docked, the rain was falling unchecked in what looked like solid sheets. Faye leaped out of the carriage, calling back, "Thanks, Ryan," and reached the gangplank just as it was beginning to draw up.

One of the crew, a tall man wearing a black slicker and matching hat, grinned. "You just made it, sir."

"Thought I'd have to swim," Faye answered. He stepped onto the deck and moved under the wide canopy that offered shelter from the sun. . .when there was sun. He felt the ferry shudder as the engine took hold. The paddles began to turn, and the huge ferry swung wide and then moved forward into the downpour. Usually Faye went inside to take shelter from the heat of the sun, but he liked the rain, and he stood watching as an occasional bolt of silver lighting illuminated the dark waters.

"You must love storms." Startled by a voice that came so unexpectedly, Faye turned to see a woman standing there smiling at him. She had a heart-shaped face and an expressive mouth that was now turned upward at the corners in a smile. Her long brown hair was exposed. She had pulled off her hat, and her hair was now turned lank by the rain. She had the most brilliant and the most beautifully shaped eyes Faye had ever seen.

"I guess so," he muttered. "I've never been scared of them for

31

some reason. My mother found me outside once when I was only four, I think, in the middle of a terrible thunderstorm. It gave her quite a scare."

"I like storms, too." The woman's voice was deeper than most women's and had a throaty quality that somehow hinted at a passionate nature, at least so it seemed to Faye. "I'm scared of snakes and spiders but never of the weather."

"Your home is here?"

"One of them. I travel a lot. My father and I have learned that any place we set our suitcase down is home."

"That must be interesting. You travel abroad?"

"Oh, yes. My father is an explorer, and he writes books about exotic lands. I go along to take care of him and help him when I can."

"That sounds exciting. Have you ever been to Africa?"

"Yes, as a matter of fact we just got back from there two weeks ago. We spent six months with the Maasai tribe."

"Savages, I suppose?"

"Yes, but they are such a fascinating tribe. Most of them are over six feet tall and lean. They hunt lions with spears, and they have a dance in which the men leap up into the air in a standing position. Some of them, I think, can leap as tall as their height."

"I never travel," Faye said. "I envy you. Oh, my name is Faye Riordan."

"I'm Marlene Jenson." She put her hand out as a man would do. When Faye took it he felt the strength of her grasp. "So, you are living here now?"

"Yes, our home is in Manorville." She gave him a penetrating look. "You take the ferry often?"

"Fairly often. I'm taking lessons in Fairfield, just across the Sound."

"What sort of lessons?"

"Oh, painting lessons." Somehow taking painting lessons sounded like a rather frail thing for a man to indulge in next to a woman who had traveled among six-foot savages in the Congo.

"Well, I wanted to paint," she remarked, "but it didn't take long to find out that I didn't have the talent for it. What do you do, oils or watercolors?"

For the next ten minutes Faye answered rapid-fire questions from Marlene Jenson. She was relentless, and her interest was almost palpable. Finally she laughed, saying, "You'll have to excuse me, Mr. Riordan. Aside from accompanying my father, I'm a writer. When I find a subject, I just can't seem to let go of it. I think I would have made a pretty good prosecuting attorney putting witnesses on the spot."

"I'm sure you would." He hesitated then said, "Painting is pretty tame after your adventures in Africa."

The two were so engrossed in their conversation for the next few moments that a blast of the whistle from the top deck startled them.

"Almost to the dock," Faye said. He tried to think of some way to ask the young woman to allow him to call, but he had had almost no experience in such things. *She'd be bored to death listening to me talk about dabbling around painting pictures!*

Suddenly Marlene, who had been looking out at the waters, cried out, "Girl, don't do that!"

Faye turned quickly to see a very young girl, no more than six it seemed. She had climbed up on the protective rail that outlined the deck of the ferry. To his horror he saw her suddenly miss a step and tumble with a scream out of sight.

Faye, without thinking, started forward, shucked out of his raincoat, kicked his shoes off, and made a running dive over the side railing into the dark waters.

Marlene couldn't believe what Faye Riordan had just done. She began to cry out, "Man overboard! Man overboard!"

She heard a sailor yelling loudly, "Cut the engines!"

The engines stopped, and Marlene ran at once to the railing. It was night, and the waters were dark as a coal pit in a coal mine it seemed to her.

The deck was alive with sailors shouting, "Man overboard!" Some had lanterns, but they made little difference in the darkness of the night.

The waters were ebony, and Marlene cried out, "Where are you?" knowing that it was useless but unable to stop herself.

The ferry stopped. The captain ordered two boats put down, and sailors tumbled into them and were lowered to the waters. They started circling the ferry, but the current at this point was very swift. One of the sailors came over and said, "I seen him go over, miss. The bravest man I've ever seen!"

Marlene nodded but asked, "How will we ever find him?"

"What I'm afraid of, miss, is that they may have been pulled into the paddles. I seen that happen once on the Mississippi. I hope it didn't get these two."

It seemed like an eternity to Marlene, but finally she saw something below moving. She strained her eyes and cried out, "There! Below! There they are!"

One of the boats was close, the men straining against the oars. Marlene watched as they pulled two bodies from the water and then pulled in close to a railing. One of the sailors came on board carrying the child, who was now crying and choking. She saw Faye get up and stagger, and one of the sailors helped him up.

Marlene could not speak for a moment, but her eyes were brilliant. She finally said to Faye, "You're coming home with me. You'll freeze in those wet clothes."

"Oh, I don't think that's necessary."

Marlene was insistent, and when the ferry docked, she pulled him off the boat, hailed a carriage, and gave the address of her home.

Faye was shaking and shivering.

She pulled him close to give him some body warmth. "We'll get you thawed out when I get you home, Faye," she whispered.

❧

The room Faye entered with Marlene was obviously a rich man's toy. He was still shivering and the soaking wet clothes clung to him, but his eyes went around the room.

Marlene pushed him onto the couch. "You've got to get out of those wet clothes."

Startled, he stared at her. "I can't do that."

"Here. Take them off. I won't look. Don't be so modest."

Faye had never undressed in the presence of anyone, especially a beautiful young woman, but she turned her back and demanded,

"Hurry up! I'll get the fire started." She kept her back to him, and quickly Faye took off his wet clothes, including his shoes and socks. Quickly he wrapped the blanket around him, which brought a welcomed warmth.

While she lit the fire in the fireplace, he glanced at the room. A George II barrister desk and matching bookshelves filled one wall. An ornate marble fireplace, where she was making the fire, was opposite with two small velvet settees facing each other across a low teak table. Along the wall, by the door, was a massive bookcase with glass-covered shelves. Several trophy heads from Africa were on the wall, including a cape buffalo that stared at Faye with glassy eyes. . .almost malevolently, it seemed. A tiger with its fangs bared watched him from another wall.

"Here. Drink this."

"What is it?"

"Never mind. It'll warm you up."

Faye took the glass that she had given him, took a swallow, and coughed.

She insisted, "Drink it all."

He drank it down, and the fiery liquid seemed to burn all the way. "That ought to warm me up."

"It should. It's ten-year-old brandy. Are you getting warmer?"

"Yes, thanks a lot."

"Well, let me hang your clothes over something." She grabbed up his wet clothes, arranged some chairs before the fire, and then came back and sat down beside him. He shivered a little, and she reached out and pushed his wet hair off of his forehead. She left her hand on his cheek and said, "Faye, I've seen men, and women, too, do some pretty brave things, but I've never seen anything more courageous than what you just did."

"Oh, swimming is about my only physical achievement."

"It wasn't just swimming. To go over in that dark water with that paddle wheel threatening to cut you in two. . .did you think about it at all?"

"Never gave it a thought. If I had, I'd never have gone."

"How did you find that girl?"

Faye thought for a moment, wiped his face with his hand, and then said, "Well, as soon as I hit the water, of course, everything was just like being in a black box with no windows. So I just began swimming around feeling with my hands. I heard the paddles churning near, but I knew the child was somewhere. Then I touched something. It was her dress. I grabbed at it, caught her, and pulled her up, but the ship had gone on by us. She was scared, and I had to hold her head up. I couldn't make much progress. It's a good thing the ship stopped and they sent those boats."

She took the glass from his hand and then took one of his hands in both of hers. "You deserve a medal for that."

"Oh no, not really."

She sat beside him, eliciting every fact about the rescue. Finally she laughed and said, "You know what I'm doing, don't you? I'm going to put this in a story. It may be in the *New York Times* tomorrow with your name and all. You'll be a hero."

"Oh, don't do that, Miss Marlene."

"A modest hero!" Her eyes arched upward, and she squeezed his hand. "That is rare."

They talked for a while until his clothes dried, and he drank several more swallows of the potion. As a matter of fact, by the time she had turned her back and he had struggled into his clothes, he was more than half drunk. He never drank alcohol other than one glass of wine with a meal. Now he felt warm and slightly dizzy.

When he stood up to leave, she put her arms around him and said, "I'll never forget what you did, Faye, never!" She lifted her face, and even a shy man such as Faye Riordan could not resist lowering his head. Her lips were soft and yielding yet firm.

Faye felt something rashly stirring between the two of them and knew he was out of his depth with this woman. As he held her, it was as if something old and something new had come into him. There was a wild sweetness here and a shock that was completely outside his years of experience. He was also startled to feel the desperate hunger of her lips, which caused a hunger of his own to meet it. He felt himself losing control and suddenly drew his head back. "I–I'd better get back. I'll miss the ferry."

Marlene stared at him, her eyes wide. Then she began to laugh. "Well, I found a bashful hero. I didn't think there was a man in America who could walk away from me at a time like this."

"Would you—would you come and visit me, and I could show you some of my paintings?"

"Of course I will. When shall I come?"

"Would day after tomorrow be too soon?"

"Not at all." She walked to the door with him and hailed a carriage. When he got in, she said, "Dream about me, Faye."

He smiled, and as the carriage lurched off, he thought, *Maybe I'm a better man than I've always thought!*

Marlene came right on the hour, and Pat Ryan met the carriage and handed her down. She started up the steps and was greeted at once by Faye.

He smiled nervously. "I wasn't sure you'd come."

"You must think I'm a fickle woman. I told you I'd be here."

"Come in. I want you to meet my family."

Faye had not prepared Marlene for the rest of his family. He introduced her to them, and Marlene saw at once that Faye was more his mother's son than his father's.

Eileen Riordan was a beautiful woman with auburn hair and light blue eyes. She came forward and said, "It's so good to meet you, Miss Jenson."

"And a pleasure to meet you. Faye's already told me much about you."

Marlene turned to Caleb Riordan and had to look up to him.

He was much larger than Faye, a strongly built man. He smiled and said, "I couldn't believe what you wrote in the paper about my son."

"It's all true," Marlene said. "As a matter of fact, I could have been even more dramatic."

She turned to greet Max and Leo, carbon copies of their father, she noticed, and then the group went in to dinner. It was an ornate dining room, and the meal itself was ornate. Marlene was perfectly at home.

The Riordans were fascinated by her career and plied her with questions, which she answered graciously.

Max was staring at her and said, "I wish I'd been there to see Faye save that child's life."

"So do I," Caleb said instantly. "I wouldn't have been surprised if Max or Leo had done it."

"Why are you surprised about Faye? He went over the side of that boat in total darkness with paddle wheels churning just like I said. I thought he was a dead man. So did the rest of the crew and passengers on the ferry."

"He won't talk about it." Eileen smiled.

"Well, if I'd done it, I'd be talking about it the rest of my life." Caleb grinned. "I never have done anything that heroic, but I'm proud of you, son."

"Thank you, Dad. Probably the last heroic thing I'll ever do."

"Don't say that, Faye." Sitting next to him, Marlene smiled. She reached over and put her hand on his head. "Once I get my hand on a hero, I make sure he comes through. I'll find you another desperate situation."

Everyone laughed.

After a fine meal and an hour's talk in the parlor, Marlene left.

"That's some woman." Caleb shook his head. "I've never seen anyone quite like her."

"Neither have I," Leo said. "She's been all over the world. Done everything."

Max grinned. "You'd better hang on to her, Faye. With her courage and daring, she'd make you a good wife."

"Don't be silly," Eileen said. "She's rather an outgoing young lady."

Caleb nodded. "Just what Faye needs."

Later Eileen talked to Faye more about the woman, and he said, "Mother, I know this sounds foolish. I've never been in love before, but I think I might be in danger of it."

"I'd be careful, son. She's not a woman that would be easy to live with."

"You mean I'd have to go to Madagascar or some wild place and shoot game?"

"I think her husband would have to be very active."

"You don't think I could do that?"

"You proved you could when you saved that child. When the courage was needed, it was there, but her kind of life wouldn't suit your painting."

That was about as long as the conversation lasted. Faye usually paid much attention to his mother's counsel, but he paid no heed to this. He was thinking about the touch of Marlene's lips as she pressed herself against him, the womanliness of her, and knew that he would see her again.

CHAPTER 3

Sunlight shed its golden beams on the bedroom that Eileen shared with Caleb. She was sitting at a Louis XIV dressing table facing a large mirror and running a brush through her abundant auburn hair.

Most of the house had been influenced by Caleb's taste, which consisted of massive, strong furniture and rather outlandish colors. But the bedroom had been designed specifically by Eileen, and she had had her way. Silks, satins, bonnets, and shoes were arranged in a large cabinet on her left, and the ribbons, laces, velvets, swags, tassels, ruffles, curlicues, fringes, and brocades dominated the rest of the room. Sometimes she felt she had overdone the bedroom as a protest against the stark, strong, masculine qualities of most of the rest of the house.

The room was furnished with delicate furniture, including a fainting couch, which Eileen had never used, along one wall. She had thought it rather amusing that anyone would have a fainting couch and had said once to a friend of hers who had just bought one, "It looks to me, Mary, if you were going to faint, you would just fall on the floor. If you have a special couch, it means somehow you have to get across the room, position yourself, and fall gracefully. I think if I faint, I'll just fall over backward. Fainting couches seem rather strange and not at all what a woman needs."

Caleb stood across the room finishing his dressing by slipping into a snuff brown coat, one of his favorites. He liked expensive clothing, but his taste was not the best in the world. Eileen had long ago given up trying to get the idea across to him that clothes should make the wearer look somewhat distinguished.

"What do you think about this affair that Faye is having with that woman, Eileen?"

Looking up quickly, Eileen saw that Caleb was studying her, a small smile on his lips. She recognized that this was the heavy-handed humor of which he was so capable. "I'm not sure it's a good thing," she replied then returned again to brushing her hair.

"Not a good thing?" Caleb exclaimed. He shrugged his heavy shoulders and cocked his head to one side, saying, "Well, she's a wealthy woman. She's got lots of spirit about her. I like that. Maybe some of it will rub off on Faye."

"I don't think so. Faye's not the kind to be influenced by that sort of thing."

"What sort of thing? What do you have against her? She's beautiful, and her father is a man after my own heart. Wades out in the jungle and fights snakes, lions, and who knows what."

"I'm sure he does, dear, and I'm sure that the woman has courage to accompany him on those safaris and journeys into dangerous places, but I don't think she's a woman that Faye could be happy with."

He came over and stood behind her and ran his heavy hand down her hair. "You know your hair is as beautiful today as it was the day I married you."

The remark was so out of keeping with Caleb's usual speeches that Eileen blinked. She felt tears come into her eyes, for she did not receive many of these compliments from Caleb. "Thank you, dear," she said. "But as far as Marlene Jenson, she's not a Christian woman."

"How do you know that?"

"Why, I asked her. She didn't make any bones about it."

"Well, she may not be a Christian, but she's dynamic and attractive and has money."

Putting down her brush, Eileen rose and turned to face Caleb. She did not have many arguments with him, for although he never abused her in any way, his personality was so forceful that she was usually intimidated by him. "She's an immoral woman, Caleb. Don't you know that?"

"Well, I have heard that she's had affairs."

"She doesn't make any attempt to cover up her past. And another thing that troubles me. . .she thinks Faye's painting is just a hobby. That he needs real work."

Caleb blinked with surprise. "Well, that's exactly what I've always said, but you've never agreed with that."

"No, I haven't, Caleb."

"But you must see a man can't spend his life dabbing paint on canvas. He needs to step out, to take chances."

"That's the way your life has been, and Max and Leo are the same, and there is a need for men like that."

"I should say so, and I've never ceased being amazed that you don't see that Faye needs some of this in his makeup. You've made him into a helpless man, Eileen, but it's not too late. This woman might change him. He could go on some of those trips with her and her father. It'd be a chance to do something great."

Eileen sighed knowing that such conversation was pointless. She and Caleb had been going over this in one form or another for most of the twenty years of Faye's life. She shook her head and said, "We've been over this again and again, Caleb. I'm not going to change. I see that Faye's got a chance to do something. . .not heroic, perhaps, but that will bring beauty into the world. He can give pleasure to people."

"You make him sound like an actor or an acrobat," Caleb protested. "A man needs to fight in this world."

"I don't think we'll ever agree, but I'm proud of Faye just as you are proud of Max and Leo. Come. Let's go down to breakfast and not talk about this anymore."

❧

The gallery was crowded, and Faye took Marlene's arm as they threaded their way through the mass of people that had come. The walls were full of art for sale. Faye was amused by some of Marlene's comments. They had stopped before a large painting that looked simply like the artist had stood six feet away and thrown small containers of brilliant-colored paint at the canvas and let it run down.

She turned to him and said, "Do you call that art, Faye? It just looks like a mess to me."

"It is a mess. You'll find this kind of phony art just as you'll find it in some books. They are phony books. They don't do anything. You can train a chimpanzee to throw paint at a canvas, I suppose, but it wouldn't be art."

"Well, I'm glad you think so. Let's find something we do like."

They moved along through the gallery, Marlene firing questions at Faye, and he tried his best to give his theory of art. "You see, Marlene," he said as they stood before a well-done painting of a fox hunt, "this painting doesn't speak to everybody, but to wealthy people who believe, especially the English, it captured a slice of their lives. They could look at it when they got old, too old to ride, and remember it, and it would be a warm memory for them."

"I can see that, but you don't paint fox hunts."

"I may. I've painted stranger things."

"Like what?"

"Come along. I'll show you." He led her through the crowd, and they came to stand before a series of paintings.

Marlene opened her eyes widely. "This is certainly different." The paintings were real-life representations of the poor sections of New York City. Marlene stared at one of the pictures, which was nothing more than a ragged young boy, obviously from the poorest section of society.

"Why would an artist want to paint that boy?" Marlene asked. "I don't see the point in it."

"Just look at him."

She looked at the painting more clearly and saw that the

young, ragged boy had a broad hilarious grin.

"Don't you see the love of life twinkling in his eyes?" Faye asked, staring at the picture intently. "He's poor, probably hungry, has been abused, and doesn't have much of a future, but he has the joy of life about him. I think people need to see things like that."

The two talked for a time about the picture and then moved on to others. In each case, in this particular group, the artist had chosen the poorest strata in American life, the sweatshops of New York. Faye and Marlene studied them, and finally they stopped before a painting of three women on a roof drying their hair.

Faye remarked, "I heard that President Roosevelt admired this painting, but he didn't buy it."

"I can see why. You can go on the rooftop of half of the tenement buildings in this city and see something just like it. It's awful. Why emphasize it?"

"It's a part of life, Marlene," Faye said. There was a gentleness and a sorrow in his voice that obviously caught her attention.

"You really feel sorry for these people, don't you?"

"Of course. Don't you?"

Marlene was uncomfortable. She had grown up in the midst of plenty, with everything she might need that money could buy, and had never really given much attention to the poorer people. They were there to serve her and were somehow in another world. "To be truthful, Faye, I've lived in a different sort of environment. I've never been around the poor, but I'm going to learn something."

"What do you mean, Marlene?"

"There's been a man who has been taking photographs of the poorer sections of the city just like these you see in the paintings.

He's starting a campaign to have the politicians pass legislation to help these poor people. As a matter of fact, I'd like for you to go with me to those neighborhoods."

"We can go, but you'd better not wear those diamonds, and you'd better get a less flamboyant dress. You won't get the right reactions dressed like the Queen of Sheba."

"I will. We'll go today."

❦

They arrived on Hester Street, one of the poorer sections of New York City, late in the afternoon. True to her word, Marlene had dressed modestly in the oldest dress she had and was not wearing any jewelry, and Faye had changed into some clothes he wore around the house when working, so they did not particularly stand out.

They stayed until the shadows were growing dark, talking to many of the residents of the neighborhood, but on their way out of the area, they were caught in what amounted to a miniature riot. Men, and some women, too, were fighting and screaming, some of them carrying clubs. Their enemy seemed to be the police and men from the upper reaches.

"We've got to get out of here, Faye."

"Yes, this is getting grim."

They started out but were caught when a man in ragged clothes carrying a short club suddenly appeared before them. He was swinging the club at anyone who moved, and the club grazed Marlene's arm. She cried out, and Faye threw himself at the man, shoving him backward. He was immediately attacked by some of the others. Frantically he fought to free himself, grabbed Marlene, and the two managed to get out.

Faye hung his head, shaking it back and forth. "I wasn't much good at keeping you safe, Marlene."

"It's not your game, Faye. Your brothers would have broken half a dozen heads, I suppose, and your father, too."

"I wish it were my game."

They did not speak again until they were clear of the crowd and had gotten into a carriage.

Marlene turned to him, took one of his hands in both of hers, and said, "We are what we are, Faye. We can't change the really important things."

It was a tender moment, and he saw a gentleness in her eyes that was not always there. Faye had never been good with words, especially with young women. He'd had no real experience. His closest approach had been in reading a few romance novels. He knew that sort of talk would not work, but he cleared his throat and said, "Marlene, I don't know how to say this. I'm not good with words at a time like this." He halted and saw she had turned to face him and was examining him with a strange stare, almost clinical. This discouraged him, but he went on and said, "I feel something for you, Marlene, that I've never felt for any other woman."

Marlene said, "I'm sure you do, but you've never had a sweetheart."

"No, I haven't, but a man doesn't have to sort through half a dozen women and go through all sorts of the games that couples play, does he?"

"That's what most couples do, and they seem to enjoy it."

"Well, I can't do that, but I tell you right now I care for you."

A thoughtful expression washed across Marlene's face. She was silent and looked down at his hands for a long time. When she lifted her eyes and met his, there was compassion on her face, and she said quietly, "Here's the truth, Faye, so listen carefully. I could have seduced you. It would have been easy. You're so innocent any woman could have done it."

Faye was shocked. "Why didn't you?"

Marlene hesitated, then a serious look came into her expression. "I don't know why. I've done it before, but I see something in you that I don't want to spoil. I'm reminded of a section of forest I once saw in the Congo. It was beautiful. . .a rain forest. I came back later, and the timber people had cut it all down. Nothing but ugly stumps and branches. The beauty was all gone. It's something like that that I feel for you. I don't want to see you spoiled, Faye. I didn't know I had any tender spots in me. I certainly haven't proved it, but I seem to have one for you."

Faye listened quietly and did not know how to reply. Finally he said, "All that may be true, but I still care for you, Marlene."

She shook her head but said no more. When she got out of the carriage at her house, he stood beside her for a moment. She leaned forward and kissed him on the cheek. She then said, "Faye, you're nothing but a baby in things like this. And the sad thing is, I've had too much experience. Try to forget about me. I wouldn't be good for you at all. I'd spoil you as those timber men spoiled that forest."

Faye watched as she turned quickly and entered the front

door. He turned and got back into the carriage, feeling somehow saddened but convinced that he would not give up. *She can come to care for me*, he thought. *I can make her do that!*

๛

Nearly a week and a half had passed since Faye had told Marlene that he cared for her. They had gone out several times, but there had been no more moments like that one. She smiled and laughed a lot. They enjoyed being together.

It was a strange delight to him to see how her mind worked. So different from his own! She was bright, intelligent, certainly physically beautiful, and he had fallen in love with her.

That morning Marlene had said, "I want us to go riding out at Central Park. It's new. We can rent some horses."

Instantly Faye felt a sudden jolt. "I–I'm not too good with horses."

"You don't have to be good. We're not going to be riding bucking horses. You know how you liked those pictures you showed me by those two men who painted pictures of the Wild West? How beautifully they brought that world to you?".

"Yes, Fredrick Remington and a man called Russell. That's what they do. They show the West as it really is, I think."

"Well, there was one with a bucking horse, and a man was on it. He was hanging on for dear life. The dust was in the air, and men were on a corral fence yelling at him and waving their hats."

"I could never do a thing like that!"

Marlene laughed and said, "Well, we won't be putting you on a wild horse. The horses they rent are fairly gentle, designed for folks who are not bareback riders in the circus."

Against his will, Faye accompanied Marlene.

When they arrived at the stables, a tall man came and smiled at them, asking, "Could I be of help?"

Marlene spoke up, "We need two mounts, sir."

"Of course. Any particular kind of animal you like?"

"Well, I like sort of a lively ride. As a matter of fact, neither of us wants to ride on horses that pull milk wagons."

The tall man grinned. "I know. That isn't much fun. Wait here. I'll bring them out."

When he had gone, Faye said, "I wish you hadn't told him that, Marlene."

"Told him what?"

"That we wanted lively horses. I've never told anybody this, but I've always been afraid of large animals."

"You mean large dogs?"

"No, I mean larger animals like horses or bulls."

"Oh, you'll do fine."

Marlene's confidence in him did not rub off on Faye. He was feeling more and more nervous, and by the time two stable hands had brought out two saddled horses, he was ready to leave but knew that he couldn't.

"This one's for you, ma'am. A fine mare. A little bit hard to handle, but you can do it."

He handed her up.

Marlene looked back to where Faye was staring at the horse.

"He's so big."

"Well, he's a stallion," the stable hand grinned. "One thing, sir.

52

Don't let him get the bit in his teeth."

"What—what does that mean?"

The stable hand looked up and saw that Marlene was smiling, and he winked at her. "Well, sir, as long you keep the bit pulled back where he can't get his teeth in it, he can't pull the lines out of your hands. But if you ever let up and he grabs that bit, he'll pull the lines right free and you'll have no control. Just keep a tight rein."

Faye started to get on, but the stable hand said quickly, "Not that side, sir. Mount from the left."

"It doesn't make any difference to me."

"It does to the horse, sir. Here. I'll hold his head."

Faye put his left foot in the stirrup, grabbed the horn, and hauled himself awkwardly aboard. He looked down and thought that the ground seemed very far away.

"That's fine, sir. Just remember to keep a tight line."

Awkwardly Faye took the reins and held them tightly as the man had suggested.

"Come along. We'll start out at a walk." Marlene smiled. "These are really fine mounts. You'll like that stallion."

The two started out, and the stallion under Faye was placid enough. They kept at a walk until Marlene, always impatient, said, "Let's try just a little faster. Not a dead run. Just sort of a trot."

"If you say so." Faye was keeping his mind on the admonition of the stable hand—keep the reins tight. The horse fell into a broken rhythm that jarred him up and down. He glanced over to see that Marlene was smiling and enjoying the faster pace.

Finally she said, "Well, a gallop is easier than a trot. Let's go."

She kicked her horse with her heels, spoke to her, and the mare started out in an easy gallop.

Faye tried to imitate her but somehow got confused. He released the grip on the reins for a moment and immediately felt something different. The reins were suddenly yanked from his hands, and all he could do was hang on. The horse was running at full speed, and he heard Marlene calling, but he could not tell what she said. The stallion was a powerful animal and ran at breakneck speed. The fear that Faye had always had of horses now had come alive. He wanted to cry out, but all he could do was hang on.

Perhaps under other circumstances the stallion would have tired, but at one point in the bridle path a thick branch hung down rather low. Faye never saw it, but he struck his head against it. It knocked him backward, and fortunately his feet were free from the stirrups already. He hit the ground flat on his back with a force that knocked all of his breath out of him. He lay there trying to breathe and felt that his head was bleeding.

Suddenly Marlene was there. She sat down beside him, raised him up, and pulled his head against her breast. "I'm so sorry, Faye. That never should have happened. Are you all right?"

It took a few moments for Faye to get his breath. Finally he said, "I'm—okay." He lay there pressed against the softness of the woman and said, "Marlene, I want to marry you." It had not been the kind of proposal he had dreamed of, but it was a tender moment, and she was holding him so close that it just came out.

Marlene leaned down, kissed his forehead, and pulled a handkerchief out. "You've got a little cut here. Let me wipe the blood away."

"Didn't you hear me, Marlene? I want to marry you."

She did not answer for a moment. Then she said, "I shouldn't have let you into my life, Faye. I knew all the time we would never be able to have any kind of relationship. I've had men hurt me, and I've left my claw marks on a few, but as I said before, some woman may let you down and hurt you badly—but it won't be me."

He lifted his head.

She kissed him on the lips and said tenderly, "I want the memory of one good man who loved me that I didn't hurt to hang on to."

No more was said.

She got him to his feet, and they walked back to the stable. When they got into the carriage, she said nothing even though he tried to speak to her. When she got out, he started to get out of the carriage with her, but she said, "No, stay here." She reached out and put her hand on his cheek, and he noticed a gentleness and softness in her eyes that he had never seen before. "I'd ruin you if we married as I've ruined other men. You don't understand, Faye. I'm not a good woman. There's evil in me, but I found that I have at least one tender spot, and that's for you. But you must forget me. Good-bye, Faye." She turned and hurried into her home.

Faye was despondent. All the way home he tried to think, but he could not. All his insecurities came flooding back. *Max could have won her, or Leo, but I didn't have the guts. I never will have.* He slumped in his seat.

When he arrived home, he entered by the side entrance and went up to his room, shut the door, and sat there until the darkness fell. But the darkness was not only a lack of sunlight but a darkness in his own soul.

CHAPTER 4

The sitting room of the Riordan mansion was a stately large room with three tall windows and a ceiling gracefully molded with garlands of flowers and flambeaux. The curtains were heavy plush, a hot crimson with thick gold fringes and ropes, which Caleb liked immensely and Eileen disliked with equal fervor. Every foot of space was crammed thick with furniture—tables incongruously jostling a mahogany chiffonier, heavy tables crowded with ornaments, Sheraton bureaus, Chinese vases, and alabaster lamps. In short it was a room filled with Victorian junk.

At least that was Eileen's idea, but Caleb had enjoyed bringing home items that he thought might please her, and she felt it necessary to show some appreciation. It was a room without taste or moderation but a part of Eileen's life with Caleb.

Caleb and Eileen had led the way to the sitting room with Max and Leo following. They all found seats in overstuffed furniture. Almost at once Caleb said, "I can't understand Faye's behavior."

"I can't either, Dad," Max said. "It's like he's a walking dead man."

Leo lit a cigar and sent purple clouds toward the ceiling. "It's that woman. She done him in somehow or other."

"I thought he was doing so well with his courtship." Caleb sighed. "He just doesn't have it in him to finish anything."

Indeed, although Eileen did not join the conversation, she was more aware than her husband or her sons of how different Faye's behavior had become since his separation from Marlene Jenson. She had noticed it almost at once, for the first sign of danger was that he, who had always been so eager, seemed to have lost his taste for painting. Whole days went by when he would not touch a brush, and when she had suggested he might try a new subject, he had merely shrugged and said, "Perhaps you're right, Mother."

He had not done so, however, and had spent his days in his room reading. He took his meals with the family, of course, but he had almost nothing to say. When his brothers or his father mentioned Marlene, he simply said, "That's all over," which closed the door finally and abruptly in a manner not often seen in Faye Riordan.

❧

One day when Faye had been walking for long hours on the property, he got back to his room and found a periodical—and the picture on the front leaped out. It was Marlene with a famous stage actor. She was looking up at him with what appeared to be adoration. His arm was around her, and he was looking down. Even the coldness of print could not conceal the fiery ardor that the two seemed to feel.

From time to time throughout the day, Faye would decide to throw the article in the wastebasket, but each time he would go back and take it out. That night at supper he was almost mute, and he went up to his room as soon as the meal was over. He was aware that his family was puzzled by his behavior, and he himself could not explain it. When he got to his room, he began to read some of the books he had begun to collect. One writer that he had read almost ceaselessly was James Fenimore Cooper, whose books reflected the sort of vigorous heroism that Americans liked to read about. His heroes were physically strong, emotionally tough, and were willing to fight to the death to overcome all obstacles. The present book was a novel called *The Deerslayer*. Faye loved reading the adventures of Cooper's famous hero, Natty Bumppo, and he also loved reading about his home state during the frontier days.

It was past one o'clock when Faye finally finished the book. A strange feeling had come over him, and he fondled the book in his hands thinking of the hero. He was still not sleepy, for his whole being was stirred by the heroic adventures of the fictional character. He finally put his head down and held it with his hands. "Why can't I be a man like Bumppo?" he whispered. The answer immediately came back that he did not have Bumppo's physical strength. He also was suddenly aware that he did not have the determination to win even if it killed him.

For what seemed like hours Faye sat in the chair, the book in his hands, his head bowed, his mind swarming with thoughts of Marlene, the failures in his life, how he had been overshadowed by his father and his brothers. A grim despair seemed to grip him, and he threw the book aside, stood, and began to pace around the room. Finally he stopped and found himself gritting his teeth. *I may not be a hero like Natty Bumppo, but I can do something!*

He prepared for bed, but once he lay down he was suddenly possessed by an idea. It came to him as clearly as black print against a white wall. "I can do something!" The idea took root, and he tossed and turned and finally got up, walked to the window, and stared out on the moonlit gardens and grounds of the estate. The idea seemed preposterous, but he was living in a desperate state since he had lost Marlene and could not face a future that only held more of the same.

He went over and picked up the paper and stared at the picture of Marlene and her lover. "I can become a man she would admire." He spoke the words aloud, and the sound of his words seemed to startle him. He fixed his eyes on Marlene's face and the poor reproduction, and the real memory of her came to him. *I can be the kind of man that she would learn to love.*

He moved quickly to his desk and pulled out a sheet of paper and a pen. He began to write, and what he designed was a list of achievements that he would have to conquer in order to be a real hero. He listed the books that spoke of such men then jotted several physical activities. His mind worked rapidly as he thought of what all he would have to achieve. "I can do it!" he said through gritted teeth.

The sun was lighting up the east when he finally put his list aside. He picked up the newspaper, stared grimly at Marlene, and then his eye caught a story he had not noticed. He began to read it. The story concerned Judge Isaac Parker who had been appointed judge in a large territory that included the Indian lands of Oklahoma as well as parts of Arkansas. The story was well written, and Judge Parker's choice of marshals had been outstanding. The marshals were described in vivid detail, all of them hard-bitten men, fearless, expert with a rifle or a side gun, ready to face danger and endure the hardships of the blistering heat and crippling snows as they pursued the criminals. He read that only the marshals were permitted to enter the Indian Territory. One of them was a man called Heck Thomas. Thomas was a family man but had sent his family away because his wife could not bear the stress of knowing that her husband was out facing killers, both red and white, in the Territory. As he read this, Faye put the paper down and thought about the stories he had read of the West. "That's the kind of man I'd like to be. One who could be a federal marshal under Judge Isaac Parker!" he decided.

The next morning Faye got up, dressed, ate a hurried breakfast alone, and went to downtown New York. He made inquiries and found a gym on the east side that he was told produced some of the best pugilists in the state. When he went in he was met by a man who had beetling eyebrows, a beefy red face, and hands the size of hams.

"My name is Kelly, sir. What can I do for you?" the man said.

"My name is Faye Riordan, and I want to learn how to box."

"Oh, do you now? Are you intending on winning the championship?"

"Nothing like that," Faye said. "Just enough to take care of myself."

"Well, if you've got the money, we've got the men who can train you."

"I can pay whatever you ask."

"All right. We got some fighting togs. Come along."

Faye followed the husky man to a dressing room that smelled strongly of smoke and human sweat and other things even more vile. He stripped, and the man watched him carefully. "How much you weigh?" he said.

"About a hundred and eighty-five."

"I wouldn't have taken you for that much. You're all packed in. Come along," he said, seeing that Faye was dressed.

He took him upstairs, and Faye found himself in the middle of rather fervent activity. There were three rings, and in each one two men were battering each other. There was a *rat-tat-tat-tat* from suspended punching bags, and men were punching them with fierce rapidity. Other men were striking at huge punching bags being held by trainers. There were sounds of grunting and cries when men were hit, and some of them were knocked completely down.

"Well, let's see. I'll tell you. It's not strength in this game, Mr. Riordan. It's speed. If a man is fast enough, he don't have to be no Samson. Now look. I'm holding up my hands, you see, and I want you to try and hit one of them."

It was the same game that Faye had played with Pat Ryan. His fist shot out and caught Kelly's big beefy hand with a sharp *splat*.

"Ho! That's the fastest I've seen in a while. Try it again."

It was the same with Kelly as it had been with Pat. If a hand stayed still for one second, Faye's hand shot out and struck it.

"Well now. You're the fastest thing I've seen around these parts. Hold your hands out now and let's see if I can hit yours."

The experiment was the same as it had been with Pat Ryan. The big man simply could not hit Faye's hands.

"Well, that's one part of being a fighter, but there's more to it than that. A man has to be able to take a punch. You're fast enough to miss most of them, but you're going to get hit. That pretty nose of yours is going to get flattened."

"That's all right. Just put me with somebody who can show me."

"Come along. I got just the fellow for you."

Faye followed Kelly to the back section of the room where a man was punching a bag. He had a wealth of curly black hair and an olive complexion—and his hands were very fast.

"Hey Tony, this here is Riordan. He wants to learn how to box. You take him in hand, will you? Don't hurt him now. He don't know nothing."

Tony nodded. "Sure, Mr. Kelly. Come along, Riordan. We'll try a little sparring."

Faye had never sparred with anyone. He had been in only one fight and had lost resoundingly. He put on big padded gloves and watched as Tony did the same.

"We'll just skip around and throw some light blows. Nothing heavy. Don't try to knock me out."

"All right."

Faye did not know a thing about footwork. He pretty well stood still, and from time to time Tony would throw a punch, which he easily avoided. He learned that when a punch came at his head, his hands were fast enough to reach up and deflect it.

"Say, you've done this before."

"No, I really haven't."

"Well, let's go at it a little bit faster, okay? This time I'm going to throw some harder punches, and you try to hit me, too."

"All right."

The Italian came in and shot a hard left, which caught Faye by surprise. It grazed his head, but immediately he threw out a hard right that caught Tony full on the forehead.

"That's a good counter punch!" Tony exclaimed. "Well, I'm not going to believe you've never had boxing lessons."

"No, I never have."

"Well, you're not going to need a whole lot of them. Come on. Let's just go at it now. I'll have to show you a few things, but you've got the speed and the build to throw a good enough punch to make it. Here we go. . . !"

❦

Faye had been back for three lessons at Kelly's gym, and on Tony's advice he had started running. "You've got to build up stamina. If you ever go up for the championship, you'll have to go fifteen rounds. Just try sometime walking around for fifteen three-minute rounds just holding your hands up not trying to hit. What kind of exercise you like?"

"I like swimming."

"That's the best! Swim all you can. Run all you can. You're doing great, Mr. Riordan."

Faye reduced his visits to the gym to once a week. Both Tony and Kelly told him he had it in him to be a professional fighter, but he had laughed that off. "No, nothing like that for me. Just to be able to handle myself, that's all I want." They had both assured him that he could, and he was satisfied.

All the heroes he had read about were experts with guns of some type. He had begun learning how to shoot by enlisting Pat Ryan and buying his own set of equipment for skeet shooting. They had gone out one day far from the house, and Pat, who had done this often for his brothers and his father, set up the equipment ready to shoot. "You holler 'Shoot,' and I'll let it go. You try to hit it. Wait a minute." Pat quickly came over and looked at the gun. "That's not a shotgun."

"No, it's a Winchester. I just bought it."

"Why, you can't hit skeet on the move with a rifle. Nobody does that."

"Well, I'm going to try."

"All right. If that's what you want, Mr. Faye."

He went back and Faye called out, "Shoot!" The circular clay pigeon flew through the air. Faye got off one shot, but the pigeon was not harmed.

"You see. I told ya. You wasted your time."

"Let's just keep going. You throw them as fast as I call. Now, shoot!"

He missed again, and for the next half hour he missed consistently. Finally he hit one, and Pat said, "Well, that's an accident."

Faye smiled. "With enough practice you can do anything, Pat."

Indeed, practice he did, until finally he became so adept with the Winchester that he could hit three out of four of the clay pigeons. By then, he knew he could hit anything on the run.

Next he knew he would have to handle a pistol. He went to a gun shop in the center of the city and looked for quite a while at guns.

The owner's name was Abe Lemmons. He seemed curious. "What will you be doing with the gun, Mr. Riordan?"

"Oh, I just need to handle a gun."

"Well, I tell you what. Most men these days want one of those .44 Colts." He reached into a glass case and said, "Here. Hold that."

"It's pretty heavy."

"Yes, it's heavy, plus your hands are small and that handle's big. Most of these are single action."

"What does that mean?"

"It means when you fire the gun you have to use your thumb to pull the hammer back before you can shoot again. As I say, you've got small hands."

"What do I need, Mr. Lemmons?"

"Well, I'd say a .38 would just about fit your hand. Here. Try this one for size."

Faye took the .38, and it did feel very comfortable. "Yes, I can hold this."

"Well, it has another advantage. It has a double action. You pull the trigger, you can fire again immediately. You don't have to cock it again before each firing."

"But it's a smaller gun than the .44."

"That it is, but let me tell you something, sir. A .38 will stop a man as quick as a .44. . .if you put the bullet between his eyes."

"Well, I'll take this one. You have a belt and a holster?"

"You're going to wear it?"

"Well, when I go into the woods, it'll be a handy way to carry it." This was not what Faye had on his mind, but it was a good enough story for Mr. Lemmons.

"Well yes, of course, we have all kinds of belts." He fitted him with one that would work fine. Faye put it on and slipped the .38 into the holster. It was about even with where his hand was hanging.

"See how quick you can get it out. That's what those big lawmen out west do."

Faye's tremendous speed came to his aid. He pulled the gun and leveled it so quickly that Lemmons batted his eyes and took a step backward.

"Heaven help us! I've never seen a man so fast! Well, you got what you need. I hope you don't ever have to use it."

"So do I. How much?"

For the next two weeks Faye went deep into the woods carrying a leather bag full of .38 bullets. He carried targets and practiced drawing his gun and shooting at them. At first he would miss the whole tree, but he had a quick, steady eye and a steady hand, and soon he was able to at least hit the tree. He improved daily, both with the speed of his draw and accuracy of hitting the target. Finally the day came when he put six bullets into a six-by-six-inch piece of paper from forty feet away. He smiled, pulled the gun up, and said, "Well, I've done that."

The next few days he went to the public library and found all the writings he could about Judge Parker and his court and especially about the marshals that represented the law in Indian

Territory. He had made up his mind that this would be a good place for him to be a man, but how to tell his mother he could not imagine. *She's going to have a terrible fit, and she's going to say no, but it's something I've got to do.*

꩜

"You want to do what, Faye?"

"I want to prove myself to be more than just a painter."

"Why would you want to do that?"

"I feel like I'm only half a man, Mother."

"You're just measuring yourself against your father and your brothers."

"I'm sure that's true and also against some other people. They're bigger than I am and stronger, but I want to prove to myself that I am a man. That I'll survive."

That was the beginning of the argument. It went on for a week but never in the presence of his father or his brothers. Always the battle took place between Faye and his mother.

As for his mother, she was shocked so greatly she could not even speak for a while. She was completely against the idea.

Finally Faye said, "I'm going away for a few days. Maybe even a month."

"Where are you going?"

"Oh, I've never gone anywhere. I want to wander around and learn to take care of myself. When I come back we'll talk some more about what I want to do."

"Yes, you think it over carefully. It would be the wrong thing, I'm sure."

CHAPTER 5

The next morning Faye left his house before breakfast, leaving his mother to explain his vacation to the family.

He took a train to upper New York State and got out at a small stop where there seemed to be nothing but three or four buildings. The trees were huge, and it was a large enough forest to intimidate him.

He went at once to the livery stable and said, "I want a very tame horse. No bucking broncos."

"Why, I've got just the horse for you, Mr. Riordan. Name is Patsy. She's just as gentle as a mother. She's never thrown a man in her life, I don't think. You're not going to win any races with her, however."

Indeed, Patsy was a gentle horse. She was strong enough and could carry his weight easily. He led Patsy down the street to a general store, and when he left he had bought a frying pan, a saucepan, salt, a knife to hang on his belt, a spoon, and matches.

He already had a blanket, some soap, a fishing line, and some hooks. He also took a toothbrush, and the biggest part of his load was feed for Patsy.

That afternoon he loaded Patsy and stepped awkwardly into the saddle. "Well, Patsy, we're going out into the woods, and I'm going to stay there for about a month. The only food I have will be what I shoot with this .38. I'll sleep on the ground, and if I don't learn to hit something with this pistol, I'll live on grass and leaves." He suddenly felt good about the whole thing and slapped her on the neck. "Come on, girl. Let's go make a man out of Lafayette Riordan!"

It was cool but not uncomfortable as Faye walked through the woods. It was two weeks into his experiment, seeing if he could survive, and now he was feeling doubt, for he had not been able to secure much in the way of food. He had learned that squirrels are quicker than a man's hand. Even when he would see one behind a tree, the creature could scoot around on the far side of the tree quicker than Faye could draw a bead on him. Up until this time he had caught two frogs and forced himself to eat them, but the only animal he had killed with his revolver was a porcupine who was a slow-moving beast to say the least. He had almost given up, but he had turned the porcupine upside down and dug out enough meat to at least fight off his hunger pangs.

Suddenly Faye heard what he thought—and hoped—was a flock of geese. Looking up, he could barely see them through the trees. They were in a familiar V-formation and crying their familiar *"K-whonk! K-whonk! K-whonk!"* To his delight, they descended quickly, and although Faye knew little about wild geese, he assumed late in the afternoon they were looking for a place to spend the night. He was fairly sure that they stayed near water.

As he moved forward, he realized that he was famished and beginning to feel a bit weak from hunger. More than once he had been tempted to give up his plan, but he had doggedly stuck with it. Once while out there, he had found a tree with berries on it that he could not identify. Hoping they were not poisonous, he ate them. They had filled his stomach, although they provided little nourishment. The other meal he had supplied himself was one he had never thought to sample. He had been moving through the woods when he heard a rattle. Whirling around he saw a huge snake in a coil, ready to strike. He had pulled his .38 and got off three shots. One of them had hit the snake in the head.

Now as he moved cautiously forward, Faye remembered how he had considered the monstrous snake. He had heard of men eating snakes but had never thought he would be one of them. Hunger had won out. He had cut the head and the rattles off, skinned it, and toasted the white meat on a stick over a fire. To his surprise it had been rather tasty and had filled his stomach at least for a period.

Trying to walk silently as the Indians did in the stories by James Fenimore Cooper proved to be a problem. According to the books, they could walk silently through a forest unless they happened to step on a twig. But now the leaves had fallen. Some of them were crisp and made a crackling sound each time he stepped on them. Taking a deep breath, he started shoving the leaves aside with the toe of his boot so he could step on the bare ground. It was a slow method, but finally he came to what seemed to be a ridge of some sort, about six feet high.

The sound of the geese came to him clearly as they were splashing, and their honking came to him on the afternoon air.

They're right over this rise down in the water.

The thought touched him, and he knew he was still too far away to get an easy shot, but he eased the pistol out of his holster and took a deep breath. *God, don't let me miss.* Faye didn't even realize he was praying, but then in one motion he came to his feet and scrambled to the top of the rise. As he had surmised, a pond fed by a small creek was filled with geese, and as he had also known would happen as soon as he stood up, a warning honk filled the air, evidently a signal. *I'm too far away for a good shot. Wish I had my rifle, but it's too late.*

The large birds rose with a flapping of wings and a hoarse cry. Faye lifted his pistol, tried to aim at one, but when he fired he hit nothing. They were rising rapidly and going farther from his range. He fired again, counting his shots, and despair filled him as he fired his last bullet. He lowered his gun, disgusted. Then he saw one of the geese falling in an awkward fashion. Quickly he shoved the .38 into the holster and ran headlong into the water. He hit the edge of the pond running, his eyes fixed on the goose, recognizing that the bird was not dead but apparently hit in the wing.

The water was shallow, and by lifting his feet high, Faye plunged rapidly toward his goal. The goose hit the water and began floundering, swimming away. Faye was breathing hard, but when he came within six feet of the wounded bird, he flew himself forward in a dive, stretching his arms as far as he could, and managed to grab a handful of feathers. The goose struggled, but quickly Faye came to his feet and wrung the bird's neck. The bird quivered once and then was still. For a moment Faye stood there holding the dead goose, and a feeling of pure joy came to him. "I did it!" he shouted.

Turning quickly, Faye made his way to the shore then ran at a trot toward the camp he had made. It amounted to little more than a lean-to he had made of saplings cut with his hunting knife and covered with branches with leaves to throw off the worst of the rain. His blanket was in there, and the fire he'd made earlier was blackened. He had, however, made sure that he always had kindling, which meant small pieces of dry wood and larger pieces to make a fire for warmth and for cooking. As he stood in the middle of his small camp, he tossed the goose down and stared at the mare, who lifted her head and considered him.

"I did it, Patsy!" he shouted again, and his voice echoed through the deep woods. "I killed it, and now I'm going to eat it."

Patsy considered Faye seriously then complacently lowered her head and nibbled at the grass at her feet.

Quickly Faye built up a fire. He had done poorly at keeping his fire at first, but practice makes perfect, and now he kept plenty of dried wood on hand and had learned how to get it started quickly.

Picking up the goose, he moved out of the way and began pulling the feathers off. It was a difficult business. The feathers closer to the breast were light and easily pulled, but getting the long ones off was a problem. He suddenly grinned and shook his head. "Well, I've eaten chickens and turkeys all my life, but never once did I think how they got dressed, cooked, and put on my plate. Now every time I eat a chicken leg, I'll think about someone having to pluck and cook the thing."

Faye spoke aloud, which he had begun doing soon after arriving in the depth of the woods. He had brought two books with him, and at times he would read aloud. One of them was the Bible, and the other was a book of the history of the southwest. The silence of the deep woods had proved to be intimidating, almost ghostly, and Faye had found that even though no one heard him, there was a consolation in the sound of his own voice.

"Now, how do I cut this fellow up?" He drew his hunting knife and began hacking away at the goose. "Bloody mess, that's what it is," he said in disgust. Finally when he had cut small pieces off the bird, he brought a small frying pan out to where the fire was now crackling merrily. He took the parts he had sheared off to the creek, washed them off, and came back. Carefully Faye placed chunks of meat into the pan. "I'm having fried goose for supper, Patsy."

Soon Faye discovered that the meat in the frying pan was burning. He turned the pieces over with the point of his knife and stirred in some water. "Hey Patsy, too bad horses don't eat goose." He laughed aloud, but his stomach had an ache in it.

As soon as the meat in the frying pan was half cooked, he stabbed it with his knife and bit off a bite. "Ow, that's hot!" he yelped. He blew on the meat, and when it was finally cool enough, although it was burned on the outside and half raw on the inside, he bit off small parts of it and chewed them with delight. "I never tasted anything so good," he murmured.

He ate slowly, devouring about a quarter of the cooked goose, and saw that the parts in the pan were softened up. "I guess I'd better save something for tomorrow." A thought came to him, and he gingerly poked through the inner parts of the goose that he had thrown aside. He found what he thought was the liver, pulled it out, and dropped it into the frying pan. When it was brown, he picked it up with his knife and waited until it cooled. Cautiously he tasted it. "Tastes kind of like chicken liver," he murmured.

Finally he spoke to the horse. "Guess I'll clean up, Patsy." He washed his pan and his knife, wrapped the remains of the goose in a piece of heavy cloth, and then sat down in front of the fire, enjoying the sensations of a full stomach. After a while he grew sleepy. He built up the fire, rolled up in his blanket, and lay down.

For a while he lay awake listening to the noises of the forest. He heard all kinds of night birds calling, and somewhere a fox was yipping at the moon. "Well, maybe Natty Bumppo could kill a wolf or a bear, but I'll bet he couldn't hit a goose on the wing like yours truly." He felt pleased with himself and quickly fell asleep, for the first time sleeping a dreamless, placid, sweet sleep.

❧

"Well, girl, about time for us to head for the house."

Stepping into the saddle, Faye settled and turned the mare's nose to the southeast. He spoke to her, and she started out on an easy walk. As they left the camp, he looked back at it. It had been home for him for quite some time. "It makes me feel a little bit sad," Faye murmured, "but it's time for other things."

The sun was coming up in the east, and as Faye swayed with

Patsy's movement, headed toward civilization and a life he wasn't sure about, he thought about the time he had spent alone. He remembered how it had taken him two and a half weeks before he hit a squirrel with his .38. That seemed to unlock some sort of ability, for he became a dead shot. He also had learned to shoot rabbits. He had missed the first ten he shot at. They were fast, and he had to learn to shoot slightly ahead of them. As soon as he found this out, he knew that he was going to be all right. He had eaten several rabbits during his stay in the woods.

He thought of the biggest kill, which had been a four-point buck he had stalked for an entire day. After standing absolutely still within the shadow of a huge tree, the buck had cautiously come out of hiding. Faye had remembered the deerslayer remaining perfectly still, making himself one with the forest. Finally when the buck stepped within twenty feet, he drew his gun with one swift motion. The bullet caught the buck just behind the front leg, killing him instantly. Now Faye smiled as he remembered the difficulty he had had dressing the deer out, but he also remembered how the animal had fed him and how he had learned to cook venison. He thought of other kills he had made, and, as usual, when he thought of the snake, he was disgusted. "Snakes are dangerous. I don't know why God made them, but they're not bad eating. Though I wouldn't want to have snake meat as a steady diet"—he smiled—"it was better than porcupine."

All morning Faye rode steadily, crossing a logging road and going past a few cabins. Finally he reached the small town where he had bought Patsy and left for the woods all those weeks ago.

When he stepped down, the owner came out to greet him.

"Well, sir, you came back."

"Sure did. Got a favor to ask of you."

"What's that?" The man was instantly on his guard, which caused Faye to smile.

"Do you know a young girl who could use a mare of her own? Maybe someone too poor to buy her own horse."

Instantly a smile came to the lips of the owner of the stable. "I sure do. My niece. She's just eighteen. She wants to be a schoolteacher. She has to walk four miles to get to school and back. Why you asking?"

"I'd like for you to give Patsy to her. Will you?"

"You mean sell her?"

"No, I mean just give Patsy to her. I can't take her with me."

"Well, mister, I sure will. That's mighty handsome of you, sir."

"What time does the train come through headed southeast?"

"About noon." He pulled out a watch about the size of a turnip. "It'll be about two hours now."

"I haven't had a good meal in a while. Is there any place around here I could get something?"

"Why, of course you can." The owner smiled. "You come eat with us. I just killed the finest pig you've ever seen. How does fresh pork chops, homemade biscuits, and beans sound?"

"Like heaven." Faye grinned. "Lead me to it." He slapped Patsy affectionately on the rump, went up, and rubbed her nose. "Thanks for the ride, Patsy."

"What about your saddle?

"Goes with the horse. Give it to the young woman."

"Why, she'll want to thank you."

"Not necessary. Just tell her I wish her good fortune with her teaching."

Two hours later Faye was sitting in the window of a narrow-gauged railroad passenger car. Cinders came in through the window, and from time to time the whistle made a shrill scream. Faye leaned back, pushed his hat down over his eyes, and wondered, *Now I've done something, but convincing Mother of the next step won't be this easy.* He thought for a while how he would tell his mother his plan and came up with nothing. Finally the clickety-clack of the wheels lulled him into a slight sleep, and as he slept, he smiled as he headed back toward his life.

CHAPTER 6

Eileen was in the kitchen talking to Kate about the following week's menus when Doris, the downstairs maid, rushed into the kitchen, her eyes wide with excitement. "Mrs. Riordan, it's Mr. Faye! He's come home!"

"Where is he, Doris?"

"He's in the foyer looking for you."

Eileen rose at once and hurried out of the kitchen. She turned down the wide hallway that divided the big house, and when she saw Faye standing in the foyer she cried, "Faye!" and ran to him.

He caught her, picked her up, and spun her around. He laughed at her protest then set her down and kissed her cheek. "How's my best girl?" He smiled.

"Why didn't you tell us you were coming? I ought to turn you over my knee and spank you!"

"You've done it before, Mother, but not since I was about six."

Eileen was almost weeping for joy. "I've missed you so much,

Faye. Why didn't you write?"

"Well, to be truthful I was a long way from a post office."

"Well you shouldn't have been." She began to fuss at him to cover her emotions but was studying him carefully. His skin was an even golden tan—something she had never seen before. His hair was long, the clothes he had on were ragged and dirty, and he seemed to have lost weight. There was, however, something new in his expression—the look in his eyes, the set of his lips. Something about him was different. "Well, come into the parlor and sit with me for a while." After catching him up on news of the family, Eileen asked Faye where he had been.

"Mother, I wanted to learn how to hunt a little, so I've been out in the woods. It was really an interesting experience for me."

"Well, I don't want you going back and doing that again." *He was heartbroken over that woman. Thank God he's gotten over her!*

Faye got to his feet. "I really need a bath and a change of clothes."

"Yes, you go bathe, change clothes, and lie down. Take a nap before supper. Your father and brothers will be glad to see you."

As soon as Faye left the room, Doris came back. "He looks like a different man, Mrs. Riordan. My, he's so tan! He must have been outside a lot."

Eileen said, "Go get Kate. She's out in the garden. We've got to have a fine meal tonight to celebrate his homecoming."

"Yes, ma'am, I'll do that."

Kate did a fine job with the meal. She had fixed a large beef roast with potatoes, carrots, onions, and garlic, but few noticed it.

Caleb and his sons were shocked at the changes in Faye and

told him so. Leo asked, "How did you get so tan, Faye?"

"Well, as I told Mother, I decided to learn how to hunt a little bit. So I was out in the woods a lot. I just wanted to travel and see the country."

"You look like you've lost a little weight," Leo said.

"I don't think so. I'm about the same."

"Did you get that woman out of your system, brother?" Max smiled.

Everyone stared at Faye who did not blink. He said, "You know, Kate makes better meals all the time. I haven't had a meal this good since I left home."

It was obvious that he was not about to discuss his personal life. Suddenly he turned to his father and said, "How have things been going at the factory, Dad?"

Caleb blinked with surprise. Eileen knew he was surprised at their youngest son's question, as Faye had shown little interest in the factory before. Caleb finally said, "Going well, son." Hope lit up his face, and he asked, "Are you thinking about coming to work with me and your brothers?"

"Not just yet, Dad. I've got a few things I need to do."

They all retired to the large parlor, and Faye talked a little about the country he had seen but not in enough detail to tell them anything. For the rest of the evening, Caleb, Leo, and Max tried to get Faye to say something about his plans, but he simply avoided their inquiries. Finally Caleb said, "Well, it's about bedtime. I can see we're not going to get anything out of you, Faye."

"I had a good time out there, Dad."

"We'll talk about it tomorrow. Will you come to the factory

and see what we've been doing?"

"I'll be glad to."

This pleased Caleb, and he left at once along with Leo and Max.

"You've gotten rather closemouthed, Faye," Eileen said. "You're not telling a thing about where you've been. It's had us all worried, and I think it's unfair of you to keep us in the dark."

"Mother, I'll tell you more about it tomorrow. All right? I'm tired now and need to go to bed."

Eileen put out her cheek to receive his good-night kiss, the same as they had done for years. Yet she couldn't help but wonder if she had lost the gentle son she had always known.

The next morning, Faye rose early and ate breakfast with the family. He promised his father to come to the factory later and lingered at the table drinking coffee while his father and brothers left.

Eileen got a cup of coffee and sat down beside him. "Now, you've got to tell me what you've been thinking. You've got to tell me where you've been."

"All right, Mother. This is going to be a shock for you, but I hope you'll listen carefully until I get through. Then you can ask me anything."

"Go ahead, son." Eileen leaned forward, her lips slightly parted, as Faye began to talk.

"I had gotten to the point when I realized that I wasn't everything a man should be." He saw her start to protest and shook his head. "Just hear me out, Mother. I know my painting is important. Art is important. Many things are important, but I had taken one part of my life and ignored the rest. I think Father and Leo and Max have ignored the opposite parts of themselves, too. They work at the big things in their lives and ignore art, music, drama. . .things like that."

He continued to speak for a long time, and then he finally said, "Well, Mother, you're not going to like this, but here it is. I've been reading about Judge Isaac Parker out in Fort Smith, Arkansas. You know anything about him?"

"No, I don't even recognize his name."

"Well, he's a judge in that district. He's over the Indian Territory in Oklahoma and part of Arkansas. He has two hundred marshals to keep the area protected. Only a federal marshal can go in and settle. It's become a hideout for bad men. Judge Parker has to send in his marshals to get them. I've been studying what they do, and I've decided to go to Fort Smith and ask Judge Parker to make me one of his officers."

Eileen stared at Faye as if she had not heard him correctly. "You mean to become a marshal?"

"That's exactly right, Mother. To become a federal marshal. I want to see if I can be any part of a man, and that's a good test, I think."

Eileen began to speak rapidly, telling him the reasons she could think of why what he had suggested was just a terrible idea.

He listened carefully and did not interrupt, but finally when she had finished, he said, "Mother, I know you're worried about me. To tell the truth, I don't think I'll ever paint again until I get this out of my system. I've got to become a whole man."

For quite some time, Eileen argued with Faye, but her pleading didn't work, and she was terribly disturbed.

"I hate for you to feel like this, Mother, but this is something I must do." He rose, went over, and put his arm around her. "Don't worry, Mother. It may not work at all. I've got an idea that the judge has pretty strict standards. I doubt if he'll have me."

"What if he won't?"

"Then I'll come home and do this thing another way. I don't know how, but I'll try to get back in the painting mode again."

The conversation ended like that. Faye knew his mother was terribly disturbed, but there was nothing he could do about it. *I'll just have to wait a few days until she accepts it.*

⌒

Eileen had not mentioned Faye's plan to her husband or to her sons. For several days, she was unable to do her work. She had difficulty following a train of thought, for all she could think of was her boy hunting a bunch of outlaws and in danger of being killed.

She had prayed about it for a long time. Every day. And finally she had an idea. It seemed simple enough, so she called Faye to sit with her. They went into the parlor and sat down.

Faye asked, "What have you decided, Mother? I hope you'll give me your blessing."

"I've decided to go along with you on this matter, son, if you'll promise me one thing."

Showing surprise that her surrender came so easily, he said, "What is it, Mother?"

"I ask that you take any job the judge gives you and stay with it, no matter how low it is, even if it's washing dishes."

Faye was obviously caught off guard. He finally smiled and said, "Why, Mother, I'll be glad to promise that."

"Good, son. Now, we'll just wait a few days, and then we'll tell your father about it."

The next day Eileen set the rest of her plan into motion. She sat down in her bedroom at the desk with paper and pen and began to write:

To Judge Isaac Parker:
Dear Sir,

I'm sure you get many letters asking you to do things for people. I suppose that's the penalty of being a public figure. I am no different, Judge Parker, and I am writing this letter with a prayer in my heart that you will at least listen.

I have three sons. Two of them are real satisfied to be in their father's business. My other son has gone another direction. My two older sons are outdoorsmen. They are tough, as their father is. They hunt and shoot and ride, but my youngest son, Lafayette, is not that kind of man. He has been a student all of his life. He is twenty years old now, and that's all he's ever known, that and his painting. I'm convinced he will be a great artist one day.

That's why I'm writing this letter. I hear that your men are in danger in their work. My son has no training, and as far as I know, no ability with a gun. I know he cannot ride a horse well. I'm afraid he will come out and waste his life and be killed, perhaps, and that would be the tragedy of my life.

Please consider this in almost the nature of a prayer, Judge. I hear that you are a father, and I know you treasure your sons. I know you wouldn't want to send one of them into a situation that would be almost impossible and dangerous. Please consider what I ask you to do, which is simply this: When my son comes to ask you to make him part of your force, agree to take him but give him the most humiliating, dirtiest job you can possibly think of. Keep him at it, and I'm sure in a short time he'll become discouraged and change his mind.

My prayer is that God will be with you as you read this letter and that you will give it your prayerful consideration.

Respectfully yours,

Mrs. Eileen Riordan

She blotted the ink, put it in an envelope, addressed it, and then left the house. She went at once to the post office and mailed the letter herself. Turning, she went back home again and felt that she had solved her problem.

❧

Judge Isaac Parker had brought a letter home with him. He sat down with his wife and said, "Dear, let me read you this letter." He read Eileen Riordan's letter and then handed it to his wife and

85

let her think it over. "What do you think we should do about this young man?"

"Why, it's clear enough." She smiled. "We have to do what she asked. This young man isn't fit to send out into the wilds of the Oklahoma Territory with the drunken Indians and outlaws. You know how many of your marshals you've already lost. It would be murderous to send this young man."

"Yes, I would never have sent him anyway, but she wants us to keep him until he gets full of this dirty side of life."

"Well, we will pray about it, Isaac, but I feel this mother's plea, and we must help her all we can."

Eileen opened the envelope, her heart pounding. She quickly read the brief letter from Judge Parker.

My dear Mrs. Riordan,

My wife and I have read your letter together. We both sympathize with you, and as concerned parents of a son, we know your heart aches. Never fear. I will do exactly as you ask, Mrs. Riordan. I will give your son such a hard time that he will not last long if he's like other young men. He sounds like he's rather spoiled, perhaps, so it will be easy to discourage him. I'll have him washing dishes, cleaning stables, all the things my men hate to do. We will pray together, my wife and I, that your son will return to his life with you.

Yours respectfully,

Isaac Parker

Faye had been escorted to the railroad station by his family. It had been a hard few days for him, for when his father and brothers found out his plan, they all were incredulous. All of them warned that he was being a fool.

"You could stay here and learn to ride and shoot if that's what you want," Caleb said earnestly.

"Yes, we'll help you," Leo said. "Don't do this crazy thing."

Faye had listened patiently, but here they were at the railroad station. The train had pulled in. The conductor was calling, "All aboard!" He shook hands with his father and then hugged his two brothers.

Faye went to his mother and said, "Don't worry, Mother. I know you'll pray for me and I'll be all right. Besides, it's likely that Judge Parker won't make me a marshal without some training. He'll probably have me learning to ride a horse better and how to track, things like that. He won't let me go out until I have some experience and can make it as one of his men."

He hugged her, kissed her on the cheek, and then mounted the train steps. Minutes later, the train left the station. His last view was of his mother and his father, both looking despondent.

He grew restive during the long train ride to get to Fort Smith, Arkansas. He read a great deal, all he had been able to find about Judge Parker's court and the marshals.

When he finally arrived at Fort Smith, he went right away to Judge Parker's office. To his surprise, he was admitted at once.

Judge Parker was standing at a window looking down at the

gallows that were in plain sight. "What can I do for you, young man?"

"Judge, my name is Riordan. I've come to ask you to take me into your marshal force."

"Tell me your experience."

This did not take long, for in effect, Faye had none. Finally he fell silent, and Judge Parker said, "Young man, I have a great many volunteers. I can only take those who are experienced, and you are not."

"Just let me work. I'll do anything you say, Judge, and I'm a quick learner. I don't expect to be sent out right away to Indian Territory."

"You mean what you say, young man, that you'll do anything?"

"Anything, sir."

"Very well. You may join my force." He lifted his voice, saying, "Mr. Swinson."

The door opened, and a short, stocky man stepped in.

"Riordan, this is Chester Swinson, my chief of marshals." He then turned to the chief. "I want you to put this young man to work."

"Doing what, Judge?"

"Whatever needs doing."

"Come along. What is your name again?"

"Just call me Riordan."

"All right, Riordan, come this way."

Carrying his suitcase, he followed the man. He had given merely his last name because he was ashamed to be called Faye, which sounded feminine to him. He always had hated the name and now determined just to be called Riordan.

Swenson led the way to a large rectangular building. He opened the door. It smelled of sweat and other nasty things he didn't want to know about. "Clean this building up until it's spotless. Clean the windows, mop the floor. . .everything. I want it shining."

"Yes, Marshal Swinson."

"All right, Riordan. When you finish this, you've got another job out in the stables. Shovel out all the stalls and put the refuse into a cart. The judge uses it for fertilizer in his garden. Dirty and nasty job. Nobody wants to do it. It'll be your job from now on."

Somehow Faye knew that he was being tested. He thought that the two men had some idea of how to make things hard on a recruit. He made up his mind right then. *No matter what they do to me or ask me to do, I'll stick it out!* "Yes sir, I'll do a good job."

After Swinson left, Faye looked around at the terrible condition of the room and then began to whistle. "I'm with Judge Parker's marshals. Maybe it'll be rough for a while, but one of these days I'll ride out with Heck Thomas and some of the other men."

PART TWO

PART TWO

CHAPTER 7

The Mexican settlement had no name and was not legally a town, just a collection of adobe huts and wooden shacks built from cast-off lumber located a few miles west of Amarillo, Texas. At night the liveliest place in the village was Pepy's Cantina. Pepy's was an exciting place for young men looking for female companionship, or vice versa.

At one end of the large room, three men were playing guitars, and a small space had been set off for those who wanted to dance. Now three couples, laughing and pawing at each other, moved around the floor. The room was filled with the shrill laughter of women, the coarse mirth of men, and the hum of constant loud voices. Rough tables and chairs were scattered around, all of them filled, and a bar ran along one wall—on the wall behind it were pictures of half-dressed, over-endowed women. One very fat man was serving at the bar, sweat pouring over his face. His filthy apron had once been white but now was a leprous gray.

The customers at the tables were served by two young men and by Rosa Ramirez. She was wearing a full skirt and a white blouse that clung to her sweaty body. Fatigue lined her face. She had been busy for over four hours, and now it was well after midnight. Most of the clientele were either drunk or soon would be.

As Rosa Ramirez threaded her way across the crowded floor, she paid no attention to the scents of raw alcohol, thick cigarette smoke, and unbathed bodies. When she reached the bar, she had to raise her voice to say, "Four cervezas and a bottle of red wine, Leon." She waited until the fat barkeep moved to fill the order.

Without warning she was roughly seized from behind, two arms pinning her. Her captor ran his hands down her body and whispered, "Rosa, you need a man to love you!"

Without hesitation, Rosa moved her head forward then flung it back and felt a satisfaction when she felt flesh crush.

A strangled voice cursed and said, "You broke my nose!"

Wheeling quickly, Rosa saw Viro Lopez, a heavyset man with dark piggish eyes, glaring at her. Blood was running from his nose, over his mouth, and dripping off his chin, and from there making an ugly blot on his emerald green shirt. Lopez cursed and reached for her but halted abruptly when he saw the six-inch blade of bright steel in Rosa's hand glittering under the yellow light of the lamps suspended over the bar.

"Touch me again, you pig, and I'll cut your liver out!"

The clientele of Pepy's Cantina was well accustomed to violence, but most of them turned now to see the knife in Rosa's hand, her face contorted with anger, and Viro Lopez, a man of blood who had killed and battered women until they could not walk.

Suddenly, almost magically, the owner of the cantina, Pepy Garcia, appeared like a ghost. He was short but broad of chest and shoulders, and his neck was thick. His eyes glittered under the lamplight, and he said quietly, "Time for you to go home, Viro. Maybe you can come back some other time." He waited for the larger man to act, but Lopez cursed, pulled out a bandanna, and began wiping the blood from his face. Pepy nodded. "That's wise. Go now, my friend. This is not your night."

Rosa had shown no fear, but she was aware now that her legs were unsteady. She showed nothing in her face, however, but a slight smile. "*Gracias*, Pepy," she said then added, "but I lost you a good customer."

"He'll be back." Pepy shrugged. He hesitated, stroked his mustache, and then said, "I don't like it when things like that happen in my place, Rosa. My customers are all drunks, and I can't control them sometimes."

"I don't complain."

"You never do. Take the rest of the night off. You look tired. Go get some sleep."

"Thank you, Pepy. I am tired."

"How is your father, Senior Ramirez? Any improvement?"

"No, sir, my father never seems to improve."

"Too bad! Too bad! I always admired him. I knew him when he was a young man and able to whip any man in the Territory, and his word, it was always strong. Whatever he said, he would do. Give him my best wishes, Rosa."

"I will, Pepy, and I'll see you tomorrow night."

Rosa left the cantina and made her way down the dark streets of the village, warily watching for men who might be lurking in the darkness. She reached the outskirts of the village and turned into a yard that housed a squat clay adobe house. Two lights were shining through the windows, a feeble yellow, and even as she reached out to knock on the door, she heard the raucous laughter from Pepy's Cantina. The distaste at the thought of the place where she had worked for two years seized her.

There was no need thinking about that, so she knocked on the door—two knocks then a single knock. This was the code that the family had created. Rough men and women were common here in the village and in Amarillo, and blood had been spilled often enough. The door opened a hair, and she pushed it open saying, "You still up, Juan?"

Juan Ramirez was a handsome boy of sixteen, tall and thin as though undernourished. He had dark hair that needed cutting and the dark eyes of his half-Crow mother. "I was worried about you, Rosa."

"You shouldn't do that. You should get some sleep."

"I saved you some supper. Raquel was sleepy and went to bed early.

Rosa reached out, hugged him, and smiled. "Good! I'm hungry." As she sat down wearily at the rough table, she looked around at what had been her home for several years and, as always, was depressed. The house had only two rooms. One was a bedroom used by her parents, and the other room was for living. It contained a kitchen, of sorts, a table for meals, and three cots with blankets, which were used as seats and beds for Rosa, Juan, and Raquel.

Juan moved toward a cabinet and brought out a plate covered with a cloth and a bottle. He set both on the table before Rosa, moved back, and got two glasses. "I saved you some beer," he said, "but it's not cold, sister."

Rosa smiled and patted his hand. She removed the cloth, picked up a tortilla, and filled it with meat. She ate without hunger, but Juan was watching her, so she said, "This is very good. What did you do tonight, Juan?"

"Nothing." The boy shrugged eloquently. "What is there to do in this place? I played cards with Chico and Carlos. We went over to see the new horse Arturo's father had bought."

Rosa listened as Juan spoke and was glad that he talked to her. They were the two that held the family together, and it broke her heart that he had so little chance to become something. She had given up on a good life for herself to work at Pepy's to bring in money for the family. Once she had had dreams, but they had faded a long time ago, and now she had to concentrate on making it through a single day at a time. "How is Papa today?"

"Not so good." Juan's smooth face showed a troubled mind. "I wish I could help him, Rosa."

"You're helping him by being a good son."

"No, that's not enough. I need to do something else. I need to get a job and go to work."

"No, there's no proper work here. We all know you would work if you had a chance at it. Just help Mama with the house. Be sure she has plenty of wood and water. You're a good son."

He shook his head and said stubbornly, "No, that's not enough."

The two sat at the table under the corona of flickering yellow light cast by a single, stubby candle. Finally Juan looked closely at Rosa's face. "You're tired, sister. Go to bed."

"Well, I am tired." She rose and put her hands on Juan's shoulders, startled to feel how thin they were. From lack of nourishing food she knew. "We have each other, Juan, you and me. I couldn't make it without you." She saw her words pleased the boy and brought color to his face. She ruffled his hair, kissed him on the cheek, and whispered "Good night, brother."

The two of them went to bed on the cots, and in the ebony darkness Rosario Ramirez tried to pray that God would give them a better life. But she had prayed in that fashion for so long that her faith was small.

☙

The sun had lifted in the west, sending pale yellow beams through the two small windows of the hut and through a large crack over the primitive woodstove. Raquel, a trim fourteen-year-old girl wearing a tattered dress too large for her, had started the fire with bits of wood that she and Juan had collected, and, as usual, the smoke made her eyes smart. "I hate this stove, Mama!" she exclaimed.

"Be thankful we don't have to cook on the floor or in a rock fireplace." Chenoa Ramirez was grinding corn with a pestle in a hollowed-out stone. She wore an ancient dress long ago faded to a dull, neutral, noncolor and held together with patches. The sunlight touched her, revealing her unusual racial heritage. Her father, Frank Lowery, was a tall American trapper, but her mother had been a full-blooded Crow Indian. The mixture of races had made Chenoa a beautiful woman. She had lost that early beauty, for now at the age of forty, after years of hard living since her youth, her face showed lines that revealed her age.

She glanced at Raquel, whose dress was almost as worn as her own, and marveled at the blossoming beauty of the girl. *Not a child. She's on the verge of womanhood.* She glanced over at Rosa, and a sadness came to her. *She's so beautiful, but what does that get her? The men of this place chase after her but for evil purposes, and it will be the same with Raquel.*

A door hinge creaked, and Chenoa turned quickly as her husband Mateo entered the room. She rose quickly and walked with him to the table. "Sit down, Mateo. I'll fix you a good breakfast."

"I'm not hungry, Chenoa."

As her husband sat down, Chenoa was suddenly reminded of how handsome he had been when she had first seen him. She had been a mere girl, and to her the young, pure Spaniard with dark eyes and lively features and an aristocratic air had been the finest-looking man she had ever seen.

A bitterness came then as she thought of how good their life had been until Mateo had fallen ill with cholera. He had been in charge of a large property owned by a wealthy citizen of Amarillo. She longingly thought of the fine wood house that came to the Segundo and how she had had a new dress for herself from time to time and how the children, who were very young, had been clothed in finery. Food had been plentiful, and she had thought this life would last forever. Mateo had finally recovered but had become so weak he was unable to work. He had lost his position, and everything from that time had become difficult.

As Chenoa began to heat a pan full of rice, she turned to see Rosa rise from her cot and throw the thin blanket back. She was wearing a thin undergarment, and Chenoa remembered how long ago she had been as shapely as this oldest daughter of hers. She turned back to the boiling rice, stirred it, added salt and a little butter, then put it in a bowl and set it before her husband. "Here. Eat this. You've got to keep your strength up."

Mateo began to eat, but he took only small bites. He did finish the bowl and smiled. "Very good, wife. You were always the best cook in the village."

Juan coughed, groaned, and rolled out of bed. He wore a pair of worn, patched jeans too small for him and a shirt that had once been colorful but now was faded. "Is there any of that pork left, Mama?" he said, yawning hugely.

"Yes, you can share it with your sisters."

They ate quickly, and then the children left the room—Juan to go fishing in the river, Raquel to visit her friend Sofia, and Rosa to work in the cool of the morning in the garden behind the house.

Chenoa had made a cup of weak tea and put it down before Mateo.

He looked at it, smiled, and tasted it. "That's very good," he said.

They sat silently, and finally Mateo said heavily, "I don't like the way our children are living." He made a thin shape as he sat watching Chenoa's face. "Juan and Raquel, they've been running with bad companions."

"Their friends are not as bad as some."

"Maybe not, but I don't like it. And I hate it when Rosario has to work in that hellish cantina." Rosario was the name given to Rosa, but her nickname had become almost second nature. Only her family used her full name at certain times now.

"I hate that she has to fight the men off. She's a good girl, Mateo."

"I know that. But what's going to happen to them, Chenoa? What in God's name will become of them? There's nothing good in this place." He lowered his head and whispered, "I failed you all."

Chenoa moved at once to his side, put her arm around him, and held his head. "You have not. You've been sick. When you are fully recovered, you will get work and things will be better." They both understood that such a future was highly unlikely, for his weakened condition grew worse, never better. "Don't worry," she said, stroking his hair now streaked with white. "The good God, He will take care of us." Her words, she saw, gave Mateo no comfort, nor did they make the sadness and hopelessness in her own breast go away.

It was two days after this that the Ramirezes had a visitor. It was late in the afternoon when they heard a knock.

"Who could that be?" Mateo asked.

"One of the neighbors maybe," Chenoa said. She got up and opened the door. She stood there for a moment in shock. "Is that you, Gray Hawk?"

"Yes, your uncle has come for a visit." Gray Hawk stepped inside at her invitation. He was full-blooded Crow, a handsome man. The Crows were the most handsome people among the Plains Indians, and he was a good example. He was near fifty but erect as a pine tree, and his muscles were still limber and strong.

"I'm glad to see you. Come in and sit down. We have some food left."

"I will eat, and then I will talk."

Gray Hawk sat down, and the family watched him as he ate. When he finished, he sat back, belched loudly, and said, "That was good. Now I'll talk. You listen."

"All right, uncle," Chenoa said. "Why have you come?"

"Your father. He is sick. He wants you to come and live with him."

The family had heard Chenoa speak of her father, who was, by all her reports, a fighting man admired among all the Indians.

"Live with him?" Chenoa said. "How could that be? He has another wife now, not my mother."

"She is dead. He has a woman to keep house for him, and he needs you he says. He has a fine ranch, a big house."

"Well, why don't you help him, Gray Hawk?" Mateo asked.

"Ah, I'm a wild hawk. I do not always keep the law. I sometimes buy whiskey and sell it." He laughed then slapped his chest. "The Choctaw Light Horse is after me."

"What is that?" Chenoa asked.

"Indian police."

For a time he talked about the house, the ranch, and what was there.

Finally Mateo, who had remained silent, said, "You are not telling us everything, Gray Hawk."

"No, I am not. Your father's ranch is in Indian Territory, which has more outlaws there than there are fleas on a dog. Evil men everywhere! Your father fought them off while he was well, but he can't fight now."

"What's wrong with him, Gray Hawk?"

"Bad heart. If you come," he said, "you will have to fight for what you have."

For a while they talked about going, but it was obvious to Rosa that they really had no other choice. "There's nothing for us here."

"Yes," Mateo said, "I can do nothing, but perhaps you can help the old man."

"But how will we get there?" Chenoa said.

"Your father has given me money. He told me if you will come to buy a team and a wagon. Some of you will ride in the wagon with your goods, and I will buy horses for the others."

"You will take us there?" Rosa said quickly.

"Yes. I must say this, though. In the mission school they talked about heaven where everybody is happy and there's plenty of food." He paused, and a grim look swept across his face. His obsidian eyes seemed to glitter. "This place where you're going, it's not heaven."

CHAPTER 8

"I'm worn down to the bone," Mateo groaned.

It was late afternoon. The sun had been beating down on them all day long, draining the strength from the horses and riders alike. They had started early in the day and had paused only an hour or so at noon to eat a quick meal. Now the party had stopped beside a small stream that gurgled over smooth stones and made a pleasant sound in the ears of the thirsty travelers.

Chenoa stood up and arched her back. She had driven the wagon all the way, and Mateo had lain down, for the most part, on the bed they had made for him in the wagon. Now she went over and dipped a small pail in the stream. As she did, she saw a group of minnows flashing silver. They all darted away then broke and made a left turn. *I wonder how they all know to turn at the same time?* The thought had occurred to her before.

She straightened up, ignoring the ache in her back, walked over, and reached down into a box in the rear of the wagon.

Taking out a quart bottle, she handed him the water then picked up another glass and carefully poured brown liquid into it. "Drink this," she said.

"I hate that stuff."

"I don't want you to drink it because you like it, but it helps you to feel better, to feel stronger."

Mateo shook his head, making a face. He swallowed the painkiller then quickly downed the entire contents of the glass. He handed it back to Chenoa and looked around at their surroundings. "This is bad country," he muttered. "I don't like it."

Indeed, this part of Texas was not known for its beauty. The land stretched away endlessly, so it seemed, flat, dull, and without any interesting hills or mountains. The strange mesquite trees that twisted their branches looked like black ghosts reaching to heaven.

Chenoa sat down beside him, put her hand on his shoulder, and kneaded his thin, wasted muscles. "It will be better when we get to Oklahoma."

"I don't think so. From what I remember of that place, it's just about as stark as this."

"It's been a long time since we've been there, and Gray Hawk says my father's ranch is much better country than this."

"I don't think that Indian would know good country if he saw it."

The two fell silent and watched as the three young people were laughing and splashing water on one another. They had taken their clothes down to the creek and were washing them, working up what soap they could from the yellow bars they had bought before they left their home.

Gray Hawk had been given enough money by Chenoa's father to buy them clothes. *He must have known*, she thought, *that we had nothing to wear except rags.* They had all outfitted themselves, and she felt better wearing a respectable dress and good shoes.

"Maybe I should try to get some firewood and build a fire for supper," Mateo said.

"No, Juan's already done that. I'll go light it. Gray Hawk ought to be back, but if he's not, he said to eat without him."

Going over, she piled small sticks into a pyramid, took a match she had brought from the wagon, struck it, and held it steady. The smoke began to rise, and as the flame caught, yellow flames leaped upward. She added larger sticks, and the fire began to crackle with almost a malevolent sound in the silence of this deserted country.

When the fire was going, she built a small base out of bricks that they moved each night. On top of it she put a steel piece of grill. It made a passable stove, and now she put water on to boil for the coffee, and right on the grill itself she put chunks of beef. Almost at once the fat began to sizzle, and the smoke billowed upward almost furiously.

"It's about time for Gray Hawk to shoot another cow," Mateo said. "This last one is almost gone."

He had no sooner spoken when Gray Hawk came in riding a small pony. He used no saddle. He slipped to the ground, tied the halter to a mesquite tree, and came over. He looked down at the meat and nodded, "I'm hungry."

"It's about time for you to shoot another cow," Mateo said.

"You better not shoot one that belongs to someone," Chenoa warned. "We'd be in a bad way if we didn't have you to lead us home."

"These cattle are wild. They're not branded. I'll shoot another one at noon tomorrow." They were pretty tough, but the beef was a welcome addition to the meat-starved diet of the Ramirez family.

"It was thoughtful of Father to send money to buy food," Chenoa said. "He must have known we were struggling."

"I think he did," Gray Hawk said. "Did you write and tell him?"

"No, I haven't written him for years."

"We left under pretty bad circumstances, Gray Hawk, if you remember," Mateo said. "He didn't want me to marry Chenoa. I thought he was going to take a gun to me."

"It was unpleasant," Chenoa said, "but evidently he's mellowed."

"I think he has," Gray Hawk muttered. He squatted beside the fire until finally the meal was ready.

Chenoa hacked off a big chunk of the beef, put it on a tin plate, and handed it to him. He dipped into the pot containing beans and scooped out a heaping spoonful. "Good," he said. "Lots of pepper. A white man don't know how to do that."

Chenoa called, "Children, come and eat."

The three came at once, bringing the wet clothes.

"I'll have to tie a line up and hang them out to dry," Rosa said. "But we'll eat first."

They all sat down and filled their plates with the spicy beans and chunks of beef.

"How much farther is it?" Mateo asked.

"A few more days. It's not too far. Not too close either." Gray Hawk looked up in the sky. "It will rain tonight. Cover everything up in the wagon with that canvas we brought." He walked over to his horse and began rummaging through the pack on the animal.

"Do you believe him, Chenoa?" Mateo asked.

"Yes, he never was a liar unless he had to be."

They all ate hungrily, dipping beans out of the pot that was boiling hot.

"These beans need more pepper," Juan said. He reached into the pocket of his new shirt and pulled out a large red pepper. Taking out his pocketknife, he cut off some small round fragments and dropped them into the beans. His eyes widened with the heat, and he said, "That's better."

Gray Hawk came back shortly with a bottle. He sat down, took a long drink from the bottle, and said, "You want some whiskey, Mateo?"

"No, it burns my gut."

"How about you, Juan?"

"Don't offer him whiskey," Rosa said. "He doesn't need it."

"Don't be foolish, woman. Every man needs a drink. What about you, Rosa?"

"What do you mean what about me?"

"You look lonesome."

"I'm fine."

"No, a woman needs a man. That's what you need. I'll find you a good one when we get to the Territory."

Rosa gave Gray Hawk a look of disgust. "I can find my own man."

"She doesn't have to go hunting men," Juan said. "They come hunting her. I think she had to take a knife to one or two of them."

"Well, a knife wouldn't discourage a good man," Gray Hawk said. He continued to drink, and quickly the alcohol made him sleepy. He went over close to the wagon, stretched out flat on his bed, and soon was snoring.

"You think he's telling the truth about these cows that wander around?" Juan said. "I thought all cattle belonged to somebody."

"It's always been that way he told me," Rosa said. "They're just wild steers. Sometimes ranchers round some up, but there are so many of them and not many ranchers. And he's telling the truth. None of these cows have brands, so they're just wild."

Soon the rain started, just a drizzle at first, and then the tiny drops began to form fat ones pattering down on the earth, settling the dust. They covered the wagon up with the canvas, and then all of them got under the wagon, out of the rain as much as possible. They had brought slickers, and each had put one on. Now they sat, waiting.

"You know, it's kind of nice sitting here with the rain falling down. I always did like that sound," Rosa said.

"It was nice of grandfather to send money for clothes," Raquel said. "Maybe he'll buy me some pretty dresses when I get there."

Chenoa's face turned sour. "He didn't buy me any when I was your age. He's stingy."

"But Mama, he's giving us a place to live. He bought these clothes for us."

"He needs us, Raquel."

"Look at Gray Hawk," Juan said.

They all looked to see the Indian lying flat on his back. His mouth was open, and the rain was falling in.

"He's going to drown."

"You better go pull him in, Juan," Chenoa said. "We couldn't do without him."

Rosa and Juan went out and dragged the drunken man under the shelter of the wagon. He coughed and snorted then went back to sleep.

Mateo began to cough, and Chenoa put a blanket over him. "We'll get you a good doctor when we get to the Territory."

"I doubt if your father will pay for that. He never cared much for me."

"I think he's probably changed. People do when they get older."

"Or when they get sick," he said.

The rain continued. It had a soporific effect. Finally Mateo dozed off. Chenoa felt her eyelids closing as sleep was coming on. She saw her younger daughter move to her older one through her half-closed eyes.

Raquel tugged at Rosa's sleeve. "Are you glad to be going, Rosa?"

"Yes, it's better than what we had." She paused for a moment and then laughed bitterly. "It couldn't be worse," she said. "Now go to sleep."

Chenoa prayed Rosa was correct as she drifted into sleep.

🐍

"How long before we get to grandfather's place, Gray Hawk?" Rosa asked. They had been traveling steadily all day, and she was tired. Riding a horse for long hours was a new experience for her. She had no split skirts, and at first the saddle had chaffed the insides of her legs, but she had taken one of her old dresses, cut it down the middle, and sewed it so that it had, in effect, legs. She had put ointment on the raw places and bound them up with underwear so that it was bearable.

Gray Hawk was riding along in front with Rosa at his side. "We've been on his land for the last hour."

"This?"

"Yes, this is all his."

"The land looks better than I expected." She had expected it would look much like the barren, sandy plains near her home, but here there were rolling hills, none of them large, but at least they broke the monotony. Some trees were scattered around, not tall, but at least they added color.

They had crossed one wide creek. Gray Hawk had told her, "That creek is spring fed. Ain't a very big creek, but it never goes dry. Got fish in it, too."

Rosa looked eagerly forward as they moved up a hill, noting the cattle running free. "Look, they've got a brand. What is it?"

"That's an anchor. I didn't know what an anchor was. He told me sailors used them to stop a ship. Don't know why he chose that." They crested the hill, and Gray Hawk motioned with his hand. "There's the ranch."

Rosa's eyes swept the vista. It made a pretty sight, at least to her. She was used to the squalid village, and here was space with trees and grass. There on a rise was a house and outbuildings. The house was wide and had tall windows. A veranda stretched all the way across the front. The roof was made of some sort of metal, for it caught the glint of the sun. "What's the roof made out of, Gray Hawk?"

"Tin. Makes an awful racket when it rains."

"I've always liked that."

When they drew closer, she saw that there were two large

barns and several corrals, all of them containing horses. The cattle were running free, and she saw two men moving around among the horses. "What is that thing?" Rosa asked, staring at a strange-looking structure.

"That's what they call a windmill. The wind blows it, turns some machinery, and pulls water up from a well. I remember when your grandfather had it built. Everybody said he was crazy, but I was there when it first started. We had to wait for a breeze. It started clanking and making noises, and then water came up from the ground. He had some troughs built so the stock could always have fresh water. The workers on the ranch use it, too."

Rosa called out, "There's our new home, Mama, Papa!"

Chenoa looked over the ranch. She turned to Mateo and said, "He added to the house. It's bigger than it was."

All of them looked eagerly at the house. There were only the two workingmen they saw, but as they got closer, they saw a man was sitting on the front porch in a rocking chair.

"That's my father," Chenoa said. She pulled up in front of the house and got down from the wagon.

Mateo crawled down, and the rest of them dismounted from their horses.

The old man got up carefully, slowly, and came down the steps. He was frail.

Rosa had never seen him, of course, nor a picture of him. He was not a tall man, and his flesh was wasted. His face was lined, but his eyes were bright and active. He carried a cane and leaned on it slightly. His eyes were on his daughter.

Chenoa stepped forward and said, "It's been a long time, Father."

Frank Lowery studied this daughter of his whom he had not seen for years. "You look like your mother when she was younger. Not quite as pretty, though."

"I never was."

Lowery moved forward and stuck his hand out to Mateo, who shook it. "Good to see you, Mateo."

"We appreciate your having us."

"We didn't get along too good the last time you were here."

"No, the last I remember you threatened to shoot me if I ever set foot on the place." He smiled and said, "Now's your chance."

"No, I'm past that. I can see you're not well. Well, that makes two of us." He grinned suddenly and laughed. "We'll see which one of us lasts the longest."

Rosa had been watching the scene, taking in her grandfather. Suddenly he turned and looked her up and down. "You look like you might strip down nice."

Rosa had heard her mother speak about how awful her grandfather's talk was.

Chenoa snapped, "That's no way to talk to your granddaughter!"

"I like that. Your grandmother was like that. She didn't mind speaking right up." He studied Rosa and said, "You're a good-looking squaw."

"I'm not a squaw."

"Well, you're part squaw. What I figure is you're one-eighth Crow. Anyway, you're good-looking enough to draw some men to help us. But you keep yourself clear. I don't need no great-grandchildren right now."

"Don't worry about me. I'll be fine."

"And who is this?"

"This is Raquel, our youngest daughter," Chenoa answered.

"Are you a good girl, Raquel?"

"Sometimes."

Lowery laughed. "I like that. Someone asked me once when I was just a boy, 'Are you a good boy?' and I said, 'No, I was born in sin when my mother conceived me.'" He laughed at the thought and said, "I don't know how I knew that scripture. I guess it about sums me up." He turned and looked at Juan carefully. "You look like your pa did when he was a young man, which is good. Hope you're as tough as he was when he came courting your mama."

"I've come to help you all I can, Grandfather."

"Good. Well, let's go in the house." He moved slowly up the steps. Rosa noticed he held himself carefully.

"Are you feeling bad, Father?" Chenoa asked.

"No, don't feel bad at all. I had me a severe spell with my heart. Never was scared in my life, but that scared me. Thought I was a goner, so I move pretty careful now. Don't want to stir that up again." He made it up the steps, opened the door, and said, "Come on in. I got a passel of bedrooms. You can take your pick, except for mine." They all filed in, and Lowery yelled in a big voice, "Ethel, get out here!"

A big woman in her forties came through the door. She was plain but strong looking.

"This here's Ethel. She's been taking care of me since I got too old. I done asked her to stay around. She makes the only good biscuits in the Territory. Ethel, I want you to fix us up a good meal. The prodigal sons and daughters done come home."

Rosa said at once, "I will help. My name is Rosa, Miss Ethel."

"I'm glad to see all you folks. He gives me trouble, but he gives me a home, too."

"You children go out and look the place over. I want to talk to your folks," Lowery said.

Juan and Raquel left at once, and Rosa went off with Ethel. She quickly discovered that the woman was blunt and plain spoken but seemed to have a kindly nature. "We got all kinds of stuff to make Mexican food. That's what he likes best. His wife was good at it, but I never was. I can do the regular cooking. If you'll do the Mexican, I'll do the rest."

"Why, you've got all kinds of things here. We can make a fine meal."

The two women set about preparing the meal.

Rosa asked finally, "How about my grandfather? He seems very weak."

"Well, he nearly died with that heart problem. He was in bed and couldn't hardly move for a long time. He had a hardworking foreman who took good care of the stock. But when some outlaws were taking our cattle, he tried to stop them, and they kilt him. I think that's really why your grandfather sent for you folks. I don't see how you can help with the killers hangin' out around here."

"Can't the law do something?"

Ethel was making a crust for a pie. She stirred the batter quickly and worked the flour in until it was pliable and said, "We're in the Territory, Miss Rosa. The only law here is the federal marshals. Judge Parker's court's got about two hundred of them, but they got the whole of Indian Territory to take keer of. They can't do everything. Then there's the Choctaw Light Horse."

"Choctaw Light Horse? What are they?"

"Indian policemen. But they only deal with Indian trouble. Don't have nothin' to do with white men." She worked quickly and efficiently.

"How did you happen to get here, Ethel?"

"A drunk Cherokee killed my husband. I didn't have no place to go, no money, nothin', so Mr. Lowery brought me out here. That was four years ago. He was a strong man then. He kept the outlaws thinned out, but now they've been movin' in, taking what they want." She gave Rosa a direct look and asked, "What kind of place do you come from?"

Rosa told Ethel how poorly they had been living. She looked up once and said, "Ethel, I'll do whatever I have to on this ranch. If anyone tries to run us off or take it from us, I'll put a bullet in his head if I can."

"That's a good thought. You hang on to it. I keep a shotgun handy by the door. In case they ever try to come in, I'll blow their heads off. Now, let's get this meal going."

꩜

Lowery was reveling in the supper. "Look at all this! Chicken quesadillas with red sauce, burritos, tamales. Everything I like and all delicious. Miss Ethel, that's the best meal I've had in a long spell."

"Well, I didn't have nothin' to do with it. Miss Rosa did all that."

Rosa said quickly, "My mother's a much better cook, Grandfather."

"Don't see how she could do much better than this."

All during the meal, Frank Lowery kept asking them questions about how they'd been living. Rosa and her mother did most of the talking, and finally Lowery said, "It sounds bad."

"It was worse than we're telling it," Chenoa said. "We needed a home badly."

"Well, I'm glad you're here."

Rosa spoke up. "Ethel's told me about your foreman getting killed by outlaws."

"His name was Sam Butterworth. He was a good man, tough and hard, but he wasn't harder than the bullets they put in him. He tried to stop Henry the Fox from taking some of our stock. Henry just gunned him down."

"Henry the Fox?" Rosa asked. "Is that his real name?"

"Partly. His last name is Beecher, but mostly he gets called the Fox."

"Did you send word to the law?"

"I sent word, but I couldn't go in person. I was too sick by that time."

"I can't really understand why you sent for us," Mateo said. "Chenoa can take care of the house, but how do you think we can help with the outlaws?"

"It's just a start. We've got to build up a little army around here. It don't have to be all that big, but they gotta be tough men." He turned and looked at Rosa and said, "Rosa, I wish you was a man, but you ain't. But you're gonna have to do a man's job. And Juan, you are second in command. We got three good hands left. They're tough hairpins, and they've stayed with me when it would have been easy to ride off. Now, you two have got to learn how to shoot, and you've got to learn horses, how to ride 'em and how to take care of 'em. You've got to be willing to shoot a man if you have to. I've talked to Captain Canno of the Choctaw Horse Brigade, that's the Indian policemen. Since you got Indian blood in you, Rosa, his band can help you, at least with Indian problems. But he's got no authority over the white man. So that's our problem."

"What can we do, Grandfather?" Rosa asked.

"Well, Mateo and me are too sick to fight. Raquel is too young. So you two are gonna have to take care of it."

Juan at once said eagerly, "I can help, sir. I can shoot a little, and I'm a good rider."

"Good boy. Now listen. Today I want you to pick out your weapons, rifles and pistols. From this time forward I don't want you to be without 'em. Sleep with 'em if you need to. I've got 'em in a room in the back of the house. We'll get you gunned up, and then I want you to go out and get Ned Little to teach you how to shoot. Blinky knows all there is to know about horses. So ask him to give you lessons, and you've got to learn quick. The first time any man comes to do us harm, shoot at him. If you miss him, fine. If you hit him, good. And listen to Ringo Jukes. He's tough as barbed wire and ain't afraid of nothin'. If you back off," he warned, "they'll walk over you. So we got four men, counting Juan, and one woman. That's our army right now. But if we make a good show, that'll keep the worst off of us until we can draw some more men. You may have to throw a wink or two at somebody, Rosa, to make 'em want to come out."

"I won't have to do that, Grandfather." Rosa smiled. She was getting used to the old man's teasing and liked him a great deal.

He was silent for a time, and then Rosa said, "I have something to say, Grandfather. I've never had a home, not a real home, but I want this to be a home for us. I wish I were a man, but a man who takes a bullet from a woman is just as dead as one who takes a bullet from a man. All of us are grateful to you, and we want to be your family."

"I can't ride or fight, Father," Chenoa said, "but I can make life easier for you."

Lowery was silent for a while, and then he said, "You know, I won't be long on this earth. I got to thinking one day what I'd be leaving behind, this house, this land, a few cattle. It'll be all gone. But then I thought a man needs a family of his own blood, and that's why I sent for you. I realized I hadn't been the man I should have been with my family, but if you give me a chance, I think I can do better."

"Lead us to those guns," Rosa said.

He led them down to a room in the back of the house where, indeed, there was a small armory. Rosa and Juan found holster belts and .38s to put in them.

"The .44s are too big for your hand. You hit a man in the brain and that'll make him dead enough," Lowery said. "Now, you go down and tell them worthless hands of mine they gotta teach you how to shoot, how to ride, and how to keep this place up."

Rosa and Juan left the house and headed for the corral where three men were sitting on the top rail. Brother and sister were both conscious of the pistols in the men's holsters and that they were holding repeater Winchester rifles. They halted, and the three men stared down at them silently.

The biggest of the men said, "You Mr. Lowery's kin?" The speaker was a tall, lanky man, around thirty, with yellow hair and hazel eyes.

"Yes, I'm Rosa Ramirez, and this is my brother Juan. Get down off that fence while I'm talking to you."

Startled, the three men leaped to the ground, and Rosa asked, "What are your names?"

"I'm Ned Little."

"My grandfather says you know guns. Your job is to teach us to shoot pistols and rifles."

Little grinned. "Who you exactly plan on shootin', missy?"

"Anybody who gives trouble to this ranch." She turned to a short rider with red hair and a mustache that was a mistake. "What's your name?"

"Blinky Mullins."

"You'll be teaching my brother and me all about horses. We don't know very much, but we can learn." She turned to face the third man who was watching her curiously. He was six feet tall, strongly,built with handsome features. His hair was chestnut with a slight curl. "I'm Ringo Jukes." He smiled suddenly. "What am I going to teach you, Rosa?"

There was a suggestion in his voice, and Rosa said, "Nothing, until I teach you some manners. You see yourself as a ladies' man?"

"Pretty much."

"All right. You call me Miss Ramirez. You touch me, I'll make you sorry."

Jukes sobered. "You ain't too friendly, are you, Miss Rosa?"

Rosa knew she had to bond with these men. "I don't mean to be hard. I'm very grateful to all three of you for staying with my grandfather. I realize I'm just a woman and Juan's just a boy, and you three can do things that we can't. My grandfather's a helpless old man, and so is my father. Gray Hawk has told me how hard this country is, and right now Juan and I aren't able to take care of this ranch by ourselves."

She paused, dropped her head, and considered what to say next. The silence ran on, and then she lifted her head. "I don't want to sound hard, but the job is too big for us. Only if you three help us can we survive. So I'm asking you, will you help us?"

Ringo Jukes said quickly, "I didn't mean to get on the wrong side of you, Miss Ramirez. I like your grandfather. I'll be glad to help any way I can."

Rosa smiled. "Thank you, Ringo, and my friends call me Rosa."

"I'll be glad to teach you about horses," Blinky spoke up.

Ned Little shrugged. "I don't claim to be no sharpshooter, but I think I can show you how to put a bullet where it will discourage a man. You ready to start?"

"Yes. Blinky, you start teaching Juan about horses while I learn how to shoot horse thieves."

CHAPTER 9

Eileen began a letter to Faye late in the afternoon before the menfolk came home from work. She wanted to have time to reread it and make sure it was worded well, for his letters to her always seemed to touch her deeply. She put the letter away in a drawer in the bedroom and went downstairs to make sure dinner was ready.

When the men came in, they had to clean up. Finally they came to the table. Their talk was of the factory and things that she knew little about, but she did sense that there was something about the way her husband did business that seemed cold and calculated. Knowing little enough about the world of business, she picked up on the fact that he was a hard man when it came to business tactics. She knew he did not mind using his power to crush a smaller and more vulnerable business opponent, and this disturbed her. But she could think of no way to change it.

When the meal was finally over and the men went to the

study to smoke and finish their talk, she went upstairs, took the letter from the drawer, and then went to the parlor. Sitting down, she unfolded it with hands not quite steady. She was not a woman easily disturbed, but the problems of this youngest son of hers occupied her mind. She prayed for him every day with all the power she could muster and hoped her letters reminded him of the home she longed for him to return to.

❧

Faye blew on the completed letter to his mother to dry the ink and then read it over to check for any errors.

Dearest Mother,

I wanted to get this letter off to you as quickly as possible because I have missed a few days. I hope you have not been worrying about me, as I am absolutely in no danger here. As I told you before, Judge Parker saw to it that I had a job, and the head marshal, Chester Swinson, sees to it that I have plenty to do.

I am learning a great deal about horses. As you know, I have never been comfortable on a horse. To tell the truth I've always been afraid of large animals, but that has been changing here. It is my job to take care of them, which includes cleaning up after them, grooming them, and seeing that they are fed properly. I've picked up quite a bit from the stable hand here. His name is Josh. He's a black man and a fine Christian. He's been after me to go to church with him, and I went last Sunday. It was a black Methodist church, and

123

the preacher was very eloquent. The singing was nothing like we have in our churches. The people all sang at the top of their lungs, some of them raised their hands, some clapped their hands. They had the best time I've ever seen any congregation have. I understand the Methodists are like this, the old-time ones anyway. Maybe I can find a Methodist church that has some of the early beginnings in it.

I've been getting plenty to eat here. There is no shortage of good food. The marshals come in at all hours after long trips. They're always hungry, dirty, and tired, so it's my job to see that they get good meals. I've even helped out by cleaning their boots and little things like that. I haven't gotten to be friendly with any of them because it's sort of like a men's club. The marshals make a close confederation and stick together, and I can see that you have to buy your way in with deeds and not just words.

I get up before daylight and work on preparing the breakfast with the cook. Afterward I clean up the dishes. Then Marshal Swinson puts me to some work that usually takes me the rest of the day. As a matter of fact, I hardly ever finish the list he gives me.

As I was saying, I have never been comfortable around horses. I told you about Patsy, the one I rode on vacation. She was a sweetheart, but there's a horse here that I've grown rather close to. Her name is Maggie, and none of the marshals will have her, or at least she's always the last choice. I found out that she's gentle, too lazy to buck, and the men think she's not tough enough to go on the scout with them. That's what they call it, "going on the scout." But I've learned she's very patient and never bucks. I've learned how to throw on a saddle and put on a bridle very quickly. I've learned to get on a horse without any problem and stay on. Well, there's no triumph there, Mother, because any ten-year-old could stay on Maggie, but I've grown very fond of her.

I must close this letter and get it in the mail. One of the men is going to the post office, and he said he would drop it off for me. I miss you a great deal, and once again I tell you there's no point in worrying about me. I'm doing nothing more dangerous than washing dishes and cleaning up after horses.

I did make one friend here. A big dog that's been hanging around, they say, marshal headquarters for a long time. He has one eye, no tail—it's been chopped off—and three legs. His name is Lucky, which I think is really poignant, but he's a good dog. I save him scraps from the kitchen, which nobody ever did, and he and I have a good time together.

I'll close this letter by asking you to continue to pray for me. Sooner or later I will be going on the scout, but I will let you know. Just give my regards to Dad and my brothers, and tell them I'm thinking of them.

With warm regards,
Faye

Faye quickly folded the letter, slipped it into an envelope, sealed it, and went to find Clyde Jordan, one of the marshals, who was headed for town. "Would you mail this letter for me, Clyde?

Here's the money for the postage."

"I reckon so." Clyde was a big, bulky man, good-natured, and not as standoffish as some of the other marshals. "This to your sweetheart?"

"In a way. It's to my mother."

Clyde nodded approvingly. "That's good, Riordan. You can have lots of sweethearts, but you only have one mother, and I'll bet she's a dandy."

"Yes, she is. Thanks a lot, Clyde. I'll save you some pie tonight before the gluttons eat it all up. What kind do you like?"

"Any kind." Clyde took the letter, and he left.

Almost at once Faye ran from his room, which was nothing more than a space above one of the stables. He had made a fairly good bed there and kept his belongings nearby. He came down the steps quickly and went to help with the breakfast. The cook was a fat, greasy man, good-natured enough except when someone crossed him. His name was Davis Beauregard. He was a French Cajun and a pretty good cook.

As soon as Riordan entered, Beauregard said, "Get started on them pancakes. You know how these sorry lawmen eat 'em up quicker than we can make 'em."

"Sure thing, Beauregard."

The men came trooping in, and Riordan put plates down and big cups. They were all hollering for breakfast, and he carried in a huge stack of pancakes and divided them up. He went back and brought another stack in and then filled their coffee cups. He ran back and forth, and finally, when the last pancake had been devoured and the last marshal had left, he drew a sigh of relief. "Well, I guess that will keep 'em fed, until noon anyway, Beauregard."

"They ain't got no manners. You sit down and eat something, Riordan. You've got to be hungry."

"I'll fix it."

"Shut up and sit down. I'll bring it to you."

Riordan grinned, for beneath the crusty manner of Beauregard was a heart that was fairly good. He ate five pancakes along with fried ham and downed several cups of coffee. He got up, took his dishes back, and said, "You make the best pancakes in the world, Beauregard."

"You'd think I was feedin' 'em hog feed, them marshals. Back where I come from in Bastrop, Louisiana, we had a few manners. We'd tell the cook he done good. They never say a nice word."

This was true enough, so Riordan always made sure he managed to say something nice about the food to the cook. "I'd better get these dishes washed," he said. For the next hour he worked hard scrubbing the plates and the silverware and putting them away. He was just finishing when Chester Swinson came in.

The marshal's face was red, as it usually was when he was upset—which was most of the time. "Quit loafing here, Riordan! You got to clean out the stables. Take the refuse over to the judge's garden. I'll be watching you to see that you don't go to sleep."

"Sure thing, Chief Swinson."

As always, Riordan was careful to give a quick word to the marshal. He had done that ever since he had been there. Never once complaining. Always ready to go.

He went out at once, and for the next hour and a half he

shoveled the stalls of the horses.

He whistled and continued to work, and when he finally finished, he walked over and washed his face and hands but knew there was no point in changing his clothes, for Marshal Swinson would have another dirty job for him.

The judge and Swinson were talking over the cases on the docket and deciding which men to send out on the scout. After they had settled all this, the judge suddenly asked, "How's that boy doing? Young Riordan?"

"Well, Judge"—Swinson scratched his head, and a puzzled look came into his face—"I've treated that boy like a dog. He should have hit me and left here. He's got determination if he ain't got nothing else."

"Well, I thought he would have quit by this time, Chester. Just keep pouring it on."

"His ma still worried about him? I don't think she has to worry. He's good at mucking stalls and washing dishes and other dirty jobs, but that ain't what we need out in the Territory."

The judge was thoughtful for a while. He tapped his chin with a pencil then ran his hand over his hair. "I'll tell you what, Swinson. Heck is going out to serve a paper on Sudden Sam Biggers. Why don't we send Riordan along?"

"Why, he ain't ready to go out on the scout."

"It's not much of a scout, as Biggers is pretty small-fry. He won't give any trouble. And you know how Heck wears his partners out. Riordan might get worn down to the knees trying to keep up with him and give up this idea."

"But he could get hurt. He might meet somebody worse than Sam."

"Well, you tell Heck to look out for him."

"Maybe you're right, Judge. Maybe a taste of what marshals have to do will discourage him. It makes me nervous when a grown man don't get mad when he's put on the way I put it on Riordan."

"Okay. You talk to Heck. Be sure you make it plain. We don't want him shot up."

"No danger of that. Sudden Sam never shot nobody. Ain't nothing but a two-bit thief."

"Well, there are other rough ones out there besides Sam. Just make it clear to Heck I don't want the boy hurt."

"All right, Judge. Maybe it'll work."

A hand grabbed Riordan, who was in a deep sleep, and he came up fighting and striking out.

"Keep your hands to yourself!"

Riordan sat up in bed, and by the lantern that the man was holding, he saw that it was Heck Thomas, probably the best of Judge Parker's marshals. He always got his man, though not always alive. "What is it, Marshal?"

"Get up. Get your clothes on and get your gun."

"What for?"

"You're going to ride with me on a little job. I'm going to give you a taste of what it's like on the scout."

Riordan at once came off the bed and began to throw his clothes on. He strapped on his pistol, his rifle, and followed Heck out.

"Get yourself a horse."

"I know which one I want, Marshal. Maggie over there."

"That ain't no horse. She's just a big pet."

"Well, she's not mean and she doesn't buck, and you know, Marshal, I'm not very good with horses."

"Well, throw a saddle on her. She looks strong enough. I guess she can keep up."

Quickly Riordan saddled up.

Heck, who was sitting down smoking a cigarette, said, "Go in the kitchen there and get us some grub. Enough to last two or three days."

"What kind?"

"Anything we can keep down."

Quickly Riordan went into the kitchen, grabbed two sacks, and filled them with things they might use on the trail. He threw in some dried beans, bacon, some hard rolls, some salt meat, and several other things.

When he returned outside, Thomas said, "Okay, let's go."

They left before the sun peeped over the western ridge. Riordan kept waiting for Thomas to tell him something about what they were after, but Thomas said nothing.

All morning all Riordan heard was, "Catch up! Put the spurs on that nag. We ain't got all day. You ride like a squaw!"

Since this was fairly well true, Riordan could hardly answer, so he kept up as best he could. When they stopped for a meal, he did the cooking, which amounted to frying some bacon and slicing some biscuits he had brought and breaking out a bottle of honey. They ate the crunchy bacon, poured honey all over the biscuits, and got their hands all sticky. As soon as they were through, they sat there drinking coffee.

Heck stared at him for a moment then said, "We're out for Sudden Sam Biggers."

"Is he an outlaw?"

"Well, not much of one. He's pretty small potatoes, but we've got to pick him up."

"You think there'll be any shooting?"

"No, Sam ain't a killer." He took another bite of biscuit and then wiped the honey from his lips and mustache. "But he's got a brother who is. His name's Hardy. He's a mean one, and they got a cousin, Dent Smith, that's rough enough to suit anybody. If we catch them, we'll serve the papers on Sam, get the cuffs on him, and bring him home."

"What if his brother's there or this cousin of his?"

"Well, we'll have to do it anyway."

Riordan began cleaning the frying pan and then stored it away, for he knew they would leave as soon as possible. "Has this Sudden Sam ever killed anybody?"

"Nope."

"What's he wanted for?"

"He's wanted 'cause he robbed Jim Tyler's widow." Heck's eyes glinted with anger. "He was my partner, Jim was, as good a man as I ever had. He got killed by Henry the Fox. I'm going to stop that gentleman's clock. You see if I don't! I'll get him sooner or later."

"Henry the Fox? What is he?"

"He's the roughest outlaw in the Territory. His real name is Henry Beecher."

"And he's the worst man in the Territory?"

"Yeah, I reckon he is, and that's saying a lot. He's got some pretty bad ones working for him. Sal Maglie, Hack Wilson, Red Lyle. A couple more. When they get together it'd take an army to stop 'em. They're all tough. They can all shoot."

After putting the remnants of the food and the utensils away in the pack and tying it on the saddle horn, Riordan climbed on his horse. When Heck came up beside him, he said, "How much did Sudden Sam steal?"

"Two hundred and fifty dollars. . .and two chickens."

The report amused Riordan. "So we're out after a chicken thief?"

"No," Heck said, his voice hard, "we're after a low-down skunk who stole from my partner's widow, and I intend to have his hide for it. We'll put him where the dogs don't bite him."

"Is he fast with a gun, this Sudden Sam?"

"Not a bit. He's slow as mud." He laughed harshly. "Why, you could get a shave and a haircut while he's pulling a gun. But his brother, Hardy, he's fast as lightning, and so is their cousin, Dent. You just let me handle them if we happen to run into 'em. They'd shoot you before you could pull a gun."

❧

Riordan was cooking the last of their bacon and heating the last of their beans. They had traveled hard for three days with no success.

Heck had spoken very little, so Riordan had kept his own counsel. Now he put the beans and bacon onto the tin plates and poured the coffee into the tin cups and walked over. "Marshal Thomas, got the grub."

Heck had been lying down taking a nap. He got up stiffly, stretched, and looked down at the meal. "That ain't much," he said.

"It's all we got, Marshal."

"Well, we got to have grub. I'll tell you what." He picked his plate up and began shoveling the beans into his mouth at a fierce rate and washing them down with boiling coffee. He seemed to have no feeling in his mouth. It was said that Heck Thomas could drink coffee boiling straight out of the pot. "We'll go over to Mason Peterson's store. It ain't but about ten miles. We can get what we need."

Riordan made sure the fire was out, climbed on board Maggie, and said, "Get up!"

Heck was amused. "One thing. There ain't no danger of that horse gettin' a bit between her teeth and runnin' off with you."

"No, she's a lady, she is."

"I never rode her, but she holds up pretty good."

"She's a strong girl."

"What are you doing out here anyway?"

Riordan was surprised. "What do you mean. . .out here in the prairie with you?"

"No, why are you washing dishes and shoveling refuse when you could be doing something easy? You got some education. You been to college?"

"Yes, a little."

"What you doin' out here then? You could work in an office."

"I did help out some in an office at my dad's factory when I was younger. Couldn't stand it. Got bored stiff."

Heck suddenly grinned. "If we run into Henry the Fox you won't be bored stiff."

"Well, have you ever gotten close to him?"

"Oh yeah. Traded shots with him, but both of us missed. He's a slick one, he is. Not very big. He's got small eyes, and they're green. He's not heavy. He's kind of built like a—I don't know, like a panther or something. That's why they call him the Fox, I guess."

They rode on for a time as Heck Thomas described Henry the Fox in his wrongdoings, and finally he said, "You ought to quit this. Go on back and do something that pays more. You're not going to be shoveling out horse stalls the rest of your life, are you?"

"I hope not."

"Why do you want to be a marshal?"

"I've never done anything hard. Everything's come easy to me, and I wanted to find out if I could do something hard."

"Well, you picked a good one. Not what you're doing now, washing dishes, but if we run into some of these outlaws, or wild Indians, you'll find out if you can take it hard. What if you can't?"

Riordan took a deep breath and looked over at Thomas. "Well, I'll have to spend the rest of my life doing something I don't want to do."

"Most of us do that anyway."

They reached the makeshift store a few hours later. Mason Peterson served them himself. They were able to get coffee, beans, salt meat, and a few other things.

After they had acquired all the goods they could think of, Thomas said, "Mason, we're on the scout looking for Sudden Sam Biggers. You seen him?"

Mason was a well-built man. He had lost most of his hair but was not bad looking. "Why, it's funny you should ask, Marshal. He was in here yesterday with his brother Hardy and Dent Smith."

"Aw, we just missed 'em."

"Well, I can tell you where he's going. I heard 'em talking. They're going for Sam's cabin."

Heck looked glum and shook his head. "I was hoping to catch Sam alone. It'd be easier to take him in."

"Well, Dent and Hardy won't take easy, but you know that."

"Thanks a lot, Mason."

The two went outside and loaded the grub and other supplies. Heck was quiet.

"What's the matter, Marshal?"

"Blast it! Seems like everything goes wrong. It'd be easy to take in Sudden Sam, but there'll be three of 'em. If we bump up against 'em, and it comes down to facin' 'em off, you try to keep Sam. Even you can outdraw him."

"You want me to shoot him?"

"Well I don't want you to powder his nose! What do you mean? Don't you know what we're up against here?"

"Well, what about the other two?"

Heck was silent. "I can't beat 'em both. I don't know what it'll be like, but that's what it is bein' a marshal."

"I wish you had a good man along instead of me."

"You keep Sam off of me, and I'll take care of the rest."

135

For the next few hours they rode in a westward direction. There was no question of getting lost because Heck knew exactly where Dent Smith's cabin was.

They stopped late in the afternoon at a stream on the lee side of a mountain. As they watered their horses, Riordan pulled some cheese and crackers out of the sack, and the two munched on them. After they had finished, Thomas brushed the cracker crumbs from his mustache and said, "We're getting pretty close. We'll reach the cabin before dark. I don't want to take 'em on after nightfall, so we'll get 'em out before then."

They continued riding, passing a herd of deer feeding off the bark of saplings, and after a while Thomas threw up his hands and said, "There it is."

"I don't see any cabin."

"That's it."

"That's not a cabin."

"Well, I guess you might say it's a cave. A dugout."

It was a small structure only about ten feet by twenty. Half of it was sunk back into a clay bank. The part that was sticking out was poles and sod and a roof of sod supported by a center pole. There was a shed adjoining it, and the horses were stamping and blowing out their breath.

"Look there. They got a fire going. Must be cooking." He suddenly said, "Take that coat off."

Surprised, Riordan took off his coat.

"Now, take a side approach. Climb up that hill, get up on top, and put that coat on that pipe sticking out up there where the smoke's comin' out. That'll go back and smoke 'em out. As soon as you get the pipe covered, come back here. We'll catch 'em as they come out the door."

Quickly Riordan did as he was ordered. The slope was not steep. He stepped out upon the sod roof carefully. It held his weight, so he put the coat over the pipe sticking up. He saw it was going to drive the smoke back, so turning he made his way back to Thomas.

"Don't stand close to me. Get over there about ten feet away."

Riordan's nerves grew tense. Soon he heard coughing, and the door burst open and two men came out.

"One of 'em is still in there," Heck complained. "That's Sudden Sam on the left and his brother Hardy on the right. You watch out for Sam. I'll take care of Hardy."

Suddenly Thomas raised his voice. "This is Heck Thomas, Sam. I'm takin' you in!"

"You ain't takin' nobody in!" The voice was rough, and it was Hardy who spoke. "Sam ain't done nothin'."

"Hardy, you stand away. I've got no trouble to pick with you, but I'm taking Sam in."

"No, you ain't."

What happened then was so quick that Riordan could not logically follow it. He was watching Sam, but then out of the corner of his eye he saw Hardy draw his gun. Heck must have drawn his own because he got his shot off first, which drove Hardy backward.

Riordan then saw, at almost the same moment, another man come out of the cabin. He knew it must be Dent Smith. He was holding a rifle up, aiming right at Heck when Heck shot Hardy.

Without thought, Riordan pulled his gun and in one practiced motion got off a shot. It caught Dent Smith in the throat. He dropped the rifle and fell back gurgling. He grabbled around on the ground, trying to speak but making only unintelligible noises.

Heck went over and kicked Dent's rifle away and looked down. "Well, you've kilt your last man, Dent Smith."

Riordan looked down at the man he had shot. He was sick, but he knew that he had done what had to be done. "I didn't want to kill him," he said hoarsely.

Heck shook his head. "You didn't have no choice." They watched as Dent Smith died, finally stiffening into that attitude of death. Heck Thomas turned and said, "Well, this bothers you, don't it, boy?"

"Yes, sir, it does."

"You never shot a man before?"

"No, I never did."

"Well, it'll bother you some. It goes like that. It did when I got my first man. But Dent Smith is a bad one. He's killed four men and one woman, and he would have added me to his score if you hadn't got him. I know it's going to be hard for you, but you done good. As good as any marshal could have done." He sighed then nodded at Sudden Sam and said, "Let's get this worthless critter in the pokey."

CHAPTER 10

Judge Parker stood at his window, staring down at the gallows. He had been responsible for condemning many men, knowing there was no appeal from his decisions. Every time there was a hanging, he stood at this window, staring down. He never missed a hanging. Most thought he enjoyed watching the men die, but only a few knew he took no pleasure from it. He just felt it was his duty. If he was going to command the ultimate sentence, he should be able to face its carrying out.

His attention was drawn to a man riding up to his building. He watched as Heck Thomas stepped out of the saddle, took a deep breath, and then made his way across the dusty street. Within a few minutes, Heck knocked on his door. "Come in."

Heck entered with his hat in his hands.

"Hello, Marshal. Have a seat."

Heck sat down heavily.

The judge poured two glasses of water and handed one of

them to Heck. "You look dried out."

"I am. This summer's got the best of me. I read a book about Eskimos living on top of the ice. I wish sometimes I had the luck to be born there."

"Well, you'd be just as unhappy there, I guess, wishing you were down here in Fort Smith with the sun burning your brains out. Well, tell me about the scout. Did you catch up with Sam?"

"We sure did, Judge, but the trouble was he had his brother Hardy and Dent Smith with him."

"That's a bad horse." Judge Parker frowned. "Were you able to sneak up on 'em?"

"Well, Judge, we had to hunt 'em pretty hard. Finally found out from a store down there that they'd gone to Sam's cabin. We took out after 'em and got there just before dark. I didn't want to tackle 'em in the dark, so I sent young Riordan to cover up the smokestack and force 'em out."

"Has that young fellow been able to keep up with you?"

Heck scratched his head and said thoughtfully, "You know he did. He's got more stamina than you'd think. He looks like he's little, but he must be made out of steel wire."

"What happened then?"

"Well, he got on top of the dugout, covered up the stovepipe, then he come back down, and we waited. Just like I knowed would happen, the smoke backed up into that dugout, and pretty soon Sam came out, and Hardy was with him. I didn't see Dent, so I told Riordan to take care of Sam. He's a slow draw and a coward anyway, but Hardy's different. So I kept my eye on Hardy. That was sort of a mistake. He went for his gun, and you know how quick he is. I pulled at the same time, and I got off a shot. But then I heard Riordan yell, 'Look out!' and knew Dent had come out of that dugout. As soon as I fired at Hardy, I started to turn, but right on top of my shot came another one. I thought Dent had missed me somehow. I turned around, and there was that young fellow Riordan with his gun out. He had hit Dent right in the throat, and that done him in. He fell down and gurgled for a while, and then he died."

"You mean that young man beat Dent to the draw?"

"I don't see how he done it. But Dent is a bad guy, and he's killed his share of folks. I wasn't sorry to see him go."

"How did Riordan take it, killing a man?"

"Not good. He's tough enough to keep up with me, and he can pull a gun quicker than I thought, and he must be a good shot 'cause he hit Dent right where it done the most good. But he was kind of green."

"Did you ask him?"

"Sure did. He said it made him kind of sick, but I remember when I killed my first man. I didn't take it too good either. But let me tell you this, that young man is better than he looks. I'll partner with him anytime, Judge."

Parker listened as Heck talked for a while. When Heck left, Parker sat down, pulled a paper from his desk drawer, took the pen, and dipped it in the inkwell. He began to write:

My dear Mrs. Riordan,

   I take this opportunity to write with what I think is very good news. I think I've told you we followed your

*advice and poured every dirty, hard job we could on
your son. It didn't do any good, however, not from your
standpoint. He stayed cheerful and did everything that
Marshal Swinson put on him. Never said a word, always
with a smile. Well, that impressed me very much. I know
you may not agree with this, but I think he's at least learned
a little bit about how to become a man. He's got all kinds
of determination. What I would like is for you to consider
letting me give him more responsibility. I don't mean to
make a marshal out of him and send him out on dangerous
missions, but there are other things he can do, for example,
delivering summons, and I'd like to try him for that. I will,
however, await your reply, and whatever you decide will be
the way it is.*

*Respectfully yours,
Judge Isaac Parker*

He sealed the envelope, put it on the desk with other mail he had answered, and then smiled. "That young man has come a long way, and I know his mother will be proud of him."

Rosa was sitting in the parlor, mending one of her sister's dresses. Her grandfather sat across from her. She looked up when he cleared his throat, obviously wanting her attention.

"Well, time for a little foolishness, I guess."

"What kind of foolishness, Grandfather?"

"Olan Henderson, a rich rancher on the Arkansas side of the

Territory not far from Fort Smith, is throwing a big wedding. He's making a celebration out of it. He's going to have dancing and drinks and food and entertainment. I think you ought to go."

Rosa had heard about the wealthy rancher and how he was marrying his daughter off. He lived so close to Judge Parker's court that for the most part the bandits stayed away from him. He had only the one daughter, and he decided it would be an event that the Territory would never forget. He had instructed his hands to build a six-inch platform, which would be the venue of the wedding ceremony itself and also be a dance floor after the wedding. He had made arrangements for music and had killed two heavy beef critters to barbecue and cut up into different sorts of meat dishes. He was a drinking man himself and would provide strong spirits for those who drank and lemonade for those who didn't. He sent out general invitations to as many of his neighbors as he knew, and one of those had come to Frank Lowery. "I'd like to. Could I take Raquel with me?"

"Why, of course. You two probably need some pretty dresses."

"I don't have much and neither does Raquel, but we'll get some material, and we'll deck ourselves out like the Queen of Sheba."

Indeed, it was a big job, but Rosa and Raquel had Chenoa and Ethel to help. They were all good seamstresses, and they had plenty of time.

When the day of the wedding came, they had the dresses ready. They put them on, and Frank and Mateo admired them.

"That's a beautiful dress, daughter," Mateo said.

Indeed, Raquel did look beautiful in a mild green dress. Her waist was tiny, and the bodice was crossed over in the front.

"Thank you, Father." She turned. "Grandfather, isn't Rosa beautiful?"

"She certainly is," he said. "You look sweet, darling."

Rosa was pleased that her grandfather was now saying gentle, kind things he would never have thought of before.

He looked at Rosa and smiled. "You are as beautiful as any woman in the Territory."

Rosa didn't think that was true at all, but she did feel pretty in the blue dress with a tight bodice defining the high richness of her bosom and the elegance of her waist. The tight sleeve of the upper arm flared out with ruffles, and the skirt flared out at the hem.

She smiled. "Oh Grandfather, you just think that because we are your granddaughters."

"Well, all I can say is you two better take your guns along. You're so pretty them men are going to try to run off with you."

"Well, they won't do that," Rosa said. "I wish you would both go."

"Somebody's got to stay here and take care of the place."

"That's why you hired two new hands." Indeed, they had hired a man called Whitey Ford and another called Felix Mantilla. This would allow Ringo and Ned to escort her and her sister to the dance. Blinky had no interest in going. He said he would stay around and watch the place.

Finally it was time to go, and they got into the wagon. It was quite a long ride, and they were glad to arrive at Henderson's ranch. They met his daughter, Hettie, who was marrying a man named William Logan.

"We're glad to see you ladies." Olan Henderson smiled. "Don't you look pretty! I can't answer all these young fellows that are coming. Some of them will be up to no good. You just watch yourself."

"Thank you, Mr. Henderson. We'll be careful."

The wedding came before the dance, so when Henderson had gotten the preacher in the front, everyone gathered around to listen as he talked about the sanctity of marriage. Finally he was through, and the bride came forward.

"Isn't the bride beautiful?" Rosa whispered to Ringo, who was standing next to her.

"All women are beautiful," he whispered back.

She laughed at him. "You don't really think that."

"Sure I do." He moved closer and put his arm against hers. "When are you going to have your wedding?"

She liked Ringo Jukes very much indeed. He was a bit forward, but she knew he admired her as a woman. They both had senses of humor, and now she said, "Well, I'll have a wedding when I find a man who will do everything I tell him."

She expected Ringo to scoff at that, but he said, "Why, you know I feel the same way."

"You don't really."

"Why, I do. You know there's a verse in the Bible that I'm partial to."

"I didn't know you knew anything about the Bible."

"Well, I know this one. It says, 'When a man hath taken a new wife, he shall not go out to war, neither shall he be charged with any business: but he shall be free at home one year, and shall cheer up his wife which he hath taken.'" He grinned at her and winked. His eyes were full of fun. "Ain't that a doozy? So you see, if you take me for a husband, I'll do nothin' but cheer you up for a whole year, Miss Rosa."

"I don't know how you found that in the Bible," she said. She was amused but also impressed that he knew such a verse. "Well, I'll tell you more about my plans after this wedding is over. Come on. The dancing's starting."

Rosa discovered that, as she expected, Ringo Jukes was a fine dancer. He was handsomely dressed in a gray suit she had not seen before, and she felt the eyes of many women taking him in. For a moment she found herself wondering what it would be like to be married to him. She was sure that he was speaking playfully about staying home for a year, but no man she had ever talked to had even such an idea as that.

Rosa was enjoying herself tremendously. She seldom lacked for a partner, if she wanted one. She did sit out a couple of dances as she needed some time to catch her breath and get a drink of lemonade.

The dance had been going on for some time when a tall man suddenly stood up in front of Rosa. "Don't know anybody to introduce me, and I don't want to be brash, but I'm Charles Rhodes. You're Miss Rosa Ramirez, I understand."

"That's right. Glad to know you, Mr. Rhodes."

"Just Charles is fine." He hesitated and said, "I've been meaning to come over and welcome you. My ranch is about twenty miles west of yours. Could I have a dance?"

"Of course." The two moved around the floor. After a couple of minutes, he asked, "Are you Frank Lowery's granddaughter?"

"Yes, I am."

Rhodes looked uncomfortable for the rest of the dance. When the music was over, he led her to the refreshment table. He seemed to be searching for words. After offering her a glass of lemonade, which she declined, he took one himself. After a long drink, he said, "I've been meaning to come over to your place, but your grandfather wouldn't like it."

"Why not?"

"Well, we had a little trouble quite a few years back. Frank got peeved at me, and of course, I got peeved at him."

"What was the quarrel over?"

"Oh, it was about a horse that we didn't agree on. But you know your grandfather holds a grudge pretty well."

"Yes, I've heard my mother say that. He's stubborn."

"Well, what I would like to ask, Miss Ramirez, is if I could come over and call on you, and maybe you could get your grandfather to forgive me about that horse?"

"Why, of course, Mr. Rhodes. You just come. Grandfather is older now, and he's mellowed quite a bit."

"Well, you can look for me then." He looked around and said, "I don't get around to many things like this. Before my wife died, we used to go out to dances and such things quite a bit. Been kind of lonesome without her."

"How long has that been?"

"It'll be four years now. She was a wonderful woman."

"I'm sorry."

"So am I. It's hard to lose someone, isn't it?"

After the dance, Ned Little, one of the hands she'd come to

like, came over and spoke to her. "I saw you talking to Rhodes."

"Yes, who is he?"

"A big rancher. His wife died a few years ago. He and your grandfather had an awful ruckus."

"He told me about it. Said it was a fuss over a horse."

"Well, it was a little bit worse than that. I never knew the ins and outs, but your grandfather despises him."

"I don't know, Ned. He asked if I'd try to make Grandfather listen to him. I think he was wanting to apologize. I told him to call on us. Maybe I can get Grandfather to forget the quarrel."

"Well," Ned said, "your grandfather hasn't set any records for forgiving folks, but now he's old and not too long for this world, I guess. Wouldn't hurt to have a friend. He's a rich man, and when trouble comes, all of us need to stick together. There's enough bad men that the good men need to do their thing together."

❧

A week after the dance, Rosa answered the door and was pleased to see Charles Rhodes. She smiled and greeted him warmly. "I'm glad to see you, Charles. Come into the house. I told Grandfather you might be coming."

Charles looked slightly sheepish. "Did you take his gun away from him?"

She smiled even wider. "No, but I told him he had to be civil."

Rhodes shook his head. "I was in the wrong about that horse deal, and I'm just too stubborn to admit it when I'm wrong."

"Well, you're doing the right thing now. Come on in."

They found Frank and Mateo, as usual, playing checkers.

Rhodes said at once, "Hello, Frank. I ask your pardon for calling without permission."

"No, my granddaughter said you might be coming." He got to his feet and stared at him and said, "Been a long time since we spoke."

"Well, it was my fault, Frank. I was wrong about that horse, and I want to apologize to you. As I told your granddaughter, I don't apologize good or easy, but I felt bad about it. Not many of us left. We need to stick together."

Frank stepped forward and stuck his hand out. "That's good enough for me. This is Rosa's father, Señor Ramirez."

"I'm glad to know you, sir. Your daughter graced the dance last week. The prettiest woman there."

"Now, that's enough of that." Rosa smiled. "Will you have some refreshment?"

"I'd really rather you show me around the ranch and any horses you might have. I'm always in the market for a good mount."

"He's got lots of money, Rosa. Be sure you gouge him." Frank smiled.

"Oh, Grandfather, I won't do that. Come along, Charles."

The rest of the afternoon was pleasant. She found herself liking Rhodes very much. True, he was a willful man. She had found that out from several sources, but he wasn't that way with her. His manners were perfect.

When he left he said, "I thank you for making the way for your grandfather and me to bury the hatchet. Next time maybe I can come without a guilty feeling."

"You're welcome anytime, Charles."

"I'll take you up on that, and I'll be back to pick up that bay stallion that I liked so much." He swung into the saddle and rode away.

She watched him go and wondered what it would be like to be married to him. *That's what all women do*, she thought. *When they see a man, they wonder if he'd make a good husband. This one's rich, good looking, got good manners. Got a quick temper, they tell me—but so do I.*

She thought about him often the rest of the day and even dreamed about becoming his wife that night.

The next day she went riding on the edge of the property, just looking things over. She was returning to the house when suddenly she saw a man riding close.

He announced himself. "My name is Henry Beecher."

Henry the Fox, she thought. *He doesn't look like an outlaw.*

Indeed, as she studied him, she saw he was well dressed. He had a gun at his side, as most men did in the Territory, but he had removed his hat when he spoke to her.

"I'm Rosa Ramirez."

"I'm glad to know you. I've come to look over your horses. I've bought several from your grandfather over the years."

Rosa did not know whether to mention she knew he was an outlaw.

He said, "I'm in the market for another mount."

"My grandfather doesn't do much business. That's why he sent for me and my family."

"Well, maybe you can show me a good horse. I'm partial to mares."

"Come this way." She rode down to the stables.

He kept beside her, speaking favorably about the ranch. She showed him the horses and named a rather high price on the mare that he liked.

He reached into his pocket, pulled out a sack, and said, "I've got these gold coins, just about the right amount." He counted them out and put them into her hand.

She slipped them into the pocket of her riding skirt.

They talked for a while, and even though she knew he did terrible things, she found herself enjoying their time together. He was a bad man, everyone had told her that, but somehow he just didn't look it. His face was pleasant. He was handsome with fair hair and pale green eyes such as she had never seen on a man.

He suddenly said, "I see they've told you about me."

"Yes, I have heard of you, Mr. Beecher."

"Just call me Henry. Well, I don't deserve any medals, but half the things they say about me I didn't do. Every time there's trouble they say, 'Well, that Henry's been at this.' I know my reputation's bad, but I hope you'll give me a chance to get to know you."

She started to speak, but then more quickly than she thought a man could move, he reached forward, put his arms around her waist, and drew her close. He kissed her before she could even react. She finally struggled back and pushed him away. She was angry and said, "That was not a gentlemanly thing to do!"

"I'm no gentleman." Henry laughed at her. "I'll take the mare with me." He went into the corral, put a loop over the mare's head with a practiced motion, and led her out. As he left, he lifted his hat. "I'll be seeing you, Miss Rosa."

As soon as he was gone, she turned and saw Ned stepping out from behind the barn. He had a rifle in his hand. "I was just about ready to shoot him."

"Is he really as dangerous as they say, Ned?"

"He's worse. You know he's smooth. Don't let that fool you. Don't ever let him catch you alone."

Rosa thanked Ned and went about her way. All that day she thought about how a man could be that attractive and be such a villain.

❧

Three days after the Fox bought the mare, most of the crew had gone to take a herd to better grass. Blinky had stayed back, along with Whitey Ford, the new hand.

Rosa was in the house talking with her father when suddenly they heard gunshots.

Then the door opened, and Blinky said, "It's raiders! They're after the horses!"

Instantly Rosa and Juan grabbed the rifles that they kept by the door and stepped out onto the porch. At least half a dozen men were opening the corral gate. Without hesitation, Rosa raised her rifle and sent off a shot.

One of the men hollered, "Shoot 'em down! Shoot 'em down!" and the men began shooting at the two, who took cover.

She was aware that Blinky and Whitey were dodging across the open ground, firing and looking for shelter. Suddenly she recognized George Pye and the two men who had tried to take their horses before. They had three more men with them and were leading some of the horses out. She was also aware that her father and grandfather had stepped outside, both with rifles, and they were pouring a withering fire. One of the outlaws cried out and grabbed his side. Then another one took a shot. Someone yelled, "Let's get out of here!"

Rosa saw Pye raise his rifle and fire, and the shot struck Blinky who was knocked over backward. All of them on the porch kept up their fire, but the men got away with half a dozen horses.

Quickly Rosa ran to where Blinky was lying. The shot had taken him in the heart. He had probably died before he hit the ground. Tears came to her eyes, for the little man had been kind to her.

Whitey came limping back.

"Did you get hit, Whitey?"

"Just pinked me in the leg. Missed the bone."

"Let's get Blinky in the house, and then I'll put a patch on it."

They carried the body of the rider into the house. She washed Whitey's wound and put a bandage over it.

There was nothing to do but wait for the crew to return. Three hours later they returned.

As soon as he stepped out of the saddle, Ringo Jukes saw her face. "What's wrong, Rosa?"

"There were raiders. They killed Blinky and shot Whitey."

Ned said, "Scatter out. They may come back."

"I don't think so. They took six of our horses."

"We'll nail things down here, and then we'll go after 'em."

"We've got to take care of Blinky first."

They buried Blinky the next morning, and it was a solemn

chore. They had all liked the small man.

An hour later, Rosa called Juan to one side. She had saddled her horse, and she told him, "I'm going to Judge Parker's to get marshals."

"You can't do that. Not by yourself."

"They won't catch me on this horse. She's the fastest one we've got. Don't tell Grandfather or Father until I've left."

"Let me go with you."

"No, they might come back. They'll need all the help they can get here. I'll be fine."

Juan argued with her for a time, but she knew what she had to do. . .for all of their sakes. She mounted her horse, waved good-bye to her brother, and rode away from the ranch.

CHAPTER 11

Judge Parker leaned forward, opened an envelope, removed the letter inside, and spread it out. His wife sat across from him, and he looked up from time to time. She was cracking black walnuts on the face of an iron with a hammer and putting the nuts into a small jar.

Parker read the letter carefully then leaned back and stared thoughtfully across the room. Finally he said, "Dear, do you remember the woman named Eileen Riordan?"

"Of course I do. She's the one who had the young son who wanted to become a marshal. How is the young man doing?"

"Well, we're very pleased with him. As you know, she insisted we give him the worst jobs we could, hoping he would get tired of it and return home. But just the opposite happened. No matter how hard or dirty the work, or how difficult it was, Riordan got at it, always smiling, never complaining. We're very pleased with him."

"Well, that's good news."

"Actually, there's better news than that. Heck usually wears young men out, the marshals that go with him. He's tireless himself, and he thinks everyone else is. So, we sent him out on what should have been an easy job. You've heard of Sudden Sam. He's a crook but not a vicious one. Never killed anybody. Never shot anybody that I know of. But he's a burglar and a robber. Heck hated him because he robbed the widow of his partner of some money and two chickens. So, we sent him out. We decided Heck could go arrest him and bring him back—and he took young Riordan with him."

"Did they catch him?"

"Well, they did, but he had two rough gunmen with him. They tried to kill Heck, and this young man shot the man that was about to do the job. Heck said he would have been dead for sure if young Riordan hadn't been there. He was amazed that the young man was so quick with his gun. And so am I."

"That sounds like he's ready for something else."

"That's what I felt, too. So, a few days ago I wrote Mrs. Riordan a letter and told her all about her son. This is her answer:

"Dear Judge Parker,

What you tell me is encouraging, although it frightens me a little. As you know I'm partial to my youngest son, Faye, and I hesitate to do anything that would put him in danger. However, it sounds to me as though he has done everything we both asked, and if you think well, I would encourage you to give him more responsibility. I'm sure you know better than I how to handle this matter. I can't tell you how much

I appreciate your consideration, and as you say, your wife concurs with this in the decision to help me bring my son to a higher part of manhood than he felt he had. So, please do your best for him.

Sincerely yours,
Eileen Riordan"

He put the letter down and said, "She's changed her mind."

"Yes, she has. Do you have any idea how you can help the boy more?"

"Well, I'm going to find some way to get him out on the field. Nothing very difficult, but I'd like to help the young man. I think he has great potential."

"Well, you must do it, Isaac. She kept the boy close, and that's the way we mothers are. But he wants to prove that he is a grown man. If I remember correctly, he had a father and two brothers who are very manly, and he feels that he's failed them."

"I can see how that would affect the boy. We'll do that. I'll give him a chance."

❧

Riordan stepped inside the judge's office and was somewhat intimidated. Judge Parker, however, smiled and said, "Sit down, young man. There's something I want to tell you."

"Have I done anything wrong, Judge?"

"No—no. Quite the opposite. Let me tell you what I've done. We were so happy with the way you conducted yourself on the job with Heck Thomas that I wrote to your mother and told her how well you had done. I told her you had completed every dirty, hard job we gave you without complaining, and then when we sent you on the scout you saved Heck Thomas's life. I told her how proud we are of you."

"Well, thank you for writing her, Judge. I've got a lot to learn, but I'd like to try a real job."

"All right, Riordan. How about this? The first request we get that I think you can handle without putting yourself in much danger, we'll send you on a scout."

"Oh, that's fine, Judge. I appreciate it."

"It won't be a big job," Parker warned, "but you need to learn how to work in the Territory."

"I promise I'll do the very best I can. Thank you for this opportunity, Judge."

Riordan did not change his ways. He stayed under Marshal Swinson's orders, still cleaning out the stables, washing the dishes, and helping the cook when he could.

He had been out one afternoon hauling the fewmets, as they called the stable sweepings, to the judge's garden and was sweaty and filthy from head to foot. He had on a floppy-brimmed hat that came down over his ears so he knew he was not much to look at.

Heck Thomas stopped him to say, "Well, Riordan, the judge tells me he's going to put you to work."

"Yes, sir."

"I wish you could go with me on this job, but it's a little bit rough."

"Maybe I can go with you some other time, Marshal Thomas."

"I'm sure you can. I told the judge so. Hang in there, young man. Your opportunity is coming."

For the next hour Riordan kept hauling the refuse of the horses' stalls to the judge's garden, which was blooming well from so much fertilizer. He was pushing a wheelbarrow toward the garden when he saw the judge and Marshal Swinson come out of the courthouse, joined by some of the other marshals. *Maybe I'll get to go on a scout soon*, he thought.

He looked up to see a young woman in a riding outfit such as he had never seen ride in at a gallop. She pulled the horse up to an abrupt halt and dismounted. Being curious, Riordan moved closer to where he could hear what was said.

Rosa climbed off her horse. It was a longer ride than she had anticipated, and she was exhausted. She had met Judge Parker at the wedding, and she glanced around to see that not much was happening. One man in filthy clothes was hauling something with a wheelbarrow. She ignored him, well aware that everyone was staring at her.

She walked right up to the judge and said at once in a loud voice, "Judge Parker, our ranch has been raided, and a man has been killed. I saw the men who did it. The leader was George Pye, and two of the men with him were Vernon Epps and Boog Powell. It was the same three men who tried to take the horses from us earlier. We took their guns from them, and George Pye swore he would get even. He killed one of our hands, and I want him and the others hanged on your gallows. We need a posse of your marshals to run them down."

Parker removed his hat and ran his hand over his hair. He was disturbed and shook his head saying, "Well Miss Ramirez, it's not quite that easy."

"Why isn't it? I saw the men who did it. I'll testify against them. I've heard you have over a hundred marshals."

"But they're out in the Territory. Our men don't stay here long, Miss Ramirez. They do their jobs, they come in, they get other assignments, and they're gone again as soon as possible. I'll tell you what, we'll send a man out to your place as soon as one comes back. Right now we don't have anybody."

"Don't tell me you don't have a single marshal to catch a cold-blooded murderer."

Parker's glance fell on Riordan, who had stopped and was listening to the conversation. He turned to Swinson and said under his breath, "We can send Riordan. He can stay at their ranch until some of our men are available to track the killers down."

"That's right, Judge. He can't get hurt just looking out for these folk. The killers have gone underground by this time. It's going to take some good men to root 'em out."

Parker nodded then put his hat back on. "Miss Ramirez, I'm sending you the one man we have. He'll stay close to your ranch and guard your folks, and then as soon as I get a few men, I'll send them. They can run down Pye and his band."

"Thank you, Judge," Rosa said. "I knew you would help us."

Judge Parker called out, "Riordan, come here!"

Rosa turned to see the man who was hauling compost in a wheelbarrow come forward. He was filthy from head to foot, had on a floppy hat, and looked young and inexperienced.

"Riordan, this is Miss Rosa Ramirez. You go with her and guard her family. We'll send a posse out as soon as some men get back."

Rosa stared at the sorry figure that stood before her. Then she turned and said, "You're sending that fertilizer hauler to help us?"

"He is better than he looks, Miss Ramirez."

Rosa was fighting hard to hold back angry tears. "I thought you'd give us somebody to help...a marshal. That dirty clodhopper might as well go on hauling refuse for the garden!" She turned, went to her horse, and started to mount.

Parker went to her quickly and said, "Just a minute. Let me explain."

Swinson ran over and said, "Riordan, saddle up, get your guns, and go with this woman."

"Don't I have time to clean up?"

"Nope, she's mad as a hornet. You stick with her. You can clean up when you get there."

Rosa waited, hardly listening to the judge who was trying to explain that Riordan was new and not yet ready for a full-time marshal's badge but that he'd help the best he could.

When Riordan rode up on a sorry-looking horse still in his filthy clothes and his floppy hat, Rosa stepped into the saddle and gave him a withering look. "You might as well stay here and clean up after the horses."

The man did not blink or smile. He said, "Wherever you lead, Miss Ramirez, I'll go with you."

She snorted and kicked her horse's flanks and rode out. Riordan followed her on his placid horse.

Marshal Swinson and Judge Parker watched Riordan and Rosa riding off toward her ranch.

"That young woman's pretty fierce, Judge. By the time Riordan's listened to her for a couple of days, he'll probably be ready to come back and clean up the stables."

Judge Parker shook his head. "She'll give him a hard time, Chester, but you remember we gave him a hard time. He never flinched. They're like fire and water, those two, but I hope they can live with each other long enough to do some good. Riordan is better than he looks, but all Miss Ramirez can see is that he doesn't look good. They'll just have to live with each other long enough for us to send some men who might do better."

"I just hope they don't kill each other," Marshal Swinson said. "I don't think it's going to work."

"It'll have to work," Judge Isaac Parker said. He gave a final look in the direction of the two who had disappeared into the distance, shook his head, and went back into the courthouse.

PART THREE

CHAPTER 12

The ranch was in sight now, but when Rosa turned and looked back over her shoulder, she saw that Riordan was far behind, his horse plodding slowly. Anger seemed to bubble within her, and she waited there, the mare shifting under her weight, flaked with sweat. She let him get close and then said, "Spur that worthless horse!"

When he did not advance any faster, she waited until he was even with her, his eyes watching her cautiously. He gave her a mild answer, "Miss Ramirez, Maggie here does the best she can."

Twilight had begun to creep over the land, the low hills to the west turning dark against the sky while the flatlands of the east slowly shadowing as night crept over them. The day had been blistering hot, sharp and bright, with no clouds to bring any relief from the sun's rays.

Now as Rosa stepped off her horse, the sun had settled westward and seemed to melt into a shapeless bed of gold flames as it touched the faraway mountains. She advanced to the porch, having seen her father and her grandfather sitting there in their cane-bottom rocking chairs. Pearl shadows had come on the eaves of the house and the barn, and the dusty road took on soft silver shadings. Soon evening's peace would magnify the distant sounds, but all the beauty of the sunset meant nothing to Rosa, for she was still furious over the treatment she had received from Judge Parker.

Shaking her head with disgust, Rosa spurred the mare, which despite being hard ridden, still had some spirit left. She rode up toward the house, and as she drew near, she saw Ned walking across the front yard. She pulled the mare to an abrupt halt, stepped out of the saddle, and said in a spare tone, "Ned, this mare is overheated. Would you please walk her until she cools off?"

"Sure I will, Miss Rosa." He started to ask how her trip went, but seeing her face set with anger thought better of it. He took the lines and moved away.

Rosa gave one disgusted glance backward over the road and saw that the man was still dragging along. She mounted the steps and seeing Ethel standing at the door said, "Ethel, I'm parched. Would you get me some cool water, please?"

"Yes ma'am, I'll do that."

Rosa looked at her father and her grandfather, but her lips were so dry it was difficult to talk. Both of them were sitting in rockers with the checkerboard in front of them. Rosa knew they were both men who were quick to pick up on the moods of others, and her mood at that moment was definitely not favorable.

Ethel appeared at the door with a large glass and a pitcher of water. "I'll just set this here, and you can drink all you want, Rosa."

"Thank you, Ethel." She drained the glass slowly, letting the coolness and the moisture of it seek out her dry tissues. She then poured a second glass half full and then put the glass down on the table.

Frank glanced at Mateo then asked Rosa, "How was your trip? Did you get to see the judge?"

"Yes, I saw him, but precious little good it did me!"

Frank exchanged glances with Mateo. It was her father who asked, "It didn't turn out well, I take it?"

"No, it didn't turn out well! I rode as hard as I could, and when I got there the judge was out in front of the courthouse. I got off my horse and walked right up to him. He was very polite, but then I guess he always is. He asked me what I wanted."

"He didn't ask you in his office?"

"I didn't give him a chance. I told him about the raid and how we lost a man to the outlaws, killed, shot dead in the dust. I told him how we were plagued with outlaws.

"What did he say?"

"Oh, he was sympathetic," Rosa said. "He said he was sorry and that he hoped he could do something."

"I told him flat out what I wanted. I said, 'Judge, we need some of your marshals to run the outlaws down.' He gave me a story about how the marshals stayed out for a long time, sometimes coming in one day and going out the next. Said he didn't have any men right now."

"Well, I expect that's true," Frank said. "This is a big territory. He's had almost two hundred marshals, but he's had about fifty of them shot down. He's got a hard job."

Rosa was beyond reason, however. She turned and looked out at the road and saw that the rider was moving along at the same pace. In a tone dripping with anger, she blurted out, "There's what he sent us."

The two men watched as the rider got off his horse, tied up at the rail, and came to stand on the ground in front of the steps.

"This is the famous marshal," Rosa said. "He claims his name is Riordan, but I just call him fertilizer hauler."

Both men were shocked at her anger, and she smiled in a humorless, bitter expression. "That's what he was doing. Dressed like he is now in filthy clothes and hauling refuse out of the stables."

Frank cleared his throat. Finally he said, "Well, Riordan, have you been a marshal a long time?"

"Just since three o'clock, sir."

His answer shocked both Mateo and Frank, but it was Rosa who snapped bitterly, "Well, he's been a marshal now for at least four or five hours, but that ought to be plenty of time to make him into a great hunter."

Mateo now cleared his throat and turned to look at the man more closely. "Didn't they have any more experienced men, Riordan?"

"No, sir, they didn't."

Rosa spoke up at once, disgust in her tone. "All they had was this famous stable cleaner, and I found out he's also able to wash dirty dishes." She slapped her hands together and knew it was not difficult to read her mood. She was still furious and gave Riordan a look of utter disgust, saying, "Go back to Judge Parker. I'm sure he misses your services. A hauler of fertilizer! I'm sure that'll be handy when Henry the Fox brings his band and kills all of us!" She whirled and went into the house, slamming the door behind her.

Frank got to his feet and walked to the edge of the porch. "She's a little bit upset, Marshal."

"Yes, sir, I can see that. I don't blame her much, but she's telling the truth. All of the marshals were gone at the moment. I've been working for the marshals for some time now, but this is the first time the judge has sent me out on any kind of a job."

Indeed, Riordan looked young and inexperienced, and his clothes were filthy, his face was dirty, and the shape of his hat shed an innocent face not at all like the hard-bitten marshals that Frank had seen coming out of Judge Parker's court.

"Why don't you get settled in, Riordan. I guess you could use a bath and some clean clothes." He lifted up his voice and said, "Ned, come here a minute, will you?"

Ned Little came quickly to stand beside Riordan, giving him a cautious look.

"This is Riordan. He's from Judge Parker's court."

"Glad to know you, Riordan. I'm Ned."

Frank said, "Ned, why don't you help him get settled in. Find a place for him to sleep, and maybe he can change his clothes and get cleaned up by suppertime."

"Yes, sir, I'll take care of that."

From the time Ned had laid eyes on Riordan he had been filled with questions. He managed to ask a few as he led Riordan around to the side of the house toward a long, low structure. "That's the bunkhouse where you'll be staying. You been with the marshals long?"

"Not too long."

"I've seen a few of the marshals. You seem younger than most of them."

"I guess that's right. The judge agreed to take me on. He let me do a few odd jobs while I was getting ready for the big ones."

"Well, this is a big one all right." He entered the door, and when Riordan followed him, he gestured with his hand. "Take that bunk over there."

The place was a mess, Ned knew, but Riordan made no comment. He simply said, "Thank you, Ned."

"Tell you what. Why don't you wash up a little bit and change your clothes. Supper will be ready soon."

"Well, to tell the truth I don't have any more clothes. Miss Rosa left in such a hurry, and the judge shouted at me to follow her. All I had time to do was get my rifle and my pistol and get in the saddle. She was almost out of sight as it was. The horse I rode is not very fast."

"So, you don't have any clothes except those?"

"Yes, this is all I have."

"Well, we lost a man in a raid. That's what Miss Rosa went to see the judge about, and that's why you're here, I guess. His name was Blinky. I'd known him for five years. Mighty good man." Ned shook his head. "He was about your size. Nobody's had the heart to clean up his things. As far as I know, he don't have any kin around. I believe his clothes would fit you; at least it's better than what you got on." He walked to Blinky's bunk and gathered a few items.

"Thanks, Ned. Where can I wash up?"

"Come here." He walked to the doorway and pointed outside. "See that windmill over there?"

"Don't see many of those."

"Well, it pumps water. There's several buckets there and a big tub. You can go splash around, get yourself as clean as you can, and put on some of Blinky's clothes. You'll be all right."

Riordan picked up the clothes and nodded. "Much obliged, Ned."

Ned stepped outside and watched Riordan walk toward the windmill. He didn't walk like most cowboys. There was nothing bowlegged about him. His legs were straight, and he walked quickly toward the windmill.

Ned turned and went to find Ringo, who was currying his horse out in the stable. "The marshal came in from Judge Parker's court."

"Well, I guess we can use him. What's he like?"

Ned leaned against the wall and watched as Ringo continued to curry the horse. "Well, you can see for yourself at supper. He's not a big man, and he looks terrible."

"What do you mean 'terrible'? He's ugly?"

"No, I reckon he looks fair. I couldn't see him, as he was wearing a floppy hat, but he looks about like a shoe clerk. You know, kind of innocent."

Ringo straightened up and stared at Ned. "All the marshals I've seen are pretty tough. This one sounds different."

"Well, he is different. But you know looks are deceiving. Remember Dirk Patrick?"

"Sure do. He was a bad one."

"Bad as they come, but you remember he had a kind of a prissy look about him, a sissified way. That got a lot of men in trouble. He didn't look like he would fight, but when someone crossed him it was like a stick of dynamite going off. He left a trail of blood all the way across Oklahoma and Texas."

The two men talked about the marshal, and finally Ringo said, "Well, he may look like a schoolboy, but maybe he's better than he seems."

"You ought to see the horse he rode in on. I watched him coming. He's just plodding along like he was on a plow horse."

"Well, there again not all gunfighters are great riders."

"Yeah, but something else bothers me, Ringo. He carries a .38 by his side."

"That's different."

Indeed it was different, for Ned knew every man in the Territory, certainly all of the marshals, carried a larger caliber, with most of them being Colt .44s.

Ringo shook his head. "Well, those little .38s won't knock a man down unless you put a bullet in his brain. Doesn't sound like Miss Rosa got a very good man out of the draw."

"No, she was mad as a hornet when she rode in. I started to speak to her but figured I'd better not."

"Well, we'll find out more about this fellow. What's his name?"

"Riordan is all I heard. Don't know his first name. I'm going to go in and tell the cook to throw on some more steaks, or whatever he's cooking, on the stove. This fellow won't eat much. He's too undersized for that, but I can eat what he leaves."

❦

Rosa came out of a fitful sleep slowly, for she was still tired after the long ride she had made, but she was aware that dawn was coming. As she sat up in the bed and put her feet on the floor, she thought of her trip to Fort Smith and how the judge had seemingly not been willing to help her. With that came the thought of Riordan, and just that one single thought seemed to trigger all the anger she had had yesterday. "What are we supposed to do with a fool like that?" she muttered.

She got out of bed, walked over to the table, and poured tepid water from a ceramic pitcher into an enamel washbowl. Stripping off her nightgown, she washed her face and hands and arms and then went over the rest of her body as well as she could. It was not a bath, but it was her habit to do this every day.

She dressed, putting on her underclothing, her divided skirt, and her white blouse. She put on the vest with the gold coins for buttons, which she had grown fond of. It had four pockets that held small things. Besides the buttons and the pockets, she thought it gave her a rakish look.

She walked over to the window and looked out. The sunrise was slow, and she had noted that the night left the land so gently that things were dim and only an outline. Now the earth was beginning to take form, the distant hills barely visible. Even as she watched, a bird began singing. She did not know what kind. "What have you got to sing about?" she muttered.

Now that she was fully dressed, she went downstairs.

As soon as she entered the kitchen, Ethel turned and said, "Breakfast will be ready soon, Miss Rosa. It's biscuits, gravy, eggs, and ham."

"That sounds good." She began moving around, setting the table, although she knew it was possible that the older men would not get up. She knew they awoke early, but many times they would just lie in their beds resting.

"Mr. Frank said you brought a man back from Judge Parker's court. What's he like?"

"He's not a man. He is little more than a dishwasher."

Ethel blinked and stood staring. "You don't like him."

"I went to get a tough man or about a half dozen to run these killers down. What do I get? A stable cleaner! That's all he's good for, that and to wash dirty dishes. Well, I told him to go back, but I suppose he's still here."

"Well, that's too bad, but maybe if we give him a chance he'll be of some use."

"He'll be of use cleaning the stable," Rosa snapped.

The food was soon ready, and she sat down and ate with Ethel. Her mother came in and joined them. When they were eating, Rosa spoke with bitterness to Chenoa, and Chenoa listened to her silently. "Better not be judging a man. He may be better than he looks."

"Well he couldn't be any worse! Filthy clothes, hands and face all smeared with dirt, and who knows what else. And you should have seen the horse he rode! I had to wait on him. I think he was riding a plow horse."

"Well, you need to give him a chance," Chenoa said, echoing Ethel's words.

"I'll give him a chance. Our stables need cleaning, and there's always dirty dishes."

She fell silent, and the other two women began to talk of other matters of the house. Her mother soon left to wake Juan and Raquel and tell them to come for breakfast. As Ethel brought in some more food for her brother and sister, an idea was forming in Rosa's mind. She finished eating and said, "I've got to go talk to the hands. I'll see you later."

Leaving the house, she noted that the sun was now climbing in the west, throwing its lambent beams down over the earth. She found Ringo, who was coming out of the kitchen shack, which also included the tables for the hands. "Hello, Ringo."

"Hello, lady. You should have been here. That Riordan, he's a better cook than we've had. Made some of the best pancakes I ever ate."

"We don't need a cook. We need a man who can shoot somebody."

"Well, Ned and me talked about it. Sure enough he don't look like much, but you never can tell."

"He rode in on a plow horse. What good is that to us?"

"Well, maybe that was all they let him have at the judge's."

"No, you can tell the way he sat on the plug he's not a rider. I want you to give him some lessons."

"Riding lessons?" Ringo laughed. "What do you mean by that? You said he rode in."

"I want you to teach him how to stay on a fast horse. Start him out with Chief."

Ringo's eyes opened wide, and he passed his hand over his face. "Chief? Why, that's a plum bad horse. He's throwed me and Ned both, and everybody else that I know of."

"Put Riordan on him. He's got to learn somehow."

"Well, that marshal might get hurt. Don't that bother you?"

Rosa smiled, but there was little humor in it. "Of course it does, Ringo. But he won't last against the outlaws if he isn't ready for it. Sometimes you have to endure unpleasant things to get toughened up to complete what needs to be done. I wish we could take it more slowly, as you all did with Juan and me, but we just don't have the time."

Ringo stood looking at Rosa, apparently searching for something to say. Finally he said, "You know, Rosa, you look sweet, but you got some toughness in you."

"All women are like that. Haven't you noticed?"

"Well, not all look as good as you, but all of 'em have a little toughness, I suppose. I don't like this, though. That horse can be plum mean."

"Don't tell Riordan he's a bad horse. Just get him in the saddle and then get out of the way so you don't get stomped."

"Well, it's your say so, Rosa, but we may have a busted up marshal on our hands."

Riordan came out of the kitchen shack. He had helped wash the dishes. The regular cook had left a week earlier, so Riordan had been glad to plunge in to fix pancakes. That was simple enough. He found Ringo Jukes waiting for him.

The husky rider said, "Need to give you some riding lessons."

"Why, I can ride."

"No, I don't mean that old pokey horse you rode in on."

"Maggie is a good horse."

"Look, sooner or later we're either going to be chasing after some outlaws or they're going to be chasing us. In either case that horse is no good. You've got to have a fast mount."

"I haven't had a lot of experience."

"Well, you're fixin' to get some. Come on. I'll pick you out one to start on."

Riordan followed reluctantly, and when they got to the corral he saw that all the hands had gathered, including Ned, who was leaning against the corral post rolling a cigarette. "Want to ride a little bit, Riordan?"

"Sure he does," Ringo said. "Here. Let me saddle this horse up for you."

Riordan had a quick mind. He saw that the men were all grinning, and when Ringo led a beautiful black stallion out of the stable, he was sure that he was in for a thumping. *I've got to do it. No other way out. I hope he doesn't kill me.*

"That horse is named Chief. He's plenty fast," Ned said. "Easy to saddle. He stands just nice and still. You see?"

Indeed, Chief did stand still while Ringo put on a blanket and saddle. He then put the bridle on. Ringo turned and said, "Okay."

Riordan approached slowly. The horse was very large and muscular. He turned and looked at Ringo, and there seemed to be a gleam in his dark eyes. "This horse is pretty hard to ride, I take it?"

"Oh, he's fine. A good horse is always a little harder to ride than your plow horses. They're lively," Ringo said. "But you'll need a lively mount around here, Riordan. Now you just go ahead. Just ride him around the corral here a few times until you get used to him."

Riordan clenched his jaw as he readied for this newest challenge.

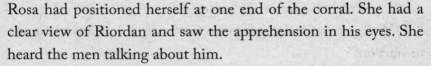

Rosa had positioned herself at one end of the corral. She had a clear view of Riordan and saw the apprehension in his eyes. She heard the men talking about him.

One of the new hands, Charlie Jones, said quietly, "Ned, that's a pretty bad horse. He plowed me up."

"Yeah. He plowed me up, too. He's a good 'un."

"I wouldn't call him a good 'un," Charlie said. "This poor fellow looks like a tenderfoot."

"Well, you know how Ringo is. Always playing a joke."

A sudden impulse came, and Rosa felt that she should try to stop what was about to happen, for it could be dangerous. Still she said nothing. *He shouldn't have come here if he wasn't ready to work.*

She watched as Riordan put one foot in the stirrup then swung his leg over the horse. He grabbed the reins from Ringo, and as soon as he did, Chief exploded with raw strength. Humping his back, he went straight up in the air and came down stiff legged. She saw Riordan jolting up and down in the saddle. He made a wild grab for the horn and missed. He was thrown sideways as Chief twisted and turned like a corkscrew. Three more jumps from

Chief and Riordan lost all control. He sailed up in the air, his arms
flailing, and turned a complete somersault. He landed flat on his
back with a distinct *whump*.

Grandfather, who had come to stand beside her, said, "That
was a bad fall."

"Sure was," Father agreed. "I hope he ain't bad hurt."

Ringo bent over the fallen man and said, "You okay, partner?"

Riordan did not answer, as he was trying to suck air back into
his lungs.

"Well, that was a pretty bad fall. No fun having the air knocked
out of you. You'll be okay. Here. Let me help you up."

Rosa watched as Ringo pulled the smaller man to his feet.

"Well," Ringo said, "maybe we'd better give you a gentler horse."

"No, that's the one I want," Riordan said.

"Oh, come on now, Riordan. This was just kind of a trick. You
don't want that horse. He's a mean one. You could get hurt."

"That's the one I want."

Rosa heard a stubbornness in Riordan's voice and saw that his
mouth was drawn into a tight line.

"Catch him up for me, will you, Ringo?" Riordan asked.

"What in the world is he doing?" her grandfather demanded.

"It looks like he's determined to ride that horse," Father said.

"Why, he can't ride Chief. None of the men can. You'd better
stop it, granddaughter."

"Let him ride."

"He's liable to get hurt."

"None of my business," Rosa said. "You break it up."

"That fellow is more stubborn than he looks." Father nodded.

Rosa saw that Riordan was stepping back into the saddle, and she watched with shock as twice more he was thrown, each time getting up more slowly.

Finally Grandfather shook his head. "This ain't right, Rosa." He entered the corral and came to where Riordan was getting up, his face pale. "That's enough of this horse, Riordan."

"I'd like to try again."

"You can try later." He turned to face Ringo and said nothing, but Ringo's face grew red. "That's all the entertainment today. Ain't there no work for you fellows to do?" he said.

All the hands scattered like quail then, and her grandfather said, "You take it easy for a while. That's too much horse for you right now." He went back, stood in front of Rosa, and bit the words off. "A woman should have some gentleness in her, granddaughter, along with the toughness. I'm ashamed of you."

Rosa flushed, turned, and left, feeling the hard truth of the statement.

❧

Riordan could scarcely move the rest of the day. That night he was so sore he could barely walk.

Ned saw him limping and said, "You know, Riordan, that big tank out there has been in the sun all day, and the water's real hot. Why don't you climb into it? I've always heard that heat was good for taking the misery out of sore muscles."

Riordan could barely turn his head to look at the tank, but he remembered how more than once he'd gotten into hot tubs to ease his aches. "You know, you may be right about that, Ned. Think I'll just go soak for a time."

"Sure, that'll set you up fine!" Ned shook his head, adding, "I didn't know Ringo had such a mean streak. He knows ain't many hands able to stay on Chief."

"I don't think it was his idea."

"Why, he's the one who put you up on that horse."

But Riordan had caught glimpses of Rosa Ramirez watching him take his fall and seeming to enjoy it. It had not surprised him, for he knew that the young woman despised him. "Oh, just guessing, Ned."

Limping out to the large tank, Riordan glanced toward the house but saw that the barn cut off anyone who might be coming from there. Slowly, with several grunts, he stripped off his filthy clothes and boots then climbed up the short ladder into the tank. He eased himself down into the water, which was very hot. Slowly he submerged himself and loosed a sigh of pleasure as his weary muscles seemed to welcome the hot bath. He kept his head above water and let the heat draw some of the aches out of his frame. For a long time he floated, thinking of what had happened. Mostly he thought of the pleasure he had seen in the eyes of Rosa when he had hit the ground with terrible force. *She really enjoyed seeing me get hurt.* The thought disturbed him greatly, for he was accustomed to women who were more gentle.

Finally he reluctantly climbed out of the tank and had put on the lower part of dirty underwear, when a voice caught him unawares.

"Don't you know our animals have to drink water from that tank?"

Turning quickly, Riordan saw that Rosa had appeared and was staring at him. He had always been a modest young man and had an impulse to climb back into the tank. A thin streak of anger touched him then, and he said, "Sorry, Miss Ramirez." He was aware that she was staring at him and saw something in her look that disturbed him. "If you'll leave, I'll put some clothes on."

Rosa laughed harshly. She had come upon him by pure accident, and her first glance of the half-naked body of Riordan had given her a shock. Now she was embarrassed and said, "Get some clothes on. We've got enough scarecrows around here." Abruptly she whirled and disappeared, leaving Riordan to stare after her.

Slowly he put on the dirty, sweat-stained clothes and returned to the bunkhouse. He found the hands sitting at a rickety table playing poker.

Ringo moved his shoulders uncertainly. He cleared his throat then said, "No hard feelings about Chief, I hope."

"Not at all."

Ringo got up and walked over to an empty bunk then gestured at a chest at the foot. "This was George Perkin's place, but he joined up with some wild riders. You might as well have his stuff. He won't be coming back for it. He was a real sharp dresser."

Riordan smiled. "Thanks, Ringo. I appreciate it."

The tension that had been in the room faded, and the card game went on as Riordan put on clean underwear and lay down with a sigh of relief. His last thought was, *That woman sure did enjoy seeing me get thrown. Wonder what she will think of next to humiliate me? Whatever it is I won't let her get to me!*

CHAPTER 13

During the days that followed her encounter with Riordan at the water tank, Rosa became more and more disgusted with him. She thought he was utterly worthless, but one thing that happened surprised her:

Her grandfather had commanded Ned to give Riordan a better horse. "Give him Big Red," he had said. "He's a fast horse. Never bucked in his life. See that the young fellow learns how to ride."

Despite herself, Rosa was interested in the experiment. She watched every day as Riordan saddled the big red gelding, who stood absolutely still as a statue for the process. Unlike other horses, he would open his mouth and take the bit without trying to bite anybody. She watched as Riordan became more and more easy in mounting and began taking Red out for rides during which he would go faster and faster.

One Thursday afternoon, Rosa went outside the house, noting that it was a lazy day and most of the work was done. She saw

Ned whittling in the shade of the big walnut tree and walked over. "Where's the big dishwasher?"

"Why, he went for a ride."

"Did he get the stable clean?"

"Oh, Miss Rosa, you couldn't expect him to do that. None of these marshals ever do anything like work on these ranches. We got a new man, a young man from Mexico to take care of that."

"Where did he go?"

"I seen him about an hour ago riding out east. Didn't say where he was going. I do know he's been studying a map of the Territory and riding over it as much as he can. Looks like he wants to know the country."

"He's just riding around to get out of work. He's a bum. That's all he is."

Her nerves were on edge as she mounted her horse and rode out. She rode for twenty minutes and got to the river. Turning the mare's head, she followed a small branch of it until she saw Riordan seated under a tree. He seemed to be writing something on a tablet.

She stepped off of her horse, tied her to a sapling, and advanced until she was within a few feet of the unsuspecting man. "What are you doing?"

Riordan was startled. He jumped up, holding the pad in one hand and a pencil in the other.

"Are you writing letters?"

"I just like to get away once in a while."

"Who are you writing to?" Rosa demanded.

"Nobody."

"That sounds unlikely." She went forward and snatched the tablet saying, "Are you writing to your sweetheart?"

She looked down at the open page and received a shock. It was not a letter but a pencil sketch of the terrain that lay to the south. There was the small stream, correct in every detail, the plains, and in a bunch of high grass, a six-point buck had lifted his head, his eyes staring, looking as real as life. Far off was the outline of the mountains. "You're drawing pictures!"

Riordan looked embarrassed. "Just a hobby."

Rosa started to hand the tablet to him, but the wind caught the pages and folded them back. She looked down and saw a sketch of herself wearing her riding outfit. Her hat was pushed back on her head, and she was frowning as if she were angry. "What do you mean drawing pictures of me?"

Riordan shrugged. "I don't know. I'm sorry. I just like to draw all sorts of things."

Rosa turned the pages and saw sketches of the ranch, of her mother standing at the cookstove, of Ringo riding a bucking bronc, her father and grandfather playing checkers. "I didn't want an artist," she snapped. "I wanted a tough man to run down some killers. I'm sick of you, you so-called marshal. Take your pictures and go back to Judge Parker."

She turned and walked back, aware that he was following her, trying to apologize. "I'm sorry, Miss Ramirez. I can promise you I won't do any more."

Rosa had reached her horse when suddenly he grabbed her from behind and swung her around. She fought loose and struck at him with a quirt she always carried, but he hardly reacted.

She was shocked when he pulled his gun in one smooth motion and fired it. Twirling she saw an enormous headless rattlesnake thrashing in the weeds.

If there was one thing Rosa Ramirez was frightened of, it was snakes, and this one was a monster. Frozen with fear, even though the danger was passed, she watched until the snake finally grew still. She suddenly realized that she had struck a man who was trying to save her life. She looked at the big snake, which she knew had venom enough to kill her. "I'm sorry—"

She broke off, for Riordan had sat down and taken his right boot off. He pulled the sock down, and she saw the twin punctures. She watched, unable to speak, as he took out a pocketknife and cut a deep etch in both wounds. The blood began to flow freely. He looked up and remarked, "I guess he got me."

Rosa had always been careful of snakes, and she had never seen one any bigger than this. Suddenly she cried, "Get on your horse. We've got to get you to the doctor."

"He's at Fort Smith. I'll be dead by that time."

Quickly Rosa ran over and pulled him to his feet and led him to his horse. "Get on your horse!"

He shrugged, and she ran to her own horse and called out, "We've got to hurry!"

"There's no hurry, Miss Ramirez. I don't think there's any cure for snakebites."

Rosa rushed as quickly as she could back to the ranch. Trying to keep Riordan awake and seated on his horse impeded their progress somewhat. When they arrived at the house, she saw Ned and motioned for him to come.

Ned responded to Rosa's summons by calling out, "Ringo, something's wrong."

The two advanced, and as they did, they saw that Riordan's face was drained and pale, that his eyes were starting to turn upward. "He's been snake bit. Carry him into the house."

There was no need to pull him off, for Riordan fell right into Ned's husky arms. He hurried to the steps and called out, "Riordan's been snake bit! We need to put him in bed."

"Put him in the bed in the front bedroom," Grandfather said. He looked down. "Are you all right, Riordan?"

"I don't—feel so good."

They took him in and cleaned the blood off of his leg as he lay in the bed, but Ned said, "From the looks of those fang marks, it was a big 'un."

"The biggest I've ever seen."

Father had come in. "What gave him that cut on the cheek? That wasn't a snake."

Memory came back, and Rosa flushed, but she said nothing. She sat down beside Riordan. People came and went, and she watched his face as it began to twist in a grimace of pain. He twitched, and his arms and legs were shaking. She reached out and held him down. Finally she was aware that only her grandfather was there.

"I'm afraid he's going to die," Rosa said.

"Well, in the case of snakebites, I guess it's up to God. I've seen men get bitten and die, and I've seen some of them get well."

The only sound in the room was Riordan's heavy and uneven gasping breaths.

She suddenly felt tears running down her cheeks. "It's my fault. I was going to get on my horse, and he grabbed me from behind. I—I thought he was trying to grab me, and I hit him with my quirt." She looked up, her face twisted with grief. "He pulled his gun and shot the snake. He was trying to save my life, and I did that to him."

"Well," her grandfather said, "some things we can make up for and some things we can't. If he don't die, you can tell him you're sorry."

The doctor came, but when he looked at the leg that was terribly swollen, took Riordan's pulse, and felt the feverish brow, he said, "He looks bad, but I think he's over the hump. How long since he was bitten?"

"At least five hours, doctor."

"Well, he'd be dead by now if that were going to happen. He just needs care."

"Tell me what to do, doctor," Rosa whispered. "I'll take care of him."

When Riordan opened his eyes, he could see a ceiling and was aware that he was in a strange room. His leg was agonizing to him, and he groaned. He then turned his head and saw that Rosa Ramirez was sitting there beside him. She had been asleep, but he had awakened her when he groaned.

"You're awake," she said. She leaned over him and said, "You're going to be all right, Riordan."

Riordan was feeling miserable, but he realized that it was the first time she had ever used his name. "Can I have some water?"

"Of course." She quickly poured him a glass of water. He received it with hands not quite steady. She held his head up and helped him drink it. It spilled, running down his neck.

"That's good," he whispered. He looked down and saw his leg, which was terribly swollen. "Not very pretty, is it?"

"But you're going to be all right. The doctor said if you'd been going to die, you'd be dead already. He wants you to try to eat and drink as much fluid as you can. I've got some broth made. I'll go heat it up." She left the room.

Riordan lay there suffering the pain and studying his leg, which seemed to be twice as big as the other one. "Well, ain't this a pretty come off," he whispered to himself.

Rosa entered the room with a bowl and a spoon. She said, "I need to prop you up." She put the bowl and spoon down, took him under the arms, and pulled him to an upright position. She propped his back up with the extra pillow. She fed him the broth and gave him more water when he asked for it.

Finally he said, "That's all I want." He laid his head back and shut his eyes for a moment before opening them again and looking to her.

Rosa put the bowl and the spoon down. She seemed to be struggling with the words to tell him something. Finally she said, "Riordan, when you grabbed me I thought you were trying to kiss me, and I hit you with my whip. Then I saw the snake, and I realized you were trying to save my life. I can't— All I can say is I'm so sorry."

"My fault."

"No, it wasn't. It was my fault."

"I shouldn't have drawn your picture."

"No, I was silly." She hesitated then said, "Maybe you should have been an artist instead of a marshal."

Suddenly Riordan grinned. "That's what my mother said."

Riordan closed his eyes again. After a few moments, he sensed that Rosa had risen from her position. He expected to hear her footsteps as she left the room, obviously thinking he had fallen asleep. But instead, she whispered some words, which he was sure she never intended him to hear.

"I'll never forget what you did, Riordan. Never."

He did hear her leave after her declaration. He kept his eyes closed as to avoid embarrassment for both of them, and his mind kept turning her words over and over.

❧

Riordan was out of bed and had put on a pair of pants with the right leg split, for his leg was still swollen. He hobbled out of the bedroom and saw Frank sitting at the kitchen table. "I'm going out to the bunkhouse. I've had your bedroom long enough."

"You don't have to do that, young feller."

"I'd feel better."

Mateo and Chenoa were both in the room. They came over, and the woman took his hand and kissed it. "You saved my daughter's life."

Mateo did not speak, but his eyes spoke volumes. Finally he said, "You are a good man."

"Anybody would have done it."

As he hobbled out, Frank said, "No, they wouldn't. Some fellows would have run like a scared rabbit when they saw that big snake."

Riordan went outside and crossed the yard, limping badly. He got to the bunkhouse and sat down on the bench outside. He leaned his head back and closed his eyes, for he was still weak. He opened them when he heard footsteps and saw Ringo coming.

Ringo sat down beside Riordan and said, "What happened? We heard all kinds of stories."

"Oh, there was a snake, and I shot it."

"That's not what Rosa says. She said you pulled her out of the way and shot the snake. That it bit you instead of her. She's told everybody on the ranch what a hero you are."

"I'm no hero."

"Well, you sound like one to me. You know. . .if you can shoot the head off a snake that quick, you must be a pretty good shot."

"Just lucky, Ringo."

Ringo rose and turned to leave, calling back over his shoulder as he walked away, "Well, whatever it was, you are a hero to everyone around here now."

After a time, Chenoa brought him some cool lemonade from the springhouse. She whispered to Riordan, sounding much like her daughter, "We will never forget what you have done for us."

Ten minutes later Rosa came and gave him his tablet. She sat down beside him. He could smell the violet scent she used. "I went back and got your tablet, and when I saw the body of that snake I nearly fainted. I'm scared to death of snakes."

"Why, you shouldn't have bothered, Miss Ramirez."

"I know it's important to you. I—I looked at all the sketches." She shook her head and said quietly, "You've got a great talent. You've got the ranch and everybody else right here in this tablet. Some of the horses. All with a pencil. Maybe you ought to learn how to paint."

Despite himself, Riordan smiled. "I thought of doing that once."

"You should do it. Can I have the picture of me?"

"Why, of course."

She picked up the tablet and found the sketch of her. "Sign it and date it."

Riordan laughed. "If van Gogh had signed one of his paintings and a fellow had it now, it would be worth a million dollars. Mine won't be worth a dime."

"Still, I'd like you to sign it."

"Well, let me fill in the details." He took the tablet and the pencil.

She sat beside him, very close, watching as the pencil seemed to fly over the paper. It was almost like magic the way details appeared, and when he gave it to her she said, "Thank you, Riordan."

For a time she tried to find out a little about his past, but he had almost nothing to say.

Finally he said, "Miss Ramirez, I know I'm not what you went for. I knew that when the judge let me come. I thought by this time they'd have Heck Thomas or some of the real marshals here, but I know I'm not what you want. Judge Parker will send you some fine lawmen as soon as he can."

Rosa sat silently for a few minutes. She finally lifted her head and looked him directly in the eye, her expression revealing sincerity. "I am not good at making apologies. I am ashamed at how I reacted by hitting you with my whip. I have realized that you risked your own life to save mine." She leaned over and put her hand on his arm. "I think you're a real marshal, Riordan. Please stay with us."

Riordan was startled. He looked at her and saw the hope and trust she was willing to place in him now. He smiled faintly, saying, "Well, maybe I will."

CHAPTER 14

The sun was falling into the west, throwing a halo of light around the faraway mountains. Rosa had been walking around the ranch looking for nothing really, feeling confused and a bit frustrated. She went into the kitchen. There her mother was sitting at the table peeling potatoes. "Let me help you, Mama."

"Oh, I'm almost done. Sit down and talk to me."

Rosa sighed, settled down on a chair, and locked her fingers together behind her head. She arched her back as if easing tired muscles then said, "I don't really have anything to talk about."

Chenoa looked up from the potato she was peeling and said, "What do you think about the marshal now, the one you referred to as only being capable of cleaning out stables and washing dishes?"

Her mother's words brought a quick glow to Rosa's face. She unloosed her fingers, leaned forward, and stared out the window for a moment then turned to gaze on her mother. "I don't know.

He's not what I thought he was."

"He still doesn't seem like he's the kind of man to be a marshal. All the marshals I've seen around have been older men, rough and knowledgeable of the land and its harshness. You can tell that Riordan's had a different kind of life."

"Yes, he's educated, and he's a talented artist. I don't know what he's doing out here in this wild country. He needs to be in the big city somewhere making a career for himself."

"I've been watching him all the time he's been here. He's a very gentle man. If you talked to most men the way you talk to him, they would have turned you over their knees and spanked you."

"Well, I made a mistake," Rosa muttered. "He looked so awful the first time I saw him at Judge Parker's, and he couldn't ride a horse. I was expecting to get one of the better marshals or maybe three or four of them, and instead I got him."

"Well, you made him pay for it. I don't know why he put up with you."

Rosa shook her head but had no answer. She reached over, picked up a potato, and started to peel it. But she just as quickly dropped it, saying, "I'm going to go outside. I feel like doing something, but I don't know what it is."

Quickly she returned outdoors, made her way to the corral, and for a while curried her mare, Beauty. She was a spirited mare, enjoying giving a good nip once in a while.

"Don't you bite me, Beauty," Rosa said. "I'll send you to the fort to be ridden by one of the marshals." She laughed when the mare whinnied slightly and tossed her head. "You're vain. That's what you are. You're full of pride because you're such a pretty animal."

She curried the horse carefully until her coat was shining and then turned her out to the pasture. "I don't know what to do with myself. I can't go out after those outlaws alone, and according to what Judge Parker says, it may be weeks or even months before he gets any men to send." Dissatisfied with herself, she made her way to the cook shack. She found Riordan in the kitchen cooking something. He had a huge pot on the woodstove, and she stared at him.

"I didn't know you were a cook."

"Well, no one else is doing it, and we've got to have something to eat."

"You should have asked me or my mother."

"Ah, it's no trouble. Just got this big roast and put it in to bake for a while. When it gets tender, it'll be ready to eat. Don't have much to go with it though."

"We have some canned beans up at the house. Maybe you can use those."

"Oh, that would be good. We're always hungry, all of us."

"I'll get some for you later."

She stayed for a while, watching him work in the kitchen and thinking, *If I saw another man cook, I would think he's nothing but a bore and not really a man. Somehow I don't think that about this man. He's different from everybody else.* Finally she got up, saying, "I'll bring the beans down."

Later that afternoon Rosa looked up to see Xeno Brewton riding up. Xeno had been there before. He was a horse trader, of sorts, and often bought from and sold to her grandfather. He paid attention to her, listened to what she had to say, and seemed to be understanding of what a hard time she had had.

"Hello, Xeno."

"Hello, Rosa. My, you're looking first rate."

"Thank you. Come onto the porch. My father and grandfather are up there arguing about something. They always are."

"They are a quarrelsome pair."

"Could you use some cool lemonade?"

"That I could. Thank you very much, Miss Rosa."

Rosa went to the springhouse and pulled out a jug. It was the only cool place during the hot summer months as it was dug back into a hill and covered over with dirt so that it was like a cave. She carefully opened the door, looking for snakes. She remembered that once she had opened the door and a big snake had nearly scared her to death as it slithered out. It turned out to be nonpoisonous, but that didn't matter at the time. She saw no snakes now, however; so she picked up the jug and then stopped at the kitchen and took it out to where the three men were sitting. "Who's telling the biggest lies?"

Xeno shook his head. "It's hard to tell between these two. Both of them exaggerate quite a bit."

She filled all their glasses with lemonade, poured one for herself, and then sat down. She studied her grandfather and saw that he was still looking very tired and weary. *He's not going to live much longer.* The thought flashed into her mind and frightened her. She had become very fond of her grandfather and hated to think about losing him. Her eyes went to her father. Mateo was looking somewhat better. The easy living, good food, and sun had helped him quite a bit. *Maybe he'll get well. I pray God he will*, she thought.

For a while she just listened to the three men conversing. Then she suddenly straightened up as Xeno said, "There was a holdup yesterday."

"Where was this?" Frank asked.

"Just north of Big Mountain. Two armed men held up two men driving a wagon. One of them put up a fight, and they shot him. They let the other one go after they took what was in the wagon."

"What was so valuable?"

"They had some money, and the dead man had a valuable ring. I don't know how the bandits knew it though."

"This country's got more bandits than it has coyotes! Come to think of it, coyotes have more kindness about them than some of these bandits. Who were these men?"

"Well, the one that the driver recognized might be part of George Pye's bunch. It wasn't Pye himself, but he recognized one of his men. I think his name is Vernon Epps."

"Epps— He's a bad one!" Frank exclaimed.

Xeno nodded vigorously. "They're all bad. I wish they'd send the army and clean out all these thugs. They did it to the Indians. I don't know why they couldn't do it to these outlaws."

Rosa said nothing as she sat there listening to the men talk about the robbery and the killing. She left after a time. The one thought going through her mind was, *If Epps was there, probably Pye and the rest of his gang were, too.* She felt frustrated, for there was nothing she could do until Judge Parker sent a group of marshals to clean out the nest of outlaws.

❧

Riordan was riding Red and watched as Brewton picked out a horse and paid for it. Then Riordan went up to him as he was leaving with his new acquisition.

"Hello, Marshal."

"Hello, Mr. Brewton. Did I hear right that you know something about a robbery?"

Riordan straightened up, and his eyes glowed. "Where did it happen?" He listened as Brewton described the robbery, and when he mentioned that it could have been a member of Pye's band, he grew more interested.

Brewton said, "I wish you had the manpower to go after them, but one man don't need to chase around after that bunch. See you later, Marshal."

"Take it easy, Mr. Brewton." Riordan rode slowly toward the stable. He didn't unsaddle Red, but instead he found a pair of saddlebags and went into the cook shack. He put in some bacon and several cans of beans and some day-old biscuits. Going to his bunk, he added a box of .38 shells and went back and put his Winchester in the saddle holster. He then mounted Red and rode out slowly.

❧

Rosa had been watching Riordan from the back porch of the house since he had talked with Xeno. As soon as he rode out, she suddenly realized, *I bet he's going after Epps and his bunch.*

She went to the house and said, "Papa, I'm going out for a ride. I may be late tonight. You and Mama go on to bed."

"Don't stay out too late. The wolves might get you."

"No, they won't. I will shoot them."

Quickly she ran out and saddled Beauty. Rosa then rode out at a swift pace, headed after Riordan. She realized she had no idea what she would say to him. She was curious, however, and wanted to know if he had any plan in his mind for capturing the gang. "Come on, Beauty. Let's go."

❦

Riordan suddenly pulled Red to a stop. His eyes were on the ground ahead, and he had a map out that showed the approximate location where the holdup had taken place. He had no idea what he would do if he saw the whole bunch. *Turn tail and run probably.* He grinned ruefully. He was weary of the life he was leading. It was actually more boring than when he was hauling fertilizer for Judge Parker. All he did now was ride around and wait. It went against his measure.

Suddenly he heard the sound of a horse approaching. "Whoa, Red." He turned around and saw Rosa riding up on her mare. He was puzzled and asked quickly, "What are you doing out here, Miss Ramirez?"

"I wish you'd call me Rosa like everybody else does."

"It doesn't sound respectable to call your boss by her first name."

"I'm not your boss. You know that. Judge Parker is your boss."

He studied her for a moment then again asked, "What are you doing out here?"

"Where are you going?" she countered.

"I'm just riding around, more or less, on official business."

"I know what you're doing. Xeno Brewton told you about the holdup, and you're going to see if you can find the men who did it."

"Well, if I could find them, I could get word back to Judge Parker. He could get up some men and bring a posse. Might catch the whole bunch."

"Your chances of sneaking up on a bunch of outlaws in the Territory aren't very good. They're all like wild animals. They have sharp instincts about lawmen. Judge Parker has already lost nearly fifty of his marshals."

"I know about that, and that's why I want you to turn around and go back to the house."

She looked at him and said, "I won't do it."

Riordan stared at her. "Miss Ramirez, I'm ordering you as an officer of the court, leave here and go back to the house!"

Rosa smiled, and then she laughed. "What are you going to do if I refuse? Tie me to a tree and leave me here, or are you going to take me back and ask my father to punish me?"

"You don't really need to be going with me. This is dangerous."

"It's just as dangerous for you. I'm going to go with you. I left word at the ranch that I might be late."

"I may not go back tonight."

"Then I won't go back either. Now let's go. We're talking too much."

Riordan threw up one hand and shook his head. "You are

the most stubborn woman, Miss Ramirez, I have ever seen!" He turned, and Red obediently began walking at a fast pace.

He glanced at Rosa, who rode beside him, and could not help but think how attractive she was. He had never pursued women greatly, except for Marlene Jenson. Rosa had clean-running physical lines. She was tall and shapely, and whatever it was that made a woman attractive, she had it as far as he was concerned. He knew she was a strong-willed woman, and the thought came to him, *If she had to, she'd draw that revolver and shoot a man down and not go to pieces afterward.* Indeed, he had seen that she had a temper, could swing from extremes of laughter and softness, and he realized that there was a tremendous capacity for emotion in her. All in all she was a beautiful and robust woman with a woman's soft depth. She had an enormous certainty in her, a positive will, and he admired the vitality and imagination that she had to hold under careful restraint. He saw this hint of her will in the corners of her eyes and lips. There was fire in the woman that made her lovely and brought the rich and headlong qualities behind the cool reserve of her lips.

"Why are you staring at me?"

Suddenly Riordan flinched, and his cheeks grew red. "I'm sorry. I just don't understand women very much, I guess."

"What's to understand? I'm just a woman like other women."

"I don't think that's true. You're not really like other women... at least the ones I've known."

"What do you mean by that? What's wrong with me?"

"Why, nothing's wrong with you. You have qualities I admire. You have a strong will, and you have beautiful hair."

She suddenly smiled. "You think so?"

"Yes, I do. I've always liked black hair."

"Well, I've wondered about you, too."

"What about me?"

"You don't fit in out here, Riordan. You couldn't even ride a horse except for that awful one you rode to the ranch. You learned a little bit, and everybody thinks you killed that Dent Smith by accident. Everybody thinks you would be killed if you got in a gunfight. You wear a gun, but you never shoot it. Never take practice."

"Hoping I never have to use it again."

There was silence except for the clopping of the horses' hooves on the hard ground, and finally she turned to him and said, "You aren't married, are you?"

"Me? Why, no. What made you think that I wasn't?"

"You don't act like a married man. I've had enough of that sort trying to make up to me." Riordan had no answer for that, and finally she asked, "What are you doing out in this country? You don't belong here."

Riordan considered telling her the story but then decided not to. "Just wanted a change. I grew up in the city and grew tired of it."

She continued to probe, but he continued to evade her questions.

They rode for several hours, and then he said, "I think we ought to go back."

"Go back? We haven't found anything yet."

"I was going to stay all night, but that's impossible."

"Why? You afraid of the dark?" She smiled at him, a sly light in her eyes.

"No, but it wouldn't look right."

"What wouldn't look right?"

"Why, a single man and a single woman out camping after dark. Your father wouldn't like it."

"He knows I can take care of myself. So does my grandfather. Let's find a creek somewhere and camp out."

"All right." They found a small branch of clear water. There was some grass, so they put the horses out on long lariats, and Riordan found enough wood to build a fire. The darkness fell quickly, and by the time he got the fire going, he pulled out a frying pan and said, "I brought some beans and some bacon but only one plate and one set of hardware."

"Let me do the cooking."

"You probably do it better than I could."

Soon the air was filled with the smart smell of bacon cooking and beans bubbling. It gave them both an appetite.

Carefully she filled the one plate full of beans and added the bacon to one side. She picked up the fork and said, "Things taste better cooked outdoors." She took a bite of the bacon and said, "Ooh, that's hot! We'll take turns. You take a bite, and then I'll take a bite."

He took the fork awkwardly, scooped into the plate piled high with beans, put it in his mouth, and then added a bite of bacon. They had their meal that way. Finally he said, "Aren't you sleepy?"

"No, I always hate to go to bed at night. I might miss something."

"You wouldn't miss much out here. Not much happens at night."

"I know." She was sitting across from him. She pulled her feet up and held them by putting her arms around them. The fire was burning brightly, and it caught the glow of her dark eyes. "What'll we do if we catch up with the outlaws?"

"Turn around and run like the devil. Go get Judge Parker and some marshals."

"I think that would be wise. I'd hate to see you get in a gunfight. Have you ever shot that pistol of yours at a man other than during the one fight with Dent Smith?"

"Once or twice."

"Are you any good? But you must be because you shot the head off that rattler."

Riordan shrugged. "Not the best in the world, Miss Rosa."

"Miss Rosa? Well, at least it's not Miss Ramirez."

"I think that's a pretty name."

"It's not my real name. It's just a nickname."

He stared at her. "What is your name?"

"Rosario."

He stared at her. "That's a pretty name. What does it mean?"

"It means rose."

They talked for a while, and then she asked him, "What's your first name?"

"I don't like it, so I don't tell people what it is. Riordan's good enough."

"Pretty formal."

Finally he got the blanket rolls off of the horses and handed one to her. "I hope the snakes don't get us."

"I don't want to hear about that. Snakes scare me to death." She suddenly said, "I've been meaning to tell you something. She

205

put out her hand, and he took it. "Thank you for all you are doing for me and my family, Riordan."

Riordan felt a jolt at the touch of her hand.

She looked at him with what could only be described as adoration in her eyes. "I've always had to be on my guard with men, but somehow I know I can trust you."

Her hand was strong and warm, and without warning, Riordan felt a warmth toward Rosa that he'd never felt for any other woman, including Marlene. At that moment the two were caught in the mystery that sometimes draws a man and a woman together—and he realized with a shock that if he suddenly took her into his arms, she would not resist.

The moment drew out, and she whispered, "Aren't you going to try to kiss me, Riordan?"

"I don't think that would be fair. I mean we're all alone, and I'd be taking advantage of you." He shook his head, saying, "Any man standing in my place would want to kiss a beautiful woman like you, but I've made a promise to myself that I'd never take advantage of any woman."

Rosa startled at his words. "You are unlike any other man I have ever known. You can explode with violence, yet there is a gentleness in you." She then seemed embarrassed at her words and withdrew her hand. "We'd better get some sleep."

They both rolled up, he on one side of the fire, she on the other, and for a long time Riordan lay there listening to the soft sound of her breathing. It was a strange situation for him. Most women he had known would not think of doing what this woman had done—spend the night, in effect, with a strange man. He knew she was afraid of snakes, but he seriously doubted that she was afraid of anything else. His last thought was, *I can't get her in a dangerous gunfight. We'll go back first thing tomorrow.*

☙

The sun was up. Riordan and Rosa ate the remains of the beans and bacon for breakfast. He said, "Let's cut around and head back toward the ranch in a roundabout way. We might run across them."

"I doubt it. This is a big territory."

The two of them rode slowly, and they came to a long ridge.

"That's Nolan's Ridge," she said. "Nobody knows why it's here. It goes a long way."

"It's not very high."

"No, it isn't."

They attained the top of the ridge, and just as they crested the top, Riordan heard a woman's voice screaming.

Instantly be became alert and spurred Red forward, and Rosa came with him. He looked down and saw a wagon with a man lying still beside it. Two men were there, and one of them had a woman down on the ground and was tearing at her clothes.

He turned and said, "Stay here, Rosa." He rode down but was aware that she had paid no attention to him.

The sound of the horses caught the attention of the two men, and the man savaging the woman on the ground got to his feet quickly. The two of them were rough looking.

As soon as they pulled their horses up, Rosa said, "That big man there killed Blinky. He was with Pye."

207

"That's right! I'm Boog Powell, and I killed him. Now what does that get you?"

Riordan studied the two.

He was a huge man running to fat but obviously very powerful. His eyes were small, and he was grinning. "You two head out of here right now and you'll be all right. If you stay around, I can't guarantee your safety." Powell laughed, saying, "What you gonna do, baby face? Shoot me with that peashooter?"

Riordan made up his mind instantly. "You two are under arrest for murder."

The woman on the ground was pale, and her clothes were torn. She whispered, "They shot the driver. Didn't say a word. Just rode up and shot him!"

Riordan said, "I'm a federal marshal. I'm going to take your guns and take you in."

"You ain't takin' nothin'!" The other man beside Boog was a tall, skinny man who was grinning. "I'm Alvin Darrow. I done killed two of your marshals. You can be number three."

"He's the fastest gun in the Territory." Boog grinned. "You better not draw on him or you'll be dead in a minute."

Darrow said, "That little peashooter wouldn't hurt nobody anyway."

Riordan was aware that Rosa was beside him and wished she were not. He was willing to take his chances, but he feared for her. "You're both going back to Judge Parker. You can go alive or you can go dead. Your choice."

Darrow laughed, and he reached for his pistol. Indeed, he was fast, but before his gun even cleared the holster, Riordan drew and fired. Darrow was still standing, but there was a black spot in the middle of his forehead. He began to go down slowly as his muscles relaxed. He fell to the ground, kicked several times, and then lay still.

Boog Powell found himself looking right into the muzzle that had just killed one of the fastest guns in the Territory. "I ain't shootin'," he whispered hoarsely.

"Drop your gun on the ground, Powell."

Powell did so, and Riordan got off his horse. He picked up the two guns and tossed them away saying, "Your friend there is going to Judge Parker dead instead of alive. You try to run away and you'll arrive at the fort the same way, as I'll get you, too. And there'll be two bodies, each tied across their horses."

Riordan turned quickly and walked to the woman who was struggling to sit up, but she was crying with pain. He saw that her face was battered and bruised and knew she had taken a bad beating rather than submit. "Be still, miss. You're going to be all right."

"My side. My side hurts so bad." He touched her side, but she said, "No, no, don't!"

"I think you've got some cracked ribs there. Hopefully they're not broken. Have you got medicine in the wagon?"

"Yes, it's in a box just beside the seat."

He looked up at Rosa, who had come to kneel on the other side of the woman. "Get it, will you, Rosa?"

Rosa jumped up and ran to the wagon. She found the wooden box and brought the whole thing back. She took a brown bottle, opened it, and smelled the contents. "This is laudanum."

"Give her a big dose of that. If it's broken ribs, I know what that's like." All the time his glance kept going back to Boog Powell, who did not move. He gave the woman the bottle. She managed to gag some of the liquid down.

"What's your name, ma'am?"

"I'm Hannah Bryant. I hired the Mexican to take me to the Blackwood Tribe school, and these men just rode up and killed him without saying a word."

Rosa asked, "What kind of school?"

The woman's face was twisted with pain as well as swollen with the blows. "I'm a Monrovian missionary."

"Never heard of that church," Rosa said.

"We preach the Gospel and teach it at the same time."

Rosa exchanged glances with Riordan.

He said, "Not very wise for a woman to cross Indian Territory." She did not answer, and he said, "I'll be right back." He went over to Boog Powell and said, "Tie your friend on his horse." He waited until Boog lifted Darrow and placed him facedown on the horse, feet sticking out.

Boog started to argue, but one look at Riordan's eyes changed his mind. "All right. Just don't shoot."

Riordan said, "Now put the man you killed on the other horse." He waited until Powell had secured both men then said, "Turn around." When Boog turned around, he said, "Put your hands behind you." Quickly he pulled a cord from his pocket that he always carried and tied the man's hands securely. Then he took the lariat off the rope, made a slipknot, and stuck it over Powell's head. "I'm tying the other end to the wagon. You try to run, you'll hang yourself and won't have to hang on Judge Parker's gallows."

"You can't do this!"

"You watch me." He went back and saw that the laudanum had taken affect on the woman. Her eyes were closed, but she was still conscious. "I've got to put you in the wagon. We'll make a bed up there. Would you see to that, Rosa?"

"Sure." Rosa went to the wagon, found some quilts and blankets, and made a bed of sorts for the woman. "We'll take her to our ranch. She'll need a doctor."

Riordan carefully picked the woman up and put her into the wagon.

"You're stronger than you look." Rosa grinned at him, got into the wagon, and spoke to the mules, but then turned to say, "This makes two men you've killed. I never saw anyone who could pull a gun as fast as you. It was the same with the snake. But you still don't look like a gunman."

"I'm not." His words were spare. He saw this upset her a bit, as she said no more while she drove toward the ranch.

CHAPTER 15

The sun was climbing higher in the sky as they rode on. But as Riordan stared down at the woman, she was crying out with pain.

"What's wrong with her?" Rosa asked, her brow furrowed with thought.

"It's the ribs. I had some broken one time. I know what to do for it, but I've never treated an injury like this myself."

"How do you treat a broken rib?"

"You make some long strips of cloth out of a sheet or something. Then you put them around the rib cage as tight as it can stand it. It will still hurt, but nothing like it is now. You see, as it is now those cracked ribs are rubbing against nerves, but this would stop some of that."

They dismounted from the wagon, and Rosa found a muslin sheet. She took a knife out, slit it, and made a long strip about two inches wide. "Is this about right, Riordan?"

"Yeah, tear up the whole sheet like that."

Rosa finished all the strips, and he said grimly, "Let's get back in the wagon. This is not going to be fun." They entered the wagon, and he said, "You're going to have to sit up, ma'am, while we wrap your ribs."

"I can't. It hurts too bad."

"I know it does, but this will make you feel a lot better." He found a box and lifted her up, paying no attention to her cries, until she was sitting. He was in front of her, and he started removing her dress.

She gasped, and her eyes flew open. "No, you can't undress me!"

"Look ma'am, we've got to get your ribs tied up."

"No, I can't let you look at me."

"Get in the back here, Riordan," Rosa said.

He saw what she intended and instantly got up. He took his place behind the woman. He also made sure Boog wasn't looking her way either.

Rosa said, "Look, Miss Bryant, all the men can see is your back, so let me take your dress down and we'll get you tied up. You'll feel better."

The woman whimpered, but she nodded. Rosa took the remnants of the dress down, and she said, "Pass me the end of one of those strips, Riordan." She took it and lapped it over, and then holding it tight, she passed it under the woman's arm.

The woman cried out more than once, but the two kept at it.

Riordan said, "It'll have to go up over her shoulders to hold it in place."

Rosa brought the strip up between the woman's breasts and

back down her back, and finally her whole body was, more or less, encased. Rosa tied it off.

Riordan said, "That's good. Take some more of this laudanum, and you can lie down."

The two got her lying down, and soon her breathing became uneven and short, but at least some of the pain was gone.

They got down off the wagon, and Rosa said, "I didn't like doing that."

"I didn't either. Broken ribs are no fun. Could you drive the wagon back?"

"Sure."

"I'll keep track of our friend out there. You want to go as slow as you can. You can't avoid all of the holes, but just do the best you can. All right?"

"Sure."

He turned and then suddenly said, "You know we're closer to your ranch than anywhere else. We can't get her to a doctor in Fort Smith. It's too far."

"No, we can make the ranch by tomorrow sometime. Maybe the medicine will help until then."

"Let's hope so," he said.

They made their way as slowly as possible. From time to time, when Hannah Bryant started moaning with pain, Rosa stopped the wagon and gave her a little more of the laudanum. "I hope I don't kill her with this."

"A broken rib makes you feel like you're dying. I remember that about it."

That night Riordan said he would keep watch on their "friend."

As he kept his eye on the outlaw, he couldn't help but be impressed with Rosa, as she stayed near Hannah the entire night, offering as much comfort as she could. She was certainly a woman with many different sides to her. And he found he was interested in learning more about all of them.

❧

It was almost dark the next evening when they arrived back at the ranch. Ringo and Ned came running out. "What's wrong?" Ned cried out. "Who is this hairpin?"

"He's under arrest for murder," Riordan said. "Lock him in the smokehouse. If he tries to get away, shoot him in the head."

Everyone in the house came out then, and Rosa explained, "We came across two men. They'd killed this woman's driver and were attacking her."

"Who are they?" Ringo demanded.

"The live one is Boog Powell. The dead one is named Darrow."

"Darrow?" Ned said, "He's a bad one! He's killed more than one marshal, and he's faster than a snake."

"How did you get the woman away from them?" Ringo asked.

Riordan said nothing, and when Rosa saw he was silent, she said, "He told them they could go in alive or dead, and this man Darrow went for his gun." She shook her head and said in a strained voice, "He never even got it out of his holster. Riordan here pulled his gun and shot him right in the forehead. Darrow was dead before he hit the ground." The scene played over in her mind of how he pulled his gun with incredible speed and shot the man exactly where he intended for the bullet to go. She had never

215

seen such a thing in her life, and it made her wonder more about the strange man that had come into her life.

"You shot down Darrow!" Ned said. He whistled. "Judge Parker will be glad to hear that. He was a bad 'un."

"We've got to get this woman in the house. Her name is Hannah Bryant," Riordan said. "She's a missionary."

"Bring her right on in," Chenoa said. "We'll make a bed for her in the back room where we can take care of her."

Hannah moaned as Ringo and Ned extracted her from the wagon. Ned took her gently as he could, and they walked toward the house. When they were in the room, Chenoa said, "Put her on the bed there." She turned to Rosa. "What happened? Who did all this bandaging?"

"Riordan and I did it," Rosa said. "We need to send for a doctor."

"I'll do that," Ringo said. "He ain't far from here. He had a case over at the Wilsons' ranch. I'll be back in two hours with him."

"All of you get out of here," Chenoa said.

But as they were leaving, Hannah opened her eyes and said, "Please don't leave me!" She put out her hand toward Riordan.

He hesitated then went to her and sat down. He took her hand and said, "You're all right, Miss Hannah. You're safe now."

"Don't leave me, please. I'm so afraid!"

"You just go back to sleep. I'll be here." And with that he sat down, determined to stay with the woman.

Rosa was watching. She left the room with the others, but later she came back with some cloths. "Her face is going to be swollen, but this cool water might help a little." She began to wet the small pieces of towel and hand them to her mother. When Chenoa put them on Hannah, the missionary opened her eyes and said, "Who are you?"

"My name is Chenoa. You're at my family's ranch. Don't worry, Miss Bryant, you're safe now."

"What about those men?"

Rosa said, "They won't bother you anymore. You just try to sleep."

"Could I have some water, please?" Hannah asked.

Rosa left and came back with some cool water from the springhouse.

"Let me help you sit up," Riordan said. He put his hand behind her back, and she cried out, but she sat up long enough to drink thirstily.

"That's so good," she whispered then lay back. She took some more laudanum, and soon she started drifting off to sleep, but she held on to Riordan's hand.

Chenoa said, "I'll go into the kitchen and fix something she can eat. Call if you need me." She left the room.

Rosa saw Hannah still holding Riordan's hand, and her eyes narrowed. "Looks like you've made a friend."

"I know. She's scared."

"She's a missionary," Rosa said. "That's kind of a preacher, isn't it?"

"Sort of, I suppose. Never thought of a single woman crossing the Territory with just a Mexican driver."

"It was foolish."

"I guess we're all foolish."

He sat there while the woman held his hand. She slept fitfully, and Rosa said, "What are we going to do with her?"

"Well, when she gets healed up, we'll take her to that school she's going to."

Rosa studied him. "You're a mystery man. Nobody thinks you can shoot, but you put one of the fastest guns in the Territory down quick as a wink. Where'd you learn to shoot like that?"

He did not answer, and she persisted, "You killed that outlaw so easy. Does it bother you killing a man?"

"Yes." His answer was simple but firm.

"Are you sorry?" Rosa asked.

"Yes, I'm sorry. I'd always be sorry for killing anybody."

Something about the situation troubled Rosa.

Hannah slept fitfully for a time, moaning periodically, her lips moving as she tried to say something in her half-asleep state.

Rosa watched her lips and made out the words: "Don't leave me. Please don't leave me..."

Riordan looked up and said quietly, "She's scared. She needs something to hang on to."

"It looks like she's going to hang on to you," Rosa said sharply.

Suddenly he looked up, and his eyes caught hers. There was some sort of anger in him, but then it turned to sadness even as she watched. "We all need someone to hold on to. I never had anybody except my mother, but I know what it feels like to need."

❦

The doctor came, looked Hannah over, and stood up. He tested her arms and her legs for breaks. "She doesn't have any bones broken that I can tell, other than those ribs. You did a good job, Miss Rosa. Where'd you learn that?"

"It wasn't me. It was Riordan there."

"I had some banged up ribs one time. That's what they did to me."

"It's about all you can do. It's going to take some time."

"She'll be all right though, won't she?" Riordan said.

Dr. Mansfield rubbed his chin. "Physically she will be, but there are other kinds of hurt."

His remark intrigued Rosa. "What do you mean 'other kinds of hurt'?"

"I'm sure you know. Did you ever get hurt pretty badly, not on the outside but on the inside, in your spirit? Those emotional hurts can be worse than a broken bone. I wouldn't be surprised if she clings to you. That often happens. You saved her, Riordan. Therefore, she trusts you."

"How long will this go on—this hanging on?" Rosa asked.

"Maybe forever." The doctor closed his black bag and left without another word.

Hannah stirred, and her eyes opened. "Is the doctor gone?"

"Yes, he's gone, Miss Hannah," Riordan said.

"He was nice. You'll stay with me, won't you, Riordan?"

"Sure. I'll be here. You just sleep if you can."

Rosa watched as the woman's eyes closed and her features relaxed.

She was still battered and bruised and had scars on her face, but she held on to Riordan with both hands.

Rosa smiled bitterly. *I notice she's not hanging on to me. I wonder why that is?*

219

CHAPTER 16

There was little they could do about the body of the Mexican who had been killed by the outlaws. Hannah had hired him but knew very little about him except that his name was Manuel. The summer was hot, and there was no possibility of keeping the body from deteriorating. They had to try to keep the body of Darrow from decaying too badly, as it had to be taken in to the judge.

Frank ordered a grave dug, and Manuel was buried quickly. A simple wooden cross with only the name MANUEL carved into it was placed on the grave.

Riordan looked down at the raw earth piled on top of the grave and studied the name. He turned to Ringo, who was standing beside him, and said, "Manuel didn't leave much behind, did he, Ringo?"

"No, but then most of us don't. A few presidents and generals, I guess, but in the war, I seen mass graves with bodies piled high and covered over with a few inches of dirt."

"But they may have left something. A child, a wife. Maybe a business. It seems wrong to go out of this earth leaving nothing behind but your name carved on a piece of wood."

Ringo said, "It don't pay to think too much about things like that. Nothing you can do about it."

Riordan turned and studied Ringo. Jukes was a roughly handsome man with a thick neck and a deep tan. He was pretty good with a gun and stuck by his friends. Aside from that, Riordan knew little about him. "I don't think that's right. I'm not much of an example myself, but my mother is. I read a book once saying the Bible wasn't true and that there was nothing to Christianity. It didn't bother me because I'd seen it in action in my mother almost every day of my life."

"Come on. Let's go get something to drink."

Ringo and Riordan walked away from the grave. Riordan felt something was wrong with what had been done with Manuel.

Rosa brought in fresh water for Hannah. Their guest was doing much better. The swelling on her face had gone down, although she had one large scratch there that would take time to heal. Her ribs were not as painful, but she was still nervous and seemed upset when Riordan was out of her sight. She had Rosa and Chenoa and Ethel to take care of her, but still she was troubled.

Riordan was sitting beside her now. They were talking about a book that both of them had read. The name of it was *Jane Eyre*. Riordan said, "There's a woman I admire."

Hannah stared at him. "She was a strong woman, stronger

than most, I suppose."

"Well, of course she was only a character in a book, but the woman that wrote the book sure knew how to draw strong women."

Rosa's brow furrowed, and she thought, *I don't know what they're talking about. They know about books, pictures, and all kinds of things, and I'm just ignorant.* She set the pitcher down, picked up the empty one, and asked, "Is there anything else you want, Hannah?"

"Oh no, Riordan's taking good care of me."

"I've got to go talk to Ringo," Riordan said.

He started to get up, but Hannah reached out and took him by the hand. "Please stay just a little longer."

"Well, just a little bit."

Rosa turned and left the room and busied herself with making a batch of fresh corn bread, which her father loved. She kept looking at the door of Hannah's room, and finally Riordan came out.

He came over to her and said, "Making corn bread. Nothing better than fresh corn bread."

"Anybody can make corn bread."

"Not me. My mother could, though. She wouldn't let the cook make it. Insisted on doing it herself."

"You had a cook?"

Riordan stared at her. "Yes, we did. A good one, too. She'd been with the family, oh I don't know, fifteen years, I guess."

"Your family had money?"

Riordan had said little enough about his family, but he had no choice but to shrug and say, "My father was a good businessman.

He knew how to make money." He waited for her to speak and then said, "Well, I've got to go talk to Ringo. If Hannah gets restless, tell her I'll be back after I run some errands."

"I'll take care of her. Don't worry."

Riordan gave her a curious glance and then left the room.

Rosa wondered about Riordan spending so much time with Hannah. *He needs to be careful that she doesn't become too attached to him or he'll be stuck with her for the rest of his life.* Rosa berated herself for the uncharitable thought, as Hannah had been through so much. But she couldn't help but feel a sense of loss when thinking about Hannah and Riordan being together for always. . .

※

Riordan crossed the yard and found Ringo helping to get a horse shod. Ned had been a blacksmith but had quit because he hated the job. Thus it had fallen to Ringo's lot. "Ringo, I've got a favor to ask of you."

"Shoot."

"I was hoping you would take Powell and the body of Darrow into the judge."

"Why don't you do it? You're the marshal. There'll be rewards out on both of them."

"Hannah's a little bit nervous. Thought I'd stay around until she got over the worst of that. That was a pretty bad time she had."

"Well, she is kind of delicate. I always like to go to town. I may have a few drinks and play some cards."

"Your sins are your own business." Riordan grinned. "Just see that the judge has the body of Darrow. And turn Powell over to him. If there's a reward, just bring it back."

After Ringo left, Riordan looked uncertainly around, not knowing exactly what to do. Finally he went back to the house and found Rosa still putting the pan of corn bread into the oven.

"You're back."

"Yeah, I thought I'd just go sit with Hannah a little bit more." He noted she gave him an odd look and said, "What's the matter?"

"Nothing. Go sit."

Riordan went in, and Hannah smiled at once. "Good. I get tired of reading, and I can't move around much."

"Well, you'll be better, but it'll take awhile. It seems like it takes ribs a long time to put themselves back together."

She made a pretty sight despite her bruised face, for she had an odd shade of red hair. It was strawberry blond, and her eyes were green, beautifully shaped, and wide spaced. Her lips were still swollen, but her features all were pleasing. She was wearing a nightgown and a bed jacket, and her head was propped up.

"Everybody's wondering what you were doing out in the middle of the wilderness by yourself. I know you said you were going to teach at a school, but you shouldn't have made that trip alone."

Hannah paused for a moment, and a pained look came into her face. "I haven't told you or anybody, but I was engaged to be married." She faltered, and tears came to her eyes. She took a handkerchief and wiped them.

"What happened?"

"He died of cholera two weeks before we were supposed to be married."

"That was rough, I'm sure. It's hard to take a loss like that. I know you cared for him a great deal."

"It—it wasn't a romantic affair. We were very good friends all through school, and we knew missionaries needed to go out in couples, so we decided to get married. Not a story like you'd read in a romance."

"Still, I know it hurts."

"Well, I decided to go alone." She paused for a moment. "Could I ask you something personal, Riordan?"

Riordan wondered what she wanted, but he still replied, "Fire away."

"Are you a man of God?"

Riordan shifted his shoulders uncomfortably and ran his hand through his hair. "That's a hard question. There was a revival in our town when I was twelve. The evangelist preached a great sermon, and I was really struck by it. I went forward and did what the preacher said, which was to call on the Lord. I did that, and I was baptized, but somehow along the way I feel as if I have strayed from it."

"You know there's a story in the Old Testament that sheds light on this. Some men had been chopping with an ax, and the head of the ax flew off and landed in a river or a pond. They went to the prophet and told him what had happened. The prophet asked where they'd lost it, and they took him back to that place. He prayed, and the axhead floated to the surface. The men picked it up. I've always thought that story meant if you lost some standing with God, if somehow you couldn't feel Him, somehow you went wrong, then the thing to do is to go back and see where you lost it, or in other words, admit what you've done wrong and make it right with God."

"I've read that story, but I never thought about it like that. Actually, I'm not sure I know how to go back. Maybe you can help me."

"We'll look for it. You can tell me the story of your life."

"Well, if you can't sleep, I will. My story is pretty dull. It would put anybody to sleep." He smiled, reached forward, and said, "You've got the prettiest hair of any woman I've ever seen. Never saw a shade of red like that."

"I've always hated my hair." Hannah smiled. "They always called me 'Red,' and I hated that."

"Well, don't. It's as pretty as any woman's hair I've ever seen."

Hannah reached up and put her hand on his and said, "What a nice compliment."

The sun was falling when Ringo rode into Fort Smith. He had spent some time there on two occasions and rode right to the courthouse. He looked out and saw that a crowd was gathered around the gallows. As he dismounted, he said, "Is there a hanging today?"

A cowboy with bowed legs and a huge chew of tobacco mumbled, "Yep, going to hang three at the same time. The judge is doing it up right."

Ringo glanced at the gallows and saw that the ropes were already attached, and George Maledon was testing them by pulling at them. He thought about Maledon, who was the official executioner. "I wouldn't want a job like that," he muttered. He went up immediately to the judge's office and knocked on the door.

When the judge said, "Come in," he entered.

"Judge, my name's Ringo Jukes. I work for the Ramirez family."

"Oh, that's where our marshal is, Marshal Riordan."

"Yes, sir, he is, and I brought two wanted men in for you."

"Well, we can lock them up and bring them to trial."

"Too late for one of them, Judge. It was Alvin Darrow."

Judge Parker opened his eyes widely. "You mean he's dead?"

"Yes, sir, he is."

"He killed two of my marshals. I wanted the pleasure of watching him hang. How'd it happen?"

"Well, it's an odd thing. All of us were a little bit puzzled about the marshal you sent out, Marshal Riordan. He just didn't seem tough enough, but he faced Darrow, and the way Miss Ramirez tells it, Darrow started for his gun, and before it even cleared leather, Riordan pulled his gun and put a shot right between his eyes."

"I wouldn't have thought that was possible! Darrow was a fast gun. Everybody knew that."

"Wasn't fast enough, Judge. Anyway, I brought his body in."

"Well, there's a reward for it. I'll give you a note, and you can draw it from the bank."

"I brought in Boog Powell, too. He and Darrow were attacking a young woman, but Darrow made a fight of it. Powell is guilty of murder, and the young woman will testify that he killed her rider. Better string him up, I say."

Ringo watched as the judge scribbled something on a sheet. He took it and put it in his pocket. "Riordan's wondering when you're going to be sending a bunch out to run that group of killers down."

"We don't have enough to send right now." Parker leaned back for a while and studied Ringo. "I didn't think I was sending a man-killer to you. As a matter of fact, I doubt if Riordan's ever shot anybody— Wait, he did shoot Dent Smith. He's got the makings in him of a man-killer. I'll see that Powell's locked up and tried for murder."

"Thanks, Judge. I'll be going now. I've got some drinking to do, and I'm going over to beat those gamblers out of some of their money."

"I would advise against it."

"I thought you would, Judge. I'm just a hopeless sinner."

Riordan entered the kitchen, looking for Rosa. "How's Miss Hannah today?" he asked her.

"All right, I guess. She's eating more and able to get around a little bit better."

"I'd better go check on her."

"I'll go with you. I need to pick up her plate." Rosa gave him a careful glance and said, "You're taking good care of that woman."

"Well, she's fragile. Not like a Western woman, like you and your mother. She needs lots of care."

They went to Hannah's room. Riordan smiled and said, "Hello, Hannah."

"I'm glad you came. Sit down, Riordan." Hannah smiled.

Riordan frowned. "You know, you've had that bandage on long enough. It's about time to change it. It's bound to be dirty, and that's not good for you. If you'll get something to make strips out of, Rosa, we'll put on a clean one."

Instantly Hannah said, "Please, I'd much rather a woman do it."

Rosa said more sharply than she meant to, "I'll put it on, Riordan."

"Okay. I'll wait outside. Come get me when she's all fit to be seen, Rosa."

Rosa had made up some bandages, so she helped the invalid sit up and then took her gown down. She began taking the bandages off, saying nothing.

Finally Hannah said, "I just couldn't help being embarrassed at having a man see me undressed."

"There was no choice the first time. I didn't know how to do this, and he did."

"I know, and I was almost out of it then. I didn't even know it, but now it's different." She grunted, and as Rosa drew the bandages tight, she said, "I appreciate so much how you've taken care of me. You'd make a good nurse."

"A rough one, I suppose."

"I admire the way you're able to ride and do all the things you do. I don't think I could stay on a horse."

"You didn't grow up on a ranch like I did, down in Texas."

"No, I'm a city girl. I'm anxious to get to my school."

"What are you going to teach the Indians?"

"Oh, how to read and write, and I also want to teach them

about Jesus." She suddenly faced Rosa and said, "Are you a Christian, Miss Ramirez?"

"I grew up a Catholic. They tell me I was baptized when I was a baby, but with the life I was caught in, I couldn't do much about that."

"Why, it's not too late now."

"I guess I don't need to hear any preaching."

Hannah blinked with surprise at Rosa's harsh words. "I'm sorry. I didn't mean to offend you."

Rosa wanted to change the subject and steer the conversation away from herself. "What about you? You have any sweethearts?"

"Yes," Hannah said. "I was engaged to a fine young man. He died a short time before we were to be married."

Rosa stared at her. What else would this woman have to endure in life? "I'm so sorry."

Hannah replied softly, "That's all right. Have you ever been in love, Miss Ramirez?"

Rosa laughed and gathered up the rest of the bandages. "I've had to fight men off since I was fourteen." She suddenly hesitated. "I've noticed you seem attracted to Riordan. Do you like him?"

"Well, I don't know how to answer that. I'm grateful to him— and to you—for saving my life. I'll never forget it."

"I think you're more attached to Riordan than you let on. I don't usually bother to give women warnings when I see them going wrong, but you two would never be happy together."

"Why would you say that?"

"Well, you're a woman of God from the East, and he's a marshal and has a rough life in front of him. I don't think you'd ever make it." Rosa left the room, knowing that what she was really worried about was that they would make it together.

❧

"Get up. Marshals don't need to take naps."

Startled, Riordan came off his bed in the bunkhouse and stared around. He saw Ringo and Heck and said, "Good to see you, too, Heck."

"I want to know something. Rosa says that Darrow went for his gun, but you pulled your own gun and shot him before he got his pistol out. You never told me you could do that. Course I haven't forgotten how you snuffed Dent Smith out."

Ringo said, "I didn't see it. I'm pretty fast with a gun myself. You think you can shade me, Riordan?"

"Yes."

That single word seemed to irritate Ringo. "Let's try it out."

"It's not a game."

Heck said, "I'd like to see it." Several of the hands had come in and were watching. Heck said, "You two men unload your guns. I don't want anybody shot."

"I don't want to, Heck," Riordan insisted. "It's not something you play with."

"Do what I tell you. I'm the boss around here."

With a sigh, Riordan removed the bullets from his gun, re-holstered it, and then stood facing Ringo, who had done the same.

"When I shout 'Draw,' go for your guns," Heck said. Both men were still, with their hands down at their sides. The silence ran on, and suddenly Heck shouted in a stentorian voice, "Draw!"

Ringo's hand went to his gun, but even as he touched the butt, he heard a click and stared down in dismay to see that Riordan had drawn, put the gun right in his belly, and had pulled the trigger.

"I never saw a faster draw in my life!" Ringo gasped. "Let's never get in a fight, okay, partner?"

"Of course not."

"Kind of funny," Heck Thomas said. "Me and the judge were afraid to send you out here. We was afraid you might get killed."

"You've been practicin' all your life, I reckon. Haven't you?" Ned said.

"As a matter of fact, I really haven't. But I've always been quick with my hands."

"What about it, Heck? Are we going out to get Beecher and his bunch?"

"No, we need half a dozen men if we run into the Fox. When we get the men, we'll go."

☙

"I want to sit up, please."

Riordan had been sitting beside Hannah reading to her from a book Frank had loaned him. It was poetry, and he enjoyed it. He got up and said, "Are you sure you feel up to this, Hannah?"

"Yes, I just need to be careful."

He pulled the cover back and saw she was wearing a nightgown with a robe over it. He helped her stand to her feet and carefully placed her in a chair. "Is that okay?"

"Yes, I feel much better." She looked at him and said, "I heard about the way you and Ringo pretended to draw on each other."

She hesitated. "Have you ever killed a man besides Darrow, Riordan?"

"I don't like to think about it. I had to shoot an outlaw once to save Marshal Heck's life."

"Did it bother you, killing Darrow?"

He looked at her, and there was pain in her eyes. "Yes, it still does. I think I could have shot him in the arm, but you were there hurt, and Miss Ramirez was with me. If he had killed me, both of you would probably be dead now, too."

"It was something you had to do. Do you think you'll do this the rest of your life?"

"I don't think so."

"What do you want to do?"

Riordan suddenly grinned. "You'll laugh at this. I had ideas of becoming a painter before I got in this line of work."

"Can I see some of your work?"

"Don't really have any paintings here. They're all back East. I've got some drawings."

"I'd like to see them."

"Okay. I'll go get them." He retrieved his tablet and placed it before her.

She opened the cover and stared at the first one. "Why, that's Ringo!"

"I don't do figures as well as I'd like."

She began to turn slowly through the pages, commenting and exclaiming about his work.

She got to one of Rosa and said, "She's so beautiful."

"Yes, she is. Would you like for me to do a sketch of you?"

"No, I'm all puffy and ugly."

He laughed. "No, I can take all that out."

He took the tablet and leaned back, putting it on the table. Taking a pencil, he began to sketch.

He was so engrossed in his work he was startled when Rosa came to the open door. She watched the two for a while. A look of displeasure came over her face. She turned and left without a word.

CHAPTER 17

A week had gone by since Riordan had done the sketch of Hannah, and she was getting better every day. She could get up now, dress herself, and move around very well. She loved the sketch Riordan had made and kept it pinned to her wall.

As for Riordan, he took the bounty money that had been on Alvin Darrow and Powell and gave it to Hannah saying, "Use this for your school."

"Why, thank you, Riordan. We always need supplies for the students."

"I just wanted to tell you that I'll take you to the school when you get able."

"I think I'd better be a little bit stronger."

"Probably best. Where will you stay when you get there?"

"I—I really don't know. I think the mission board expected a couple coming out, and of course I thought William would make all the arrangements."

It was evening, and the two were standing on the front porch. Riordan often did this, sat outdoors at night, looking up at the sky and admiring the beauty displayed among the stars.

Hannah asked, "You like to watch the stars?"

"Yes, I do."

"I wish I knew the names of them like sailors do."

"I know some of them." He began to name the stars.

Finally she exclaimed, "You know so much! You went to college, didn't you?"

"I don't know as I learned all that much that was helpful."

The two were standing close together. She moved and said, "I'll be glad when my ribs get well." She inadvertently leaned against him.

He felt the soft pressure of her body. He smelled the rose scent that was in her hair, and by the light of the huge full moon, he could see her face. She had a tender expression, and Riordan did something he had not thought he was capable of. Without another word, he put his arms around her, held her gently, leaned over, and kissed her. He felt her surprise, and for a moment she resisted. Then she seemed to melt against him, and her lips moved under his.

When he lifted his head, she said, "I'm so ashamed."

"No, I don't want you to feel that way. It was all my doing."

"I don't know. I feel different toward you than I've ever felt."

"The doctor said that would happen. That you'd be dependent on me and Rosa because we helped you when you needed someone."

"I don't think that's it, but I'm ashamed that I would kiss a man so easily." She turned and left.

Suddenly Rosa's voice came in the darkness. "You comforting the patient, Riordan?"

Quickly Riordan turned and saw that she had been sitting in one of the cane-bottom rocking chairs usually occupied by her father. He hadn't dreamed she was on the porch. He was embarrassed and could not think of a thing to say. Finally he said, "Rosa, I feel sorry for her. She's helpless. She's lost the man she was going to marry, and she's afraid."

"And that's all there was to it?"

"Yes."

Rosa rose and came to him.

He was taken off guard when she reached up, put her arms around his neck, and pulled his head down. He felt the softness of her form and was suddenly aware that old hungers had been stirred.

Her lips were soft, and she pulled him closer, and then suddenly she stepped back. "You see? You were after her, and now you're after me. If a cheap saloon girl walked by, you'd be after her, too." She turned and walked quickly away.

Riordan wanted to talk to her, and he called her name.

She turned around and came back. "What is it?"

"I loved a woman once, but she didn't want me. She was the only sweetheart I ever had. I'm not a woman chaser, Rosa. I may have made a mistake with Hannah. It won't be the last mistake I make."

Suddenly Rosa felt sorry that she had tormented him. "I apologize. I'm the one that was out of order. Just forget what happened."

But all Riordan thought about was how he was supposed to forget about holding Rosa in his arms.

Gray Hawk rode in the next day and ate as if he were ravenous.

He listened to Rosa as she explained what had happened with the outlaws and how they had killed a man and that a federal marshal was now on the spot. She told him about Riordan.

"I've heard about Riordan. He's the one that gunned Dent Smith and Alvin Darrow down."

"Yes, he did."

"Must be some gunman."

Rosa took Gray Hawk to see her father and her grandfather.

After catching up on the news, the conversation turned once again to the outlaws. Rosa said, "I want George Pye brought to justice for killing Blinky."

"That was Powell who shot Blinky," her father interjected.

"Pye was shooting, too. He's just as guilty," she countered.

Gray Hawk's eyes suddenly gleamed. "I know where he is."

"Where?" Rosa demanded.

"He's holed up in Spivey Town. It's a rotten little hole full of bad Indians and outlaws. No decency in it."

Later on, Gray Hawk hunted Riordan down and wanted to know about the killing of Darrow. Finally he told the marshal what he had told Rosa. "Pye's and Beecher's gang are in Spivey Town, but you'd better stay away from there. Wait until you get a whole band of marshals. It's got more bad men and killers than a dog has fleas."

"Well, maybe the judge will send out a troop to clean out that rat's nest."

"It'd take a troop," Gray Hawk grunted.

"I'll send word to him. We'll see what can be done."

"You'd better tell him to get some good ones. The Fox is out there with his band. It's like a small army, Riordan."

Rosa walked up then. "I heard what you two were talking about. Riordan, you go back to the city where you belong. You're educated, and you've got a good family with money. You can't win out here."

"You're probably right," Riordan said. He said no more but turned and walked away.

The next morning Gray Hawk saw Rosa at breakfast. "Riordan rode out early this morning."

Rosa stared at him. "Where was he going?"

"Probably to Fort Smith to see the judge about getting the marshals," Mateo said.

"No, he didn't head toward Fort Smith. He rode due east headed toward the hill country."

They were silent, and it was Gray Hawk who said what they were all thinking. "I wouldn't be surprised if he was going to Spivey Town to root out that fellow who shot your hired hand."

"He wouldn't be foolish enough to do that!" Rosa exclaimed.

"Men do foolish things. He didn't ask me to go with him. We could have gotten a bunch up here, I think, but it looks like he's determined to go it alone."

Rosa groaned, and a couple of tears escaped her eyes. "I was the one that got him here to hunt up Pye and his murderers. I wish I had never done anything now."

Riordan spoke to Red, as he often did, "I'm just being a fool, Red. A horse wouldn't do a fool thing like this." He had formed a habit of talking to the big horse when he was alone. "I know I ought to get to Fort Smith and beg the judge to send at least two or three marshals, but I guess I just really haven't proved I'm as tough as I need to be. Maybe I can catch Pye out alone, just me and him. It'll be easy."

He had heard the directions and seen a map that pointed out Spivey Town. He arrived there late in the afternoon and saw that it wasn't much of a town. A few unpainted shacks and a line of businesses all built of warping boards—a general store, a livery stable, a feed store, and too many saloons for any place to remain decent.

He came to the edge of town, rode in, stopped in front of the livery stable, and dismounted. He tried to think of some way to find Pye, draw him out, and then get him alone. He was certain that if he tried to take Pye with his gang around, there would be a battle he could not survive.

Finally the sun went down, and still he could not come upon a plan. He took a deep breath and said, "I've got to do something." He started down the street, staggering, pretending to be drunk.

He stumbled into a half-breed who said, "Watch where you're going!" with a curse.

"I've got to find George Pye," Riordan mumbled. "Got some money for him."

The man's eyes narrowed. "Money? He's with his woman. Give

me twenty dollars, and I'll show you her place."

"Sure." Riordan fumbled the money out and gave the man the cash.

"Come on," the man said.

Riordan followed him down a street. They stopped in front of a saloon with a sign saying THE BELLE IRENE.

The man pointed up to the second-floor window. "That's Sally's place. If George ain't gambled all his money away, and if he's drunk, he'll be in her room. He ain't, he'll be in that saloon."

Riordan mumbled his thanks, and the man left.

Slowly Riordan tied Red to the hitching post. The street was almost empty now. Just a few people walking along and going into different stores. *Maybe I'll get lucky and he'll be there alone or with the woman.*

He entered the door that led to the upstairs section. When he got to the top, he saw there was a short hallway. Each wall had a door. He looked at one, and it was empty. Going to the other door, he lifted his ear and heard a woman talking and a man grunting some answers. *That's got to be him.*

He quietly opened the door, which was unlocked, and saw a woman wearing a dirty robe standing. She whirled to face him, and he drew his gun and mouthed the words *Shut up*! She turned pale and backed over against the wall. He looked at the bed and recognized Pye. He had heard the description and saw the ragged scar going down the left side of his face and down his neck. Pye was mumbling something, but his eyes were closed.

Going over to stand beside him, Riordan reached down, grabbed him by the collar, and pulled him upright. He put the muzzle of his gun to Pye's head and said, "You're under arrest, Pye. You're coming with me."

Pye woke up and started to holler, "Hey, there—"

But Riordan slapped him with the barrel of his gun and pointed it at his head. "You're going, dead or alive! Just one more bit of noise and it'll be dead. And I'm not particular. Now, get out of that bed."

Pye scrambled out of the bed. He was obviously drunk.

"Put on your boots." Riordan watched him put on his boots, and at the same time he took Pye's gun and shoved it into his belt. "We're going now. You make a sound, and I'll kill you."

Pye was rapidly sobering up. He saw the gun in Riordan's hand. He had heard of how Riordan had put a bullet exactly in the middle of Alvin Darrow's eyes. He swallowed hard and nodded.

They went down the stairs, but by the time they got to the horses, the woman had stuck her head out and was screaming, "There's a marshal here!"

Riordan said, "Pye, get on that horse." He waited until Pye mounted, and then he got on his own horse. But even as he did, the bat-wing door of the saloon flew open and five men came out. They lined up before Riordan, and one of them said, "I'm Henry Beecher. Turn that man loose, or we'll make a dead man out of you."

"I'm Riordan, Beecher. I'm taking him in."

"You're a dead man!" Henry Beecher's eyes seemed to glow in the darkness.

"That's the one that killed Alvin Darrow, Henry," one of his men said. "He's plenty fast."

Beecher shook his head and smiled. "He's smart. He sees he's outgunned. Isn't that so, Riordan?"

Riordan drew his gun in a flash of movement, and it was pointed right at Beecher's face. "You make one move or one of your men makes a move, and I'll kill you, Beecher. And then I'll take some more with me."

"You can't bluff me."

"Go for your gun, Henry. See if I'm bluffing."

Beecher's eyes opened, and he saw the expression on Riordan's face and the gun pointed at him. The muzzle was entirely steady.

One of his men yelled, "He's bluffing!"

"No, he's not bluffing!" Henry exclaimed. "He means it. He'd die, but so would some of us. Not worth it."

Riordan smiled. "That's smart, Henry. Now you get on a horse."

"You're not arresting me."

"No, I'm not, but you're my free pass to get out of here with my prisoner. You go with me until we're clear of the town, and then you can come back."

Beecher grinned sourly. "I'm supposed to trust you?"

"It's that or some of us are dead. I give you my word, you'll be the first. I give you my word also you can come back as soon as I'm clear with my prisoner."

"Don't do it, Henry," one of the men said. "He's lying."

Henry studied Riordan and finally said, "I think he's got us." He advanced, got on one of the horses, and said, "You boys wait here."

Riordan kept his eye on the men watching him and was aware that other men had come out of the saloon and were staring at him. He put himself on the far side of Beecher and Pye and said, "Let's go."

As they left town, Riordan was careful to keep his two prisoners between him and the men on the sidewalk. He felt the muscles of his back tighten as he rode out of town, expecting a bullet. None came.

They reached the town limit, and he said, "Spur those horses." They rode at a fast gallop and rode for five minutes. "This is good enough." They all pulled up, and Riordan said, "You can go back now, Henry."

Henry turned and stared at Riordan as if he were viewing an alien species. "You know I can't live with this, Riordan. I have to pay you back or I'll be laughed out of the Territory."

"You take your shot, Henry. I've got nothing against you, but if you come after me, better make sure you do a good job of it."

Beecher suddenly laughed when he saw that he was out of danger. "All right, Marshal, I'll be seeing you."

Riordan watched him go.

Pye said, "He'll kill you. I hope he does."

"I expect he'll try. Now, we got a hard ride. Let's go."

☙

Henry rode back and found his crew milling around.

"Let's go get him," Hack Wilson said. "There's plenty of us to get one man."

"No, that would be too easy." Henry was silent for a time. Finally he smiled evilly and said, "I've got to think of a very special ending for Marshal Riordan. Something that will hurt him worse than a bullet. . ."

The ranch seemed to come alive as Riordan rode in with his prisoner. He dismounted, and they all gathered around him, Ringo keeping an eye on the prisoner.

Hannah was one of them. She came and put her hand out. "You're safe," she whispered.

"For a while, Hannah."

"How'd you do it, Riordan?" Frank asked. "Nobody ever got one of the wild bunch like this."

"Well, I had a little help from Henry the Fox," Riordan said. They demanded to know his story, and he said, "It wasn't all that much. Ringo, you and Ned put Pye here under guard."

They went inside, and Frank said, "I don't know what you did, but if you made a fool out of Henry, he won't forget."

"That's what he told me, but he can't kill me but once, can he?"

"Don't say that!" Rosa said sharply. "You must be hungry. I've got some stew and beans on the stove. Sit down. The rest of you leave."

Rosa fixed him a meal, beans and a tender chunk of beef and fresh biscuits. She watched him as he ate. She sat down across from him and said, "I've said some hard things, but you did what I asked. You brought in the killer." She put out her hand, and he took it. She stared at him with a strange look in her eyes. "No man has ever kept his word to me or did what he promised. I guess I can always remember you as being one that did, Riordan."

Riordan was aware of the warmth and the strength of her hand. "You know, as I was bringing Pye back, I was thinking about you."

245

She stared at him. "What about me?"

"Well, there was a touchy situation, and the thought came to me that if they killed me, I would never see you again, and it made me sad."

Suddenly she smiled, and her face relaxed. She put her other hand down and held his prisoner. "You have your moments, Riordan."

PART FOUR

CHAPTER 18

Caleb Riordan sat in his favorite easy chair, staring across the room. His eyes were fixed on an ormolu clock. He was not studying that object but was merely giving deep thought to his son Faye.

It was a hot day. The windows were open, allowing a slight breeze to come in and stir the flowers that Eileen had set in the window. From far off came the sound of servants laughing as they trimmed the yard and worked in the flower beds.

None of this entered into Caleb's thinking, and finally he shook his shoulders together in a gesture of helplessness and looked over to where Eileen was sitting on a divan, knitting. "Eileen," he said, "Faye never writes to me." He had not intended to say this, but it had been on his mind for some time now. When Eileen looked up at him, he said defensively, "It seems like he could write his father once in a while."

Eileen smiled slightly and ceased knitting. She studied Caleb and finally said simply, "You two were never close, Caleb."

Caleb gave her a sharp look and shook his head. "No, we weren't."

"None of us were really close to Faye," Max said. He was wearing a pair of blue trousers, highly polished shoes, and a snow-white shirt. "I should think he would be considerate enough to write to us, though."

Leo looked up from the book he was reading. "Well, Max, I'm not really expecting a letter from him. I didn't pay much attention to him while he was here, and I suppose he thinks I haven't changed."

"He may be sick or hurt," Caleb said. "Surely he'd write if he were." He suddenly straightened up in his chair and passed his hand over his thick hair in a gesture of despair. Then he said, "Eileen, he writes to you."

"Yes, he does. He tells me a great many details of his work there."

"Well, why don't you read the letters to me?" Caleb complained.

"I didn't think you'd be interested, dear."

Shaking his head, Caleb growled, "He's wasting his time out there playing cowboy."

"I don't think so," Eileen said calmly. "I believe he's doing something he thinks needs to be done."

"But he can never make any money out there riding around on a horse. He's never done anything a man should do at his age."

"That's right. He never makes any money," Leo said.

"And he could, too. He could come to work at the factory."

The men waited, but Eileen went back to her knitting.

Finally Caleb got up and left the room, his back stiff with displeasure.

The carriage stopped, and Caleb and his two sons got out and started up toward the steps that led to the wide front porch. Caleb had put in a long day at the factory and was surprised when he saw a distinguished-looking man leaving the house. He was tall, well dressed, and had a pair of sharp black eyes.

"Who is that, Father?" Leo asked.

"Never saw him before."

As they passed, the man nodded pleasantly and said, "Good afternoon."

"Hello," Caleb said. He wanted to ask the man who he was, but that seemed somewhat rude. He turned and watched him go into a landau carriage, and as the man rode away, Caleb shook his head. "I don't like strange men coming to the house."

They went inside, and Eileen met them with a smile. She kissed Caleb on the cheek, having to reach up and pull his head down, and said, "Did you have a good day, dear?"

"It was all right." Caleb waited for Eileen to say something about the visitor, but she simply began chatting about what she had been doing. Finally Caleb could not refrain from saying, "We met a fellow coming out of the house. I didn't know him."

"Oh, that was Mr. Samuel Steinbaum."

The men all waited for her to say more, but she didn't. Finally Caleb said, "I don't believe I know him. What was he doing here? Is he selling something?"

"Not at all. I asked him to come. You go along and wash up. We'll have dinner early tonight."

"But why did you ask him if he isn't selling anything?"

"He's the director of the Mellon Museum of Art."

"Well, why did he come here?"

"Why, I invited him."

Leo said, "That's unusual, Mother. You don't usually invite people that we don't know."

"I've exchanged letters with him several times, so I thought I'd invite him and we could talk." She laughed and said, "Are you jealous, Caleb?"

"Don't be foolish! I would like to know what he was doing here, though."

Eileen shrugged her shoulders and said, "It concerns Faye's work."

"What work?" Leo demanded.

"Why, his painting, dear. I asked him to come and give me his opinion of Faye's paintings."

All three men stared at her, and it was Caleb who finally demanded, "Well, what did he say?"

"They couldn't be worth much," Leo shrugged.

Eileen pulled a slip of paper from her bodice. "Here's his offer on the paintings that he looked at."

Caleb stared at the paper fixedly. He did not speak. His mind seemed to be moving rather slowly. "The first one says, 'Woman With Small Girl—four hundred dollars.'" Looking up, he blinked with surprise and said, "I remember that painting. If I remember right, Faye painted that in two days."

"That's right. Not many young men make four hundred dollars in two days, do they, dear?"

"Let me see that list," Max said. The two brothers flanked their father and read down the list. They named off the paintings that they remembered and finally looked at the figure at the bottom, the total offer.

"Why, this adds up to five thousand dollars!" Leo declared.

"Yes, that's good, isn't it? Mr. Steinbaum wants to have a one-man show of Faye's work. He'll handle it all for a fee of ten percent."

"You think people will buy the kinds of paintings Faye does?" Max asked dubiously.

"Well, Mr. Steinbaum says painting in Faye's style by artists with not half his talent are selling very well."

All three men were speechless. Finally Max said, "Two hundred dollars for one day's work? Why, that's more than I make."

"Yes, I suppose it is." Eileen smiled. "Mr. Steinbaum thinks Faye has a brilliant future. He wants to act as his agent."

Caleb could not take his eyes off the list. He ran up and down it with a steady gaze, trying to find something wrong with it.

He was interrupted when Eileen said, "I need some money, dear."

"Of course. Will twenty dollars do?"

"Oh no, I need a lot of money."

Caleb had always been generous with Eileen where money was concerned, and she very seldom had to ask, for he saw to it that she had spending money at all times. "What do you want that costs so much? Some new furniture?"

"No, I'm going to Fort Smith." Eileen smiled as the shock registered in all three men's faces. "Faye needs to hear about this wonderful news—and I need to see him. I miss him so desperately."

Caleb's thinking seemed to have slowed down. He would not have been much more surprised if Eileen had said, "I'm going to the moon." The idea of her going west never had occurred to him. "Well," he said abruptly, "we'll both go."

"Let's all of us go," Leo said. "I'd like to see this world he's thrown himself into full of cowboys and guns and rattlesnakes, I suppose."

"Right," Max said. "We need a vacation."

Eileen was pleased, but she asked, "What about the factory? Who'll take care of that? You can't leave your work."

"My manager Charles can handle it. He knows as much about the place as I do." He stared back at the list and said, "I'd like to see these pictures."

Eileen was pleased. "Yes, of course. All of you, come on. I've still got them out on display."

☙

"I really need to go to Forth Smith," Hannah said.

"Why would you need to go there?" Riordan asked. The two were standing on the front porch. Riordan had come in to get something to drink, and she had joined him.

"I need to send a telegram to my superior in the church."

"I'll take you."

Rosa had been standing in the doorway and had turned to leave, but then she abruptly stopped and said, "I'll go with you. Boog Powell and Pye are going to hang for killing Blinky. I want to see it."

Ringo had arrived to stand beside Riordan just as Rosa spoke. At once he said, "I'm going, too."

"All you want to do is go get drunk," Riordan smiled. "You stay home and behave yourself."

"No, I'm going with you. I don't think you understand Beecher, Riordan. He knows people all over the Territory are talking about how you rode right in big as life and took away one of his gang. He's like a snake, Riordan. He may be quiet, but he'll strike when you least expect it. Your life's not worth a dime as long he's alive."

Riordan put up some argument, but Rosa said, "We'll take Zack and Ned with us. That'll be enough to handle Henry the Fox. I hate that name!"

"I think he sort of likes it," Ringo said. "Takes pleasure at being seen as some kind of a hero, which he is to a lot of people."

"A hero?" Hannah exclaimed. "Why would they admire a man like that?"

"Well, that's the way it is out here, Miss Hannah." Ringo shrugged. "They admire strength and courage, and you have to admit Henry's got those two qualities."

In the end, they took the whole crew except for two men.

They arrived in Fort Smith late Saturday afternoon. Hannah sent her telegrams and then joined Riordan and Rosa at the hotel for dinner. The hands spread out to various distractions. Rosa knew they wouldn't be seen again until it was time to go home.

Rosa noticed that men recognized Riordan. She heard one of them whisper to a companion, "That's Riordan. They say he's as fast as lightning with that gun of his."

This both pleased and disturbed Rosa, for she knew that Ringo was right. That Beecher would never rest until he got his revenge.

Rosa and Hannah shared a room. After they were ready to go to bed, Hannah said, "Are you really going to that hanging?"

"Yes, I am."

"I don't know why you'd want to see such a thing."

"They killed one of my men who was liked a great deal and who had done nothing to deserve it. The poor fellow didn't even get to live his life out. Call it what you want. I want to see justice done."

❦

There were three men to be hanged, and a crowd, as usual, had gathered.

Riordan stood beside Rosa and nudged her arm with his elbow. "Look up at the window on the second floor. That's Judge Parker," he said. "It's a way he has, so I hear. He watches every hanging from that window."

"Why would a man enjoy a hanging?"

"I don't think he does. At least that's what the marshals all say. They say he sees himself as an agent of the government dealing out justice, but he hates the hangings themselves."

They studied Parker, who was standing still, until finally they heard a murmur run over the crowd that filled the square. They watched as George Maledon led three men with their hands tied behind their backs to the gallows. He stood there and helped steady them as they climbed the few steps and then placed them very carefully in their positions.

As for Rosa, she was already beginning to wish that she had

not come. It was one thing when violence explodes and somebody's shot unexpectedly. But this was different. These men were all alive and well and knew that in a few moments their hearts would stop, their blood would stop flowing, and they would be no more.

When the men were in place, Maledon said, "If you have anything to say, go ahead."

The first man was small and looked sickly. Neither Pye nor Powell spoke, and Pye seemed frozen by what was happening to him. Boog, alone of the three, did not seem to be afraid. He stared arrogantly out at the crowd and said, "Some of you deserve hanging as much as I do. Now get on with it, Maledon."

Maledon shrugged and adjusted the ropes around all three men's necks. He stepped back and without hesitation pulled the lever. The trapdoor opened, and the three bodies shot downward. As the bodies drew the ropes taut, a sigh of some sort went over the crowd.

Riordan shook his head. "Let's get out of here, Rosa. That's enough of this."

As they left, Rosa found herself shaken. She had thought herself ready for this, but now she realized she was not. She felt sickened by what she had seen.

Riordan said, "It's too late to go home tonight. We'll go in the morning."

"All right. Suits me."

Rosa got up in the morning and saw that she had overslept. She had slept very poorly, as a matter of fact, and now wished she had not come to the hanging at all.

Hannah was already up and dressed and now turned to her

and said, "Let's go get some breakfast."

"I'm not hungry."

"Well, you can have some coffee before we leave." She hesitated then said, "I'd like to go to church. Would you go with me?"

Rosa automatically began to frame a reason why she could not go, but later when Riordan joined her and Hannah for breakfast, he said, "What would you think about all of us attending church this morning? After witnessing the events of yesterday, I feel the need for something spiritual in my life."

"Okay, that sounds good." Her answer shocked even her, for she had not had any interest in being religious before. Somehow she felt the same as Riordan. She needed something like this to maybe bring peace to her heart and mind.

❦

Beecher was sitting at the table with a bottle of whiskey in his hand. He now poured a tumbler full and drank it down. Red Lyle said "You're worrying too much about that Riordan."

"I'm not worrying about anything!" Henry snapped.

"Well, that's good. You know the best thing to do is just lay back until Riordan gets off the ranch. Just shoot him in the back. Kill him out of hand. I'll do it myself for a price if you'd like."

"You'd have to, Red. You couldn't beat him to the draw."

"Well, he may have a faster draw than I do, but he ain't faster than a thirty-thirty slug in the head."

The two men sat there drinking until Sal Maglie entered. He took his hat off, beat the dust off of it, and then walked over. "Got all of them supplies, Henry."

"You go to the hanging?"

"Yeah, I went. He went pretty good, Boog did, but he always did have nerve. You know Riordan was there with that woman, the Mexican, at the hanging, I mean."

"They were? How'd he look?" Henry said, lifting his eyes.

"Well," Sal scratched his head, "I heard some folks talkin'. They say Riordan's sweet on the Ramirez woman."

"Can't blame him for that," Maglie said. "She's a good-looking woman."

Beecher was silent for a time. Finally he looked up, and there was a smile on his lips. "You know Riordan took something of mine. The only way I'll feel like I beat him is if I take something of his."

"Like what?" Red said in a puzzled tone.

Beecher knew none of the men understood him. He was a mystery. They knew he was deadly, and none would dare cross him, but he was a deeper thinker than any of the hands.

Now Red said, "I don't understand you, Henry. What can you take of his?"

Beecher leaned forward with his smile broadening, his eyes glittering. "Here's what we'll do. . ."

CHAPTER 19

As soon as Rosa stepped into the small wood-framed church, she felt some sort of strange pressure. Religion had played almost no part in her life. She was told that she had been baptized in the Catholic tradition when she was a baby, but as she had grown up, her life had taken a different turn. During the last year, she had been working in saloons, fighting off lustful men, and simply trying to make some sort of a life for her family.

"Come along. There are some seats," Hannah said. She put her hand on Rosa's arm, and for a moment Rosa resisted, but then it was too late. She walked with Hannah down the aisle between the two rows of wooden pews, which were already, for the most part, occupied.

A quick glance around revealed that the church was filled with men and women and children from all walks of life. Some of the men and women wore expensive clothing and looked well groomed. On the other hand, some of the men were wearing what looked like work clothes, overalls, and they had the look of poverty on their faces. Their wives wore the cheapest sort of gingham dresses, and the children were dressed as well as the parents could afford.

Moving into the vacant space, Rosa sat down. Hannah sat down beside her whispering, "I heard this preacher is a wonderful speaker. I know we're going to enjoy the sermon."

At that moment, a tall, thin man stood up and in a deep voice said, "We will now sing 'Old One Hundred.'"

The entire congregation stood up, and not wanting to be noticed, Rosa stood up with them. They sang a song that was very simple:

"Praise God, from whom all blessings flow;
    Praise Him, all creatures here below;
Praise Him above, ye heavenly host;
    Praise Father, Son, and Holy Ghost. Amen."

The song leader smiled and said, "Now we'll sing my favorite hymn, 'When I Survey the Wondrous Cross.'"

There were no hymnals, but everyone seemed to know the song. Rosa listened and found herself being strangely moved by the singing. Of course, the singing itself was not exceptional. Some of the people sang off-key and some too loudly, but the words came through to her.

"When I survey the wondrous cross
    On which the Prince of glory died,

261

My richest gain I count but loss,
    And pour contempt on all my pride.

Forbid it, Lord, that I should boast,
    Save in the death of Christ my God!
All the vain things that charm me most,
    I sacrifice them to His blood.

See from His head, His hands, His feet,
    Sorrow and love flow mingled down!
Did e'er such love and sorrow meet,
    Or thorns compose so rich a crown?

Were the whole realm of nature mine,
    That were a present far too small;
Love so amazing, so divine,
    Demands my soul, my life, my all."

The singing went on for almost twenty minutes. Finally the song leader stepped back and took a seat on the rostrum.

A short, well-built man with brown curly hair and direct blue eyes stood up. "We are glad to welcome you to our church. Those of you who are visitors, feel at home. We welcome you."

He laid his Bible on the pulpit, flipped it open, and said, "The sermon this morning will be very short. I'm going to pray that if there be one in here who does not know the Lord Jesus Christ as Savior, that he or she will leave this building as a part of this family of God."

He had a pleasant look on his face. His voice was clear and carried well in the small building. "My sermon this morning," he said, "if I had a title for it, would be 'A Woman Who Found Jesus.' As a matter of fact, if you were to go to most foreign countries where paganism rules, you would find women treated worse than animals. But when Jesus came, he lifted women from a lowly status to a place of honor. This morning I want us to think about one of those women who encountered Jesus."

He picked up his Bible and began to read:

" 'And a woman having an issue of blood twelve
years, which had spent all her living upon physicians,
neither could be healed of any, came behind him, and
touched the border of his garment: and immediately her
issue of blood stanched. And Jesus said, Who touched
me? When all denied, Peter and they that were with
him said, Master, the multitude throng thee and press
thee, and sayest thou, Who touched me? And Jesus said,
Somebody hath touched me: for I perceive that virtue is
gone out of me. And when the woman saw that she was
not hid, she came trembling, and falling down before
him, she declared unto him before all the people for what
cause she had touched him, and how she was healed
immediately. And he said unto her, Daughter, be of good
comfort: thy faith hath made thee whole; go in peace.' "

The minister closed his Bible and began to speak with excitement in his voice. He obviously believed his message and did his best to communicate that feeling. "Isn't that a wonderful story! This poor woman was unclean, for according to Jewish law any woman with an issue of blood was as unclean as a dead person. No one could touch her without becoming unclean. And for years she had sought to be healed and spent all her money on physicians but was no better."

Rosa had come prepared to ignore the sermon, but she found herself caught up with the story the minister had read. She had never heard it before, and he went on to describe the woman so well that she was absorbed in the drama of it.

"This poor woman, who had been failed by man on every hand, thought, 'If I could just touch the hem of the garment of Jesus of Nazareth, I will be healed.' Ah, now there is faith, my friends. There is faith! And you have heard how she did touch just the hem of the garment of the Lord Jesus and instantly she was healed. Bless the Lord, O my soul! That's what happens when people come to Jesus. They are healed. That's what I would like to present for you today. A savior who is Christ Jesus, the Son of God."

The minister continued discussing the story in great depth, drawing a picture of the poor woman who had struggled for so long and was so sick and how she had found healing in no place except in touching Jesus Christ.

Finally the preacher said, "Let me mention one other woman who found Jesus. It's found in the eighth chapter of the Gospel of John. 'And the scribes and Pharisees brought unto him a woman taken in adultery; and when they had set her in the midst, they say unto him, Master, this woman was taken in adultery, in the very act. Now Moses in the law commanded us, that such should be stoned: but what sayest thou?'

"The law indeed had such a verse, but Jesus did a very strange thing. He answered them not a word, but He 'stooped down, and with his finger wrote on the ground, as though he heard them not.' Finally he looked up, and He said words that I have treasured and have kept very carefully. Jesus said, 'He that is without sin among you, let him first cast a stone at her.' Well, dear friends, the Bible says that they were 'convicted by their own conscience, went out one by one, beginning at the eldest, even unto the last: and Jesus was left alone, and the woman standing in the midst.'"

The preacher ran his hand over his hair and said, "The Bible doesn't say this, but I like to think this dear woman, who was the sinner but yet a beloved sinner, came to Jesus and bowed down and held to His feet. We do know what Jesus said. He said, 'Woman, where are those thine accusers? hath no man condemned thee? She said, No man, Lord. And Jesus said unto her, Neither do I condemn thee: go, and sin no more.'"

This story went straight to the heart of Rosa. It was as though she could see the poor retched woman ready to die for her sin, and she could hear the voice of Jesus saying, "Neither do I condemn thee: go, and sin no more." A longing somehow such as she had never known before began to build within her, and as the sermon went on, she found her hands trembling. She held them to conceal it from Hannah.

Finally the sermon ended, and the preacher said, "We're going to sing a few verses of an old hymn, and if there be one of you out there who does not yet know the Lord as personal Savior, and perhaps you are in the same condition as this woman, you have a sickness. You have sinned, and you don't know where to go. I call upon you to look to Jesus of Nazareth, the Savior of the world. He died to save sinners, and that means all of us. So come as we sing."

Everyone rose and began to sing a hymn that Rosa, of course, didn't know. She saw two people go down and speak with the preacher, then another who knelt at the altar, and she could not control the emotions that flooded through her. She stood there, her head bowed and her eyes closed, thinking about the two women that Jesus had touched. She felt tears come to her eyes, a very rare thing for her.

Finally the preacher dismissed with a short prayer.

As they left the building, Hannah, whose face was radiant, said, "Wasn't that a wonderful sermon?"

Rosa could not answer. It had been such a moving experience she did not know how to identify it. One thing she felt sure of was that her thoughts of Jesus Christ had been wrong. She had seen statues in Catholic churches of Jesus, but they were not Jesus. They were merely statues. But the man the minister had read of was living and full of love and compassion, and she knew that she would never forget this morning.

❧

Judge Parker was poring over documents on his desk, but when the door opened and four strangers entered, he rose at once. "Good afternoon," he said. "I'm Judge Parker."

"Oh, Judge Parker, I'm so glad to meet you," the woman said. She was an attractive woman in her mid-forties with auburn hair and light brown eyes. "I'm Eileen Riordan."

"Why, Mrs. Riordan, it's good to see you."

"This is my husband Caleb and two of my sons, Leo and Max."

Parker came around from behind his desk, shook hands, greeted them all, then turned his head to one side, and smiled. "I expect you've come all the way out here to the frontier to visit your son."

"Yes, we have. We just got off the steamboat, but we don't have any idea where to start looking, so I thought we'd come and ask you."

"Well, you're fortunate, Mrs. Riordan. Your son is in town today."

"Where has he been?" Caleb asked curiously. "We'd like very much to see him."

"I've had him stationed out on a ranch. The owners have been threatened with outlaws, and I haven't had the men to send a crew in to quiet them, so I sent Riordan." He stopped and said, "I don't even know his first name."

"It's Lafayette," Eileen said, "but everyone calls him Faye."

"Well, it's a small town. Let me call one of my marshals."

Parker went to the door and said, "Marshal Thomas."

Heck Thomas stepped inside, put his hazel eyes on the visitors, and listened as Parker explained who they were. He smiled briefly and said, "You know your son saved my life."

"You don't mean it!" Caleb said. "How did that happen?"

"I was going out to arrest a minor criminal, and I thought I'd take Riordan with me just to get him used to the Territory. When we got there, the man I wanted as prisoner had two of his kinfolk with him, both of them gunmen. One of them drew on me, and I just had time to get off a shot. I really expected to take a bullet in the head, but another shot rang out echoing mine, and I saw the other outlaw fall. I turned around and saw that Riordan was holding his gun. None of us had any idea he had that quickness or was that certain a shot."

"He—he killed a man?" Eileen asked tentatively.

"Yes, that's the way it goes out here in the Territory. Thomas, they'd like to find their son. Do you have any idea where he might be?"

"He was with Miss Ramirez fifteen minutes ago. They were in the general store. Probably still there. They seemed to be loading a wagon with supplies. I'd be glad to take you over there," he said to the visitors.

"Good. We're so anxious to see him."

"Are you planning to stay over?" Parker asked.

"Yes, we planned to make a lengthy visit of it."

"You may have trouble finding a place to stay. The hotel's full."

"Yep, we had a multiple hanging today. Two of them were killed for murdering one of Miss Rosa's hands."

"Please take us to him," Eileen said.

"Come this way. It's just down the street," Heck Thomas said as he started out the door.

☙

"Why don't you get some more apples? I like those apple pies," Riordan said. He had been helping Rosa stock the wagon, and he picked up a large red apple. "I love apples."

"All right. Get a dozen of them. We'll have apple pie tonight. Maybe tomorrow."

Riordan obtained a sack, filled it with the fruit, and then he followed her around as she wandered through the store. "Did it bother you seeing that hanging, Rosa?"

"Yes, it did."

"I know something that bothered you worse."

"What?"

"The sermon that preacher laid on us."

Rosa shot a quick glance at Riordan. "Well, I had never heard anything like it before. You probably grew up hearing sermons like that."

"Yes, I did, but you know there was something in that man that's not in most preachers. To tell the truth, he shook me up quite a bit."

"But I thought you said you were converted when you were twelve years old."

"Well, I thought I was, but I got away from my raising. Never got into any trouble. . .until I got out here."

They were alone at one end of the store, and Rosa said quietly, "I don't know what to think. I never thought much about God and heaven and hell, but I know they're real."

"Maybe we ought to go back and talk to that preacher, just you and me."

"No, I'd be embarrassed. I don't think God—"

"Faye!"

Riordan looked up and was shocked to see his mother, father, and two brothers had entered. His mother ran toward him, and he held his arms out. He caught her. She smelled of lemon and lavender, like always, and there were tears in her eyes. "Mother, what in the world are you doing out here?"

Caleb stepped forward. "We came out to visit with you, son." He looked his son over, up and down. "I have to say I am impressed with you, son. You are so tan, and there's a steady look in your eye now."

"Father's right, and besides, we wanted to see the cowboy in all his glory." Max grinned.

Riordan pulled Rosa toward his family and said, "This is Miss Rosa Ramirez. I've been staying at her ranch for quite a while now."

"I'm so happy to know you, Miss Ramirez," Caleb said. He could have a gentlemanly manner when he chose, and he smiled saying, "Has this young man been behaving himself?"

"Oh yes, he has." Rosa was overwhelmed with the family. One look at them told her that they were aristocrats. They dressed entirely in the fashions of the East and were all fine-looking people. She did not see much resemblance between Riordan and his father and his two brothers, but some of his mother was in his features.

Caleb said, "I hear it's going to be hard to find a place in town. I don't know where we'll stay unless we buy a tent."

"No need to do that, Mr. Riordan," Rosa said quickly. "You need to come back to our ranch. Your son will be there. It's quiet, and you can visit as long as you'd like. Plenty of room at our big old ranch house."

"We wouldn't want to impose," Eileen said.

The entire family continued trying to protest, but Rosa said, "It will be an honor to have you. You can meet my family and have plenty of time to visit with Riordan. What do you call him? We don't even know his first name."

"His name is Lafayette, but everyone calls him Faye."

"Now you know why I don't use my first name," Riordan said. He was recovering from the shock of seeing his family, and he watched Rosa carefully and saw that she was on her best behavior.

Finally she said, "We'll have to rent a buggy to get you to the ranch. I'll go see about that. Riordan, bring them down to the livery stable when you're ready to go. I'll also let Hannah—she is a friend who has been staying with us—know that we will be leaving soon." She turned to the store owner who was listening avidly. "Fred, load these in the wagon outside, will you?"

"Sure will, Miss Rosa."

She left, and Leo said, "That's a good-looking woman. Is she Spanish?"

"Part Spanish with a little Crow mixed in."

"You mean the Indian kind of Crow?" Max lifted his eyebrows.

"That's right. Her mother was half Crow. I guess that makes her one-fourth. They say the Crow are the best-looking Indians on the plains." They stood there talking, and finally Riordan said, "Where are your bags?"

"We left them at the wharf. We didn't know where to take them."

"Well, let's go see if she's found a buggy. We'll get you out to the ranch. You'll see a side of life you've never seen before, I expect."

Marshal Swinson was outside, and he said, "Well, Mr. Riordan, I want to congratulate you on this son of yours. He don't look it, but he's got the bad men in this territory scared of him. You heard how he saved Heck Thomas's life, and he had to shoot another one that was going to harm Miss Ramirez. He was an outlaw, too."

Caleb stared at the marshal and shook his head. "He never did anything like this at home. All he did was paint pictures."

Swinson grinned broadly. "Well, you watch how the bad ones act around him. It's like they're walking around a keg of dynamite that's liable to go off at any minute. Come along. I'll help you."

Riordan said, "Let's go. And that's enough talk about me."

Rosa and Hannah saw Riordan and his family approaching. Rosa introduced everyone to Hannah, who told the story of how Riordan had saved her, with Rosa's help, which further embarrassed Riordan.

Rosa had rented a two-seat buggy with a top. "That'll keep the sun off you, Mrs. Riordan."

"Thank you, dear. That's so thoughtful of you."

"I'll drive the buggy, and you can sit in the front with me."

"Riordan, why don't you take the wagon?"

"All right, Rosa. I will."

Rosa drove by the dock to pick up the baggage. The men loaded it in the wagon, and they all started on their way home.

Rosa and Eileen chatted easily as they traveled. They talked mostly of the countryside and what brought Rosa and her family to this territory.

Rosa finally broached the subject she hoped to elicit some new information about: Riordan. "You know I made a terrible mistake about your son when he first came."

"How is that, my dear?"

"Well, I needed help to run down some outlaws that killed one of my hired hands. I rode into town to asked Judge Parker if he had any men available. All the regular marshals were gone, so he assigned your son. You should have seen him. They had given him the hardest jobs they could find, the dirtiest."

"I know. I asked Judge Parker to do that."

Rosa looked at her. "Why did you ask him that?"

"I hoped he would get tired of it, come back, and pick up his life again."

"What was his life like back East?"

"He spent most of his time painting pictures," Eileen said. "His father and brothers were pretty disgusted with it. Caleb thought he should have gone into business with him at the factory."

"Does he still feel that way?"

"Not really. We discovered Faye's paintings are very good, just as I always thought. But of course, Caleb thought I was just speaking as a mother. Anyway, he could have a very fine career as an artist. Do you think he will stay here?"

"I don't know. You'll have to ask him," Rosa said. She slapped the line on the horses and they broke into a fast trot.

They continued to chat, but Rosa was unable to get any more information about Riordan from his mother. She really liked the older woman and could see where Riordan got some of his nicer qualities.

They finally arrived at her grandfather's property. "Well, there's the ranch," Rosa said.

"How picturesque. You raise horses?"

"Horses and some cattle. Come along." She looked back and saw that the mounted hands who had gone along for protection were following behind Riordan who was driving the wagon next to her buggy. As they approached the house, a tinge of uncertainty ran up Rosa's spine. The house was too quiet. Something was definitely wrong. "Where is everyone?" she turned and asked Riordan.

Riordan looked around. The fear in his gut reflected what he saw on Rosa's face, but he did not want her to see it from him, so he forced himself to remain calm and answer in a light tone, "I don't know. Looks vacant."

The entire party rode up to the front of the house. Before anyone could dismount, the front door opened, and Henry "the Fox" Beecher stepped out. He was wearing gray trousers and a light blue shirt with a dark blue handkerchief around his neck. His low-crowned hat was shoved back on his head, and he was smiling like he had some inner amusement.

"What are you doing here, Beecher?" Riordan demanded.

"Well," Beecher said, "I've been thinking about you and about the way you took a man away from me, Riordan. Doesn't sit well with me. I can't put up with it. People are laughing at me, so I decided to do something about it."

Rosa's fear showed in her voice. "Where is my family?"

"Safe and sound. Bring 'em out, boys." Beecher's men brought out Mateo, Chenoa, Raquel, Juan, and Frank Lowery. "See. They're all right. I'm not a bad fellow. I wouldn't hurt such fine people." Beecher smiled and shoved the hat farther back on his head. "Let me show you something. You notice all my men here have guns, and I want for you to look at the barn over there. My men are going to be all right as long as your fast gun behaves himself." He pointed toward the barn and said, "Riordan, look at that second story. I've got two men there with rifles. Both of them are aimed at Miss Ramirez. You may be fast with that gun of yours, but you can't beat this hand."

"What are you saying, Henry?" Riordan asked.

"Why, I'm saying that Rosa is going with me. I'm taking her away from you as you took my man."

Riordan felt the chill of fear. "You can't do that. You'll never get away with it."

"Oh, I think I can and I will. I could have shot you off your horse, but I'm giving you a chance." He took a step forward and spread his hands out in an eloquent gesture. "Here's the way this will play out. I'll take the woman with me, and you come and take her from me like you did George. Just you. No posse. I'll give you three days. You come alone. We'll be waiting for you. You come now and see how much good that fast gun will do you."

Riordan tried to think, but he knew that Beecher was not joking. There probably were rifles aimed directly at Rosa, and the men on the porch all had their guns out. "You harm Rosa, and Judge Parker will put fifty of his marshals on your trail."

"Well, you'll have to stop that from happening, Riordan. As soon as you're dead in the dust, we'll let her go. What do you say, fast gun? From what I hear you can draw and shoot me down right now, but if you do, then my men will cut down the rest of your folks."

Riordan thought quickly and knew what he must do. "It looks

like you got the best of the argument, Henry."

Beecher laughed pleasantly. "I knew you'd see it that way. Bring the horses, Wahoo."

A Mexican rode around holding the reins of several horses.

"Get on that horse, Miss Ramirez. We'll see if Riordan values you as much as he does his hide. Oh, one thing more," Beecher added as Red Lyle pulled Rosa off the buggy and led her to her mount. "You have three days, as I said, to come. After that, I'll take your woman for myself. I'll treat her right." He raised his voice, "Okay, you fellows, come out of the barn."

They all watched as two men with rifles exited. Hack Wilson was one of them. He said, "Lots of doings, Henry. I say just burn him right now."

"No, everyone says he is some kind of a white knight in armor ready to save poor folk. Let's see if he is. Come on." They all turned to ride out.

Riordan couldn't resist the itch to pull his gun. But he stopped from actually pulling it from the holster.

Rosa must have seen his action as she cried out, "Don't do it, Riordan!"

"Now, that's smart, Rosa. Your knight will come and get you, but he'll get killed doing it. All right. I'll be out there somewhere waiting for you. Three days."

Riordan watched as the men rode away.

At once a babble of voices broke out. Ringo said, "We'll have to follow them. We can beat 'em, Riordan."

"No, Henry's too smart. The first thing he'd do if he saw a bunch coming would be to kill Rosa. It'll have to be his way."

CHAPTER 20

The journey Rosa was forced to make with Henry Beecher and his outlaw band was torture for her. They went at an easy trot, and all she could think was, *With every step the horses make, I'm getting farther away from home.*

"Don't worry, Rosa. I'm sure your hero will come through." Henry had pulled up beside her and was grinning at her. "After all, he is the white knight coming to save the fair princess, isn't he?" He kept up such talk for some time, and finally when Rosa simply refused to answer him or even look at him, he shrugged and said, "You'll be friendlier after a few days with us."

They rode for four hours, stopping only to rest the horses once, and finally they came into a stretch of what could only be described as badlands. There were no trees to speak of, just scrubs hardly higher than three feet. The land rose slightly into hills, which they had to ride around. Overhead, the sky was a dull gray, and the feeble rays of a waning sun cast the entire location to Rosa into a grim light. Finally they pulled up, after crossing several arroyos and making their way through several canyons, some barely wide enough to permit the passage of a horseman. Henry spurred his horse and came back to her. "Well, there it is. See, up on that hill there. There's your castle, Rosa."

The "castle" was a weather-beaten frame house with rusted tin for a roof. There was a porch running the length of the building, the roof of which was propped up by six-inch saplings. There was a run-down look about the place. The barn was leaning, and it received the same kind of treatment as the roof—six-inch logs dug into the ground and pushing against the top kept the whole structure from falling. The fences were in bad shape, barely good enough to keep the herd of horses that looked up and whinnied as they approached.

When they reached the house, Henry stepped out of the saddle, reached up, and pulled Rosa down. "Don't be bashful, sweetheart. This is your new home."

Rosa felt the strength of his arms as he pulled her up the steps, and when he opened the door, several chickens came fluttering out, clucking and ruffling their feathers. "Maybe you can do a little housekeeping. Me and my boys, we're not much at that." Beecher smiled. He pulled her inside, turned back, and said to his men, "Unsaddle those horses and grain 'em and see that they have plenty of water drawn for them. They've had a hard trip."

Rosa glanced about noting that it was about as unlovely a room as she had ever seen. The floor had been painted some bright color once but now was a leprous gray, scarred by spurs and with boards nailed over holes to keep the livestock out, which it had failed to do. The room had a cast-iron stove at one end with the stovepipe wired together and the door to the oven sagging. A three-by-ten-foot table served for meals she supposed, and some of the dishes from the last meal were still there with the food hardening and flies swarming everywhere.

"We don't stay here much, so we don't keep it up," Henry said.

He came close to her, and when he stood directly in front of her looking into her eyes, Rosa felt a trace of fear. She knew this man was ruthless, that he thought nothing of killing any more than the other members of his band. Now she forced herself to stand straight and meet his gaze. "It looks like a pigsty."

Beecher laughed suddenly. "I like a woman with spirit, but you can clean it up. Make yourself handy while we're waiting on Riordan to follow us here. Come on. I'll show you where you'll stay."

He walked across the room, and she followed him. There was a hallway, with rooms on each side, she supposed.

Beecher walked to the end, opened a door, and said, "Right in there, sweetheart."

Rosa moved inside the doorway and was disgusted. "This place is filthy!" She stared at the bedstead with broken springs and a mattress losing its padding. There was a washstand with a chipped pitcher and bowl, and a bucket over in the corner.

"Well, it's not the Waldorf, but you'll like it here. I'm going to have to leave you awhile now. I'll have to lock you in. Not that I think you could get away. If you try to run away, Rosa, it'll just make it hard on you. You saw what the land is out there. From up here on this hill, we can see ten miles, so just make yourself comfortable." He waved toward a chair that was broken but had been fitted with sticks and boards to make it sit up. "I'll be back, and you can cook a good supper for us." He looked at her and said, "I guess you're pretty scared."

Rosa looked at him. "I know you'd do anything, Henry, so of course I'm scared."

"I'm not such a bad fellow," Beecher said, his eyebrows rising in surprise. "As long as I get my own way, I'll look out for you." He waited for her to reply, and when she said nothing, he turned and walked out.

She heard the door close, and then she heard a bar being dropped to prevent her from opening the door. Quickly she walked over to the window, which was barred. The bars were so close together that there was no hope of wiggling through them. A child might do it but not a grown woman. She looked out over the landscape and noticed that with the exception of one clump of three walnut trees grouped together over to her left, the trees had all been cut down. She lifted her eyes and noted that the house was up on the highest point around. The land fell away for miles, it seemed, and she realized that Beecher had chosen this place because, with a lookout, no one could ever take the man off guard.

She turned and for a long time paced the floor, which was rather dangerous because it had broken boards that she could step through. The thought came to her that maybe she could remove the boards at night and crawl down under the house, but she found they were nailed securely, and she had no tools to remove them.

Finally Rosa sat down in the patched-up chair. Her mind was in a state of confusion. She tried to calm herself, but everything she could think of had a grim ending. *Riordan will come*, she thought. Then immediately she whispered, "Don't do it, Riordan! They'll kill you!" Realizing the futility of speaking, she simply sat in the chair. After a time, she heard the men laughing and banging in the next room and dreaded when she would have to go out and be subjected to their crude talk and manners.

She surprised herself when she suddenly began thinking of the sermon that she had heard. She had a good memory, but this was different. It seemed she could hear every sentence that the minister had spoken. It was a relief to think of something other than Henry Beecher and his murderous band. She thought about the scripture that the preacher had read, the woman with the issue of blood, and how she had sought Jesus out, and how she touched Him and was healed instantly. She thought of this for some time, and then her mind moved to the other illustration, the woman caught in adultery. Rosa had a vivid imagination at times, and she could almost see the scene. The woman being dragged before Jesus, before the whole town, she supposed. She thought about how the men had insisted that she be killed. Rosa went over the whole scene, thinking about how the men had left and Jesus stood up and asked the woman where her accusers were. *She must have been weeping. She says, "They're gone." Jesus then says, "I do not condemn thee," and the woman reacts with tears to that*, she thought.

The noise from the other room grew louder, and she knew soon she would be called out to cook for the men. She was used to being around rough men, but always she had had control of them. These men had control of her now, she realized. She was totally at the mercy of Henry Beecher, and it was not beyond him to throw her to his men for their entertainment.

She forced herself to think again. *I'm like that woman taken in adultery. I haven't done that, but I've been a sinner all my life. If I could just hear Jesus say, "Neither do I condemn thee," I think I'd be the happiest woman in the world*, she thought. She remembered the invitation that the preacher had extended. He had said at one point, *"A person can find God anywhere. In the middle of the desert with no one there, in a crowded room, on the streets. It doesn't matter. It's when you believe that He's the Son of God and you're ready to yield your life to Him. That's when He'll say, 'Neither do I condemn thee,' and you'll become a part of the family of God."*

Suddenly the door rattled and opened, and Henry said, "Come on, sweetheart. You can do some cooking for us. We butchered some beef. Reckon you can cook steaks, can't you?"

Knowing that she had no choice, Rosa got up and walked into the room. The men were leering at her. She walked over to the stove at once and began cooking their meal, ignoring them as best she could.

⁂

Riordan knew his father was a man accustomed to being able to solve any problem, but as Caleb Riordan watched Henry Beecher and his men disappear into the distance raising huge dust clouds, he must have felt totally helpless. Riordan understood the feeling all to well.

"We've got to do something!" his father cried out desperately. "We've got to go back to Fort Smith and get a posse!"

"That won't do, Father," Riordan said. "You heard what Beecher said, and he's just cruel enough to do it, too. He'd kill Rosa in a minute if he saw a band of marshals coming."

Eileen came over. "But you can't go after them alone. They're all killers. You're just one man."

Riordan put his arm around his mother and said softly, "Well, it's not what I'd like to do, but the question is—is it the right thing to do?"

Mateo Ramirez said, "Go get my daughter. You can do it." He looked sickly and pale in the fading sunlight.

Chenoa came to stand beside her husband and said, "That's asking too much of anyone, Mateo."

"No, it's not," Riordan said.

The ranch hands all stood watching the drama. Ringo finally said to Riordan, "They can talk all they want to, but I can tell you right now I know you and you are going after that girl."

"I think you're right, Ringo. I don't think you can get her, Riordan. No offense, now. You're fast with a gun, but there's too many of them, and you can bet they'll be holed up in a safe place."

"I need a little time to think," Riordan said.

Chenoa took charge. She introduced herself and her family to the new guests. "Now, everyone come into the house, please. I know you are all tired and hungry. We'll fix something to eat and then try to figure out what to do."

Riordan turned and walked away from the house. He was aimless, for it mattered little where he went, as the situation wouldn't change. Riordan had never faced such a dilemma as this. He tried to think of a way to get Rosa back, but Henry was too

283

clever. *He knows he's got me, and he knows I'll come. I don't think I can do it by myself, though.*

Finally he arrived back at the house. Twilight had come. There were sounds of talking in the house.

Riordan looked up and saw Hannah coming out to the porch. "What are you going to do?" she asked in a solemn tone.

"I know I've got to go after her, Hannah."

"I knew you'd say that, but I want you to know God before you leave."

"It may be too late for me."

"No, you've got a good spirit in you. You told me how you made a profession of faith when you were a boy and that you'd gotten away from it. I think you've been in God's family all this time. You just need to come back."

"How do I do that?"

Hannah moved closer to him and put her hand on his arm. "You remember the story in the Bible of the Prodigal Son? How he went bad, went away from home, and ruined his life? And what did he do?"

Riordan smiled briefly. "He decided he'd had enough eating with the hogs and wanted to go home and just tell his father what he had done and that he was sorry."

"You remember it well. And what happened when he got home? Did his father curse him and tell him to leave?"

Riordan dropped his head and thought. "No, the Bible says, if I remember correctly, the old man looked up and saw him when he was a long ways off, and he ran to meet him. He threw his arms around him, and the boy tried to tell him how badly he had messed up his life. The old man wouldn't listen to it, though. He said, 'Kill the fatted calf. Make merry for this, my son, was lost but now he's found again.' Something like that."

"That's very close to word for word," Hannah said. "But you need to come back to your Father, too. Don't you see?"

Riordan had been touched by the sermon much in the same way that Rosa had. He said quietly, "I need God. I know that."

"We'll pray, and you must dedicate yourself to Christ. Will you pray with me?"

For a moment Riordan seemed to be swayed between two choices, and then he whispered. "I've got to."

The two bowed their heads, and Hannah prayed fervently a long prayer, an encouraging prayer. Finally her voice fell away.

Riordan was silent for a moment. Then he said, "Lord God, I'm not worth anything. I haven't served You, but I want to." He went on to confess about his life away from God. Finally he said, "Lord, I want to be in Your family, so just like that wayward boy that came to his father, I come to You." He waited for a long time.

Hannah didn't speak. The two of them were totally silent.

Then something happened. Riordan had been disturbed and confused, his thoughts like the waves of the sea without purpose. But now there seemed to be a calm that was creeping into his heart, and he realized that this was what he was looking for.

"God's welcoming you home, isn't he?"

Riordan's throat was thick, and he could barely speak. He felt the tears in his eyes. "I may not have much life left, but whatever I do have, I give it to God."

The next morning Riordan ate breakfast with the family. When they were almost through, he spoke to them as a group. "I've got to go get her. You all know that. There's no other choice."

Caleb said, "Son, you're just finding yourself, and I'm just discovering what a good son you are. You can't throw it all away."

Riordan rose to his feet and looked at his father and his brothers. "I wouldn't be a good son if I let Beecher have Rosa, would I now?"

No one said a word in answer.

Riordan finally said, "I prayed last night for the first time, really, in years, since I was a boy. I told God I would do whatever He commands, so now I'm going to do it. I'll be leaving in a moment, as soon as I get saddled."

Caleb said, "I can't think. I've always been able to fix things, but I can't fix this."

"I think God is fixing it," Eileen said. "Come. We'll all pray while he is gone and trust God for the outcome."

They all went out to the corral, and Riordan began strapping the saddle down on Big Red.

His mother came to him, and when she looked up at him, he saw that there was pride in her eyes. "I'm proud of you, son. You might not live through this, and that would be a terrible tragedy for all of us, but I know you're doing it because you love that woman. Is that right?"

"Maybe I do. I'm not really sure yet. But I'd go even if I didn't."

Caleb had been silent for a while. Finally he said, "You know.

I don't know how this is going to turn out. I always wanted a son that was strong, and I didn't think you were, Faye, but now I see that you are stronger than all of us." His voice took on a bit of sadness and regret as he added in a whisper, "And I wish I'd been a better father to you."

Riordan had to hold back tears. He simply hugged his father and said, "I love you, Father."

He then shook hands with his brothers and was amazed, as he thought he saw tears in their eyes.

He turned to his mother last. He looked straight into her eyes, communicating how much he loved and appreciated her. He kissed her on the cheek, stepped into the saddle, and then rode away at a fast pace.

CHAPTER 21

Riordan straightened up stiffly and resisted the impulse to turn around. He had been riding steadily, looking down at the ground for signs of Henry Beecher's passing. When he had the eerie feeling that he was being watched, he tensed up, waiting for the gunshot, to feel the bullet crashing into his spine.

Suddenly a voice said, "You'll never make it this way, White Eyes."

Twisting around the saddle, Riordan saw Gray Hawk, the relative of the Ramirez family. He was riding a big lanky bay without a saddle but with a twisted rope for a bridle. Riordan had seen him only once, but he was not the kind of man that one forgot. His skin was bronze and drawn tightly around his face, making his high cheekbones more prominent. His eyes were obsidian, as black as night.

Riordan was surprised to see a little smile twist the corners of his mouth upward. "What are you doing here, Gray Hawk?"

"Tryin' to keep you from getting killed." Gray Hawk kicked his horse and rode up even with Riordan's gelding. "You don't think you can find Beecher by yourself, do you?"

"I'm going to try."

"You're going to get yourself killed, as I said. Now I'm going to help you."

Riordan felt the tension leaving his muscles and said, "Well, I guess I can use all the help I can get. I'm no tracker."

"I am. Best tracker in my tribe. I can help you find Henry, and we can get the woman. We could even kill Henry if you want."

"I don't really want to kill anybody."

"That's not what I hear about you. You've killed a couple of men."

"Sometimes a man has to kill to save."

Gray Hawk glanced down at the ground and said, "Pretty easy tracking to here, but this ground gets hard farther on past those draws. Takes a good eye to follow their trail. Besides, I think Beecher probably is going to do a lot of dodging around to throw you off for a while."

"I don't think so. I think he wants me to find him."

"Maybe you're right. He's made it pretty clear that he's going to kill you."

"I guess he'll have his chance."

The two rode along silently, Gray Hawk glancing down at the ground from time to time. They did hit hard ground quickly, and more than once he had to get down, lead his horse, and lean over, scrutinizing the hard earth carefully. "They came this way." He straightened up and looked off into the distance.

It was a hazy day, and Gray Hawk did not speak for such a

long time that finally Riordan said, "Well, what are you thinking?"

"I'm thinkin' I must be crazy helpin' you commit suicide like this. If they get you, they'll get me, too."

"I'm hoping that God will keep us safe."

Gray Hawk turned and stared at Riordan. "You're a Jesus man then."

"Yes, I am. I didn't always act like it, but that's what I am, a Jesus man."

A broad smile came across Gray Hawk's face. "Well, from what I hear it's good to have God on your side. Did you notice the trail turned back there, about a quarter of a mile headed over toward those rocks?"

"No, I didn't notice."

"You better start noticin' or you're going to find yourself dead."

"Do you think their hideout is that way?"

"No, not in a hundred years. He's just moving around. As a matter of fact, he's probably got somebody watching us right now. They could knock us right out of the saddle."

"Well, it'll be dark soon. If they don't kill us before we get there, maybe we can do something."

Gray Hawk shook his head. A sober look flitted across his bronze face. "I don't believe in happy endings."

"I do this time," Riordan said grimly.

❧

Rosa had cooked several meals, for it had been two days since they had arrived at the house. None of the men had offered to touch her, but that was because Henry had warned them against it. He hadn't warned them, however, against making crude jokes at her expense. She had been exposed to rough male talk before, but nothing like this. Gritting her teeth, she determined to show no sign that she was afraid.

"These are good pancakes, Rosa," Henry said. She had found supplies enough to make pancakes, and they had blackstrap molasses to pour over them. She had been working hard, for they ate like starved wolves. "You'd better sit down and eat some yourself."

"I'm not hungry," she said.

"Do what I tell you," Henry said. "I don't want a sick woman on my hands here."

Rosa put the last pancake on a tin plate and picked up a fork and a knife. She sat down as far away as she could get from Henry, who grinned and said, "You won't always be so standoffish."

"Yes, I will." She cut the pancake up and poured syrup over it, but it might as well have been sawdust. She was exhausted, as she had slept very little. When she wasn't cooking or trying to clean up some, she felt alternately calm and uneasy as she thought of the sermon she had heard. She had the feeling that she was under some sort of magnifying glass and that God was looking at her to see what she would do.

Henry finished his pancakes, drained his coffee cup, and said, "Get me some more coffee, Sal."

Maglie got up, moved to the stove, and brought the coffee back. It was thick and black, and Henry drank it without any sugar or cream. He was studying Rosa and said, "You know, Riordan is a tough fellow, but I've got the feeling that he's smart as well."

"What does that mean?" Rosa asked.

"Why, it means that he'll never come for you. He'll run to Judge Parker and get a big posse. That's what any man would do with any sense. I get the feeling he's sweet on you. Anything between you two?"

"No." She felt this was the wrong answer, but she could give Henry nothing to build on. "All I want is out of here," she said.

"Well, you heard my terms. Riordan comes and we knock him off, then I'll see you get back to your family. You see, I'm not such a bad fellow."

Wahoo Bonham, a short, barrel-shaped outlaw with a round face and a short beard, giggled. He had a strange high-pitched giggle that sounded ridiculous from such a muscular man. "Maybe you ought to marry her, Henry. She's a better cook than anybody else and keeps the place clean."

"That's just like you, Wahoo," Mordecai Bailey said. He was as tall and lanky as Wahoo was short and round. He had only one good eye, the other covered by a black patch. "You don't have to marry her. But, maybe one of us could do the marrying if you do. I thought about becoming a preacher once. That ought to qualify me."

"You, a preacher?" Hack Wilson said. "You're about as far from a preacher as a man can get."

"What about you?" Wahoo grinned. "You'd make a pretty good preacher, a nice-looking fellow like you. Got an education. You ought to quit this robbin' and stealin' and shootin' and get you a job as a preacher in some town. They got an easy life."

Hack shook his head. "Not for me. I don't believe in God."

"I do." Everyone suddenly turned to look at Henry. He was

staring at his men and said softly, "A man's a fool not to believe in God."

"Why, Henry, you never said nothin' about having a religion!" Wahoo said in astonishment.

"No, I never said anything because I don't have any, but you just go out sometime and look at the stars. No, there's a star-maker somewhere, and I'm pretty sure it's the one in the Bible. I'm not scared of dyin', but I don't like to think about when I have to meet God and give account."

Sal Maglie said, "My grandpa was a preacher. He was a good man. He believed in God all the way through. I can't forget about him."

The talk went around the table.

Finally Rosa got up and began to collect the dishes. No one ever offered to help wash them, but she didn't expect it.

Henry watched her and waited until the men started a card game and then went over to where she was standing by the dishpan washing the sticky plates. "Rosa, I don't want to see you disappointed. I keep men watching, and as soon as they see that posse, I won't kill you like I said I would. But you'll be my woman. There's plenty of places in this territory to hide. I'll keep you until I get bored with you, and then I'll pass you along to one of my men."

"He'll come for me." Rosa was astonished at the assurance she felt as she said this.

She saw that Beecher was surprised as well. "You believe that in spite of everything?"

"I do. I'm not a Christian woman, but I believe in God, and I know Riordan's family is praying for him. . .and for me."

293

"Well,"—Henry yawned and stretched—"they'd better be good prayers." He went over and joined the card game. When she finished the dishes, he got up and said, "Come on. Get on to your room." He walked with her, and when he unlocked the door, she started to step in, but he grabbed her instead. His strength was frightening. He held her to his chest, his eyes inches away from hers. "You're a good-looking woman. I never had much of a weakness for women, but I like you. If he don't come tomorrow, you'll be mine."

"I'll never be yours!" Rosa tore away and stepped inside the doorway.

He stared at her then laughed and pulled the door shut.

She heard the bar fall into place. Rosa paced the floor, and fear came like an armed man. She had never known fear like this, and she was thinking of what Henry had said about God. *He's not afraid to die, but he's afraid to face God and give account.* The words came floating back to her, and she slumped down on the side of the bed, put her face in her hands, and suddenly began to weep. She was not a weeping woman, but things had fallen apart, and now here in this darkness, with only the candlelight flickering, she knew that she had reached the end of her resources. She wanted to run and scream, but there was no place to run and no point in screaming. The beast that held her there would merely laugh at her.

Finally she grew quiet, but the words of the minister's sermon came floating back to her again. She remembered a great deal of it, and the part that stuck in her mind was when Jesus spoke the words *'Neither do I condemn thee.'* That was what caught her attention, that Jesus, the Son of God, didn't condemn that woman who was obviously a sinner. She thought on that for a while, getting up from time to time and pacing the floor. She leaned against the wall, put her head back, and shut her eyes. "I can't go on like this," she whispered. "I've got to believe God."

She walked over to the bed, knelt down, and began to pray. The words were hard to get out. She'd never had so much trouble, but she had no practice. She nearly gave up, but she kept thinking, *That other woman took a chance. She didn't know Jesus would help her. She was desperate.* And then it came to her, and she realized that she was fully as desperate. Finally, weary, she whispered, "God, I don't have any right to ask You for anything, but I'm reaching out to You, just like that sick woman. She needed physical healing, and I need the other kind. I sinned against You terribly. There is no reason why You should forgive me, but I'm asking You to do that. Do for me what You did for that woman."

She grew quiet then and waited. From time to time she would try to pray again, but there was a stillness that had crept into her soul now. "Lord, I don't know of anything else to do. That preacher, he wanted people to believe in Jesus and to follow Him and obey Him, and, Lord, that's what I intend to do. No matter what happens tomorrow, I'm going to follow You." She lay on the bed then and after a time grew utterly still. She could hear a night bird crying out and a coyote singing its plaintive song way out on the prairie, but all she could think of was herself and God.

Time ceased to exist, but there came a moment when she whispered, "Lord, I don't deserve it, but I feel that You've done something in my heart. I'm still a prisoner, but I know somehow that I can ask You and You'll help me and Riordan. Get us out of this terrible situation." She fell asleep then, exhausted emotionally, and lay as still as if she were paralyzed.

Riordan and Gray Hawk had tracked Henry's party to a difficult place. Actually Gray Hawk had done the tracking. He had passed over ground that Riordan could not see a single mark on. It was hard, stony ground, but the Indian had eyes apparently like a microscope.

"How do you know we're following them?" Riordan asked.

"Because Rosa's horse had one shoe off. Ringo was going to put the shoe on. I've been followin' that track. She won't be far from Henry or his men."

They were paused at the foot of a hill. It was late afternoon, and the rays of the sun were feeble. Gray Hawk said, "Well, there it is. That's where they are. There are their horses in that corral."

"Well, there are at least six or eight of them. How do we go about this?"

Gray Hawk laughed silently. "I got you here. Now it's your turn. You're the tough man with the fast gun. You tell me what you want, and I'll do it."

Riordan had been thinking ever since they had paused and located the band. The house was on a rise, and he realized they would have a scout out on a moonlit night. They could spot anybody coming from any distance. He stared over at the large barn. As he stared, the door opened, and Rosa came out carrying a bucket. At the sight of her Riordan felt a sudden gladness. "She's all right."

"Yes, but look. They're watchin' every move she makes."

"We'll have to wait until dark. Wait until they all go to bed."

"That part's easy. What's the next part?"

"I'll think of something."

The sun went down, and the night creatures began calling softly. It was easy to spot the scout, for he made no attempt to hide himself.

They waited, listening to the noises from the house. Apparently the men were gambling and drinking.

"Maybe they'll all get drunk and pass out," Gray Hawk said.

"No, they won't do that. I don't know what to do, but it'll come to me."

"You've got a lot of confidence. I don't know if we're going to do any good here at all except to get ourselves killed, and I'm not ready for that yet."

They did not speak often, but slowly the night wore on. The noise in the house ceased, and it was past midnight when Riordan said, "Here's what we'll do. We've got to create a diversion."

"A diversion? What do you mean?"

"We've got to get them out of the house, all except Rosa. I'm sure they've got her locked up. So here's what I've come up with. I want you to go over to that guard out there by the barn. He's got to be put down."

"You want his scalp?"

"I wish you didn't have to kill him, but if he gives the alarm too soon, we're done. You go in there and, except for Rosa's horse, let the horses out at a walk. Bring Rosa's horse back here to me."

"And then what?"

"Then you go set fire to the barn, and when it's burning good, fire off a couple of shots."

Gray Hawk chuckled. "You white men have crooked minds. What's going to happen then?"

"The men will come to put the fire out, and when they do, I'll go in and get Rosa. You come back and meet me here, and we'll get out of this place."

"It's too complicated. It'll never work."

"It's got to work, Gray Hawk. Now get to it."

Gray Hawk disappeared, silent as a shadow. Riordan sat there. The house was clearly outlined in the moonlight. He had been all the way around, and he saw that there was one window with bars on it. "That must be where she is. I hope they all get out of there so I don't meet any of them."

Time seemed to stand still, but finally Gray Hawk came back leading a horse.

"Tie him with ours, Gray Hawk." He waited until the Indian had tied the horse, and then he said, "Now, go back and set the barn on fire. Let it get to blazing fairly well, then fire off a couple of shots and holler and then run back here as quick as you can."

"And you're going in?"

"I'm hoping they'll all come to put the fire out so that the barn won't be burned up with the feed."

Gray Hawk was enjoying all this. "This is the kind of life I like, lots of entertainment." He disappeared again into the darkness.

Fifteen minutes later Riordan saw a flickering light and knew that it was the barn. It grew higher and higher, and then he heard several shots and somebody hollering. He knew it was Gray Hawk. He straightened up and moved in closer.

The door opened, and men began tumbling out. Henry was yelling, "Get the horses out of there. They'll burn up! Put that fire out!" They all ran toward the barn.

Riordan knew his moment had come. He made a dead run for the house. Glancing over his shoulder, he saw the men fighting the fire. He burst in with his gun in his hand, but the house was empty. "Rosa, where are you?" he shouted.

"Back here!"

He ran to the sound of her voice and saw the barred door. He ripped the bar off, threw it down, and opened the door.

Suddenly she was in his arms. "I knew you'd come, Riordan," she said weeping. "I knew you'd come."

"I had to come, but let's get out of here. They may come back any minute."

The two fled, and when they got back to the horses, Gray Hawk was there. He was grinning and said, "You're a good man, Riordan. You should have been an Indian."

"Too late for that. Let's get out of here. Gray Hawk, could you take us another way? They won't be able to follow our tracks tonight, but they'll pick them up in the morning. By that time we'll be gone."

The Indian nodded and jumped on his horse.

Riordan and Rosa mounted up. He looked at her and said as he picked up his lines, "I came to realize I couldn't live without you, Rosa."

She gave him a smile and moved her horse closer. When he leaned over, she kissed him. "Let's get out of here," she said. "We'll not get another chance."

CHAPTER 22

"Looks like it might rain tonight," Riordan remarked, looking up at the sky. "Those clouds look like they've got some rain in 'em maybe."

Rosa shifted in her saddle and glanced upward. "I hope it does. It'll wash out any tracks we make." She looked over her shoulder and added, "I keep thinking I'll look back and see Henry and his bunch right there, coming at us."

"I don't think so. Gray Hawk gave them a false scent to follow. They'll follow it for a while, and then they'll figure out that it's not us. But they will be coming after us. You know that."

The two were riding in a canyon that twisted and turned, and when they emerged at the far end, they found a small stream with what looked like good, clear water. "We might as well wait here. We can't travel tonight, and besides, the horses would give out."

"I'm pretty tired myself. . .Faye." She grinned at him.

Giving Rosa a quick look, obviously due to the use of his old name, Riordan nodded. "I am, too. We've got a little food left in here. Let's tie the horses and let 'em feed on that grass. We'll leave before daylight in the morning."

The two stepped off their horses and removed their saddles and blankets. Then they staked the two, using lariats to tie them to the tops of young saplings. They were separated so that each of them had plenty of grass, and they began chomping at once hungrily.

"I'll break some of that dried wood off of that fallen tree. You look through the saddlebag and see what we can come up with. It won't be much."

"We'll make out." Rosa watched Riordan as he moved away toward the dead tree that had fallen and began breaking small branches off. Then with a sigh she pulled off his saddlebag and found two cans of beans, an end of bacon, and a quarter of a loaf of bread, which was already hard. *We'll soak it in the beans with juice*, she thought.

Thirty minutes later they were both seated before the small fire. Rosa was heating the beans up in the skillet. She had added some water to make it more like soup and was dropping the bits of bread in. The bacon was frying in another pan and sent a tingle of smoke upward.

Rosa looked up and followed its track then remarked, "Look. There's just one star in the sky. I wonder where the rest of them are."

"They took the night off." Riordan grinned.

Rosa knew he was weary and tired, and worried for her. She knew that Henry would kill them both if he found them.

"That's Venus," he said, nodding his head toward the star.

Rosa looked at him and asked, "How do you know that?"

"Oh, my head is packed with useless knowledge. Venus is called the evening star. Anytime you look up at night and all the stars are gone except one, that's Venus."

"I wish I knew as much as you do. It must have been nice to go to school and then go on to college."

"I was bored out of my skull most of the time," Riordan said. He picked his fork up, stirred the beans, and cautiously lifted a few to taste. "Still not hot enough," he said. "I like my food hot."

The two sat there in silence. From far off came the mournful howl of a coyote.

"That sound always makes me sad," Rosa said.

"Well, he's probably having the time of his life. Coyotes have an easy life. Something to eat, a little water to drink, and a little family life to make little coyotes. We should have it so good."

Rosa shook her head. "I don't think anybody has that easy a time in this life."

"No, I don't think so either."

She glanced at him and studied his face carefully. "Something happened to me at Henry's house."

A look of concern hit his face. "What did he do to you?"

"No, nothing like that. I mean something spiritual."

"Well, that's a great thing. I gave my life to God before coming after you. I have felt so much freer since then."

"Well, I feel so. . .guilty still."

"You mustn't do that. My grandfather used to say, when you ask forgiveness for a sin, God always gives it. That's in the Bible, in the book of First John. 'If we confess our sins, he is faithful and just to forgive us our sins, and to cleanse us from all unrighteousness.' You can take that to the bank. God Himself said it. Grandpa said, too, that you could take your sin out in a boat in the ocean, drop it in the deepest part, and then put a sign up somehow out there that says 'No Fishing Allowed.'"

"I think the beans are done. We have one plate."

"You take the plate, and I'll take the pot."

She divided the meal up. She had a spoon, and he had a fork.

"Bacon's about done. Wish there was some more of it."

"You know. I want to do something, Faye. I know families pray over food before they eat it. I've never done that, but I'd like to start."

"Well, go ahead and start. We did it all the time at my house."

"You do it then."

"All right." Riordan bowed his head and said simply, "Lord, we thank You for this food, we thank You for every blessing, and we ask You to give us safety, in Jesus' name. Amen."

"Amen," Rosa echoed him. "Is that all there is to it?"

"That's it. You don't think God expects a long oration for a blessing over food, do you?"

"I don't know. I don't know anything. I don't know how I'm going to live the kind of life I know a godly woman does."

"You *are* a godly woman, Rosa. That's what God made you when you called on Him." He took a mouthful of beans, moved it around in his mouth, and then immediately began to make a face. "These are hot!" He took a sip of water from the canteen that they shared and said, "I've been having thoughts myself about how I started out with God when I was just a boy, but I got away from it somehow and got interested in art. Things were so easy at our house. Never wanted for anything, but I see now that I did. I needed God, and I wasted a lot of my life."

The two continued to eat the beans and the bacon, washing it all down with cool water from the brook.

Finally they sat back, and Riordan said, "We'll wash the pot and the frying pan in the morning. I'm too tired."

Rosa put two more small pieces of wood on the fire. She listened to it crackle, and the movement sent fiery sparks upward. "Look. They look like tiny stars going up to the heavens."

"They do, don't they? Here. We're going to have to make some arrangements." He got up and went to where he had thrown his saddle and got the blanket he carried behind the cantle and brought it back. "Here. Let's sit on this. It'll be more comfortable." They sat down close together.

Rosa was very aware of his presence and his arm pressing against hers. "I have to tell you that I haven't been a good woman."

"You don't have to tell me, Rosa."

"I guess I do. I want you to know. A man came into my life, and I thought he loved me. He said he did." Her voice was unsteady, and she looked down. The light from the fire flickered on her face, and she added, "He was unfaithful and left me, and I grew bitter. I'm like that woman that preacher preached about, the one that committed adultery."

"Well, that's all over now. Both of us have made a decision to serve God. I guess we're at some kind of fork in the road, and we've got to be sure we don't take the wrong way."

"How can I be sure what God wants?"

"Lots of scriptures talk about that. It says to wait on the Lord. Don't rush ahead. Pretty hard for some of us to do."

They fell silent for a time.

Rosa broke the silence, "I think Henry Beecher is going to come for us."

"No doubt. He's that kind of man."

She turned to him suddenly and put her hand on his forearm. "I think you need to go back East, Faye. He couldn't get you there."

"One thing I've learned is that you can't run from trouble. You have to trust God and face it. Sooner or later things come back to haunt you."

"Faye, you've led such a simple life. I don't know what could haunt you."

"You know, Rosa, when people talk about the big sins— murder, adultery, theft—that's not been my problem. I've been troubled by the spiritual sin."

"What kind of sin is that?"

"Something that you do that's wrong, but other people don't see it. God says it's wrong, but it's on the inside of you. People could look at you and never know it. Like envy. You could envy somebody's possessions. Nobody would know it, but that's a sin. So I've had trouble with sins on the inside."

She was quiet for a long time. "I still think you ought to go back East. You can be a great painter."

"I'll probably be a painter wherever I am. I've grown to love this country, Rosa. I didn't think I would. It looks so barren to some people, but I like it. That's the way God made it. And there are plenty of subjects to paint. Indians, for example. Nobody is really doing that."

"But Henry will hear about it. How would you feel if you had to shoot him?" A long silence passed, and Rosa could see that he was thinking hard.

Finally he said heavily, "I don't want to kill anyone, Rosa. I'd rather save someone, and that's all I can say." He thought for a while and then added, "My mother asked me why I had to leave to come after you. I told her I had to do it because it was the right thing to do. . .and I thought, too, that I might be falling in love with you."

Rosa grew absolutely still. She did not know what to say, for no man had ever affected her like this.

Finally he reached over and pulled her so that she turned to face him. "Rosa, I can only tell you what's in my own heart. For me, you are the only woman on earth. I love you for your beauty, but that's not who you are. That may fade sometime, as it does for all of us, but I tell you what. When this beautiful dark hair is white, I'll still love you, and when this strong figure is dim and bent with age, I'll love you even more than I do now. After you've lost the bloom of life, I'll love you, Rosa, for you're the one woman, I think, that God has made for me."

Rosa was moved. She leaned toward him, and he brought her to him with a quick sweep of his arm. When he kissed her, she felt the desperate hunger, a feeling that came to her as it never had before. She knew she had this power over Faye, this way of lifting him out of the ordinary, to touch the vague hints of glory a man and woman might know.

She moved to catch a better view of his face, and when she saw the heaviness of his lips, she thought she knew what he was telling her. And something like a pair of shears seemed to cut a restraining cord.

He put his arms around her and drew her into himself.

Even though he was saying all of these wonderful things, she was not yet completely sure of him, of how he felt, and she had a dread of making a mistake with him. For a moment, she watched him. She felt no anger and offered no resistance.

He lowered his head and kissed her again.

It was what Rosa wanted. She could sense that he felt the luxury of it as well. For her, it was a need that she could neither check nor satisfy. She knew the pressure of his arm and his mouth was too much for her, yet her own arms were tight about him, holding him as he held her.

Finally, with an effort, Riordan removed his arms and ended the embrace. He said simply, "I want to spend the rest of my life with you, Rosa."

She was shaken by the kiss, and she said, "Your family wouldn't like that, and I'm not sure I could live in the East. People would make fun of you for taking a Spanish woman, especially one who is also part Indian."

"I think all couples have to make some adjustments when they come together, but God will help us. And if I could have my way, I'd live out here half of the year. Buy a ranch with some peace and quiet where we could come and be close to your family. And then have another home in the East where I could go to visit my family."

"You think that's possible?"

"I think it is. We'd better get some rest. Well, we only have one blanket. You wrap up in it."

"No." She smiled. "We'll share it. I trust you, and I never thought I'd trust any man."

They lay down on the blanket and pulled it around them.

Rosa felt him relax as he fell into sleep. She whispered, "I love you, Faye." Then she went to sleep, a smile fixed on her face.

"Did you get Hannah on her way, Ringo?" Eileen asked.

"Yeah, I hired four men to take her to her new post. With that many watching her, she'll be fine. Shame to waste a good woman like that. She'd make a fine wife."

"She's doing what she thinks is right," Eileen said. They had finished breakfast, and no one spoke for a while, but she knew they all had the same thoughts—that Faye might be hurt or even dead. Eileen said, "I want us all to pray for Faye. He's come a long way, but he's in trouble, and I want us to ask God to keep him."

She bowed her head, and the other members of the family did the same. Afterward the men left, and Eileen turned to Chenoa. "What do you think about my son marrying your daughter?"

Chenoa gave Eileen a direct look, and there was pain in her eyes. "You can't know what a hard time Rosa has had. She had to give up everything that she wanted to keep the family together. We would have starved, Eileen, if she hadn't helped us. She had to work in a terrible, despicable saloon just to make money to feed us."

"I treasure her for that, Chenoa. She's a fine woman. All she needs is to let God come into her life." The two women had begun to grow close during the Riordans' brief stay. Eileen had never been around people of the Ramirezes' class, but she saw fine things in all of them. "You know, Faye loves Rosa, whether he fully realizes it yet or not. How would you feel about it if they married?" she asked again.

"We're from two different worlds, Eileen."

"I know, but if they love each other, God will make a way."

Riordan and Rosa were so happy to see the familiar ranch come into view. As they rode closer, Riordan saw Ringo and knew the hand recognized them. He ran into the house, and Riordan imagined his telling all inside that their loved ones had returned.

Sure enough, there was a stampede as everyone rushed outside.

When Riordan and Rosa dismounted, Caleb grabbed Riordan. "Son, you're back! Thank God, you're back!"

Riordan was shocked. His father had never shown this sort of appreciation or love for him. It seemed to sink down into his spirit. "I'm back, and I'm all right."

"As I told the boys and Eileen, the first thing I want to say is how proud I am of you. You are a real man, and I'm proud to have you as my son."

Eileen was standing close. Riordan put his arms around her and saw the tears in her eyes. "You brought her back, son."

The Ramirezes were gathered around Rosa, all of them trying to hold back the tears. Rosa could not.

"He brought you back," Juan said. "I didn't think anybody could."

"He saved me, but I think I knew already what kind of a man he was."

"Come on into the house," Chenoa said. "The food's ready. I know you two are starved."

"We're pretty hungry." Riordan smiled. "Your daughter's a pretty good cook, but even she can't make beans and bacon burnt over a campfire taste very good."

They all went to the table, and when they were all gathered, Rosa said, "There's something I must tell you. While I was being held at Beecher's house, they locked me in a room. I had time to myself, and I began to grow afraid. Not of what Henry would do, but of what I had been." She went on in a steady voice, and finally she said, "So I asked God to save me, and He came into my heart and gave me peace."

"Well, hallelujah!" Chenoa said. "That's wonderful news!"

Leo demanded, "How in the world did you do it, brother?"

"Well, it was mostly Gray Hawk. He found me and guided me to them and helped me get her away." He went on to tell the entire story. When he finally finished, everyone agreed what a wonderful thing it was that God had delivered them.

Finally Riordan said, "One other thing I want to make clear. I haven't had a chance to talk to you, Mateo, to ask you to give me your daughter as my wife, so I'm asking you now, you and Chenoa. I love her, and I always will."

His announcement brought smiles and cheers and applause and congratulations.

Finally Caleb said, "We'll be happy to welcome you and your wife to our home, won't we, Eileen?"

"Of course we will. We love her already."

Caleb nodded. "I've been critical of you, Faye, but I'm so proud of you now I'm about to bust."

Suddenly Mateo said, "What about Beecher? He'll be after you for besting him again."

"I don't want to take a man's life, and I'm not going to do it unless he absolutely makes it necessary." He shrugged and said, "I'm handing in my badge as marshal, and Rosa and I are going to start a new life."

Rosa came and stood beside him.

He put his arm around her and looked down at her. "Well, we've got everyone's permission. Now all we need is somebody to marry us, and we'll have our whole life together."

CHAPTER 23

A slight breeze brought some comfort from the heat of the day as Caleb and Eileen sat on the front porch. They had spoken for a long time of the problem that Faye was facing, but no matter what, they could think of nothing that seemed certain to bring a solution.

Chenoa came up and leaned against one of the pillars of the post. She gazed out into the distance and said nothing.

The silence grew so heavy that finally Eileen said, "What's troubling you, Chenoa?"

"I'm worried about Rosa and Riordan."

Caleb instantly said, "You're worried about their marriage."

"Yes. Your son is a fine man, and we all have the utmost respect for him, especially since he risked his life to save our daughter, but I'm not certain that the marriage between them would be a good thing."

Caleb shifted uneasily in his chair and glanced over at Eileen.

Finally he said, "Why would you say that? Faye can give her a good life."

"We're hoping he'll go back to the East with us," Eileen said. "He's becoming well known as a painter and could make a good living for her. Besides, we would help them."

Chenoa turned and faced them both. There was a troubled look on her bronze features, and she said reluctantly, "I think it would be hard on Rosa because white people look down on other races."

Mateo joined them now. He stood beside his wife and listened intently to what was being discussed.

"I think that depends on the people," Eileen said. "Some dislike other races, but others have no problem with people of different ethnicities."

Mateo said, "If they lived here, it would be different. No one makes anything of a white man who marries a woman who has Indian blood, but it would be different in the East."

"You can't know that, Mateo," Eileen said quickly.

"You know it's so, though, don't you?" Mateo said, his dark eyes fastening on Eileen. "You've seen it happen, I'm sure."

Eileen glanced at Caleb, knowing both of them had the same thought. They both had memories of people from their social class marrying outside the white race. Even though it was a European race, there were still problems.

"Rosa would be unhappy among the rich, white people," Mateo said. "Many would not accept her. You know that's so."

A silence fell across the four of them, and finally Chenoa said, "Will your son want to take our daughter to the big city?"

"I haven't heard the plan, Chenoa," Eileen answered, "but I've got a plan of my own."

Caleb instantly turned to face her. "What kind of a plan? You haven't said anything to me about it."

"I have my secrets, and besides, nothing may come of it. Let me think on it a little."

❧

Riordan and Rosa came in from a ride. They dismounted, tied their horses to the rails, and started into the house.

"Let's go get something to drink," Rosa said. "I wish we had some ice. At least the water will be wet."

The two went inside.

Rosa went out to the springhouse and brought in a cool pitcher of water. "We've got enough lemons and sugar for lemonade."

"Sounds good."

Rosa made the lemonade efficiently and handed him a glass. "You always had ice available in the city, didn't you, Faye?"

"Pretty much. I don't miss it all that much, though." He drank several swallows and said, "There. That washes the dust down."

They sat there talking idly, and finally he reached over and took her hand. He looked at it.

She watched him, wondering what he was thinking. Her hand was strong and showed signs of work.

He smiled at her and tightened his grip on her hand. "You've got strong hands," he remarked. "I like that. How do you feel now?"

She smiled and said, "For the first time in my life, I'm content,

Faye. I never knew where I was going. All I could see was another day in that vile saloon where I had to fight men off. But now it's different."

"I'm glad, but you still looked concerned about something. Please tell me about it."

"Well, I'm a little worried. If we stay here in the Territory, it'll be simple."

"You mean nobody pays any attention to intermarriage here."

"That's exactly right," Rosa said. "But if we go to your home in the East, some people would be unkind. I'd bring shame to you."

"You think that bothers me?" Riordan said at once. He extended his other hand and held her in a grip. "I love you, Rosa, and if we have to live at the North Pole, that'll suit me fine."

She laughed and shook her head. "I don't want to live in all that ice."

"Our parents have talked about this."

"What do they say?"

"Well, they say that they're so glad to have me back alive they'll be happy to see me married."

The two sat there sipping the lemonade.

Finally Rosa said, "We haven't had time to think about it. I'd like to get you away from this place. Somewhere it will be safe. Beecher won't stop until he kills you, Faye. You know that."

"That's the kind of man he is. I hate to run, though. It seems cowardly."

"It's either that or face him, and you said you didn't want to shoot another man."

"I don't. I don't want to ever kill another human being. So I talked to my mother, and we've come up with a plan. She is a very wise woman."

"What sort of plan?"

"We'll get married, and then we'll go to the East, but not for very long at our home. I'd like to go somewhere in the Smoky Mountains. It's beautiful there. We could have a fine honeymoon." He grinned. "Did you know that the Bible says that when the Hebrews married, the man didn't go to work for a year?"

She stared at him in disbelief. "What did he do?"

"The Bible says he just made his wife happy."

Rosa suddenly laughed. "I like that a great deal. Yes, we'll do that. You can just please me for a year."

"I'm serious, Rosa. We'll go to the Blue Ridge Mountains, and we'll do two things. We'll have a great time just being in love with each other and enjoying the scenery and just being together. And I'll be painting, and you'll be in my schoolroom."

"What does that mean?"

"Well, there are ways that Easterners have that you'll need to know about. Nothing too difficult—what to wear, what utensils to use at a meal, things like that."

"You consider yourself an expert in women's clothing?"

"Oh, definitely!" Riordan grinned broadly then dropped Rosa's hands and rubbed his palm across his chin. "I could teach you which fork to use. We'll be among some high-class people there. So when we go back to my home, everyone will fall in love with you, just as I have."

"It sounds too good to be true."

"Well, here's what I'd really like to do. I'd like for us to have a house here somewhere. Not a fancy one. Just someplace we could come. I love the West. I'd like to do some painting here of the people, the cowboys, the Indians, even the outlaws and the marshals. We could spend half our time here and then have a house somewhere close to my parents and go spend time with them. That way both families will have their grandchildren close. By the way, I'd like to have a great number of children. We'll talk about that. How do you like my plans, sweetheart?"

"I love them!"

"Good. Now about these children. I'd like to have at least four. You can have them one at a time or all at once. . . ."

❧

The house was busy with people getting ready to make the trip to Fort Smith. Riordan had gotten up that morning and said, "I want to get rid of this badge. It's like a weight on me."

"You sure you want to do this?" Mateo said. "It's quite an honor to be a marshal."

"Yes, they're great men, but it's not for me, Mateo. I want to give this badge back to Judge Parker and put this gun away for good."

"I think that's wonderful." Eileen beamed.

"You've proven what you are—a real man." Caleb nodded. "Now, it's time to move on to a new life. I love the idea of you two spending half your time close to us, and half here. That'll make all of us happy. Won't it, Mateo?"

"I think we'd all better take the hands with us," Rosa said.

Instantly Riordan looked at her. "You're thinking we might

run into Henry along the way and his bunch?"

"I think he'd like nothing better than to catch you out alone."

"All right. We'll all go. Just leave a few hands here to take care of things."

They left as soon as they had finished packing and made the trip in record time. When they pulled the buggies up in front of Judge Parker's office and tied their horses, Riordan went upstairs at once. His parents and Rosa followed.

They found Judge Parker at his desk, as usual. He rose at once and said, "Well, Marshal, I'm surprised to see you." He came around and shook Riordan's hand. "The whole Territory is talking about how you took this young lady away from Henry."

"It was mostly Gray Hawk," Riordan said.

"Well, in any case you got her back. I was trying to scrape a big posse together to go after her, but you never know about Henry. He might have killed her just out of spite."

Riordan reached up, unpinned his badge, and said, "I appreciate you letting me serve with you, Judge Parker, but I'll be leaving now. We're going back East for a time."

"Well, I think that may be a good idea. Sooner or later we'll catch up with Beecher. Nothing would please me better than to see him hang on that gallows out there."

"Judge, I want to thank you for taking care of my boy," Eileen said.

"Why, it's more like he took care of us." Parker smiled. "I'll be losing a good man, but you were meant for a different kind of life. Besides, it's good that you're leaving the Territory. Beecher won't ever forget you made a fool of him. I've been talking to Heck

Thomas. We've got a number of marshals available. They're going to leave soon and run the Fox into the ground. We'll get him. Don't worry about that."

"Thank you, Judge. I'll see you again before we leave."

"Write me when you get settled. I'd like to see some of those pictures of yours sometime."

"I'll paint one and ship it to you." Riordan smiled.

They made their good-byes to the judge and went back to the street.

"You feel better now, Faye," Rosa asked, "I mean not being a marshal?"

"It was getting to be a heavy thing. They're noble men, most of them, but just not for me."

They were headed for the restaurant, both families, and suddenly a shock ran through Riordan, for Henry Beecher stepped out of an alleyway. He had his gun drawn, and it was pointed directly at Riordan.

"Don't move, Riordan. I've got my men posted along the street."

"You're making a mistake, Henry."

"No, my mistake would have been if I tried to match draws with you. I've heard about that draw of yours, and I don't care to test it."

"I don't have a gun on me, Henry."

"I don't believe that. You always have a gun."

"Not anymore I don't, and I'm not a marshal anymore."

Beecher scowled. "I know you've got a hideout somewhere."

"No, I don't. I don't ever want to shoot anyone else."

"You're a liar!" Beecher shouted. "I'll give you a break. I count to three, and on 'three' you go for that hideout."

Judge Parker's voice came, "Beecher, you're under arrest."

Beecher looked up and saw Judge Parker leaning out the window. "You won't get me this time, Judge. All your marshals are gone out on a job. I found that out. I'm taking Riordan out."

"You'll hang if you do."

Beecher merely laughed. His eyes were alight. It was the kind of situation he liked. "All right. On the count of three. One—two—" On the count of two, Beecher fired.

Riordan thought he could feel the hiss of the bullet passing close to his ear. He did not have time to move, but he suddenly realized that there was another gunshot right on the heels of the first. He saw a black spot appear in the center of Beecher's forehead. Beecher's eyes went dead, and he simply collapsed, dropping his gun in the dust.

Riordan whirled and saw that Ringo was pulling his gun up. "You owe me for that one, Riordan." Ringo grinned. "I'm going to claim the reward on this scoundrel, and then I'm going to have me a high time."

"He died like he lived," Caleb said. "A cheat and a liar."

Beecher's men began to scatter. They mounted their horses and rode out.

"Well, they'll break up now. Henry was the brains of the outfit," Riordan said. He turned to face Rosa and saw her face was pale. "Don't be afraid. It's all over."

Rosa whispered, "God kept you from killing him."

"Yes, and I'm thankful for it. All I want is you and some peace."

"You can have me, and we'll see about the peace." She giggled.

A crowd was gathering. Some were bending over Beecher, but Riordan said, "I don't want to see him. Let's get out of here. We're safe now. God has answered our prayers for peace."

❧

Rosa and Riordan got out of the buggy and stood looking at the small cabin. "Not much of a honeymoon spot."

"But the mountains are so beautiful," Rosa said. She turned to look at the rolling hills that seemed lost in a blue haze. The air was clear, and the forest was thick. "This is such a beautiful place."

"I'm glad you like it."

"Whose house is it?"

"Well, it's ours for a week." Riordan reached over and put his arms around her. "I've got just one week to teach you how to be a good wife."

Rosa laughed and threw her arms around him. She drew him down and kissed him and said, "It's going to take longer than that for me to teach you how to be a good husband."

"Come on. Let's look at the inside." They went to the door, and he opened it then turned and suddenly swept her into his arms. "An old custom. The groom always carries the bride over the threshold." He walked inside and put her down. They stood looking around. "Looks like a palace to me."

"Plenty of peace here. That's what you wanted, Faye, me and peace."

"Right."

They found another door and saw a large bed. "This is the

bedroom. I hope you like it." He smiled at her. "You'll be spending a lot of time here."

She hit him on the shoulder, laughing.

"I'll go bring the things in. You can cook me a fine meal while I rest up. Getting married is hard work." He looked thoughtful then said, "Which case has the white silk nightgown my mother bought you?"

"Never mind. Just bring it all in. I think I'm going to wear my old flannel gown. It's sort of ratty, but after all, you should have to work to get the white silk one."

They suddenly reached for each other, and he kissed her gently and then with fervor. "We're going to have a wonderful life."

"Yes, and four beautiful children—one at a time," she smiled.

They clung to each other as they rested in the peace God had provided. A peaceful place to begin their married life together, a peace from having to fight outlaws, and the most important peace. . .the peace residing in each heart given to God in faith and love.

SABRINA'S MAN

PART ONE

PART ONE

CHAPTER 1

Little Rock, Arkansas, 1864

The late summer sun, which had been hiding behind a silver cumulus cloud, illuminated the face of Waco Smith as he stood staring up at a large sign glistening with fresh paint. Here at the north end of Little Rock, the businesses framing Main Street were, for the most part, framed structures, but others made a more permanent statement with their façade of brick and marble. Waco turned and looked down to his left to the Arkansas River that dissected the town and lent its own dark odors to the sense of the southern part of Arkansas.

Waco noticed with a degree of sadness that many of the men walking the street to his right wore parts of the Confederate uniform. Many of them were missing arms, and others hobbled along on crutches or on one leg. *This war is going to ruin the South.* The thought was bitter in his mouth, for he was tired of the war as were most people in the South.

He thought with bitterness of the year that he had served in the Confederate Army. He had joined up in a fit of patriotism when Fort Sumter had fallen but had signed up for only one year.

He had fought at Bull Run, but when his year was up, he had left the army and determined never to fight in the Civil War again.

Waco's train of thought about the war was broken when a voice behind him said, "That's a right nice sign you got there, Waco."

Waco turned and smiled at the speaker, Micah Satterfield, and paused, studying the police chief.

Satterfield was a heavyset individual with a square face, a pair of sharp blue eyes, and a neatly trimmed mustache. He had served Little Rock as police chief for three terms and kept a tight lid on the city. "You're getting to be a respectable citizen."

Shaking his head, Waco gave Satterfield a brief grin. "Never thought I'd be one of your taxpayers, did you, Chief?" He was six feet two inches tall and had to look down on Satterfield, as he did on most men.

Satterfield glanced up at the large sign that announced SMITH & BARTON HARDWARE. "Hope to get rich, do you, son?"

"I doubt that. All I've ever done is raise horses." He shrugged his broad shoulders, adding, "Will—he's the smart one."

"So I understand. You two must have been friends for a long time."

"Nope." Waco studied the sign and murmured, "I worked on my grandparents' horse ranch most of my life. My grandfather died, so I ran the ranch for Grandma. Last December she died. Since I was the only kin, she left the ranch to me. I sold out and made straight for the big city. I was tired of cleaning up after horses and aimed to waste all that money I got on wild women and whiskey."

Sheriff Satterfield studied the tall man. "Well, you didn't do that as I thought you might. What stopped you, Waco?"

Smith took off his hat and ran his hand through his stiff black hair. "Well, I would have, but when I went into the bank to deposit the money I got from the sale of the horse farm, I met Will Barton. I guess I was boasting about what a fool I was going to make of myself, and he talked me into putting off such foolishness. We got to know each other, and somehow he convinced me to go into business with him." He stuck the hat on his head, pushed it back, and said, "I still don't know how it all happened, but the first thing I knew we took my money, Will quit his job at the bank, and for the next six months we just about killed ourselves working twenty hours a day getting that hardware business started."

"You put up all the money?" Satterfield had some doubt in his voice. "That's unusual."

"Oh, Will had a little money. Mostly he took care of the finances of the business. He knew how to keep books, and he knew hardware. I just turned out to be a strong back and a weak mind. You know, Sheriff, I thought breaking horses was hard, but running a business. . .that's worse. Sometimes I wish I was back there in the simple life."

Suddenly a voice called out, "Well, are you going to stand and stare at that sign all day, or are you going to come in and give me a hand?" Both men turned and saw that Will Barton, Waco's partner, had emerged from the store. He was wearing an apron and shook his head. "I can't pick up those kegs of nails. That's your job."

"My master's voice." Waco nodded toward Satterfield, bid him good-bye, and with a rolling gait moved to the front door. "When are we going to hire somebody to do all my work, Will?"

"Not anytime soon." Will Barton smiled then and added, "If you think handling stock is hard, you ought to try balancing a set of books for a new business that's out of money. Put those nail kegs over by the wall, will you?"

"Sure." Waco moved over where six nail kegs were stacked,

picked one of them up, and carried it easily with a strength that surprised most people. He moved the rest of the kegs then leaned against the counter and sighed. He opened one barrel and pulled out a cracker and then reached into another and pulled out a pickle. He took a bite of the pickle, made a face, and said, "These things are sure sour."

"Well, stop eating them. That's my profit."

"I wish I had never run into you, Will. If I had gone right down to having my fun, I could be living it up with the hostesses down at the Golden Nugget."

"Hostesses! That's a nice word for 'em."

"Well, it doesn't do any good to be nasty. That's what they call themselves."

"If you had done that, you'd be broke and probably in jail."

Suddenly Waco grinned, which he'd been told by several ladies made him look much younger, and reached out and put his hand on Will's shoulders.

The man was his opposite in almost every way. Barton was only five feet eight and was almost fragile. He had blond hair and hazel eyes, and his face was composed of delicate features. Waco's hair lay thick and black and ragged against his temple. He had high cheekbones, and minute weather lines slanted out from his eyes across smooth bronze skin. His mouth was broad below an aqualine nose, and his eyes were a shade of gray that was almost blue.

Will had been to college for a year when his father had died. There had been no inheritance. Will had found a job as a clerk at the bank and had done well enough.

"I was just kidding, Will," Waco said. The feelings of his partner were easily hurt, so he had to be careful.

Instantly Will gave Waco a smile. "Take the cash from the sales to the bank, will you? I don't like to keep it at the store."

"Sure."

"And take the pistol. You might get held up."

"I'll be right careful." Waco moved to the drawer behind one of the counters, pulled out a .44, checked the load, stuck it in his waistband, and sighed. "Do you reckon business will pick up after this war's over, Will?"

"Bound to, and it can't last much longer," Will declared. "Grant's got Lee penned up in Richmond."

"I wish it would end today. I lost some good friends in that fracas." Waco turned and called out as he left, "I shouldn't be long."

"Sounds good."

Waco left the building, but not before hearing Will turn back to the books with a sigh.

❧

As Waco left the bank, he was greeted by a blond woman who grinned at him. "When you coming down to visit me, Waco?"

"Oh, I'll be there. You just hang on, Rosie."

Stepping outside, he looked up and studied the sky, then muttered, "There's some rain in those clouds." He walked down the street to the train station. When he got there, he stopped to talk to Oscar Riggs.

"You still aim to go hunting after a deer with me this weekend?" Oscar asked. He was a muscular man with a pair of sharp black eyes.

"Yep, we need some venison at our place."

"We'll go on Sunday morning."

Oscar shook his head violently. "I'm plum nervous about hunting on the Sabbath."

Waco was amused. "Well, you're a sinner just like I am, aren't you, Oscar?"

"Yes, but I don't want to make it any worse." He took a match out of his pocket, stuck it in his mouth, and began chewing on it. "Don't it scare you to think about what's gonna happen to us when we die?"

"Some. I try not to think about it much."

Oscar suddenly turned and said, "Well, there comes the 2:15. I hope there's no baggage for me to move."

The arrival of the train always drew visitors to the station. Men with nothing else to do, many of them veterans crippled up, gathered, and Waco idly watched as three men got off.

Then a woman stepped down, and the conductor reached up to take her hand.

"That's a right nice-looking woman," Oscar said.

"Sure is," Waco replied.

The two watched the woman as the conductor helped her locate her luggage, which she set down on the platform. She looked around as if confused.

Waco would have left, but he had gone only a few steps when Oscar said, "Uh-oh, that's trouble."

Waco turned and saw that two men had bracketed the young woman and were giving her a hard time.

"Those two ought to be run out of town."

Waco recognized Jasper Landon and Orville York. Both of them had served short terms in prison, and Waco had beaten Orville in an oozing fistfight in the Golden Nugget Saloon. The sight of the two giving the young woman a hard time brought the quick flare of temper that lurked somewhere below Waco's smooth surface. "Those fellows need a lesson in manners," he remarked.

"Better watch yourself, Waco," Oscar called out as his friend left. "They been spreading it around they're gonna wipe you out."

Moving to where the three stood, Waco paused.

Instantly the two men turned their attention on him. Both of them had anger in their expressions.

"You two be on your way. Leave the lady alone."

"What makes you think you can give me orders?" Jasper Landon said. He was a tall, lanky man with a lantern jaw.

Orville York was shorter but muscular. He spat out the words, "You might as well move on! We're doing right well without your help here."

Waco ignored them as he turned to the woman. "Young lady, you're probably going to the hotel. I'll be glad to escort you."

"Thank you very much." The woman was very attractive, with blond hair and blue eyes and dressed better than most.

"I'm going to wipe you out one of these days," Jasper said. "I hear you think you're a tough man."

Waco kept his eyes fixed on both and was not surprised when, without warning, Orville threw a swift punch. Waco had been expecting it. He blocked it with his left arm and struck the man a tremendous blow on the nose. Orville wheeled, cried out, and fell backward in the dust. Instantly Waco wheeled to see that Landon was reaching for a gun. With one quick move he pulled out his own gun before Landon could free his own weapon.

"I ain't drawin'!" Landon said quickly.

"Second thoughts are usually best. You two move on. I'm tired of the sight of you."

Orville scrambled to his feet. Blood was staining his shirt. "You won't always have that gun."

"I'll always have the gun, Orville. I'm not telling you again. Move on."

The two cursed but left.

Waco watched them to be sure they were out of the way.

The woman said, "I can't thank you enough."

Waco said, "Sorry you'd get such an introduction to our city. I'm Waco Smith. Could I help you with your luggage?"

"I—I don't know exactly where to go. I need a room for the night."

"Well, there's the Majestic Hotel. The name's more stuck up than the hotel, but it's clean."

"If you wouldn't mind, I'd appreciate it."

Waco picked up the two suitcases and then nodded. "Down this way, miss. I don't know your name."

"I'm Alice Malone. I'm very grateful to you for you help, but won't it make trouble for you?"

"Oh, those two will make trouble wherever they go, but they won't bother you."

They reached the Majestic Hotel, and Waco waited while the woman signed her name to the guest register.

The desk clerk instructed, "Room 206 up on the second floor. Got nobody to carry your bags."

"I'll take care of that," Waco said pleasantly. "Got a key, George?"

"Right here." George leaned over and pulled a key from a board and handed it over. "There you are, Miss Malone. Glad to have you in our city."

"Thank you."

Waco moved up the stairs with the young woman. When she got to the room, she unlocked the door, and he walked inside and put the suitcases down. He took off his hat and said, "Well, like the man said, welcome to Little Rock."

She hesitated and bit her lower lip.

There was some sort of fear in her, at least Waco thought so. "Look, it's a little early, but those train rides can get you pretty hungry. Be proud to have you go down with me. We'll have an early supper or late lunch. Whichever."

"Oh, I am hungry, but it would be a bother."

"No bother at all. Come along."

The restaurant was only a quarter full. Waco pulled a chair out, and when she sat down, he moved across from her.

A woman came up and said, "Hello, Waco, what can I get you?"

"What's good today?"

"Got some good beef."

"Bring us some of that and any vegetables you can find. That suit you, Miss Malone?"

"It sounds wonderful."

The woman moved away, and Waco managed to make small talk as they were waiting. The meal came, and she ate hungrily. Waco, who was always hungry, downed his meal quickly.

Finally Alice seemed to be troubled about something and said, "I don't know exactly what to do, Mr. Smith."

"Waco's fine, ma'am. What do you mean you don't know what to do?"

"Well, I was living with my sister and her husband. They have a large family and a small house, so I felt like I needed to give them some freedom. I have another aunt that lives here. I need to find her. She invited me once to come and stay with her, but I haven't talked to her in some time. I'm just a little bit nervous."

"Well, be good to have you here. What's your aunt's name?"

"Bessell Gilbert."

"Don't know the lady, but we'll find her."

After they finished their meal, Bessell Gilbert turned out to be easy enough to find. At least her house was.

Sheriff Satterfield had been their source. When the two had found him in his office, he was slapping flies with the swatter, but he rose at once and nodded when Waco introduced Alice.

"My aunt's name is Bessell Gilbert. Do you know her, Sheriff?"

"Yes, I do, but I'm sorry to tell you she's not here."

Dismay swept across Alice's face. "I haven't heard from her. I wanted to come and stay with her. I really don't have any other place to go."

"Well, we'll find something. She got married and moved away out to Kansas somewhere. Perhaps we can find her."

"That won't do any good, I'm afraid," Alice said. "If she's not here, I'm sure she's sold her house."

"Yes, she did, and folks are living in it now."

"Come along. We'll figure out something," Waco said. "Let's go down and sit on the bench and watch the old Arkansas River flow by."

She did not answer, and he saw that she was upset. He himself had never had such a problem, and he felt an urge somehow to help her. "Here. Sit on one of those benches there, and we'll watch the steamboats."

Alice sat down, and he sat beside her. She was quiet for a long time.

Waco did not know how to handle the situation, but he felt that somehow she had to have help. "I'll tell you what. We'll find you a place to stay, and then you can decide what to do."

"I—I don't have very much money."

"We can probably find you a place with low rent. Don't let it worry you. Things like this always look bad when you're in the middle of them." The two sat there, and Waco spoke to her as cheerfully as he knew how.

Finally she rose and said, "I'm tired. I think I need to rest." Waco stood beside her, and she turned to look at the river. A steamboat was making its way up the stream, and she watched until it moved around the bend. "I'm really afraid. I've never had to really take care of myself in a situation like this."

"If you want to work, I'm sure we can find something for you to do."

She did not answer, but he saw that tears were in her eyes. She began to tremble.

Waco put his arms around her, drew her close, and said, "Don't worry about it. I'll see you're all right."

Alice did not move. She was looking at him with her face lifted, her lips motionless. The fragrance of her hair touched his senses. He saw the quick rise and fall of her bosom, and then an impulse took him. He drew her closer, bent his head, and kissed her.

He'd had little enough experience with a woman of this nature. Most of his women friends were rougher, but as she lay in his arms in an attitude of trust, he felt a sweetness and a richness that filled the empty places in him and allowed him for this short fragment of time to know what completeness could be. The best of life suddenly took him, but a sadness came, for he knew this would soon pass away.

She lay quietly in his arms, the rhythm of her breathing growing calmer. "I shouldn't have let you kiss me."

"Not your fault. Men are pretty selfish."

"You're not, Waco." She smiled suddenly, pulled out a handkerchief, and wiped away the tears. "Take me to my room, please."

He walked with her to the hotel and left her there, but she turned at the foot of the stairs and gave him a sweet smile. "Will I see you again?"

"Why don't we have breakfast? I'll come to call for you at the hotel."

"That would be nice. Good night, and thanks for helping me."

Waco nodded, put on his hat, and left the hotel. He went back to the hardware store where he and Will had made a temporary bedroom to serve until they could do better.

He found Will sitting at the table eating something from a bowl. "Have some of this stew. Not bad."

"I've already eaten."

Will looked up. "Why'd you do that?"

A sharp, uncomfortable feeling touched Waco as he told how he had met the young woman. "Will, you know all the businessmen in town. She's got to find something to do. We've got to help her."

Will held the spoon in his right hand, looked at it for a moment, and then said, "I don't know the lady, but I know you. Be careful, Waco."

Waco stared at him. "Be careful about what?"

"Well, you've had some experience with another kind of woman. This one is apparently different. You'd be right for the plucking."

"She's not that kind."

Will Barton smiled faintly. There was a doubt in his eyes, and he said, "They are all that kind sooner or later. Just be careful."

"Sure. But she's not that kind."

CHAPTER 2

Will Barton walked to the sheriff's office.

Micah Satterfield sat in one of the rockers in front of his office reading a week-old paper. The news displeased him, evidenced by the creases along his forehead. With a twisted mouth he muttered, "The Yankees are going to get us. Ain't no doubt about that." He continued reading the paper, but a movement caught his eye and he looked up at the man who had approached. "Hello, Will. What brings you to my office today?"

Will Barton nodded to the sheriff. "I wanted to talk to you about something that's got me pretty worried. Are you gonna put a special guard on the bank, Chief?"

"Why would I want to do that?"

"Well, the First State Bank over at Jonesboro was robbed. That's not too far from here. We might be next. I don't want a bunch of outlaws to be getting the money I worked so hard for."

"Don't worry about it, Will. The thieves didn't get much over at Jonesboro if what I hear is true. Sheriff Conners has got a posse out running them down."

"Well, can't be too careful." Barton leaned up against the post and glanced at the paper in the sheriff's hand. "Not good news about the war, is it?"

"There ain't no war left, son. It's just a matter of survival, and the Confederacy won't do that very long."

"I'll be glad when it's all over. I wish we had never got into it."

"So do a bunch of grievin' widow women and men, too."

The two chatted about the war; both of them, like many Southerners, had practically given up on the Cause. Finally Satterfield folded his paper and tossed it into the chair next to his. "What's going on with Waco and that woman that come to town?"

"I never saw a man so dazzled by a woman," Will said sourly. "I thought Waco was a pretty steady man, but he's not. She's been here a month, and Waco just acts like a man bewitched. He'd run into a fence post if she was close."

"Well, you reckon he's going to marry her?"

"Might be, but I'd hate to see it."

"Don't you like the woman?"

"She's the wrong woman for him." Barton shrugged his shoulders. "They're different. She's a city woman. Waco doesn't know anything but horses."

"Well, he's learning the hardware business. That'll make him a city man."

"I don't think he'll ever become a city man. He does what I tell him, but he's not really got what it takes to make money."

"Well, you do, so I guess he'll be the strong back, and you can be the sharp mind."

"I don't think it's exactly like that. I'll see you later, Chief. You be sure you keep an eye on that bank."

"I'll take care of it, Will."

Stepping up out of the dust of the street onto the wooden plank sidewalk, Waco glanced up at the sign that said THOMAS'S JEWELRY STORE. He hesitated for a moment and shook his head. Then, taking a deep breath, he walked across the sidewalk and entered the store. It only took him ten minutes to make his purchase and exit the store. When he stepped onto the sidewalk again, he was still confused. He walked along until he approached the sheriff, who was, as usual, sitting in the rocker outside his office. "Hello, Micah."

"Hey, Waco. Say, I been meaning to talk to you. It might be a good time." Satterfield leaned forward, spat out an amber stream of tobacco juice on the floor, stared at it thoughtfully, then shrugged. "I've been needin' a new mount. You know horses, son. I want you to look at that stallion that Bill Green wants to sell."

"Already seen him. He's a fine horse. Can't go wrong with him." The two men talked about the virtues of the horse in question. Waco realized he knew more about horses than any other man in Little Rock, or in Arkansas for that matter. It was his strong point. Finally Waco glanced down at the newspaper. "What's the latest news?"

"Did you hear about Cold Harbor?"

"No. What's that?"

"Why, it's a place, son. Been a big battle there."

"I don't really keep up with the war. Just hopin' it'll be over soon," Waco remarked.

"Well, this was a bad one for the Yankees. Grant's followin' Lee's army all the way to Richmond, I reckon. He caught up with him at Cold Harbor."

"Is that pretty close to Richmond?"

"Not far. That's what Grant's aimin' for." A look of satisfaction swept across the sheriff's craggy face. "But Grant got more than he was askin' for this time."

"What do you mean?"

"Lee beat him to Cold Harbor and got his men in an entrenched position. They was just lyin' there waitin' behind them trees and rocks. Grant always thinks he can lick Lee anytime he can catch up with him. Well, he caught up with him, but he wished they hadn't! He sent his whole army in, but General Lee was in an impregnable defensive spot. Paper says seven thousand Union soldiers were killed in less than an hour. They're calling him 'Butcher' Grant now."

"I guess that's the kind of man the North needed."

"Guess he is. He can lose four men to our one, but if he loses a thousand men, he just sends word back to Lincoln and asks for a thousand more. Lincoln reaches out and makes a call to one of the states, and they send a thousand men without even thinking about it. Every time we lose a man it leaves a gap. No one to fill his place."

Sheriff Satterfield studied Waco's face and finally asked, "How's that Alice girl you been courtin'?"

Waco shot a quick glance at the sheriff. He had taken considerable ribbing about his courtship of Alice. "She's doing fine."

"How's it working out her working there in the hardware store with you and Will?"

"She's doing fine. She didn't know much about hardware, but then I don't either. She's smarter than I am though. She's learned all the prices, and Will's satisfied with her."

"I'm surprised that Will would let a woman work in the store."

"Well, I had to keep after him, but he finally caved in."

Waco shifted from one foot to another.

"What's the matter, son?"

"Well, I guess I've got a problem, Chief."

"You want some advice? I'm mighty free with that."

Waco grinned. "I guess I do." He reached into his pocket and pulled out a small box. He lifted the lid and said, "I just bought this ring."

"Why, that's a right fancy article," Micah said. "I'll take a wild guess and say it's for Miss Alice."

"Yes, but I'm not sure I ought to give it to her."

"Why not?" Micah asked with some surprise.

"Well, I bought it for an engagement but to tell the truth, I'm feeling pretty shaky."

"It don't take much advice here. You love that gal, don't ya?"

"Yes, but I'm not sure she cares for me."

Micah chuckled. "Take a run at it, son. Marry that girl. Get you a house full of kids and settle down."

Waco was not quite satisfied with Micah's advice. He looked at the ring for a long time, closed the lid, and then put it back in his pocket. "Doesn't seem right to get married with this war still going on."

"Well, it'll be over soon. Everybody knows that."

"Yes, but what'll happen to the South then?" Waco demanded. A stubborn look crossed his face, and he added, "The Yankees will come down here and tell us how to do everything. They're going to make life tough on us Rebels."

"There's always something to wait on, Waco. There ain't never a perfect time to get married or do anything else. If you love that gal, then grab her and tell her so and get hitched."

Waco suddenly smiled. His broad lips turned upward at the edges, and he said, "Well, that's just what I aim to do, Micah. Thanks for your advice."

Waco moved away, walking down the sidewalk rapidly, now sure of his decision.

Waco and Alice were walking along in front of the Olympic Theater. They stopped to look at a bill outside. A heavy rain had fallen earlier, and the smell of more rain was in the air, which carried the spongy odors of spring. The violent rain had stopped, but the stubborn clouds rolled overhead like huge waves from a rough sea breaker. It was late in the afternoon. There was little light in the day, and lights were shining up and down Front Street as the two paused and looked at the poster.

MINSTRELSY, BURLESQUE, EXTRAVAGANZAS,
ETHIOPIAN ECCENTRICITIES.
Nothing to offend ladies or children,
for all are done in the most sensitive taste.
Tickets fifty cents. Orchestra chairs one dollar.
Boxes three dollars.

Alice stared at the sign and then turned to face Waco asking, "What's an Ethiopian eccentricity?"

"I don't have no idea. You want to go in and find out?"

"It might be fun."

"It's early yet. Let's go. Maybe we can get something to eat later."

"All right."

Waco paid a little shriveled-up woman with bright black eyes the admission fee, and the two went inside. The room was filled with stale smoke from cigarettes, cigars, and pipes. Their seats were halfway to the stage. The show started almost at once, and they found it mildly amusing.

When it was over they left, and Waco said, "I reckon I could get along without seeing something like that every night."

"Oh, I think it was fun. I still don't know what an Ethiopian eccentricity is though."

The two walked down Front Street until they got to the Royal Café. They went inside.

A heavyset waitress with stains on her apron said, "What can I get you folks?"

"How about some roast beef?" Waco asked.

"Nope. Special is pork tonight. We got pork chops and pork ribs and pork roast."

"I'd like to try the ribs," Alice said. "I always like pork ribs."

"I'll have the same. Bring us some vegetables if you got any."

The two sat there talking about the show while the heavy waitress moved away.

Waco was nervous, which Alice noticed, and she asked, "Is something bothering you, Waco?"

"Why, no. Not really." He searched his mind for something to say. He finally said quickly, "I don't know much about you. Do you have much family?"

"No, I don't have any parents. My father was a gambler, but my mother didn't like that. My father left when I was only ten. Mother had to work hard to provide for the two of us."

"What did she work at?"

"Oh, whatever she could find. She was a good seamstress and

did that for a while. We moved around a lot."

Waco picked up one of the ribs. Chewing thoughtfully, he swallowed and said, "What about sweethearts? You have a lot of them?"

A smile came to Alice's lips. "I'm not supposed to tell about things like that, am I?"

"Oh, you can tell me." He studied her carefully.

She seemed to have a spirit glowing in her that showed self-sufficiency. But at the same time she always seemed on guard. She was a beautiful and robust woman with a woman's soft depth that could scarcely conceal a woman's fire. Alice's face in habitual response had an expression that stirred Waco. Finally he found himself trying to find a name for what it is. It was something like the gravity that comes when someone has seen too much, like the shadow of hidden sadness. There was also some sort of strength in her. She seemed to be the kind of woman who could, if necessary, draw a revolver and shoot a man down and not go to pieces afterward. She was past her first youth, but there was a beauty about her that drew him as no woman ever had.

"What about you?" she said.

"What about me?"

"What have you done all your life? How old are you, Waco?"

"Twenty-five."

"So am I. Did you go to school?"

"Oh, for a little while. Never got past the sixth grade. Most of what I know is horses."

"Yes, everybody says you know horses better than anyone. You ever have a sweetheart?"

Waco stirred and could not seem to find an easy answer. Trouble clouded him, and he cleared his throat then shook his head. "I've known a few women, but nothing serious. I guess I know more about horses than I do about women."

Alice obviously found this amusing. When she smiled, two dimples appeared at the corners of her mouth. "I'm glad to hear a man admit that he doesn't know everything there is to know about women."

A silence fell over the two. Finally the meal was finished, and he said, "I've been wanting to ask you something, Alice."

"Well, go ahead."

"Have you ever thought of me as a man you might marry?" The words were hard for Waco to get out.

Alice stared at Waco for a long moment. "I think a woman wonders that about every man she knows, Waco."

"I care for you more than I can say. I wish I had the words, but all I can say is I love you and you'll never know meanness from me. Would you think about marrying me, Alice?"

Alice reached over and covered his broad hands with hers. She rubbed the calluses that were on his palm and said nervously, "How strong these hands are." She grew silent and seemed to be thinking deeply. Finally she smiled. "I'll think about it, Waco. I will definitely think about it."

☙

"Well, I wish I'd been the knight in shining armor to save you, Alice. Waco has all the luck." Will Barton spoke simply and with obvious sincerity. Alice had just told him that Waco had asked her to marry him.

"Why did you never come courting me?"

"Because I saw Waco was in love with you." He moved forward then and put his arm around her in a protective fashion. "If he doesn't treat you right, I'll shoot him, and we'll run off to the South Seas and eat coconuts."

Alice laughed.

She had once told Will that she liked his light sense of humor. He smiled, lost in thought. He suddenly came to himself and said, "But Waco would never mistreat a woman."

"No, he wouldn't."

An hour later, Will encountered Waco. He immediately said, "Alice has told me that you want to marry her."

"Yes, that's right."

"Well, congratulations."

Waco ran his hand through his hair with a troubled expression. "It's not exactly settled yet. She's got to think about it."

"I don't understand having to think about things like that," Will said, shrugging his shoulders in a gesture of disgust. "If you love someone, that's all there is to it."

"No, I don't think so, Will. A man and a woman have got to have something different, almost like magic. Or else why would they stick together no matter what?" Waco suddenly saw something in Will Barton and asked quickly, "Did you ever feel like marrying a woman, Will?"

Finally Will dropped his head and turned away muttering, "Just once."

"Why didn't you do it, then?"

Will's voice was no more than a whisper. "She favored an-other man."

☙

"Come along, Alice. I've got something to show you."

"What is it?" Alice had been standing outside the hardware

store when Waco had walked up with a smile on his face. "Come along. I'll show you."

Alice looked puzzled but walked along. They cleared Front Street and turned and walked to where a few houses had been built on large lots.

"Come on and look at this." Waco led the way up on the porch of a painted frame house with gables and two windows covered by curtains.

When Waco reached for the door, Alice exclaimed, "You can't just walk in there, Waco!"

"Why can't I?"

"Because we'd be trespassing."

Waco laughed. "No, we wouldn't. This is our house."

Alice stared at him in disbelief. "What do you mean *our* house?"

"I took what was left of the money from the sale of the horse ranch and put it on this house. It'll take awhile to pay for it, but it's for us, Alice. Come on in and let's see if you like it."

Alice followed Waco inside. They went through the house room by room, and finally when they got to the spacious living room with the large fireplace, he walked over and put his elbow on the mantel and stared around the room. "I wonder if there was ever a murder in this room."

"A murder?" Alice stared at him in disbelief. "What are you talking about?"

"Well, lots of things happen in houses, Alice."

"But not murders."

"Maybe so. No telling what the history of this place is. Might have been a fellow standing right here where I am. A woman came in the door. He took one look at her and fell in love. They married and had children and grandchildren."

"That's much nicer than a murder."

"I just imagine things like that sometimes. Maybe there was a couple that lived here, and one of them was unfaithful and ran off with the hardware salesman or an insurance salesman."

"You know, Waco, you're a much deeper thinker than most people take you for."

He came to her and brought her to him with a quick sweep of his arm. He'd kissed her before, but lightly. This time he felt not only the desperate hunger of her lips, but running through him was an emotion almost like wildfire. She had this power over him, lifting him to a wild height so that he could know the vague hints of glory a woman and a man might know. When he lifted his lips, he said, "Marry me, Alice. I'll make you happy."

Alice put her hands behind his neck, drew him down, and kissed him again. "All right," she whispered. "I'll marry you."

❧

"Alice has agreed to marry me, Will."

Will was adding up figures in a book. He looked up and said, "Well, that's fine. Of course that's no surprise to me. My congratulations. You're getting a fine girl."

"You mentioned you loved a woman once, but you didn't explain what happened."

Will shook his head, his lips clamped together. "No sense talking about things like that. When is the date of the wedding?"

"As soon as we get the house ready."

Will closed the book. "All right," he said. "Are you sure you love her?"

"I am."

"And are you sure she loves you?"

Waco did not speak for a moment, and Will saw uncertainty in his face. Finally Waco said, "She doesn't care for me like I do for her, but I can make her love me, Will. You just wait and see!"

CHAPTER 3

A violent rain had swept through Little Rock earlier, leaving the pungent odors of spring that followed a downpour. It was late in the afternoon, and there was a small light in the sky. Already some businesses were lighting lamps, but Front Street had become a muddy yellow street through which wagons, weary riders, and small groups made a river of mud illuminated by the street's gas lamps.

Alice had left the house and held an umbrella over her head to catch the few remaining remnants of the rainstorm. She moved along past Jackson's Confectionaries and next door smelled the dry, faint fragrance of cotton goods at John Maddox's shop. There was a jam of wagons locked hub to hub, and she heard the curses of the teamsters. She made her way to the shop that had become very familiar to her and arrived at the hardware store barely touched by the earlier rain.

As she collapsed the umbrella and shook it dry, a group of young men passed by and called out to her. Their raw comments brought only a look of disdain from her, and she did not bother to answer them.

Folding the umbrella, she entered the store and was greeted by Will, who put down a box that he was lifting up on the counter. He turned to face her. "Surprised you come out in all this rain," he said, smiling at her.

"Oh, the worst of it was over. Is Waco here?"

"No. I sent him out with a load of equipment to Walnut City. Should be back fairly soon. What are you doing out in this weather?"

"I was going to get him to go with me and pick out a wedding dress."

Will came over and leaned against the counter and studied her thoughtfully, a slight smile on his face. "You excited about getting married, Alice?"

"Why, of course." Her remark was perfunctory, and she had a calm look about her.

"You don't look excited."

"Well, do you want me to jump up on the counter and do a dance?"

Will laughed. "That would liven things up. Customers would like it, I'm sure."

Alice turned to smile, then said, "Well, I guess I'll have to go alone."

"James is here. He can handle the place for a while. I'd like to go with you."

"Shopping?" Alice looked surprised. "Not many men would want to help a woman go look for a dress. Most men, I understand, hate shopping."

"Oh, not me," Will said cheerfully. "I like shopping with pretty women. Why, I shopped with my mother all the time."

"Will, why is it I have trouble believing you when you make statements like that?"

"Because I'm such a nice fellow. Let me get my coat, and we'll go find you the prettiest wedding dress in Little Rock. Money is no object."

"Oh, it is, too."

"Nope. This will be on the store." He slipped into a lightweight coat, picked up her umbrella, and said, "We might need this before we get back."

They left the store and walked down the rain-soaked street.

"I love the smell that comes after a rain," Will said. "It's even better when you're out in the country somewhere."

"You aren't a country boy, Will."

"No, I wasn't. I have at least been there after a rain. Which store we going to?"

"We'll go to Maddox's. He has some nice things."

The two made their way down the main street of Little Rock, which was less crowded than usual, for the rain had kept people in.

When they passed by one of the saloons, Alice glanced in and saw the men playing poker around a table. "You never seem to have any fun," Alice said. "Don't you ever go out and play cards or something?"

"I'm a terrible poker player. Terrible gambler for that matter. I always lose more than I win. Cheaper to stay out of it."

"I'm a pretty good poker player."

Will glanced at her with surprise. He turned his head to one side and asked, "Where in the world did you learn to play poker?"

"I had an uncle who was an inveterate gambler. I must not have been over twelve years old, and he taught me how to play." She laughed. "He was surprised when I beat him. We were just playing for matches, and he told me I was a bad girl to beat her old uncle."

"He sounds like a pretty nice uncle."

"He was the only one I had. He used to take me places. His name was Luke Carmody." She did not speak for a while, and then she said, "When he died, I cried for a week it seemed like. I was closer to him than anybody."

"What about your folks?"

"Oh, I had my mother. My father left sometime when I was very young, so it was just Mother and me and Uncle Luke. He was her only brother, or at least the only one she knew about."

They reached Maddox's store, turned, and went inside.

Alice at once went to the section set apart for women's dresses and began pulling them off of a table and holding them up. She held one up that was obviously too large. It had large figures on it and was fairly hideous.

"Oh, that'll be the one." Will grinned. "You'll get fat enough to fit into it one of these days. You won't have to buy any more dresses."

"It's awful!" Alice put it back and began going through other dresses. She was amused by Will, who did not seem at all embarrassed by the looks he got.

The owner, Mr. Maddox, came over and said, "Well, good afternoon, folks. Some storm we had."

"We needed the rain. We got plenty of it," Will said.

"What do you need today, Miss Alice?"

"Going to buy a new dress. A wedding dress."

"Oh, that'll be back here if we have any that'll fit you. If we don't, Minnie Stover could make you one. She's right good with a needle."

They moved back to where Maddox had indicated the dresses might be, and for the next half hour they looked at different dresses. Finally they got one that Alice remarked about slowly, "I rather like this one."

"Well, go try it on. Let's see what it looks like."

"You don't have to wait around, Will."

"I wouldn't miss it. Go on now. Let's see what you're going to look like on your wedding day."

Alice moved into the room that was set apart for women to try on clothes and wondered where the men tried theirs on. For the most part, the men of Little Rock wore rough clothes. It was still a frontier town, more or less. She slipped out of her dress, into the new one, fastened it, and then stepped outside. There was a full-length mirror. She came in front of it and examined herself critically. "What do you think?"

"It doesn't do you justice. It's not gaudy enough. You need to get something that will knock everybody's eyes out when you walk down the aisle of that church. I wonder if they have any bright red dresses."

Alice laughed. "You fool! Brides don't wear red dresses."

"Well, you can set it in motion."

He kept teasing her, and finally she gave up and said, "I guess it will have to be Minnie Stover."

"Well, let's go down and tell her we've got to have it in a hurry."

They left Maddox's and walked down Third Street, where they turned left and found Minnie Stover's shop.

There was a dress in the window that caught Alice's eye. "Now that's the dress I like."

"Not bad. About your size, too."

"I wonder how much it is."

"Don't worry about it. You only get married once. The store

has made a better profit than usual this month. We'll get the dress if it fits."

The dress did fit except for a few minor alterations. Minnie Stover, a short, round woman with bright, merry blue eyes said cheerfully, "Might have been made for you, Miss Alice. I'll have it ready for you tomorrow."

"Oh, the wedding won't be for a week."

"Well, you can pick it up tomorrow anyway."

The two left the store, and Alice noticed that Will had fallen silent. "What's the matter? Cat got your tongue?"

"No, I was just thinking. You ever heard that old saying about brides? You need something old, something new, something borrowed, something blue?"

"Yes, I've heard that."

"Well, I want you to have this to wear." He reached into his pocket and pulled out a box. "I've been carrying it with me since yesterday. I found it in my things."

She opened the box and saw a beautiful pearl necklace. "Why, this is wonderful, Will!"

"It belongs to my grandmother. Very old."

Alice looked up and saw that there was a sadness in his face that he could not hide. "You should keep this for the woman you marry."

Will Barton seldom showed his emotions, but there was some sort of grief in him. "I doubt if that will ever happen."

They continued on their way, and Alice glanced at Will several times. When they reached the store and went inside, she said, "Tell me what's the matter."

"I can't hide my feelings very well. I guess that's the reason I'm not a good poker player."

"What's wrong, Will?"

"I guess I feel left out somehow."

"Left out of what?"

"I don't know. I had a partner. Now I don't."

"Why, you'll still have Waco."

"No, I won't. You'll have him, Alice." Will turned, picked up her hand, held it, and looked at it for a moment. "You have beautiful hands." Then he said with a note of gloom, "The way marriage is, at least as I understand it, one man, one woman. They make some sort of group."

"Don't feel that way." Her hand tightened on his. When he looked at her, she reached up and put her hand on his cheek. "Don't be sad, Will. You know we both love you."

Will Barton stiffened and seemed to find something in her words that he needed to hear. "That's good to know," he said softly. "Now we'll have to find you something blue and something new."

❧

Waco sat in the parlor of Reverend James Stoneman's house next door to the framed Methodist church. Stoneman was a middle-aged man with iron-gray hair and smooth cheeks. He wore a black suit, the typical uniform for a Methodist pastor of the day, and he had been speaking for some time about the general arrangements for the wedding. Finally he said, "I wish Alice were here."

"Why is that, Pastor?"

"Well, I like to have meetings with the bride and groom together before the wedding."

"Meeting for what?"

Stoneman leaned back and ran his hand over his gray hair. "I want to warn 'em that things won't be easy. Usually when a couple come in and want to get married, they have stars in their eyes. They see nothing but a long road filled with only good things and joyous days passing as they grow older."

His words troubled Waco, who leaned forward in his chair and asked, "Isn't it like that?"

"Well, no. There are difficulties."

"I don't think Alice and I will ever have any."

Stoneman suddenly laughed. He had perfect teeth, and they showed against his tanned complexion. "Even Adam and Eve had problems. Every couple I know has some."

"You and your wife, you have problems?"

The question seemed to disturb James Stoneman. He half turned away and looked out the window. "The birds have been building a nest out there," he commented. "You see it? I've told my wife to leave it there. The mother bird comes every day and sits on those eggs. I'm looking forward to the time when she brings their supper to them."

Waco did not speak for a while. Finally he said, "You're not telling me about the trouble you had."

"All right," Reverend Stoneman said heavily, and a sober look chased away the good cheer that seemed to be habitual with him. "Well, my wife and I were deeply in love when we married, but we separated."

"I never knew that, Reverend."

"Not many people do. It was a long time ago in another town."

"What happened? I don't mean to be nosy, but—"

"It's all right, Waco. Maybe you need to hear this. My wife left me."

"Well, why did she leave you?"

"My fault. I became infatuated with another woman. Ran off with her."

The news was somehow shocking. He had never thought of a preacher having that kind of a problem. "I can't believe it. You're still a minister."

"It wasn't easy. I soon found out I had made a terrible, terrible mistake. I had to go back and beg my wife's forgiveness, and she forgave me, and I had to go before the church to confess what I had done. I was out of the ministry for five years. I was too ashamed to even speak to God. My wife helped me though. I got her forgiveness, she stayed with me, and the church members were kind. None of that was easy." He turned and said, "There are a great many ways for a marriage to go wrong, and only one for it to go right."

"What's that one way?"

"When you both love each other so much that nothing else matters."

❧

As Waco entered the store, he found Will and Alice putting up stock. Will said, "Well, about time you got back. You deliver the goods?"

"Sure. What have you two been doing?"

"Oh, Waco," Alice said, her eyes shining. "I found a wedding dress." She began to describe it.

Will shushed her, saying, "Don't tell him a thing. When you walk down that aisle, let it be the first glimpse of it." Will had been sitting on the counter chewing on crackers. He was a cracker addict and kept the barrel pretty well filled, but now he slid off and shook his head. "You know you have everything, Waco. You got a good business, and now a fine wife."

Waco did not know exactly how to answer that and was troubled by it.

Will said, "I've got to go to the bank. You two watch the store."

After his friend left, Waco turned to Alice and said, "You know, I feel bad about Will."

"I know. He was telling me how he would be all alone."

"Well, he'll have us."

"He said a marriage was sort of a closed corporation, a man and a woman, and nobody could really get inside."

"Why, that's foolish! They could have friends. They should have. I'll tell you what. Maybe we could find a young woman for Will to court and marry."

Alice suddenly laughed. "It's not like buying groceries, Waco, or a loaf of bread."

"No, I guess not. You know I've never been a Christian man, Alice, but I can't help but believe that God put us together, you and me."

Alice smiled and put her hand on his chest. "You are a romantic, Waco. I never knew that before. I'll bet you like stories with happy endings."

Waco reached out and drew her to him, holding her tightly. "Don't you?"

Alice suddenly grew serious. She bit her lower lip and then said quietly, "I don't think that happens very often."

❦

"Look, Alice, horses could be your friends."

"I've always been afraid of them, Waco."

The two had come out to the livery stable. Waco had determined to teach Alice to ride. He had been shocked when he discovered she had never ridden, and now as they stood before the chestnut he had saddled for her, he said, "You shouldn't be afraid of horses. They're really nice." He patted the horse and said, "Aren't you nice?"

The horse threw its head up and drew its lips back.

"Haven't you ever been hurt by a horse?" Alice asked.

"Well, a few times, but I always thought it was my fault. Horses are good until somebody hurts them."

"Well, I'm sorry to give you your first disappointment in marriage. I know you love horses, but I'm going to be too busy being a wife. You'll have to get a buggy for the honeymoon."

Waco grinned, shoved his hat back, and said, "I'll make you a fine rider, Alice."

Alice shook her head. "You know, I noticed something about you. You think you can change people, but I don't think so."

"Why, sure you can. Haven't you ever changed?"

An odd look crossed Alice's face. "I don't think so. I always knew I needed to change, but I never could." She turned abruptly, saying, "Let's go back to the store."

They made their way back to the store, and when they walked in, Will showed them a new line of boots that he had managed to get. "Our men are walking around in worn-out boots falling to pieces. Some of them they had in the army."

"Well, what's happening to General Lee?" Alice asked.

Will shook his head. "The Confederate Army is whittling down. I'm afraid it's only a matter of time until the South is forced to give up."

They discussed the war until Alice insisted they turn the conversation to lighter topics. The talk turned again to the wedding and who they were going to invite.

Waco finally said, "Invite whoever you want. I will just be happy when we are married."

Alice replied, "Don't let yourself get too happy, Waco. Nobody should. Usually when a person does, something bad happens."

"Never happen to us." Waco grinned.

He had no sooner spoken than a man entered. He was a sullen-looking man with one pant leg pinned up and a crutch. He hobbled in.

Waco said, "Hello, Jake."

Waco knew Jake Callahan resented the fact that Waco and Will did not serve in the Confederate Army. He knew that Waco had served as a soldier for a year at the very beginning, but to Callahan that did not count. Confederate men served until they died or were injured so badly they could no longer fight, and he always let his feelings be known. Callahan had a thin face with a pair of muddy brown eyes. "Gettin' hitched, I hear, Smith."

"That's right."

"This your little woman here?"

"Yes, it is."

"I guess you ain't been by the post office today, have you?"

"No, I haven't."

Callahan grinned. "You won't like it."

"What is it, Jake?" Will asked.

"You don't know either? Well, the notice just went up, and I talked to Colonel Johnson in charge of the troops here in Little Rock. It's a new law."

"What kind of new law?" Waco asked cautiously. "What's it all about?"

"It's called the Conscription Law."

"Conscription? What does that mean?"

"It means that the Confederate Army's got to have men, and at least one of you is headed that way. Conscription Law says every able-bodied man's got to serve in the army. I guess that means you."

Waco could not answer for a moment. There was a triumphant look in Jake's eyes as he said, "You will be gone pretty soon. You'll catch up with General Lee somewhere in Virginia. Let me know how you make out."

As he turned and left, the three were quiet for a time.

"Look, there's Micah. He'll know about this," Will finally said. He went to the door and hollered, "Sheriff, come over here, will you?"

Micah Satterfield came in and looked at the three. "How're the bride and groom?"

"Never mind that," Waco said. "What's this about a Conscription Law?"

"Well, that just came out. The notice is on the post office wall."

"Is there any way to get out of it?" Will asked.

"Sure. Run. I guess if you make it to the North, you won't have to serve."

"It won't be too bad," Waco said.

"I knew something like this would happen," Alice said, her voice tight and a tense look in her eyes.

"It ain't as bad as it sounds," Micah said. "This war can't last too much longer. You fellas just go on and stay out of the way of any bullets."

Alice turned and ran out of the store even before Micah.

"She's plumb disturbed," Satterfield said. "Women are crying all over the Confederacy, I guess. She'll feel better, Waco."

"I don't know. I don't think I will."

"Well, one of you might be able to stay to run the store. It's a pretty lame excuse, but it might work."

Waco quickly replied, "I'll be going back for sure."

"You didn't believe much in the Confederacy, did you, son?"

"No, I didn't, Sheriff. Oh, I did at first when the bugles were blowing and the flags were flying and we were winning, but it became pretty obvious that we couldn't win this war. I knew that a long time ago."

"Well, you better go talk to Alice," Will said. "Women are weak, but she'll stay with you."

⁂

Waco's world had been shaken. He had talked to Satterfield several times and to the commanding officer of one of the Confederate groups and got the same story.

The major was a tall man with a fierce mustache. "Lee's penned up, and Grant will get Richmond surrounded. That'll be the end of it. Your woman will wait for you."

He did not go back to the store for some time but just walked around town.

Finally when he returned, Will said, "Where have you been, Waco?"

"Thinking." He stopped and gave Will a sober look. "I can't marry Alice, Will."

"Why, of course you can."

"What if she got pregnant? Who would take care of her and the baby? When I come home, I may be blind or crippled. She needs a whole man."

"You've got to do it, Waco. I wish you didn't have to go. Just trust the Lord. He'll bring you through."

"You don't believe that any more than I do. I don't know about you, but I've ignored God so long He's forgot about me."

Later in the afternoon, Waco and Alice were in the store.

Will had gone on one of his errands, and he came back with his face alight. "I've been talking to the major. He says a man can pay a substitute to go into the army in his place."

Waco stared at him. "That's a pretty sorry kind of man to hire somebody to do his fighting for him."

"No, listen. Here's what we'll do. I'll be your substitute. Then you can stay here, get married, and take care of the store."

Waco shook his head firmly. "You know I couldn't take care of this store. We'd be broke in a week. But you're right. One of us has to stay."

They argued about the situation most of the day, and after closing time, Will said, "You may not like it, but one of us has to stay here and take care of the store and Alice."

"You're the only one to take care of the store, Will."

"And you're the only one who can take care of Alice. Here's what we'll do. We'll cut cards for it. The high card goes to the army. The low card stays here and takes care of things until this war is over."

"I don't like it," Alice said. "It doesn't seem right."

"I don't like it either," Waco added.

In the end, though, Will had his way. He walked over and took a deck of cards out of the drawer and said, "Here. Alice, you hold the cards out, and I'll pick one and Waco will pick one."

Waco watched as Will picked a card out and showed it to them. "The nine of spades."

Waco reached out and said, "It'll take a high card to beat that." He picked a card out and stared for a moment. When he turned it over, he said, "Queen of hearts. I guess I'm going after all."

"I still think it should have been me," Will said.

"We did this your way, which was fair. As I said earlier, the store needs you anyway."

"Well, it shouldn't be for long. You'll go off to the army and get the fighting done. When you get back, the store ought to be doing well, and you and Alice can get married then."

Seeing the stricken look on Alice's face, Waco smiled and said, "Well, that's the way it's got to be. I'll be back before you've even missed me. Now I'd better be getting you home."

Alice and Waco left the store and walked together. She said, "I knew something would go wrong."

"Wars break up things, Alice. I'll be careful. I'm no hero."

"You can't promise that."

"Well, there are ways to keep from being shot. Take one of the wounded men out of the battle back to the hospital. It won't be for long. You can fix the house up. Will will help you."

Alice said sadly, "I thought my life was planned. Now it's a wreck."

"Your life is all right, sweetheart." He stopped, turned her around, and held her tightly. "I'll be back, we'll be married, have a house full of kids, and grow old together."

"If you say so, Waco."

CHAPTER 4

The law office of L. G. Simms was cluttered to such an extent that Waco wondered how any work ever got done there. All the walls had shelves going up to the board ceiling, which were packed with books, magazines, newspapers, and souvenirs. The big desk, with its back to the single window, was illuminated by sunlight, and the surface was filled with artifacts, books—some of them open, some of them closed—and old newspapers.

Simms himself was a large man bursting out of his clothes almost. He had a large stomach decorated by a gold chain that led, no doubt, to a gold watch in his pocket. His white shirt had the sleeves rolled up, and the buttons seemed ready to burst off. All in all, L. G. Simms was a disappointment.

Waco had not known the man, but he and Will had come in to have him do some work.

"So, you're going off to war. Is that right, Mr. Smith?"

"That's right," Waco said sparingly. "We have a little legal matter we want to take care of before I go."

"Very well. That's my specialty, little legal matters." Simms grinned, pulled a half-smoked cigar from a desk drawer, stuck it in his mouth, then struck a match on his thumbnail and sucked the blue flame in. As soon as the purple smoke was rising as if from a miniature engine, he said, "What can I do for you, gentlemen?"

Will spoke up at once. "Mr. Simms, we went into business, a hardware store, as partners. We're doing real well, but then this conscription thing comes up and throws us into a bind."

"I should imagine it does." Simms had small eyes and glasses that were propped up over his head.

"Yes sir, it really does." Will nodded. "But only one of us has to go."

"So I hear. So what's your decision?"

"We cut cards for it, and I won, I guess you might say." Will made a face. "I didn't like it. I still don't like it. It's not right. It's not fair, and I hate the whole idea."

"Will, we already thrashed this out." Waco shrugged. He turned to look at Lawyer Simms and said, "What we want to do is put everything in Will's name, the business and a house we recently bought."

"Well, that should be simple enough. You have the papers here?"

"Here are the Articles of Partnership," Will said, opening up a folder. "And here's the papers for the mortgage on the house. Still a little bit owing on it."

"Well, this will be fairly simple. You gentlemen just wait one minute. I'll get this matter out of the way."

Waco watched as the lawyer worked on the papers. He appeared to be rather messy and almost turned the ink bottle over once, but he got through the business without total disaster. "Here, you two gentlemen sign right where I have marked. That's all that will be necessary. You'll need to go to the court with this at the capitol building."

Will shook his head but leaned over and signed his name carefully. He handed the pen to Waco, saying, "I still don't like it, Waco."

Waco shook his head. He signed his name and said, "How much do we owe you?"

"Ten dollars ought to cover it, I reckon."

Waco fished in his pocket, but Will beat him to it. He came up with cash and said, "Thank you, Mr. Simms."

"Well, good luck to you both." He turned to Waco. "And you dodge them bullets now."

"I'll do my best."

As soon as they were outside, Waco said, "I guess we might as well head for the train station. From what I hear, the train will be pulling in sometime this afternoon. Trains don't run on schedule with this war going on."

The two walked along the boardwalk, and finally Will said, "Waco, can I ask you something?"

"Sure."

"Are you scared? I mean scared of getting shot?"

"Not right now, but they're not shooting at me." Waco managed a grin. "I will be when about five hundred Yankees are trying to kill me." He glanced over and saw a flight of blackbirds circle the town, making their harsh, guttural cries, then disappear behind the taller buildings. "I remember when I served the last time. I didn't like it a bit."

Will was quiet for a while and said, "We've never talked about this, but do you believe in God?"

"Of course I believe in God. What do you take me for? Just

look around you. With a world like this, there's got to be a world maker."

The two trudged silently on, threading their way between the people going to work and soldiers wandering the town, and finally Waco said, "You know I'm not afraid of dying."

"I would be."

"Well, it's what comes after that bothers me."

Will shot a quick glance at his partner. "Maybe you'd better go talk to the minister."

"No, I reckon not."

"I expect he can tell you how to get right with God."

Waco turned and shot a hard glance at Will, saying, "Will, I've been ignoring God all my life. Now you think if I run to Him and tell Him I've been a bad boy, He's going to let me into heaven? That would be like trying to buy insurance on a house when a house was on fire. I may be a sinner, but I'm no hypocrite."

They continued their walk, and when they approached the train depot, Waco said, "Look at that crowd."

Will shook his head. "They don't look like much, do they?"

"No, the Confederacy is skimming the bottom of the bucket."

The two of them moved back and leaned against the station house, and Waco's attention was drawn to an older man.

A woman was hanging to him and weeping, and a young woman with a small boy was standing by, watching with a worried look in her eyes. "You'll be all right, Carl," the young woman said.

"Sure I will."

The boy perked up and said, "Are you going to kill the Yankees, Grandpa?"

"I reckon as how I'll do my best."

The woman was weeping violently. "Why'd they have to take

you, Les? You're fifty-five years old. You're too old to be a soldier."

"Well, I got to go, Liz. That's all there is to it."

The scene disturbed Waco, and he shook his head in despair. "That old man doesn't need to leave his grandson and his wife."

"No, it's not right, but it's the way it is."

Ten minutes later, a very young lieutenant with rosy cheeks and bright blue eyes and dressed in a new Confederate uniform appeared. He shouted out as if everyone were deaf, "I'm Lieutenant Burl Gibson. When I call your name, sing out." He began calling out names.

When he called out Waco Smith, Waco raised his voice: "Here, Lieutenant."

The officer called out several more names, and then he called, "Charles Abbott." The lieutenant waited. "Charles Abbott, are you here?"

There was no answer, and one of the men said with a wry smile, "He lit out last night, Lieutenant, headed for the West Coast, I guess."

Lieutenant Gibson turned rosy, blushing furiously. "He'll be sorry when we catch up with him."

An older man, obviously seeing a younger son off, said, "You ain't gonna catch Charlie, Lieutenant. He's going all the way to the West Coast, sign on a clipper ship, and get down to the South Sea Islands. I wish I was going with him."

Gibson stared furiously at the older man, completed the roll call, and said, "You men stay where you are. The train will be here any minute."

He had no sooner spoken than Alice came, almost out of breath. She was holding a fairly large box. "I fixed you something to eat on the train, Waco."

Waco took the box and said, "Feels heavy. What you got in here?"

"Cake and sandwiches and pickles. Everything I could get in there."

"Thanks, Alice. That'll come in handy, I'm sure."

Alice looked around, her eyes falling on the older couple, and then she burst out, "I hate this war! I hate everything about it!"

"I reckon we all do, Alice."

"Grant wouldn't let this bunch in his army," she said.

"No," Waco said, "but Lee has to use what the South has got. This is it."

"You know the best of the men went off in the first excitement," Will said thoughtfully.

"That's right. Most of them got killed. I was in that bunch. We were all excited. Thought we'd be home before Christmas. Pretty soon it'll be the fifth Christmas."

They stood there talking awkwardly as none of them knew exactly what to say. Finally Waco lifted his head. "There it comes. I heard the whistle."

They stood waiting, and everybody watched as the old wood burner pulled onto the narrow-gauge rails. It huffed and puffed and let loose a tremendous blast of steam and the wheels made a grating noise as it came to a stop.

Lieutenant Gibson shouted, "You men get on those flat cars!"

Alice threw her arms around Waco and pulled his head down. Her lips were desperate, it seemed to him, and he held her close, aware of the soft contours of her figure.

When he lifted his head, he whispered, "I've got to go."

She said, "Be careful! Oh, be careful, Waco!"

"Sure." He turned around and put his hand out, but Will

ignored it and put his arms around him and hugged Waco. He had
to reach up, of course, as Waco was so tall. "Take care of yourself,
partner," he said huskily. "Don't worry about this. I'll take care of
everything. You get home. You'll be a rich man. You'll have your
wedding, and things will be good."

"Thanks, Will. I know I can count on you."

Waco moved to one of the flat cars, noting that the riding
stock was filled already. He clambered on board and sat down
and heard his name called. He turned around and saw a young
man with bright blue eyes and a cowlick in his red hair. "Howdy,
Mr. Smith."

"Why, it's Chad Royal, isn't it?"

"Yes, sir. My dad worked for you on your horse ranch. Ain't
this great?"

Waco stared at the young boy. It was as if he went back in
time and saw himself in this sort of attitude back when he had
first signed up just before Bull Run. He had been excited, and
the train had stopped at stations. Young women had come out
with lemonade and cake, cheering them on. Suddenly he felt a
pang to think that most of the young men who had been with
him on that train were now in shallow graves. "It's good to see
you," he said.

"I'm glad we're going together. I'm a little bit scared to tell the
truth."

The two sat there talking, and a man named Roger Sanders
was sitting by listening. When he heard Waco mention that he
was engaged and had to put his wedding off, he said, "Well, I hope
she's faithful to you."

Waco turned quickly, anger in his eyes. "She will be."

"Sorry. I've already served three years. Got invalided out, and now here I am going back. I tell you this. . .I'll run the first chance I get."

"You can't do that," Chad said.

"You hide and watch me, sonny."

The train gave a lurch forward and then began to move slowly out of the station. The last sight that Waco Smith saw as it pulled out was Alice and Will standing together. Will had his arms around her, and she seemed almost ready to faint. He watched until they faded from view then turned grimly and glanced into the direction of Richmond, where he knew he would be likely to be buried in a narrow grave.

"Well, here it is April," Les Dickson said. The old man had stayed up with the younger men even more than others had thought. Waco had become fond of Dickson. He was a good man; he didn't complain, did his job. He and Dickson, along with Chad Royal and even Roger Sanders, who complained constantly but had never run as he had threatened, had stuck together through all the months of warfare.

It had been a dance of sorts. Grant would bring his army down, attack Lee, and there would be a battle. The first one was The Wilderness, which was a horror. It was a thicket of trees, grass, and vines, and somehow it caught fire. Men burned to death, screaming as they were consumed by the flames. Then came Spotsylvania and Cold Harbor, all butcheries. Grant lost five thousand men in Cold Harbor in less than an hour, but he was grinding Lee down.

"What do you hear from that gal of yours, Waco?" Sanders asked.

"Haven't heard lately. The mail service is not too good in the army, if you noticed."

"Nothing else is."

"Where we going?"

"I heard Lieutenant Gibson say we was going to some place called Appomattox."

"What for?" Chad Royal asked. "Are we going to fight the Yankees there?"

"I don't think so," Les Dickson said. "We don't have enough to fight a battle."

"We'll fight 'em until we can't fight no more," Chad said.

"I think that time's gone," Waco said. Indeed, the talk was that the war was over. Lee had evacuated his army from Richmond, and it was now in the hands of the Union. They were headed along a dusty road toward some little place called Appomattox.

Finally they reached it and found there a courthouse, but there were more people gathered around a white house with a front porch that ran the length of the house. There were all kinds of officers there.

"Looky there. Some of them men are Union," Chad said. "I could hit one from right here."

"Better not," Waco said. "You could hit him, but they got plenty to take care of that. No, this is the end."

They were halted and told to be at ease. Time passed slowly, and finally Roger Sanders said, "Look, there's General Lee."

Indeed, as Waco looked, he saw Robert E. Lee riding Traveler, his favorite war horse. He rode up to the house and dismounted, and one of the soldiers took his horse. Lee turned to look at the ragged scarecrows left of the Confederate Army and said nothing, but his eyes were sorrowful. Turning, he walked into the house.

"We lost even with Robert E. Lee," Waco said.

"Well, we were outnumbered in every engagement," Roger said.

The two waited, time passed, and finally Chad said, "Look, who's that?"

Everyone turned to look at a short man in a Union uniform but with no insignia except four stars on the shoulder. It was dusty and grimy, and Chad said, "That's General Grant, I bet. He's come to take Lee's surrender."

Grant hurried into the house, and there was a long time of waiting. There was nobody to tell them what was going on, but finally Robert E. Lee stepped in the door, looked out, and said, "Men, the war is over. I've done my best for you. Those of you who want horses are permitted to take them home." He turned, mounted Traveler, and rode slowly away without looking back.

Captain Dorsey Hill came over quickly and said, "Hey, Waco."

"Yes, Captain?"

"Pick you out a good horse."

"Why, I'm no horse thief."

"No, the Yankees gave us our horses from what I hear. Pick you a good one and get home to that girl of yours. Marry her. Just remember to name your first child Dorsey after me."

"I'll do it, Captain. I'm going home, getting married, and selling hardware." He quickly turned and went to the horse herd, where he picked a tall, rangy gray stallion, slapped a saddle on it, and rode out, headed toward Little Rock as straight as an arrow.

CHAPTER 5

Waco had made the trip back from Appomattox to Little Rock in company with his two fellow soldiers. The young man, Chad Royal, had stuck close to Waco from the first day in the army, as had Les Dickson, the grandfather whom all called "Gramps."

Dickson glanced across at his two fellow travelers and said, "Well, I'm going to leave you fellows here. That road leads to my place. That wife of mine will be mighty glad to see me."

"You go on and have some more grandchildren, Les," Waco said.

"I ain't ever going to forget you fellows."

"I guess I'll take off, too," Chad said. "I'll ride a ways with you, Gramps. My folks got that place over in Windy Hollow. They'll be right surprised to see me."

Waco moved his horse around closer to Chad and stuck his hand out. "Chad, I haven't forgot how you saved my bacon when the Yanks had me pinned down."

Waco noticed how the young boy's face had become mature. In a year's time, solid battles all the way from The Wilderness to the last fight at Fort Steadman added more than just time, and he knew that Chad and Gramps, like he, would never forget their time together.

"You fellows get on. We'll all be in the same area. Come into my store, and we'll go out and have a meal."

"We'll do that." Les kicked his horse into a run.

Chad followed, waving and shouting, "I'll see you later, Waco."

Waco had gotten a good mount, a tall, rangy roan that he called Sarge for no reason except his face kind of resembled his first sergeant, long and sober. "Come on, Sarge, let's get home."

As he rode, the skyline of Little Rock showed itself over the horizon. He kicked Sarge into a lope, but all the time he was thinking about the last time he had said good-bye to Alice. He had never forgotten how she whispered, "Waco, I can't bear it! How can I wait? I love you so much." He remembered the firm pressure of her lips on his, the urgency in her voice, and her arms around his neck. It was a memory that he had lived on for the last year. Suddenly he kicked Sarge into a dead run.

He approached Little Rock and rode down the main street, noting that the war that had wrecked so many Southern towns had not hit Little Rock so hard. There were many soldiers wearing Confederate uniforms, or part of them. He remembered a line of poetry he had heard somewhere: *All things are passing.* He muttered, "They sure are, and I'm glad the war has passed!"

He rode down Main Street eagerly and pulled up in front of the hardware store, but when he looked up, he got a shock. Instead of the old sign SMITH & BARTON HARDWARE, the new sign, still white with paint, said SAUTELLE HARDWARE. As he stood under the sign, he had an odd feeling. *Something's wrong about this.* He had not heard from Will or Alice for months now, but there could be letters he had missed. Mail service wasn't too regular in the Confederacy.

He dismounted, tied up his horse, and opened the door leading to the office. He noticed that it had been enlarged and redecorated. It had been a combination office for him and Will where they did their book work and kept supplies. Now there were three large rolltop desks along the center of the room. Filing cabinets were neatly ranked along the back wall with a series of charts and maps on each wall.

As Waco entered, a man looked up. He was tall and expensively attired. Turning to a younger man, obviously a clerk, he said, "We'll finish this later, Ray." Then he turned and said, "May I help you, sir?"

"Well, I'm looking for Will Barton."

A flicker touched the man's gray eyes. "Well, I can give you his mailing address."

"Mailing address?" Waco frowned. "Isn't he here?"

"No, I'm Ralph Sautelle, the owner."

The alarm that had been very faint suddenly grew very evident in Waco's head. He settled back on his heels, studying Sautelle's face. Finally he said carefully, "I'm Waco Smith. That name mean anything to you?"

Sautelle shook his head. "No, I'm afraid not. Have you done business with me?"

"I own this place. My partner is Will Barton."

Suddenly the man nodded to his clerk and said quickly, "Leave us alone, Ray." After the door closed, Sautelle said carefully, "You're out of the army, I see."

"Just out." Impatience stirred Waco, and he said, "What's going on here?"

Sautelle nervously pulled a cigar out of his pocket, his hands unsteady as he lit it. After taking a few puffs, he jerked it out and said, "I bought this place from Barton two months ago. He never said anything about a partner."

Waco froze. Finally he took a deep breath then expelled it, holding on to his temper. "He didn't say anything to me about selling the place."

"I think we'd better check into this, soldier," Sautelle suggested. "Do you have a lawyer?"

"Yes, I do."

"Go see him—and then, unless I'm mistaken, you'd better go to the police."

"The police?"

"Yes, that's right. I went over this business very carefully before I bought it. There's always a chance that a lot of debts aren't listed in the books. For example, I made sure the title was clear. According to my lawyer, Will Barton was the legal owner."

"We put the place in his name when I went into the army to make it easier for him to handle the business."

Sautelle's eyes flickered, and he shook his head slowly. "Mr. Smith, go see your lawyer and then come back. It looks like you've been taken."

"I don't think so," Waco replied.

"He's not living at his old address," Sautelle said. "I know that much. A month ago I needed to talk to him about something that had come up. Sent a man around, but he returned saying that Barton had moved, apparently right after he sold the store. I have the address he left with his landlady." He turned, walked over to a file, opened it, and pulled out a slip of paper. "Not much help, I'm afraid."

Waco stared at the note. *General Delivery, New York City.*

"Soldier, take the advice of an older man. Go to the police at once. Your friend has sold you out."

"I'll be back." Waco whirled and walked out, mounted Sarge, and headed down toward the house he had bought. He felt like when he had almost taken a bullet in battle. It had left him empty in the stomach and his pulse beating rapidly. He pulled up in front of Will's house and saw that it looked basically the same. He dismounted, walked up to the door, and knocked.

When the door opened, a woman greeted him. She was in her midthirties, he thought, with a wealth of brown hair and brown eyes. "Can I help you?"

"I'm not sure," Waco said slowly. "Is the man of the house here?"

"No, my husband, Samuel Trent, works for the railroad. He won't be back for two more days. I'm Hattie Trent. Is there something I can help you with, Mr. . . . ."

"I'm Waco Smith. May I ask when you bought this house?"

"Well, we moved here only three months ago. The house was such a bargain. Mr. Barton said they were leaving to go east, but he didn't say where."

"He didn't leave an address of any kind?"

"No, I'm afraid not. Is something wrong?"

"Did you meet his wife?"

"Yes, I did. They hadn't been married too long. I did find that much out."

Waco knew that further questioning of this woman was useless. The truth was sinking in on him, and he had a hollow feeling in his chest. Slowly Waco said, "Thank you," turned, and walked away. He mounted his horse, moving slowly. He did not urge Sarge but let him walk slowly down the street. When he came to the sheriff's office, he was relieved to see that Micah Satterfield still held the position. Waco dismounted, tied Sarge to the rail, and then walked inside.

Micah was sitting at a desk. When he looked up and his eyes lit on Waco, he jumped to his feet and cried out, "Waco!"

"Hello, Micah."

"It sure is great to see you back from the war safe and sound."

"I'm afraid I've got some trouble here, Micah."

"What's the matter? You got wounded?"

"Not by a bullet, but I found out Will sold the store and house and ran off with Alice."

"Well, I knew they left together." Micah looked down at the floor as if he hated to look into Waco's eyes. "I sure did hate to have to face you with it. I guess they got married just before they left town. I heard about them selling the house and the business. Have you been down to talk to the new owner?"

"Yes, I have."

Micah said, "Well, I don't know what charges we can bring. The lawyer who handled the sale said that Will was the only name on the property."

"That's right, Micah. I signed it all over to him so it would be easier." He grinned wryly and said, "Of course I didn't realize he'd be taking it all anyway."

"We'll see if we can run him down."

"I don't guess it would do any good." He hesitated as if he wanted to say something else, then turned and said, "If you hear anything of them, let me know."

"Where'll you be staying?"

"I'll get a room at the hotel." Waco left, but instead of going to the hotel, he rode down Main Street. His mind seemed to be closing. He couldn't think clearly. "I can't believe I was so wrong about a man—and a woman."

He glanced down the street and saw the sign THE GOLDEN NUGGET. It was an old saloon that had been there for years, and although Waco was not a drinking man in any sense of the word, he turned Sarge toward the saloon. He tied the horse up at a rail and went inside. He was struck by the acrid smell of alcohol, stale tobacco smoke, and unwashed male bodies. Walking over to the bar, he hesitated.

A heavyset barkeeper nodded and said, "What can I serve you?"

"Whiskey."

"Sure." The bartender put a shot glass on the surface of the bar, poured it full from a bottle, then started to take the bottle away.

"Leave the bottle here."

"Right."

Picking up the bottle, Waco went over to a corner of the room where there was a table with two chairs. He sat down in one, put the bottle down, then held up the shot glass. He studied it for a moment, and bitterness seemed to flood him. He was not by nature a bitter man, but he had been dealt a harsh blow. This was worse than being called back to the army! Worse than anything he'd ever had happen.

For a time he drank the whiskey off, bracing himself as the fiery liquor bit at his throat then warmed his stomach. He filled the glass again and downed it quickly. He sat there alone until one of the women who frequented the bar came over. But when he shook his head, she sneered and walked away from him.

An hour later, Waco knew he was drunk. He dropped some coins on the bar and was aware that there was a dullness of sound and knew that he had lost it. He got up, walked over to the barkeep, paid for the drinks, then left.

He knew he had very little money left, but he went to the hotel and got a room. Going inside, he lay down on the bed and closed his eyes, making the room seem to swim. The bitterness had turned into hatred, and he lay there thinking of his "friend" Will Barton and his new bride, Alice Malone. He could not turn his mind away from the two of them, and he finally passed out, still thinking of how he would get his revenge if he ever saw them again.

❧

"That young man sure got a rotten deal," Micah Satterfield said. He was talking to his deputy, Zeb Willis. They were both seated in the sheriff's office.

"He sure did." The deputy was a tall, lean man with a ferocious mustache and a pair of mild blue eyes. "As I see it, he let himself in for it. Must be a trusting sort of fellow, signing his business and house over to Barton like he did."

"Yes, I guess he was trusting. He always was an easygoing man. Don't know if he'll ever trust anybody again."

"Well, trusting someone to keep something for you is dangerous business. I think he'll have trouble getting his money back."

"He thought Barton was his friend," the sheriff said. He remembered now how Waco had unloaded to him, and the sheriff knew there was really no recourse for Waco Smith to regain his business or his woman. But he had to check out every opportunity.

A silence fell between the two men. Then Willis said, "I hear he's staying drunk most of the time."

"Yes, he is, and that's different, too."

"Well, I don't know where he's getting the money, but he's sure trying to drink the Golden Nugget dry."

"Waco never was a real drinking man. Never any trouble in that way."

"I reckon he thinks he's got a good excuse. Bad enough to have to go to that war, but to come home and find your best friend skipped out with your cash and your woman. That's tough." Zeb leaned back and said thoughtfully, "You know he's got a pretty hard look in his eyes. I don't blame him a bit."

"Well, he's been hurt pretty bad. Last night I went by to try to talk him out of drinking, and he said, 'They done me in, Sheriff, but they won't do it again.' You know, I don't think he was talking just about Barton and that woman. He's not going to trust anybody for a long time."

The deputy got up and left, leaving Satterfield to his thoughts. He sat for a long time, trying to think of a way to trace Barton, but knew there was little he could do.

Finally he looked up to see Waco and called out, "Come and sit."

Waco stopped, hesitated, then came and lowered himself into a chair. He said nothing.

Finally Satterfield said, "Well, you got to put this behind you, Waco."

"How do you do that?" Waco's voice was harsh and had an edge to it.

His eyes, as the sheriff had noticed, were hard and sharp, something unusual for him. "You need some money?"

"No. I got a little grubstake. My grandmother left me a little plot of land. I sold it. My partner didn't know about it, or he'd have that money, too."

"Well, why don't you go back into business, Waco. The town is booming and—"

"Nope, I'm pulling out."

"But you've got friends here."

"It's not the same anymore. I need to get away."

"I sort of figured you might. Where will you head for?"

"Someplace far out in the woods where the only company will be squirrels and timber wolves."

Micah Satterfield was a student of men, and he studied the stubborn cast to Waco's face. The two had been close, and with a heavy heart he realized this was not the same happy young fellow he had known before the war. The easy ways and the careless manners were gone. What he saw now was a man filled with cynicism that obviously was turning into something much worse.

Finally Waco shook his head and said, "I've had enough of people to do me for a lifetime. This is probably good-bye. I'm leaving early in the morning."

"Keep in touch. Drop me a line when you can."

"I won't promise that. I never was much for writing."

Something much like grief touched Micah Satterfield. He hated to see a man go wrong, and if he ever saw a man on the way down, it was Waco Smith. "Look, boy, it's not the end of the world. Not everybody's a crook like your partner was. Not everybody's a hussy like that woman was."

Waco shook his head and said, "No, I'm going to get out of here. Far away from everything I know. I don't know where I'll go. Maybe get on a ship and go to England or somewhere."

"You won't like it there."

"Probably not." Waco put out his hand and gripped the sheriff's hand hard. "You've been good to me, Micah. I know it won't please you, but I think I found a place where I can just live and won't have to fool with any man or woman."

"Where's that?"

"Indian territory. Out in Oklahoma at the edge of Arkansas. Judge Parker is out there now, but he's got some marshals. It's a huge territory. A man can do anything he pleases."

Satterfield shook his head. "No. No man can do that. There's still laws and rules."

"I'm through with all that," Waco said. "So long, Sheriff." He turned abruptly and walked outside.

Satterfield stared at the door, shook his head, then murmured, "He's headed the wrong way, and there's not anything I can do to stop him."

❧

Waco had pushed his way slowly westward, and as long as he had money, he stopped at small towns and drank himself insensible at bars. He would then carry a bottle with him and get drunk on the way.

The whiskey destroyed something in him. He had not known alcohol could have this much effect. All he knew was that he had lost his good opinion of men, and at some point on his journey he reached a conclusion that he never would have thought of back in earlier days. "I'll take what I want as long as I live." That was the sum of his philosophy. It gave him a grim satisfaction to realize that he was headed for the one place in the United States where that would be totally possible—the Indian Nations where the only law were a few scattered marshals who could not possibly keep up with all the wrongdoers.

He was almost to Oklahoma when he drew up and saw that a wagon was pulling up close behind him. He pulled Sarge over and hid behind a bush. He saw that it was a Union Army wagon.

They're bound to have some money on there. At least those soldier boys will have, he thought. *I'll get what they've got in their pockets.* Pulling his pistol, he waited until they were close enough then stepped out and called loudly, "Pull up there, or I'll shoot!"

One man was driving the wagon; two more were on horseback. One of them immediately reached for his gun.

Waco fired, not to kill but just close enough where the man might have heard the bullet whizzing by his ear. "If you want to die, go ahead and pull for that gun," Waco called out and was gratified to see that the man stopped. "No shooting," he said. "Now, you two drop your weapons and get off your horses. You get out of that wagon, sonny." He waited until all three men were down and were disarmed. "Okay, you head back down the road. If I still see you in five minutes, I'll shoot you."

The three stared at him and saw something in his face that kept them silent. "Come on," the oldest of them said. "Let's get out of here. We're not going to die for this."

Waco watched until they were mere blue dots down the road, and then he climbed into the wagon. He found more than he bargained for. There was a strongbox there. It was locked, but he shot the lock off and opened it up. "Look at that," he said. It was filled with papers, but there was also a pile of gold coins. He looked at the papers and discovered that this was the payroll for a small fort almost in Oklahoma. He found a sack, put the gold coins in it, cut the horses loose, and then mounted Sarge after tying the gold to his saddlebag. "Come on, Sarge, we got financing."

The horse leaped ahead, and Waco Smith, for one moment, had some sort of guilt. He had never stolen anything before except for some livestock, mostly chickens, when he was in the army. But this was a different Waco Smith. He reached into his saddlebag, got out the whiskey bottle, drained it, and threw it away. "Well, here's my new rule," he announced to the air. "I'm going to do what I please and take what I want!"

CHAPTER 6

Indian Territory, April 1870

Trey LeBeau leaned back and threw his cards on the table. There were several men there, including the James brothers, Frank and Jesse. His band included five other men, but only Al Munro and Zeno Shaw were at the card table.

Trey let his eyes go over to the woman who sat at the table, not playing cards but just simply sitting and watching. Calandra Montevado, whom everyone called Callie, was the most beautiful woman he had ever seen. She had a pure olive complexion and large almond-shaped eyes with long lashes. The color was blue, a particular shade of blue. He had seen a stone that was called lapis lazuli. Her eyes were that particular shade of blue. She had hair as black as the darkest thing in nature and sensuous lips.

He let his eyes rest on her, admiring her figure as usual. She lifted her glance and met his gaze coolly. They had been together now for nearly a year, and he had never gotten the best of her in any way. In any case, she added something to his life that was missing.

"We got to pick up somebody to take Butch's place," Al Munro said. He was a small man with pale blue eyes and hair that was prematurely white. A deadly man with a gun, a knife, or any other weapon.

"I don't know where we'd get one," LeBeau said.

Zeno Shaw was the biggest man at the table. He was six feet two and weighed well over two hundred pounds. He had brown hair and brown eyes and was a ferocious saloon fighter. He was not particularly accurate with a gun, but in any activity requiring brute strength he was a good man to have. He glanced over at LeBeau and said, "You might think about that fellow Waco Smith. I've heard lots of talk about him."

"He wouldn't be interested," Callie said. "He's a loner. He takes what he wants, but he's not a killer. Not like you fellas."

The insult, if that was what it was, did not move the other men from the table. Frank James said, "Why don't you look into it." He glanced over and said, "Jesse and me are going to be leaving pretty soon. We're going back to civilization."

Jesse James smiled slightly. "Yeah, this is hard living here, Trey."

"Pretty safe though. You go back to Missouri or somewhere, you'll have sheriffs and deputies and all kinds of lawdogs on your trail all the time. Here all we got is a few marshals."

"I don't like it here," Jesse James said. "You better look into this fellow Smith. What's he like?"

"Well, he's evidently pretty tough. I've never met him. I don't think many have. He stays in the territory mostly with Indians. I hear Judge Parker has put a special price on his head."

"If he ain't a killer, I don't know how we can use him," Al Munro said.

"The man will do what he needs to do if there's enough money involved." LeBeau nodded. "But anyway it's a good idea. I wonder where he is?"

Frank James said, "I heard some talk about him when I was over at Travis's store. He's around there somewhere. He comes in for supplies."

"That's not far from here," Trey said. "What do you say we go look him over, Callie?"

"That sounds good to me. I'm bored with watching you men lose at cards."

LeBeau laughed and said, "Come on. We can be there in two hours."

As they were on their way, LeBeau said, "You watch out for Waco Smith. Stay away from him."

Callie laughed. "You don't own me, Trey. Don't tell me what to do."

❧

They reached Travis's store and were surprised at how easy it was to find the man called Waco Smith.

"He comes in here pretty often, but he's got a camp over by Red Canyon." Travis, the barkeep, explained how to get there. "I wouldn't try to sneak up on him though. He's as quick as a snake with that .44 of his."

"Oh, it's just a friendly visit."

The two mounted again, and two hours later, as Travis had said, they came upon a camp, but they did not get far before a voice said, "Hold it right where you are."

Immediately Trey LeBeau held up his hands. "No trouble. We come friendly."

Callie glanced around and saw a man emerge from behind some bushes. He was very tall with black hair and a tapered face. He had a coppery tan, and he held a .44 loose in his hand. Not pointing it at them, just saying that it was there.

"I'm Trey LeBeau."

"I'm Waco Smith."

"Sure," Trey said. "We come looking for you. This is Callie Montevado."

"I'm glad to know you, Miss Callie. Why are you looking for me?"

"Is it all right if we get down and talk?"

"Sure. Just be careful that you don't make any moves that would set me off. I'm a nervous type."

"I doubt that." Trey smiled, and his eyes crinkled when he did. He stepped off his horse, as did Callie, and kept his hands carefully away from the gun. "The thing is, I've got a pretty good bunch of boys. We've taken in quite a bit of coin. Somebody said you might be interested in joining up with us."

"I don't think so. I'm doing all right on my own."

"Well, we can talk about it, can't we?"

"Sure. Come on and sit on the front porch."

The three sat down in front of a shack that at least had a porch with a roof on it.

Waco brought out a bottle and three glasses. "If you're dry, this is pretty good whiskey."

"Any whiskey is good whiskey," Trey said. When he swallowed it, his eyes flew open, and he gasped. "That's like liquid fire."

"Yeah, the Indians like it."

"What are you doing out here all by yourself?" Callie asked.

"That's what I am. All by myself. I got tired of people back East. Here I do as I please."

"You couldn't be making much coin selling whiskey to the Indians."

"I don't need much."

"Of course you do. Every man needs a lot. Look, you go in with us, and in six months you'd have enough cash you wouldn't have to sell whiskey to the Indians."

"Well, tell me about it."

Trey was a good talker, and for a while he outlined the plan for making money. "Robbing trains, that's where it's at. My boys are good at that, but like I say, we lost a man."

"You don't know me."

"Well, you don't know me either. You watch me and I'll watch you."

"I wouldn't do it if I were you, Smith," Callie said.

Her remark obviously interested Waco. "Why not, Miss Callie?"

"You just look like a loner."

"That's what I intend to be."

"Callie, you keep out of this," LeBeau protested. "We need some help."

The conversation went on for an hour, and Trey was pleased to see that Waco was interested.

Waco said finally, "Well, I'll come along with you, and we'll see if I fit. If I don't, I can always come back."

"Sure. We're not too far away from here. You can come back anytime." As they shook hands, Trey was mentally counting all the money Waco Smith was going to help them take from all those unsuspecting trains.

❧

Waco had been welcomed by LeBeau's band. Frank and Jesse James were gone, but the rest of them seemed to find him acceptable. It was not that he did anything, but they were careful in their movements around him for they had heard he was deadly with a gun. He did not have the reputation of a killer, but he had pulled and drawn on several men before they could even move.

One interesting thing was that Callie seemed to be fascinated by him. They went on several brief hunting trips together, and on one of them she said, "You have many sweethearts, Waco?"

"I almost had one once, but she didn't love me."

"Did she say that? Tell you she didn't love you?"

"No, she waited until I was gone to war, and then she ran off with my best friend. He was my partner in business." A wry expression touched his face. "He took all I had."

She was quiet for a while before she said, "Trey is jealous of me. Haven't you noticed how he looks at you when we go out together?"

"I've noticed."

"Are you afraid of him?"

He grinned. "All LeBeau can do is kill me, and he couldn't kill me but once."

"Doesn't that bother you?"

"No."

She suddenly said, "What do you feel for me?"

"You're the most beautiful woman I've ever known."

They were sitting under a tree, and he read an invitation in her eyes. He reached forward, pulled her close, and kissed her. She lay soft in his arms. Then she put her arms around him and drew him closer. Her warmth became a part of him, and her nearness brought up a constant, never-lessening want. He was conscious of her in a way he had never been conscious of any woman, not even Alice.

The effect of the kiss worked at him. They were along the edge of the same mystery every other man and woman face, neither of them knowing what good would come of it, nor what tragedy. As she pulled him closer, she knew what they shared was physical and not a thing of the spirit.

✺

LeBeau was being taunted by Al Munro about losing his woman. "You shouldn't have let that good-looking guy come in. Callie is crazy about him."

"Shut up, Al!"

Munro knew better than to go too far, but humor was in his eyes, a sly humor that LeBeau did not miss. Thirty minutes later, Waco and Callie came in, returning from one of their trips. As soon as they were inside, Trey said, "Everybody sit down. We're going to make a big haul. We're wasting time robbing trains for watches and rings. This one is going to have a good gold shipment."

"How do you know that?" Rufo Aznar said. He was Mexican, trim with an olive complexion and dark eyes. He had a knife scar on the right side of his face. "They didn't send you an invitation, did they?"

"No, I paid a lot of money to find out."

"Money to who?" Waco asked instantly.

"A man who works for the railroad. He knows if he lied I'd kill him. Anyway, we'll do some planning here."

✺

The plans were all made, and Callie warned Waco as the men left. "Don't turn your back on him."

"I won't."

They rode out, and as always Waco kept to one side where

he could watch all the men. Trey had made a good plan pointing out that there was one spot where the train had to slow down practically to a stop in order to make a sharp curve.

"You and me will get on that train, Waco," Trey said. "We'll go up and force the engineer to shut down. The rest of you go through and find that gold."

Waco did not particularly like it. He didn't like working with other thieves. He made up his mind he would leave after this particular robbery.

The heist went as planned. The train had to slow down, and it was no trouble for Trey LeBeau and Waco to get on board. They made their way along the top to the engine, jumped down and put their guns on the engineer and the fireman, who was holding a shovel and staring at them with wide-open eyes.

"You fellows be still, and nobody'll get hurt," Waco said. But no sooner had he spoken than he heard a shot.

Trey had shot the fireman, then turned and shot the engineer. Even as they were falling, he had raised his gun and brought it down on Waco's head.

As everything began to fade to black, Waco realized he had been betrayed yet again.

❧

Out of the darkness Waco came, and he heard voices. He felt something tying his arms, and when he opened his eyes, he saw that he was a captive. A man with a star on his vest said, "Well, I hope you enjoyed your robbery. You're going to hang for it."

"I didn't shoot anybody."

"I'll bet," the lawman said. "We'll let the judge decide about that."

❦

Things moved much more quickly than Waco had ever known legal matters to. He spent two weeks in a vile jail, then was brought up before Judge Parker. During the trial, the fireman, who had survived his injuries, testified that it was another man who had shot both him and the engineer, who had died. "He hit this fellow in the head, but this man didn't shoot anybody."

"Well, the longest sentence I can give you for holding up a train is ten years," Judge Isaac Parker said. "I wish it were for life. If you give me the names of the rest of the robbers, I'll make it five."

For a moment he was tempted to do it, but then he said, "No, I won't squeal."

"Honor among thieves," Judge Parker said cynically. "All right. Go on to jail then."

❦

The days passed in his cell, then the weeks, the months, and finally the years. Time had crawled by more slowly than Waco could have imagined. He had put in days on a road gang chained to other prisoners. Sometimes he had been locked up in the cell for months without getting out to the sunshine.

Finally one day Mel Batson watched him scratch on the wall and said, "What's that for, Waco?"

"My anniversary. I've been here five years today."

"Well, you only got five more to go," Batson said. "You won't get no parole. You've been a bad prisoner. Me, I'm trying to be a good boy."

"I'm not licking anybody's boots. I'll do my ten." Waco lay

down and thought of the five years that lay ahead of him. He had
been beaten and mistreated, but his spirit had never been broken.
I'll do five more, he thought bitterly, *and then I'll go looking for
Mr. Trey LeBeau. . . .*

PART TWO

PART TWO

CHAPTER 7

Memphis, Tennessee, 1870

"Dulcie—you've got this water too hot!"

Sabrina Warren had stuck her toe in the zinc bathtub and jerked it out immediately. Glaring at her maid, her voice filled with irritation as she went on. "Can't you even draw a bath right?"

Dulcie, at age twenty, was as black as nature would allow. She was an attractive young woman, but now her lips drew tightly together as she glared at her mistress. "I doin' the best I kin. If I don't get it hot enough, you raise a ruckus! I get it too hot, you do the same thing. How I'm supposed to know what you want?"

Sabrina glared at Dulcie. "You're supposed to have a little sense! Test it yourself before I boil my feet off!" Sabrina Warren knew she was tall for a woman at five ten. She also knew she was quite beautiful with her auburn hair, green eyes, and peaches-and-cream complexion. To top this off, she had a splendid figure. No one had ever questioned her good looks, but she readily admitted, to herself anyway, that her temper was more volatile than one would expect of a young woman in her position. "Well, pour some cold water in there and cool it off!"

"Then it'll be too cold. You watch what I says." Nevertheless, Dulcie picked up a bucket and dumped half of it into the tub. "All right. See if that suits you. Nothin' else does."

"You're getting too uppity." Slowly Sabrina stepped over the edge of the tub, and when she stuck her toe in she found it suitable. She stepped over with the other foot and, holding on to the edges of the tub, lowered herself down into it. A look of relaxation came to her eyes then, and she forgot about Dulcie, her fit of temper quickly over. She slid down into the tub, luxuriating in the warm water, and as she did, she looked around the room that had been converted from a large bedroom into a spacious bathroom.

Many houses had taken this method of adding a bathroom, for most of the mansions in Memphis had not made provision for bathing back when they were built in an earlier day. She glanced around and saw that the ornate gas chandelier had been left in place so that it shed its luminescent beams over the marble floor. She knew it had come from Italy for she had ordered it herself. Her father had almost fainted when he saw the bill, but she had patted him on the cheek and said, "Now, Daddy, you know we've got to have a good bathroom."

She eased down more into the tub and thought, *I'm going to get rid of this zinc tub. It's ugly.* As a matter of fact, it was rather ugly. It had a flat bottom and a raised back, but it did not suit her sense of decorum. The walls had once been papered, but the steam from the hot water had caused the paper to begin to peel. So she'd had to work to take it all off and put instead wooden panels that she had had painted a beautiful shade of orchid. There was an ornate dressing table over to one side and two chairs in front of a full-length mirror. As she closed her eyes, she thought, *Must have been awful not to be able to take a bath back in the old days.*

She lay in the bath until it grew tepid then said, "Get some of that rainwater, Dulcie. I want you to wash my hair."

"You done washed it yesterday."

"Well, wash it again!" Sabrina snapped.

Grumbling under her breath, Dulcie found the bucket of pure rainwater, and selecting a soft soap, she wet Sabrina's hair down and worked up an ocean of suds. "Don't see no need in all this washin' anyhow," Dulcie grumbled. Actually she did not mind helping Sabrina. She knew she had an easy place and was not at all unhappy in her situation.

Sabrina sat up in the tub, and as Dulcie washed her hair with the soft water, she began thinking about Lane and the ball she was going to attend. *I wish Lane were more dashing.* The thought came to her mind, and it was not the first time. Indeed, Lane Williams was not a dashing man at all. He was, as a matter of fact, two inches shorter than Sabrina. He had brown hair that he kept carefully trimmed, along with a brown mustache and mild brown eyes. He was neat in all of his ways but had never taken a risk in his life.

Sabrina sighed and relaxed while Dulcie finished her hair. Finally Dulcie rinsed the soap out with several buckets full of soft water then began to dry it. "There. Get out of there, and I'll dry you off."

It was difficult to get out, for she had relaxed almost to the point of going to sleep, but finally Sabrina stood.

With a huge, fluffy white towel, Dulcie dried her off carefully.

"Don't dry me off so hard," Sabrina complained.

Dulcie ignored her curt words. "You sit down there, and I'll fix your hair."

"All right." Fixing hair right was the one thing Dulcie

could do excellently. Sabrina knew that many society belles of her station had to put up with much worse, and she sat quietly, thinking about the ball, smiling slightly. As a matter of fact, her life was made up of parties, balls, teas, an occasional trip to the Memphis symphony, and a traveling opera on occasion. Her family was not in the upper regions of society but just in what was not far from it. Sabrina had grown up with never wanting for anything, and now at the age of twenty-four she was one of the belles of Memphis society. "Don't pull my hair out by the roots!"

"I ain't pullin' nothin' by no roots. You just set still."

Finally, when her hair was fairly well fixed, Sabrina sent Dulcie off to get some perfume, and while she was gone, she slipped into her underwear that Dulcie had laid out. The garments were all made of silk or fine linen.

When Dulcie came back, she stopped dead still and stared at Sabrina. "You ain't got yo' corset on."

"No, I don't, and I'm not going to wear that old thing," Sabrina said. "I don't need it." Indeed she did not, for her waist was small. She smiled at Dulcie and said, "You don't have to wear one. You don't know how uncomfortable those things are, and the bustles are just as bad."

"All the respectable women wear corsets to them balls."

"I don't need one. It rubs me wrong."

"You know your momma ain't gonna let you go to no ball without a corset."

Sabrina laughed. It made a pleasant sound. She knew well how to work her parents. "We just won't tell her, Dulcie."

Dulcie was shocked. "Maybe you won't—but I will."

"No, you can't tell her."

"Why not?"

"Why should I wear an old corset? I look well enough without it." Indeed she did, but corsets were standard equipment for young ladies of her station. An idea came to Sabrina, and she said, "I'll tell you what, Dulcie, if you don't tell Momma that I'm not wearing a corset, you can have that red dress of mine that you covet."

"It's a sin to covet," Dulcie said righteously. "I ain't studyin' no red dresses."

Sabrina drew closer to the young woman and said, "And you can have the petticoat and the shoes that go with it."

Sabrina was amused as she watched the struggle going on within Dulcie's soul. She knew that the girl had longed for that particular dress, but this came in conflict with her idea that her mistress needed to wear a corset. She said nothing, and finally Dulcie threw her hands up in a gesture of despair. "Well, if you's bound to dress like a hussy, I guess I can't help it."

Sabrina laughed and said, "You can take it today. Maybe there'll be a party you can wear it to. You'll have to take it up a little bit."

"I ain't studyin' no parties." Dulcie pouted. "I'm thinkin' 'bout how you treat your poor momma and daddy. You ain't never minded them a day in your life."

"Of course I do—when I want to."

"Well, I'll tell you one thing," Dulcie said, "you better start being nicer to Mr. Lane or that Aldrich girl is gonna take him away from you."

"Melissa Aldrich couldn't take anything away from me." She was confident and knew that none of her friends could take her gentleman friend away from her. "Well, finish my hair."

"All right. I'll finish it, but you better ask forgiveness for foolin' your poor old momma. If she knew the stuff that goes on in your mind, she'd be shocked, and your daddy, too."

"Oh, I never tell them things like that, and you don't either, Dulcie."

"I don't reckon I can, but you're gonna get caught one of these days."

As Dulcie finished her hair, Sabrina was thinking of the ball, though not with any particular excitement. It was just another ball, and she had been to a thousand of those it seemed like.

❦

Mick Sullivan pulled the buggy up in front of the Warren mansion and clambered down to the ground. He was a ruddy-faced Irishman, sturdy, with huge hands, and was known to be the best horse trader in Memphis. He walked up to the front steps and knocked on the door.

A butler came to the door and said, "May I help you, sir?"

"I've got a horse here for Miss Sabrina Warren."

"Well, you can't bring the horse in here," the butler said.

"All right, but I've got to have her sign for it."

"You take the horse around to the stable. I'll tell her you're here. You wait until she comes."

"I ain't waitin' forever," Mick growled. He went back, unhitched the beautiful bay mare, and led her around the house. This was what was once the center of Memphis and now was merely a neighborhood. There was plenty of room, and the grass was green. Mick shook his head. "These folks got too much. Spoiled rotten is what they are, especially that girl." He had sold horses to Sabrina before and knew there would be no question about money. He found Morris Tatum, the groom, sitting on a barrel whittling.

"Got a horse here for Miss Sabrina."

Morris jumped down and said, "Well, she's a beauty, ain't she? How much did you gig her for?"

"I give her a fair price. Don't you worry about that."

Morris was a small man. He had spent some time working as a jockey. Now his blue eyes sparkled. "The last time you gave anybody a fair price, Adam and Eve was in the Garden of Eden."

"You got anything to drink here?"

"Soft or hard?"

"Just whiskey."

"When's the last time you had water?" Morris made a face. Nevertheless, he disappeared inside the stable and came back with a bottle. "Here. Don't drink it all."

Mick took a long drink, then another, and handed it back to Morris. "That girl. She's spoiled to the bone."

"Well, I can't help that. You're right though. I don't think she's ever wanted anything in her life her momma and daddy didn't get for her."

"One of these days," Mick said, "she's gonna want something she can't get. We'll see what she does then."

Five minutes later Sabrina came out and said, "Hello, Mick."

"Hello, Miss Sabrina. Here she is. Prettiest mare in Memphis."

"Oh, she is a beauty," Sabrina crooned. She stroked the smooth hide of the mare and said, "I'll take her."

"We ain't settled on a price yet."

"Well, I know you'll name a price, and I'll tell you it's too high, and you'll come down. Why don't we just skip all that."

"All right. Price is eight hundred dollars."

"I'll give you seven hundred."

"Seven-fifty."

"Oh, that's all right. I hate these things."

"Okay. Here, sign this. These are the papers on the mare." Sabrina signed the papers, and then Mick nodded, saying, "Thank you, Miss Sabrina. I'll let you know when I get some more good-looking stock."

"Thank you, Mick." Sabrina stood there stroking the silken nose of the mare then said, "Morris, rub her down and be sure to watch her diet. I think I'll take her out for a ride tomorrow."

"What about today?"

"Oh, I've got to go to a stupid ball. I'd much rather go with you, sweetheart."

"Is that what you named her? Sweetheart?"

"No, I haven't given her a name yet. I think I'll call her Cleo for Cleopatra."

"Well, she's a beauty, Miss Sabrina. I'll take care of it."

Charles and Caroline Warren were entertaining Sabrina's escort, Lane Williams. They were in the larger of the two parlors. There was a large fireplace of polished marble at one end, and the pictures on the walls were either seascapes or Dutch pastoral scenes with cows.

The long green velvet curtains splayed out on the floor and sagged with braided sashes. There was a large cut-glass bowl of roses on a low mahogany table between two chairs, and all in all the room had all the Victorian clutter that had been so popular and still was.

"I expect there'll be a crowd at that ball, Lane," Charles said.

"Everybody I know is going except us."

Lane Williams was a small young man, shorter than Sabrina. "There probably will be, but I'm not going to stay for the entire ball."

"Well, you'll have a lovely time," Caroline Warren said. At the age of forty-seven she was an attractive woman with the same auburn hair and green eyes that she had passed along to her daughter.

"I hate balls," Charles Warren said. He had a square face, was six feet tall, and weighed over two hundred pounds. He was forceful and stubborn. Founder and owner of Warren Steel Mills in Memphis, he loved his family, his church, and his business, in that order. He had planned on having sons to help him with the business, but that had not happened, so he always thought what sort of partner one of the girls' suitors would make.

They were interrupted when Marianne Warren came into the room. She was nineteen, with beautiful smooth blond hair and blue eyes. Her parents had long ago learned that she was very romantic. She read romances by the ton it seemed, and once her mother had said, "Marianne, you're waiting for a knight in bright shining armor to come and sweep you off, but there aren't any white knights in armor these days." She had realized, of course, that that would mean nothing to Marianne.

She was wearing a beautiful bright green satin dress trimmed with glittering black lace and black velvet ribbons. Three black feathers were arranged in her blond hair, held on by an impossibly large emerald and a diamond stick pin.

"You look beautiful tonight, Marianne. You'll be the belle of the ball." Caroline Warren smiled at her daughter.

"Oh no. Sabrina will be the belle of the ball."

411

Charles grinned, and then a thought came to him. He turned to Sabrina's suitor. "I can't keep up with you two. Are you engaged or not?"

"We were yesterday, but this is another day." Lane smiled wryly. "I ought to keep a record or a journal or something. You can ask her, and then we'll both know."

Even as he said this, Sabrina came in. She was wearing a beautiful dress of her favorite Nile green color, and it was as elegant as the water in the sun. It was stitched with silver beading and seed pearls. The waist was tiny, and the bodice crossed over in front with the bosom cut low.

"You look beautiful, Sabrina." Lane smiled. "You'll be the belle of the ball."

"She always is," Marianne said. "I wish I could be just once."

"Well, when we're married, your competition will be gone," Lane said. "By the way, your father wants to know if we're engaged. What's the score on that?"

It was a question that came up often, and Sabrina stared thoughtfully at Lane. "I'll let you know before the evening's out. If you step on my toes, the engagement's off."

"Well, let's go," Lane said.

They left the house, and as soon as they were gone, Charles said, "I don't know about that young man. He doesn't have much strength it seems."

"You think everybody who's not as driving and forceful as you are doesn't have enough strength, Charles. He's a fine young man. He'll be good to Sabrina."

"She'll wear him out just like you wore me out."

Caroline came over and put her arm around his waist. "No, I didn't. You always get anything you want from me."

Charles laughed and said, "That's the way it's supposed to be in a marriage."

❧

The ball at the Steens' mansion was held for the betrothal of their daughter. It was glittering, glamorous, and grandiose. At the entrance to the ballroom was a long table covered with a snowy white tablecloth, and gentlemen's silk top hats, canes, and gloves were arranged in militarily precise rows. The strains of a slow waltz filtered through the twelve-foot-high double doors, which were open but still guarded jealously by two gigantic footmen.

Inside the great ballroom the scents and sounds and sights were overwhelming. Women glowed in hundreds of butterfly colors. All of the men were striking in full evening dress of white ties and tails. The flowers smelled luscious, the chandeliers glittered like diamonds, and the music of the twelve-piece orchestra resounded magnificently.

Almost as soon as they were inside, a tall, handsome man with a beautiful beard came and said, "I'm going to have to ask for a dance from your fiancée, Lane."

"All right. You try to steal her at every ball. Go ahead, Harold."

As the two whirled off to the music of a waltz, Lane said, "It seems a shame to spend all this money on something as frivolous as a dance."

Marianne looked around. Thousands of flowers lined the walls in great stone urns. There were old ivies, deep green, long, trailing, curling up the walls. "It is rather frivolous, I suppose, but it is exciting."

"May I introduce myself?"

Neither Lane nor Marianne had heard anyone because of the music, but when she turned quickly, she saw a man six feet tall, very trim, and very handsome.

"My name is Gerald Robbins. I'm here on business. I hardly know anyone at this ball, so I thought I'd ask the most beautiful woman here for a dance."

"There you are, Marianne," Lane said, smiling. "You're already attracting the men." He said, "I'm Lane Williams, and this is Miss Marianne Warren, daughter of Charles and Caroline Warren."

"And may I have this dance, Miss Marianne?"

Marianne was flustered. He was the best-looking man in the hall as far as she was concerned, and there was something dashing about him, always an extra for a man.

He led her to the dance floor, and soon they were moving around smoothly. "You dance beautifully, Miss Warren."

"Why, thank you, Mr. Robbins. You say you're new in town?"

"Yes, just here on some business."

"Well, where is your home?"

"Oh, out West. I deal in cattle quite a bit. Have a large ranch."

"Oh, how exciting!"

Robbins laughed. "Well, that's one way of looking at it, but taking care of a thousand cows is not very exciting. That's why I come East every once in a while just to have some real culture."

Marianne was fascinated and peppered him with questions about his ranch and his life. He had a smooth voice and had all the wit that one would expect in a man. "You don't look like a cowboy."

"Well, I don't wear spurs and chaps and a ten-gallon hat to a ball like this." Robbins smiled. "What does your father do?"

"He owns an ironworks here in Memphis. Actually, it's called Warren Steel Mill."

"And you have brothers and sisters?"

"Only one sister. She's around here somewhere."

For the rest of the ball, Marianne either danced with Gerald Robbins or else waited for another chance.

When Lane prepared to see her and Sabrina home by going outside and sending for the carriage, Robbins said, "I'm a lonesome bachelor and usually wouldn't be this forward, but there's a concert tomorrow in the park. I just wonder if you would accompany me."

"Oh, I'll have to ask my father. But I'm sure he'll say yes," Marianne said.

Robbins bowed slightly. "I'll pick you up, if you'll give me your address, tomorrow. I think the concert begins at two o'clock."

Marianne watched as he walked away.

After he had returned to the party, Sabrina joined Marianne with their coats.

"Oh, I wanted you and Mr. Robbins to meet before we leave. He is so wonderful, Sabrina. I know you will just love him. He is taking me to a concert tomorrow. That is, if Father agrees to his taking me."

"You know how to work Father. Just give him that pitiful look you do when you want something, and he will give in as usual. Now let's go. Lane is waiting for us."

"But Mr. Robbins. . ."

"I'll meet him some other time, Marianne, all right? Come along now. My feet hurt. Let's go home and relax."

Marianne relented. "Well, I think you will have many other opportunities to meet him as I plan on seeing Mr. Robbins many more times after tonight." She sighed contentedly as she left with her sister. She knew she would in fact see him in her dreams that very night.

CHAPTER 8

July had brought a heat wave into Memphis. Dulcie had washed some of Sabrina's finer clothes and was now hanging them out on the line. She mumbled to herself as she often did. "There comes that no 'count Caesar. He's gonna try to get next to me just like he always does, but he ain't gonna have no luck."

"Well, hello. How's my favorite young woman?" Caesar, the carriage driver, was a tall, well-built, handsome black man. He had a beautiful smile and graceful moves that had made him a favorite with the ladies. Now he came and stood next to Dulcie and said, "What you been up to today, Miss Dulcie?"

"I've been eavesdropping."

Caesar blinked his eyes. "Well, that ain't nice. Who was you eavesdropping on?"

"I was listening to Miss Sabrina and Miss Marianne. Then I listened to what Mr. Charles and Miss Caroline had to say about them daughters of theirs."

Caesar reached over and put his hand on Dulcie's shoulder. "That's always nice to be able to listen in on the rich folk." This

416

was his term for the Warren family. "I don't get to eavesdrop on nobody except you and some of the other ladies around this neighborhood."

His grasp tightened, and Dulcie suddenly looked up with her eyes flashing. "You get your paws off of me, Caesar!"

"Why, honey, I'm just being affectionate."

"I know what you're being. You're trying to get next to me like you always do."

"Why, you can't blame me for that," Caesar protested. "After all, you're the prettiest lady in this whole town of Memphis. As a matter of fact, I came over to give you an invite."

"Humph! I know your invites. What is it this time?"

"Well, it's so hot I thought later in the afternoon when it cools off, we go down to the river. You know where the big trees overhang and there's a nice grassy bank there. We could take something to eat and have a little picnic."

Dulcie glared at Caesar. She knew his reputation, and although she was tempted to give in to his invitation, she knew better. "I remember," she said loudly, "how Clara went to the river with you, and she got a baby out of it."

"Well, that's so, but ain't that boy baby handsome? Just like me."

"You think mighty well of yourself, Caesar, but I'm a Christian woman, and I'm not about to put myself in any kind of a way with you."

"Well, I goes to church every Sunday."

Dulcie bent over the basket, picked up one of Sabrina's gowns, and clipped it onto the clothesline. The breeze stirred it slightly, and it smelled of lavender, for Sabrina liked her clothes to have this scent. "Bein' inside a church don't make you no Christian—no more than bein' inside a stable makes you a horse."

Caesar grinned and shook his head. "You is a mighty clever woman, Dulcie. Just think what it'd be like if you and me had some children. They'd be handsome like me and pretty like you. They'd be smart like you. They'd be nice and easy to get along with like me. Now, tell me what you heard them women and Mr. and Mrs. Warren talkin' about."

"Mostly they was talkin' about that new man that Marianne has got on her mind."

"What did they say?"

"Well, Miss Sabrina tried to tell Marianne how foolish she was to make that much of some man that ain't goin' to be here. Mr. Charles and Miss Caroline said about the same thing. They's worried about her."

"Well, what do you think, Dulcie?"

"That girl Marianne, she's a sweet child, but she ain't had no experience with men to speak of, and right now she got some romantic notions. Them things is bad for a person. They can get her into bad trouble, and Miss Marianne don't need no trouble with a stranger, which is what that man is."

Caesar listened carefully as Dulcie talked on. When she finished, he pushed his case for a picnic again. He looked surprised to hear her say, "All right. I'll go to the riverbank with you, but I'm takin' one of our knives from the kitchen. You try to put your hands on me in a way that ain't proper, and I'll cut your fingers off."

"I'll be just as good as the driven snow. We'll have us a time, Dulcie."

🐍

Sabrina was sleeping peaceably, but the door opened and then closed, waking her up. She sat up in bed and looked startled, then said, "What are you doing interrupting my nap, Dulcie?"

"You done had enough nap. You won't sleep tonight."

"You want to run my life. You're my maid and sometimes you act like I'm the maid and you're the mistress."

"You need to get up. Miss Marianne done had a long talk with your momma and your daddy."

"You always listen to people."

"Well, why shouldn't I? White folk treat house servants like they was furniture. What do you think, we don't hear nothin' or see nothin'? You just plumb forget about us. You better get dressed. You need to talk to Miss Marianne about that man she's been seein'."

Sabrina took a deep breath and nodded. "I guess you're right about that, Dulcie. Help me get dressed."

Sabrina had almost finished dressing when Marianne burst in. "I'm going out with Gerald late this afternoon. We may go out to Rudolph's Restaurant. That's the nicest place in Memphis."

Sabrina turned so that Dulcie could fasten the buttons on the back of her dress. Her mind worked rapidly. She had thought a great deal about this man whom Marianne was seeing, and when she turned around, she said, "That's fine, Dulcie. Why don't you go take some of those clothes that you washed this morning and iron them."

Dulcie gave Sabrina an insulted look. She well knew that this was her signal to leave.

Marianne waited until Dulcie had left the room then said, "I'm so excited. You're going to have to help me pick out a new dress. I don't have a thing to wear."

"You've got plenty of dresses, but let me tell you, Marianne, you don't need to be thinking about Gerald as a man you could marry."

"Why not?" Marianne demanded instantly. She was not a quarrelsome girl. As a matter of fact, she was far more docile than either their mother or Sabrina, but she was sensitive about Gerald and defensive.

"Well, in the first place you don't need a man who is not a Southerner."

"Well, he is a Southerner."

"Where is his home? I don't know anything about him. Neither do Father or Mother."

"He grew up in Mississippi. As a matter of fact, he served as a cavalry officer in the war. Fought under Robert E. Lee." She shook her head and said defiantly, "He and Lee were close friends."

"That's what he told you?"

"Yes, and the man couldn't be a close friend of General Lee unless he was a good Southerner."

"Where is he from? What does he do?" Sabrina said. Now as she looked at her sister whom she loved dearly, she saw a vulnerability there that, for some reason, frightened her. Sabrina herself had always been forthright, saying pretty much what she thought without apology, but Marianne had a far gentler attitude. She could not bear to hurt anybody or anything.

As Sabrina stood before her sister, she studied her face and saw there a quiet calmness that she herself did not possess. Sabrina had always been outspoken, forthright, and willing to argue with anyone, even her parents. But Marianne had a gentleness that she envied. Marianne's face was a mirror, which changed as her feelings changed, and she had never showed herself capable of robust emotion. But now that seemed to be what Sabrina was seeing in her.

Marianne's hair had a rich yellow gleam, and she was wearing a gray dress that deepened the color of her eyes and turned her hair into a more shining color. She had a pleasantly expressive mouth, one that, Sabrina had learned, showed her emotions very easily. She was growing up now, and Sabrina saw that her hips, which had been straight as a boy's only a short time ago, were rounded, and the light from the windows ran over the curves of her shoulders, and the light was kind to her, showing the full, soft lines of her body, the womanliness in breast and shoulder.

Suddenly Sabrina said, "Marianne, I think you're paying far too much attention to this man. He's not going to be here long, is he? Didn't you tell me he'd be leaving for the West?"

"Not for two weeks, and he asked me to go with him tonight to see *Hamlet*." Marianne's face was as clearly expressive at that moment as Sabrina had ever seen it, graphically registering the light and shadow of her feelings. Pleasure and wonder and the fullness of her youthful heart seemed to flow, and a strange small stirring of hope followed. She wasn't smiling, but the hint of a smile was at the corners of her mouth and in the tilt of her head.

Sabrina sought vainly for something to say that might change Marianne's mind. She was a little bit surprised, for she had always been able to guide Marianne's thinking, for the younger woman was easily led, but now there was a strength in her and a manner of decision. Sabrina saw there a new strong and self-assertive pride.

"I'm sorry you don't like him, but I don't care why. I'm going to keep seeing him. Besides, you've never met him."

"Well, I'll meet him soon enough, I guess. I do hope you have a good time tonight."

"Thank you, Sabrina. I'm sure you'll change your mind about Gerald once you do meet him." Marianne left the room.

Sabrina suddenly sat down. She was discouraged and not at all happy with the way she had handled the situation. She took a deep breath, released it, and sighed. "Somebody needs to be able to talk to that girl. She doesn't know what in the world she's getting into."

❧

"I don't think this man playing Hamlet is much of an actor."

Marianne looked up at her father, surprised. "Why, you don't ever go to the theater, Father."

"No, but I listen to people. They say his father was a great actor, but the rest of his family are second rate."

"But he's so handsome. I saw him in *Julius Caesar*."

"Yes," Caroline said, "but that's not everything."

"I wish you'd go with us to the theater."

"I'm not going to see any play. I don't want to," Charles said. "And I wish you wouldn't go. I'm disturbed about this man you're seeing. We don't know anything about him."

"But I do," Marianne said. "He's a fine man. He's got a big ranch out in the west part of the country. He's built it up to where it's hundreds, maybe even thousands, of acres."

"Well, why don't you invite him to dinner one night so we can get to meet him?" Caroline said.

"He's been very busy, but I'll ask him."

❧

After Sabrina came home that evening, Dulcie told her about Marianne's going to the theater.

"I heard you went down to the river with Caesar. You need to be more careful, Dulcie. You know what a bad man he is."

"He ain't bad. He's just a man."

"Well, you don't let him take any liberties."

422

"I reckon I know how to take care of myself. You don't need to give me no sermons."

✤

Frank Morgan, at the age of twenty-eight, was a trim young man almost six feet tall and athletic. He had fair hair and dark blue eyes and had worked for Charles Warren for a long time. He had become an indispensable man at the factory.

Charles sat back and listened as Frank went over a new method he had discovered that would make them money. "You could sell this for a lot of money to U.S. Steel, Frank."

Frank shook his head. "I don't work for U.S. Steel, sir. I work for you."

"Well, you deserve something for your work. I'd like to make it right with you."

"No need of that, Mr. Warren."

"It's a business, and I insist on paying you outright or making you a stockholder."

Instantly young Morgan's eyes lit up. "I'd like that very much, sir, to be a stockholder."

"Fine." The office was quiet now for it was after office hours and all the help had gone. Charles Warren studied the young man and thought, *I've done at least one thing right.* "You know, Frank, I started this company with a son in mind to take over when I'm gone, but I have no son and never will now. As a matter of fact, Frank, you're closer to being my son than I had ever thought anyone could be."

"Well, I'm glad you feel that way, sir." Frank nodded. "I've never been able to thank you for all you've done for me."

As a matter of fact, Charles had practically raised young

Morgan. He was the son of Charles's second cousin, and when both of his parents died of cholera, Charles took him into his own family. He sent him to college, and now one of the chief prides of his life was the way Frank Morgan had turned out. He looked out the window at the buildings of the factory, took a pride in it, then said, turning back to face the young man, "I worry about my family, Frank. If I were killed, nobody would know about the business. That's why I decided to make you executor of my estate."

"Why sir, I never thought of such a thing." Frank was genuinely surprised.

"Well, one of my friends died. His money was all used poorly. I know you've got a solid head for business and you'll take care of my wife and my daughters. You know, my wife and I had always hoped you and Marianne would make a match of it."

Suddenly Frank flushed. He had a fair complexion and hated it when a flush revealed his true deeper feelings. "Well, that's what I'd like, but I'm not the kind of man she wants."

"Why not? You're not bad looking. You're smart. You know the business. You've got a good future. Why don't you just go ask her, Frank?"

"I wish I could, but Marianne is interested in a more romantic fellow than I could ever be."

Warren got up, walked around, and put his hand on Frank's shoulder. He said quietly, "I'm sorry, son, but she may change her mind."

"I don't think so." Morgan smiled at Charles, turned, and left the office.

After he left, Warren stood there thinking of how a man's plans for his life seldom worked out.

Dulcie knew Sabrina was leaving early but was pleased she came in to see how Dulcie and Marianne were getting along with the new dress. It was a beautiful satin gown of a china blue color that matched Marianne's eyes.

"I look awful," Marianne said.

"No, you don't," Dulcie insisted. "You looks fine. Just fine."

Sabrina agreed. "Yes, it's a beautiful dress. I picked it out myself. Now, you sit down and let Dulcie fix your hair. I have to leave, but before I go, I thought you'd like to wear some of my jewelry. Here's this sapphire necklace and earrings that match." She put the earrings in then put the necklace around her sister's neck and said, "Now you truly look wonderful."

Marianne touched them and smiled gratefully. "Can I have some of the perfume that Lane gave you that he bought in Paris?"

"Of course you can. You know where it is."

As Marianne left the room, Dulcie said, "I wish you wouldn't run off. That girl needs somebody to look after her."

"Well, she's got you. You try to boss everybody on the place."

"He may be fine-looking, but he's a man."

Sabrina left, headed for the horse race in which she had a mount that she thought would win.

Dulcie went back and watched as Marianne eagerly applied the perfume behind her ears and in other strategic locations. "Don't you let that man take no liberty with you, Miss Marianne."

"He wouldn't."

"Yes, he would. He's a man, ain't he? I'm going to pray that you come home as sweet and innocent as you leave here."

"Oh, you worry too much." At that moment Clara, another

servant, came and said, "Your gentleman friend is here, Miss Marianne."

Marianne got up and left the room, excitement aglow in her face.

Dulcie shook her head. "I just hope that man is decent."

Clara stared at her. "Seems to be. Just for the night, ain't it?"

"That's all it takes—one night."

∾

Marianne had enjoyed the drama tremendously. Her father would not let her go to many plays, and she had been conscious of Gerald's arm pressing against her. They left the theater, and he took her to have a light meal then drove her home.

He got out of the carriage, and she waited, knowing that he would come around and help her down. *He has such fine manners,* she thought.

When he took her hand as she stepped down, he didn't release it but held it for a moment. "You've given me great pleasure tonight, Marianne."

"It's been wonderful."

Suddenly something changed in Gerald's face, and Marianne, though inexperienced, knew that he was going to kiss her. She had thought long and hard about how she would handle such a situation, but she had no choice. She had nothing to do but surrender. Whatever plan she had left her, for she felt the lean strength of his body, and he was smiling in a way she had never seen in a man's eyes. She breathed more quickly, and as the moonlight highlighted his face, he pulled her closer and then lowered his head and kissed her.

Marianne knew nothing of actual passion, but she learned it

426

at just that moment. The full growth of woman came into being at that time, and she knew that she cared for this man in a way she had never felt for any other man. She felt fragile in his embrace, but he was not rough.

When he lifted his head, he said huskily, "You're sweet, Marianne. I've never known a sweeter young woman in all my life."

The kiss had been an experiment. She discovered she had the power to stir this man and found herself feeling a wave of emotion she had not anticipated. She put her hand on his chest and stepped back.

He smiled at her. "I shouldn't have done that," he whispered.

"It's all right."

"I ask your pardon, yet the fault was not entirely mine."

She knew that this was absolutely true, and when she turned to go into the house, she knew she would not forget that kiss for a long time.

CHAPTER 9

"I really don't think you should be running off on a shopping trip, Sabrina." Caroline Warren had come up to Sabrina's room and had at once begun speaking about her proposed trip to New Orleans. "It's just not a good time for you to go."

Sabrina, as usual, was headstrong and merely smiled, then came over and patted her mother on the shoulder. "Mother, I've planned this trip for weeks now, and I have friends who will be expecting me there. I really have to go."

"But at such a hard time. Neither your father nor I know what to do about this man that Marianne's been seeing."

Frank Morgan had come in to stand beside Caroline, and he added his plea to hers. "I really don't think you should go, Sabrina. Ordinarily it would be all right, but this is different."

"Oh, Frank, you and Mother, and Father, too, are just worried too much. Marianne will be all right. I'll only be gone for a few days. Maybe two weeks. And then when I come home, I'll meet that man and decide what he's like."

"Every day your sister falls more in love with him," Frank said quietly. "You really ought to show more consideration."

The remark touched off Sabrina's temper. "I think I am better aware than you of what my sister is, Frank. I know you mean well, but this is just not possible. I'll come back, and it'll take me a few days, but I'll get Marianne to see her foolishness."

"She's never been this serious about a man," Caroline said. Her hands were unsteady as she reached up and pushed her hair away from her forehead. "I've never seen her like this."

"He's romantic from what I hear. That's what she's always been looking for. She reads too many of those romance novels," Sabrina said then added, "She just needs to wake up."

Frank shook his head and for once dared to cross Sabrina. "She's not like you, Sabrina," he said quietly, but there was a steadiness in his voice that was unusual.

The argument went on for some time, but in the end Frank and Caroline left, and Dulcie entered. "You ought to listen to your momma. She knows what she's talkin' about, and Mr. Frank, he knows, too."

"Dulcie, I'm not going to argue with you. I'm going on this trip, and you're going with me."

Dulcie was sullen for a while; then as she continued to help Sabrina pack, she said, "You always think you can fix things."

"Well, it's true. I can fix things. All it takes is a lot of determination. Nobody's really showed any of that with Marianne."

"I don't know how you think you'd do anything about it. You ain't been listenin' to her. She's really gone on this man. We don't know nothin' about him. None of the family does."

"Well, when I get back I'll handle it."

"How you gonna do that?"

Sabrina threw a petticoat into the trunk that was already

packed then turned to say, "I'll meet this man and decide about him. If I don't like him, I'll hire a private detective to find out what kind of a man he is. Now help me get the rest of this stuff packed. We've got to be on that steamboat by two o'clock today."

❧

Marianne had met Gerald for lunch, and after he watched her carefully, he said, "You've got something on your mind, Marianne. What is it?"

"I was wondering if you would come and have dinner with us tonight."

Gerald smiled. He had a good smile, broad, and humor sparkled in his eyes. "I guess your parents want to see what kind of a man you've been running around with. I've been wondering when this would come up."

"I wish you wouldn't tease me, Gerald. I've never been as serious about a man as I've come to feel about you."

"I didn't think your family would let you."

Marianne's eyes blinked; then she nodded slowly, realizing the remark was true. "They've always been very protective of me. Very careful about what I do and who I see."

Gerald leaned back in his chair, sipping his tea. "Not like that sister of yours, are you?"

"No, she's very strong."

Gerald set the cup down and stared at the young woman. He was quiet for one moment; then he turned his head to one side and said, "What if you had to choose between the man you loved and your family? Would you go against their will?"

Marianne was troubled by the question. She looked down for a time and said, "I just don't know, Gerald."

Leaning forward, he took her hand and held it. "If you love a man, Marianne, you give him everything. Just as he'd give you everything he had in him."

"That's sweet, Gerald. That's what I've always thought."

"One thing you have to understand, Marianne. I'm not a rich man. Not like your father. You'd have a comfortable life here if you choose to stay. You'll find some man, and your father will give you more than I ever could."

Marianne suddenly smiled. "I don't care about that."

"It's hard living out West. Not like living in a big city. You can't run down to the store every morning to get a pound of butter."

"It'd be like at pioneer times. I've read so many stories by James Fenimore Cooper about how difficult the pioneer life was. It would be like that, I think."

"Well, it's pretty rough all right. As for tonight, I'll be glad to come to dinner. This may be the last time we meet together. I fully expect your father to see me as a greedy man after his money through his daughter."

"They'll love you after they get to know you, Gerald."

Gerald Robbins had come to dinner dressed in the latest of fashion. Caroline Warren saw there was a roughness about him, but he was also able to put on a fine manner and was pleasant. Her husband had probed carefully around, trying to find what kind of man he was, but had not been very successful.

Charles now asked their guest, "I understand you are in the cattle business."

"Yes, Mr. Warren, that's about all I know. I've done well at it." He took a bite of the steak on his fork, chewed it, then said,

"Of course I haven't done as well as you have. It's hard to make a fortune in the cattle business unless you're someone like the King Ranch with unlimited space and money to go into it."

"Where do you sell your cattle?"

"Well, now that the railroad is in, we just take them down to the stockyard. Some of them get shipped to Chicago. I would imagine some even come here. We try to grow the finest cattle in the world."

"I imagine that's a lot of hard work, isn't it, Mr. Robbins?" Caroline said. She had been impressed by Gerald Robbins's manners, and for some reason had been expecting less.

"Yes ma'am, it is a lot of hard work, but I've got a good crew. They've been with me a long time, so we make out very well."

"Is your ranch very far from town?"

"It's not around the corner, but of course we have plenty of good horses and carriages. No trouble to go once we make up our mind."

"I imagine it's pretty lonely out there, isn't it?" Mr. Warren said.

"Well, you know, you get used to that and you get to where you even like it. As a matter of fact, I get to feeling all crowded in when I'm in a big city like this one. From the ranch you can look over to the west and see the peaks of the mountains. Beautiful mountains. I go there for a hunting expedition once in a while. Plenty of deer and any other kind of game you like to shoot, but then out on the flatlands that's right pretty, too. In the springtime the wildflowers make a riot of color. Very beautiful. The country gets to you."

Marianne had said little. "Oh, that sounds so beautiful. Just like I read about in the books."

The dinner went on for some time, and then they adjourned to the drawing room for coffee and more talk. Finally Robbins took his leave.

After he left, Marianne came to them at once, her eyes sparkling. "Isn't he a handsome man, Mother?"

"Very attractive."

"But he's talking about a hard life that you've never had." Marianne's father sought for the words. Caroline knew he felt deep in his soul that something was wrong here, and finally he said, "I don't believe you ought to see him, Marianne. You're infatuated with him."

"I am not. I actually care for him."

That was the beginning of the closest thing to a quarrel that Marianne Warren had ever had with her father. Caroline and Charles were determined that she should stop seeing Robbins, and she was equally set on seeing him even more. Marianne finally left the room in tears.

Charles shook his head. "This is a real problem. I wish Sabrina hadn't gone off."

Caroline shook her head. "I don't think it would make any difference. I've never seen Marianne this stubborn before. It's just not like her."

❧

"You got two letters?" Dulcie asked.

"Yes. One from momma and one from Marianne." She opened the first letter and began reading.

Dulcie asked, "What does she say?"

"She's worried about Marianne, of course, but we went over that before I left. She'll be all right." Sabrina opened the second letter and was quiet as she read it.

"What did Miss Marianne say?"

"She is besotted with that man Robbins."

"I told you! Didn't I tell you? We ought to go home."

"No, I've got more shopping to do, Dulcie. I may not get back here for a year. We'll leave Wednesday. Now don't argue with me anymore about it. Things will be all right. When I get there, I'll see to it that Marianne settles down."

CHAPTER 10

Waco lifted the eight-pound sledgehammer over his shoulder and was about to swing it down and break a large rock into fragments when the shrill whistle of one of the guards stopped him. He could have gone ahead and smashed the rock, but he was determined not to do one thing that he was told to do if he could get out of it. Carefully he lowered the sledge and looked over at Cecil Petit, his cell mate. "There's the whistle, Cecil. Let's go wash this dust off and maybe get something to eat."

"Sure, Waco." Petit was a small man no more than five-seven and thin. He had been unable to handle an eight-pound sledge so the guard had furnished him with a five-pounder. Even this was too much for the young man. He was barely past twenty years old and was the typical Southerner with light greenish eyes and tow hair and a Southern accent.

The guard rode by, his shotgun in the crook of his arm, his eyes darting here and there. "Okay. Get on in and wash that dirt off."

Waco turned wearily and slapped Cecil on the shoulder. "That's about enough for one day." Indeed, it had been a terrible day. The blistering sun had burned those who had light-colored skin. Fortunately for Waco, he had his tan from his work on the horse ranch and his years in prison out under the sun.

The prisoners all formed a single line and went by an outdoor shower of sorts. It was simply a hose that was attached to a well that ran on a windmill sort of pump. Waco pulled his shirt off, and when his turn came the tepid water seemed almost cold it was in such contrast with the blazing sunlight. He would have liked to take off all his clothes, but he knew that the guard wouldn't let him.

"Okay, Smith, move on. You're clean enough."

Waco stepped outside, pressed the water from his hair, and waited until Cecil had gotten his shower. The two of them made their way to the long building that contained, among other things, the mess hall.

"Sure wish they'd have something good to eat tonight," Cecil said. He was almost gasping for breath, for the hard manual labor was almost more than he could take. "You know," he said, "I was down in New Orleans one time. We had shrimp, fish, and gumbo. Sure wish I had a mess of that. Or even some catfish out of the Mississippi River."

"Shut up or I'll break your head, Petit."

Quickly Waco turned to see that Ring Gatlin, a hulking brute of a man, was glaring at Cecil. "Take it easy, Ring," he said.

Gatlin was the bully of the prison. He had whipped everybody except Waco Smith. The two had fought it out under the hot sun, and the guards had merely laughed and watched. Waco had walked away, but Gatlin lay unconscious, his face cut and slashed.

"You makin' this your fight, Waco?"

Waco didn't answer. He just simply stared at Ring to see if he would make a move. Then he shrugged and said, "Come on, Cecil. Let's see what we've got to eat."

The two men filed into the mess hall, which contained six-foot-long tables with benches. At one end there was a mess line, and the prisoners were lining up in front of it. When Waco looked down at the food that was in metal pans, he said, "Well, Cecil, no good old fish or gumbo tonight."

"No, I didn't reckon there would be."

The two men filled their plates, walked back, and sat down at a table. Waco stared down at the food, which amounted to a tough piece of pork, beans not fully cooked, and rough bread. There was also a small amount of cold rice. Cecil went at his food like a starved wolf, for as skinny as he was he ate ferociously. As the two men ate, there was little talking.

After all the men had been fed, the guard blew a whistle. "All right. Get into lockup."

Cecil and Waco made their way out of the mess hall and under the watchful eye of one of the guards went with other inmates down through a long corridor. On each side were steel bars fencing in a small cell no more than ten by ten. They stepped inside, and Waco sat down on the lower bunk. He was so much larger, and Cecil found it easier to scamper up into the top bunk.

For a while the two men rested up. Waco felt even the bad food allowing strength to flow through his body. He said, "You ought to sleep good tonight, Cecil, after a day's work like that."

"I reckon I will."

The two lay still for a time, exhausted by the hard labor. Finally Waco heard a scratching sound, and a bluish light illuminated the cell.

Cecil had the stub of a candle that he had obtained somehow, and now he came down from the top bunk and set it down on the edge of Waco's bunk. "I've been readin' here in the Bible somethin' that you ought to know about."

"I don't guess I'm interested."

"You ought to be. It's about a guy like us."

Waco looked at Cecil with what little fondness was left in him. The two had grown close, especially after Waco had saved Cecil from a beating by Ring Gatlin. "Why don't you give up on me? You've been preachin' at me for three years now."

Indeed, Cecil had been converted when a visiting minister had spoken. He had become a fervent Christian and had obtained a Bible, which he read in all of his free time.

"God ain't never give up on nobody, Waco. Now you just listen to this." He began to read. "This is when they crucified Jesus. Nailed Him up on a cross, and it says here in Luke 23, verse 32, 'And there were also two other, malefactors. . .' That means criminals, Waco. They were 'led with him to be put to death. And when they were come to the place which is called Calvary, there they crucified him, and the malefactors, one on the right hand, and the other on the left.' Then, Waco, the Bible says people made fun of Him, the rulers mocked Him, and the soldiers made fun of Him, too. They called out, 'If thou be the king of the Jews, save thyself.' And here's the part I want you to hear. Starts on verse 39.

" 'And one of the malefactors which were hanged railed on him, saying, If thou be Christ, save thyself and us. But the other answering rebuked him, saying, Dost not thou fear God, seeing thou art in the same condemnation? And we indeed justly; for we receive the due reward of our deeds: but this man hath done nothing amiss.'

"Now listen to this, Waco. Are you listenin'?"

"Yes, I'm listening, Cecil."

" 'And he said unto Jesus, Lord, remember me when thou comest into thy kingdom.' Waco, you've got to remember this guy lived like us. He was a criminal, and Jesus was the Son of God, but he asked Him to help him. 'And Jesus said unto him, Verily I say unto thee, Today shalt thou be with me in paradise.' " Cecil chortled, shook his head, then slapped Waco's broad shoulders. "Ain't that somethin' now. There's a guy no better than us. He was in jail just like we are, and he was gonna die that day, but Jesus said he would be with Him in heaven. Ain't that a great story, Waco?"

Waco closed his eyes. He had grown accustomed to Cecil preaching to him, and actually he did not mind. He had developed a fondness for the young man and was determined to see that he was not bullied. "I've heard that before. An evangelist came to town, and my grandpa and grandma took me to hear him. He preached the same text."

Cecil considered this, and then he said, "Well, why didn't you get saved, Waco?"

"Don't ask me, Cecil. I don't know. Maybe I'm just too lost to be saved."

"No, that ain't right. Jesus said, 'Whosoever will may come.' "

The two men sat there by the feeble, flickering light of the candle until there was a sound of a whistle, which meant everybody had to be quiet. The guards had ways of enforcing this, so Waco said, "Better put that candle out. We don't want to burn the place down."

Cecil laughed. "Couldn't burn down this place. It's made out of stone." Cecil put the candle out and said, "You think about that criminal, Waco."

"Sure," Waco agreed. He waited until Cecil had scampered to the top bunk then stretched full-length on his cot. It had nothing but a straw ticking, and for a long time he lay there.

It had become his habit to go to sleep as quickly as he could and to avoid thoughts of what life was like before he had been thrown into prison. But tonight sleep eluded him and he thought back on the time when his grandfather taught him how to break horses. Then he thought of the meals his grandmother cooked. Every morning biscuits six inches in diameter and fluffy.

He finally began to doze off, but suddenly he came wide awake. He shifted in his bed and sat up, looking around, but he could see nothing in the darkness.

"What's the matter, Waco?" Cecil whispered.

"I don't know. Something's wrong."

"What's wrong?"

"Can't say, but if anything happens, you stick close to me, Cecil."

"Ah, nothin's gonna happen."

"Probably not."

Waco lay back, but five minutes later he heard the sound of a voice, and then the steel door at the end of the corridor that led to the cells opened. He sat up at once, for he knew that this was not something that happened every night. Suddenly a voice broke the silence, and a man shouted, "Wake up! We're getting out of this place!"

Waco stood up then.

Cecil joined him as they looked out. "That's Ring Gatlin," Cecil said.

"Yeah, and his two buddies, Tad Mason and Shortie Tyler. They're all three troublemakers."

"How'd they get out of their cells, Waco?"

"I don't know."

Ring had keys in his hands and started unlocking the doors. "Come out of them cells."

When Waco's cell door opened, he stepped out to face Ring. "What's up, Ring?"

"We're gettin' out of this place." Gatlin had a wolfish-looking expression. "I done killed one guard, so I'll kill whoever I have to. They can't hang me but once."

"You can't get out of here. There are guards everywhere," Waco protested. He saw the wild light in Gatlin's eyes and knew that the man would stop at nothing.

"We're going to shake the warden down and get the key to the weapons room. We're gonna get a gun in the hand of every prisoner here, and we're gonna shoot our way out. Anybody gets in our way, that's their tough luck."

Waco shook his head. "You'll never make it. Count me out."

Suddenly Ring snarled, "Get out of that cell, Smith. You're either with me or against me." He held the revolver up, pointed directly at Waco's face. "You either help us do this or I'll kill you now. And I'll kill that cellmate of yours, too."

Waco knew Ring, and he was not entirely sane. He had no idea how the big man had worked this, but he knew that he was telling the truth about shooting him. He took a deep breath and said, "Well, you've got the best of the argument, Ring."

"All right. We'll get you a gun, and then we're leaving this place." All the cell doors were open, and there were at least twenty inmates in that cell block. Ring hissed, "Everybody be quiet. We're going to the warden's office."

Waco kept his eyes open. The three men were all carrying lanterns throwing a feeble yellow light over the scene. They passed the body of the guard whom Ring had killed, turned down a corridor, and stood before a door that said WARDEN CRAWFORD.

Ring lifted the gun and said, "All right. Get ready." Ring opened the door and stepped inside, and his two friends shoved Waco through the door along with Cecil. Waco saw that Warden Morgan Crawford was shocked. He stood up immediately, a small man with dark hair and dark eyes. "What's going on?"

"We're bustin' out of this place, Warden. Give us the key to that weapons room where you keep the guns."

"I won't do that, Gatlin."

"Then I'll shoot you and take it off your body."

Waco was shocked to see one of the guards go for his gun in spite of being under the guns of the three inmates.

Ring shot him down, and he lay kicking for a moment then grew still. "You're next, Warden."

"Wait a minute, Ring. I'll get the key," Waco said. He walked over to the warden, who was standing with the remaining guard. He had his eyes on the gun that was at the guard's belt.

Ring laughed. "Give him that key, Crawford, or you'll be dead. Get that guy's gun. Find the key to the weapons room."

Waco's mind was working rapidly. He knew he had no choice, but he also knew he couldn't go along with Ring. This could never work. He walked across the room. His eyes met Warden Crawford's. He took the gun from the guard then stepped in front of the warden. "Drop your gun, Ring. You're not going to do this."

Ring lifted his pistol and fired two shots as Waco knew he would. The first shot grazed him, but Waco felt the other bullet strike him. He then shot off three rounds, one at Gatlin and the other two at his companions, before he felt the world turning black. He then fell, conscious only of the smell of gun smoke then of nothing at all.

Dr. Simmons was talking to Warden Crawford. "He's going to be all right, but those two slugs hit him. I guess if you have to be shot twice it was pretty good. One missed the lung and lodged in the shoulder. The other creased his head. If it had been an inch to the right, he'd be dead."

Warden Crawford had come to the prison hospital and watched as Simmons had patched Waco up. Waco's shots, to the warden, had been miraculous. He had put all three men down, Ring dead and the other two so badly wounded that the guards were able to come and overpower them. "He saved my life, Dr. Simmons. Do your best for him."

Waco came out of a deep darkness. He was conscious of pain, and when he opened his eyes he saw a face peering down at him. "Well, Warden, he's going to live."

The face disappeared, and Warden Crawford's face appeared. Waco could not put it all together. "How'd I get here?"

"Well, you got here by saving my life and maybe the lives of half a dozen others. You got Ring dead center. And the other two, after they shot you, you kept firing until they both went down. Waco, I want to thank you for saving my life. I owe you for that, and I always pay my debts."

Waco was weak and felt himself drifting off. He tried to put it all together but could not think. He knew somehow that Warden Crawford was saying something very important. He tried desperately to remember it as he drifted off into sleep.

CHAPTER 11

Sabrina looked around the room as Dulcie shook her head. The room was piled high with packages of all shapes, and dresses and other garments were hanging from anywhere the two could find a place to put them.

Finally Dulcie said, "You don't need no more new clothes. You couldn't wear all you got now in a year."

"Hush, Dulcie," Sabrina said. She held up a dress that she had not been sure of, and now she shook her head. "This is just a little bit too daring. Look at that neckline. I would never wear it."

"Then what you buy it for?" Dulcie shot the question. "I told you when you tried it on it showed too much of you, but would you listen to me? No, you never listens to me."

Sabrina suddenly laughed. "I don't know why you're fussing so much," she said, staring at the dress. "You get all my old clothes."

"You ain't got no old clothes."

"What are you talking about? I always have clothes that I give you when I buy new things."

"You give 'em to me, but they ain't old. You ain't never wore out a dress or a petticoat or a pair of pantaloons in your whole life."

"Well, you probably have the best wardrobe of any servant in the United States."

Indeed, this was true. Sabrina knew Dulcie did not keep all the clothes, for she had friends who needed them, and there were certainly not enough places for her to go where she might wear the fancy dresses. But still she grumbled. "You got enough stuff here to start a store."

"Well, come on. We're going to go out to one more place."

"One more place for what?"

"There's one more place that makes stylish dresses. Just one of a kind. Come on. I want something absolutely different."

The two left the hotel and walked down the streets of New Orleans. It was the city that Sabrina loved, for it was so different from any other town or city that she had ever seen. They passed down a street where there were organ grinders and a fair where they were selling all kinds of things that nobody in the world had a need for but bought anyway. They went by the square where Sabrina glanced at a cathedral. It seemed to be doing not nearly so much business as the shops.

Dulcie followed her as Sabrina went into one of the stores, looking around. "They ought to have something here for me."

"I reckon they do," Dulcie grumbled, "and it's gonna cost you an arm and a leg."

Sabrina had long ago given up looking for bargains. Now she simply bought what she wanted. She noticed that there were, strangely enough, couples there, men with women. The women were Creoles, beautiful women, and she suspected they were the mistresses rather than the wives of the men they accompanied.

She was interrupted when a man who had come up to stand

beside her said, "Well, I don't believe we've met."

Sabrina turned and studied the man quickly. She had become quite a student of males for she had been pursued since she was in her midteens. She was wise enough to know that some of the pursuers were simply after her father's money, and she had quickly learned to identify that species instantly. "No, we haven't met, and I don't think we will."

She was studying the man, who was tall and darkly handsome with black hair and eyes a deep brown. He had a trim mustache and a clean-cut jaw, and his clothes were absolutely everything except cheap. The quality and cut of his suit, the perfect-fitting shoulders, the smooth, flat lapels—all were impeccable. He was dressed in a pure white soft silk shirt and a wide, flowering cravat tied meticulously, and his jacket was a fine wool. The price of his boots would have fed a poor family for a month.

He was a handsome man with a face full of humor and undisciplined imagination. "I take it you are a visitor in New Orleans."

"Yes sir, I am."

"Well, we are happy to welcome you. My name is William Blakely." He hesitated for a moment then said, "At this point it's customary for a lady to give her name."

Sabrina ordinarily would do no such thing, but she knew she would not be seeing this man again, so she said, "I am Sabrina Warren from Memphis."

"Fine. Now we are acquainted, and I think we should have lunch."

"Don't you have work to do?"

"No, not a bit."

"Well, what do you do for a living?"

"Nothing."

His honesty and mischievous look attracted Sabrina.

"My father made a pile of money, so all I do is flit around going to social events."

He was a charming, witty man, obviously with plenty of money. Most women would have been flattered with his attention, but Sabrina was merely amused. "Doesn't it embarrass you to come right out and tell people you're a parasite?"

"Not a bit," Blakely said. "Dad knows when he goes up the flue I'll have to take over the business. Then I'll become a boring businessman like all the rest."

"Are you married?"

"No. And I hope you're not either. . ."

"I'm also unmarried."

His smile widened. "Great. I'll tell you what. I think it would be suitable if you and I would go to lunch as a welcome to our fair city."

Men did not often amuse Sabrina. He was obviously a scoundrel and a wastrel but a wealthy one and a witty one. She turned and said, "Dulcie, you go back to the hotel. Can you find it?"

Dulcie gave her a disgusted look. "You think I get lost in this place? Of course I can find it."

"Well, you go on back and wait for me there."

After Dulcie left, Blakely said, "Come on. I'm going to take you to the finest restaurant in New Orleans, and I'm an honored guest. They'll give us the best they've got."

They moved outside, and several minutes later he led her into the Boudreaux Café. The tables were covered with snowy white tablecloths, the silver glowed with a richness and a warmth almost alive, and the lights illuminated the richness of the décor.

A man dressed in a fine black suit came forward. "Well, Mr. Blakely, we haven't seen you lately."

"Hello, Franklin. This is Miss Sabrina Warren. She's a visitor in our city, and I brought her to the best restaurant in New Orleans."

"Kind of you to say so." Franklin beamed. "Come. I'll give you your usual table."

A few minutes after they were seated, Franklin extended a menu, but Blakely said, "Just bring us the best you have. It'll be good." He leaned forward and said, "I've never gotten a bad meal yet."

"Thank you," Franklin said. "Your food will be out very quickly." He turned and left their table.

"Well, now. Tell me about yourself, Mr. Blakely," Sabrina said. "If you don't work, what do you do?"

Blakely turned his head to one side and seemed to think. "Well, I suppose my chief occupation at the present time is looking for a bride. As a matter of fact, I've got a list of prospects for the job. My mother and father made it out. The usual things for a rich wastrel like myself. She must be not hideous, have lots of money, come from a good family, and be respectable. As I say, my parents made it out. I'd like to add you to the list."

"It would never work, Mr. Blakely."

"Just call me William. Now, why wouldn't it work?"

"Because we're both used to getting everything we want."

"Well, that doesn't matter. We've got money enough between us to take care of that."

"We'd fight constantly."

"I'd rather like that. Every couple needs a good fiery argument at least once a week. Then they can have fun making up. What about you, Sabrina? Has your family tried to marry you off to a suitable candidate?"

Ordinarily Sabrina would not have spoken to a stranger about her life, but something about William Blakely made her open up. She said honestly, "My family feels like yours, except they're looking for a suitable husband."

"Well, this is going to work out fine." Blakely smiled. He leaned forward and whispered, "After we eat we'll go to my house. You can apply to my parents for the position of my wife. I think they'll give you a high rating. I'm afraid," he said sadly, "they're trying to marry me off to Emma Gibbons."

"What's the matter with her?"

"Well, she's rather homely, to be truthful. Stacks of money. Comes from an old-money family, and lots of poor men without money are after her. Oh, I think you can beat Emma out."

Sabrina laughed and said, "That's very tempting, but we're too much alike. Both spoiled to the bone."

"Well, I like being spoiled, and I expect you do, too, right?"

"Pretty much."

"Any brothers or sisters to inherit the money?"

"I have one sister, but she's younger than I am. As a matter of fact, she's very romantic, which I am not."

"Oh, I think you might be if you had the proper...encouragement."

"No, I've had the proper encouragement. I'm very practical. My sister is expecting a white knight to come riding in and carry her off. She's being courted by a handsome one right now. My parents are afraid of him." She went ahead to explain the situation, and finally she shrugged. "My parents are worried sick, but I can handle it."

"What will you do, shoot the poor man?"

"Oh, there are ways of getting rid of fellows like that. I've had quite a bit of experience."

Blakely smiled and stroked his mustache. "Well, it occurs to me maybe I could go back with you for a double purpose. I could shoot the fellow, maybe not kill him, just wound him and persuade him to leave. Then I can persuade your parents that I'm just the sort of son-in-law they need."

"I don't think that would work out. My mother's not very astute, but my father's sharp. He got rich by knowing men. He'd see you, William, in a minute as a poor choice for a son-in-law."

"That breaks my heart, Sabrina, but let's at least enjoy the lunch. Then tonight we'll go out together, and I'll have another chance with you."

Sabrina enjoyed the lunch and enjoyed the chatter, but immediately following the meal she said, "Good-bye. It's been nice talking to you. You're a charming fellow, but I'm looking for a man with a little bit more backbone."

"I don't have much of that, I'm afraid." Blakely shrugged. "If you change your mind"—he reached into his pocket and gave her a card—"here's my name and address. Just write me, and I'll come on that white horse to carry you off."

Sabrina took his hand. He offered to accompany her, but she said, "No. This is good-bye forever, William."

When she got back to the hotel, Dulcie was waiting for her. "Well, did you get rid of that triflin' man?"

"Why, he's rich, handsome, and charming."

Dulcie said sourly, "He's a trashy man. You don't need no trashy man, Miss Sabrina. You needs a good man."

"Well, I'm trying hard. I seem to have run through the available list in Memphis."

"But there's plenty of good men out there, and one of them would be a good man for you, but you is too picky."

"Well, let's look at these dresses now." She threw herself into the task of trying on dresses again, knowing full well she would send some of them back.

☙

The following day, Sabrina was awakened early by Dulcie, who said, "There's done been a telegram come for you."

"A telegram?" Sabrina sat up in bed and blinked her eyes, trying to come awake. "Where is it?"

"It's right here." Dulcie handed her a single slip of paper.

She peered at the signature. "It's from Father."

"What does he say?"

Sabrina scanned the telegram. "It says: 'Sabrina, Marianne insists on marrying Gerald Robbins. It's a tragedy. Please come home at once and help us change her mind.'"

Sabrina threw off the bedcovers and got up. "Help me get dressed, Dulcie," she said. "We've got to leave today."

"I told you so! Didn't I tell you? You didn't have no business leavin'. Now you got to go home, and I don't think you can do nothin' about Miss Marianne."

"Yes, I can. Now help me get packed."

"Gonna take an extra railroad car to get all this junk back," Dulcie muttered, but she began stuffing dresses into suitcases and trunks.

☙

As the carriage drew up to the front door of her home, Sabrina got out. The footman was there to help her. She turned and said, "Dulcie, you take my things. See that it's all hung up."

"Yes, ma'am," Dulcie said.

Sabrina was met by her mother, who threw herself at her daughter. Sabrina held on to her, patting her back and saying, "Now don't cry, Mother. It's going to be all right."

"No, it's not going to be all right. It's going to be awful. She won't even listen to her father and certainly not me. You've got to change her mind and tell her about this man."

"Well, I haven't even met him."

"He's not a man for her. You'll find that out."

"Where is she?"

"She's up in her room. We had an awful fight. She went off and told me she didn't want to see anybody."

"Well, she'll see me," Sabrina said grimly. She released herself from her mother's embrace and headed up the stairs. As she did, she tried to make up a speech. *I've got to be firm. She's too young to get married. She's not mature enough to marry anybody. Not this knight in white armor she's been looking for.* She had already formed a poor opinion of Gerald Robbins without having met him. She had heard him described well by her parents and ecstatically by Marianne, and none of it pleased her. She reached the top of the stairs, went to the door of Marianne's room, and knocked. "Marianne, I need to see you."

"Go away!"

"I'm not going away." She opened the door and saw Marianne lying across the bed.

Her younger sister raised her head. Her eyes were red with weeping. "Leave me alone, Sabrina."

"I'm not leaving you alone. I'm going to talk sense to you."

For the next ten minutes Sabrina did her best to "talk sense" to Marianne, but it was like talking to a dead stump.

Marianne would do nothing but shake her head and say, "I

love him, and I'm going to marry him."

"You're not going to marry him. Why, I haven't even met him."

"Your mind is made up against him. So is Mother's and Father's, but I don't care. I love him, and I'm going to have him."

Sabrina was set back somewhat. Marianne had always been the gentle, easily led one of the two. Sabrina had been the bossy, demanding type, but now she had run up against a problem she had never encountered before. Marianne was obstinate; her mouth was set in a stubborn fashion, and she was glaring at Sabrina with resentment and anger. "We don't really know this man," Sabrina said. "We don't know anything about his family."

"I know one thing. I know I love him."

"You're just in love with romance."

"Don't start on me, Sabrina. I'm not going to listen."

That, in essence, was Sabrina's effort to cause Marianne to listen. But after ten minutes of total silence from her sister, Sabrina gave up. "We'll talk about this some more when you feel better." She waited for Marianne to answer, but when she still refused to speak, Sabrina got up and left the room. She went downstairs and found her father and mother waiting for her.

"What did she say?" her father demanded. His face was lined with care. He obviously expected her to have a good word.

"She won't listen to me now, but I'm not through yet. We can't give up."

"She's like a different young woman," Caroline Warren said. Her face was swollen from weeping, and she said, "Can't we just bundle her into a carriage and take her away?"

"She's not a child," Charles Warren said.

"She is behaving like a twelve-year-old," Sabrina said angrily. She was disturbed at having failed in her first attempt. Always before, whatever she pleased, she could get Marianne to agree to it, but this was a different young girl, and Sabrina's mouth set in a stubborn line. "I'm going to stay here and not let her out of my sight. And I'm going to meet this Gerald Robbins. I've got a word or two to say to him."

"We've said everything we can think of to him and to her," her father said. "It's a hopeless case."

"No, it's not hopeless. I can fix it," Sabrina said stubbornly. She turned and walked out of the drawing room and up the stairs.

She found Dulcie sitting in the midst of a pile of her clothes, waiting. "Did you talk her out of marrying that scoundrel?"

"You don't know he's a scoundrel."

"I bet he is. He ain't no good man."

"You wouldn't think any man was good enough."

"That doesn't change that he's a scoundrel. You mark my words on that."

"I'll make up my own mind on that," Sabrina said. "I'm going to see him tomorrow."

"You might have met your match this time. I don't think the Good Lord Himself could change Miss Marianne's mind."

☙

Sabrina could not sleep well that night. She woke up late. Dulcie was not there, so she put on a simple dress, brushed her hair, and started down the stairs.

She was met halfway down by her father, who had a sheet of paper in his hands. His face was pale.

"What is it, Father?"

"Read this."

454

Sabrina took the paper and read it in one glance. It was in Marianne's handwriting, but where her handwriting was usually neat, this was obviously scratched at a moment's notice.

I know you're all going to hate me, but I can't help it. I love Gerald, and I'm leaving with him. I would like to be married here, but he says we can be married after we get to his home, that he knows a good parson there. Please don't try to find me. Gerald is my life. I love you all, but I must do this.

Marianne

"When did she leave, Father?"

"Nobody knows. She went to bed early, and she was gone this morning. She must have made arrangements for Robbins to take her in the middle of the night." He slumped over against the rail and looked as if he were about to fall.

"Don't worry, Father. We'll find them."

"How? We don't know where she's going. We know very little about the man."

"We'll find him. Don't worry. This isn't the end of this thing yet." But even as Sabrina spoke, she knew that somehow something had ended in the life of their family. It was almost like a death, and Sabrina, for the first time in her life, felt helpless.

She had tried her best to change Marianne and failed. Now the thought that if she had stayed it might have been different came to her. She slowly descended the stairs, determined to give her mother all the comfort she could—which wasn't a great deal.

CHAPTER 12

Caesar was sitting in the kitchen eating a huge piece of cake, stuffing his mouth full.

Dulcie glared at him. "You eat like a hungry dog. Take little bites."

"It's so good I can't hep it. You the best cook there is in addition to being the best-lookin' one around."

"Don't you come at me with none of your ways. I ain't gonna stand for it, Caesar."

Caesar's eyes opened wide. "Why, I was just being appreciative. You is good-lookin', and you is a fine cook."

Dulcie did not object to these two descriptions of herself, but she plopped herself down, and her head drooped. "This place is a madhouse."

"Sho' enough is. They all act like Miss Marianne died. She didn't die."

"About the same to them. She says she's going to marry that man, but he ain't said one word to Mr. Charles 'bout marryin' her. I don't think he's got marriage on his mind. He didn't look like a marryin' man to me."

"Well, he was a fine dresser and good-lookin' gentleman."

"Gentleman? He ain't no gentleman."

"How can you tell?"

"I've been around enough gentlemen to know one when I sees one. Mr. Frank Morgan, now he's a gentleman. Mr. Charles, he's a gentleman. Even that Mr. Lane Williams that been courtin' Miss Sabrina is a gentleman. But that fellow Robbins, he wasn't no gentleman. He's gonna ruin Miss Marianne, that's what."

Caesar took a small portion of the cake and put it in his mouth. At once it was gone, and he took a larger portion. He washed it down with a glass of milk and said, "Miss Sabrina, she's plumb upset. I took her downtown today, and she snapped at me like I wuz a snake."

"She's worried. First time she's ever been worried about anything."

"She knows it's her fault."

"How could it be her fault? It was her sister who run off."

"If she had stayed here and helped, she could have done somethin'. No, she had to go to New Orleans and spend a lot of money on clothes that she didn't need nohow."

"She surely was upset. She didn't even look like herself."

"Her father is going to have to have a doctor for his wife. She about to lose her mind."

The two sat in the kitchen, continuing to discuss the plight of Marianne.

❧

Downstairs in the larger of the two parlors, Charles was trying to comfort Caroline, who was weeping. "Dear, you simply must get ahold of yourself. I think we'd better have the doctor."

"What could he do?" Caroline wailed. "He couldn't bring Marianne back."

"No, but he could give you something for your nerves."

"What are we going to do? What can we do?"

"I tell you what I'm going to do right now. I'll leave Sabrina here to care for you. I'm going down to the police."

Caroline's eyes widened. "Do you think he kidnapped her?"

"I'm sure we couldn't charge him with that since she went willingly enough, but at least the police will know how to find her. . . I hope. I'll go get Sabrina. You try to lie down and get some rest."

Charles Warren left the drawing room and went at once to Sabrina's room. When he knocked on the door, she opened it up. "Sabrina, I'm going to town. You stay with your mother. Try to keep her calm as you can."

"Why are you going to town, Father?"

"I have no idea how to find my daughter. I'm going to the police."

Sabrina at once said, "That's a good idea. Let me go with you."

"No, you stay here with your mother. I don't know how long I'll be. If your mother gets worse, call Dr. Simpson. Have him come. Have him give her something that'll make her sleep. And make her stop worrying so much."

"I'm not sure there is anything like that." Then she said bitterly, "I need some myself."

Warren looked at his daughter and saw with surprise that her face showed signs of tears. "I haven't seen you cry since you were seven."

"It's all my fault! I should have stayed here."

"I don't think it would have made any difference, but you do what you can now by taking care of your mother."

"Come back home as soon as you find out something."

"I'll do it, daughter. Try not to worry."

"I won't do that. I should be worrying. I should have been more careful." It was an admission that his strong-willed daughter did not often make.

As Charles left the house he thought, *This thing has broken Sabrina. That shows how bad it is.*

⁂

"I'm sorry that we're not able to do more, Mr. Warren."

The chief of police was a personal friend of Charles Warren. His name was Louis Stone, and he was a good policeman.

It was the day after Warren had come and laid his problem before the chief. Now Stone shook his head. "I've had my best detectives out, and they can't find a trace of the man. Nothing solid. I don't think Robbins is his real name."

"Any leads at all?"

"Well, they found the hotel where he lived. Several people knew him, but he didn't talk about himself. We did find out one thing. . . ."

"What's that?" Warren asked eagerly.

"Strangely enough it was from a boot black. He was polishing Robbins's shoes, and Robbins started talking to a man sitting next to him. The boy's name is Jason. Seems like a reliable witness. He told my men one thing that might give you a lead."

"What's that?"

"He mentioned Robbins going to Oklahoma."

"Well, that's a big place. It would take forever," Warren said sadly.

"Well, he went a little bit more into detail," Chief Stone said.

"Said Robbins mentioned Judge Parker's territory. You know what that is?"

"I don't believe I do."

"Judge Parker is the judge over the whole Indian Territory. It's supposed to be just for the Indians, but every hard case, gunman, and crook running from the law in the country goes to Oklahoma Territory. Jason said this fellow laughed and said he could hide out there for a hundred years and nobody would ever find him."

"It sounds like he thinks somebody might be coming for him."

"That's what I thought, so I tried to find a confirmation on trains leaving, but no luck so far. I think this fellow is a criminal of some kind, and he's run off to Oklahoma Territory."

"Thanks, Chief."

"You might go see Donald French. He's the best private detective I know. If anybody can find out anything, he will do it."

"I'll go right there. Where's his office?"

"In the Hall Building."

"Well," French said, "I've done my best, Mr. Warren. I did find someone, after interviewing a hundred people, who saw a couple get on a train headed for Oklahoma. Couldn't be sure, but he gave a brief description of the man. Said he had blond hair and was well dressed."

"What about the woman?"

"She was small with blond hair and blue eyes. And the witness said she was hanging on to this man. It's not much, but I did find out from the conductor that one of them asked him how long it would take to get to Oklahoma."

"Well, that's what Chief Stone said."

"I think that's where you'll find them."

"Thanks, Mr. French."

"Well, I didn't earn the money, but I'll take it. And I'll tell you this. If he's taken that girl of yours to Oklahoma Territory, he's no good."

The chief's words discouraged Charles Warren, but he went home and repeated them to his wife. He softened the blow as much as he could, but it sent her into another torrent of grieving. He told Sabrina to put her to bed, and when Sabrina finally came back down, she saw an odd look on his face. "So the police and the private detective think this man's taken her to Indian Territory?"

"That's what they both said."

"What are you going to do?"

"Hire more detectives."

"What can they do?"

"Well, not much. Even if they found he had taken her there, they couldn't go in after her. It's against the law."

"But they do have some law, don't they?"

"Judge Isaac Parker is judge over the whole territory. He has about two hundred marshals. They go in and hunt the criminals down, but they're badly outnumbered, and he's lost about fifty of them."

"What do you mean, lost?"

"They were killed. It's a dangerous place." He hesitated. Then when he looked up, he saw an odd look on Sabrina's face. "What is it, Sabrina?"

"I'm going to find Marianne."

Warren's eyes flew open with surprise. "Why, you can't go into Indian Territory. In the first place, it's against the law. In the second place, you're not a marshal."

"I'll hire one of the marshals. I'm going to find her, Father."

That was not the end of Sabrina's announcement. The next day she left the house. Dulcie was crying and begging to go. Sabrina hugged her and said, "It won't be any place for you."

"Who's going to take care of you?"

"I'm going to find me a man," Sabrina said. "And we're going to go get my sister and bring her home."

There was more talk and more weeping on the part of Caroline Warren.

Her father pleaded with her not to go, but Sabrina Warren was cursed with a stubbornness that was almost endemic in her spirit. At two o'clock that afternoon she was on a railroad car. As it pulled out of the station headed West, she said under her breath, "I'll find me a man, and we'll find that scoundrel and bring my sister home!"

PART THREE

PART THREE

CHAPTER 13

The narrow-gauge coal-burning engine that touched into Fort Smith emitted a scream that sounded to Sabrina like a banshee. She was weary of her trip and had scarcely ever been more uncomfortable. The hard seats in the carriage car that she sat upon forced her into either an upright position or slumping down with a curve in her backbone. The windows were open most of the time, for it was hot. They admitted mostly hot desert air and cinders from the locomotive that chugged along toward its destination.

She had brought few clothes with her, and the garments that she wore were rather prim and severe, at least for Sabrina's taste. Her dress was a chocolate brown velvet, and she wore only a pair of earrings for decoration. Three black feathers were arranged in her hair, but they were now drooping and looking as if they were ready for the garbage heap.

Relief came when the conductor, a small, scrawny, ill-looking man in a crumpled black suit and a stiff-billed cap, came through shouting, "All out for Fort Smith! Everyone out for Fort Smith!"

Quickly Sabrina rose and straightened her back with a grunt.

She had expected a rough ride, but nothing as uncomfortable as this relic from the Civil War days that made the daily run from Fort Smith.

Passengers began filing off, and when Sabrina stepped down, the scrawny conductor was there. He reached up his hand, and she looked at it then shrugged and took it. When she stepped down to the brick surface, she said, "I need to find the courthouse."

"Oh, anybody can tell you about that. Just start walkin'."

"I have luggage."

"Yeah, I seen that. Well, let me get it for you."

He waited until the car was empty; then she guided him by saying, "That gray one is mine and that dark brown one—and the large one."

"You must be coming to stay for a spell, miss." The conductor waited to be enlightened about Sabrina's intention.

She merely nodded, murmuring, "Thank you, sir." She looked around and saw the ticket office, and leaving the luggage, she went inside.

She walked up to the window where a very fat man with a pair of startling green eyes peered at her and grinned. "Howdy, miss. Just get in I see."

"Yes, I need some directions."

"Where you be going, ma'am?"

"I need to see Judge Parker."

"Oh, well, the courthouse is right down that street to your right. You follow it, and you see the biggest building there three stories high. You'll find the judge somewhere around in there, I reckon. What do you need to see the judge for?"

"Private business!" Sabrina snapped. "Can you have someone put my luggage in a safe place?"

"Well, I don't know as there is a safe place around here."

Sabrina took a deep breath and withheld her comment on that. She saw a man sitting with a small wagon and said, "Does that man carry passengers?"

"Yes, ma'am, he does. His name is Zeke Cousins. He fit in the big war, he did. He'll take you anywhere you want to go."

"Thank you."

Zeke Cousins turned out to be a tall, lanky man dressed in a pair of bib overalls with a worn straw hat pushed down over his eyes. He moved slowly as if he were crippled getting out of the wagon but had no sign of a wound. Sabrina said, "I need to go to a hotel, and then I need to go to the courthouse."

"Yes'um. It'll cost you two dollars though."

"That'll be fine. My luggage is over there."

"I'll jist get it fer you."

She watched as Cousins moved slowly, carefully, as if he were about to step on dynamite, and wondered how a human being could move that slowly. The heat from the July sun was pouring down, and she was wet with perspiration, her clothes droopy.

Finally Cousins brought all three pieces of her luggage and said, "Just hop right in there, ma'am."

Sabrina was accustomed to being helped into carriages and vehicles. She saw that Cousins was not about to offer that service so, gritting her teeth, she stepped on one of the spokes, clambered onto the hard seat, and sat down. She found she was sore from sitting for many hours on the hard railroad seat, but there was no point complaining to her driver. "Take me to the best hotel."

"Sure, I'll do that, ma'am. That'll be the Starlight Hotel. It's run by Mr. and Mrs. Jamieson. They get along purty good 'cept they had a fight some time ago, and he lit out. But he come back, and they made it all up. Never did know what it was all about. Sure was sad for a while."

Such talk continued about people Sabrina had never heard of, and Cousins attempted, from time to time, to pry her name and purpose in coming to Fort Smith from her. Finally he pulled up in front of a two-story building. "That there's the Starlight Hotel, ma'am. You tell 'em Zeke Cousins brought you. They'll give you a good deal."

"Well, could you carry my luggage in?"

"Oh, that'll be an extra quarter."

"Fine." She handed him three dollars and said, "Keep the change."

"Why, that's right thoughtful of you, ma'am. I do appreciate it." He hopped down, but as soon as he touched the ground, his feet grew slower as if they were magnetized to the earth.

Finally the luggage was inside, Cousins left, and Sabrina walked up to the desk.

A young man, no more than eighteen it seemed, with his hair parted in the middle and wearing a string tie and a white shirt said, "Yes, ma'am, can I help you?"

"I need a room."

"Just for one night or for several days?"

"I'm not sure."

"Well, you better hold on to it for two or three days. Rooms are kind of scarce right now."

"Yes, that'll be fine. Three days."

She waited while the young man pulled out a leather-bound register, opened it, and said, "If you'd just sign your name right there, please."

Sabrina signed her name.

He turned it around and stared at it. "Miss Sabrina Warren—or is it Mrs?"

"It's Miss. Now, is there any chance at all of getting a bath in this hotel?"

"Yes ma'am, but that's extra. I'll have to have some boys bring up some hot water."

"That'll be fine. What's the room? Give me a key, please."

The young man turned and said, "My name's Joel Barnaby. Anything you need you just let me know. Here's your key. Room 206. Boys will be up with the hot water as soon as they can get it het up."

"Thank you."

"We ain't got nobody handy now. Let me help you with your luggage, Miss Warren."

Sabrina picked up the smaller suitcase, and the clerk carried the other two. When they got to the room in the middle of the hall, he put them down, opened her door, and then carried the suitcases in.

She entered behind him, said, "Thank you very much," and handed him fifty cents.

"You don't have to do that, ma'am."

"I appreciate it."

"Well, I'll have the fellers bring the water up as soon as they can get it."

"Thank you."

Sabrina waited until the door was closed and then took off the lightweight jacket. Her hair seemed to be drooping, and she knew the heat had done that. She looked around the room and saw it contained the bare necessities: a double bed with a corduroy-looking spread and a small table with a pitcher of water and a basin, the basin being cracked and the pitcher being broken at the lip. There were no closets, but there were nails driven into the wall. "I suppose that's where my clothes will go."

There were two chairs in the room, both with hard seats, and the wallpaper was sort of a leprous gray so ancient it was impossible to tell what it really was. She walked over to the window, which was open, and even as she did, two flies came zipping in. She shooed them away and looked down on the street. "Well, Fort Smith, there you are, and you're not much," she said grimly.

She watched as people moved below, noting that it seemed to be a typical Western outpost. The men wore pants tucked into high-heeled boots. Many of them carried guns and holsters, and all of them wore big hats. The women were dressed mostly in plain calico or printed cotton. They wore bonnets, and some of them carried umbrellas. "Well, here I am."

For a moment she felt a sense of despair. She knew her errand would not be easy, but she was a determined young lady. When she made up her mind, she ran at the job as if her life depended on it. She sat down on the bed instead of on one of the hard chairs and waited impatiently.

Finally there was a knock on the door, and three men came in. One of them was carrying what appeared to be a brass bathtub, an elongated affair. The other two both had two buckets of water. "Got your bathwater here, ma'am," the leader with the tub said. "You want it right here?"

"Yes, that's fine."

"Fill her up, boys."

Sabrina watched as the two men emptied the water out of the buckets into the tub and noted with satisfaction that at least the water was steaming. She thanked them all.

The tall man carrying the tub said, "If you need any help, just holler." He leered at her.

She stared at him disdainfully. "Good day, sir."

"Well, good day, ma'am. Enjoy your bath."

Sabrina recognized the look in his eye and knew that she was in rough territory.

After the men left, she opened one of the suitcases, took out a fresh outfit, then stripped down. The door did not seem to be locked, so she put one of the chairs under the knob and hoped for the best. She touched the water cautiously, and sure enough it was far too hot. She also realized she didn't have a washcloth or a towel, and none were furnished. "How am I going to wash?" Fortunately she had brought some soap with her.

She waited until the water had grown almost tepid. She stepped inside and sat down slowly, sighing with pleasure as the water lapped over her. She let her body slip down under the water. As she lay there soaking, she grew sleepy but knew she had to hurry. She stayed as long as she could, then got up and dried off as best she could with the dress she had worn. It was dusty, and she hated having to use it this way. She made a note to buy some washcloths and towels. As she dressed, she thought, *I've got to see Judge Parker, and he's got to help me!*

She went downstairs and said, "I need to see Judge Parker."

The clerk shook his head and said apologetically, "Well, ma'am, that ain't going to be possible until after the hanging."

"The hanging?"

"Yes ma'am, there's a hanging. Takes place in about thirty minutes. They're going to hang five men."

"At the same time?"

"Yes, ma'am. Go on down the street, and you'll see the

471

courthouse, and right across from it you'll see the gallows. The town's fillin' up. They always come for a big hanging. There ain't been five men hanged here in a spell."

Sabrina left and moved down the street, aware that indeed a crowd had come. The street was packed with wagons and mounts with saddles, and there was a babble of voices in the air. She finally saw the courthouse and had to endure the pressure from the crowd. She thought, *Do I want to see a hanging? It must be horrible.*

She almost left, but she said to a woman who had come to stand next to her, "Does Judge Parker come to the hangings?"

"Oh, he does. Look up there."

Sabrina looked up where the woman's gesture indicated, and the woman added, "That's him right there in the window. He comes to every hangin' right there at that window. I don't know how he stands it, all these men dying and all on his conscience."

"Well, he's a judge. That's what his job is."

"I reckon so, but I'd hate to be meetin' my Maker with Isaac Parker's record." It was only a few minutes later before a group of men came out of the courthouse. "The jailhouse is down underneath the courthouse," the woman said. She was a middle-aged woman with a wealth of freckles and reddish-blond hair. She was well padded and nodded, saying confidentially, "Looky there. They're all going to meet God. Ain't that a shame."

Sabrina watched the men. Indeed they were a mixed crew. One of them, the first out, was a hulking giant who glowered at the crowd. *He has some Indian blood in him,* she thought, for his skin was dark and bronze. The man next to him was small and neatly dressed. Beside him were two men of medium height. Both of them were terrified. It showed in their eyes. The fourth man was tall and spindly, and the fifth man was a Mexican apparently, who looked down at the crowd as if they had come to be his entertainment.

"That's him right there! That's George Maledon. He's the hangman for the judge." She was a talkative woman, and she began to say, "My husband owns the store, and Maledon came in to buy some rope to hang men with. Nothin' suited him. He ordered it all the way from El Paso. He found the thickest hemp he could, and he buys linseed oil, and he spends hours working it by hand into the fibers until those ropes are plied just as well as your hair is. It will just glide around the prisoner's neck, and he ties a monstrous knot and puts it right behind the right ear. When the man falls, the neck snaps like a bit of celery."

The gruesome information disgusted Sabrina, but her neighbor was not through. "He makes up two hundred pounds of sandbags like they use to dam up the Arkansas River. He ties those ropes, and he throws the trap. You can hear 'em *squee-thump* almost day and night like he takes pleasure in it."

Maledon wore two guns at his side and was a small, sour-looking man with a pair of dead eyes it seemed. He did not speak except to say, "You fellows can talk."

All five of the men had something to say. The Mexican said, "I am not afraid to die. I have found the Lord Jesus Christ as my personal Savior, and He will take me right to heaven."

His was the only gentle speech. The rest of the men were angry. One of them who stood next to the giant said, "There's worse men than me I see out there in that crowd. Some of you ought to be here hangin'. Not me."

As soon as the last man had spoken, Maledon moved down, putting a hood over each man's head and arranging the hangman's knot behind his ear.

Sabrina began to grow a little sick and wished she were not there, but she was. When the last knot was tied, Maledon, without further ado, caught Sabrina off guard. He simply turned and pulled the lever, and all five men dropped through a trapdoor.

She distinctly heard the popping of necks, and then she heard the most horrible sound of her life. One of the men had not died but was strangling and kicking. Blindly she turned and made her way out of the crowd. *I can't stand this anymore,* she thought and went directly toward the courthouse.

ॐ

"I'm sorry, ma'am, but you can't see the judge until after the court has dismissed."

Sabrina stood in the judge's courtroom. Now she looked around with disgust and saw that the courtroom was as plain as art can make it. There were rough-hewn benches made from warping pine.

Judge Parker, the presiding judge, stood upon a slight platform behind a desk. She stood there while he went through the process of handling the business at hand, and he seemed to be a man without feeling. He appeared to be in his early fifties, and there were white hairs in the brown hair that he kept neatly combed. She noticed that Parker had dark smudges under his eyes that looked like bruises. He was a dignified-looking man, handsome in a way.

Finally the last case was dismissed. The judge got up and left, but Sabrina hurried after him. "Judge Parker," she said, catching him, "my name is Sabrina Warren. I've come all the way from Memphis to see you."

Parker turned and bowed slightly in a courteous manner. "Why yes, Miss Warren. Come on up to my office." He led Sabrina up to the second floor and down a hall then opened a door. There was a man seated over to one side, and Parker said, "Heck, would you excuse us, please."

"Sure enough, Judge." The man got up, an ordinary-looking fellow wearing a gun as most did. There was a marshal's badge on his vest.

As soon as he left, Judge Parker smiled. "That was Heck Thomas, the best of my marshals. Would you have a seat, Miss Warren, or is it Mrs. Warren?"

"No, I'm not married."

Parker waited until Sabrina was seated.

She took a quick look around the room. It was barely large enough to contain a black walnut desk as large as most dining tables, several chairs, shelves, and a credenza, but every flat surface was piled high with papers and bursting portfolios. The air was stagnant, redolent of tobacco long since chewed and expectorated and murky with the exhaust of cigars. A revolving bookcase to one side leaned drunkenly, threatening to fall, and mustard-colored bound case histories filled one complete bookcase.

"Now, what can I do for you, Miss Warren?"

"I've come to get your help, Judge. My sister's been kidnapped. She's in the Indian nations, and I've come to enlist your help in rescuing her."

"Tell me all the details," Parker said.

Sabrina went on to tell how her father had hired private detectives, but they had not been able to find her sister. "Finally," she added, "Marianne managed to get a letter brought out. I received word from my father on my way here. Apparently she gave all the money she had to a traveling cowboy. He promised to mail the letter, which he did. In the letter Marianne said she is being held captive by a man named Trey LeBeau."

Parker sat watching his guest with a pair of steady, warm brown eyes, and finally he said, "You've come at a rather awkward time, Miss Warren. At the present time I only have a single marshal, and I have to keep one here. I don't have anyone to send after your sister."

"But I thought you had two hundred marshals."

Parker shook his head sadly. "No, I did have at one time, but over fifty of them are gone. Some killed, some turned outlaw."

"Marshals turning outlaw?"

"Oh yes, ma'am. The Dalton boys, they were marshals. Now they're out robbing trains and holding up people. If I catch them, they'll see the end of a rope."

"But you must have somebody."

"Well, it's like this. This very day I might have five or six rangers come in, but there might not be one for a month. They have to follow the outlaws until they catch them. And that takes longer. There's no schedule to it."

Sabrina grew angry. "I've come all this way to get help. You're the man in charge of law and order in this territory. You've got to help me!"

"I can't help you, Miss Warren, not now. I will as soon as I get some men who will go, but I wouldn't send one man out to capture LeBeau."

"Why not?"

"Because he's got a band of armed outlaws at his beck and call. One man wouldn't stand a chance. It will have to be a posse, maybe at least a dozen men, and I honestly can't tell you when we'll have that kind of personnel."

Sabrina stood up. Her temper, which had gotten her into trouble before, flared out. "Well, I'll find some men who will do the job if you won't do it!" She turned and started for the door.

Judge Parker got up and said with alarm, "Ma'am, you don't know these men. I advise you to wait."

"I won't wait! I'm going to get my sister!" She left the room.

Heck Thomas was sitting outside. He grinned as she stormed by. She knew he was "laughing" at her expense, but she didn't take the time to stop and upbraid him. She was determined to find her sister and get out of this territory for good.

❧

Sabrina was not accustomed to having to wait for anything. Her father's money and the family's position had always made it possible for her to get her own way. This, however, was not working in Fort Smith.

She knew no other way to find help than to simply stop men on the street and ask them. She received many indecent proposals, for men in the frontier of Fort Smith assumed that when a good-looking woman stopped them on the street, she had something special on her mind. They simply grinned and said things like, "Well honey, let's you and me go somewhere, and we'll talk this thing over."

On the third day she was seated in the restaurant having a lunch consisting of a greasy pork chop and a limp salad when two men came in. They were both tall and well built. When they identified themselves as brothers, she saw the resemblance.

"I'm Asa and this is Roy. Denvers is our name. I hear you are looking for someone that will go into the Territory and do a chore for you."

Instantly Sabrina grew excited. "Yes. I haven't been able to find anybody. Men in this part of the world evidently don't need money or else they're afraid of the Indians."

"Well, that's a shame," Roy said. He had the same pale blue eyes of his brother, and both men were sunburned. There was a lupine aspect in the two. They looked rather like hungry wolves, but Sabrina had expected this.

She said, "Sit down." The two men sat down and drank coffee while she explained about her sister being kidnapped and being held by a man called Trey LeBeau.

"That's bad news," Asa said. He was evidently the older of the two. "LeBeau's a bad man."

"Are you afraid of him?" Sabrina glared at him, waiting for his answer.

"It pays to be afraid of rattlesnakes and men who'll kill you for a quarter."

"Well, then you can't help me."

"Wait a minute." Roy Denver, the younger of the two, seemed to be the brighter. "We can do the job, but lady, it's gonna cost a lot of money. We've got to buy horses, equipment, supplies, ammunition, and guns. Pretty expensive."

"I've got the money, but you've got to guarantee me that you'll get my sister."

"All we can do is say we'll find her and we'll try to get her back from LeBeau. He don't let go of things easy." Roy Denver shrugged. "It'll take some persuading."

"Yes," the older Denver said. "A man could get killed."

"Well, how much money do you want?"

"To buy the equipment? Well, we'd have to have at least five hundred dollars just to get started."

"All right. Let's go to the bank, and I'll get a check cashed." She thought for a minute then said, "When can you leave?"

"Oh, we can buy the equipment today and leave at first light," Roy Denver said.

"All right." She went with them to the bank and gave them the money.

Roy said, "We'll be leavin' in the morning before you get up."

"No, I'm going with you."

The Denver brothers stared at her and then at each other. Roy Denver shook his head. "Ma'am, that is a terrible idea."

"I'm going, and that's all there is to it."

The two argued halfheartedly, but finally they said, "Well, it's going to be a rough ride."

"I don't care how rough it is. I'm going."

"Well, then you'd better get yourself outfitted. You can't wear a pretty dress like that on the trail."

"I'll take care of that. Come and get me at the hotel when you're ready to leave in the morning." She watched the two leave then went at once to buy some rough clothes. She found a riding skirt, for she knew she would have to ride a horse astride, a white lightweight shirt, and a vest with silver pesos for buttons. She found a black hat that had a small brim and a low crown but would be good for heading off the sun.

As she went back to the hotel with her possessions, she glanced up at Judge Parker's office. "I'll show you, Judge Parker, you're not the only fish in the ocean!"

❧

Sabrina was absolutely exhausted. She had ridden for two days now, and the Denver brothers seemed to be made out of leather and steel. They never seemed to be tired.

At the end of the second day, she said, "I can't go any farther."

Asa Denver shook his head. "Got to go a little further, missy."

"No, we'll camp here."

"All right. If you say so."

She stared at him. "I'm not happy with your work. You don't seem to know where you're going."

Both men grinned broadly. "We know where we're going, but I hate to tell you we're going without you."

Sabrina stared at them. They looked like two lean timber wolves at that moment. "What—what are you talking about?"

"We're going to leave you here, and you better count yourself fortunate. Worse things could happen to a nice lady like you with a pair of men like us."

"You can't leave me here!"

"Why can't we?" Roy Denver grinned. He dismounted, came over, and pulled her off her horse. She carried her money in a leather pouch. He reached down, snatched it, and said, "You have a good time out here."

Horrified, Sabrina watched the two get on their horses that contained all their equipment, her money, and all she had. Roy Denver was leading her horse. "You can't leave me here!" she cried out.

"Just go back to where you came, honey. You'll find it."

Sabrina watched them go, and for the first time in her life, real paralyzing fear seemed to grip her in a frozen clasp. She wanted to cry out, but she knew those two men would never return. Slowly she turned and started walking back. She had not paid particular attention to the landscape or the signs and the hills and trees that could have been landmarks.

By the time the sun was low in the sky, her legs were trembling. She sat down on the ground, drew her knees up, and held them with her arms. She put her forehead down on her knees and began to weep.

CHAPTER 14

Sabrina awoke and found she was shivering. The two villains she had placed her confidence in had taken everything, even the heavy coat that was tied behind the saddle on her horse that they had stolen. She hugged herself and shut her eyes tightly, aware that the sky was beginning to light up the east. A sharp pain came to her when a stone that she had lain down on penetrated her thin jacket and the white shirt she wore. She tried to escape into sleep again, for the moment she woke up, at least partially, her plight came to her.

I'm lost in the middle of the desert. I don't have any horse. Nobody knows where I am except the two men who put me here. I'm thirsty, and I'll starve out here in this desert unless someone finds me.

Shifting around, she found that she could not hide in the pavilions of sleep anymore. With a groan she sat up and hugged herself to try to control the shivering. The light indeed was breaking, and she saw the landscape as a ghostly affair with cacti casting hideous shapes, or so it seemed to her. From far off a coyote howled, a lonesome song that somehow made her feel even worse.

She sat for a moment then turned to face the east.

Suddenly an icy hand seemed to run down her back, and fright came with such a powerful force that she could only sit and stare at the Indian who stood no more than ten feet away watching her. *He's going to kill me!* The thought seemed to freeze her mind, and she stared at the savage, waiting for him to come forward and cut her throat or worse. She had heard of the cruelty of the Indians and had never given it any thought. Now, however, a black veil of fear and dread seemed to envelop her.

The silence ran on, and when the Indian did not speak, Sabrina climbed to her feet. She was sore from head to foot from the cold and the hard ground, but she did not take her eyes off of the Indian. He was a handsome enough fellow, judging from the sorry specimens she had seen hanging around Fort Smith. He was no more than medium height, and he wore a pair of white man's jeans and a green-and-white-checkered shirt. His face seemed to be carved from steel. He had a prominent nose and wide lips now compressed, but it was his eyes that held her. They were obsidian, blacker than any eyes she had ever seen, and they stared at her unwaveringly. He had a rifle in his left hand, and ten feet farther off was a horse with a red blanket tied to a mesquite tree. He wore a wide-brimmed hat, but the black braids of his hair hung down his back, red ribbons tied in each of them.

Finally Sabrina tried to speak and found that her throat was dry. She cleared it, coughed, licked her dry lips, and said, "Hello."

Whatever she expected did not happen. She had no idea that the Indian would speak English, but he said, "You are lost."

Glad that he could speak English and that he made no move to threaten her, Sabrina nodded violently. "Yes, I hired two men to help me, and they took my horse and everything I had."

"What two men?"

"Their names were Denver. Asa and Roy Denver."

A slight movement of the Indian's lips might have been a smile. "Bad men," he said simply.

"I—I need to get back to Fort Smith. Could I hire you to take me?"

"My name is Gray Wolf. You were foolish to come with those two men. Everyone knows they are not good."

"I know that now, Gray Wolf, but I'm helpless. If you'll help me get back to Fort Smith, I'll see that you're well paid."

Gray Wolf was examining her from head to foot. He came forward, and she stiffened up for she could not read his intentions in his features. He came and stood in front of her saying, "Yes, I can take you to town." Without another word he seized her by the arm and began to pull at her.

Sabrina's first impulse was to resist but she knew that would be useless. He was strong as an animal, she felt, and for the first time in her life she was completely at the mercy of another human being, one whom she did not know and who owed her nothing.

Gray Wolf stopped beside the horse, which had no saddle. "Get on," he said.

There was only a woven leather bridle around the horse's neck, not even between his lips as a proper bridle would be. "I—I can't get up there."

"Here. Put your foot here." He locked his fingers together and stooped over, and she tentatively stepped in. He heaved her up, and she managed to throw her leg across. There was nothing to hang on to, for the bridle he used, such as it was, was tied to the tree. Gray Wolf said nothing but untied the bridle and began to walk toward the east.

Sabrina felt a great gush of relief flow through her. *He's not going to kill me!* She was not a praying woman, but at that moment she felt that if she were she would give thanks for her deliverance. *I'm not going to die,* she thought, and the thought gave her a sensation of relief such as she had never known before.

For the next four hours the Indian moved steadily forward, tirelessly so, it seemed to Sabrina. She had nothing to do with her hands, no horn to cling to, no bridle to hold, so all she could do was sit there. She recognized none of the territory that they were passing through, but finally she said in a voice that was a croak, "Do you have any water?"

"Over there." Gray Wolf pointed over to the right and turned the direction of the horse that way. He led her two hundred yards on. He stopped, tied the horse, and said, "Water here."

Sabrina slipped to the ground and saw a tidy rivulet of water running over rocks.

"Spring here. Always cold no matter how hot," Gray Wolf said. "Drink."

Awkwardly Sabrina leaned down and, cupping her hands, waited until they filled up. She drank noisily, awkwardly, and thirstily, and repeated that several times until she rose up and wiped her lips with her sleeve. "Thank you. That was good."

Gray Wolf shrugged, reached on his back, and pulled out what seemed to be some kind of a canteen. He filled it up then leaned over and drank himself. "We go now."

Sabrina was exhausted. She had had nothing to eat all the previous day except a small breakfast, and she was beginning to feel the pangs of hunger. "You have any food?" she asked timidly.

"Soon." The monosyllable was all that Gray Wolf offered her, but he put her astride again and walked away.

They had traveled about thirty minutes when suddenly he lifted the rifle in one smooth motion and fired.

The sound of the shot startled Sabrina, and she looked wildly around but saw nothing.

She sat there as Gray Wolf led the way, leaned over, and picked up something. "Food."

It was, Sabrina saw, a large rabbit.

"Get down." She got down, Gray Wolf tied the horse, and then, picking up some small twigs, he pulled some matches from his pocket, struck one, and touched it. The fuel was dry, and he kept adding wood until there was a blaze, its crackling a cheerful sound.

Gray Wolf pulled a knife, stripped the fur off the rabbit, and skillfully cut it into two pieces. He found two sticks and impaled half on each stick. He handed her one, and without another word stuck his own half over the flame.

Almost instantly the smell of cooking meat caused Sabrina's stomach to knot. She quickly followed Gray Wolf's example.

Five minutes later Gray Wolf pulled the rabbit out of the fire, tore off a strip, and put it in his mouth. "Good," he grunted. "You eat."

The meat was only half cooked, but she was ravenous.

He saw she did not know how to eat it. He took it from her and, pulling out his knife, stripped off small portions.

The food was better than anything Sabrina, who had eaten at the finest hotels in the country, had ever tasted. She ate hungrily, and then when they were finished, they both drank.

"We go now."

"How far, Gray Wolf?"

"Another hard day's travel. We get there in the morning if we travel at night. If not, later."

That was all the conversation Sabrina had with him for the rest of the day. The pony seemed to be tireless, as did Gray Wolf. She herself was exhausted by the time dark fell.

Seeing this, Gray Wolf pulled off and said, "We'll rest here." He pulled the blanket off the horse and grunted, "Sleep."

Willingly Sabrina wrapped herself in the blanket and lay down. As sleep descended on her exhausted body, she once again had an impulse that she should give thanks, but she was not a woman of God and knew that she was not a fit subject to ask God for anything.

❦

The sun was high in the sky when Silas Longstreet, who was sitting in a chair tilted back against the outer wall of the courthouse, came to his feet and said, "Well, by gum, I ain't seen a sight like that. That woman's had some trouble." He knew a bit about Sabrina's story, for he was the oldest of Judge Parker's marshals. Parker had told him about the woman and expressed his concern. Now he looked and saw the two, and getting out of his chair, he pulled his hat off. "Howdy, ma'am. My name's Silas Longstreet. Looks like you had some trouble."

Gray Wolf laughed softly. "She's a foolish squaw. She hired the Denver brothers to help her, and they took all she had and left her in the desert."

Silas, who was a small man with a shock of white hair and pale blue eyes, said, "Ma'am, you had some luck there. They could have done a lot more than let you go. Let me take you to the hotel. You can get some rest."

"I can find my way." She turned and said, "Gray Wolf, you saved my life. I have no money here, but I'll get some from the bank. Later on today I'll see that you're well paid."

"Good." Gray Wolf watched the woman go and seemed amused. "She's a proud woman but not so much anymore."

"You'd better keep an eye on her, Gray Wolf. She ain't got much judgment. She's a city woman obviously. She could get mixed up with somebody worse than the Denver boys."

"Yes. Give me money. I want something to eat. All I've had is a stringy jackrabbit."

Silas stood before Judge Parker, who was seated at his desk, and was just finished telling him the story of Sabrina. "So, sure enough, she got cleaned up and she gave Gray Wolf fifty dollars. More money than he's ever had in his life, I reckon."

"He's probably drunk by now."

"No, he ain't drunk. He went to the mission school. He's a Christian Indian. Don't act like it sometimes, but he is."

"Well, she could have been raped and killed out there. I'm glad Gray Wolf found her. I don't know what she's going to do."

"What did she come here for?" Silas listened as the judge repeated the story of how she had come to get her sister free from the clutches of Trey LeBeau and his band.

Silas shook his head then whistled softly. "Well, that's a bad one."

"I told her I didn't have no marshals to send. You're the only one here."

"We don't need to send one man out to get LeBeau. He's got at least a half dozen killers."

"That's right, but I've got an idea. She's not going to quit on this thing, Silas. She's going to hire somebody, but I think her only hope is one she'd never meet if we didn't help her."

"Who's that, Judge?"

"Waco Smith."

Silas was surprised and showed it. "Why, Judge, he's in the penitentiary at Yuma."

"I know it, but I've got a plan. I'm a good friend of Warden Crawford, the warden of Yuma Penitentiary. He wrote me a letter and told me how there was a breakout and he could have been killed. There was a man ready to do the job when Waco jumped in front of him and killed the man with a gun he'd taken from one of the guards. He got shot a couple of times, but he made it. Warden Crawford is right grateful to him."

"Well, I don't see how he can help her if he's in prison."

"He's the only one I know who would even have a chance against LeBeau. Let me have a talk with that young woman. Have her come by my office."

"I'll do that, Judge."

❧

"I think I may have found a possible man for you to hire."

"Just one man?"

"That's all we've got right now, but this one can help if anybody can. His name is Waco Smith."

"Well, I'd like to talk to him. I'll hire him if you say he's a good man. Where is he?"

Parker smiled slightly. "You won't like this. He's a prisoner in Yuma."

"He's a criminal?"

"I guess he was when he went in, but sometimes prison changes a man. He's the only man I know who's tough enough to go with you into the Territory. We can maybe find some more, but you'll need one man like this."

"I can't hire a criminal."

"You don't know the Territory, miss," Silas Longstreet said. He had brought her in and now leaned against the wall. "Waco knows it like the back of his hand. He's a hard man."

"I can't hire a criminal! He's a dangerous man, I'd think."

"Yes, he is, but he may have changed since he's been in prison. Prison either makes a man better or worse or kills him. From what Warden Crawford says, I think we might work something out."

"How could he help me if he's in prison?"

"Well, he saved the warden's life. I think I could let him out on a conditional pardon, and the warden would agree to it. Then you can talk to him and see if you want to take him on."

Sabrina nodded slowly. She was not happy about the decision to hire a criminal, but yet the opportunity was the only one that seemed to be opening its way up.

"All right. I'll talk to him, but I can't imagine going into the Territory running around with a criminal."

"You need to get rid of that idea," Silas said. "You don't need to be going into the Territory with Waco or anybody else."

"I'm going," Sabrina said flatly and put her eyes on Silas. "There's no argument about that. It's settled."

"You are a stubborn young lady, but the Territory changes folk."

"Well, I'll talk to the man."

"We'll have to go to the prison."

"How long will that take?"

"Just a day's ride from here. It ain't far."

"All right. When do we leave?"

"We'll leave first thing in the morning. We may have to stay overnight."

"Silas, you go along with Miss Warren and see she's all right."

"As you say, Judge." Silas nodded. "We'll be ready first thing in the morning. You want me to rent a buggy?"

"That might be best, or a wagon in case we bring him back with us. But I don't think that's likely."

⁂

The sun beat down on the men who were working clearing rocks and breaking them into smaller chunks where necessary. Waco swung the sledge, struck a rock, broke it in two, picked it up, and threw it to one side. He was covered with dust, as were all the men out working on the road, and as always, he was hungry and thirsty. He drew his forearm across his face. He was working without a shirt and had sunburned at first, but now he was burned a bronze color almost like an Indian. He did wear a cap with a bill that shaded his eyes, and now he looked over and said, "Cecil, you okay?"

"Doin' fine, Waco."

The young man, Waco saw, was about past going. He was frail, and the road work was more than he could handle. Fortunately the guard, a man named Roberts, was one of the gentler ones at the prison.

Waco had said, "Mr. Roberts, I'll do some more work if I need to, but Cecil there. . .he's just not fit for this."

"Yeah, I'll try to get him a job in the office somewhere out of this heat. You're right. He ain't fit to be breakin' rock."

Waco had thanked him, but he still kept a close watch on Cecil.

The two worked until noon, and then the whistle blew and the water wagon came with the noon meal, which was bread and slices of ham that made them thirstier, but the water was worth it all.

"I sure hope there ain't no roads to do in heaven." Cecil sighed. He had eaten the bread but had only nibbled at the ham, knowing that it would give him a raging thirst.

"I expect they got angels doing that." Waco grinned. He had resented Cecil's preaching at first, but now it merely amused him. "The Lord wouldn't let a good man like you break rock in heaven. Besides, I heard the streets were made of gold. Like to have a shot at that."

"That's right, and the gates are all pearl, bigger than you'd think. Imagine a pearl big enough to make a gate out of."

"Sounds sumptuous."

"Oh, it is, Waco. Heaven's a good place. I'm going to see you there one day."

Waco smiled. "I doubt that. God wouldn't want a maverick like me dirtyin' up His heaven."

"He's gonna do things for you. He's gonna make you all clean and pure and clothed in the righteousness of Christ as the Bible says."

"Well, I've always heard God could do anything, so I reckon if He wants to do it, He could do that for me."

The two went on until the whistle blew again. Waco got to his feet, pulled Cecil up, and said, "Don't try to break any rocks. Just go through the motions. I talked to Mr. Roberts. It's okay with him."

"Why, that wouldn't be right."

"He's gonna try to get you a job inside. I'm kind of a favorite of Warden Crawford now. If Mr. Roberts can't do the job, I'm gonna ask the warden to do it."

"Well, he owes you a favor. You saved his life."

"Yeah, he hasn't said anything about it except thank you when

I was first comin' out of it. Men forget, I guess."

"Maybe not. It just takes time."

Ten minutes later Roberts came out and said, "Waco, come on with me. You've got to go see the warden."

"Well, what have I done wrong this time?"

"Nothing, I don't think. It might be somethin' good."

"You think that, do you, Mr. Roberts? I've about given up expectin' on something good."

"You've had it tough, Waco, but Cecil's givin' you the right advice. I ain't much of a Christian myself, but he is. I've seen the real thing enough to know that it can happen."

"Well, you sure been a gentleman and a Christian to help Cecil out. I appreciate it."

"Nothin' to it. Come along now."

Sabrina was sitting in a chair in Warden Crawford's office. She turned when the door opened.

"Here he is," the man in the blue uniform said. "Call me if you want me, Warden."

"I'll do that, Roberts. Thank you."

The door closed, and Sabrina fixed her eyes on the man who stood there. He had on a shirt and wore a pair of worn jeans. He had black hair and eyes almost as dark as those of Gray Wolf, her Indian rescuer. His face was broad at the forehead and tempered down to a determined jaw, and a slight scar on his right cheek went down to his neck. He was burned by the sun and had wide shoulders and a narrow waist. His eyes went to the warden then came over to take her in. He said nothing but simply stood waiting.

493

"Waco," Warden Crawford said, "I've been talking with this young lady. This is Miss Sabrina Warren. She needs some assistance, and Judge Parker and I think you are the man that could help her."

"She's not going into the prison, is she?" Waco smiled slightly.

Sabrina saw that he had very white teeth. The teeth of most of the men she met were stained with tobacco from chewing and smoking.

"No, I'll let her tell you what her problem is, and then we'll talk about it. Have a seat."

Waco dragged a chair over and sat down facing Sabrina. He was alert as a wild animal, Sabrina saw, and there was a toughness and a wildness about him that she recognized would be excellent qualities in a man-hunter, which was what she wanted.

"I have one sister, Mr. Smith."

"Just Waco, ma'am. I lost my mister along with other things when I came to Yuma."

"Well, Waco then. She's very fragile and naive. She ran off with a man named Trey LeBeau and is being held captive." She waited and said, "Have you ever heard of him?"

"I know Trey."

"You know him? How do you know him?"

"Well, I had dealings with him a few years ago. He did me a bad turn. He's not exactly a friend of mine. What do you want me for?"

"I need somebody to go into the Territory and get my sister away from him."

"Well, that's Judge Parker's job, or his marshals'."

Crawford said, "You know how many marshals he lost, and those he has left are just bogged down, Waco. He just doesn't have anybody to send. He's the one who suggested we might get you to help Miss Warren."

"How can I help her in prison here?"

"You can't, but here's what Judge Parker came up with. He said if I agreed, the two of us together could give you what is called a *conditional* parole."

"Never heard of it."

"Well, that's because it's never been done. What it means is this. We release you to Miss Sabrina's custody. You will help her get her sister back. When the job is done, if you've been faithful and done your best, we'll make the parole a full-fledged parole. You'll be free."

Sabrina was interested in the workings of the man's face. She saw at once that he was interested and said quickly, "I'll also be willing to pay you to help me. My father has means, and we can pay almost any fee."

Waco was quiet, and finally Crawford said, "What's the matter? Don't you like the deal?"

"Not that. I just can't believe it."

Silas spoke up. "It's true enough, son. You've had some jolts along the way, but this woman's the real goods. We checked into her family. You do what Judge Parker and Warden Crawford ask you to do, and you can get a new start."

"Well," Waco said, sighing deeply, "I can use a new start. Sure, I'll do it, Miss Warren. Can't guarantee anything, you understand. LeBeau's a tough hairpin."

"Well, one man doesn't seem like enough," Sabrina said.

"It won't be one man. You're gonna have three men," Silas spoke up. "I'm going along and so is that Indian that saved your life, Gray Wolf. He can track a buzzard over the desert floor. I swan he can. We'll be going along so that'll give us three guns. Maybe pick up some more."

"The odds are still against us. He's got a rough bunch, Miss Warren," Waco said. "I've met most of 'em, all killers, and they might not be as nice to you as the Denver brothers. Might not be enough to just rob you."

"I'm going along, Waco, so don't argue with me."

"Just sayin'." Waco closed his mouth and nodded. "I'll take the deal, Marshal."

"Good. I'm releasing you right now. Go get changed into some decent clothes."

"I don't have any."

"Well, we'll find you some. You can't go looking like a tramp."

"Thank you, Warden."

Sabrina smiled, went over to the warden, and offered her hand, which Crawford rose hastily and took. "I wish the good Lord to help you."

"That's kind of you. I'll thank Judge Parker when I see him."

"We brought a buggy, so I guess we'll take him back."

"Might be best."

CHAPTER 15

"You think you'll be able to get along with that woman, Waco?" Silas asked. He had come to the general store and found Waco buying supplies.

The tall man turned to him and grinned suddenly, which made him look much younger. "No, I don't reckon I can—and I don't reckon anybody else can."

Silas could not contain his smile. "Well, you read her about like I do. She's had her own way pretty much. Comes from a rich family. Her parents probably spoiled her to death. I been tryin' to talk her out of this fool notion she's got of traipsin' around the Territory."

"So have I, but she's stubborn as a blue-nosed mule, Silas." Waco shook his head and looked up at the ceiling for a moment. His face was relaxed, and he was silent, staring at a hornet's nest that was built in the ceiling. "We had a hornet's nest in Grandpa's house where I grew up. I offered to get rid of it for Grandma. She said, 'No, let 'em alone. They catch flies.' I never did get to feeling easy around hornets though." Taking a deep breath, he said, "I'm gonna have one more try at talking some sense into her, but don't hold your breath."

"Well, we need more men. Just me and Gray Wolf ain't gonna be enough, even with you along."

"I talked to Judge Parker about that. He's pretty stubborn. He said he won't have any more men for at least six months. Not enough to send a band out to get LeBeau."

Silas studied the tall man carefully. "You ever meet LeBeau?"

Something crossed Waco's face. It brought a tension, and his eyelids half dropped as if he were staring at a specimen that he didn't particularly care for. He reached up and ran his hand through his black hair and said briefly, "I've met him."

"You didn't take to him, I guess."

"No, I didn't. I owe Mr. LeBeau something. It wasn't only to help Miss Warren get her sister back. I've been promising myself when I got out of prison to pay LeBeau a visit. I figure he owes me something. I'm gonna take it out of his hide."

"Men have tried that before and didn't make it. He's quick with a gun. Quick as a snake they say, and no more feelings in him than a snake either. He'd be a good one to decorate Judge Parker's gallows. Let Maledon have a hand at him. He could break his neck with one of them big knots of his."

"That'd suit me fine," Waco said flatly. "Here. Finish getting this list together, but watch it. I figure we'd take a light wagon. Don't know how long we'll be gone. Won't have time to run down to buy groceries every day."

Silas took the list and shrugged. "Well, go have a shot at it, boy. Maybe you'll have luck."

❦

Waco left the general store and walked down the main street of Fort Smith. It was a busy day. The streets were crowded with wagons of all sizes, buggies, horsemen, and mule trains. The sounds of voices filled the air, some acrimonious and angry and others laughing. Getting to the hotel, he turned in and went to the desk. "I need to see Miss Warren."

"Well, she's upstairs."

Waco got the room number and walked up the stairs. When he got to the door with the number he was seeking, he knocked, perhaps harder than he had intended.

The door opened, and Sabrina Warren stood facing him. "What is it, Waco?"

"Can I talk to you?"

"I don't see any point in it, but come on in if you must."

Waco came in, took his hat off, and turned to face her. "I am gonna make one more try to talk you out of going on this hunt, Miss Warren. It's not like you think it'll be."

"I'm a good rider. I've been riding since I was twelve years old."

"I'm sure that's true, and I admire that in a woman, but there are other things besides riding a horse. It's gonna be a hard trip, and when the marshals go out it wears them down, and they're about the toughest men on earth."

Sabrina shook her head. "I'm not going to argue about this. We've settled on a price. I'm going, and you can just move on out now and let me get some sleep."

Waco, for a moment, seemed inclined to argue, but he saw the hopelessness of it. He stood for a moment staring at her, wondering what it would take to break her spirit down. He knew that there was a pride in this woman that could sweep her violently and set off a blaze in her eyes. He had already seen it more than once. He, more or less, admired the fire in Sabrina. It brought out the rich, headlong qualities of a spirit otherwise hidden behind the cool reserve of her lips. She had an enormous certainty in her, a positive will, and if things had been different, Waco felt he could have been drawn to her. But he had a job to do and he was not interested.

"We'll be leaving early." He turned without waiting for a word, stepped outside, and shut the door. He put his hat on, walked downstairs, and crossed down the street until he found Silas making the last purchases. "Well, that ought to be enough, Silas," Waco said. "It looks like we're going on a vacation instead of a manhunt."

"Never know how these things will turn out. We might be out there two months just huntin' for LeBeau. He's harder to find than a flea on a long-haired dog."

"You got that right. All right. We'll pull out real early."

"Gray Wolf is movin' around town here. I'll see if I can find him. We'll be ready when you say, Waco."

A voice broke into Sabrina's sleep, and at first she did not know where she was and thought perhaps she was home again with her father speaking to her.

And then the voice spoke again. "Time to get up, Miss Warren."

Instantly Sabrina sat up, all ideas of sleep gone. Moonlight filtered through the window, and she saw the tall form of Waco Smith standing beside her bed.

"What are you doing in my room?"

"You told me to get you up when it was time to leave."

"Can't be time to leave. I haven't slept more than a couple of hours."

"Well, we're leavin'. If you want to stay and sleep, that would probably be a good idea."

"You get out of my room!"

"Are you goin'?"

"I'll be there. Give me time to get dressed, and don't you ever come in my room again!" Sabrina waited until the door closed behind Waco, and then she leaped out of bed and began dressing. She was angry that he had intruded her privacy. "He's a beast! No more manners than a grizzly bear!" she muttered. She dressed, got her personal things in a small canvas bag, and went downstairs. She was hungry but knew that the restaurant would not be open.

The three men were standing beside the wagon, three horses tied to the back. "Well, you ready to go this nice, cheerful morning?" Silas asked.

Sabrina still felt the gritty sensation in her eyes that came from a sleep interrupted. "Why are we leaving at this ungodly hour? What time is it?"

Waco answered her. "It's about two o'clock, I reckon. I got a lead on LeBeau and his bunch. We're gonna go check it out. May be a false alarm. You could just stay in town here, and when we find out if it's true or not we'll come back for you."

"No, I'm going, and I don't want to hear anything else about it."

"Well, all right. Get on board then." He climbed up into the driver's seat of the light wagon.

Sabrina scrambled to get into place, tossing her bag in the back. She saw the wagon was filled with supplies, including extra rifles.

"Be mighty nice if you stay here and rest up," Waco suggested.

She did not answer him. She knew he was trying to discourage her, but she was determined not to complain.

The trip was harder than Sabrina had planned. She wished she had brought a pillow or a pad, for the hard seat paddled her rear. She was sore before they had ridden for an hour. The road was nonexistent, nothing but potholes and ruts throwing her from one side to the other. Once she was thrown over against Waco.

He grinned and put his arm out. "Maybe I'd better hold you in before you get thrown out, boss."

"Take your hands off me!"

"Just tryin' to be a help," Waco said.

Turning, she looked back and saw that Silas was practically asleep in the saddle. "It's cruel of you to make an old man like that keep a schedule like this."

"I didn't invite him, boss. I told him it would be rough, and he said he'd been on rough hunts before. Tell you what. I could let Gray Wolf take you and him back, and then he could come back and meet me. We could go on this hunt then. You two can wait, and I'd come and get you in time for you to watch me kill LeBeau."

"Kill him?" Sabrina bounced in the seat and grabbed to hold on. When she turned to face him, her eyes were large with shock. "What do you mean kill him?"

Waco turned and looked at her with surprise. "Why, I thought you knew that. He won't be taken, Miss Warren. He'd rather take a bullet than hang." He saw the truth sinking in and realized that this was the first time that she had thought that far ahead. "What did you think would happen when we caught him? What was your plan to take care of him?"

"Why, to capture him and take him into Fort Smith. He could

go to trial in Judge Parker's court. He'd pay for kidnapping."

"He's got a lot more than kidnapping to pay for," Waco said. "He's killed four men that I know of. Two of them in a robbery where he's been identified. There's been a paper out on him a couple of years now. None of the marshals have been able to catch him."

"All I want to do is get my sister back."

"You think all you have to do is face Trey LeBeau and say, 'Mr. LeBeau, would you please give me my sister back?' Nothing like that is going to happen."

"He might. I'll offer him money."

"You could offer it if he gave you a chance to talk. But when he sees me he might start shooting."

"Why would he do that?"

"Because we didn't part on the best of terms. I owe Mr. LeBeau something."

"You're not hired for that. I would just ask him to give me my sister back."

"You might as well ask a hungry wolf to give up his dinner." He slapped the lines on the team and they sped up.

Sabrina noticed that his eyes were never still. He looked from point to point and each side constantly. She had seen Gray Wolf do the same thing and even Silas. They were men on edge. She realized she was in a world that she had never imagined.

Finally Waco said, "These men are killers, boss. They'd think no more of killing a human being than killing a deer."

The day wore on, and finally, when it was just before dark, they pulled up beside a small stream that Gray Wolf knew about. It was all Sabrina could do to climb out of the wagon. She felt like she had been beaten with a flat board, her muscles were so sore.

She had missed practically an entire night's sleep and now she was so groggy she staggered when she hit the ground.

She leaned up against the wagon and watched the men quickly and efficiently go to work. Gray Wolf gathered up some sticks and built the fire, adding dry wood to it that he found from a fallen tree. Silas was busy with the supplies, getting out some food to be cooked.

It was only half an hour later that she was offered a pancake in a tin plate. "I make the best pancakes in Fort Smith. Better than the restaurants," Silas said. "Try these, missy."

All of them had pancakes, and Silas suddenly said, "I reckon we'd better ask a blessing on this food."

Sabrina was watching Waco and saw a smile turn his lips upward. "My cellmate at the prison in Yuma always said thanks over the meals. Personally, I didn't think some of 'em were worth thankin' anybody for, but he was real faithful."

"Well, he was a child of God, I take it," Silas said.

"That's what he said."

"Did he try to make one out of you?" Sabrina asked.

"He tried, but it was a hopeless task."

"Let's eat these pancakes. I brought some sorghum molasses to make 'em sweet."

They all sat around eating pancakes and eating the bacon that Gray Wolf had fried, and when they were through, they washed their tin plates in the small stream that was fed by a spring.

"I'm gonna hit the sack. I'm plumb played out," Silas said. He got up and limped over to the wagon, pulled a blanket out, moved away, and rolled up in it. He seemed to go to sleep almost instantly.

Gray Wolf watched him and said, "He is one tired man."

Silence reigned for a time, until Waco looked to Gray Wolf, who stood peering out in the night, and said, "Why'd you leave your tribe, Gray Wolf? You never told me."

The Indian turned and gazed down at the two of them, who were still seated on a log. "I was too pretty. The squaws wouldn't leave me alone."

Waco suddenly grinned and winked at Sabrina. "Well, I've had that problem myself."

Suddenly Gray Wolf turned and loped out into the darkness. He was soon hidden, and Waco said, "That's an Indian for you. That's what they like. Prowling around looking for something to shoot or skin or scalp."

"But he's a Christian Indian."

"Well, that may be so. Gray Wolf's a Christian, I think, but he'd kill his enemies quick enough. Mission school can't take that out of him."

Overhead the stars began to come out in a magnificent fashion. Sabrina noticed that Waco was looking up at them and asked, "What did you do to get yourself put in prison, Waco?"

He turned to face her, and a serious expression swept across his face. "A woman put me there, boss. I guess that's why I don't put too much stock in the breed. They always get a man in trouble."

Sabrina stared at him. "Did you—did you kill her?"

"No, I didn't kill her. I might have, but I didn't have a chance."

"Well, how did she get you put in prison?"

"I had a friend. . .or at least a man I thought was my friend. I left town for a while. When I came back, my friend and my woman were gone. Took everything I had. Left me with nothing. A thing like that takes the strength out of a man. I didn't care what

I did, so I got into trouble. Got in with a bad bunch. I was charged with train robbery. Lucky I didn't get charged with murder. Came near to gettin' killed."

"One woman hurt you, and now you hate all women?"

"Tells the story completely," he said, allowing admiration to shade his tone. Then he asked, "You married?"

"No."

"Why not?"

"That's none of your business."

Waco leaned back and stared at her. "Might be." The solid moon was bright, and the flaws on it were obvious. "Why boss, we might fall in love just like in the romance books. You've read them stories. Rich, beautiful city girl falls in love with a handsome outlaw; then she makes a man out of him. Then they get married and live happily ever after."

"That's something in a book. That'll never happen, especially not with you and me."

"Just a minute." He got up, walked over to where she had put her blanket down on the ground, picked it up, and shook it.

"Why'd you do that?" Sabrina demanded.

"Well, to get rid of scorpions or rattlesnakes."

His words sobered Sabrina, and she looked fearfully at the blanket. "Do—do they get into a bed?"

"Pretty often. Some fellows believe if you put a rope in a circle around a campfire, snakes won't cross it."

"Does that work, Waco?"

"Nope." His answer did not cheer her up. He came over and handed her the blanket, and as she reached her hand out to take it, he held on to it. "You should be scared right now, boss."

"Why?"

"Snakes and scorpions aren't as dangerous to you as a man like me."

Instantly Sabrina grew angry. "I'm not afraid of you!"

Waco stepped a little closer, still holding the blanket. He could see the fear in her eyes and said so. "Yes, you are, boss. I can see it in your eyes." He reached out with his free hand and held her by the forearm. "You need to learn to be afraid of things, Sabrina Warren."

Fear touched Sabrina, for although Silas was there and Gray Wolf was somewhere around, she knew that this man had the power to hurt her if he chose. Suddenly he smiled and said, "Go get some sleep. I'll keep the snakes off of you."

Snatching the blanket from him, she went back away from the fire, laid it down, and rolled up in it. But as she lay in the darkness tired, weary, and sleepy, she remembered the strength of his hand. "I'm not afraid of him," she whispered, but she knew deep down she had been afraid.

❧

By sunup they had risen, eaten pancakes, had coffee and bacon, and started in on a day's ride. Sabrina did have judgment enough to make a pad out of her blanket and affix it on her seat.

"These hard seats sure hurt a woman's bottom, don't they?" Waco asked.

"Some things seem impolite. Don't talk about that."

"About what?"

"About my bottom."

"Well, you've got one, I take it, and I know what it is to get sore."

"Just don't talk."

"All right."

He kept his word, and as they traveled all day, stopping only once for water and some beef sandwiches, they finally reached the outskirts of Hayden, a small town.

"We'll pull up here and stay for the night. I'm going into town. I've got a fellow here who might know where LeBeau is."

"He wouldn't tell you, would he?"

"With a little persuasion he might."

Silas said, "Bring some good grub back. Maybe some good candy."

They had a good supper with beans and bacon and the last of the fresh bread they had bought. Sabrina went to bed but was awakened at some time in the night by a horse whinnying. She sat up and saw that Waco was stepping off of his horse and tying him to a mesquite tree.

She got up at once. She was dead tired. She said, "Did you find out anything?"

"Maybe. Silas, get up."

Gray Wolf had been awakened by Waco's coming. "You know that man's too old for this kind of thing."

"Yes, but he's here and he has to come along."

"Let the old man sleep a little longer," Sabrina said, putting a gentle note in her voice.

"Sure."

"You will?"

"Yeah. I'll go do some poking around and see what I can stir up. You all stay here and wait for me."

"No, I'm going."

"You are the stubbornest woman I have ever run across."

"And you are the hardest man I've ever met. Don't you feel anything for anybody?"

Silas was not yet up, and Gray Wolf was hitching the team. They were on the far side of it. Suddenly he moved toward her. When she saw something in his face she said, "You stay away from me."

"Well now, boss, in those romance books at a time like this it gets real romantic. The hero kisses the girl, and she just can't resist him."

Suddenly she drew the .38 she had brought and carried in a holster and pointed it at him. "Stay away from me or I'll shoot."

Waco said, "Well, our romance isn't making much headway, but it'll pick up." He nodded and added, "And that gun isn't loaded."

Sabrina looked down at the gun, and suddenly he snatched it from her. "That was your best chance to shoot your lover. Here. The gun's loaded. Just don't believe everything I tell you." He laughed at her, and she shoved the gun back in her holster and started making a fire for breakfast.

CHAPTER 16

As Marianne stood on the front porch of the house, she lifted her eyes and saw that sunlight burned against the earth, catching at the thin flashes of mica particles in the soil. The day was already hot, the heat dropping on the tin roof layer on layer until it was a substance that could be felt even in the bones. Heat was a burning pressure in this country, she had discovered, and sometimes the gray and burnt-brown desert and heat rolled back from the punished earth to make an unseen turbulence. She took a deep breath and noticed that the smell of the day was a rendered-out compound of baked grass, sage, and bitter dust.

This was one of the few times she could relax. As she stood there, over in the east the land at first had been only a looming in the darkness, dim and vague, but now night was leaving, and the features of the land began to show themselves. At first it was only a darkness beneath the shine of pale stars. Finally low clouds began to appear, and timber far off stood massed solidly with a brooding atmosphere that seemed to haunt her. Slowly the light arose as she stood there, and the earth began to take on form. She waited until the sun rose and the whole eastern sky was alight. Far down by the creek, birches stood whitely in their cleanliness, and squirrels trilled high up in the oak trees. It was a time she had learned to steal from her situation. Now she glanced overhead, noting that the stars, gold and brilliant, were disappearing, nothing but faint pulses of light. Daylight then flowed over the land. The smell of dust lay rank and still upon the earth, and Marianne could not help but let the memories, bitter as gall, come to her.

The worst memory always came, bringing with it something almost like a physical pain. The day that she had arrived at the ranch, she and the man she now knew was Trey LeBeau had gotten off a train. He had obtained a wagon and a team, and they had left Fort Smith in the early hours. Even then it had seemed to her he was anxious and was somehow careful and stealthy in his movements.

She remembered how excited she had been when they left town and began crossing the prairie. She asked him questions along the way. What kind of tree is that? Does that river have a name? He had smiled and answered her. She did not notice at the time, but there was a sharkish, dangerous look about him. However, she had not the experience to see it.

After two days' travel, he pulled up and said. "There it is. Your new home, Marianne."

That moment came back to her now, and she felt all the keenness of the disappointment. She had seen pictures in books of fine ranches with corrals, barns, and cattle browsing in the background.

There was none of that here. High on the rise stood a house with a tin roof that was red with rust and almost past reflecting the sunlight. It was a small house with a porch running along the front with windows in the upstairs. Perhaps it had been painted at one time, but now the rain and the wind and the blowing dust had rendered it a pale gray so that there was nothing artful, beautiful, or romantic about it. She remembered how her heart had sunk and how she was aware that he was looking at her strangely. "Not what you expected, is it?"

She had managed to say, "Not exactly."

He had laughed and then driven the horses down, and as they approached the house, men came out. She remembered running her eyes from one to the other, and when they pulled up the team he said, "Boys, I want you to meet my new wife. That small fellow there, he's Al Munro." A short man with pale blue eyes and prematurely silver hair stared at her. There was something deadly about him.

"That big fellow there. That's Zeno Shaw. Don't ever get him mad at you. He'll crush you like a bug."

Shaw was a man whose face was scarred with the memories of many fights. He grinned at her and said, "You got you quite a good-looking woman there, Trey."

The use of the name, she remembered, was the first time she had found out that this was Trey LeBeau.

The other three men were introduced. Rufo Aznar, a Mexican with a terrible scar on the right side of his face, Breed Marcos, a muscular half-Apache, and Boone Hagerty, a big, fine-looking man, but with a cruel look about him.

"Well, this is Marianne. Marianne LeBeau for a while anyhow."

As she stood on the porch watching the sun slowly illuminate the land, she felt again the keen pain of that revelation that had come to her like a bolt of lightning. She remembered thinking,

Mother and Father were right, and Sabrina was right! I've been a fool!

Unable to bear the memory, she went out to where someone had put up a wire fence and a few chickens cluttered around. She opened the gate then opened the cabinet, took out some chicken feed, and began to scatter it, calling to them. They came clucking and fluttering around her feet, and she watched for a moment as they were fed.

"Let's have one of them for lunch."

Quickly Marianne turned and saw that the man she had once loved but now hated, Trey LeBeau, was leaning against a post grinning at her. The sight of him that once had pleased her so much was now hateful, and now he said, "Come on out of there. I'll have Zeno pluck a couple of those chickens."

She hesitated, and Trey's smile disappeared. There was a lupine expression in his face. "Did you hear me, Marianne? I said come out here."

She came out slowly and locked the gate, and he came over to her, threw his arms around her, and held her figure against his. He kissed her roughly, and she could do nothing.

"You ain't got much spirit for a bride. I expect a little action out of a good-lookin' woman like you. Sleepin' with you is like sleepin' with a dead woman."

Marianne was used to such talk. It had pained her to the heart when she had first heard it, but she had to learn to endure it.

He said, "Come on in the house."

She followed him in, and the fetid odors of male sweat, tobacco, and alcohol were rank. The place was a wreck. "Clean this place up. Make yourself useful."

"Looks like a man could get more use than that out of a good-lookin' woman." Breed Marcos, the half-Apache, was grinning.

He was thin and muscular and carried a knife that he constantly whetted when he was sitting still.

Al Munro was the smallest of the men. He had pale eyes, and there was something carnivorous about him. Marianne realized he reminded her of a panther she had once seen in a zoo.

She began to clean the house, knowing it was futile. LeBeau seemed to get pleasure out of tormenting her and found ways to do it. Her mind was dull, and she tried to make it so. Whenever she got close to one of the men, he might reach out and grab at her until LeBeau said, "Find your own woman. This one's mine."

❧

Sunset was approaching, and a visitor had come to the house. He was a half-breed, but the Indian side of him did not show. Marianne did not know what business he had with LeBeau, but she knew it was something dirty. Desperation had caused her to think up the only plan that seemed at all possible. She had written a letter and sealed it and taken what money she had, thankful that LeBeau had not found it. When the man left, she could hear the cursings and laughing of the men inside. They were engaged in a wild poker game.

"Please wait a minute."

The half-breed turned and stared at her suspiciously. "What do you want?"

"I have some money here and a letter. If I give you the money, will you mail the letter for me?"

"Why don't you get Trey to do it?"

"No, I can't. The letter's to my father, and then I asked him to send you five hundred dollars more. All you have to do is post the letter at a post office."

"I'm not gonna get LeBeau down on me. He'd kill me like a snake."

"He will never know. I'll never talk. There's nearly two hundred dollars here, and you'll get five hundred more. My father's a wealthy man. It says in the letter he's to mail it to you if you'll write your name on it. You could pick it up at the post office in Fort Smith."

The half-breed hesitated and glanced at the house. The noise was increasing. It seemed they were all getting drunker by the minute. He took the money and the letter and said, "This could get me killed, but I need the money. Don't ever say nothin' to nobody."

"I promise I won't. My father will be happy to give you the money. He would give you even more if you asked for it. You'll just have to wait until the letter gets to Memphis, and he'll probably wire you back. Just tell him your name."

The half-breed stood irresolutely then turned and walked away. She watched him go, knowing that this was her only hope. Looking back, she remembered that LeBeau had left no trail. He had used a false name until they got back to the Territory, and now she watched the man ride away. She found herself praying that he would mail the letter and not drink it up as she feared.

❧

Calandra Montevado had been angered by Trey's action in bringing another woman. "I thought I was your woman," she said acidly.

"Why, you are. This one's just for fun."

When he came over to put his arms around her, smiling, she

suddenly produced a knife and held it poised over his stomach. "You take one more step, and I'll open you wide, Trey. You keep your hands off of me. Have all the women you want, but don't be comin' to me."

Trey knew that the woman was totally capable of cutting his heart out. He had seen that in her, and he had said, "It's your call, Callie."

Later on Callie found the captive young woman sitting in a chair. The men were gone on some errand, and Trey had told her to keep an eye on her. She sat down and studied the girl, who looked about sixteen years old. "What's it like to be rich?" she said.

Marianne blinked with surprise. "I don't know what you mean."

"I've never been rich, but I'd like to be. I think it probably beats this life."

"Have you been with— Have you been here long?"

"Too long." Callie continued to stare at the girl. "I'm not surprised Trey was able to win you. He can do things like that, win women, me for one."

"Why do you stay here? You could get away."

Callie Montevado's lips turned bitter. "Where will I go?" she asked. "Who would have me now? Don't try to get away. They'd find you and make it worse for you." She got up and left the girl. Actually she felt sorry for the young woman, but her life had not left much room for grief or sorrow.

❧

The sun had been sharp and bright and blazing all day. Now it was settling westward and seemed to melt into a shapeless bed of gold flame. Far off the mountains broke the horizon, and the desert seemed to cool off instantly. The sun slanted down to the west, and the late summer's light was golden, and already the night birds were beginning to make their lonesome calls.

Gray Wolf had gone hunting and come back with a fat young deer. He and Silas were cutting it up. Silas grinned. "This will go down pretty good. I'm about half-starved."

"Where did Waco go?"

"Oh, he said he had an idea. That man don't talk enough. I don't know what's going on in his head half the time."

"Well, probably out looking for LeBeau." He glanced over and saw that Sabrina had put her blanket down and was lying there curled up sound asleep.

Silas shook his head. "That girl's in bad shape. She's wore plumb out."

"She's had some good years." Gray Wolf shrugged. "Now she has some bad years. You know, at the mission they told us about a story in the Bible about a man called Job."

"Yeah, I've read that book."

"One thing I read in it I agreed with," Gray Wolf said as he stripped the flesh from the bones of the deer. "A man is born to trouble as the sparks fly upward. I ain't sure about the rest of the Bible, but that's true enough."

"I guess we all know that. You know," Silas said thoughtfully, "I heard an educated preacher once say that Job was the oldest book in the Bible, but I never really liked it."

"What's not to like?" Gray Wolf looked up with surprise. "It's a pretty good story."

"No, it's not. Job was a good man. As a matter of fact, the Bible says he was a perfect man and upright."

"You can't get no better than that. I expect he went straight to heaven when he kicked off."

"Well, it always bothered me that Job was probably the best man on the face of the earth, and God experimented with him. The devil told Him, 'The only reason Job serves You is because You're good to him. You made him rich and gave him a family. Who wouldn't serve You?' "

"I remember that." Gray Wolf grinned. "God said to the devil, 'Well, that ain't so. You just take it all away from him. Just don't touch his body.' And that's what the devil done."

"Stripped him down to nothin'. He had everything in the first chapter and from then on out he had nothin'."

"Makes you think, don't it?" Gray Wolf bit off a chunk of the raw venison, chewed it thoughtfully, and swallowed it. "That's good, tender venison. Let's get some of it to cookin'."

They built a fire quickly, and as they were cooking the steaks, Silas said, "You know, makes you wonder about LeBeau. He's got everything. All the money he wants, and does what he pleases. He's a wicked, evil man, but he's got everything most men want."

Gray Wolf looked up, and his eyes seemed to glitter. "Well, he'll lose it all one day."

"You're right," Silas said. "He will. We got to remember that, me and you. Them two with us, they're not Christians."

"You figure to convert 'em?"

"Gonna do my best, Gray Wolf. You might give it a try, too."

❦

The sound of hoofbeats awoke Sabrina. She sat up and saw that Waco had come in. She watched as he tied his horse to a mesquite tree and got up and went to meet him. He was weary to the bone she saw, and she asked, "Are you hungry?"

"Yes."

"Well, sit down. Gray Wolf killed a fat deer. The best thing we've had."

"I can use it." He moved over toward the wagons and slumped down cross-legged, leaning back. Fatigue was in his every movement, and she knew that he was exhausted. He had slept less than any of them, and now she was well aware of the discipline that he imposed on himself. She studied the shelving jaws of his big-featured face. His eyes, she knew, were sharp with a light in them, but there was a recklessness and something in him like a hidden heat. He was a tall man, and his shoulders were broad. His high, square shape made an alert form against the shadow of the wagon. There was a toughness to him and a resilient vigor all about him. He had discipline, she knew that, and as she pulled a chunk of meat off of the grill and put it before him, she said, "There's two biscuits left from breakfast."

"Sounds good."

Sabrina watched as he ate the meat, hungrily tearing at it with his strong white teeth, and saw that he had plenty of water. Finally she asked, "Did you find anything, Waco?"

"Not really." He gave her a sharp look. "Are you wantin' to give up?"

"No."

"I didn't think so." He finished his meal, put it to one side, then came to his feet. He moved slowly at times, but there was a hint of speed and power in him. "Come along." He walked out of the camp, and she followed him with some trepidation. He walked quickly for all his fatigue. Finally he stopped and said, "Look at that."

It was growing darker, but she moved closer and saw a stone

flat and upright. "That looks like a tombstone," she said.

"That's what it was, but the wind and the sand and the rain have eaten it all away. Look. Whoever buried him made an outline of where the coffin is." He pointed down, and Sabrina saw that there were a few stones that marked a rectangle. She watched as Waco suddenly moved forward. He began to pull his boot through the line of stones, digging a little trench. When he had gotten all around it, he kicked the stones back in the trench.

She could stand it no longer. "What are you doing, Waco?"

"Don't know. Maybe trying to put off what has to come."

"Like what?"

"Whoever this is, they had the same kind of dreams I have, I expect. Maybe a husband that found a wife and loved her. Maybe a wife that found a husband, but she only made it this far. I don't know. It makes me sad."

"You didn't know whoever it is."

"No, that's true," he said slowly, and she could see he was thinking deeply. "But whoever it is, when they were alive, they have the same hungers I do and the same problems probably. Maybe it was a husband whose life was cut short. His wife had to bury him out here in this wilderness."

"Could have been a woman."

"That would be even sadder to me." He began to move away from her and traced the line of small stones that marked the grave into a trench with the toe of his boot. Then he carefully put the stones back in there.

When he stood up, she asked, "Why did you do that, Waco?"

"Don't know. Feel sort of down, I guess."

Suddenly she said, "Waco, I wish you could put that behind you. If you don't, you'll be like those men who took Marianne.

Like you say LeBeau is. I wouldn't want you to be that kind of a man. Don't nurse grudges and hate until you are rank inside. You'll be your own worst enemy. You weren't meant to snarl at the world, be against people, be cruel."

He took her hand and looked into her face. "When you lose something it hurts."

"You're thinking about the woman who ran out on you."

"Guess I'll never forget her. How she betrayed me."

Again a wave of pity came as Sabrina was very much aware of his hand, the warmth and the strength of it. "I'm sorry, Waco."

He shook his head. "Funny thing, Sabrina. I haven't been thinking much about the hurts of other people. Too busy pitying myself—but I hate to see you hurting over your sister."

Sabrina did not know what was happening, but she waited there, saying nothing, when suddenly he reached out and pulled her to him. He put his arms around her, and she looked up at him. The feeling of his kiss went through her, and it was a goodness without shame. She was stirred and did not know why it was, but it was what she wanted. She felt the luxury of it as well as he.

She felt that Waco was on the near edge of rashness. His impulses were clear. He was a strong man, and she was a beautiful woman. She saw the battle take place, and then with some sort of joy, she saw him shake his head and step back. "I'll do my best for you, Sabrina, to find your sister. . .even if I have to die for it."

❧

The deer meat was about gone, and that night it was Waco who said, "We're going to have to go get more grub. We're worn down to nothing."

It was night, and they had just eaten the last of the canned beans they had brought along with the last small chunks of bacon. They hungered for bread, for something solid.

Silas had been quiet, and as they sat there finishing their meal, he said, "You know, I still miss my wife, Lottie."

"How'd you meet her, Silas?" Sabrina smiled.

"Well, I was no good, but I took one look at her and fell in love with her just like in the storybooks. She wouldn't have anything to do with me. I'm glad she wouldn't. She was a pure woman."

"Well, how did you ever get her to marry you?"

"I went off and I looked for God. I had some trouble there," Silas said thoughtfully. "I signed a trade with God. I'll be a good man if You give me that woman. I found out pretty soon you don't do business with God like that. Finally I said, 'God, whether You ever give me Lottie or not, I'll serve you.' So I got saved out behind the church with the service goin' on. I was too ashamed to go in, so I listened to the singin' and the preachin'. When the preacher made an altar call, I went in. Been servin' Jesus ever since." He turned and said, "Gray Wolf, how'd you find Jesus?"

Gray Wolf had been listening carefully. He grinned, and it softened his features. "I was a real bad man. I was on a horse-stealing raid and got captured. The chief was a tough hombre. I was on the ground tied, and he had a spear in his hand. He lifted it up, and I knew he was going to run it through my heart." He grew quiet then.

Finally Waco said, "Well, he didn't kill you obviously."

"No, he didn't. He stood there looking at me, and something came into his eyes. He had hard eyes, I tell you, that Indian did! But after a while he threw his spear down and walked away. I couldn't understand why he let me live. For a long time I wondered about it, but I know one thing. . .only God could have made that man spare me. So I promised I'd live like a Christian."

Silas said, "I'm going to tell you two sinners how to get saved."

"That's what I like. You're a real Southerner with your preachin'." Waco grinned. "Go ahead. Turn your wolf loose."

Silas began to quote Scriptures, almost all of them about the death of Jesus. "It's His blood that washes us from sin. The Bible says God puts our sins behind His back. He blots 'em out of the Book. We become a part of His family, and all you have to do is give Him everything you've got, which most people can't do," Silas said.

He spoke for a long time, and finally Sabrina was forced to admit, "I don't know what he's talking about. I've been going to church all of my life, but I don't have anything in me like Gray Wolf and Silas."

The next day they pulled out, and as they did, Sabrina turned to Waco and said, "What did you think about what Silas said?"

"Funny you should ask," Waco said. "I'm a pretty hard nut, but I can't forget what he said about Jesus."

"Do you think you'll ever be a man of God?"

Waco dropped his head. "I hope so," he whispered.

CHAPTER 17

Heat lay like a thin film in the windless air as Sabrina stood with her back to the campsite looking out into the distance. The sun was a white hole in the sky, and the deep haze of summer had lightened so that the land was a tawny floor running immeasurably away into the distance. The Territory frightened her, for it was not the kind of climate or the kind of world that she had been born into. There was no security in this land. None by day and none by night. It was a country of extremes, of long silence and sudden wild crying, a bone-searching dryness followed by a sudden rush of cloudburst torrents down in the narrow canyons. It was raw and primitive, and she had already seen it scoured the softness out of a man and made him into something sometimes frightening.

"I've been wanting to talk to you, Sabrina, about Marianne."

Instantly Sabrina turned to him, for she heard a somber tone in his voice. "What is it? What do you want to tell me?"

"I don't think you're going to be happy, Sabrina, even if we find her." There wasn't the faintest hint of tension in his body or voice.

"I think we'll find her," he said finally. "But you come from a family that's well off, and your parents are religious people. Well—"

"What is it?" Sabrina asked. "What do you want to tell me, Waco? Just say it."

"All right. I know LeBeau. He's using your sister like he uses all women. That's what he does, Sabrina. He never loved a woman in his life. To him they're something to be used and thrown aside. He'll throw her aside, too, as soon as he gets tired of her."

Thoughts of this nature had come to Sabrina in many forms, but she refused to agree. "I don't care. I don't care what's happened or what she's done. Marianne's my sister."

"You may love her, but what about the way she feels? You think she can just walk away from this? When these things happen they leave scars."

"You're wrong." She held her hand up and said, "See that scar?"

Waco nodded.

"I almost cut that finger off, and it bled and it hurt. Even after it was bandaged it hurt for weeks, but look at it now. Touch it. See? It doesn't even hurt. I know it's there. I know that something happened that day, but the pain's not there anymore. Just the memory. And that's what it'll be when we get Marianne back. We'll take her home, take care of her and love her, and she'll be all right."

Waco smiled slightly. "You always think the best, don't you, Sabrina? Well, I'm glad you do, and I hope you always do."

Their talk was interrupted when Gray Wolf rode up on his pinto pony. He slid off of the horse, walked over, and grinned at the pair of them. "I found them!"

Waco looked up and exclaimed, "LeBeau!"

"Yes. My cousin, he come from the north. Cherokee nation.

Says he saw LeBeau three days ago close to Grand River."

"Come on. Let's tell Silas."

Quickly they held a council of war, and when they heard what Gray Wolf had to say, Waco said, "Why, I know where that is. I'd forgotten about it. LeBeau doesn't use it much. Sometimes he goes out and robs a train; then he ducks back in there. It'll be hard to get at," he sighed. "They can see for miles in every direction. If too big a bunch comes after them, they split up and fade in the hills. Then they'll come back together somewhere else."

"What do you think, Waco?" Sabrina asked. "You think we can go after them?"

"Yeah, we can. We'll travel tonight. Be cooler that way."

The party pulled out shortly before dark, just as the air was beginning to cool, and traveled most of the night. Waco called a halt just before dawn. The horses were beginning to tire. They rested there all morning then started again after eating at noon. They traveled hard all that day, making quick camps and taking short rests.

Waco was glad to see that Sabrina was standing the trip better than he had hoped. "I believe we're going to make it," he remarked to Silas. "She's doin' better than I thought she would."

"I guess so." Silas nodded. He took off his hat. A slight breeze lifted his fine white hair.

Waco saw that the old man was tired and looked even more frail than ever.

"I wish she weren't here, Waco," he said. "This ain't no place for a woman like that. She could get killed."

"I've thought of it, but I don't know what to do with it. That woman's got more determination than a hungry mule." The two stood there for a moment looking off in the direction they were headed. "What do you think of her? Sabrina, I mean."

"A good-looking woman. Stubborn though."

"Always liked a woman with grit in her," Waco remarked.

They rode hard, and the next day Waco sent Gray Wolf ahead to scout. The Indian left at three o'clock while the others made camp. Darkness fell as they were finishing the evening meal, and Waco lifted his head. "Somebody's comin'," he said in a low voice. He picked up his Winchester and moved over to a large rock, listening carefully. After a moment he lowered the rifle and said, "Gray Wolf." The Indian rode in, excitement lighting his smooth face. "Found them!"

"You saw him? LeBeau?"

"No, LeBeau's not there, but a woman is there and Boone Hagerty."

"It's them then." Waco nodded.

"A woman?" Sabrina asked curiously.

"Yes." Gray Wolf grinned. "Name is Calandra Montevado. I always liked her name. People just call her Callie though."

"Did you see my sister?"

"Small woman with blond hair?"

"It's Marianne. We found her!"

Silas was excited. "Found 'em at the right time, too. If there's only two men there, the rest of 'em must be out on some kind of a raid. What do you think, Waco?"

"Sounds good. We'll take 'em in the morning. Tonight might be better. Catch 'em off guard."

"I'd say morning," Silas said. "You get to shootin' in the dark, no tellin' who could get hurt. Tomorrow we get there and we surround that cabin at daylight. As soon as the men come out, I'll take one, you take the other. With only two, we can kill 'em the first thing. They won't be causin' no trouble."

His words seemed to send a chill over Sabrina. "You mean kill them without warning?"

Silas stared at her. "You didn't think we'd get your sister back without shootin', did you?"

"Well no, but don't we need to give them some warning? Give them a fair chance?"

"You're thinking like a woman that lives in a fancy house in Memphis," Waco said. "Don't you understand? We let 'em know we're here and one of 'em will grab a pistol and put it to her head, threatening to kill her if we don't leave, and they'd do it, too, Sabrina. They don't think any more of taking a human life than you think of taking a drink of water." He hesitated then shook his head. "I know it sounds rough to you, but out here it's different. These men you have to treat like wild animals."

Sabrina walked away and began cooking over the fire.

Later on Waco came and sat down cross-legged in front of her. He put aside his hat. "You all right?" he asked.

"I'm worried about tomorrow."

"Yeah. I knew you would be, but Silas is right. The important thing is to get Marianne out of there. If you give those men one chance, they'll kill her, Sabrina."

A heavy stillness seemed to hang in the air, and as Sabrina stared into his face, he knew she was wanting comfort. "I—I just can't think straight," she whispered. "It goes against everything I've ever thought that I know."

He stood up then and stood before her, his face impassive. She was very beautiful as she stood close to him, and the vulnerability of her spirit was reflected in the troubled lines of her face. Her eyes were enormous, and they glistened in the ghostly light of the moon. She was trembling, and Waco muttered, "I wish you didn't have to go through with this."

Suddenly Sabrina stepped closer to him. Finally she whispered, "I just don't know what to do." Unconsciously she reached out and touched his arm as if to gather strength from him.

Waco was starkly aware of her closeness and the aura of femininity that seemed to emanate from her. Sabrina was a woman, shapely, beautiful, full of vigor, and her nearness made him desire her in a way he had never wanted a woman before.

Seeing desire in her eyes, Waco put his hands at her hips, pulled her upright against him, and kissed her full on the lips. His mouth bore down hard and heavy on hers, and he could feel her wishes joining his. Her response touched the deepest chord within him, and he had never known such exhilaration.

Suddenly she drew back. "I don't know why I let you kiss me." Her voice was distraught. "This must never happen again."

"It probably will," Waco said calmly. Then he shrugged his shoulders. "You've got to decide, Sabrina. What will we do?"

She stood absolutely still for a moment, and then she whispered, "All right. Do what you have to do. I want my sister back."

❧

"I know you don't want to shoot nobody, Sabrina," Silas said. He handed her a rifle and said, "You just point this up in the air. Make a racket with it. Here are some more shells. Make it sound like we got twenty marshals out here."

The small group stood facing Waco, and he said suddenly, "Sabrina, you sure you want to go on with this? We can back off right now. We can take you back, and me and Gray Wolf and Silas will get at it another way."

"No, I want Marianne back now."

"All right," Silas spoke up. "We're going to surround the house. If anything happens, remember you just fire off as fast as you can in the air. We want to make 'em think they're outnumbered. Waco, let's you and me and Gray Wolf take up a position beside them rocks. As soon as those two birds come out, we'll pop 'em, and it'll be all we need to worry about. You think we need to worry about the woman?"

"No, she's an old friend," Waco said evenly. "I think we can leave her alone. What if the men come out one at a time?"

"No good," Silas said. "We've got to get both of them. They'll have to come out together sooner or later."

The plan seemed simple enough. They arrived, and at first light a lantern came on inside. Almost at once a man stepped outside. "That's Boone Hagerty," Silas said. "He's as bad as the rest of them, but his mother was a fine Christian."

Time crawled on, and Hagerty did nothing but smoke and stare out across the desert. Suddenly the door opened, and Marianne came out. Sabrina almost cried out. She seemed to devour her sister with her eyes. Finally she went back into the house, and for nearly an hour Hagerty sat on the front porch smoking and staring out at the desert. Finally he rose and got a drink of water.

"I wish that other bird would come out," Waco whispered.

He did not, but the woman came out. Sabrina, who had stayed beside Waco, saw a strange expression on his face, and then her eyes went back to the woman.

She was very attractive, with black hair and a shapely figure. She went to the barn and came out ten minutes later mounted on a beautiful black mare. Calling out something to Hagerty, she spurred the horse and rode off into the west.

The time dragged by. It was now close to dark, but the two men never appeared at the same time.

Waco moved over closer. "What do you think, Silas?"

"I don't know. I never could stand waiting."

"Always that way, I reckon. I remember once before that charge at Gettysburg. I was as nervous as a June bride."

The two spoke quietly, and finally Gray Wolf called out, "They're coming back. Callie and another one. Now there's three men for us to worry about."

"That's not Pratt. That's Al Munro. He's the worst of the crew," Waco said. "We can't hang around here, Silas. That bunch could come back at any time."

"You're right," Silas said with finality in his voice. "Here's what we'll do, Waco. I'll sneak down front. You go around the back. You peep in the window, and if you can see the men in there, you break the glass and let 'em have it. I'll rush the front door when I hear your shots. It's risky, but so is hanging around like this."

"I don't like it, Silas. Those men are quick on the shoot."

"Well, let's try to get closer anyway. They've got to come out sooner or later."

As they crept closer, Waco said, "You stay here. I'm going to go catch a look at the layout of the cabin. If it looks bad, we'll pull back and wait for morning."

"Go do it, son."

Waco moved toward the cabin, taking a roundabout way. He moved carefully across the ground until he reached the side of the house and flattened himself against it. He could hear the muted voices inside, and removing his hat he cautiously lifted his head. He saw the girl he had been seeking. Boone Hagerty, Al Munro, and another man were sitting at a table playing cards. He didn't see Callie anywhere. He assumed she was in one of the bedrooms. It was almost pitch dark now, and Waco decided he couldn't take the risk.

Suddenly he started, for the sound of gunfire screamed through the night somewhere in front of the house. He leaped to one side, cleared the window, and saw several men shooting. *They're back!*

The men inside burst out the door, and Al Munro shouted, "Over to the side, Boone. They're over there. Get 'em!"

Waco ran forward and the men opened fire on him. He heard the shots whistling through the air and tossing up dust almost at his feet. He laid a heavy fire but knew he had missed because he was shooting blindly. As he neared the hiding place, he said, "It's me. . .Waco. Don't shoot!"

Instantly Gray Wolf was at his side. "No good! No good! We leave now!"

"Yeah, let's get out of here. Let's move, Silas."

"I'm comin'." Suddenly Silas said, "We can still—"

Waco's heart seemed to sink. "I think they got Silas. You wait here, Gray Wolf." He found Silas. "Are you hit bad?" he asked.

"Don't—know. Somewhere low down."

Waco knew he couldn't help him there. Crouching down in the darkness, he picked up the old man and slung him over his shoulder. "This is going to hurt, but we've got to get you out of here." He ran across the open spaces. "Don't shoot!" he called. "They'll know where we are if they see the muzzle flashes. Come on. Let's get back to the others."

They made their way back, and Gray Wolf helped carry the old man. Waco saw vague outlines, and he let off a round. Instantly he heard a shout of pain and someone yelled, "This way! Come on, we got 'em, Trey!"

LeBeau's voice ordered, "Spread out now! Surround 'em!"

Waco grimly lifted his rifle and began to lay down a heavy fire, but knowing he was being quickly cut off, he retreated. The two men made their way stumbling, and they found Sabrina.

"What happened?" she asked.

"LeBeau got back," Waco said. "He surprised us. Silas got hit. We've got to get out of here and get Silas to a doctor." They lowered the old man into the wagon, and he said, "Sabrina, you'll have to drive. Just head on out. We'll find you."

"I'm staying."

"You get going. We'll take care of this end."

Waco and Gray Wolf reloaded their rifles. "We'll hold 'em for a while and give her a chance to get a clean start."

"Too many." Gray Wolf shook his head. "No."

"We'll have to hold 'em just for a little while."

The fight began in earnest, and at some point, after they loosed a volley of shots, Waco heard someone call out, "I'm hit! I'm hit!"

"We've got to get out of here," he heard another voice say in panic. "We've got to get out of this. There's too many of 'em. They got Hagerty. He's a goner."

"Pull back then!" LeBeau's harsh voice called.

It was the moment Waco and Gray Wolf had been waiting for. "Let's go," Gray Wolf gasped. "Let's get back to the others. They won't be coming after us."

"They'll be after us as soon as it's light enough to track us. We can be clear by then. I want you to stay here, Gray Wolf. There's no way LeBeau will stay at this place. They'll go to a new hideout. You find out where it is and meet us in Fort Smith."

"Yes, now go. Back soon." Gray Wolf melted away into the night, and Waco hurried, his heart heavy as he realized that Silas was badly hurt.

❧

"We've got to get back to Fort Smith," Sabrina said desperately. She had drawn Waco aside near where Silas was lying flat on a blanket. They had taken him out of the wagon. The sun was now high in the sky, and the horses were pretty well winded by the fast pace of all last night and half the day.

They reached a small creek and decided to rest the wounded man. "How far is it? How long is it going to take?"

"Best part of two days." Waco shook his head. "And we can't go too fast. It'd shake him to death. But you're right, we can't stay here."

"Do you think Silas will be all right?" Sabrina asked.

"I don't know, Sabrina. He wasn't too strong to begin with, and that bullet hit something in his lower back. Last time he woke up he said he didn't feel any pain. Bad sign."

They stood paralyzed by indecision, and finally Waco said, "All right. We'll rest here until it cools off. We've got plenty of food but no grain for the horses. I'll take 'em out and find some graze and rub 'em down and let 'em rest tonight. We can make it in two days, I think." He turned and looked at Sabrina. "I'm sorry we didn't get your sister. I made a bad play."

Sabrina looked at him. "No, Waco, it wasn't your fault."

They stayed beside the cool trickle all day. Early in the morning they loaded up and headed out.

They had not gone far when Waco said, "Pull up! Stop the horses!"

As she obeyed, Sabrina said, "What is it?"

"I don't know. We need to check on Silas."

He pulled the stretcher down and looked at his face. "Something's gone wrong. I'm not even sure he's breathing."

Holding his breath, he put his hand over the frail chest of the old man. Silas did not move. "Heart's beating like crazy. Real fast and not at all. I don't know what that means."

"Let's get him in the shade," Sabrina said. "I'll bathe his face with some cool water."

When they got him into the shade and she had bathed his face, she whispered in anguish, "He looks awful."

"I always feel so blasted helpless. If we only had a doctor."

Sabrina turned to him. "I'm not sure a doctor would help now." She continued to bathe the old man's face.

Waco pounded his hands together in a gesture of helplessness. "Well, I guess we'll stay here until he comes to. Or maybe I'll ride on ahead and bring a doctor."

"No, don't leave us," Sabrina said. She was more afraid of the country and the predicament than she let on.

The afternoon passed slowly, the burning raw heat changing into a cooling breeze. Waco did not get far away from the wounded man. He fed the fire, and they made a pot of coffee. It was black and bitter, but it was hot and refreshing.

The hours passed, and finally a faint sound came from Silas Longstreet. Like a cat, Waco sprang to his feet, and almost as quickly Sabrina was there. "Can you hear me, Silas?" Waco asked.

At first there was no answer; then Waco saw the old eyes

slowly open. He cried out, "Silas, can you hear me? Are you in pain?"

"Water."

"Here." Quickly Sabrina knelt at his side and held the canteen. He managed to drink a little as most of the water ran down his chin.

"That was good." He stared at Waco and then at Sabrina. "Well, I guess I've torn it this time."

"You'll be all right. We'll get you to a doctor."

Silas shook his head slightly. "Can't feel nothin' except my head. Ain't that somethin'? It feels like my whole body has gone to sleep." His eyes began to droop, and they were afraid he was drifting into unconsciousness. "Sorry about your sister, missy."

"Don't worry about it." Sabrina reached up and gently brushed a lock of his white hair back from his forehead then lightly wiped his forehead with the handkerchief she had dampened. "We'll find her, Marshal, and you'll be all right."

"No, not this time," Silas whispered.

Waco glanced at Sabrina then said, "Sure you will, Silas. You've taken bullets before."

"No," Silas said, "this is it for old Silas." There was a peacefulness on his face and in his eyes. "I'm on the receivin' end this time." He looked up and said, "Don't you cry now, missy. Don't you cry for old Silas."

"I can't help it," Sabrina sobbed, biting her lip. "It was all my fault."

"I was here 'cause I wanted to be, missy. I've been on lots of hunts that I wasn't proud of, but this time I was proud. Wish we could have done it."

The dying man was silent, and finally he said, "I ain't been the man I should have been. Hard to be a Christian in this line of work. I tried to be fair and honest, but I had to handle some rough characters. That takes rough ways, don't it, Waco?"

"That's right, but everybody knows you're a good man," Waco said gently. He felt helpless kneeling beside him. He loved the old man. He had known him and respected him, and now he saw life slipping away like sand through an hourglass.

The moon crept fully across the sky; the stars twinkled and burned quietly against the velvet black curtain of night. The desert silence was broken from time to time only by the cry of a night bird or the howl of a coyote. As the old man's life flickered weakly and seemed to be fading away, Waco was struck dumb by the awesomeness of the moment.

Finally Silas roused and whispered, "One thing—one thing." He faltered, but then his voice returned stronger than before. "One thing I done a long time ago. I took Jesus as my Savior. I ain't been faithful to Him always, but I always loved Him, and I always studied His Word. And now I guess when I go to meet my God, all I'll be able to say is Jesus died for me."

The old man's voice trailed off, and then he opened his eyes. "Son, I'm going. I'd like to know if you are going to find God, and you, too, missy." His faded blue eyes closed, and for a moment there was silence.

"He's gone," Waco said angrily. "One of the best I ever knew shot by a no-good dog!"

Very carefully Sabrina lay Silas's head down, crossed his frail arms across his chest, stood to her feet, and walked away to stand in the darkness.

Waco walked over to her. "We'll leave as soon as you're ready, Sabrina. I know how hard it is. You loved that old man, didn't you?"

"Yes, I did."

"Me, too. I've known lots of men but never known one more faithful. He was the kind of man I wish I was. The cards didn't turn up that way."

Sabrina turned and looked at him, wiping the tears from her cheeks. "Not too late, Waco. Maybe this all happened so you can see what it's like. I know it's made me see. I call myself religious, but I couldn't go out to meet God like Silas did. I'd be scared to death."

Waco searched her face, his expression puzzled and questioning. He was disturbed by her confession, but he muttered, "I can tell you one thing. I'm coming back, and I'll get LeBeau. I'll put a bullet right between his eyes, and I'll get your sister."

"No, don't talk like that," Sabrina said quickly.

"Why not? It's what you want, isn't it?"

"I want Marianne, but if you turn out to be a man who does nothing but kill—why, it's all for nothing, Waco."

"I don't know any other way to get the job done."

They put Silas back in the wagon and headed for Fort Smith.

Waco did not say so, but he had been moved and shaken by the old man's death. Not just the loss of his friend but thinking of his own walk before God. . .or lack of it. He had tried to avoid thinking about things like this, but now it had happened, and he knew he would never forget that moment. "Maybe it's my time," he muttered as he rode forward into the darkness.

CHAPTER 18

The journey back to Fort Smith was a terrible time for Sabrina. The farther she and Waco went, the blacker the pall seemed to become as it hung over her heart. She still grieved terribly for her sister, but now she knew that the price that had been paid was terribly high, and it wasn't fully paid yet.

As they finally entered Fort Smith and headed down the main street, Sabrina was shocked to see her parents coming toward her. Both of them rushed forward and surrounded her, and Sabrina saw that her mother was weeping.

"You're safe," her father said, his voice tight. He held on to her, squeezing her. He was not a demonstrative man, as a rule.

"Are you all right, Sabrina?" her mother asked.

"Yes, but we didn't get Marianne back. It almost worked, but it didn't."

"Did you see her at all?"

"Yes, from a distance. It broke my heart."

Father turned to face Waco, and seeing the question in his eyes, Sabrina said, "This is Waco Smith. He's the man who set out to help us."

"I didn't do the job, Mr. Warren. Sorry."

They were interrupted then when Judge Parker came out, accompanied by Heck Thomas. The two men had waited until the family had greeted Sabrina, and then Judge Parker paused and said, "What happened, Waco?"

"We got ambushed, Judge. They got Silas."

The judge's eyes flew to the still form on the wagon. He turned to say, "Heck, take him down to Roberts. He'll take care of him."

Heck climbed up into the wagon, and it moved away.

"I'd like to hear all of the story," Judge Parker said. There was pain in his voice. "I hate to see it. Silas was a good man. Who did it?"

"Can't be sure." Waco shrugged. "Most likely LeBeau. If it wasn't him, it was one of his men. All the same."

An ominous light glowed in the eyes of the judge, and his lips drew into a thin white line. "We'll nail his casket shut." He turned to her father and said, "If I can do anything, Mr. Warren, let me know."

"I expect it's going to take you in this thing, Judge. I'll be depending on you."

Parker turned and walked away.

Her father turned back to Waco. "So you're Waco Smith. I've been looking into your character. Asking around, you know. Way I hear it you're a rangy wolf with long teeth and whiskers of metal shavings. Scare little children in the night, do you, and make the girls scream and run for cover? That's what they say. What's the other side of you?"

Waco replied, "Isn't any."

"Well, just as well you think so then." Her father had an ability to make decisions about people. When he did, he seldom changed his mind and almost never made a mistake. "I know you feel bad about your friend Marshal Longstreet."

"He was straight. Never let a man down. Never broke his word." Waco shuffled his feet then said, "Well, I don't guess you'll be needing me anymore."

"Oh no, you're not getting off that easy, Smith," her father said calmly. "We're going to get that girl of mine back, and you're the one who's going to have to do it. I can't go because I can't sit on a horse and can't shoot. So let's make some plans."

"Come on into the café. I imagine you're hungry." They all went inside, and for some time they discussed the possibilities.

Finally her father said, "There's nothing else we can do now. I know you're both dead tired. So let's eat, and then I'll get you a room here, Waco."

"No need spending your money on me, Mr. Warren."

"Got more money than I have good sense. You're going to do this job. I want you to be fresh. You go get some rest. When you get up in the morning, we're going to get together and decide what to do. I'm going to ask the good Lord for an answer, and if you know how to pray, you might do the same." He got up abruptly and walked away, her mother following him.

As soon as they were gone, Waco stared after him, saying, "He's quite a fellow, your dad. Is he always like this?"

"Yes, he's the kindest man I've ever known, but it's taken something out of him. Mother's suffering, too."

Waco's expression suddenly went grim. "The best thing would be to get twenty marshals and throw a chain around that bunch."

"But what would happen to Marianne? Could she get hurt?"

"She can get hurt any way we go about it, but you're right. The first sign of something like that, and LeBeau's going to threaten to kill her." He looked at her and saw her weariness. "You're worn out. Go to bed."

"All right, but do you think we have another chance, Waco?"

"Always a chance," he told her. "Your dad said something about praying. He's a praying man?"

"Yes, he is, and my mother, too. Do you ever pray, Waco?"

"No, wouldn't be right."

"Not right? What do you mean?"

"A fellow like me, I never think of God, never do anything for God, then out of the blue I start beggin'. Seems pretty small to me."

Sabrina chose her words carefully before she spoke. "I think all of us have to reach some point where the only thing we can do is ask God. Until we get there, we're pretty likely to stay stubborn—at least that's what I've been. I'm turning in. We have a lot facing us tomorrow."

❧

"What do you think about this fellow Waco, Sabrina?"

"Think about him? Why, I don't know." She had come to her father's room early in the morning to talk to him, and now he said, "Well, you must have some thoughts, girl. You trusted him enough to go gallivanting around the desert with him."

"I—don't really know, Dad. He's a strange man."

Charles Warren knew this elder daughter of his. She never had acted like this about a man before, and her difficulty in speaking of Waco Smith made him want to ask more, but he decided not to press her. "Well, I've discovered one thing. He's tough as a boot heel. Far as I know he's not vicious."

"He's had a hard life," Sabrina said. "I think if he'd had more chances, he would have made something out of himself. He's very quick. Not educated, but he knows things. He's what you used to call 'country smart.' "

"He's quick-witted all right. You know, he looks kind of like a wolf. His eyes are sharp, looking right through you."

"I dread the funeral. I don't do well at funerals, but I've never lost anyone that I was close to like I was to Silas."

"Well, funerals are never happy affairs."

❧

Waco accompanied the Warrens as they left the hotel and went to the small, weather-beaten white church. The funeral was heartbreaking.

The minister was a well-built man with greenish eyes and curly blond hair. He had known Longstreet for many years, and he preached a sermon about how wonderful it was that Silas Longstreet had stepped from one world into another one. "In an instant's time," he said, "he stepped from earth to heaven. And however many problems he had, he doesn't have them anymore."

The mourners left the church after the sermon, went out to the cemetery, and gathered around the grave. "Would you care to say a few words, Judge Parker?" the minister said.

Parker cleared his throat. "I'm not a preacher, but I am a believer, and I want to say something about Silas my friend. Well, that's what he was to me. He was more than a marshal, you know. He had a hard job, and he always did his duty, but even when he was doing the hardest things, he stood by the way of Jesus Christ. He was a faithful servant, and his greatest desire, as he told me many times, was to stand before God and to be with his faithful wife, Lottie." He hesitated and then looked around the crowd. "One of the last things Silas said to me before he went on this trip concerned some of you standing here. He was worried and concerned about your souls."

The preacher then read Scripture, and the wooden coffin was lowered.

Waco turned and left, but Sabrina caught up with him. "I've cried myself out, Waco."

"I wish I could cry. I know I'd feel better."

Waco heard someone call his name, and he turned to see Judge Parker approach him. The tall man's face was grave, and he said, "I didn't want to call any names in public, and it was you, Waco, and Miss Sabrina here, that Silas was concerned about. Before he left, he asked me to pray for you, and if I had a chance to give you an encouragement to turn to the Lord."

"How kind of you, Judge," Sabrina said. Tears filled her eyes again. "He was such a good man."

Waco escorted the Warrens back to their hotel. He began to walk a bit aimlessly down the street. He was hard hit by the death of Silas Longstreet, and his grief was mixed with a bitter, fiery anger against LeBeau. He finally encountered Heck and said, "I don't think a posse will ever catch up with LeBeau."

"No, he's pretty sharp. When he sees a bunch comin', he'll kill that girl or threaten to."

"Somebody's got to pay for Silas," Waco said, then turned and walked away without another word.

❧

Later in the day, Charles and his family were seated on the front porch of the hotel.

"There comes Waco," Sabrina said. "He has that serious look on his face. He's thought of something."

"You think so?"

"I know that look, like he could bite an iron spike in two. He's stubborn about things like that."

"Hello, Mr. Warren. Mrs. Warren. Sabrina."

"Sit down. Tell us what you've been doing, Waco," Charles said. Now he saw what Sabrina meant about the steady look on Waco Smith's face. His features seemed to be set in metal somehow. There was a dark preoccupation in his face, and Warren saw that he was a man taller than the average, heavier boned, more solid in chest and arms. His life, perhaps even the life in prison, had trimmed him lean. Exposure to rain and sun and cold had built within him a reserve of vitality. Warren knew without being told that never in his life had he known real peace. *There is a sorrow shining through this man,* Warren thought, *guiding him into strange ways.*

"I've been thinking, and I have a plan for getting your daughter back."

Instantly all three members of the family straightened up. "What is it?" Sabrina asked quickly.

"Well, we've talked about how it's hard to sneak up on LeBeau. He's ready for that. But you know if somebody was there on the inside, a member of the gang, well, he could make a chance to get your daughter away, Mr. Warren."

"Are you thinking about yourself?" Charles Warren spoke sharply.

"I can't think of anybody else," Waco replied offhandedly. "I know LeBeau. All he really knows about me is that I've had my share of run-ins with the marshal. As a matter of fact, we rode together for a while. He trusted me then."

"That will be pretty dangerous," Mr. Warren said. "If they found what you're there for, they'd kill you in a blink. You think he knows you were in that shootout when the marshal got shot?"

"No, it was dark. I didn't say anything. I was hid real good."

Sabrina said plaintively, "Waco, how could you do it? I mean, even if you were there, they'd be watching you. They'd be suspicious, wouldn't they?"

"They're suspicious of everybody, that bunch is." Waco shrugged. "But like I say, if I was right there, I could make a chance for Marianne. They'd ride out sometime and leave just a man or two with her. I might be one of those men they leave. Then I'd just take Marianne and ride out with her."

Silence fell over the group, and every face except Waco's was troubled. After a while Charles Warren said, "I've thought of everything in the world, but not one idea that would have a chance. Maybe, just maybe, this one would, but it's dangerous. I'd pay you for it though. Real well."

Waco did not act as if he had heard.

"How could the rest of us help? You can't go out alone."

"Better that way." Waco looked at Sabrina and said, "So if you agree to it, I'll pull out as soon as Gray Wolf comes in. Probably a couple more days."

"But we've got to make a better plan than this," Sabrina protested. "You propose just to disappear into the desert. You can't get in touch with us. We won't know what's happening." The vehement flow of words stopped, and her eyes narrowed.

Charles Warren knew his daughter's determined expression. "What's going on in that head of yours, girl? I know that look."

"I just had an idea, but I'll have to think about it." She got up suddenly and left without another word.

"Well, there she goes. We've seen her look like that before, haven't we, Caroline?"

"Yes, we have."

"I don't know what she'd be able to think about in this kind of a situation." Waco shook his head. "Anyway, I'll see you again before I leave."

☙

The sun lit the tips of the eastern mountains, touching the ragged rim of the hills. Then livid red balls began to break out, spilling over the spires and peaks and rough-cut summits of the mountains far to Waco's left. He looked quickly as light flashed a thousand sharp splinters against the sky, creating a fan-shaped aurora against the upper blue. He had watched the mountains since he had left Fort Smith an hour earlier, and now hot silence covered the summit as he stared. He heard only the staccato beat of a woodpecker pattering rocking waves of noise out in the distance.

Suddenly, as if he had received a clearly spoken warning, a sense of danger overtook him. He had had this sense before, and it had saved him more than once. He drew his horse in sharply and took shelter behind a large outcropping of rocks. Dismounting, he tied his horse to a small sapling and crept back. Inching his way on his belly, he worked his way up to the top of the outcropping of rocks. He lay flat, his outline invisible to any onlookers, appearing only as a darker part of the stone. There was enough light to see, and now he heard what he thought he had heard more than once that morning, a sound of hoofbeats coming from the same direction he had traveled.

Lying as motionless as the rock beneath him, every nerve in

Waco was tingling with a familiar sensation, one he had always felt at the approach of danger. More than once since he had left Fort Smith he had sensed that someone was following, but never until now had he heard the sound of pursuit.

The hoofbeats of a single horse sounded along the trail that wound directly beneath the rock. With extreme caution, Waco moved into a crouch, his legs gathered beneath him, his boots gripping the rough surface. He could have used his gun, but he was wary of the sound of gunshots carried to other ears.

Suddenly a horse appeared with a single rider. Waco tensed his muscles. The animal slowed to a trot. Waco's nostrils flared as he tried to judge the distance. The rider would pass within five feet of him. He could easily ambush the stranger without having to arouse any unwanted attention.

When the shadowy figure appeared directly in front of him, he released himself in a powerful spring, the muscles of his legs thrusting him forcefully, his arms outstretched. Knocking the rider from the saddle, the two of them hit the ground. The horse reared and neighed shrilly, and from underneath Waco heard a muffled grunt. He pinned the rider down, and his hand went down the side of the coat looking for a weapon.

"Who are you?" he demanded. "Why are you following me?" Even as he spoke, he caught the faint wisp of delicate scent. He whirled the rider around and knocked the low-brimmed hat back, then stood in shock. "Sabrina!"

Sabrina was gasping desperately for breath. "You didn't have to do this."

Hot anger coursed through Waco, and a chill of fear gripped him over what might have happened. "You crazy, fool woman!" he shouted. "I almost shot you!" Clutching the lapels of the jacket she wore, he pulled her to her feet and bellowed, "What are you doing out here? Don't you know you could get killed? Assuming I didn't shoot you first, there are Indians and outlaws around here."

Sabrina was finally able to draw a deep breath. "I was following you."

In disgust Waco muttered, "Fool woman! You could have gotten killed." He looked up at the sky in disgust and then asked, "Are you hurt?"

"No, just the breath knocked out of me. I know you are furious with me, but I had to come. I had to. You're going into danger, and I didn't like—I mean, I didn't think it would work."

"Does your dad know you're here?"

"Yes, I left him a letter telling him what we're going to do."

"What *we're* going to do?" Waco jerked to a stop. "*We're* not going to do anything. *You're* going back to Fort Smith."

"Wait a minute. Please, Waco," she begged. "Just let me tell you my idea. Just give me a minute, please."

"Oh, for crying—" Waco blew an exasperated breath. "Well, let me go catch your horse. He's probably halfway to the next territory by now."

He turned and scrambled up the steep rock outcropping, went to his horse, and swung into the saddle. It was an easy job to catch her mount, for the little bay had not gone far before she stopped. Waco found her dawdling around nibbling at some scrub brush. On the next rise he could see the form of a rider, and he recognized Gray Wolf's familiar mount. Grabbing the reins, he went back to Sabrina. "Well, let's go riding. Gray Wolf's up ahead."

"All right," Sabrina said meekly. She swung up into the saddle.

Waco relentlessly searched the horizon. "I hope Gray Wolf doesn't shoot us. Now what's all this about?"

Eagerly Sabrina began to speak. "I thought of a way that would be better. You were going in blind without any plan at all, and I don't think it would have worked, Waco. You could have been found out. They could watch you every second. You know they're suspicious."

"Well, what's your plan, Miss Sabrina Warren?" He was still angry at her and couldn't keep it from his voice.

"All right. I thought about this a lot." She took a long, deep breath and then spoke rapidly. "You take me into the outlaws' camp. You tell LeBeau that I'm the daughter of the manager of the Western Express Company over at Durango. I was in New Orleans when LeBeau came to our house, and he won't know who I am. We never met. Anyway, they ship gold coins usually by train."

"How do you know that?"

"Some of the men were talking at the hotel. That's what made me think of it."

Waco thought then said, "What's next?"

"You tell them that you kidnapped me and you're going to make my father give you the number of the train and when it's due to leave with a big shipment of gold, a million and a half dollars or something like that."

Despite himself, Waco smiled. "Well, that ought to be enough to get Trey's attention. So how does this work?"

"We'll locate some place out here in the desert and plant a sealed bottle there. Your story will be that my father's going to send us a message about the train."

"And what then?"

"You tell him that you've got this big shipment of gold located, but you don't have a gang to hold the train up. Trey's got the gang; you know when the gold will be shipped. You see?"

"What will Marianne say when she sees you? Won't she accidentally reveal who you are just because she is excited to see her sister?"

"I think if you tell everyone who I am before she has a chance to speak that it will work. She catches on to things pretty quickly."

Waco couldn't help himself and muttered, "She didn't with LeBeau."

"She was blinded by his loving attention."

Waco had an active imagination. He rode along without speaking, the clopping of the horses' hooves on the dusty ground the only sound. The dust rose in the air, and Waco could sense the spicy aroma of sagebrush and the thousand other indefinable scents of the desert that he had grown to love. His mind toyed with what Sabrina had told him, and at length he said reluctantly, "Well, it might work. It has possibilities anyhow. Look, there's Gray Wolf. I guess I'd better ask him not to shoot us." He called out, "Gray Wolf, come in here."

"Will you try it, Waco?"

Waco was of a divided mind. It did sound like a good plan, but it would put Sabrina into danger, and the last thing in the world he needed was for her to get hurt or even killed. He said, "I'll think on it as we go. If I decide it won't work, I'll have Gray Wolf take you back."

"You can't do that," Sabrina said, and suddenly there was that streak of stubbornness that Waco had noted many times. "I'm going to help with this, and you've got to let me do it."

Waco suddenly grinned. "I probably will. Tell me, woman, was there ever a time when you didn't get your own way?"

"Yes." Sabrina smiled brilliantly. "I think it was when I was six years old. Let's go. I'm anxious to get started."

PART FOUR

PART FOUR

CHAPTER 19

A storm seemed to hover over the land late in the afternoon. The air was filled with streaked lightning and long, booming drums of sound. The sky itself was gloomy and dark, and the wind made a howling noise to accompany it.

This kind of storm Sabrina had never seen before. She lived in a city where the buildings made barriers to cut down on the wind, and she was always indoors when the storms that they did have came. Now the thunder clapped loud and sharply because there was nothing to serve as a barrier, and the sound reverberated endlessly, rolling off into the distance. The thought came to her that this must be something like battle, cannon shots, suddenly deafening and shattering then clattering on, dying by slow degrees. The sound left her stunned, and her ears were dull. The shock seemed to rock the earth.

Lightning suddenly reached down from out of the dark clouds and seemed to fork and branch and grab the ground. The lightning flashes burned and leaped upward, crackling and vivid, dangerous it seemed to her. It almost seared the eyes, and she wanted to cover her ears when the thunder boomed and the white streaks blinded and burned.

She clung to the pommel of her saddle, and slowly the storm seemed to move on. The wind was still there, sounding like the tearing of soft silk, and then without warning rain fell fiercely in slanting lines of light. Glancing over at Waco, she saw that he sat upright in the saddle, appearing to ignore the rainstorm. The fat rain came down on both of them. She noticed it was soaking his clothing, and her own clothing was sodden and uncomfortable.

Waco walked the horses at a medium pace, but now the afternoon was so dark it could have been night. The sky was thick and furred like a blanket. To her the air seemed heavy just to breathe, and there was still the sharp, metallic taste of the storm. For the next half hour the rain did not slacken, and the wind continued to blow, sending before it, high in the sky, vast swollen cloud rollers that slashed earthward in crusted, gravel-core sheets and then in ropey gouts and then in whirling balls of wind.

"Are we ever going to stop, Waco?"

She saw Waco turn to her. He wore a wide-brimmed Stetson with the top creased and filling up with water then running down over the brim. "We're not far from where I told Gray Wolf to meet us." He gave her a slight grin. "You ready to stop and rest?"

"Who could rest in rain like this?"

"It'll stop pretty soon. Look. The clouds there, they're about blown away."

His words came true. Within half an hour the air cleared, and it smelled clean and pure, unlike the dusty smell she was accustomed to in the rolling plains of Oklahoma. She was wearing a lightweight divided skirt that had soaked through, and the rain had now run down into the tops of her boots so that she was miserably uncomfortable.

She was glad when he finally lifted his arm and said, "There's where we're going, right over there."

Sabrina lifted her gaze to follow his gesture and saw, no less than a mile away, a rising cone-shaped hill. The hills of Oklahoma were rough and irregular, but this one seemed to be shaped by human hands. "That's a funny-looking hill."

"Yes, everybody travels this way uses it for a landmark. Come along. We'll try to get some dry wood to light a fire and dry ourselves out."

They rode at a slow pace, the horses' hooves making splashes in the puddles left by the driving rain.

Waco looked around and said, "You know, this'll be pretty in a couple of days. Rain like that always brings out the wildflowers. You wouldn't know this place. The prettiest time of the year, I do think."

The rain had stopped completely, and finally they reached the foot of the cone-shaped hill. It was much larger than it seemed in the distance, and there were lower hills around the base of it.

"We've got to get dried out," Waco said. "We'll freeze to death. You got any dry clothes?"

"Yes."

"First we'll fix a fire. I'll rig something to dry these wet ones out. The blankets are pretty well soaked, too."

For the next hour they gathered firewood, such as could be located. Waco found an old tree, broke it open with his knife, and dug out the inside. "This is called punk. It burns real good. You see if you can find some small branches. Shake 'em out until they're as dry as we can get 'em. I'll look for something larger."

That was the way they built the fire. She found a double handful of small branches that seemed to be fairly dry, and he came back with several larger chunks. He laid the punk on the ground, surrounded it with the branches she had, then took a box of matches out of his saddlebag, struck one of them, and held it to the punk. The yellow tongues of fire leaped up immediately. He carefully added wood, and finally they had a large fire going. Taking his knife, he trimmed off two of the saplings that were close to the fire and tied a piece of string to each of them. "There. We'll tie the blankets on these and get them dry. It's gonna be cool tonight."

After they had hung the blankets up, he dug into his saddlebag and pulled out two cans of beans and then reached into her saddlebag and got a large chunk of bacon. Taking out his knife, he sliced it into thick portions, put the frying pan on the fire, and let it all begin to simmer.

The odor of the cooked food hit Sabrina almost like a blow. She had not known real hunger, but they'd had only a small breakfast and nothing for lunch. She watched eagerly as the bacon sizzled and the beans began to smoke.

He stirred them occasionally with his knife, adding a little water from his canteen. Finally he said, "Okay, let's eat."

"I'm starved."

"Pretty hungry myself. Here." He dumped half of the beans in a tin plate, added some of the crisp slices of bacon, then handed her the plate and a fork. He fixed his own, and Sabrina did not wait but began eating at once.

They had finished eating when suddenly a voice scared Sabrina. "Food." She looked up and saw that even Waco was startled as

Gray Wolf stalked in. "You better start givin' some warning before you walk into a camp, Gray Wolf." Waco grinned. "You might get shot."

"You white eyes can't hear anything. You don't have any ears. I want something to eat."

"Well, we have to fry up some more bacon and beans. Sit down, and while it's cookin' I'll tell you what the plan is."

Waco prepared more meat and beans and handed them to Gray Wolf on a plate. "Here. I'm gonna write some notes. I've got a jug hid where only you can find it, a glass jug with a top, but I've got to write some notes."

He took out a pencil and a small pad of paper and began to scribble. He looked up once and said, "Here's the first one. I want you to put this in the glass jug as soon as we leave."

"What does it say, Waco?" Sabrina asked.

"Says I won't pay until you give me evidence that my daughter is safe."

"I see. That'll give us some time, won't it?"

"Yes, we take that note in and prove to LeBeau that we've got a good thing going. The second one is supposed to be written from her father. It says the gold will be shipped on August 3 on the 2:20 train out of Lake City. The gold will be in a locked car, and you won't be able to get inside. I'll have one man on the train. He's short, stocky, and will be wearing a gray suit and a white hat. As soon as you turn my daughter over to him, he'll go and tell the man inside to open the door. Then he and my daughter will leave and you can get the gold." He folded it over and said, "We'll put the other one in before we leave. They'll send me out with somebody to find it, but then after we get this one out, you put the second one in."

Gray Wolf listened stolidly but ate furiously like he was a starved wolf indeed. He got up and said, "Sleep now." He lay curled up away from the fire, wrapping up in a blanket that looked sodden, but it did not bother him.

Sabrina looked at Waco. "You think this will work?"

"It better. It's the only chance we've got."

"What if something goes wrong?"

"Nothing we can do to make sure everything is right." He got up, felt the blankets, and said, "Well, these are nice and warm. Better wrap up, and I'll keep the fire going pretty well all night." He got up and came back with some larger wood and built the fire up so that it blazed, sending golden sparks like stars into the sky.

She sat there thinking what a strange thing it was that she would be out in a place like this with a man she ordinarily would not trust for a moment. She stared at him, but he was looking at the fire and appeared to pay no attention to her. He sat with his elbows on his knees, his head dropped forward, and his lip corners had a tough, sharp set. She watched him with the closeness that could come only of deep personal interest. Everything about him fascinated her, his expression, his mannerisms, the way his long fingers hung down. He had a man's resilience and a rough humor she had seen at times. She was relatively sure she saw in his face the marks of old wounds and a white scar from some encounter with horses, cattle, or even men.

She picked her blanket off the string, and moving back a little from the fire, she rolled up in it. She was exhausted. She continued to think about him as her eyelids grew heavy, and she knew that for some strange reason she could not explain, she was attracted to him in a way that no man had ever drawn her. *It's just that he's different,* she thought wearily. And then she thought no more but fell into sleep.

❧

It was one of those strange dreams when consciousness is there. . .but not there. Sabrina felt herself dreaming of a huge man coming toward her, his hands held out, a cruel smile on his face, and she cried out, "No, leave me alone!"

Suddenly she felt hands on her arm, and when she opened her eyes, she was instantly awake. She saw Waco bending over her. Freeing one of her hands, she clawed at his face and raked her fingernails down his cheek.

He grabbed her wrist and said, "Wake up! You're having a bad dream."

Waco released Sabrina, and she sat up at once, trembling and staring around her wildly. "I—I thought somebody was—"

"I can imagine what you thought. No wonder. Not many women would try what you're doing. You're a nervy one all right, Sabrina."

She glanced over and saw that the light from the fire was enough to reveal a bloody track down his left cheek where her fingernails had raked him. "I'm sorry," she whispered. "I didn't mean to do that."

"No problem. You just had a nightmare." He got up, went to the canteen, washed his face off, and dried it.

"I'm so sorry," she whispered again.

"Don't worry about it, Sabrina. If we get out of this with no more damage than that, I'll be happy. We got enough grub left for breakfast. I gave Gray Wolf the notes he's supposed to put in the jar and told him where to find the glass jug. Let's eat a bite, and then we'll get on our way to find Mr. Trey LeBeau."

꩜

They had made their way across the broken land until they finally came to a deep valley that sloped downward and then rose again. Up on the top of the hill was an ancient house made of unpainted wood and capped by a tin roof that was red with rust.

"Well, there she is. You sure you want to do this, Sabrina?"

Sabrina gave Waco a steady glance. "That's my sister we're talking about."

"Okay. Just remember I'm gonna have to treat you roughly. We'll be lucky if they give us a chance to say anything. I didn't make this plain to you, but LeBeau and I didn't part on the best of terms. He did me a bad turn, and I expect he knows I haven't forgotten it."

Sabrina suddenly wondered what would happen if they killed Waco. She had no other source of safety. "Be careful," she said nervously.

"Okay. They're not going to believe me. The only thing we can do is convince them that we've got a scheme that'll make them money. Money is all they care about."

She nodded, but he could see she was nervous. Suddenly he turned and said, "What would you do if I slapped you?"

"I—don't know. Nobody ever slapped me."

"Well, I may have to do that. You can't be what you have been, Sabrina. You're a young woman who's been protected all your life. Now you fear for your life. That's the role you have to play. You're not strong. You're weak, and you're scared to death of LeBeau, and I don't think that's all bad. If you're scared enough, you won't have to do much acting. You've got to convince these outlaws you're terrified."

"I'll do it, Waco. I'll do it."

"All right. Let's go." He spurred his horse, and the two of them rode down the slope. When they were halfway across the bottom of the valley, Waco said, "There they come. I told you we wouldn't sneak up on 'em."

They started up the hill, and when they were halfway up the rise, a group of men rode quickly down and framed them in by forming a half circle around them.

Waco spoke first. "Well hello, Trey. I haven't seen you in a while."

Trey LeBeau scowled. "If you've come to get even with me, you picked a bad way to do it. We'll shoot you out of the saddle if you make one move, Waco."

Waco shook his head and grinned. "No, I'll admit I had a pretty bad feeling about you. You left me in bad shape on that train robbery."

"Didn't plan it that way. It just happened."

Waco shrugged his shoulders. "Water under the bridge."

"Who's the woman? You haven't up and got married on me, have you?"

Waco laughed. "Not likely, and if I did, it wouldn't be this one. We're pretty hungry."

"You didn't accidently come this way. You knew about this hideout," LeBeau said. "What do you want?"

"I want to make you a business offer."

Suddenly LeBeau laughed. He was an attractive man and could charm anyone when he wanted to. "That's like you, Waco. Come in makin' boasts that you can't carry out. What kind of business could you throw my way?"

"Not just you. All you fellows." Waco leaned back in his saddle, shoved his hat to the back of his head, then said, "I've got a good thing that I need help with."

"What kind of help do you need?" LeBeau demanded.

Al Munro, Trey's most trusted man, suddenly drew his .45. "I say kill him here. He's just trouble."

"I guess you just don't want to be rich, Al," Waco said. He looked around and saw Zeno Shaw, Rufo Aznar, and two men he had not met. Both of them were large men, and one of them appeared to be half-Apache. The other one was a strong-looking man who watched Waco steadily.

It was Rufo Aznar, a trim man with an olive compexion and dark eyes and a terrible scar on the right side of his face, who said, "Hold on, Al. Maybe you don't want to be rich, but I do. We ain't had no luck lately."

"I heard about that train, Trey," Waco said. "Didn't you get rich off of that?"

All the men suddenly looked disgusted, and LeBeau said, "We got some gold watches and a few wallets, but there wasn't any gold."

"Why don't you invite us in, and we can make some medicine together."

"Take his gun, Al." Al spurred his horse forward. He reached out and plucked Waco's gun and stuck it in his belt.

"Okay. We go up to the house, and we'll listen to what you have to say."

Waco and Sabrina had both been worried about Marianne. The sight of her sister might be the end of the plot. If she called out Sabrina's name and showed that she knew her, there was little chance for any of them to get out of this alive.

As they rode up to the house and dismounted, Waco saw a

young woman come out and knew this was Marianne. He held his breath, but after one glimpse at him and then one no longer at Sabrina, she just stood and watched.

"Get off that horse, Helen!" Waco said. Sabrina/Helen did not move, and he reached up, grabbed her by the arm, and cuffed her. "Didn't you hear what I said?"

"You're not treating her like a lady friend," Trey said. "Who is she?"

"That's part of the business deal, but we need something to eat."

"All right."

"But I've had to take a quirt to her once or twice."

"Take it easy, Waco," Al said suddenly. "If you really got somethin' that'll make us rich, let's have it."

"After we eat."

"We'll have to cook somethin' up." At that moment, a woman left the house and walked toward them. She stopped dead still and stared at them. "What are you doing here, Waco?"

"Hello, Callie. Maybe just came to visit you."

"You're a liar! Who's the woman?"

"We'll talk business after we have a little something to eat."

Trey watched the scene between Calandra Montevado and Waco with obvious interest.

Waco knew Callie had been Trey's woman until he had come along and she had turned from Trey.

Trey's eyes narrowed. "We'll get something to eat, and then we'll know what you're here about—and whether we let you live or not."

Waco laughed and seemed totally relaxed. "You love money too much to let anything happen to me. I'm your one shot at getting you enough money where you can live like you want to instead of out here in this hole."

After they entered the house, two of the men started stirring up the fire, and Marianne began cooking a meal.

"That's a good roast," Zeno Shaw said. He was over six two, a brute of a man, with scars of fights of the past on his face. "Got some taters left over here, too."

Soon Waco started to sit down and said roughtly, "Sit over there, woman." He was glad to see Sabrina had somehow, although she had not spoken a word, showed her fear. It wasn't all acting he knew. She was afraid. He reached out, grabbed her by the arm, and threw her into a chair. "Eat something."

"I'm not hungry."

He reached out and grabbed her by the hair and said, "Eat something or I'll shove it down your throat."

Callie was watching all this. "She's not your woman, I take it."

"Well, in a way she is. I'll introduce you to her after we eat."

The cabin seemed to be charged with electricity. Only Waco seemed to be at ease. He kept slicing pieces of the roast off and eating it with great enjoyment. "Your woman is a good cook, Trey. We've been eatin' prairie dog lately. About ready to eat a hawk."

Calandra was watching Sabrina carefully. "She's scared to death of you. What are you doing with her? Did you steal her?"

"Now Callie, don't be hasty. This is going to be a long night. I've got lots of business to talk to you."

They ate, Waco eating heartily and Sabrina picking at her food.

As soon as Waco was finished, Callie sat down across from him and said, "All right. What's all this about, Waco?"

"He's threatenin' to make us rich," LeBeau said. "I think he's just a lot of hot air."

"You won't think so after I tell you the whole story. Let me have some of that coffee, and I'll lay it out for you." Waco smiled as if he had not a care, but he saw the hatred in Trey LeBeau's eyes, and understood that with one false move he and Sabrina would be doomed.

CHAPTER 20

From the moment she had faced Trey LeBeau, Sabrina had been truly afraid. It had occurred to her for the first time that since LeBeau had been in her home, he might well have seen one of the pictures of her, for there were many in the house. But when he stared at her with no sign of recognition, she suddenly realized, *I don't look much like I did then.* Indeed, the trip had worn her down and her hair was now stringy and she looked very little like the Sabrina Warren who had come on this quest.

She noted that Waco, after one glance at Marianne, paid her little attention, but finally he put his gaze on Marianne and said, "Well, Trey, I see you got yourself a new lady friend." His glance went to Callie, who merely smiled at him. "It looks like you got your time beat, Callie."

"No, nothin' like that, Waco. I picked this little girl up back East. She's got a rich daddy, and you don't have to talk about makin' me rich. As soon as I get tired of her, I'll sell her back to him. I expect he'd pay a pretty good ransom for you, wouldn't he, honey?"

He had spoken to Marianne, who refused to answer.

"Not very talkative, is she, Trey? Well, this one of mine's not either."

"You two aren't on a honeymoon. I can see that, Waco."

"Why, it is kind of a honeymoon. She's not used to the idea yet, but she'll be fine when she is."

Trey was watching Waco carefully and said, "Well, this ain't exactly a hotel for honeymooners, Waco. Was you thinkin' to stay the night?"

Waco drank from his coffee and leaned back and nodded with sleepy satisfaction. "Good meal. Thought we might, Trey."

LeBeau said, "You're losin' your bedroom tonight, Breed. We'll let the lovebirds have it. You go sleep in the shack."

All the outlaws were waiting to find out what Waco was up to, and finally Trey said, "Well, what's this all about?"

"So you didn't get rich on that train robbery?"

"No, I've told you we didn't. It's not my fault."

"We wasted our time. It wasn't worth the trouble," Zeno Shaw said. He stared at Trey with discontent in his eyes.

"I can't guarantee what a train's carrying," LeBeau snapped.

Waco studied Callie carefully and openly.

She held his gaze and said, "What's on your mind, Waco? We've got no secrets here."

Waco said, "All right with me. How about you, Trey?"

"Just say what you got on your mind," Trey said. "For all I know Parker might have got you out of jail to be one of his marshals. You might be wearing a badge under that vest."

"No badge," he said, pulling his vest away from his shirt, "but if Parker wants me to work for him, that shows you what a good cover I have, doesn't it? I've got a job coming up, Trey, but I'm not sure your bunch is able to handle it. You're down a few men, aren't you?"

"We're able to handle any job you come up with, Waco. What is it? Spit it out."

"All right." Taking a deep breath, he said, "Here it is. My lady friend is Miss Helen Richards. Her father's name is Charles R. Richards. That mean anything to you?"

Nobody spoke, and Waco grinned. "Mr. Richards is in charge of the Express Company over in Durango."

Suddenly everybody in the room grew alert. They obviously were well aware that the Western Express handled large amounts of gold and silver. There were no mines where the offices were located, but they received shipments of gold and silver coins from the Treasury in Washington and transported them over different parts of the country.

Al Munro's eyes gleamed. "Western Express! You're not dumb enough to hold that place up I hope, Waco. They've got enough guards to furnish an army."

Waco grinned at Munro. "No, nothing like that. What I've got in mind is helping the 'transport' end of things."

Trey said impatiently, "You know every train robber in the country has tried that, Waco, but they're clever. They ship out empty boxes one day. Then boxes loaded with rocks the next day, and any day they might or might not ship the real stuff. Anything to throw us off. Nobody ever knows what or when."

Waco leaned back in his chair and ran his fingers through his dark hair. He glanced over at Trey and said, "That's right. We don't know—but Helen's dad knows." The silent tension built up in the room. "Her dad's in charge of the shipping. He always knows."

An electrifying current went around the room. Rufo Aznar

said, "Why, if we knew which train to hit, we'd all be rich."

"Shut up, Rufo!" Trey snapped. He leaned forward and stared at Waco. He was silent for a moment then stared at Sabrina. "That's right, is it? Your daddy runs that express?"

Sabrina said, "Yes, but he'll never tell you about the shipments. Men have tried to get at him before. You wouldn't believe how much money he's been offered just to tell them when things are shipped."

Waco laughed broadly, his eyes gleaming in the twilight. "But they didn't have his only daughter held in Indian Territory away from the law, did they, honey?"

"He'll see you hanged if you do this!" Sabrina muttered. "You won't get away with it."

An excited babble rippled through the room, everybody talking at once. Sabrina watched them. Each one of them was visibly excited. *This is going to work*, she thought triumphantly. *They're going for the bait.*

Suddenly Callie's voice commanded the attention of the room. "And how do we know all this is true?" Her dark eyes were a feline glow in the lantern light, reflecting its yellow flame. Coolly she stared at Waco and Sabrina. "These two come out of nowhere and have this big scheme, and I don't believe a word of it."

LeBeau gave Callie a thoughtful glance. "You may be right," he said. He turned back to Waco. "You've never done anything like this before. You may have done a little holdup work, but you've always been a lone wolf."

"What have I got to show for it?" Waco shrugged. "A horse, a gun, and a blanket." Every eye in the room was locked on him. This was the moment in which they would stand or fall. His voice grew rock hard as he said to LeBeau, "I'm not proposing to join you, Trey." Looking around scornfully, he went on. "I don't want to live in a shack out in the desert somewhere running from Parker's marshals. Not me! I'm gonna do one job, make a pile, and buy a ranch somewhere far out of this forsaken territory." There was a loaded silence in the room, and Waco banged his cup down on the table and told the group curtly, "But I can see you're more interested in listening to Callie than anything I've got to say." He rose to his feet and said, "Come on, honey, let's get a little sleep. Tomorrow we'll pull out of here and see if we can find somebody else. I've been thinking about Jack Chambliss."

"Jack could do the job," Callie said.

Callie's words infuriated Trey.

"We can do anything Chambliss can do!" LeBeau snapped. "But we don't need you, Waco."

LeBeau was on the verge of pulling his gun and shooting Waco, at least so it seemed, but Al Munro said, "Wait a minute. We can do this job, Trey."

"All right, put these two in the room, Al."

Munro led them to a room at the end of the hall. "You two can stay in here tonight."

"Get in there, Helen!" Waco said and pushed Sabrina through the door. He shut it at once and took a deep breath. "Well, all right so far."

"Oh, Waco," Sabrina whispered. She was feeling weak, and she put her hand on his arm. "I was so scared."

"That's good. I wanted you to look scared."

"I think they all believed you. . .except that woman." She watched his face as she mentioned Callie, but Waco's expression didn't change. She thought for a moment then said, "I saw how she stared at you. She hates you."

572

"How do you know that?"

"A woman doesn't have that kind of animosity unless she loved a man once."

Waco ran his hand through his hair and wiped his forehead. "We were friends at one time," he said briefly.

From that one sentence Sabrina knew what she had suspected was true. *Waco and Callie were lovers. That's why she hates him. He must have walked off and left her or done something awful.* Bluntly she asked him, "So you were lovers?"

Strangely enough, her words seemed to embarrass Waco. He looked into her eyes and asked, "Why do you care, Sabrina?"

"I don't care." Even as she said it, she realized that she *did* care. Resolutely she thrust the thought away from her. "But she was in love with you once. You may have to use her to get us out of here."

"No."

The refusal was so flat that Sabrina knew instantly there was no use in pursuing it. She was embarrassed by the scene and agitated by her own show of jealousy when faced with Waco and Callie's relationship. Confused and conflicting thoughts crowded her mind. She said, "Well, Marianne's here and she's all right, so we have a chance."

Waco breathed out heavily. "Yeah, we got a chance, and I don't want to mess this up, but it's going to be tough. They're gonna be watching us like hawks no matter what we do." He pushed himself away from the door, walked to the window, and looked outside. "They've already put a man out front. We've got to be careful because they could sneak up here. He's probably watching through this window, and someone will be watching it all night. They're not about to let us leave here unexpectedly."

Sabrina's shoulders drooped. The hard ride and the immense

strain of the past few hours had begun to affect her.

Waco glanced at the single bed. "You take the bed, and I'll take the floor." It was early, and they were both tired. "I'll blow out the light, and you can get undressed."

"I'll just sleep in my clothes," she said hastily.

Waco didn't reply. Finding a blanket in the gear they had brought in, he made a bed beneath the window, took off his boots, and started to lie down. Instead he rose, walked over to the single chair in the room, carried it to the door, and shoved it underneath the doorknob. "Somebody might want to come bustin' in here, Sabrina. They'd expect us to be in the same bed."

Sabrina didn't reply as Waco lay down. For days now she and this man had slept within five feet of each other beside a campfire, but somehow being in a bedroom with him was totally different. She was apprehensive, almost afraid. She lay down on the bed, pulled the blanket over her stiffly, and lay unmoving and tense until she heard his even breathing. Then she relaxed.

Sleep didn't come all at once though. Sabrina lay quietly thinking of the strangeness of it all. Her other life, her life of teas and parties and balls and fancy dresses—those all seemed a million miles away. With a mental start, Sabrina realized that she could not easily go back to such a life. It would seem so tame after all she had gone through.

She began to worry about the next day, when suddenly Waco's voice came quietly. "I'm glad Marianne's all right."

"Yes, I was afraid. She's going to have a hard time even when we get her away. She's ashamed of what she's done."

"Never easy to get over your bad deeds."

His words intrigued Sabrina. "You're speaking from experience."

Waco didn't answer her for a few moments, but finally he

said, "We're not on this earth here for very long, and sometimes I think it doesn't mean anything. But then once in a while I meet someone who's found more meaning and purpose than I ever thought about. Like Silas." His voice grew soft as he spoke of the marshal. "I've thought a lot about him. He was a good man, and his life meant something."

"He did die well, didn't he? I've admired him very much." When Waco didn't reply, Sabrina turned over and allowed sleep to claim her.

"All right. Tell us how this thing works. How are we supposed to know when that train with the gold moves?" LeBeau said.

They were all in the main room, even Sabrina and Marianne.

Waco said, "All right. Here's the way it will work. I've got a man out there, an in-between sort of fella. But I don't know about your bunch. It's going to take all of us. What about these women?"

"I'll take care of mine. You take care of yours."

"Who will take care of me?" Callie grinned like a cat.

"Here's what'll happen," Waco said. "I got us a man between me and Helen's father. As soon as her father finds out she's all right, he'll send the information about the shipping."

"So he's got to have proof that she's alive. How will we do that?" Trey demanded.

"All she has to do is write her dad a letter. Tell him to send the money. That she's been treated good."

They were talking for some time about the plan, and finally Trey said, "How are you going to contact him? You're stayin' with us until we get the job done."

Waco leaned back and said, "Well, Trey, if I told you everything I know, you might not need me. So I'm not telling you, but I've got a meeting place and I'm not telling who he is, but I will tell you this. When I get the lowdown, which is what train to hit, I know the place to hit it."

"They're bound to be carrying plenty of guards with a big shipment," Al Munro said.

"Nope. That's one thing I found out about Richards. They don't send out a whole lot more guards when they ship the real stuff. They figure it'd be sort of like posting a sign saying that gold and silver are on this here train." Amused laughter ran through the room. "Sometimes they don't even send out one guard more than usual, and that's what's going to happen this time."

No one said anything for a time. Waco was leaning back in his chair, and he dropped it with a crash and slapped the table. "Come on, Trey, look at it! No guards, lots of money, one train. Hit it, we're gone, and that's the last you'll see of me. Any of you."

A thick silence fell over the room, and Waco knew they were greedily weighing the possibility. His eyes surveyed all their faces. "What do you think, Al?"

"I put no trust in any man," Munro said. "But I think Waco's hungry enough to pull it off." Then his voice changed slightly, and his heavy lips twisted with cruelty. "We're going to watch you, Waco. You're going to be in the crosshairs at all times. One thing goes wrong, you get a bullet in the brain. You got that?"

"Sure, Al. I know that. But don't you forget. I want to be rich more than any of the rest of you." His tone couldn't have been milder, but every person there recognized the seriousness in his words.

"All right. Let's do it then," Rufo Aznar said. "I'm tired of penny ante stuff."

LeBeau said, "All right, but one thing more. I get some cash out of this girl. I'll get word to her man to lay his hands on some cash and give it to me or I'll send her head in a sack."

"That'd be hard to do two things at once," Zeno Shaw said.

But Trey was adamant. "I'll send a telegram to her old man. Tell him to have the cash in Fort Smith and we'll hand the girl over."

Finally LeBeau turned to Callie. "You've been awful quiet, Callie. What about it? You for it?"

"It's all right with me. I think it'll work."

"When's this message coming?" Callie asked.

"I got a spot staked out. I'll have to ride out and check it every day until we hear from the old man."

"You ain't goin' alone," Trey said.

"No, he's not. I'll go with him," Callie said.

"I don't think I trust you either."

"Shut up, Trey," Callie shot back. "You do your job, and I'll do mine. That's the way it'll be."

"Might as well ride out today," Waco said. "I don't think it'll be there, but I don't want to risk missing it." He nodded to Callie. "Whenever you're ready, Callie, we'll take a little ride."

"All right, Waco."

The two were ready at once, and as they left, Marianne came up to Sabrina and said, "I can wash your clothes if you need some help."

"Oh, thank you," she said.

As soon as they were alone, Marianne fell against the other woman, crying out, "Oh, Sabrina, I'm so glad you're here! But what are you doing here?"

Sabrina was holding on to Marianne and felt the tears come to her eyes. She was so glad to see her sister, and there was at least a hope of getting her away. "We've come to get you out of here."

"Who is that man that's with you? He looks like an outlaw himself."

"His name is Waco Smith. He's been made into one of the marshals, and his job is to get you out of here."

"Just one man?"

"We have another man outside there, and we've got a scheme. But you and I, we're going to have to be sure that they don't suspect that we're sisters."

"I don't see how anybody can do it, especially with that man. He looks so rough."

"He's a good man, Marianne. He's been—well, a little wild, you might say, but now he's risking his life to get us out of here."

"I'll have to lock you in, but I've got to go clean up. Why don't you lie down and get some rest, and we'll have time to talk tonight."

Marianne clung to Sabrina fiercely and began crying. "I'm so glad to see you, sister. I thought I was lost forever."

"No, we're going to get out of this. You lie down now."

Marianne said, "I'm afraid. What if Waco goes away and doesn't come back?"

"He'll be back," Sabrina said briefly.

Looking sharply at Sabrina, Marianne said, "Well, who is he? What kind of man is he? The others talked about him and Callie being sweethearts once."

The words cut Sabrina much deeper than she cared to admit, but she gave no answer.

"I suppose he's just another hired killer like everybody else around here," Marianne said bitterly.

"A man should learn to fight or let him put skirts about his knees," Sabrina rasped, trying to hold her anger in check.

Marianne had never seen her sister so passionately defend a man. "I'm sorry, Sabrina. I didn't mean it, but I'm so scared."

Sabrina closed her eyes and forced herself to calm down. Finally she said, "Don't worry about Waco. He's a hard man, and in this situation I think that's a good thing. He will get us out of here. He will." She stared at the two riders disappearing into the distant shimmer of the heat on the horizon. "I don't know what he'll do after that, but I know he'll never quit until he does what he sets out to do." They continued washing, and all Sabrina could think of was the long ride that Callie and Waco would take and what that ride would entail.

⁂

Waco said little as he and Callie rode steadily east, but her presence had a powerful influence on him. From time to time he turned slightly, and vivid memories came trooping through his mind.

She broke the silence, saying, "Well, Waco, do you ever think of when we were together?"

Waco was startled and could not come up with an answer. He was shocked when Callie laughed, and when he turned he saw that her dark eyes were alive with an emotion he couldn't name.

"It's an easy question," Callie said and waited for an answer.

"Sure I do," Waco said slowly and faced her as he added, "but it's ancient history, Callie."

"Is it?"

"I don't think people can go back where they once were."

"You're wrong about that."

Her blatant reply startled Waco, and he demanded, "Would you want to go back to that time?"

"It was a good time, wasn't it?"

For a moment he was silent and confused, then he said slowly, "I remember the good times."

"We could go there again."

"You're Trey's woman."

"I'm not his woman. I'll never belong to any man as I did to you."

The cry of a far-off bird came to Waco, and he could not remember a time when he'd been so shaken. He had never once thought that he might find what he'd once had with Callie, and now she was offering him herself.

"I don't think it would be smart to go back to that time—not with this job in front of us. It's going to be tough, and no matter what you say, Trey won't let anything of his go."

"Maybe he is, but you're a strong man, Waco. I'm a strong woman." She kneed her mare, and when they were close, she put her hand out and gipped his arm. Her touch startled Waco, and she whispered huskily, "We had something once—and we can have it again. . . ."

At that moment, Waco Smith realized he was not as strong as he had thought himself to be. *She can stir me up—and I don't know if I can say no to her!*

CHAPTER 21

Waco Smith had always considered himself to be basically a simple man able to make up his mind quickly and then follow through. But something had happened to change all that when Callie had urged him to pick up their love affair where it had left off years ago. It had caught Waco off guard so that he spent long hours simply walking alone out on the territory surrounding the hideout house, and he did so now this Tuesday afternoon. He glanced up and saw the horizon fading as the late afternoon sun seemed to be melting into the earth. He had always had an appreciation for the world of nature and had taken an unspoken delight in the sky, the woods, the animals and birds, but now they seemed to give him no pleasure.

"Waco, just a minute."

Quickly Waco turned to see Sabrina, who came walking toward him. She had some wet clothes in her arms, and she was headed for the wire stretched between two posts to dry them out. Waco glanced toward the house and saw that Breed Marcos, the Apache halfbreed, was watching carefully. Turning quickly, he walked toward her and said, "Be careful, Sabrina, you're being watched."

"I know. I'm always being watched. I feel like I'm an animal in the zoo."

"You better start putting those clothes on the line or they'll send somebody out here to see what we're talking about."

"All right. I will."

Waco stood back, ignoring the hideout and Breed watching from the porch. He knew what she was talking about, for he himself had been under surveillance ever since he had arrived with her at LeBeau's house. He turned so that he seemed to be facing away from Sabrina and said softly, "Are you all right?"

"Yes. I'm just afraid."

"I guess we all get afraid of some things."

She was pinning a dress on the line and she didn't turn, but after a moment she said, "I wouldn't think you'd be afraid of anything."

"You'd be wrong there."

"What are you afraid of?"

The question caught Waco off guard, and for a moment he had to stop and think. "Lots of things. Afraid of growing old and nobody with me, nobody to take care of me. Afraid of getting crippled so that I can't take care of myself."

"Are you afraid of death?"

"Well, not so much death. I face that pretty often. It's what comes after death that scares me."

She continued to hang up the clothes, and finally she picked up a petticoat and, hanging it on the line, said, "You're worried about your soul, then?"

"I never put it like that, but I guess that's right."

"I know what you mean, Waco. I've been so selfish all my life, and now that I've hit something really hard, I just don't know how to handle it."

"We have to take it as it comes, Sabrina."

Suddenly her voice changed, and he turned to face her fully. He had always considered her a weak woman, softened by the life that she had led, but now he saw that there was something different. In her eyes and lips lay flexible capacities carefully controlled as though she was determined to do something, and Waco felt he had a view of the undertow of her spirit. For that moment she forgot her reserve and was watching him with the fully open eyes of a woman momentarily and completely engrossed. The lines of physical fatigue showed in her face, and the hard usage that she had taken had made her shoulders sag, but he saw in her, despite this, a fire burning that had not been there when he had first met her. Her skin was lightly browned by the sun, and her lips were broad and on the edge of being full, the lips of a giving woman but not a pliant woman. He asked her, "Sabrina, have you ever been truly in love with someone?"

"No," she said, and bitterness tinged her voice. "I've been in love with myself. I didn't know it until I lost Marianne. What about you?"

"I thought I was once."

"With Callie?"

"Her and the other woman who betrayed me. I guess I don't learn very quickly."

"You have a distrust for women. Two women were dishonest, and you're afraid to trust any other woman."

"I guess you're right. I don't like to admit it."

"Do you think you'll ever find a woman you can trust?"

"I don't know, Sabrina. Sometimes when I'm riding along and

dark is falling, I pass a cabin, and I can see the yellow glow from the fire inside. Sometimes I can see people laughing, can hear them, and it never fails to make me sad."

"Why should that make you sad?"

He shifted his shoulders, and his lips tightened. "Because they have everything, those people, and I don't really have anything."

She continued to hang clothes, and finally she asked, "But you thought you loved Callie."

"It wasn't the kind of love you could build a marriage on."

"What kind of woman would that take?"

Waco suddenly had a moment's insight. "I thought it might be you, Sabrina."

His words startled her, and she exclaimed, "Me? Why, we're as different as night and day!"

"I guess so, but still, who can explain what a man sees when he looks at a woman? I guess," he said slowly, "every man carries a picture in his head or in his heart or wherever things like that take place, and they carry a picture of a woman, the one they want. But I thought that sometimes it was a picture built up of many women, not just one."

"Well, that's not very fair for the woman a man finally gets. How can a woman be everything a man wants?"

Suddenly Waco smiled. It made him look much younger. "I guess when a man finally gets the right woman, he sees all the things in her that he wants to see."

"That's a whole lot like saying that love is blind."

"No. I'd say it's like a very strong light. It makes a man see things he otherwise wouldn't. There's some sweetness, some honesty in the woman and things that he always admired, and he suddenly realizes that this is the woman he's been looking for, although he didn't know it."

"Until she hurts him."

"That goes with love, I guess."

"Even people in love hurt each other, don't they?" She hung up the last garment and now picked up the basket and said, "I'd better get inside."

He said suddenly, "I never would have imagined that you had thoughts like this, Sabrina, and I guess I embarrassed you by telling you that I have feelings for you that I never thought I'd have for any other woman."

Sabrina was shocked. She had felt the masculinity of Waco Smith. It was the kind of strength that a woman loved to see, but she had not featured herself being in love with this man so different from herself. "I guess we're both surprised then."

Suddenly he caught a glimpse of movement on the porch and saw that Trey and Callie had come outside. "They're watching us," he said. "I'm going to have to treat you rough. I'm going to have to push you around. Act like you're hurt. I'm going to tell 'em you won't write the letter."

"Go ahead. Do what you have to."

Without looking toward the two who were approaching suddenly, Waco reached out and seized Sabrina by the arm. He saw her eyes open wide, and he swung his open hand and slapped her on the face. She cried out slightly, and then he slapped her again. "This has to look good," he muttered.

"What's going on here?" Trey asked.

"This woman's getting some kind of religion. She said she wasn't gonna write that letter, but she knows now she will or she'll be sorry."

"I'd hate to have you mad at me." Callie laughed. "Of course, if you slapped me around, I'd shoot you."

Waco suddenly grinned. "I expect you would. Well, let's get that note written, and I'll take it."

"I'll go with you."

Waco shrugged. "That's fine." He went inside and found a piece of paper, had Sabrina write a note simply saying to her imaginary father that she was well but that she was frightened and needed him.

Waco took the note and shoved it in his shirt pocket and stepped outside. "I've got it."

"I'm going with you this time," Trey said.

"You stay out of it," Callie said. "We'll do what we've been doing."

Temper flared in Trey LeBeau's features, and he glared at her, but she merely laughed at him. "We don't need you along. I'm not your woman anyway."

"You will be when we get out of this," Trey said.

"Come on. Let's go get this note in the bottle, Waco."

The two left at once, and as they were riding out, Waco said, "You're going to go too far with LeBeau. He's capable of hurting any woman bad."

"He'll never touch me. He knows I'd kill him if he did."

They rode slowly, and she asked finally as they approached the site of the bottle, "Did you think about what I said?"

He was silent for a while, and then he said, "You know, a friend of mine was kind of a scholar. He liked to read the old Greek writing. He read about one Greek philosopher that said you can't step in the same river twice."

"I don't understand that."

"Well, it means the rivers are moving all the time. You step in them and ten minutes later that river's gone and another's come. I always took it to mean you couldn't start all over again with anything that's dead."

She pulled her mount up close, reached out, and grabbed him, and he leaned toward her. She kissed him and laughed. "I'll show you what's dead! What we had wouldn't die. It may have been asleep for a while, but it'll come back."

The two found the bottle, and she watched as he put the note in it. He concealed it and said, "Now we just have to wait until we get the information we need on that train."

"Let's take our time going back. That place depresses me."

During the ride back, more than once, Waco was aware that she was trying him out. She made several allusions to the love they had had, and despite himself he had memories, sharp and keen, of how she had come to him in a way that a woman comes to a man that he never forgets. He tried to shake it out of his mind, but he found himself instead thinking of Sabrina and their brief conversation. *I don't see any good in that*, he thought. *No matter what I try to do she's above me.*

Judge Parker looked up, for the door to his office had opened with no knock and Charles Warren and Frank Morgan entered. "We need to talk to you, Judge."

"Sit down," Parker said at once.

"This is Frank Morgan."

The judge saw that the young man looked soft but had a determined look in his eye. "Sit down and we'll talk about this thing."

For the next half hour, Parker managed to get both men

calmed down as he told them of the plan he was working out with Waco and Sabrina. "We've been exchanging notes. Waco and Miss Sabrina have convinced LeBeau that she's the daughter of one of the officials of the railroad in charge of shipments of gold and silver. They've told him that they can find out which train the shipment will be on and that there'll be no guard."

"You think they'll believe that?" Frank Morgan demanded.

"Depends on how good a front Sabrina and Waco put up."

"So what we're doing now is waiting on a signal," Warren pressed.

"Well, it's farther along than that. There's an Indian that's been helping them out. He brought this in yesterday." He opened his desk drawer and pulled out a piece of paper much folded.

Warren took it and stared at it. It said:

Daddy,

These men are going to kill me if you don't help me. I'm all right now and they say they'll let me go, but you have to tell them the time for the next gold shipment. Please help me.

Helen

"There won't be any gold on that train. Instead of that, we'll have every marshal, and I'll hire some new posse members. We'll load that train up with men who are good with guns. We'll stop Trey LeBeau's clock."

"I'm going along," Warren said.

Instantly Frank Morgan nodded. "Get me a gun. I'll go, too."

"Could be dangerous. You could get shot."

"I don't care. I've got my wife here, and I'm staying until we get both our girls back. If I get shot in trying it, it won't bother me.

I've got to do what I can for my family."

Parker studied the two and finally said, "Well, we can always use more guns. I've already written the answer and sent it by way of the Indian." Parker studied the two men and said gently, "I'm sorry for your trouble, but I'm hopeful that it will come out all right."

༄

LeBeau looked up and saw Callie and Waco coming back. It had been three days, and they had sent the letter from Helen, and now he got up and said, "Well, at last here they come. They better have somethin'.

"Sometimes I think this whole thing is gonna blow up in our face," Al Munro said. "There's something I don't like about it."

"The one thing I don't like about it is Waco Smith." The anger and rage had been building up in LeBeau, and when the two got off and entered, he said, "What did you find?"

"Answer to the letter." Waco handed him the bottle with the paper inside. "Won't need to be any more letters passed."

Taking the bottle at once, LeBeau fished the paper out. He read it out loud. " 'Two ten out of Lake City will be carrying a huge shipment of gold. There will be no guards on the train. There will be one man on board wearing a blue suit. You give my daughter to him. He will get you into the gold car. They'll open the door for him. Please let my daughter go.' "

"I know that train," Waco said. "And I know a good place to hold it up. There's some sharp bends in the road there, so they can't make much speed."

"What are we going to do with these women while we're doing the job?" Al Munro demanded.

"I know what we can do with them," Waco said. "I don't want

any murders in this thing. None of you need it either. There's a deserted cabin not far from where this hook in the railroad is that makes the train slow down. It's less than a mile away. It's empty now. We can lock 'em in there while we're doing the job and then we can turn 'em loose."

Trey was staring hard at Waco, but finally he nodded his head slowly. "All right. That's the way we'll play it, but I'm telling you, Waco, I'll kill you if you even blink."

"I won't be blinkin'. I want this gold as much as you do—more, I think."

"Well," Trey LeBeau said, "the note says it'll be in two days. We'd better get everything ready and be on the spot."

◈

The gang spent most of the time getting their guns oiled and polished and packing ammunition. There was a sense of expectation about it, and Rufo Aznar moved close to Waco saying, "Don't think you can pull anything on us, Smith. You're tough, but you're not tougher than the whole band here. Everybody will be watching you."

"They better be watching that train."

"We can do both at the same time."

◈

The hours crept by. Marianne and Sabrina found a few moments alone to talk in whispers about what was going to happen.

"I'm afraid it won't work," Marianne said. "Even if it did, they may just kill us. These men are all murderers."

"Waco won't let them do that."

"He's only one man."

"I know, but he can do things. I have confidence in him."

Marianne stared at Sabrina. "Why do you feel like that about him? You've known him only a short time, and you know he's a criminal."

Sabrina could not answer. She dropped her head and said, "I don't know, but there's something in him that I trust."

The next day as they were pulling out, Waco was saddling Sabrina's horse. When she came to mount up, he whispered, "There's a way to get out of that house. If you can get out, fine. There's some woods over to the north of it. I'll come for you if I make it."

"Don't take any chances."

He suddenly grinned. "Life is a chance, but if I don't make it, I want to tell you, Sabrina, I've never felt about any woman like I have about you. I know it's useless. We have no future together, but if things were different, I could see it would be great for me."

"Maybe for me, too. Oh, be careful!"

As the band rode off, Callie rode up to ride beside Waco. "We're going to get that gold," she said quietly so that it could not be heard over the sound of the horses' hooves hitting the hard ground. "I mean we'll get all of it."

"Your plan could get us both killed."

"No. We'll get that gold. We'll leave, and we'll find a place where we can spend the rest of our lives doing whatever we want. We'll have a new life." She suddenly looked very young, and there was something like joy in her face that Waco had never seen. "I can change, Waco."

"I guess you can. I guess any of us can."

"I'm tired of being what I've been all my life, a bad woman."

She laughed and said, "Wouldn't it be something if we got married and had a house full of kids? Can you see me changing diapers?"

"Can you see me doing that?" He grinned and said, "Both of us need a change, but we'll have to be careful. If LeBeau even suspects either one of us, he'll kill us in cold blood. Stick close after we get the gold."

"We don't have much of a plan."

"Impossible to plan for a thing like this." Waco felt a sharp pang as he realized that he was being as deceitful to this woman as a woman had once been to him. He knew he did not love Callie, never had really, but when he saw the joy in her eyes, he felt like a traitor. He said no more. The troop headed steadily toward the site of the holdup.

CHAPTER 22

The room was crowded, but Heck Thomas, the chief marshal, wanted to see all of the men he had chosen at one time. He looked over the room and saw that at least four regular marshals were there plus six more that he had recruited. These were men who he knew were tough and could shoot and would not hesitate in a fight to take Trey LeBeau and his bunch down.

Thomas started to speak, and then his eyes fell on Charles Warren and Frank Morgan. They stood out blatantly against the other members of the posse. Both were wearing suits and looked like what they were, businessmen ready to go to work in an office but hardly fitted to go up against hardened, cold-blooded outlaws who would kill them without a second thought.

Shaking his shoulders in a gesture of dismissal, Heck spoke up in his husky voice. "All right, you men, we've been over this war plan, I like to call it, several times. Let me repeat. There will be no passengers on this train. This a special train designed to do one thing—to wipe out LeBeau and his band once and for all. Now I put most of the men in the car next to the mail car where the gold and silver is usually hauled. Nothing in there now, of course, except two of you who will be ready in case LeBeau does get the door open. They think only one man will be waiting for them, but I think they're going to come with all guns blazing. That's the way they always do, and they're convinced that they've got the inside track on the biggest train robbery since there were trains. All right. Any questions?"

For a moment there was silence; then one of Isaac Parker's marshals, Ted Summers, said, "You want us to try and keep 'em alive, Heck?"

"No. Put them down any way you can. If they live, they'll be hanged. If they get shot in the heart, that'll just save the judge an extra trial. All right. If there are no more questions, we'll meet at the train. I've already assigned you your places. When the train slows down, that'll be when they'll send a man to go up and stop the engineer. The train will stop, and that's when they'll come in. All right. Let's get at it."

The men started to leave, but Heck said, "Mr. Warren, you and Mr. Morgan, just a word."

Charles Warren and Frank turned and faced Heck. "What is it, Mr. Thomas?"

"Just Heck will do. I'm gonna tell you one more time. This ain't a good idea."

"Don't try to talk us out of it, Marshal. We're going. Those are our folks that LeBeau is holding. We're going to get them back." Frank's face was paler than usual, but his jaw was set. He glared at Heck Thomas, daring him to reply.

"Well, I can see your mind is set on this, Mr. Warren, and you, too, sir, but let me bring this up. How would you feel if I came into your business office and tried to take over your duties there? You wouldn't permit it for a minute."

"Not the same thing," Charles Warren said abruptly. "This is a matter of family, and you know it."

"Can you shoot?"

"I can shoot this." Warren reached over to the wall and picked up a double-barreled shotgun. "I've got plenty of extra shells. If they get within range, I can blast their heads off."

Despite himself, Heck smiled. "That'll do the job, I guess. What about you, Mr. Morgan?"

"I spend my winters hunting ducks. Not the same as hunting men, I know that's what you're going to say. But I've been in several shooting matches. I've got this rifle. I don't think I can hit anything with a handgun, but with this rifle I won't miss."

Heck paused and tried to summon another argument, but one look at their stern faces and the determined light in both their eyes and he finally shrugged and said, "Well, some of our men are liable to get shot, and you may be the ones."

"We're going to get our womenfolk, Heck," Charles Warren said grimly. "Whatever it takes."

"All right. When the shootin' starts, just be sure you shoot one of them and not one of us."

※

The mounted party arrived at the cabin where the women were to be kept. It was set back in deep woods, and the path had almost grown over. "This house hasn't been used in a long time," Waco said. "Nobody ever comes here."

"I still don't like it," Breed Marcos said. "They could get loose."

"No, they can't," Waco spoke up at once. He stepped off his

horse and saw that LeBeau had done the same and the outlaw was eyeing him with a hard look.

"Why'd we bring all these extra horses?" Rufo Aznar said. He required a big horse himself since he was over six two and weighed well over two hundred and thirty pounds.

"We want fresh ones," LeBeau said, not taking his eyes off Waco. "When this is over, they'll be sending a posse after us. We've got to outrun everything."

Waco said, "That's good thinking."

Le Beau said, "Well, let's see the inside of this place." The men all dismounted, and Waco stepped up to the door. It was a solid door made of two-inch-thick oak. "They're never gonna break this down," he said. He shoved the door open, and they stepped inside. LeBeau saw that there were only two windows, and a large fireplace dominated one side. The furniture was simply a battered old table, a few chairs, and what was left of a bed.

"This won't do, Waco," LeBeau said. "All they have to do is shove the door open. It locks from the inside."

"We're going to nail it shut on the outside. I already thought of that," Waco said. As a matter of fact, he had not, but he could not show a moment's hesitation. The men were walking around, and Zeno Shaw said, "They must have been expecting Indians or something. This place is like a jail."

"That's right. They can't get out of here. That's why I thought of this place. We can fasten them in, come back after the job's over, and turn 'em loose."

Waco walked over and pulled Sabrina off her horse. "Come on, sweetheart," he said.

Marianne slid off her own horse, and the two walked inside.

Waco said, "Don't be tryin' to bust out of here. If you do, it'll be bad for you."

"We won't do anything," Sabrina said, staring at the rough outlaws.

"No, you won't," LeBeau grinned. "I'm leaving a guard here."

"You can't do that," Munro protested. "We need all the fire-power we got."

"No, Callie will watch these women."

Callie said, "No, I won't do it."

"Do it or I'll shoot you in the leg," LeBeau snapped. "Somebody has to watch these two, and you're the right one."

Waco said, "That's a good idea, Trey." He was facing Callie and winked at her. She caught his meaning and nodded, saying, "All right, I'll do it."

Waco said, "Let's get out of here. We don't have all that much time."

They started out, and Waco saw to it that he was last. He said, "Oh, I forgot something." He turned and came to stand before the two women. "You two women don't try anything funny. You'll be all right if you do what we say."

Sabrina was watching his eyes, and he winked at her, his back to LeBeau. "If you try anything funny, you could get killed, both of you."

"We won't do anything," Sabrina said quietly.

Waco turned and walked outside.

"We'll leave the horses here in that corral right there, tied out back here," LeBeau said.

It took a few minutes to get the extra horses tied out so they could get to water in a trough, and then they all mounted up. "Let's do it," LeBeau said. He turned to Waco and said, "This better work, Waco, or you'll pay for it."

"It'll work." Waco nodded and said, "Go this way." He led the band to the place that he had selected. He pulled up and said, "There. You see that steep curve. Every train that goes through here has to slow down to no more than ten miles an hour."

"Why'd they make it curve like that?" Breed Marcos asked.

"Because they couldn't run it through that big rock formation over there, so they just laid the tracks around it. It slows the train up, and then they have to get up speed again."

"Where are we going to hide out where they can't see us?" LeBeau demanded.

"Right over there in that patch of trees. By the time the train slows down, it won't be going over more than fifteen or twenty miles an hour. So all you have to do is put one man on that train; he goes up and puts a gun on the engineer and makes him stop the train. As soon as the train stops, go for that gold, LeBeau."

"Well, you're always wantin' to show off, Waco." LeBeau smiled, but it did not reach his eyes. "It'll be your job to stop the train."

"I can probably do that better than anybody I see here," Waco said, holding LeBeau's glance.

"All right. Let's get the horses hidden."

"I'll stay here, and the rest of you get on down about a hundred yards. It'll take that long for the train to stop. You can hide out behind those oak trees."

"If anything goes wrong, I'll put a bullet in you, Waco."

"Nothing will go wrong." Waco stepped off his horse, tied it up, and said, "All we have to do is wait."

LeBeau stared at him for a moment then said, "All right.

Let's get on down there and get ourselves ready. How long will it be?"

"It'll be another hour," Waco said, "but we'll need to stay under cover."

"Don't tell me how to run my business," LeBeau said.

~

LeBeau led the troop up to the clump of oaks that offered shelter. "Get those horses tied down. When we rush the train we won't need them," LeBeau said.

Breed spoke up. "According to what that letter you got said, there'd only be one man on there, but he's expecting us to give the girl to him."

LeBeau grinned. "Let him wait. He can expect anything he wants, but if he argues, we'll give him a bullet in the head."

"Better not do that," Al Munro said. "According to the letter, he can give the word to get us in to where that gold is."

"We won't kill him, but we'll hold a gun to his head and make him think so," Trey said. "Now everybody knows what to do. Scatter out here."

The others moved to both sides from where LeBeau was standing, all except Al Munro. The two men were silent. LeBeau said nothing for so long that his lieutenant said, "What's on your mind? I know you're thinkin' about somethin'."

LeBeau turned and grinned at Munro. "I tell you what, Al. It grates me to have to split all this money with Waco."

For a moment Munro looked startled, and then he grinned. "I don't reckon we have to do that, do we, boss?"

"One of us will take care of it. Once we get the money, take him out."

"What about those women?"

"I guess we can let 'em out of that house and let 'em walk wherever they're goin'."

"Well, they can identify us. Maybe we ought not to give them that chance."

That Al Munro was suggesting that the women be killed to keep from testifying did not seem to shock LeBeau. "Might come to that. Let me think on it. Now let's wait it out here."

❧

Waco had been waiting impatiently, and finally he heard a faint whistle. He got on his horse and said, "Okay boy, get me on board that train, and then you can do as you please." He checked the loads in his guns and pulled his horse out almost to the clear.

Five minutes later he saw the train appear, puffing black smoke, the drivers churning. It began to slow down as it always did, and as it made the curve, the speed lessened even more.

When it came out at its slowest speed, Waco kicked his mount in the side and said, "Get 'em, boy!" The horse shot out like a racehorse opening a race and soon was galloping beside the engine. Waco looked up and grabbed the handles that led beside the stairway. When he got on he saw that the engineer was a tall, lanky man wearing a marshal's badge.

"You must be Waco Smith. I'm Marshal Fred Gierson. He grinned and said, "I used to railroad before I became a lawman. How's it lookin'?"

"Pull it down to a stop, Fred, right now."

Instantly Gierson threw the brakes on, and the screeching of the brake's steel began to sound like a banshee.

"The men all in place?"

"In every car. Mr. Warren and his employee Morgan, they're there, too."

Waco climbed over the coal tinder and entered the first car behind. The first man he met was Heck Thomas, who suddenly grinned and shouted over the noisy engine. "Well, I thought you might be joinin' us. Are they waitin'?"

"They'll jump us as soon we're up by those trees."

"I got men in every car. As soon as they come out, we'll catch 'em in a crossfire. What do you want to do?"

"I'll wait until the train stops. I'll drop out on the other side. I'm gonna run down to that express car. That's where LeBeau will be. I'll try to nail him. Promise me you'll take care of him. By the way, there's a house about three miles northeast by a big cut, an old stone house. Anybody can tell you where it is. The Warren girls are there. You get 'em out if something happens to me."

"Sure, Waco. We'll take care of it. You watch yourself. That LeBeau is a wolf." Pulling his gun, he looked out.

Waco leaped out on the other side. He had not gone ten steps before he heard shots ring out. *Something's gone wrong. They were supposed to go to the man inside. I think somebody's trigger happy.*

The train ground to a complete jolting stop, and Waco crawled beneath it. Before coming out, he saw that the band, all of the men, were shooting at the car, and fire was being returned.

He looked quickly to find LeBeau and saw him stooping down. He fired a shot but didn't have much of a target.

He could tell that the windows were open and Heck's men were throwing a blistering fire on the outlaws. They were completely unprepared for it, and even as he watched, Zeno Shaw was knocked backward, his face a bloody mess. The next to go down was Breed Marcos. The half-Apache was firing rapidly, but a bullet took him and knocked him backward. He tried to lift his gun, but two more slugs struck him. That left Aznar and Al Munro, as well as LeBeau.

Al Munro said, "Let's get out of here. It's a trap."

Munro and Aznar started to run but were cut down by the withering fire. He could hear the boom of a shotgun and couldn't imagine who would be firing it.

Scrambling out from under the car, Waco met Heck, who was reloading his pistol. "I think we got 'em all."

"All except the one we wanted."

Heck looked startled. "You didn't see LeBeau?"

"No. I got a feeling he might have stayed back and let the other men take the risk. The rest of them are dead or wounded."

The men were piling out of the cars, checking the bodies and putting cuffs on the two who were alive and able to stand up.

Suddenly Waco said, "LeBeau's gone to get those women."

Heck shot him a startled glance. "We'd better get there."

Waco said, "I'll take care of it." He ran back to where his horse was standing with the reins dragging. He moved quickly to the saddle and said, "Let's go, boy. Let's have a fast trip." The big horse strode out with a sudden lurch that nearly threw Waco off, but he leaned forward, and although the fight had caused him no fear, he knew what that was now.

The thought passed through his mind. *LeBeau will kill 'em just to get his revenge.* He leaned forward and urged the big stallion to a full driving run and prayed, "God, let me get there in time!"

❧

Heck Thomas walked the length of the train, stopping to look down at several bodies. He stopped when he saw Charles Warren holding the 12-gauge shotgun and staring down at the body of one of the outlaws. Warren's face was pale, and he turned to ask, "What's his name, Marshal?"

"Breed Marcos," Heck said. "He was a real bad one. Four murders that we know of."

"I think I killed him."

Heck shook his head. "No, you didn't."

"How can you tell?"

"Because those are bullet holes in his chest, not wounds from that shotgun." He saw that Frank Morgan was standing off to one side, a bitter expression on his face. "He's taking it hard, I reckon. When I was a soldier with Lee, I noticed that most of us felt pretty bad after we killed our first Yankee. Almost made me sick! But as time went on, we learned to live with it." He hesitated then added, "You didn't kill this man."

Warren sighed with obvious relief. "I'm glad of that. I just pulled the trigger and reloaded." He stared down at the bloody corpse. "I know he was a bad man, but it's a tragedy for a man to wind up like this."

"He chose his way, Mr. Warren."

"I know, but I can't help feeling sorry for him. If things had been different, he might have had a better life."

"He would have killed your two daughters and thought nothing about it."

Warren looked up abruptly. "I guess he got what he deserved."

"He would have been hanged along with Rufo Aznar if we'd taken him alive. But the bad thing about all this is that the big fish got away."

"You mean LeBeau?"

"Yes." Heck shook his head, an angry expression on his

sunburned features. "I'd rather we got LeBeau and the rest had lived. He's the kingpin, and he'll get another bunch of outlaws, and we'll have it all to do again."

"What about my daughters?"

"Well, Waco told me they were kept in a cabin not too far from here." Heck's mouth drew into an angry line, and he continued, "Waco had his horse, and he's on his way there now. I hope they're all right. Waco said they left that woman that hangs out with the gang to guard them." Heck suddenly called to one of his men and walked away, and Frank came at once to stand before Warren. His face was strained, and he said, "I'm glad that's over. Did you hit any of them?"

"Marshal Thomas said I didn't, not a killing wound anyway. How about you?"

Morgan's mouth became a tight line, and he said, "I killed the one they call Al Munro. He was LeBeau's right-hand man. I shot and hit him right in the heart."

"I know you feel bad about that."

"Not as bad as if he'd hurt Marianne or Sabrina."

"Well, we've got to go to them as soon as Heck's men locate the horses."

"Charles, I've got to tell you something."

"What is it, Frank?"

"I'm going to marry Marianne." Morgan took a deep breath then said, "I've loved her for a long time, but she wanted another kind of man. She's going to have a hard time getting over this, and I'm going to be right with her."

Warren said, "Why, Frank, Caroline and I have wished for a long time that you and Marianne would make a match of it. We'd be proud to have you in the family."

Even as he spoke, a rider emerged from the timber leading

three mounts. "There's our horses," Heck said. "Mount up and we'll go to your girls. Waco told me how to get there. The place ain't far, but LeBeau is a wolf. He got beat, and he'll try to get even."

The three mounted, and Heck led them out at a driving run. It was all Charles Warren could do to stay in the saddle, but he could only pray that his girls were all right.

"Somebody's coming in. It must be over," Sabrina said.

"I hope Waco's all right and the rest of the men, too," Marianne said.

Sabrina called out, "Waco, is that you?" There was no answer and finally the door itself swung open, but instead of Waco, Trey LeBeau stepped inside. His face was red, and he was furious. "Well, you two pulled a fast one."

"What are you talking about?" Sabrina gasped.

"That train was packed full of lawmen. They got all of us except me, so that leaves me with you."

"Just let us go, LeBeau," Marianne said. "You can't take us with you."

"I can do it all right. Waco Smith will be here soon if I know him. You stand inside there. You make a funny move I'll kill you."

The two women moved back and watched as LeBeau loaded his six-shooter. He put it in his holster but stood behind the open door looking out.

Callie said, "We can ride away from this, Trey. Leave these women alone."

"Not likely. We're leavin', you and me, but not until after I kill Waco Smith."

At that moment Sabrina Warren knew how much Waco meant to her. She had not recognized it until now, and she was convinced that LeBeau would shoot him down without warning. She knew it would be a dark hour for her.

"There he comes. You women get over there!"

"Let me go out and talk to him," Callie said.

"Nothin' doin'. You're all soft on him. I knew it all the time. He won't get you now. We'll get out of here and start a new life." LeBeau suddenly turned and said, "There he is." He watched as Waco pulled up and stepped off his horse twenty feet from the cabin door. He raised his revolver.

Suddenly Callie ran past him. She moved across the yard, calling, "LeBeau's inside, Waco! He's going to kill you!"

Waco stopped and put one bullet through the open door. He could see the shape of LeBeau. No sooner did he fire than LeBeau returned the fire, and he felt it rake his ribs. Not a bad wound. He knew he was a dead target there, for LeBeau was in the shadows of the house and he was afraid to fire for hitting Marianne or Sabrina.

Suddenly Callie put herself against him, and even as she did, Waco felt her body shudder as a bullet struck her. "Callie!" he cried and lowered her to the ground. He saw LeBeau come running out of the cabin, firing as he came. He had time to lift his gun and fired one shot. It caught LeBeau in the chest. It stopped him, and LeBeau stared down at the blood that stained the front of his shirt. He looked up and tried to speak but couldn't. He tried to lift his gun, but it was suddenly too heavy. It dropped from his fingers, and suddenly he collapsed and fell to the dust.

"Are you all right, Callie?" He knew this was a foolish question. He could feel the blood on his hand where he was holding it behind her back. He was aware of the two women who had come out of the cabin, but he leaned forward, for Callie was trying to speak. "What did you say, Callie? I didn't hear you." He put his ear down to her lips and felt her hand on his face. Her voice was feeble, and suddenly she whispered, "We won't be going on that trip, will we, Waco?"

As Waco held her, she died in his arms. When her body went limp, emptiness and despair filled his heart.

CHAPTER 23

As soon as he pulled up his horse, Charles Warren saw the lifeless body of LeBeau and Waco sitting on the ground, holding a woman in his arms. Then he saw Marianne and Sabrina, and crying their names, he fell out of his saddle and ran to where they stood. As he caught Marianne in his arms, she cried out, "Dad! You came for us!"

"Of course I did!" Warren tried to speak, but his throat was tight and he felt tears running down his cheeks. He held her close and felt her body trembling, but she was safe! "Are you all right, daughter?" he whispered.

"I—I'm fine now."

Warren turned to embrace Sabrina. "You did it, Sabrina!" Warren said. "I'm so proud of you!"

"It wasn't me, Dad. It was Waco."

"But you found him and you stayed with him. What happened?"

Sabrina did not speak at once but finally said, "Waco planned the whole thing, Dad. I once thought he was pretty dense, but he's smart! He had to convince LeBeau and all the other outlaws that he had a plan to make them all rich. Some of them wanted to shoot us, LeBeau for one, but he just sold them all on his scheme."

"Were you afraid?"

"I was scared to death, but Waco had told me what to do. He told them I was the key to getting the information about the gold and the train it would come on. Dad, he never showed anything like fear. He has more nerve than any man I've ever seen!"

"How did he treat you?"

Sabrina smiled. "Like dirt. He had to convince them that I was the key to the whole thing, and he treated me terribly. Once he slapped me after asking me if he could for the act, and it helped convince LeBeau."

Warren studied Waco and saw that his features were twisted with grief. He hesitated then asked, "Were they lovers—Waco and that woman?"

"Once they were, a long time ago."

"Looks like he never got over her."

"He did, but he had to use her to get Marianne and me away."

"Use her how?"

Sabrina hesitated then said, "It's complicated, Dad."

"He looks like he's grieving. Doesn't that mean he still loves her?"

Sabrina shook her head. "He used her to keep LeBeau and the others fooled. But he told me that he felt nothing for her any longer, that he had never really loved her. But he never told her that."

Warren shook his head. "I don't understand why he's so shook up over her death if he didn't love her."

Sabrina knew that it would be impossible to convey to her father all that had gone on with Callie, but she had to try. "She saved his life," she said simply.

"How did she do that?"

"When LeBeau came back, he told us he was going to kill Waco. He meant it, too. You could see it in his eyes."

"What about the woman? What's her name?"

"Her name is Calandra Montevado, but everyone called her Callie."

"If she was in love with Waco, wouldn't LeBeau have known it?"

"I think he knew, and it gave him one more reason for killing Waco. I think he planned all the time to kill him."

"But how did she die, Sabrina?"

"When Waco rode up, LeBeau stayed inside, but he had his gun out. We all saw he meant to shoot him down. Callie ran outside, and she was calling out, 'LeBeau's inside, Waco! He's going to kill you!' Then she got in front of Waco, and when LeBeau fired, his bullet hit Callie in the back. Waco caught her, and when LeBeau ran out the door firing, Waco got off one shot, but it killed LeBeau."

Warren turned to stare at the big man holding the dead woman. "So she saved his life and lost her own doing it. She must have loved him greatly."

"Yes, I think she did." Sabrina nodded. "I ran out to where she was lying in Waco's arms, dying, and I heard her say, 'We'll never make that trip now, will we?'"

"Which trip did she mean?"

"She had begged Waco to run away with her. She said she was tired of the life she's been living."

"I see. So that is what's bothering him."

"Yes. He promised her they'd have a life together, but he never meant to do it. And that's why he's sitting there in the dirt holding her. He knows he can never make it up to her."

"Maybe he'll get over it. Most men do."

"I don't know, Dad. He's a rough man, but he feels things more deeply than you can guess. He may not be able to put her death behind him." She turned her face away from him, but not before he saw the stricken look on her face.

※

"I can't tell you how I feel, Marianne," Frank said. He had come to stand beside her while Warren spoke to Sabrina. "I don't think I've had a full night's sleep since you were kidnapped."

"I wasn't kidnapped, Frank," Marianne said in a spare tone, devoid of feeling. "I ran away with an evil man, and all the time all of you were telling me how foolish I was."

Morgan shook his head. "You were inexperienced, Marianne, and thought you were in love. We all behave foolishly over love." He waited for her to speak, but she said nothing. It was this silence that troubled him, that and the deadness he seemed to see in her eyes. He desperately wanted to take the pain away from her, but he was wise enough to know that only time and true, godly love would make a difference to this woman he loved so greatly. He looked toward Waco, wondering at how he held to the dead woman, and then he noticed how Sabrina was standing a few feet away, her eyes fixed on him. "Sabrina looks terrible," he said. "Why do you suppose that is? She didn't know that woman all that well, did she?"

"She's not grieving for Callie," Marianne said. "She sees what's happening to Waco."

"What do you mean?"

"She's fallen in love with Waco."

"No! That can't be so."

"Why not? He's a strong man."

"But they're not alike, Marianne, not in the least."

"I think they may be more alike than you think. She had no

use for him when they first met, but they went through some hard times, and that changed Sabrina."

"They come from different worlds," Morgan said, shaking his head. "And it looks to me like he cares for that woman. Look how he's holding her."

"She died for him, Frank," Marianne whispered. "When someone dies for you, I don't think you can ever walk away from that unscathed."

"It's all over, Marianne."

"No, it will never be over."

Frank said, "Time will help," but she looked at him with tears in her eyes. He said softly, "You've got a whole life ahead of you, Marianne, and I intend to be in it."

❧

Waco had once been struck a violent blow in the stomach that had taken away his breath and rendered him unable to speak or move. Now as he sat holding the dear body of Callie, he was unable to think or to speak. He was aware of people moving and speaking, but none of it made any sense to him. All he could do was try to think of how he had failed Callie, and a sense of deep hopelessness cloaked him, profound and frightening.

He heard his name spoken and looked up to see Heck Thomas standing over him. "What did you say, Heck?" he asked, his voice thready and uncertain.

"We've got to get back to the train, Waco." Heck squatted on his heels and stared into Waco's eyes. "It's time to get away from here."

Waco turned his head and saw that they had tied LeBeau's body facedown on his horse. "You're not tying Callie on a horse like that," he said flatly.

Heck said softly, "We've got to get her into town, son."

"Not like that."

Waco glanced across at Sabrina, who had come to stand and watch. She stooped down and asked, "What do you want us to do, Waco?"

Her words seemed to confuse Waco, but then he said almost roughly, "Bring me my horse, Sabrina."

At once Sabrina rose and walked quickly to the line of horses that were tied to a rail in front of the cabin. Quickly she loosed Captain's reins and led him back to where Waco held the dead woman.

Waco looked for a long moment at Callie's still face then carefully laid her down. He rose and stepped into the saddle, then said, "Hand her up to me, Heck."

At once Heck bent and picked up the limp body of Callie and lifted her up. Waco took the body and placed her in front of him, and with his left arm, he held her close to his chest. He touched Captain with his heels, and the big stallion moved forward at a slow place. Waco did not look back nor did he speak.

◈

As Waco rode away, Sabrina said, "Marshal, I know I should be rejoicing. My sister and I are both safe and LeBeau and his outlaws are gone—but I feel like crying."

Heck turned and said softly, "Know what you mean, Miss Sabrina. I never saw a man take anything so hard. It's like that bullet that killed that woman hit him right in the heart. I just don't understand it. Waco is a pretty tough man, but this has brought him down. He must have loved her a lot."

"No, he didn't love her," Sabrina whispered. She watched as Captain bore his burden out of the tree line then added, "He didn't love her enough." *He'll never forget her,* she thought, *not after this.*

She turned quickly and went back to stand beside her family. They seemed mystified by what had happened, but no one questioned her.

"Well, we've got to get the bodies and the prisoners back to Fort Smith." Heck walked to his horse, mounted, and moved forward slowly. The others all got into the saddle, and as they left the clearing, both Sabrina and Marianne turned and gave the cabin a last glance. Sabrina knew that this day would not be easily forgotten—if ever.

As the procession reached the train, Heck waited until Waco halted. Then when the big man simply sat there silently holding the limp form of Callie, he knew what he must do. He dismounted and said, "I'll be right back, Waco."

Heck moved quickly to the car that ordinarily would have carried mail and gold. He stepped inside and found three of his men sitting around laughing. Heck said roughly, "You fellows clear out." His words were sharp, and the three left without waiting for any other word.

Heck had remembered that the car held a cot for the use of the mail clerk who traveled for the railroad. He found a clean blanket, laid it carefully over the cot, then moved to the sliding door and opened it. He saw Waco still holding the woman and called, "You can put her in here, son."

He saw Waco move his shoulders and give him a strange look.

"Hand her up to me," Heck said, and at this word, Waco spoke to the big stallion, who came to stand at the sliding door. "I can take her," Heck said, and for a moment he thought that Waco would refuse, but then he nodded and lifted the lifeless woman. Heck took her and said, "Come on in, and I'll put your horse in the cattle car with the other mounts."

"All right, Heck." Waco simply stood up in the stirrups, then with an agile move rose and, catching the side of the opening, lifted himself into the car.

"You can put her on that cot," Heck said. When Waco lifted his arms and took the woman, he said, "I'll take care of your horse, and then we'll be on our way."

"Thanks, Heck," Waco said woodenly.

Heck left the car and shut the door. Taking Captain's reins, he walked down the track and loaded the big stallion into the cattle car.

As soon as he closed the door, Sabrina came to ask, "Where did you put her, Marshal?"

"The railroad furnishes a cot for the man who handles the mail. I expect Waco will put her on there."

"Did he say anything?"

"Not much. Reckon I'll go back and see if everything is all right."

He moved back, mounted the steps, and entered the mail car. He saw at once that Waco had laid the body of Callie on the cot, had folded her hands over her breast, and was smoothing her hair.

"This okay, Waco?"

"Sure." Waco finished arranging Callie's hair, then turned suddenly and asked, "Did you ever do a friend a bad turn, Heck?"

Heck Thomas was caught off guard but nodded slowly. "I'm grieved to say that I let my partner down. Ain't ever been about to put it out of my mind, and that was over twenty years ago."

"What happened?"

"I was in the Texas Rangers then, and my partner was Sollie Bacus. We got jumped by a Kiowa war party. We lit out, but Sollie caught an arrow in his back. He hollered at me to keep going, said he was a goner."

Heck fell silent then said, "The Kiowas swarmed all over him. I was about to stop and help, but he called out, 'Get out of here, Heck!' " A sad expression came into Heck's face, and he said, "I should have gone to him, Waco. I know the hostiles would have gotten both of us, but I've grieved over what I done for twenty years."

Both men were silent, lost in a deep sadness, and finally Heck said, "No going back, Waco. We both of us got regrets, but all we can do is go on livin' and make sure we never let anybody else down."

Waco sat beside the body of Callie. Heck came and sat beside him and tried to make him feel better, but Waco would not be comforted.

Finally Heck said, "Well son, one person in this world loved you enough to die for you. That's one more than most folks have."

෨

As soon as the train pulled to a stop at the station in Fort Smith, Charles Warren stepped down and gave Sabrina and Marianne a helping hand. Caroline had been waiting and rushed forward to embrace both her daughters. She was weeping for joy and could not speak.

Heck saw Judge Parker standing to watch the train and went at once to him. "Well, Judge, we got the whole bunch. All but two of them are dead."

"What about LeBeau?"

"Dead as a hammer."

"Who got him, Heck?"

"Well, it's a right sad story, Judge." He told Parker the story of how the woman Callie had taken a bullet for Waco and how Waco had killed him.

"I'm sorry it didn't work out for Waco, but LeBeau was the kingpin. I'd say we owe Waco Smith something. I hope he'll join up with us."

Heck shook his head, saying, "Doubt that will happen, Judge. The bullet that killed the woman—it was like Waco took a bullet right in his heart but didn't die."

"He'll have to get over it."

"I ain't sure he can ever do that."

❧

Judge Parker stood before Waco. "I'm sorry for all this Waco, but let me say we have a place for you on the force."

"Judge, I'm through with all this."

Parker nodded and said, "Let me take care of your friend."

"No, I have to do it all, Judge. Who takes care of things like this?"

"I thought so. You need Caleb Felton. His place is right across from the courthouse. He's a good man, and he'll take good care of your friend."

Waco picked up Callie's body and carried her down the street. He was aware that people were watching but could only think of the loss her death had caused him.

He was met at the door by a tall man with dark blue eyes who said, "I'm Caleb Felton. I heard about your loss."

"My name is Smith. This is Calandra Montevado. Do your best for her."

"I'll do my best for the lady. Bring her this way."

Waco followed Felton down a hall and placed her body on a padded table. He took one look at Callie then walked rapidly away.

CHAPTER 24

"Marianne, I've got to talk to you."

The sound of Frank Morgan's voice had caught Marianne off guard. She had been overwhelmed by the almost hysterical happiness of her mother, and her father seemed unwilling to let her out of his sight. She knew they had been terribly hurt by what had happened to her.

She had been standing in the twilight of the afternoon watching the sun drop beneath the horizon. It made a golden glow, but her emotions were anything but cheerful. Over and over again she went over how foolish she had been to ignore her parents' advice about LeBeau, and then following that was the utter misery thinking how he had used her and abused her. She turned quickly and said, "I can't talk to you now, Frank."

Morgan moved closer and saw that tears stained her cheeks. "I know you're all upset," he said, "but I've got some things I need to say to you."

"Not now, Frank, please!"

Morgan almost turned and walked away, but he set his jaw

and shook his head. "I know it's not a good time, but probably it will never be a good time, or at least a better time than right now." He reached out tentatively, for she had turned away. He turned her around until she was looking up at him.

She studied him with an odd intensity, and then her lips began to tremble and she knew that there was nothing he or anyone else could do to change what had happened.

"We're going to have to talk about this, Marianne." His voice was gentle, and suddenly she began to sob. Reaching out, Morgan pulled her in and held her. She put her head against his shoulder and for a long time could do nothing but give great gasping sobs. Slowly she began to grow calm, and Frank waited until she was. Taking out his handkerchief, he wiped the tears from her face and said, "I know it's going to take some time, Marianne. What happened to you was terrible, but it's over now."

"No, it will never be over." Her voice was tense, and she looked up at him and whispered, "No man could ever forget what's happened to me."

"Don't be foolish. A good man wouldn't think twice about that. It's not your fault, Marianne. It was against your will."

"Doesn't matter."

"It matters to me. You know I've cared for you a long time, and when you were in such trouble, my love seemed to grow. What I want us to do, Marianne, just as quickly as you can do it, both of us together, we'll shut the door on this. I want you to marry me. I know it's too early to talk of that, but we'll spend time together. We'll be going home soon. I'll go back to work, and you'll live in your house. We'll begin doing things together. We'll take rides in the park. We'll go to the zoo. We'll read books together, and all the time God will be giving us both peace."

"You think that could happen, Frank?" Marianne's tone was wistful, and she felt like a small child as she stood in the encirclement of his arms.

"Of course it can, and it's going to."

Sighing suddenly, she put her cheek against his chest and savored for a brief moment the strength she felt there. "I'll never forget how you came to fight for me, Frank. That was something I didn't expect."

"Well, I'm hoping you'll see a lot of things in me you didn't expect."

The two stood there until the sun suddenly dropped and they were standing in the shadows.

As the sunlight faded, Marianne felt another light begin to dispel some of the darkness in her heart.

❧

Judge Parker looked over at Heck Thomas, who was sitting in his chair tilted back against the wall. "Waco is still acting like he's a dead man."

Heck shrugged his shoulders. "I did some askin' around. Found out a few things. He and that woman had quite an affair goin' a few years ago. Sweethearts, you know. The way I get it, he was gonna use her to make his getaway, and then when she got killed, well. . ."

"You're right about that. He stays in the saloon all night and hides out in the daytime where nobody can get at him. I've tried to talk to him, but he just won't listen."

"Well, he's too good a man to waste. I never thought we'd bust up LeBeau's bunch, but he did the job. As you know, I wanted him to become a marshal, but he declined my offer." Parker sighed.

"He just seems so lost."

"Well, that's what a woman can do to a man. When I was talkin' to Miss Sabrina, though, somethin' came out. I could tell she feels somethin' for Waco."

Parker looked up with surprise. "Why, she's rich and comes from a fine family. Waco hasn't got anything but the clothes he's standing in."

"I don't think that's the whole story. I'll keep an eye on him, Judge."

"You do that. He's too good a man to waste."

"Sabrina, I need to talk to you."

Turning quickly, Sabrina gave her father a quick look and saw that he was in deep thought. She had learned to read him fairly well and saw that he was troubled. "What is it, Dad?"

"Something I have to ask you about."

Sabrina sighed. "I'm tired of talking about it. I thank God He got us out of that by His grace. Just a miracle that Waco wasn't killed, and I think LeBeau pretty well decided to kill me and Marianne, too. He just kept us alive to trap Waco."

"Sit down a minute and let's talk." They were on the front porch of the hotel, and the walkway was empty. It was midday, and the sun was beating down on Fort Smith, bringing with it the intolerable heat.

Sabrina shrugged but followed his request and sat down in one of the rockers.

He pulled his chair around to where he could see her face and said, "I've got to know something, daughter."

"What's that, Dad?"

"Well, you can tell me if it's none of my business. I'm used to that. But I've had some long thoughts since all this happened with Marianne and then almost losing you. It shook me up some."

"You never were much shaken by anything," Sabrina remarked. She studied her father's face and saw that there were lines that she had never noticed before. "What is it that's bothering you?"

"Well, I may be all wrong," Charles Warren said slowly and rather reluctantly. "But I've got the feeling that you feel something for this man Smith. Your mother feels the same way. Now, I don't know about a father poking into his children's private lives, but this thing has made me love my family more. I don't want to miss any signs. What do you think of this man?"

Sabrina dropped her head and was silent for a while. When she looked up, Charles Warren saw that her face was tense. "It's hard to say. He's not what I thought he was."

"What do you mean by that?"

"Well, he was in prison, and to tell the truth I was a real snob. I just used him, but we were together alone quite a bit, and I got to know him. He's had a terrible life. Betrayed by his best friend and a woman that he loved. He's never gotten over it."

"That can cut a man pretty bad."

"Well, it almost destroyed him. He just gave up and became an outlaw. But he's got more to him than that. I know he has."

"So you love the man?"

"I—I feel something for him."

"What about him? Does he care for you?"

"It's hard to say. I think he does, but since Callie died, he's been sunk in some sort of deep depression. He drinks all the time, and from what I hear that's not like him."

"Well, I can kind of understand that. She took a bullet for

him. From what you told me, it would have killed him if she hadn't jumped to save him."

"I know. He's very bitter, and I don't know anything to bring him out of it."

"Well, we've got the woman's funeral to go to."

"Are you going?"

"Yes, we'll all go. She wasn't a good woman, but she did a good thing there at the last, and I want to honor her for it."

Waco did not want to attend the funeral of Callie. More than anything else he longed to just get on his horse and ride away and try to put all the thoughts of her and everything else about this sorry affair behind him. He knew, however, that he would be a long time, maybe forever, trying to forget her.

Pastor Mordecai Jones read a long list of scriptures, but they meant little to Waco. Finally he heard the pastor say, "One thing I may conclude my remarks with. Most of us live for ourselves. We take care of ourselves, we're worried about our problems, and very rarely do we find a human being who steps outside of that pattern." Jones hesitated for a moment then said, "But this woman, who had struggled with a hard life, at the last moment gave the gift, the greatest gift. The Bible says that Jesus came to die for the sins of all of us, and we are eternally grateful for that. Now every time I think of this woman, I will have the thought she had her problems but at the end she gave the most precious thing she had, her life, for her friend."

At these words Waco bowed his head and closed his eyes. He wanted to get up and leave but could not. He stayed until the service was over and then followed the funeral procession. When they reached the cemetery, they surrounded the open grave. The pastor read a few scriptures and then dismissed.

Finally Waco turned and stumbled away. He heard Sabrina calling him, but he did not hesitate.

Sabrina followed him, saying, "I have to talk to you, Waco."

Waco stopped, turned, and saw that the crowd was dispersing. "I've got to get away from here." He turned back and began walking.

"Then I'll go with you."

Waco gritted his teeth and said harshly, "Go away and leave me alone!"

"I can't do that."

Finally they reached the edge of town. There were few people stirring that afternoon.

Sabrina said, "Waco, I know you're sad and grieved over Callie's death, and you should be. It was the bravest thing I ever saw anybody ever do. She loved you very much indeed."

"Don't say that!"

Sabrina's eyes opened with surprise. "Why shouldn't I? It's true enough."

"Don't you understand, Sabrina? I was using her. I let her think I loved her. That after the robbery she and I would run away together. I knew all the time that was a lie. I'd give anything if I could do it all over again."

Sabrina knew she was standing on precarious ground. She said quietly after a long pause, "You were trying to do a good thing in the best way you could. Think about what it means to my family, especially to Marianne. I think she'll marry Frank and they'll have a family. That never would have happened if it hadn't been for you. I think LeBeau would have killed me. I saw it in his eyes, and it didn't happen because you were there."

Waco stood with his head bowed, listening as Sabrina spoke on. Finally he said, "I can't live with this thing."

"You can have a good life, Waco."

"How can I live a good life? God can't use me."

"God doesn't need to use any of us. You know what the Bible says God wants of us?"

"I guess to work hard for Him."

"He doesn't need anybody to work for Him. He's almighty. He can do what He pleases. But there's one thing we can give Him, and I'm just now finding out what it is."

Waco lifted his head and saw that there was a tremendously sober look on her features. "What's that?"

"God created us to do one thing. To worship Him. To love Him. If we do that, we've satisfied Him. Anything we could do for Him, that's fine, but to love God, that's what Jesus said. 'Thou shall love the Lord thy God with all thy heart, with all thy soul, and with all thy might.' That's what I'm going to try to do for the rest of my life—and I would like it very much if you would do the same thing."

Waco did not answer. He heaved a deep sigh and said, "I'm not sure I could do a thing like that."

"I would like to see you try, and I'll help you all I can. You've made so many friends here. Judge Parker and Heck and my family. We all care for you. But we don't care for you as much as God cares for you."

Waco stood stock still, and he whispered, "I just don't know, Sabrina. Let me alone." He turned and walked quickly away and was relieved when she did not follow him. He walked to the stable and was surprised to see Gray Wolf standing in the shadows.

"Hello, Gray Wolf."

He said in his direct manner, "God's giving you another chance. If that woman hadn't got in the way, you would have been dead, and you wouldn't have any way to make it right with God. But she bought you some time. Now act like it. Don't act like a fool."

Waco felt a flash of anger, but then it passed. He shook his head slightly. "I'm not worth saving."

"Yes, you are as much as any of us. Climb out of that whiskey bottle and act like a man."

Gray Wolf suddenly faded back in the shadows, and Waco stood there silently, thinking of Sabrina's words and then of Gray Wolf's warning. He got his horse and went for a long ride, but he could not ride far enough to avoid the thoughts that came to him. He thought of Callie's face as she lay dying in his arms, and it was a razor cutting him to pieces on the inside.

Finally, when darkness came, he went back and for a moment thought of going to talk to Sabrina. But instead he turned and walked into the Lone Eagle Saloon. He began to drink and knew that he was a lost cause.

Time passed, and he knew he was so drunk he could barely walk. Suddenly he felt something on his side. He turned to see that Heck Thomas had pulled his gun loose. "Don't take my gun, Heck."

"Come along with me. You're under arrest."

Waco had trouble speaking his tongue was so thick. "For what?"

"For being a fool. Now come on." Heck hauled Waco out of the saloon, and Waco could barely walk. When he got to the jail, he hardly knew it when Heck shoved him into a cell and down onto a cot. "Stay there for a while."

Waco wanted to protest, but he was so drunk he fell into a stupor.

"Well, are you sober enough for me to turn you loose?"

Waco looked up, and his head was throbbing. "Let me out of this place."

"I'll let you out, but first you've got to talk to a man."

"What man?"

Thomas did not answer. He led Waco out of the cell and took him to a small office.

Waco saw that Charles Warren was sitting there. "Hello, Waco," Warren said. "Sit down. I've got to talk to you."

"You can pick up your gun when you leave, Waco," Heck said. "You listen to this man. He's got sense."

Charles Warren said nothing but watched as Waco sat down in a chair. Waco's hands were trembling, and Warren said, "I know you feel awful. Hangovers are no fun."

"No, they're not. What do you want to talk about?"

"What are you going to do with yourself, Smith?"

"I got no idea."

"Are you going to become one of Judge Parker's marshals? He told me he'd be glad to have you."

"No, I'll never do that again. I've had enough of that sort of thing."

"Then you'll have to have a job."

"I can get a job somewhere takin' care of stock or on a ranch. I can handle cattle."

Warren fell silent, and Waco blinked. "What else do you want to talk about besides my future?"

"I want to find out how you feel about my daughter."

"Your daughter?"

"Yes. Sabrina. You remember her?"

"What do you mean how I feel about her?"

"I think she cares for you."

"Well, that's impossible. We're too different."

"Women choose men who are different sometimes. My wife did. I was no good when I met her, but she saw something in me. If it hadn't been for her, I'd be in the poorhouse or worse. I was no good for her. Maybe you're no good for my daughter, but I need to know how you feel about her."

"It doesn't matter," Waco said quietly. "She'd never care for me."

"I think she does."

Waco said, "You're a smart man, Mr. Warren, but you're wrong this time."

"You'll have to talk to her. If she cares for you, and you walk away from her, you'll hurt her terribly. I think she's been hurt enough, and I'm asking you to overlook some things in her. I know she's proud, she's spoiled, but she's got good stuff in her. She's a good woman."

"No question about that. The question is me."

"I guess I know more about men than most, and I see something in you that needs to come out."

Waco laughed. "I don't know what that would be."

"You talk to her, and you two decide which way you're going. If you decide to tell her you love her and you'll share each other the rest of your life and she tells you the same thing, we'll talk some more."

"I'll talk to her, but it seems a waste to me." Waco got up and left the room. He picked up his gun, strapped it on, and looked at it with disgust. "I hope I never have to shoot you again," he said.

He made his way toward the hotel where he knew the Warrens were staying. When he walked up on the porch, he saw that Sabrina was sitting there.

"Did you talk to Dad?"

Surprised, Waco said, "Yes, I did. How did you know?"

"Because I told him to talk to you. Sit down, Waco."

Waco sat down feeling as uncomfortable as he ever had in his life. "Your dad's got some funny ideas."

"Funny like what?"

"He thinks—" Waco could barely say the words. "He thinks we're in love."

"What's funny about that?"

Waco suddenly grinned. He felt miserable, but this woman always had something to throw at him when he wasn't ready. "Nothing much except you're rich, from a fine family, and used to good things. I'm nothing but a bum, never done anything really good in my life. Why shouldn't we fall in love?"

Sabrina suddenly rose and said, "Stand up."

Waco stood up at once and stood to face her.

She suddenly reached up, put her arms around his neck, pulled his head down, and kissed him.

Waco felt something turn over in him. He knew that he had had some feeling for this woman, but the tragedy of Callie had driven it all away. When she released him, he looked down at her and said, "I guess I'll have to tell you, Sabrina, I love you. Never thought I'd say that."

"Well, I love you, too, Waco. I know we're different. I know there's going to be hard times. I'm a spoiled brat, and some of that's still in me, but I ask you to help me to become a godly woman and a good wife."

"Well, who's going to help me?"

"Everybody. My father will help you and my mother. Marianne, too. She worships you almost. You know you saved her from death. And I care for you, too. I love you, Waco."

Suddenly Waco Smith found himself unable to speak. "One thing, Sabrina. . .I've been thinking about God for some time now. I don't know how to go about it, but I'm going to become a servant of the Lord."

"Waco, I'm so glad. Come on. Let's go tell my family that we're engaged."

"Why, we can't just bust in and tell them that."

"I can. Come along."

The two walked into the hotel. "I saw Father come in a minute ago. He'll be with Mother." Sabrina smiled. "They'll be waiting on a report of our matrimonial expectations."

"It'll be mighty poor doings if we get married. No honeymoon."

"As long as we have each other, Waco, that's all I ask."

The two walked upstairs and paused in front of a door. Sabrina knocked on the door, and Charles Warren's voice said, "Come in, daughter. Bring him with you."

As soon as they stepped inside, Waco felt that he was trapped. He saw the whole family was there, including Marianne and Frank Morgan.

"Well, what's the status? Did he say he loved you, daughter?"

"He said so."

"And Sabrina, do you love him?" her mother asked anxiously.

"Yes, I do."

"Oh, that's wonderful!" Marianne said. She was standing

beside Frank Morgan, and her eyes now glowed. "You saved my life, Waco, and I'll never forget it."

"Neither one of us will. This is good news," Frank added.

"Not very good news," Waco said. "I never heard of a more unlikely pair. I don't even have a job."

Charles said, "You sure this is what you want to do? You love my daughter?"

"Yes, I do, Mr. Warren. That's the one thing that's sure."

"Well, let me tell you something. I've been investing in fine horses for a couple of years. I bought some land and hired three louts to take care of the horses. They don't know one end of a horse from the other. You think you got sense enough to make it pay?"

Waco laughed. "It's the only thing I did growing up, take care of horses. It's the only thing I'm good at."

Mrs. Warren came over and put her hand on Waco's cheek. "Do you *really* love Sabrina?"

"Yes, I do, Mrs. Warren, with all my heart. She'll never know anything but love from me."

"Well, I'll have to have a little bit more than that," Sabrina said loudly.

Waco's eyes opened wide. "What do you mean?"

"We're going back to our home. You're going to show us you know something about horses, and you've got to come courting me. You've got to buy some nice clothes and learn how to say sweet and lovely things. Say something sweet to me now just to get into practice."

Waco suddenly laughed. He winked at Charles Warren and said, "Marshmallow."

Sabrina laughed. "Well, that's sweeter than anything you've

ever said. Come on, let's go have our engagement party."

"Judge Parker will be sad," Warren said. "He's losing a marshal."

"Yes, but you're gaining a good son-in-law," Sabrina said. She took Waco's arm and said, "Come on, husband-to-be, let's start our courting."

RAINA'S CHOICE

PART ONE

PART ONE

CHAPTER 1

November 1891

The room was nothing but four walls with no windows. The eight bunks lined up against the edges were filled with six Mexicans and two Americans. It was one of ten small prison cells that were blazing hot under the sun in the summer and freezing when the weather turned bad as it had now.

Ty Kincaid tossed restlessly and came out of a fitful sleep at the sound of the guards, who were playing poker and shouting and cursing each other. They usually got drunk during the night when they were off duty. Ty tried to block the noise out of his mind, but he could not. He had no idea what the time was, for without windows in the prison hut there was no way of telling. There was only one door, made of solid oak, with three bars across a small window.

One of the prisoners began to curse under his breath. Not loudly because none of the prisoners wanted to call attention to themselves.

With an effort Ty rolled over and lay on his side. He was taken with a coughing fit as he did, and pain like ice picks going through his chest struck him. He finally gained control.

His cell mate, Jim Adams, whispered, "Are you okay?"

"I'm all right," Kincaid muttered. This was not true, for he was ill and had been for several days. It had begun with a runny nose and a mild but persistent cough, but each day's toil in the bowels of the earth working in a copper mine in the unseasonably cold weather had taken its toll on him.

"You sound terrible," Jim said. "There ought to be a hospital or a doctor for you to go to."

Kincaid did not answer, for both men were well aware that the Mexican prison system paid little attention to the ailments of convicts. Many of them were allowed to die when a little medicine or a doctor's care might have saved them. When they did die, they were simply thrown into a hole and covered with lime. Ty had seen this happen more than once in the three months he had been in the prison.

"I don't think I'm going to make it, Jim." Kincaid's voice was feeble and scratchy. He rolled over on his back, threw his forearm over his eyes, and tried to control the coughing that was constantly tearing him to pieces.

"You'll be all right. We're going to get out of here."

"No, we never will."

"Don't talk like that. It's pretty grim right now, but we're gonna make it."

"I don't know what makes you say that."

"The Lord will get us out of this."

"I'm glad you believe that, Jim, but I don't." Kincaid again began coughing, and even as he did a whistle split the dawn air.

Then there was a rattling at the door, which opened a crack, and a raucous voice shouted, "Get up! Get up! Get your scrawny rear ends out of those bunks!"

Using all his strength, Ty managed to sit up, then paused, hanging on to the edge of his bunk. The mattress was made of coarse feed sacks. The straw had not been changed in weeks, and the stench of urine and rotting food was enough to make a well man sick. He tried to stand. Suddenly Ty was so weak he couldn't do it.

Adams, who had the bunk next to his, said, "Get up quick, Ty. You don't want the Pig on your case."

Ty again struggled to rise.

The door swung open, and a big man filled the opening. In the growing dawn Bartolo Azner stepped inside. He made a huge, ominous shadow and was called "the Pig" by the convicts. Not to his face, of course. "What are you doing on that bunk?"

"I'm sick," Ty whispered and coughed scratchily.

The Pig laughed. "You're not on a vacation. Get up!" He suddenly swung the short billy club made out of hard oak and caught Ty across the chest.

It knocked him back onto the bed, and he struck the back of his head on the wooden wall. The blow sent a myriad of sparkling colors like fireworks through his head and before his eyes.

"Get up, I told you!"

Ty felt the huge paws of the Pig grab him and drag him out of the bunk. He fell on the floor and received a kick in the back.

Ty was stunned and had no strength as Azner reached down, jerked him up, and held him upright as if he were a child. "You gringo dog! You come to my country and try to destroy my government!

You'll stay here until you rot! Why don't you die?"

Ty was shoved toward the door then fell against Jim Adams, who caught him and held him upright. The two men joined the other convicts who trooped out into the frigid night air. All of them wore simple cotton garments. The biting air of winter was like a knife cutting through Ty's chest.

"Get going, you dogs!" the Pig shouted.

The men joined the prisoners from the other prison huts and headed toward a larger building.

Tyler Kincaid hardly knew whether he was awake or unconscious. There was a murky light in the east, but as he stumbled into the mess hall—so it was called—he had to be held upright by Adams, who took him firmly by the arm.

Adams was a big man and had lost weight as had all the prisoners, but still he was not sick and he was stronger than Ty. He eased Ty down onto one of the benches, and then he joined him. "Hang on there," he whispered. "Maybe we'll get a hot breakfast this morning."

Ty was too sick to answer. He just sat there trembling. Finally when one of the prisoners who served with the cook came by and put a bowl in front of him, Ty opened his eyes and saw that it was a bowl of thin rice gruel with beans floating around the top. It was the typical breakfast and would have to do them through a hard morning's work. . .until the same dish would be served at noon, and then again, when it got too dark to work, it would provide the evening meal.

"Eat up, Ty," Adams whispered. "It's rotten, but we've got to get as strong as we can. Need to keep your strength up."

"What for, Jim?" Ty took a spoonful of the rank mixture,

chewed, and managed to swallow it. The taste was atrocious, and he had to overcome a sudden urge to throw up. "We're gonna die in this place anyhow. Why don't we go on and do it?"

Adams leaned over. He had piercing, dark black eyes, and his hair was as black as the darkest thing in nature. He was basically an Irishman through his mother and had been strong as a bull before he was captured along with Ty. "We're gonna get out of here."

"I don't know what makes you think that. Nobody ever does."

"God's going to help us."

"I already told you I don't believe that."

"You need to believe it, Ty. God's our only hope in a place like this."

Ty ate slowly, but other men were scraping the bottoms of their bowls when he was only half through. He washed the rest of it down with tepid water that had a terrible taste and then said, "I didn't know you were such a fervent Christian until we got in this mess, Jim."

"Well, I was going with a woman, and she talked me into going to a revival meeting with her in Arkansas. I went and got saved." He reached over and punched Ty lightly on the arm. "Of course, I ain't always lived like I should since then. I let the Lord down several times, but I know I'm saved. That's what you need, Ty."

"Too late for me."

"Don't be foolish."

"It's not foolish. Why would God be interested in a reprobate like me? I've broken every one of the Commandments a hundred times."

Adams had been through this many times with Tyler Kincaid,

and he never seemed to tire of it. "Well, I did, too, but the Bible says God forgives us when we do what He says."

"You mean get baptized?"

"No, I don't mean that. Getting baptized never saved nobody. It's what you do before."

"I don't believe that anymore. I had some faith at one time, but it's gone now," Ty muttered.

The Pig hollered, "All right, on your feet, you dogs!"

As Ty rose, he grew dizzy.

Jim once again had to grab him to keep him from falling. "When we get in the mine you kind of get over behind me. Those guards don't pay no attention to who's doing the work."

"I can't let you do that, Jim."

"You can if I say so. Now come on."

The two walked outside, and it was all that Kincaid could do to walk the quarter of a mile to the mountain and the hole that enclosed a set of miniature tracks. On the tracks ran small carts that the prisoners filled with the rock after they'd broken it with picks.

Ty went in, and as soon as they were put into place, he reached for a pick.

They were in a side tunnel, and Jim whispered, "You just get there and move every once in a while. They don't pay any attention to us."

"I feel bad," Ty whispered, "letting you do all this because I don't do anything for you."

"Well, when we get out of this, you can buy me a good supper to pay for it."

Ty knew Jim was trying to be lighthearted, but the copper

mine had become his version of what hell must be like. True, it was somewhat warmer in there at this time of the year than outside. In the summer it was a welcome coolness. But now the freezing weather that swept over northern Mexico was phenomenal. No one could remember when it had been this cold. There had been snow in strange places, and in some areas it had even piled up to several feet, which was unheard of in this territory.

Ty tried to swing the pickax, but it was all he could do to bring it over his shoulder. It made a pinging noise as it hit the rocks on the side of the wall, but it made no imprint.

"I told you. You just stand there. That guard ain't looking at me. I get enough rock for both of us."

Ty wanted to argue, but he was too sick. The last thing he remembered was getting dizzy. He felt Jim lowering him, and he slumped against the rocky wall as unconsciousness pulled him down.

୭

Time had no meaning for Kincaid, but then he heard Jim whisper, "Come on, Ty. Time to go get something to eat."

Kincaid had to struggle to get up, and in the end it was Jim Adams who pulled him upright.

One of the prisoners stared at him by the light of the flickering lanterns. "He's going to die, Adams."

"You shut your mouth or *you'll* die."

The Mexican, a little man with a weasel face, shrugged. "He'll die no matter what you do to me. I've seen it before."

"Don't pay any attention to him, Ty."

"He's probably right."

Ty and Jim staggered out of the mine and went back toward the mess hall. There was somewhat more talking there as the prisoners whispered to each other.

The Pig wandered around ready to crack their heads if they showed any sort of resistance. He was a monster, and Ty Kincaid knew hatred for one of the few times in his life. The man loved to inflict pain, and he had killed more than one prisoner with that stick of his.

"Eat up, Ty," Jim urged.

"I guess I'll have to." Ty began eating the same weak, watery stew, and this time there was a crust of hard bread to go with it. It was almost impossible to bite it, but Ty soaked it in the soup and softened it. Once again he was nauseated, but he knew that Adams was right. If he didn't eat, he would die.

They had only fifteen minutes to eat, and quickly the Pig yelled, "Get out of here! You're not on a vacation!"

The two Americans were the only white-skinned men in the prison. The two of them had been working for a Mexican railroad when they were arrested. Revolutions shook Mexico on a periodic basis. Neither Jim nor Ty had any feelings about Mexican revolutions, but they had been caught in the middle of one. They had been working on the railroad when the revolutionaries suddenly appeared yelling and screaming.

They killed most of the crew members, but they took the white men prisoners. Ty could never figure why. Jim had said they probably thought they could get a ransom for the two white men. But this had seemed unlikely to Ty, for no one had ever attempted such a thing as far as he knew.

They had worked on the train, teaching the revolutionaries

how to fire up the engine, but it was only a short time before the *federales*, the Mexican police, took over with a large troop of well-armed and fairly well-trained soldiers. They made short work of the revolutionaries and had taken Jim and Ty along with a few other prisoners to the copper mine. "You'll work in the mine until you die," the officer said. "This is what you get for interfering in my country's politics."

There was no answer for that, so the two men had been thrown into the brutal routine of working from dawn until dusk on such meager rations that over time they became almost like human skeletons.

The work went on, but Ty could not do it.

Bartolo Azner kicked him and then said, "Throw him in his bunk. Lock him in without food or water. He'll work or he'll die."

Adams and two of the other men picked Ty up, carried him to the hut, and laid him on his bunk. Adams leaned over and whispered, "You just stay here. I'll smuggle you some water back somehow."

Then Ty Kincaid was left alone. His lungs seemed bound with an iron band, and every time he coughed it felt like he was being stabbed. He coughed and gasped for some time before finally falling into a coma-like sleep.

"Wake up, Ty. I've got something for you."

Ty had been asleep for some time. He knew now that it was dark, for the prisoners were locked up in the hut. "I bribed a guard and got some food and a jug of water. Sit up and eat."

Ty struggled up, ignoring his desire to cough as it tore him in two. He ate slowly. "How'd you get this food, Jim?"

"Oh, I had a little money on me that they didn't find, so I bribed a guard. It ain't much, but it's better than nothin'."

"It's good. Thanks, Jim."

As he ate, Adams sat beside him. "You need to see a doctor."

"You know Mexican doctors and how they treat gringo prisoners."

"Yeah, that's right."

The two men were silent until Ty finished the food, which seemed better than the usual fare they received, although Ty realized this was probably just due to his state of hunger. He drank deeply of the tepid water and said, "You could have gotten in big trouble for this if the Pig had caught you."

"Ah, he's too stupid to catch anybody."

"He's caught two or three. You saw what happened to them."

Adams shook his head. There was at this time one feeble light, a candle that burned in the center of the room. The sanitary arrangements were two buckets, one at each end of the hut, and the smell was overpowering. "You feel pretty bad, don't you, Ty?"

"Pretty bad."

"I don't guess you've ever been in a mess like this."

"Not this bad. Have you?"

"No, I never have. What about people? Have you got a family?"

"I ran away from my home when I was just a young man, seventeen years old."

"Why'd you do that?"

"It's not a pretty story."

"I can't think you'd do anything real bad."

"Well, I did. I got a young woman pregnant. She was only

fifteen. When she found out she was going to have a baby, she told me, and I knew her people. The brothers were all mean as snakes. They would have killed me in a minute if they had found out, so I've been moving ever since."

"Well, that's not a very good story."

"No, it's not. I wondered a hundred times if she had that baby and what happened to her. I was nothing but a coward."

"You were just a kid. Don't worry. We'll get out of here. Maybe you and I'll go find him. Wouldn't it be somethin' if you found a young fellow who was your own flesh and blood?"

"I don't believe good things like that happen."

Adams leaned forward and studied Ty's face in the dim light of the flickering yellow candle.

Ty Kincaid knew he was a fairly good-looking man, but disease and ill treatment had stripped the excess flesh off of him so that his face must look almost skull-like.

Adams reached out and laid his hand on Ty's shoulder. "We're going to get out of this."

There was a silence in the room, and Adams looked around carefully before whispering, "I hadn't told you this, but we got some help outside of this prison."

"What kind of help?"

"I got a friend in the Mexican government. You may have seen him. He came when we were working on the road a few times. I did him a favor, and he always was grateful. When he came in to see me, he said he was going to help me get out."

"How is he going to do that?"

"Well, he tried to do it through the court to prove that we weren't the enemies of Mexico, but Mexican courts ain't known for their kindness and generosity to gringo prisoners."

"So that's out."

"That is, but you remember when I was gone for about an hour a couple of weeks ago?"

"Yes, you're the only one that's had a visitor."

"Well, some of the Mexicans have. But anyway this friend of mine came. He told me he hadn't given up. That he was still going to help."

"How can he do that?"

"He's going to get us two guns and some ammunition. Then all we have to do is knock our guard over the head when we get a chance, grab a couple of horses, and then cross the border."

"You think that guard will stay bribed? He could take the money and then tell the Pig what's going on."

"My friend says he can handle it. He won't give the man all the money until we're away."

"So you think we can shoot our way out of this?"

"I think we've got to do something, Ty. We're gonna die here sure enough. Not just you, but me, too." Jim Adams once again put his hand on Ty's thin shoulder. "God's going to get us out of this. He'll help us."

"You keep saying that, but nothing's happened."

"You remember that psalm I read to you that time? The psalm of David?"

"Yes, you read it more than once."

"Well, you may have forgotten. Your mind ain't too clear. But David had everything. He was the king of Israel. He had money. He had a good family. He had everything a king has, but Absalom, the son he loved most, rebelled against him and raised an army.

David had to run out of Jerusalem trying to keep his son from killing him."

"I remember you told me that."

"You may not remember this. David was in the worst shape of his life. He had lost everything. And then he said, 'I cried unto the Lord.' And then he said, 'The Lord comforted me and I lay down and slept.' Ain't that a wonderful thing that when a man has lost everything he can lie down and sleep!"

"You believe that, don't you, Jim?"

"I sure do, and you need to believe it, too."

"I just can't do it, Jim. Things look too bad right now."

"Just hang in there, Ty. We're gonna make it!"

❧

Two days later Ty woke up in the middle of the night. He knew that much because the door had swung open at least a crack. He saw Jim Adams outlined against the door.

Jim reached out and took something, then came back. The door shut, and the key turned in the lock, making a metallic sound. Jim came back down between the cots and whispered, "You awake, Ty?"

"Yes. What was that?"

Jim leaned closer, and his whisper was barely discernible. "We've got guns and ammunition."

"But the minute we use them, they'll shoot us down," Ty argued.

"No, they won't. Here's what we'll do. We'll do the day's work, and you know how it's always dark when we come out of there. The guards don't pay much attention to us. They can't imagine a prisoner staying in that mine, so we'll let everybody else leave, but we'll stay. As soon as the guards march the prisoners to the mess shack for supper, we'll take two horses."

"Where are you going to get horses?"

"I kept my eyes open when they brought us in here. There's a corral about three hundred yards from the mine. We'd have to go quiet, but there's no reason for anybody to be around at that time of night."

"What then?"

"We saddle us two horses, and we mount up and walk them out of here until we're out of hearing distance. Then we drive those horses straight for the American border."

"I don't know if I can make it, Jim. I'm just too sick right now."

"You'll make it if I have to throw you over that horse and tie you down," Jim said. He slapped Ty's shoulder. "Don't give up, buddy. God's going to help us!"

※

The guards yelled, "Come on. Get out of here! Leave those tools where they are."

"Stay here," Adams whispered to Ty.

Ty, who was almost past going, slumped against the wall. There had been a feeble lantern, but one of the prisoners leading the way took it out as he always did. Utter darkness seemed to fill the mine. Kincaid listened as the steps grew fainter. He and Adams then found their way out.

Adams said, "Come on. Here, take this."

Ty took the gun and held it in his hand. There was no place else to carry it.

"Don't drop it. I've got bullets in a sack tied around my neck. We're getting out of this place."

They crept through the darkness, and finally Ty heard the nickering of horses. "I can't help you, Jim. I'm as weak as a kitten."

"Some of these horses are pretty tame, and there are saddles here. You wait right here. If anybody comes, don't let them see you."

In the velvety blackness of the night, Ty sat down and heard the footsteps of Adams as he left. He had little hope and no faith at all that God would help him. He had listened to Jim's testimony many times, but it meant nothing to him.

Finally Jim came back leading two horses.

"I can't go, Jim," Ty whispered. "I'll just slow you down."

"We're both going. Get on this horse."

Ty got to his feet and with great effort lifted his foot into the stirrup. He swung into the saddle.

Jim said, "That's good. I'll go first. You just hang on to that horn, and I'll lead your horse."

"Go without me, Jim."

"We're both going."

The sound of the horses' hooves seemed very loud to Tyler Kincaid, but he knew that they were at least three hundred yards away from the house where the guards stayed.

Ty said, "Jim, if anything happens, I want you to know I never had a friend like you."

"You'd do it for me, Ty."

"I hope we never have the chance to find out about that."

They had gone no farther than the edge of the camp when suddenly two guards rode out. There was a bright full moon shining, and one of them called out, "*Hola!* Stop where you are!"

"We've got to run for it, Ty!" Jim turned his horse, and as the two guards rode full speed toward him, he aimed and fired.

The guards began firing, too, and although Ty could see little, he lifted his own gun and threw a few shots. The guards halted. One of them fell out of his saddle; the other turned and rode away.

"We've got to get out of here, Ty!"

"Let's go."

The two rode hard for some time, and then Jim said, "Gotta stop, Ty."

"What's the matter?"

"They got me." Jim suddenly swayed in the saddle then fell off. He hit the ground with a thud.

Ty's head was swimming. As weak as he was, he came off his horse at once. He was dizzy and sick, but he knelt beside Adams and said, "Where'd they get you?"

"In the back." The words were feeble.

Ty leaned down, and even in the darkness he could see the blood beginning to stain the prison garments that Adams wore. "We'll have to take you back to a doctor."

"No, I ain't going to make it, but I want you to." The words came slow.

Ty Kincaid leaned forward. "Don't die on me, Jim!"

"It's a good thing I went to that revival meeting and got saved." Adams coughed, and his voice began to fade. "I'll be with God, but you get out of here. Ty, make your life count."

Ty at once held him, but the life went out of the man. Tears ran down Ty's face. Finally he laid the body down gently, took the gun that was beside Adams, and went back, loosed the lines, and mounted his horse. "I'm too weak to bury you, Jim. I wish I could." He turned his horse's head, and his heart grew darker as he rode off into the gloom, knowing he would never forget Jim Adams.

CHAPTER 2

The steamy swamps of the southern coast of Louisiana put out an unseemly heat during the late summer. This pattern had been broken, however, for it was the middle of December, and a cold spell unlike anything the inhabitants had ever experienced had dropped down from the north. The populace of La Tete were fortunate that the worst of the winter storms were north of them, but they found themselves shivering. Men and woman alike put on heavy coats before going out to face the stiff winds and the dropping temperatures. The Cajun people, who were thickly settled in La Tete, fared no better than anyone else but kept fires burning in their huts in the swamp and in the larger towns to the north.

The feeble candle that Raina Vernay had lit barely enabled her to read the book she held. It cast a yellow flickering corona of light over the pages. Raina was so intent on the story that she hardly heard the door swing open, but she suddenly felt hands placed on her. She uttered a small cry of alarm and with a violent start came to her feet.

She saw her sister's husband, Millard Billaud. He was a big, brutal man with coarse features. As usual he was carelessly dressed.

Raina jerked away from him and moved to get away out the door, but he blocked the entrance. "Get out of my room, Millard!" Raina said loudly. "I told you never to come in here."

Millard was not alarmed by her anger. He smiled, and his thick lips had a brutal cast. His hatchet face was dark, and his flat black eyes gleamed. For all his size he was very quick, as Raina had learned to her sorrow, and she retreated until her back was pressed against the wall.

"Don't be so shy, Raina," Billaud said. "You've been up in this cold room long enough. You need to get downstairs where we got some fire."

"Next time you come into my room, knock on the door," Raina said, knowing her words would have no effect at all.

Suddenly his eyes glowed with anger, and ignoring her protests, he advanced and seized her by her shoulders.

Raina cried out as his mighty grip cut into her flesh like steel hooks.

"You never learn, do you, Raina?" Billaud said. He made no attempt to disguise the pleasure that her gasp of pain gave him. "If you had any sense at all, you'd know that I'm never going to let you get away from me."

Raina struggled mightily, but she was not a strong woman, certainly not one to match Billaud. "You're a yellow cur, Billaud," she said. She was unable to avoid the ringing slap that caught her on the cheek. She gasped, and her eyes watered with the pain. "You can hit me, but you can never have me."

"Oh yes, I'll have you. What's the matter with you anyhow? You ought to be happy that a man finds you attractive."

Raina kicked his leg, and he gave a grimace of pain and let out a sudden gasp. "Get out of my room! Or maybe you want me to scream to let Roxie know what's going on with you."

Billaud stared at her, studying her for a moment. His expression was a mixture of anger and admiration. He was accustomed to having his way with the lower class of women that frequented the saloon that his wife had inherited part ownership in, which he now owned. His eyes wandered over her and took obvious pleasure in her appearance.

Raina recoiled in revulsion. She knew she was considered attractive by many with her large eyes, which were her most prominent feature, well shaped and of a peculiar shade between green and blue. Her hair was jet black and fell in lush profusion over her shoulders. She had an olive complexion, which came from her Cajun mother. Although she was barely five feet five inches in height, her carriage was so erect she seemed taller. She wore a faded calico dress of some indeterminate brown color, but it did not conceal the full-bodied figure that was rather common in young Cajun women. Her curving lips and smooth oval face made a striking combination that had brought her the unwelcome attention of many men since she had been a teenager.

Billaud stared at her with a lustful look in his eyes and shook his head. "You didn't learn anything the last few days, did you?" He slapped his hands together and said, "You tried to run away, but you didn't make it and you never will."

Indeed, Raina had tried to run away. The saloon was the only world she knew. Her mother had owned it and willed it to her sister, Roxie, and herself. Roxie, a plain woman unlike Raina, had made a foolish marriage with Billaud. She had quickly learned that he cared nothing for her but was determined to own the Silver Dollar Saloon.

Frantic with fear, Raina had tried desperately to run away. She had risen in the middle of the night and taken what clothes she could carry and what little money she had saved. She had begun to walk north, but Billaud had been too careful for her. He had guessed her route and had sent James Farmer, the county sheriff, after her, promising him a reward if he brought her back. Farmer had indeed caught her, and Raina had pleaded with him. "Let me get away. He's going to have me," she said.

"I'm sorry, Raina," Farmer had said. He was not much of a sheriff but was a creature of Oscar Butler, who owned most of the land in this part of the world.

Standing before the huge form of Billaud, Raina thought of how she had walked through the cold and had a brief thrill as she thought she would get away, but then Farmer had caught her and brought her back. "I've done nothing," she cried. "He can't force me to stay."

Farmer shook his head. He had some of the aspects of a bloodhound. "I got a warrant signed by Oscar Butler. It says you're charged with grand theft."

"I didn't steal anything!"

"I expect you didn't, but that's the charge."

Farmer had brought her back, and now as Billaud stood looking at her, he read her thoughts. "If you run away again, I'll let them put you in a women's prison at El Paso. You'll like that even less than you like it here, and you'd come out an old woman.

Why don't you listen to reason? You don't want to waste all those good looks."

Raina could not think of anything to say. She knew she would never change Billaud's mind. He was a stubborn, willful man and a womanizer. He had ruined several young girls, and now it was her turn. "I'm not such a bad fellow," he said. "Try to like me. I'll make it nice."

"You're my brother-in-law. You're married to my sister. That's reason enough for you to stay away from me."

"That's not your problem. You're going to have to accept it, Raina. And Roxie knows better than to question anything I do," Billaud said carelessly. He took her by the shoulder, pulled her against him, and tried to kiss her, but she turned her face, and he merely touched her cheek.

"Just leave me alone!"

"I'll never do that. I've got to have you." He turned toward her, but she drew back, and he said, "I want you to go downstairs and wait on the customers tonight. Need a good-lookin' woman down there."

"I can't. I've got to cook."

"Roxie can do the cooking. You wear that dress I bought." He pointed to the one hanging on a peg on the wall. "You'll look nice in it. Hurry up now. The crowd's starting to come in."

A wave of relief came to Raina as Billaud left. She expelled her breath and felt so weak that she had to sit down on the side of the bed. Tears came to her eyes, and she helplessly began to weep.

She heard the door open, and her sister, Roxie, came in. Roxie had worn her life out serving, cooking, and making a saloon work. She stopped abruptly, and her dull brown eyes said, "Is he after you again?"

"You've got to help me, Roxie. He's going to get me."

"There's nothing I can do."

"He wants me to go entertain the customers. Last time he told me I had to sleep with one of them."

"You know how he is."

"He says you'll do the cooking, but you don't like it."

"I don't like anything about Billaud. I don't like anything about this place."

After her sister left, the words echoed in Raina's mind. *I don't like anything about this place.* She had grown up in the Silver Dollar Saloon, knowing no other world. Some of the Cajuns who came in were kind, but most were heavy drinkers, just the kind who would find their way into a saloon. When she was only fourteen, men had begun trying to put their hands on her, and Billaud had only laughed. Finally she had persuaded him to let her do the cooking, and for two years she had done that. Now he wanted more than that from her.

Slowly she got to her feet, knowing that there was no way out. Moving across the room, she picked the dress up, staring at it with dislike. She shook her head in disgust. "Just the kind of dress that man would buy." She slipped off her worn dress and put on the new one. It was low-cut and too tight. She stared at herself in the mirror and tried desperately to think of a way out. Perhaps the reading she had done about romances had given Raina a false idea of the world. Her own life was drab and painful, and she spent hours thinking how life could be different if she were somewhere else. But the Silver Dollar was her universe, and Billaud was her curse. Slowly she moved over to the chest with a small mirror on top and put on a trace of makeup. She did not need it, for her coloring was fine as it was. Her eyelashes were long and shaded her eyes. Taking off her old shoes, she put on a pair of patent slippers that Billaud had bought with the dress. They were too tight and hurt, but she had no choice but to wear them.

Leaving her room, she went downstairs and into the kitchen, which was at the back of the large room that served as a bar and a gambling establishment. She could already hear the noise of the men who had come to gamble and drink, and a grimace swept the pleasantness from her features. Going into the kitchen, she saw her sister cooking at the stove. "I want to stay and cook."

"Doesn't matter what you want or what I want. You know what he's like. If you tell him no, he'll just beat both of us."

"Why did you ever marry him, Roxie?"

"Because I was a fool." Roxie's eyes grew bitter, and her mouth twisted into a scowl. She had long ago given up on trying to look presentable. She usually wore a shapeless dress and kept her hair tied behind her back.

Roxie's own father had been a drifter whom their mother had simply taken up with, but she'd discarded him. When their mother married again, it was to an Irishman who was working on a railroad in the vicinity. He had been the man who had fathered Raina. She couldn't even remember him. No one cared about ancient history like that.

"He's going to try to get me to do evil things, Roxie."

"I can't help it. You know I can't."

Raina sighed and looked at the floor. "What was my father like?"

"After all this time you're asking that?"

"I can't remember him."

"No, I guess you can't. He left when you were just beginning to walk."

"What did he look like?"

"Well, he had red hair. But you didn't get that. You got Mother's black hair. He was not a big man, but what I remember most about him was he was crazy for God."

"I don't know what that means."

"It means all he could talk about was what God had done for him. Somehow he had gotten the idea that God had put special favor on him. Of course our mother didn't want to hear that, and she ran him off after a time."

"Do you know where he is?"

"No, I don't. What difference does it make?"

Raina stared at her sister and knew that there was no help to be had from her. *She's worn down. She's not going to be able to fight Billaud off. I wouldn't be surprised but what he'll kill her one of these days.* "We'll try to talk him into letting me cook and then you can rest."

A brief smile touched Roxie's face. "You're a good girl, Raina. I'm sorry I married such trash, but there's no way out of it."

That phrase entered into Raina's thoughts repeatedly. *"There's no way out of it."* As she passed into the saloon, the odor of alcohol, strong tobacco, and sweat struck her. She had always been sensitive to things, loving the scents of flowers and of a bottle of perfume that she had used sparingly.

A small white-haired man was banging away on a piano, and a woman in a scanty dress was trying to sing along with him. Both of them were half drunk, so the music was not exactly beautiful.

Raina made her way across the floor toward the bar.

The bartender, a heavyset man with muddy brown eyes and black hair, said, "Hello, Raina. Billaud tells me you'll be serving tonight."

"I guess so, Juan."

"Here. Take these drinks over there in the corner. Gonna be busy tonight."

Raina took the tray and threaded her way across the crowded floor. There were tables around an open space, and couples were trying to dance. The noise was horrendous, women's shrill laughter and men yelling across the room at each other. She knew that sooner or later a fight would break out, for Cajuns were hot tempered. All she could do was stay away from them.

"Well, thank you, sweetheart." The customer looked up and grinned at her. He was a bronze-skinned man with a shirt that had once been white. It was open to his belt, and he was hairy as an animal it seemed. "Why don't you sit down and help me drink up this stuff?"

"I can't do that. It's against the rules."

"Rules are made to be broken." He reached out and grabbed her hand.

She wrenched it away. "I can't do that. The boss wouldn't like it."

"Why, I'll make it right with the boss."

"Just leave me alone," Raina said sharply.

"Think you're too good for me, do ya?"

At that moment, the bartender, Juan Rolando, suddenly appeared. He was a huge man, running to fat but strong as a bull. He grabbed the arm of the man who was reaching for Raina, squeezed, and said, "Drink your booze, and leave the help alone!"

"I just wanted—"

"I know what you wanted. Now here's what *I* want—get out of here or I'll break your neck!"

Raina watched as the customer staggered out. Then she turned to Juan. "*Gracias*, Juan."

"If you have any trouble, just give me a call."

She moved back toward the bar and got another order. For the next half hour she filled her time with serving the customers. The smells, the odors, and the profanities that rose in shrill voices all were an offense to her.

She had read a book once about a meal in a fancy New York restaurant where everything was quiet except the man with a violin who played beautiful music during the meal of the heroine and her lover. A longing rose in Raina, and she knew she would give all she had to have one meal like that where the men weren't drunk and the women were pure and the music was sweet.

That'll never happen to me, Raina thought, and all the joy of life faded from her as she continued to serve the drunken patrons. She saw that Billaud was scowling at Juan but said nothing.

She passed by a table where a tall, well-dressed man was sitting, and smiled at him. "How are you, Mr. Channing?"

"Fine, Miss Raina." Mason Channing was the one decent man Raina had encountered in the cantina. He was a lawyer and had the respect of everyone in town. He always called her "Miss Raina" and was ever polite. "A little trouble, Miss Raina?"

"Oh, nothing unusual, Mr. Channing."

Channing studied her and said, "A pretty tough life you have here. Did you ever think of trying something else?"

"What else is there?"

"Not much in this town, I know."

"If everyone were as nice as you, life would be a lot easier."

Channing considered her words then said, "I'm sorry it has to be so hard."

"Not your fault."

"No, but I hate to see a fine young lady have to put up with the trash that comes in here."

"I'll be all right."

"Did you ever think of getting married?"

"To who? One like Juan threw out the front door a little while ago? That's about all we get—except for you. And you're already taken. How is your wife, by the way?"

"She's doing just fine. In fact, I should be getting home to her now. Well, if I can ever help you, just let me know."

Raina would have been suspicious if any other man she knew made the remark, but she smiled. "That's like you, Mr. Channing." She walked away, hopelessness filling her completely.

CHAPTER 3

Tyler Kincaid pulled his worn shirt closer around his neck then buttoned up the top button of the heavy mackinaw coat he wore. The sky overhead was a dull lead-colored canopy that pressed down upon the earth. It was late morning now, and the temperature was dropping rapidly.

When Ty had left Houston, the weather had been mild enough, but as he'd traveled toward the northeast, the cold seemed to lower itself upon the earth, chilling him to the bone. Tiny granules of what would turn into snow were already falling, and he blinked his eyes to clear them then stared up ahead. Somewhere he would reach the Louisiana border, and his goal was to make it to Baton Rouge where he could continue his journey on a paddle-wheeler.

His horse had been a poor one to start with. Now he felt the animal tremble with the cold. Ordinarily Ty would not have ridden a horse in this condition, but there had been little choice for him.

Suddenly he was seized by a spasm and began to cough. The

cough from his imprisonment had returned when he had left Houston. He had gone there after his escape and worked at odd jobs to earn barely enough money for this trip. He muttered into the stiff wind, "Getting sick again. Better not be too serious this time."

He rode for another thirty minutes, and when he felt the horse's pace faltering, he knew that he'd have to rest her. He found shelter in a grove of hickory trees and tied the horse up, although there was little danger of her running away in her condition. He studied the animal closely and then shook his head. "Never make it, I reckon."

He turned to the task of fixing some sort of breakfast. He found a fallen tree and was able to break off small fragments of the dead limbs. He made a pile of them, and taking a match from his inside pocket, he struck it, waited until it burned blue, and then pushed it down into the pile of dead wood. "Come on, burn, blast you!" he muttered. His words had little effect, but soon the wood caught and a tiny yellow blaze flared up. Carefully he added larger pieces until he had a respectable fire going. The warmth of the flame would have cheered him, but it was so small and the weather was so bitter that it did little good.

Going back to his horse, he pulled a skillet and several small bags out. One of them carried grain, and he put it on the horse's head. Tired and weary and sick as the horse was, she began to eat. "That's about all we got, girl," he said. "You'll have to make out until we get somewhere to get some more."

Going back to the fire, he broke wood and made a pyramid. He balanced the skillet precariously on top. As soon as the skillet got hot, he dropped in three thick slices of bacon, the last of that store, and dumped a can of beans beside it. There was a small end of a loaf of bread, which he put on top of the frying bacon, letting the grease soak in.

As the meal sizzled and sent a good aroma to Kincaid, he squatted there, trying to estimate how he would be able to make it all the way to Arkansas. That was his master plan, to get from Houston to Fort Smith, Arkansas, which was a difficult thing under any condition. He was a man of silence, but he was planning ahead how he could, perhaps, sell the horse for at least enough to get a ticket partway up the Mississippi. The big river didn't go to Fort Smith, but the Arkansas River cut into the Mississippi, and the smaller paddleboats and sternwheelers made it all the way up to the Indian Territory and Fort Smith.

Ty ate slowly, chewing thoroughly, pulling his coat around his shoulders and his hat down to avoid the tiny fragments that stuck to his face and burned like fire. Finally he straightened up, put the skillet and the pitiful remains of the food into the saddlebag, and studied the horse. "You got to go a little bit farther, girl. Sorry about that." He was a man who cared for horses and had no use for men who mistreated them. He knew that the horse could not last long, but he stepped into the saddle and urged the animal forward. "Come on, girl, you can do it." The mare started forward, and in short steps they headed northeast.

The cold wind was sucking the energy out of both man and horse, and as Ty looked down the road, he shook his head. He had been told at the last stop that the small village of La Tete lay in front of him, and it wasn't far from the river itself. He rode slowly, and finally the horse stumbled and nearly fell. Stepping out of the saddle, Kincaid grasped the bridle and leaned forward. "Come on, now. Without all my weight you ought to be able to make it." As the two plodded along, the wind whistled a dirge like a funeral hymn. It was a depressing moment for Tyler Kincaid, but there was no way he could do anything except continue on his way.

⁂

La Tete was indeed small, and as Ty staggered into it at almost noon, he saw a sign that said CECIL'S LIVERY STABLE, halted the horse, and dismounted.

He was greeted by a tall, lanky man who appeared at the livery's door. He was bundled up against the cold, his red hair extending beneath his hat. He had a pair of sharp blue eyes. "Bad weather to be travelin', my friend. My name's Cecil."

"I'm Kincaid." Ty was almost too winded to answer, but he took a deep breath and began coughing again. When it finally stopped, he said, "I need to leave this horse with you until she gets rested and then find me a room."

"It sounds like you need a doctor more than any of that."

Kincaid smiled. "You know one that works for nothing?"

"Well, not really, but you could maybe work it out. Albert Vance is a pretty good fella for a doctor. How far you come?"

"All the way from Mexico."

Cecil whistled and shook his head. "That's a far piece on a horse like that. What were you doing down there?"

"Went to work on a railroad, but I got caught in one of their revolutions. And I was on the wrong side, at that."

"You headed far?"

"Headed for Fort Smith, Arkansas."

"Well, you're going in the wrong direction, you know."

"I know. Fort Smith is northwest of here, but I was hopin' to get to Baton Rouge. I could get on one of those sternwheelers and head up that way."

Cecil shook his head, took a toothpick out of his pocket, and stuck it in his mouth. "I doubt if this hoss will make it." He wiggled his toothpick up and down. "And the Mississippi don't go to Arkansas."

"No, but the Arkansas cuts into it. They got boats go all the way to Fort Smith, I hear."

"I guess that's right, but I doubt if this hoss will make it."

"No, I'll try to sell her."

"She ain't worth much, you know." The toothpick wiggled up and down again. He turned his head to one side and added, "The fare is pretty high on those paddleboats."

Kincaid wanted to get in out of the cutting wind. "I planned to work my way. Where can I get a room and something to eat?"

"Down the street there. The Silver Dollar Saloon. It ain't nothin' but a saloon, but they got some rooms, and they cook some meals. You can sure get some whiskey, maybe warm you up."

"Well, grain this horse, Cecil. Get her out of the cold."

"Sure, but I doubt she gets you very far."

"Well, maybe I can swap with someone."

Cecil shook his head doubtfully. "I'll ask around, but you ain't got much to swap with."

Kincaid paid Cecil then started down the street toward the saloon and did his best to keep from coughing. His chest was already sore from the wrenching it took with each spell. He reached the Silver Dollar, identified by a handmade sign. He walked inside and was struck at once by the heat. A woodstove blazed at one end of the saloon, and several tables were gathered around it, their occupants taking advantage of the heat. He started for the stove and noticed that a pretty girl with long black hair was singing a song, but he was too beat to pay much attention.

A large man with coarse features approached. "Help you, mister?"

"I'm Kincaid. Can I get something to eat and a room?"

"Yeah. This is my place. I'm Millard Billaud. You be stayin' long?"

"No, I'm heading for Baton Rouge then headed up north to Arkansas."

Billaud shook his head. "The weather is gettin' worse. Got a fellow that came in from the north just a little bit ago. He says the snow is fallin' thick and fast up that way. Better stay here until it clears up."

"What I need right now is a room."

"Go up the stairs. First door on the left. Ain't no locks. People carried the keys off a long time ago. Just put a chair under the knob if you want to, but nobody will bother you."

"Thanks." After giving the man the cost of the room, Kincaid climbed the stairs. He felt the weakness of his legs and struggled to restrain the coughing. He felt hot and knew that he had a fever coming on, and that made it worse.

Entering the room he saw that it was about as primitive and ugly as a room could get. It was papered with yellowed sheets of newspaper, some of it peeling off now and hanging by strips. There was a bed with a sorry-looking mattress that appeared as if it had been slept on since the Flood, one chair, and a table with a pitcher and a basin on it. He poured the cold water into the basin, washed his face as well as he could, then moved over, took his boots off, lay down, and pulled the dirty quilt and a blanket, equally dirty, over him. He began coughing and knew that the fever was going up. Finally he went to sleep, but the coughing woke him from time to time.

When he woke up it was dark outside, and the room was freezing. Kincaid felt awful. He summoned what little strength he had, pulled on his boots, and went downstairs. He went up to the bar.

A balding man, who was obviously the barkeep, had a filthy apron on. He turned to Ty. "Something for you?"

"Whiskey." As soon as the man handed him the drink, Ty threw down some coins, took the glass, and swallowed the liquid down in one gulp.

"The woman will cook you something if you're hungry."

"That'd be good. Whatever she's got will do me."

The girl who had been singing was now moving from table to table, carrying drinks on a tray. She stopped in front of him.

He glanced up and saw that she had a beautiful complexion, but he was not at all interested in women at the moment. The smell of cigarettes, stale smoke, unwashed bodies, and alcohol flavored the air, but it was that way in all saloons. He chose a table and sat quietly, paying little attention to what was going on.

Finally the girl came over and said, "Here's your breakfast."

He looked down and saw that it was ham with some eggs and thick-sliced bread. "Can I get coffee?"

"Yes, I'll get it for you."

There was something odd about her speech, and Kincaid wondered what. And then he realized that this was Louisiana country, full of Cajuns who spoke French and English, but French better than the latter. "Thanks," he said and began eating. He ate slowly and managed to withhold his cough.

The table next to him was occupied by three men, all of them wearing lumber jackets, heavy coats, and fur hats. One of them said, "Wanna sit in on the game, mister?"

Kincaid looked over and shook his head. "I don't have much money."

"Ah, it's just penny ante poker to kill the time. I'm Beaudreux. This is Johnny. That's Conroy. Come on, set in while you thaw out and maybe have another drink."

Kincaid did not feel like gambling, but neither did he want to sit alone. He joined in the game and listened to the men talking, figuring out they were lumberjacks and most of them had grown up in swamp country. One of them was telling the story about how he had landed a twelve-foot alligator with his bare hands.

"Oh Conroy, you always tell the best lies," the tall man called Beaudreux said. "What's your name, mister?"

"Tyler Kincaid."

"Well, pretty cold out there to be travelin'. You headed far?"

The young woman came with drinks, and he took his and looked up and nodded at her. "Thank you, miss."

His politeness seemed to shock her. For a moment she stared at him, then said, "You're welcome."

Kincaid turned back to the men and the game. "I'm heading for Indian Territory."

Beaudreux asked, "What for? They say that ain't much of a place."

"Oh, I thought I could trade with the Indians. Do something. Maybe become one of Judge Parker's marshals."

The man called Johnny shook his head mournfully. "I hear that's a rough crowd. Been more than fifty of them marshals kilt chasin' around after bad men and Indians."

"That's right," Conroy said. "Every crook in the world winds up in that territory. Hard on them marshals. I heard about that Judge Parker. Feller said he'll hang 'em half a dozen at a time." Conroy shook his head. "He must be a hangin' judge."

Kincaid noticed that the girl did not get far. She apparently had lingered to listen, but he could not understand why. The talk seemed mundane to him. He continued playing poker, and finally he said, "Well, too rich for my blood. I lost nearly two bits."

At that time an older man with a star on his vest came over and said, "I'll have to take your gun, mister. I'm Sheriff Farmer."

"My gun? Why would you do that?"

"I got a poster with your picture on it. You're a wanted man, even got a reward out on you."

"Who's offering a reward for me?"

"Mexican police put it out. Claims you shot a national big shot down there."

Ty stared at the sheriff. "That was one of their revolutions I got caught in."

"You did some shootin'?"

"I got caught in one of the fights between the nationals and the revolutionists. I defended myself and got out of there."

"Have to hold you, Kincaid. Maybe you can get some help from our government."

Ty saw that argument was useless, so he handed the sheriff his gun, and the two of them left the Silver Dollar.

The sheriff led Ty to the jail, and as he locked him in a cell, he said, "Sorry about this, son, but I've got no choice."

As soon as Farmer left, Ty collapsed on the bunk. A bitterness filled him, and he muttered, "I'll either die of whatever sickness I've got or rot in a Mexican prison."

An old man with bleary eyes came into the room and stopped to peer into Ty's cell. "Guess you could use some grub."

"Not too hungry."

"I'm Gabe Hunter. We got some stew left over, and I'll get you some fresh water."

"I appreciate that."

"Whut you in fur?"

"Got mixed up with a shooting down in Mexico. They put out a reward on me. Guess I'll be in jail for a long time."

"Hope not," Gabe said. "It ain't no place for a young feller like you. Life's too short as it is."

Ty felt miserable, but when the jailer came back with a bowl of stew and a pitcher of fresh water, he took it.

Gabe stood and watched, and when Ty had a coughing fit, he shook his head sadly. "Sounds like you got something bad."

"Hope it's just a bad cold."

"No, hit's down in your chest. You need something to break that up. I've got some medicine that might help." He reached into his hip pocket and brought out a half-pint bottle. "Try a bit of this."

Ty took the bottle, took two swallows, and then went into another coughing spasm. He managed to say, "Thanks, Gabe."

"You want me to get a doctor or maybe a preacher to pray over you?"

Ty stopped coughing long enough to whisper, "No thanks, Gabe." Then he lay back and tried to sleep.

CHAPTER 4

The night had drawn on forever, or so it seemed to Raina. She had tossed and turned and gotten up more than twice to get an extra blanket, for the room was not well sealed. Frigid air blew in from the cracks around the window and through the other passages.

While she had been tossing and turning, suddenly an idea came to her. It was like nothing that had ever happened, but she had been thinking for days now about how to get away from Billaud. The thought startled her. At first she put it aside and tried to go back to sleep, but she did not succeed. The idea kept coming back, and she kept building upon it and found herself growing excited about the possibility that her plan might hold.

Finally dawn broke, and although the sky was a dull gray and the sun was only a feeble light as it came through her window, she got out of bed and quickly dressed, putting on her woolen underwear and her warmest dress. Going downstairs, she stirred up the fire in the stove and quickly cooked a supply of ham and

676

then scrambled eggs. These she put into a basket along with half a loaf of bread that she sliced carefully. No one was stirring yet.

She had taken on the job of feeding prisoners in the jail for the small pittance that it paid. Putting on her heaviest coat and a shawl over her head, she left the Silver Dollar and made her way down to the jail. When she got there the door was locked, but she knocked and soon it opened.

Harry Jackson, the night man at the jail, looked at her out of sleep-filled eyes. "What are you doing here so early, Raina? You're not usually stirring around at this hour, are you?"

"Well, I just woke up early today and decided to go ahead and get breakfast ready for the prisoner and for you, too, Harry."

"Well, that's right nice of you, Raina. Come on in. Get out of the cold."

She stepped inside and put the tray down then suddenly turned. "Oh, I forgot."

"What's that?"

"That beer you like so well. I was going to bring you a bottle of it, and I just walked off and forgot it."

"Well, tell you what. Why don't you go back and get it?"

"It's so cold. Would you mind going for it? If you'll go, you can get two bottles of the beer for having to make the trip."

Harry's eyes lit up. "Well, sure I'll be glad to do that. I'll have to lock you in here though."

"That's all right. The prisoner can't get at me. I'll slip his breakfast under the bars."

"Okay. Where's the beer?" Harry listened as she told him the location of the beer, and he left at once whistling a cheerful tune.

As soon as she heard the door lock, she moved out of the main office back to a row of four cells, two on each side of an aisle. There was no one in there except the one prisoner. She saw that the man was lying on the bed and said quickly, "I brought you some breakfast." She watched as he got up and saw that his face was flushed and that he moved carefully. "You're sick," she said.

"I guess I am a little bit. Nice of you to bring breakfast."

She slipped the tray into the space underneath the bottom row of the horizontal steel bars. "I brought some coffee, too." She put the cup between the bars and he took it. He sat down slowly, and she saw that he had started eating, but he did not act hungry. "How long have you been sick?"

"About a week. I hope it's not pneumonia, but the doc said it probably is."

Raina hesitated and then, knowing her time was short, said, "I heard you tell some of the men in the saloon that you were headed north to Indian Territory."

"Well, that's where I was going. Doesn't look like I'll make it now though. From what everybody says, I'll be in jail for a long stretch."

Raina took a deep breath and stared at him. He did not look at all trustworthy. He had a rough look about his face. There was a scar, she noticed, on the left side pulling down his eye into a partial squint and his mouth open to what looked like a sneer. The scar spoiled his looks. It gave him a sinister appearance, but she knew she had no choice. "If I get you out of this place, would you take me with you to the Indian Territory?"

He looked up. "Why, I never thought of such a thing, but it won't work. You can't get me out of here."

"I can get you out, but you'll have to promise me two things."

"What's that?"

Quickly Raina said, "First, you have to promise to take me with you all the way to Fort Smith."

"Well, if I can get there, I'll get you there."

"You have to promise to—to leave me alone. Not to put your hands on me."

"Sure. I'm not much on forcing myself on women. But I don't think it can be done."

Raina was afraid that Harry Jackson would return. "I can do it."

"I don't see how."

"I'll come by late tonight. The jailer, Ben Hogan, is a real drunk. I'll bring some whiskey by and tell him it's my birthday and I want him to help me celebrate, but the whiskey will be drugged with laudanum. It'll put him out. Whiskey does that to him anyway."

"What then?"

"Then I let you out and we leave."

"You might get me out of here, but they'll be looking for us."

"Remember, you do anything I ask no matter how crazy. Let's just get you out of here tonight; then I'll tell you the rest of my plan."

He smiled briefly. "I'll be here. I won't be going anywhere."

❧

Mason Channing said, "Why, Raina, good to see you. Won't you come in?"

Raina walked into Mr. Channing's office. She had been there before. He was a lawyer and often sent for meals from the saloon, and she had brought them.

Channing gave her a warm smile. "What can I do for you, Miss Raina? Most people come to see lawyers because they're either in trouble or about to make trouble for somebody else."

She glanced down at the floor and then she looked Channing straight in the eyes. "I've got to get away, Mr. Channing. If I don't there'll be trouble."

Channing studied her face. He picked up a letter opener, balanced it on one finger, and then said, "Who's going to be in trouble?"

"You, I'm afraid, Mr. Channing."

Channing laughed. "You'd have to get in line for that. There're so many people who don't care for me. They'd have to wait. What's the nature of this trouble you're going to give me?"

"I want you to buy my half interest in the Silver Dollar."

"Why, I thought your sister and brother-in-law owned that."

"My mother divided it before she died. It was in the will. We each got half interest. But she married Millard, and she found out pretty quickly he was just interested in getting her half of the business away and then mine."

This did surprise Channing. "Why would it be trouble for me?"

"Because if you bought my half, you'd be a partner with Billaud, and he can be troublesome. He's a mean, cruel man."

Channing said mildly, "No, I don't think so, Raina. If anyone has trouble, he'll have it with me. How much would you want for half of the place?"

"I don't know what it's worth, but I must have two thousand dollars cash to get away from here."

"It's worth more than that," Channing said.

"I mean I want the money right now, and I want it in cash."

"You mean today?"

"I mean in one hour."

Channing said, "Everybody expects lawyers to cheat their clients. I wouldn't want you to think that. Half of that place is worth at least three thousand."

"I know, but I just want enough to get away, and I want you to get paid for your service. Will you do it, please?"

"You want to tell me anything else about your plan?"

"I'm going to find my father. All I have is a letter with his picture that came some time ago from Arkansas. It was written to my mother, but she had died by the time it got here. I found it by accident. He asked her to let him come and see me, but she never told me about it."

"All right. I'll help you. Now let's talk about this." They talked for fifteen minutes, and in the end he went to the safe and got some cash out. "Most of this is in small bills. That'll help. Now you'll have to sign a paper. Let me make one out."

Raina waited while he wrote out a paper, and then he had two men come in whom she didn't know. He didn't tell the men what the paper said. "Just witness this signature." He dismissed them, and as soon as they left the room, he said, "Here's your money, Raina. Go with God."

"Thank you, Mr. Channing. I'll think of you often when I get away. You've been very kind to me."

She left the office and went at once to a small house on the outskirts of town. She knocked on the door, and it was opened almost at once by Antoine Doucett. He was a slim man with dark hair and black eyes. Unlike most of the men in the area, he had always treated her with respect. "I need your help, Antoine."

"Surely. Won't you come in?"

"Are Lena or the kids in the house?"

"No. She's away for a few days with our kids visiting her parents."

"All right." Raina entered and said, "I want you to help me get away." She went on to explain how she was running from Billaud.

Antoine's face darkened. "He is a cruel man. He cheated me out of my money on that stallion I sold him. But Billaud won't let you go."

"He won't know it. I'll pay you for this, but I want you to go buy a wagon and a team." She went on, giving him instructions about where to put it, and told him that she would be leaving late that night and needed him to be waiting for her with the wagon and team. "And another thing, it must be loaded with hay."

"That will not be hard. It's bad weather to be traveling though."

"But it'll be bad weather for those who try to find me, too. I appreciate this, Antoine."

"That's what friends are for. Don't worry. I know where I can get a wagon and team cheap." She gave him cash and then left. She went at once back to the Silver Dollar and started cooking breakfast. That day she made everything as usual. She cooked and served and managed to stay away from Billaud all day long. Finally night came, and she asked Roxie, "Where's Millard gone?"

"He's after some woman. He won't be back until tomorrow probably. I wish he'd stay gone forever."

Raina went up to her room and gathered together what she wanted to take. She didn't have a suitcase, so she tied her things in a bundle using a blanket. She did not have many clothes anyway, but she did throw in six of the small romance novels that she loved especially.

She sneaked down and got a bottle of whiskey and went to the place where Roxie kept the medicine. She found a bottle of the laudanum they all used when they had aches and pain and poured part of the whiskey out and filled it to the top with the strong sedative.

Finally the saloon grew quiet. She looked at the clock and saw that it was after midnight and the town was shut down in the midst of the storm. Quickly she left the saloon and went to the jail. She knocked on the door.

A voice said, "Who's there?"

"It's me, Ben. Open the door."

The door opened, and Ben stared at her. "What are you doing out this late?"

"Why, I've been having a birthday party, Ben. I've come by to get you to celebrate with me." She held a bottle up.

Ben Hogan's eyes livened. "Come on in out of the cold!" he exclaimed.

"Get us some glasses. We're going to have a good time."

Getting Ben Hogan drunk was the simplest part of the whole plan. He drank quickly, gulping the whiskey down. She had been pretending to drink with him but actually did not swallow any.

Finally his eyes began to shut. He said, "I don't feel so good, Raina."

"You sick?"

"I think so."

"Well, here. Lie down on this cot. You'll feel better in a minute." She helped him over to the cot.

He practically collapsed. He put his feet up and began snoring, his mouth open wide.

Quickly Raina got the key off the wall, entered the jail section, and saw that the prisoner was waiting for her. "We've got to hurry," she said. "Get as far away as we can." She unlocked the door, and he stepped outside.

His face was flushed, but he smiled and said, "If this works, it will be a miracle. I've got to have my gun." He found his gun and gun belt, strapped it on, and said, "What now?"

"Come along. We've got to be away from this town as soon as we can."

She led him down the alley to Antoine's house. She was glad to see, even in the darkness, that Antoine had lit a lantern and was standing there in front of the house.

"That you, Raina?"

"It's me. And this is the man I told you about."

"You're the fellow that was in jail?"

"That's right. I'm Tyler Kincaid."

"He's taking me away from here, Antoine. You get everything fixed?"

"Sure did. I built a little kind of a box on the wagon. You get in there and shut the door. It'll be pretty dark, but you don't have to stay in there too long, I hope. And here, I had this much left over from the money you gave me."

"You keep it, Antoine."

"I'm going to drive you to my cousin's house. I'll borrow a horse from him to get back here."

Raina nodded. "Thanks so much for doing this for me."

"It's no problem. I'm glad to help you get away from a man

like Billaud. I just wish you had come to me sooner."

"I never saw a way out until now."

Antoine looked up at the continuing storm. "You were right about the weather. There won't be anybody out looking for you at this time of night and in all of this." Antoine turned to the bed of the wagon, scraped some of the hay away, and opened the small door. It was about five feet square. He said, "Put your blankets in there, and I brought some extra ones. It's going to be cold tonight."

Ty stared at the hiding place and smiled. "Well, I never done anything like this. You want to go first, Miss Raina, I believe is your name?"

"Yes." She got in, and they spread the blankets around to make the floor somewhat softer and then wrapped up in them.

"I'll stop when we get to my cousin's house. If somebody stops me, just don't pay any attention. But I don't think they will. They don't know you're out, do they, Kincaid?"

"No."

Antoine shut the door, and they heard him piling loose hay over it. Then the wagon sagged as the young man got into the seat, and the wagon jerked as the horses pulled out.

"Are you scared being here in the dark with no light at all?" Kincaid asked.

"There are things that are scarier than this."

Kincaid replied, "I guess you've had it pretty hard."

"I can tell you know why I have to get away. My brother-in-law that's married to my sister. He—he's been after me for a long time, ever since I was fifteen. He's going to get me, too, one way or another. I've got to get away."

"Well, we're on our way. I guess Billaud's a bad man to cross."

There was silence for a time, and finally Raina said, "God will take care of us."

"Well, that's a good thing to think. But why do you trust me?"

The wagon jolted and threw her against him. He made no attempt to touch her, and she immediately moved away. "I have nobody else, Kincaid."

The wagon rumbled on, and both of the passengers inside the small box wrapped up and kept warm under the hay and with their covers.

Raina wondered if she had done the right thing. Finally she asked, "*Can* I trust you?"

"You've just about saved my life. I'm not much good, but I always pay my debts, so yes, you can trust me."

"I've not had much luck with men being honest with me."

"Sorry to hear that, but I promise you I'll keep my word to you. Not too many people would have helped me the way you have."

They both fell silent.

Once the wagon stopped, and Raina whispered, "I hope it's not the sheriff."

"Not likely in this kind of weather."

Raina held her breath, but then the wagon lurched on. "Guess we're all right." Raina heard Ty's uncontrolled coughing. "We need to get you to a doctor."

"I'll be all right," he muttered, but Raina knew a little about sickness and wondered if he would live long enough to get her to the territory.

CHAPTER 5

Even though Kincaid could feel the wagon swaying and hear the whistling of the wind, he knew that his fever was rising. His forehead was beginning to feel like a furnace.

He longed to be out of the rather small cocoon where they were hidden from the eyes of men. Close places had always troubled him, and this was a tight one and pitch black, with trouble on the outside. Everything was wrong with it.

"What's the matter, Kincaid?" Raina's voice was soft in the darkness.

He said nothing except, "Well, this fever of mine's going up."

The wagon jolted on and suddenly Ty felt her move closer to him, felt her hand on his shoulder and then up on his forehead. "You're burning up with fever. Here. You need to drink all the water you can."

They had put two water bottles in the hiding place, and now Ty groped for one and felt it. It was cold, but his lips were cracked and parched with the fever. He drank all he could hold, put the

687

top on, and murmured, "That was good."

"Maybe we need to get out of this thing. We may be safe now."

"I don't think so. We'll wait until we get to Antoine's cousin's place. That ought to be good enough."

"I wish this storm had held up. It sounds as if it's getting worse."

The wagon rolled on, and Kincaid continued coughing at times. Then he heard her say, "Here. Let's wet this handkerchief and put it on your face."

"All right." He waited until she had moistened the large handkerchief that she wore around her neck and began to bathe his face with it. "Feels good," he muttered. "I would have to pick this time to be sick."

"You didn't pick it. Sickness just comes on."

From time to time Raina moistened the handkerchief. It would grow almost hot from the fever that was running through him. "What's your plan after we get out of this thing, Ty?"

"We'll immediately head for Indian Territory."

"It might be hard to get there, don't you think?"

"I expect so. It's an out-of-the-way place. I'm hoping we can catch a steamboat at Baton Rouge."

"Does the Mississippi River go all the way to Fort Smith?"

"No, we'd have to get off where the Arkansas River feeds into the Mississippi, but steamboats go up the Arkansas all the way into Fort Smith. The trouble is I don't know if we can do that."

"Why not, Ty?"

"I think Sheriff Farmer will send out word with our descriptions. We'll have to sneak in somehow." He suddenly hacked a raw cough.

She said, "You're so sick. I'm afraid."

"I'll be all right. I've been sick before."

🐍

Sometime later Raina heard Antoine say, "Whoa!" and the wagon ceased to heave and pitch. "Here we are, Ty." She got no answer and realized that he was asleep. "Ty, wake up!"

Ty came awake slowly, and his voice was thin. "Are we here?"

"Yes. Antoine will let us out now."

A few minutes later they heard the scraping at the door of their hiding place and then it opened. A freezing blast of air mixed with snow swirled in, and Kincaid murmured, "That's real winter there."

The two got out, and Raina said, "You did a good job, Antoine."

"Well, come in to my cousin's house and get warm, and I'll fix you something to eat."

It was a welcome break for both of them. They went inside, and Raina saw a heavyset woman with black eyes and a man who looked somewhat like Antoine.

Antoine said, "Give them something to eat. They'll be moving on."

"We don't have much."

"Anything. Heat up some beans or bacon or whatever you can find."

"We've got some ham and some corn."

"That'll be good."

Thirty minutes later the fugitives were standing beside the wagon. The wind was rising now. It was winding around the house corners, and it had blown down the chimney, making the smoke whirl inside the house.

The whole world was cold, and Raina saw that Ty was using all his strength just to hold on to the wagon. "Get on into the wagon, Ty. I'll drive. We'll cover up with these blankets." She turned to Antoine and said, "Thank you, Antoine. You may have saved our lives. Stay out of Sheriff Farmer's way though."

"You do the same. But he won't likely be out in this kind of weather. Everyone will just think I went to see my wife and kids overnight. I'll be fine."

Raina climbed into the wagon and picked up the lines. She had driven a few times. The horses were sluggish, so she took the whip and touched them with it. They pulled forward, throwing her back into the seat. "You all right, Ty?"

"Sure."

"Wrap up in these blankets. It's getting worse all the time."

As they moved on, Raina saw that Ty's head was nodding. *He looks terrible,* she thought. *I've got to get him in some shelter.*

They drove for a while in the driving wind, and the weather was getting worse.

"Ty, there's a house."

"We probably don't need to stop there. If anyone is tracking us, they would stop and ask at houses about us."

"No, it's vacant. Antoine told me about it. Folks sold out last week, and it's for sale, so it'll be abandoned. Nobody will be out looking at a house to buy in this storm. And there's a barn to put the team in."

"All right."

Raina drove the team up to the barn, got out, and had to struggle to open the doors that were crammed with snow. She did get them open wide enough and drove the team in. She noted that Ty was only able to fall out and hang on to the side of the wagon.

"Look, Ty. They left some feed here. The horses will need it. Let's go in, and I'll come back later."

"I wish I was more help. I hate being sick."

"It'll pass." The two of them made for the house, and Raina said, "Look. They've got a lot of firewood stacked up against the side of the house here."

"We'll probably need it in this storm."

When they went inside, the faint light came through the windows, but there was a lantern with coal oil in it. Raina lit it and set it on the table. "Here. You come on in and lie down. I'm going to get a fire started."

"Let me do that."

"No, you lie down. We've got to take care of you."

"Whatever you say."

Raina was glad that the wood box was filled. There was even some rich pine kindling there. She got the fire started, and while it was catching she went out and fed the horses and unhitched them. Going back to the house, she looked in the wagon and got the box of groceries and took it inside. The snow was falling thick now so that she could barely see the house. She stepped inside and felt immediately the difference that the small fire had made. *I've got to be careful with the wood. It's got to last.*

She went over to the stove and got out the frying pan and a saucepan. She quickly cooked some grits, added condensed milk and some sugar, and then she fried up some ham and added two eggs. She fixed a plate for Ty and said, "Just stay in your bed. You can eat there."

"I can get up."

"No need to. Here." She watched him struggle in the bunk,

691

leaning back against the wall. His face was flushed, and his eyes were bleary. When he took the food, his hands trembled, but she said nothing. She ate her meal and watched as he tried to get some down. "You need to drink all the water you can."

"I don't know why I'm not eating like I should."

"Fever does that. Especially pneumonia."

"Well, it's bad news if I've got that. I think more people die of it than live through it. Can't eat any more." He handed her the plate.

She saved the food. She then saw that he had slumped back. A spirit of fear came to her. She was alone in the middle of a snowstorm such as she had never known. She saw that Ty was unconscious. His breathing was irregular, and the violent coughing came at fairly regular intervals.

I got Ty into this, she thought. *I wish I hadn't. He may die here. . . .* The thought frightened her, and she tried to pray, but she was not a woman of prayer and could only say the Lord's Prayer that she had memorized. It didn't seem right, but she didn't know what else to do.

She rationed out the fire, built it up, and put a pallet on the floor. She lay down on it, wrapped up in two other blankets after covering Ty. The warmth of the cabin soon got to her. She tried to pray again but failed and dozed off to sleep.

Raina was awakened by the coldness of the room. The fire had died down. She shivered, got up, and built up the fire again.

Going over to the bunk, she looked down and said, "Ty, are you all right?"

He did not stir nor speak.

She saw that his lips were crusted over, and his breathing had a frightening rattle to it. She had seen pneumonia before, and to be alone with a dying man and no one to help was the scariest moment of her life.

She remembered that the horses needed water, and taking a bucket she went outside and returned. She filled a dishpan with snow until it was full then set it on the stove. As the snow began to melt, she stirred it to hurry the process. Finally she got a large fruit jar and began to dip it out into the bucket. It took her four trips to get the horses satisfied, and she had to keep on heating the snow as it was the only water available.

She returned to her makeshift bed and wrapped up in the blankets, continually repeating the Lord's Prayer as she slipped into a fitful sleep.

❧

The storm went on for two more days, and it was a Herculean struggle for Raina to exist. She had to keep the horses watered and fed, and just getting to the barn took a mammoth effort. When she came back each time, she was so weak she had to sit down and pant like a dog. Keeping the fire going with what wood was available was also a chore. Each time she had to go break the firewood loose where it was frozen and bring it into the house so it would thaw out before it could burn.

Her worst problem, though, was with Ty. She knew for sure now that he had pneumonia, and there was nothing she could do for him except to help him sweat it out. She would warm the blanket at the stove and put it on him. He tried to fight her for he was blazing with the fever, but there was nothing else she could do.

She had brought some of her romance novels. On one of her return trips from the barn, she had brought one inside. It was called *Ivanhoe* and was written by Sir Walter Scott. She had read it more than once, but now she sat down and passed the time reading. There was a sufficient supply of coal oil to keep the lantern burning dimly, and she read the story of the knight and the fair lady and the dark lady again. Finally she closed her eyes and held the book to her breast. *I wish life was like that. That some man would come along and care for me and tell me the things I want to hear, but I don't think that will ever happen.*

On the third day, the wind dropped and the snow stopped falling out of the sky. She went over to Ty and said, "The storm is falling away, Ty." She saw that he was unconscious, but he was burning up. She pulled the cover back, wet some cloths in the dishpan where she melted the snow, and covered his body as best she could. The cloths grew almost hot to the touch, and she dipped them again into the cold water. Finally the fever came down, and he fell into what seemed like a normal sleep.

Once again Raina tried to pray, but it was a failure. "I wish I knew God," she whispered, "but I don't. So God, hear somebody's prayer. Help this man and help me to get out of this place." She waited for some kind of answer, but all she heard was the silence and the crackling of wood in the stove. She said wearily, "It'll just have to be like it is."

She sat down beside Ty, picked up his hand, and held it. She stayed that way for a long time. She felt alone. . .without a future, with a bad past, and no present. Tears began to roll down her cheeks, and she gave in to the sorrow and grief that had been building up. As the storm abated outside, so her spirit seemed to grow weak and weary.

CHAPTER 6

The day had passed and the night, and now getting up from the floor Raina saw that the fire was practically down. The room was freezing cold, and she had to start with the few pieces of kindling she had made by breaking one of the drawers to a small cabinet. As soon as she got a blaze going, she picked the smallest bit of firewood and laid it carefully and then added two more pieces on top, leaving room for it to draw. The sight of the yellow flames flickering and the sound of the crackling was cheerful.

She rose and went to the door. She opened it, looked outside. She felt smothered somehow by the coldness, the terrible, awful coldness of the weather. She shut the door then laid her hand against it. It made a solid wall of walnut, but it was a feeble thing against the onslaught of the bitter cold.

She listened closely and heard the wind rising again. It whirled around the house corners and blew down the chimney, making the stove smoke. She felt the chill bite into her shoulders, and with the fire burning it only made the temperature bearable.

She knew she had to go make snow water. Finally when she went out, she found the horses stamping. They looked pitiful to her. She fed them from the grain that had been left and some of the hay. She gave them two buckets of water each and then went back inside. She took the dishpan and made enough snow water to fill buckets. Then there was nothing left to do.

Finally she saw Ty turning from one side to the other and coughing. "Are you all right, Ty?" she said.

"It's cold."

"Let me wrap you up in another blanket." She took one of her own blankets, put it over him, and tucked it in closely so that the air could not get through. She had thought to put one of the blankets underneath him so that the cold rising would be barricaded off. "I'm gonna fix you something to eat, Ty."

"Not hungry."

She ignored his words and cut off two slices of ham and made more of the oatmeal from their diminishing supplies. There was a little piece of pork fat, and it made the skillet greasy. The ham sizzled in it as she warmed a small skillet full of the oatmeal. She poured it onto a plate, went over, and said, "Sit up, Ty. You've got to eat." He said nothing, and she helped him into a sitting position, and then she fed him. "How do you feel, Ty?"

"Rotten." He opened his eyes and stared at her. His eyes seemed to be hollow, and he whispered huskily, "I'm no help to you, Raina."

"That's all right. We're going to make it."

Ty said, "That's what Jim said, but he didn't."

She got up and put two small logs on the fire. "I can't use up all the firewood, but you know, Ty, I think it's warmer on the floor."

His teeth were chattering, and she pulled the blanket off, made a thick fold, and said, "Come on. Lie down here." She helped him out of the small bed.

He lay down as close to the stove as she dared allow, and then she covered him up with all the blankets. "That feels good," he whispered. His eyes shut.

She said, "Are you thirsty?"

"Yes, I feel like I need water all the way through me." Indeed, his lips were chapped, and when she fed him he sipped the water gratefully. When he had drunk enough, he laid his head back and whispered, "I wish I could help you, Raina."

"We'll be all right."

"I'm not sure about that."

The day passed, the night, and another day and another night. The woodpile was going down alarmingly, but she could not afford to have no fire. It had helped some to put Ty on the floor, for the heat radiated outside the woodstove for a few feet. Finally she lay down with him, and the warmth of her own body seemed to help him.

Later that day she went outside, and to her surprise she heard a faint sound. She looked over and saw a hen staggering out of a small building. She walked over to the building, looked inside, and saw that there were four more, but they were skinny and all trembling with the cold. She picked up the one hen, shut the door, and taking a sharp knife, cut its head off. She went to the barn and got some of the feed for the horses and scattered it inside for the chickens, and while she was there she found just outside that there was some cracked corn. It could be eaten if it was soaked, but the chickens could eat it, too, and that thrilled her.

She walked inside carrying the chicken and said, "Something good, Ty."

"What's that?"

"There are five chickens out there. We're going to have us a nice chicken stew."

She worked hard making the stew, which was really nothing more than chicken soup. She dressed the chicken and boiled it. For the next day they ate chicken, chicken, and chicken, even the gizzard and the liver.

The food seemed to help Ty, for his eyes grew brighter, and he said, "How many chickens did you say there were?"

"There's four more out there, so we can last a week on that."

"I feel sorry for the poor chickens."

I feel sorry for us, Raina wanted to say, but she did not. She watered the horses, fed them, and saw that the feed was going down rapidly. *What will we do if the feed goes and the horses die?*

The next day she went out, and the chickens were huddled in a far corner. Their feathers were drooping, and their eyes were glazed over, but they were alive. She had found a narrow pan and knew they must be thirsty, so she took the bucket of water and the pan and filled it. One of the chickens came over at once, clucking feebly, and began to peck at the water, and then the others came. "You poor things. You're starving, aren't you? I'm afraid you're going to have to die for us." She realized she had never felt sorry for a chicken before, and she had had fried chicken all her life. Finally she left and went back.

Ty was sitting up in bed. "You know you could bring those chickens in here. It's warmer than it is in that henhouse."

"I think you're right, Ty." At once she left, and it took her four trips, but the chickens were inside. She brought some of the feed and the pan out, and soon the warmth of the fire helped the birds. One of them seemed to be dying, and she managed to pour a little water down its throat. The bird began to perk up and finally ate a little.

"How much firewood is left, Raina?"

"About half of it."

"How long do you think it will last?"

"Well, it all depends. We can't have big roaring fires like I'd like to have."

"No, but this cabin and that firewood is saving our lives and now those of the chickens." His voice was somewhat clearer, and she moved closer and put her hand on his forehead. "Your fever's about gone!" she exclaimed. "That's wonderful."

"Well, I do feel better."

"Could you eat some more chicken soup?"

"I believe I could."

She stirred up the fire and put the pan right on the coals from the front where she usually loaded it. Soon the soup was bubbling, a full stew pan. She poured two bowls of the soup, went over to Ty, and said, "Can you feed yourself?"

"I think so."

She gave him one bowl and a spoon, and then she took the other. "This is good," she said.

"Sure is. I thank the Lord for those chickens." He hesitated then said, "That's what my friend would have said. Jim Adams. He always believed in the Lord, even when things were at the worst."

"Have you known him long?"

"Just a few months. We worked on the railroad together." He

then told her how they had been captured by the army and thrown into a prison. He ended the story by saying, "He gave his life for me, Raina. He could have gotten away if he had left me there, but he didn't do it."

"What a good man he must have been."

He suddenly changed the subject. "That wind's picking up."

She had finished her soup, and she went over to the door and cracked it. "It's blowing hard. I don't think—" She suddenly stopped.

Ty asked, "What is it?"

"There's a deer out there. He's coming this way."

"You'll have to shoot him, Raina."

"I'm not much good."

"There's that shotgun. You can't miss."

"All right, Ty, if you say so."

"Bring me the shotgun."

She took it to him.

He checked the load and said, "Get as close as you can and pull one trigger. If he doesn't fall, pull the other one."

"All right, Ty." Raina took the shotgun, moved to the door, and closed it behind her. She half expected to see the deer run away. The poor creature was weak and did not seem to see her. She walked on the snow, and when she was no more than five feet away she lifted the gun. She pulled the trigger. The deer was knocked backward. It lay there bleeding in the snow. Raina felt tears come into her eyes, but she knew that this was life or death. She took the shotgun inside and said, "It's down."

"I wish I could help you dress it."

"I helped my brother-in-law dress a deer once. I think I can do it. I'll cut off some steaks and bring them in. Then I'll get the rest of it."

The deer was indeed lank and had lost most of the fat, but it was the closest thing to a feast that they had had. She worked hard getting the deer cut up, and finally she had all the meat inside. She was panting with fatigue. Ty had fallen asleep again. She put the meat over to one side of the cabin and cut it into smaller pieces so she could fry it.

When Ty woke up a few hours later, she told him what she had done. "We're gonna have a steak now. I cut a couple out." She put two pieces of small wood in the stove, and when it got popping she took the two steaks and put them in the large frying pan. They sizzled for a while.

Ty said, "That smells better than anything I've ever eaten."

Indeed it was good. The two of them ate slowly, chewing the tough meat.

"Did you save the liver?" he asked.

"Yes, I did."

"It would make a good soup. The liver is the best part of a deer, I think."

"We'll have that for supper."

They sat there with the odd sensation of being full and not hungry.

"You know we've got enough food here for a couple of weeks if we take it easy," Ty said. His voice was thin, and his weight loss was obvious by the hollows in his cheeks and in his eyes.

"We'll be all right. I think your friend was right."

"He said God was going to get us out of it. I never believed him. I guess I need to now."

They were quiet for a time, and he slept. When he woke up she left him and looked outside. "I've never felt cold like this," Raina said.

"I did once, up north in Michigan. Went up to work as a timberman, but I was no good at it. It got even colder there."

The next three days passed without incident. Raina had found the well and was able to get water from it. She fed the horses and watered them and was glad to see that there was still a bag of feed that would last another week or maybe two on short rations.

The deer had been thin, but she used every bit of it, and they had fresh meat every night.

A couple of days passed, and their supplies were low.

Ty had awakened that morning and taken a deep breath. "My lungs feel good," he said.

"Oh, Ty, that's wonderful."

"Let me get out of this bed and sit up like a human being."

She helped him out of bed, but he didn't really need it. She saw that there were hollows in his throat where he had lost weight. "Our wood's not going to last much longer," she said.

"Well, now that I'm strong we can get out of here. How are the horses?"

"I've kept them on low rations, but they look strong."

"We'll need 'em to get us out of this place."

"I expect so." She had sat down on the floor, soaking up the meager heat the stove threw off. "Do you think God had anything to do with leading us to this place?"

Ty looked at her and said, "We'd be dead if we hadn't found it.

And then that deer coming and the chickens. . . Makes me think God is in some things."

"I think so, too."

The two sat there quietly talking, and he said, "Give me two more days and we can go. As long as no more bad weather comes."

They waited the two days, and the weather was clearer. "We can go now. We'd better take any supplies left, including food for the horses. We should also kill the last chicken and take it. Don't know how long it will take us to get to Baton Rouge."

"Well, the sun's shining. I think God has helped us," Raina said. "I'm thankful that we made it."

Ty suddenly turned and faced her. "You saved my life, Raina. Thank you for that. I hardly think I'm worth saving, but you did it."

Raina felt a warmth. She had learned to trust this man, and in his weakness he had revealed that he was a good man. She had not really doubted it before, but now she knew it beyond any doubt. "I'm glad for both of us."

The sun was shining even brighter as they left. Ty had managed to hitch the horses to the wagon, and they had watered and fed them. As they left the cabin, they got into the wagon, and Ty looked back. He stared at the house and shook his head. "I'll never forget that place, Raina."

"Neither will I. Thank God for that house."

"Amen," Ty said. "I'll say amen to that."

CHAPTER 7

A loud screeching noise brought Raina out of a fitful sleep. She sat straight up in bed and looked around wildly for a moment, then realized the sound came from the street below. The room was cold, but she threw the cover back and dressed in her warmest clothes. As she dressed, she looked down where Ty had slept, and a start of fear ran along her nerves. *What if he's left me?* The thought frightened her more than she had thought it would, for she realized that she was helpless without him. As soon as she was dressed, she began pacing the floor. She was ordinarily able to handle a crisis, but the strain of the storm, the imminence of possibly freezing to death, and the crisis of running away from all she knew to some destiny that she could not even think of—had all worn her down.

Finally she stopped and walked over to the window. The street was muddy, and a man was driving a wagon pulled by four mules. He was striking them steadily and methodically with a whip. She could hear his curses clearly.

She roamed the room restlessly, then finally she walked over to her baggage and pulled out a copy of one of the romances she loved so dearly. She had read it at least five times, but she found some sort of comfort in pulling the blankets off the bed, wrapping them around her, and reading the story again. It was a story she loved about a young girl who was pursued by an evil man. She snuggled deeper into the cocoon she had made out of blankets, and as always, she was able to turn her mind away from the immediate and very real problems into the world of fiction.

I read too much, and I know these stories aren't true, she thought. *But it gives me some sort of pleasure. I don't see anything wrong with it.* Her sister had criticized her endlessly about reading what she called *trash*, but Raina had paid her no mind at all.

She was so deeply engrossed in the story she paid little heed to the footsteps, for it was apparently busy in the hallway. But then she heard the two knocks, a hesitation, then three knocks. She came out of the chair quickly, throwing the blankets back on the bed, and tossed the book back into the box she had taken it from.

She got to the door, unlocked it, and opening it, she stepped back. She had no idea what to say to Ty. He looked tired, and the sickness had worn him down. He had not shaved so he looked scraggly and rough. "Come in," she said. "But it's cold in here."

"Well, we'll be leaving anyway." Ty stepped inside, glanced at the bed for a moment then back to her. "We're going on. We're not too far from the Mississippi River. There's a little town on the bank there. We can sell the wagon and the team, and we'll take the boat up to where the Arkansas feeds into the big river."

"What if somebody hears about us and recognizes us?"

"They'll be looking for a couple. I'll get the tickets, and I'll go in by myself. There's always a lot of activity on those boats when they pull out. People leaving, others hurrying on. You just hide yourself in there. The cabin is room number 206."

"Do you really think that we'll be safe?"

"I think so. When you get in the cabin, I'll get some food and bring it to you. We won't be seen together."

"All right, Ty," she said timidly. "You've done well."

"We'll be all right," he said finally. He shrugged his shoulders. "I'll carry your stuff down to the wagon."

Thirty minutes later they were eating a breakfast of ham and eggs and homemade bread in the single restaurant the town possessed. After they finished their meal, they went outside. She climbed into the wagon, and he mounted to sit beside her.

He picked up the lines, slapped the horses' backs, and the team at once lurched forward. "If I got it right, we ought to be at the river sometime before noon."

Raina said quietly, "It's been hard on you. You're not fully recovered yet with that sickness you had."

"I'm all right."

They stopped once to rest the horses and then proceeded at an even pace. When they reached the river town, Raina saw it was even worse than the one where they had spent the night.

He nodded toward a small steamboat tied up at the wharf. "That's the ship, I expect. I'll go find out about the rooms. You stay here in the wagon."

"All right, Ty."

Raina sat in the wagon watching him move away. He was moving slowly, and she knew that he had lost some of the vitality that she had first noticed in him. Sickness would do that. The fever had drained him, but he doggedly moved forward.

He was back in thirty minutes. He said, "I'll show you the rooms up on the second deck. When you get in there, I'll bring you food."

"Thank you, Ty."

He hesitated, then for the first time that morning lifted his eyes and stared at her. "You won't have to worry about me bothering you again, Raina."

Raina was on the verge of apologizing, but his manner was so stiff she could only say, "Thank you, Ty."

❧

"Almost time for the boat to leave, Raina," Ty said. He had sold the wagon and the mules and bought a trunk that could carry more of their things in it. He stood beside it now down on the wharf and said, "I don't think there's any danger. We'll go on together."

"All right."

She was relieved when he picked up the trunk. She carried the valise. She had to struggle to get up to the second deck, but when they got to the room and he shoved the door open, he stepped back and let her go in first.

It wasn't much of a room, but the ship was rough and years past its youth. It might have been finely finished at one time, but now everything looked worn and pitiful.

Putting the trunk down, he said, "We'll be leaving right away. Maybe you ought to stay in here until I come for you."

"I will."

"There's a lock on the door. Don't let anybody come in until I knock like I did before. We'll go eat after we're under way."

"Where will you sleep?"

"There was an extra room. Somebody canceled their trip."

The trip up the Mississippi had been tense at first. Raina had been terrified that they would be caught, that Farmer had put arrest papers out on them. But the boat was small, the passengers were few, and nobody paid attention to them. They had their breakfast, the noon meal, and then there was nothing to do.

Ty stayed on deck mostly, up in the bow looking ahead, his eyes searching the banks. She could not tell what he was thinking, but she was low-spirited.

The boat stopped several times as it went up the Mississippi, taking on passengers and letting off some. The tension left her as she became less and less worried about getting caught.

Most of the time she read one of her romance novels. She stayed for long hours in the room and from time to time would take a break.

Once Ty had come to get her in the middle of the afternoon and said, "The cook's just made some fresh donuts. Let's go treat ourselves."

"That sounds good. I always love donuts." The two left the cabin and walked down to the kitchen.

The cook, a fat, greasy-looking man with a broad smile, winked at them. "You smell them donuts, do ya?"

"I can resist anything except temptation and fresh donuts." Ty smiled.

"Well, here. Sink your teeth into one of these, and you, too, ma'am. I'll have to tell ya I'm renowned for my donuts."

Raina bit into the donut. "These are so good!"

"My ma taught me how to make donuts. Never thought I'd

wind up bein' a cook, but there are worse things to be."

They ate two of the donuts apiece with fresh coffee, then she said, "I think I'll go up to the front."

"Pretty cold still. That breeze is stiff."

"I don't mind."

Ty followed Raina as she moved toward the bow. He watched as she put her hands on the railing and stared out at the broad Mississippi.

She stood for a long time. The breeze was cold, and she shivered a little.

He said, "You ought to wear a heavier coat."

"It's all right. I don't mind. It's good to be out here."

They stood together, and from time to time one of them would notice something on the bank. Mostly it was nothing but forest and cotton fields right up to the river itself. "Mighty flat country," Ty said. "I always liked to see hills and mountains."

"I've never really seen any big ones."

"You'll see some up around Fort Smith. That's Ozark country up there. Some of it's right pretty. Oklahoma's got pretty things and ugly things."

Raina was quick to ask what he was expecting next.

"The next thing is we'll get off this boat and find a smaller one going up the Arkansas."

"Does it go all the way to Fort Smith?"

"Well, there will probably be some stops, but yes, pretty well. What will you do when we reach Fort Smith, Raina?"

"I'm going to look for my father."

He turned to study her face in the growing dusk and was once again impressed with the qualities he saw in her. Her hair was raven black, but her eyes were blue and made a pleasing contrast. She was, as far as he knew, as thoroughly alone in the world as if there were no other thing alive on the planet. He knew she was hungry for color and warmth, and he had seen the solace she seemed to take from her romances. Here in the falling darkness a spirit glowed in her like live coals, but as always, she was on guard.

She looked at him silently, and a woman's silence could mean many things, Ty knew. He was not sure what it meant in Raina, but it lay on his own solitary thinking. When she drew away, there was a curtain of reserve, and he suddenly felt that she was the kind of woman who could, if necessary, draw a revolver and shoot a man down and not go to pieces afterward. He had seen her courage and willingness to face danger, and he knew that she had a temper that could swing to extremes of laughter and then turn instantly to softness or anger.

He could not help but appreciate the supple lines of her body. She was just past the stage that follows girlhood, and he realized, for all her youth, she was a beautiful and robust woman with a woman's soft depth and a woman's spirit and a woman's fire. "What if you find your dad and he's not a good man?"

"I don't know. I don't have any other plan."

"Well, I guess we better turn in." Raina nodded in agreement, and Ty escorted her to her room before going to his own.

A restlessness settled over Ty. He finally left his room and moved toward Raina's. Seeing a light through the crack at the bottom of her door, he knocked.

Raina opened the door slightly. "What is it, Ty?"

"I couldn't go to sleep and wanted some company. But if you

want to go to bed, I'll leave you alone."

"No, that's all right. Come on in."

Ty entered the room. He saw that Raina had been reading one of her books and asked her about it.

She began to tell him the plot. He got lost in her words and in the way her eyes lit up when she talked about one of her stories.

Ty saw that she was only wearing a thin robe over her nightgown. The beauty that he had ignored struck him hard, like a raw force. She was looking up at him, her lips slightly opened. Ty had been under pressure for a long time, and now as Raina smiled, he felt a sudden gust of freedom. He was aware of his vow to this young woman, and it had not been difficult to keep himself from even thinking of her as a woman—but now as the desires of a lonely man drew him to beauty, he suddenly felt a sense of joy.

He made no conscious decision, but without thinking he reached for her with a suddenness that caught them both by surprise. Her firm body came against him, and old hungers awoke with a force that shocked him. He lowered his head and kissed her, again without thought, and at that moment she was for him like cool water to a thirsty man.

❧

Raina surrendered herself to Ty's sudden embrace too easily. She was a woman of strong emotions, but a hard life had forced her to keep them under iron control. Now, however, as his lips pressed against hers, she was aware of a passion that shook her. She had longed for love from a man, and the long hours she had spent caring for Ty had gone deeper into her spirit than she had suspected.

Perhaps if Ty had released her at once, the kiss would not have struck Raina so hard. It might even have been a moment for her to treasure, for even in that instant she sensed in his caress something different from the crude advances that she had spent a lifetime avoiding.

Then she felt a flash of anger—mixed with disappointment—and her self-defense flared. He was a strong man, and she was alone and in his power, just the kind of situation she'd learned to avoid. She struck Ty in the chest and cried out, "Leave me alone!"

Ty was shocked and started to respond. "Raina. . ."

Raina was shaking, and her emotions were a mixture of fear and loathing. He tried to explain, but she was beyond listening and moved away from him until her back was against the bulkhead as she cried, "You're no different from all other men, Tyler Kincaid!"

Ty said, "Raina, it was just a kiss. Nothing more."

She crossed her arms in a defensive gesture, and her tone was hard as steel. "I've heard that before."

Ty stared at her for some time with a sad look on his face. Then he lowered his head and said flatly, "I'll see you tomorrow, Raina."

Raina saw the determined look on Ty's face as he turned and left the room. She began to tremble and paced the floor for a time before finally getting into bed.

She lay awake, unable to forget the encounter with Ty. She had a fleeting thought that maybe she'd misjudged him, but her old defenses returned in strength. *He's just like the others!* She finally fell into a fitful sleep with the sense that her future lay before her like a black tunnel whose end she could not see.

Raina woke with a start, and at once the incident with Ty flooded her mind. *I'm all alone now!* She knew that she and Ty had lost something, and the sense of loss was sharp.

She shook off the depressing thoughts, then rose and dressed. She was startled by a knock at the door.

It was Ty, but the sight of him was troubling. His features were stern. "We have to have breakfast," he said, his voice revealing nothing.

Raina hesitated and said, "I'm sorry I spoke to you so sharply last night, Ty."

"The fault was mine, not yours. It won't happen again." His voice was flat.

Raina went with him to the dining room, and the meal was a misery for her. Ty didn't speak, and it was all she could do to swallow the food. When they rose, Raina followed him, hoping they could talk, but the glance she got of his features convinced her that they were now two strangers with nothing to say to one another.

"We're there, Raina."

Raina was in the stateroom. She heard Ty's knock and opened the door at once. "Do we get off now?"

"Well, we'll get our things together. It won't be long."

"Here. Take the money."

"No, you keep it. You'll have to find a place to live."

After they had packed their few belongings, Ty carried the trunk up and they moved their baggage. Finally they sidled into a wharf, and a plank board was let down. He shouldered the trunk, and she followed him off the boat.

When they got on land, he put it down and turned to face her. "We'll have to find you a place to live."

"I have to thank you."

"No, I'm in your debt. I'd have been in prison if it hadn't been for you." He hesitated and pulled off his hat and ran his hand through his coarse black hair. His face looked rough, but she had learned that the roughness was all in the outer man. "I'll be around, Raina. If you need me, let me know."

"That's good of you, Ty. But I hope I don't have to call on anyone."

"Come on. I'll carry your trunk."

It did not take long to find housing for there were several boardinghouses. The first three had no rooms, but at the fourth one, the landlady had two available. Raina chose one.

When he carried her trunk upstairs, he took his hat off and said, "I'll be going."

She hesitated then put out her hand.

He was surprised but took it.

She was aware of the bluntness and the strength of his grip. "Good-bye, Ty."

Ty was shocked at her gesture, but he said, "We'll be seeing each other."

Raina watched as he turned and left the room. She felt a sense of loneliness. He had been her hope of protection, and now he was gone, forever, she was convinced.

She went to the window and saw him walk away. Suddenly she was filled with a sense of loss and was terrified at what lay before her.

PART TWO

CHAPTER 8

Raina awoke when the storm that had been threatening the day before finally broke. A boom of thunder brought her awake, grasping at the bed covering as if for safety. She was very afraid, and for a moment could not think where she was. Finally a drum of thunder came to her.

She got up and walked to the window. The sky was very dark, and the wind was blowing hard. She stood looking out while the thunder clapped loudly and sharply and reverberated endlessly, rolling off into the distance. She wanted to go back to bed, for the weather had turned cold, but she knew she would not sleep through the storm.

She looked out the window and blinked as the lightning forked in the sky. It seemed to grab at the ground and burn and leap upward, crackling. While the thunder boomed and struck her ears, the bright streak blinded her eyes. Then the rain started, a few drops and then increasing as if someone had poured a huge bucket of water over the town.

Finally Raina went back to bed and managed to sleep until dawn. She got up, shivered, and quickly put on the warmest clothes she had. When she was fully dressed, she went to the window and stared out.

On the damp ground a flight of sparrows were searching for food. Taking a piece of a sandwich that she had had the night before, she tossed it out. Immediately the birds began to fight over it, and she remembered a romance she had read and a character who had said, "Birds in their nest agree, so why can't we?" And through her mind came the thought, *No, no, even birds have fights.*

She lit the lamp. The room was dark with the one tiny window. The yellow blaze, small as it was, cast its glow on the darkness of the room. She went to the washstand and discovered that there was a film of ice on the water in the pitcher. She broke it with her fist and poured the basin half full. She forced herself to wash in the cold water, then she looked up and saw that her hair was not as neat as she usually kept it.

She thought of a set of mother-of-pearl combs and a brush that had been her mother's—and hers. It was all she'd had of her mother's, and she felt the loss of it. She had misplaced them or someone had taken them. In any case, it was one of the many things that she had lost, and it made her sad. She felt dirty. Her clothes were filthy. She always hated that, but there was no other choice.

When she was fully dressed she sat down on the bed, and fear swept over her like waves. She thought abruptly of Ty and was disturbed to find that she missed him. She couldn't help but think of their time in the cabin and how they had been so close.

Then another thought came to her of the time he had kissed her and how she had lashed out at him. *I wish I could do it over again. He wasn't that bad. It was my foolishness.*

She tried to brush the thoughts away but had little success. Finally she stood and gave up on her hair. She took one more look out the window and saw that the morning was white with frost. The trees outside stood stiffly as if reaching for something they could not have, and some of the roofs were lightly quilted with frost. At that same moment the wind began to utter a long, low whine from the eaves of the building, and tiny flakes of snow began to dance before her eyes. This disturbed her, so quickly she went downstairs to the kitchen.

Mrs. Mullins, the lady who owned the house, said, "You're just in time for breakfast. I've got some biscuits made."

"Oh, I can fix my own breakfast, Mrs. Mullins."

"That would be a help."

Raina found a basket full of eggs, and being hungrier than usual took two of them and three slices of thick bacon. She turned the bacon over until it was well done and then made her eggs over lightly. There was a jar of some sort of jelly on the table, rather dark. She tried it and found that it was delicious. "This is good fig preserves."

Mrs. Mullins was a large woman with lines of fatigue in her face from running a boardinghouse. "My husband planted that tree. We always had a good crop of figs." She made a face and shook her head. "It was the only thing he could ever do well. No farmer at all." She poured herself a cup of coffee and filled Raina's cup again. "Have you come far?"

"Yes, pretty much."

"Well, you picked bad weather to travel in. You got business in Fort Smith?"

"One thing I have to do is find my father. I'll show you a picture of him. I only have one. His name is Ed Vernay."

"Well, I don't believe I know the man, but you can ask around and somebody's probably heard of him around here. He's in this part of the world, you say?"

"The last I heard—which has been quite awhile ago."

"Well, are you going to stay here long?"

"I don't have much money."

"Well, there's a Chinese man here who does washing. Your clothes probably need it after that long travel."

"Oh, I couldn't afford to hire somebody."

"Why, you can use my tubs. You'll have to heat the water on the stove before I start cooking lunch."

"Thank you, Mrs. Mullins." The kindness of the woman pleased her, and she spent the next hour heating water and washing all of her clothes. She asked Mrs. Mullins if she could hang them close to the fire.

She said, "For the next hour you can, then I have to start cooking dinner."

After she washed her clothes, she borrowed Mrs. Mullins's iron and pressed them.

Two of her boarders came in, rough-looking men, and one of them winked at the other one and said, "Hey, sweetie, how about you and me goin' out tonight?"

Mrs. Mullins entered as he spoke and said, "That's enough out of you, Bill. Leave this lady alone."

Both of the men laughed, not at all intimidated. "We'll be

back. We'll work on that goin' out together."

When the two men left, Raina said, "Thank you for taking up for me."

"Well, what are you aiming to do now?"

"Well, I'll start trying to find my father."

"How will you do that?"

Raina suddenly realized she had no idea about how to find a man who had disappeared from her own life years before. "I don't know," she said. "I'll just have to start asking around."

"That won't be easy," Mrs. Mullins said. "People comin' and goin' here all the time. Most of 'em is trash and wouldn't help you unless there was money in it for them."

"I don't have enough money for a reward."

"I didn't reckon so. Just didn't want you to get your hopes up."

Raina shook her head. "I don't have much hope, but I have to try to find my dad. I don't have anyone else."

"Sad to have no folks."

"Do you have a family, Mrs. Mullins?"

"Me and my man had five children—but two of them died and the others went off."

"You don't know where they are?"

"No, I wished I did."

The two talked for a while, and then Mrs. Mullins said, "You ort to go to the hanging."

"A hanging? Why would I go there?"

"Why, you might see your pa there."

It was a thought that never would have occurred to Raina, but she decided at once that she would go. *I might not know him if I saw him. All I have is this one picture, and he's a lot older now.* She got her coat and left the boardinghouse.

The flakes of snow had fallen enough to whiten the ground. As Raina walked down the main street of Fort Smith, she was not overly impressed. It was not a beautiful town. The main street had businesses on both sides, usually in framed buildings, many of them unpainted. The bank itself was made out of brick, as was the courthouse, but aside from them, the buildings were mostly warping lumber.

She had almost reached the end of the street, and she saw a crowd had gathered. They were talking loudly. She went closer to watch.

A woman stood next to her. She was wearing a scanty-looking dress and over it a coat not fastened in the front. The woman turned to her. She had a hard look about her. Her early beauty had faded. "Do you know the fellow?"

"What fellow?"

"The one being hanged."

"No, I'm new to town. Who is he?"

"Mack Wilford. He killed his wife and her cousin and a marshal who came to arrest him. Ought to be a good one. Mack's a tough man." She laughed shrilly and said, "We'll see how tough he is with a rope around his neck."

Raina had nothing to say to this. She had never seen a hanging and suddenly had an impulse to leave, but for some reason she stood in place waiting to see what would happen.

"My name's Alice."

"I'm Raina."

"So you're new around here. . . ."

"Yes, I just got in town yesterday. I'm looking for my father.

I've lost touch with him, but I know he's somewhere here in the territory." She reached down in her reticule and pulled out the picture. "This is him. You ever see him?"

"Nope," Alice said, "but to a dance hall girl, all men look alike—" She broke off suddenly and glanced up. "Look, there's the judge."

Raina looked up and saw a dignified-looking man standing in the second-story window. The window was up, and he ignored the cold weather.

"Who's that?"

"That's Judge Parker. They call him the Hanging Judge."

"Don't all judges hang people from time to time?"

"Not as many as Parker. He never misses a hanging. He must have hanged forty men. How do you think a man would feel if he hanged forty men?"

"Pretty bad I would imagine."

"Look, there's Jack Maledon."

"Who's Maledon?" Raina asked.

"He's the hangman. See, he's got that rope. He went all the way to Saint Louis to get the rope he uses to hang men. He's very fussy about his job."

Maledon was a small man with a large, long-pointed beard. His eyes were a cold gray, and he appeared to be completely uninterested in what was going on.

"He tries to pretend he don't like it, but he does. One time they hanged six men all at the same time. They made quite a racket when they pulled the trapdoor. See that scaffold there? They can hang as many as eight men at once. I doubt if there's another gallows like that in the whole country."

"I don't see how a man could live with himself knowing he had hanged men like that."

Alice laughed again, her voice shrill and yet without humor. "Can you imagine when he goes home and his wife says, 'How was your day, Jack?' 'Oh,' Jack would say, 'I only hung two. Not a very good day.'"

"Look, that must be the man they're going to hang."

Everyone in the crowd began to murmur as a man came out. His hands were tied behind his back, and he was kicking and cursing at the two jailers who dragged him out.

One of them said loudly enough to be heard, "Now Mack, be nice."

"Be nice nothin'!" Mack Wilford cursed the jailers, Maledon, the judge, and the people who were watching. He was practically dragged up the stairs and held in place.

Maledon came forward with a hangman's noose in his hand, pulled a black mask over Wilford's face, and then adjusted the rope.

"I often wonder why they do that," Alice said. "What don't they want 'em to see?"

Raina watched in horror as Maledon tightened the noose so that it was just under the man's left ear. He stepped back then and without warning pulled the switch. The trapdoor opened beneath Wilford's feet. He shot downward, and she heard plainly the snapping of his neck.

"Well, he was a tough one," Alice said. "Some of them faint."

The execution sickened Raina. She turned to leave.

Alice said, "You go see the judge. He knows lots of people. He may know where your pa is."

"Thank you, Alice." Raina left and made her way to the court-house. The crowd was dispersing. She walked in and asked a man who was also entering, "Where would I find Judge Parker's office?"

The man was not imposing. He had a pair of direct blue eyes and a mustache and a big pistol on his side. "Well, it's upstairs, but you won't be able to see him now. He's behind with his court. You can try later."

"Do you know him?"

"Yes, ma'am. My name's Heck Thomas. I'm the chief marshal."

"I'm here looking for my father. Would you look at this picture to see if you've seen him?"

Heck waited while she pulled out the photograph, and he stared at it. "No ma'am, I don't recognize him, but that don't mean I ain't seen him. There are so many folks here, and I see lots of 'em. If I see a face on a Wanted poster, I don't forget it, but I don't recollect your pa. You got any copies of this picture?"

"No, I don't."

"There's a picture man here. Takes portraits, you know. He could probably make some copies. You could pass 'em around. I got a hundred and fifty marshals, and they see lots of folks."

"Could I see the judge later?"

"I 'spect so. He's a mighty polite man, and he'll help you if he can. What's your name, miss?"

"Raina Vernay."

"Right pretty name, Miss Vernay. You come on back. I'll mention it to the judge."

"Thank you, Mr. Thomas."

Raina made her way back to the boardinghouse, not knowing what else to do.

Mrs. Mullins had a harried look. "My helper is sick and will not be able to assist me for a while. Can't pay much, but if you want to help me with the cooking, you can get your meal and fix up a storage room in the attic. That is, if you'll help me with the cooking and maybe some cleaning."

"I'll be glad to do that." The work did not sound terribly hard, and Raina was a fine cook. She peeled the potatoes and baked the bread.

That night, Mrs. Mullins, whose first name was Emma, said with satisfaction, "You'll do real well, Raina."

Later Raina served the table. There were eight men there. One man, about as rude and dirty as a man can get, made a remark equally rude.

Emma Mullins said, "Jack, if you can't be decent, you can get out and find someplace else to stay."

"Didn't mean nothin', Emma."

Mrs. Mullins said, "Miss Raina, show 'em your pa's picture."

Instantly she went to get her bag, got the picture, and passed it around. They all examined it but said they didn't know him.

The lack of response dampened her spirit. She helped Emma clean up.

The old woman then took her upstairs to the attic. The room was small, but it did have a window. It had a bed but lots of junk. "This is a catchall. I've got another place you can store all this stuff. You might make it fairly presentable. You'll need some bedding though. I can fix you up with that."

"Thank you, Emma. I appreciate your help. I feel kind of lonesome here. No people, no friends."

"Oh, you'll make lots of friends. These men are great at makin' friends with pretty women," she said sarcastically.

For most of the next day, Raina did her best with the room. It was indeed dirty and full of dust, and by the time she had moved out all of the extra stuff, washed the window, swept the floor, beaten out the rug that covered part of it, moved in her things, and fixed the bed, she was tired.

The room was cold so she put on her warmest clothes, lit the lantern by the bed, and then picked up one of the romances she had brought with her. She got in the bed and pulled the blankets over her and read the old romance again.

Finally it was time to go help Mrs. Mullins. She got up and went downstairs. She peeled potatoes, fried ham, shelled peas, and made coffee.

At the meal, the men were pretty much the same except there were two new faces. She showed them her father's picture, but neither of them had seen him.

After the meal was over and she had helped Emma with the dishes, she said, "I'm tired. I think I'll go to bed."

"Why don't you have some coffee before you go. It'll warm you up."

"Thank you, Emma." She drank the coffee, chatting with Mrs. Mullins.

She then went upstairs and, not bothering to undress, simply pulled off her shoes and got under the covers. She read some more of the novel but found it strangely unsatisfying this time. She realized she was longing for a real romance, one that provided more than those she read about in the pages of her books.

CHAPTER 9

A fly crawled across Ty's face, and he slapped at it unconsciously. The straw that he had slept in fitfully all night exuded a rank odor. Slowly Ty brushed his hand across his face and then opened his eyes to see the sunlight coming through a crack in the roof, putting a bar of yellow illumination on the livery stable.

Slowly he rose up to a sitting position, reached over his head, and stretched his muscles. The straw had been better than sleeping on the floor, but not a great deal. The lack of a bath troubled him, and he reached up and tried to scratch between his shoulder blades but did so ineffectually.

He got to his feet noting that his wardrobe was sparse. His jeans were worn and patched over the left knee, white with many washings. He dusted himself off as best he could.

Reaching into his pocket, he found a dollar and twenty-seven cents. He stared at the money as if by observing it he could make it multiply itself, then shook his head dolefully and stuck it back in his pocket. He took off his shirt and shook it violently, getting the straw and the dust out of it. He put it back on and buttoned it. Then he picked up his coat and shrugged it on. It had been an expensive coat at one time, but that was many years ago. Now it was merely shabby and did little to cut out the cold. His hat was hanging from a nail in the rafters, and he plucked it off and jammed it on over his head. Slowly he left, and not seeing anybody in charge of the livery stable, he filed it in his mind that he might have to come back and spend another miserable night in the straw.

He walked along the boardwalk, noting that the town was only gradually coming to life. A few stores were now opening up, and glancing up, Ty saw that a darkness lingered beneath the stars.

He moved slowly and noticed the sun was just beginning to glow in the eastern sky. He passed by some birds that were noisy with a wild joy, twittering and calling. They were not yet singing but ecstatically greeting the day.

Sunlight soon ran fresh and fine throughout the town, flashing against the windowpanes and cutting long, sharp shadows against the dusty velvety carpet. "Going to be cold today," Ty muttered, but it was not a complaint. He had expected no less.

He reached a café and was glad to see that it was open. When he entered, he saw that he was the only customer. He sat down at one of the tables covered with a dingy red-and-white-checked tablecloth.

A woman came over. She was past her prime but still attractive, somewhat overweight but with a figure that drew men's eyes. "What'll you have, hon?"

"I guess bacon and eggs, if you have it."

"Sure do and some fresh biscuits, and how about some coffee?"

"That sounds good to me."

"Be right back." He watched as she left, swaying in a practiced gait that she had obviously assumed would attract men's attention.

As soon as she disappeared through a swinging door, Ty leaned back and closed his eyes. The night had been fitful, and he had slept little. Now he felt the grim arm of weariness and despondency drawing him in. He was not a man who gave in easily to such things, and finally he put the matter out of his mind. *I'll get out of this somehow,* he thought. *I always do.*

Ten minutes later the woman brought out a platter of eggs and bacon and a cup of coffee. "I'll get your biscuits, hon."

"Thanks. That will be just fine." He began to eat slowly.

When she brought the biscuits, she had a chunk of butter on a saucer. "This is fresh butter. Just put some of that on them biscuits, and I'll bring you some jelly to go with it. Blackberry jelly, I think."

"That would go down real well."

She turned to leave, then stopped to turn and face him. She flirted with him wantonly. Ty knew that she was one of the many women he had met who outlasted their first flush of beauty and began to degenerate.

He answered, but mostly he paid attention to the food. He ate slowly, chewing as well as he could, and he did find that the biscuits with the blackberry jelly and butter were as good as any he had ever had. When he had finished, he asked, "What do I owe you?"

"Seventy-five cents, I guess."

He put a dollar down, smiled at her, and nodded. "Mighty good food," he said.

"I get off at six o'clock."

"Maybe I'll see you then."

"I hope so, hon."

Leaving the café, Ty walked down the plank boardwalk. The earth began to warm up, not a great deal, but it was better than the coldness of the livery stable. He was thinking about what to do next when he saw a man wearing a star leaning back against the wall of a two-story building. Glancing up, he saw the sign said City Hall. Slowing down, he walked over and said, "Howdy."

"Hi there. Gonna be warmer I reckon today."

"I'm new in town. Come a long way. I'd like to be one of Judge Parker's marshals."

"I'm Frank Dillinger. I'm one of the marshals." A gloominess occupied the man and marked his face with a doleful expression. "You better think on that."

"Why had I better do that?"

"Why, it's a dangerous line of work." Dillinger reached into his pocket, pulled out a plug, took a bite, and stared at the remains joylessly. "Mighty dangerous work. The judge used to have two hundred marshals. Over fifty of 'em have been killed. Dangerous line of work."

"Well, I guess I'm ready for that."

"Your choice." Dillinger shrugged. "The judge's always lookin' to hire more marshals but can't find many who can do the job."

"What kind of qualifications is he looking for?" Ty smiled.

"Somebody that's tough. I guess that's the biggest thing. Bein' smart don't help a lot. Got to be tough to be a marshal these days. Just last week there was two of our men got waylaid and shot not ten miles out of town. They never even seen the killer, I reckon. Nobody knows why they was killed, but you make enemies in this line of work."

"Well, I'd like to see the judge."

"Guess you'd better wait until after the hanging. He's in a bad mood on hanging days."

"What time will the hanging be?"

"I think this one will be at ten o'clock. You'll see the judge standing up in that second-story window. He never misses a hanging."

"Pretty hard man?"

"Hard as you ever seen. I guess I'd feel kind of jumpy myself if I'd hanged forty men. I wonder what he thinks about at night. . . ."

"Probably about the next forty men." Ty walked away from the courthouse and stopped long enough to take a free cup of coffee from the blacksmith's shop. He was watching the blacksmith shoe a fine black stallion, and he commented, "I never could do that. It takes a special man to be a blacksmith."

Tim Carver, the blacksmith, was a bulky middle-aged man. He grinned and said, "You've got to have not much sense and tough muscles. That's about it."

The two fell into a conversation about the art of shoeing a horse. A crowd began gathering.

"It looks like that hanging is about ready to take place," the blacksmith said. "Sure hate to see it."

"Do you watch 'em?"

"No sir, not me! I got bad enough dreams without some of them comin' into it. Most people do though."

The blacksmith was correct, because by the time ten o'clock rolled around, a large crowd was gathered around the gallows.

Ty had no interest in seeing a hanging. He had seen two and had not liked either one—but he was shocked to see Raina. She was standing back in the crowd. His eyes fell on her, but he didn't move toward her.

He was aware that a man had moved in beside him and turned to see a well-built individual wearing a gray suit and a fancy checkered vest. "You new in town?" He had a pair of intense gray eyes and was watching Ty carefully.

"Just got in."

"I'm Sid Driver. I own the Lucky Star Saloon. Come on over and try your luck."

"No, I won't be doin' that. I'm flat broke."

"You lookin' for work?"

"I'm hoping to get a marshal's badge."

Driver shook his head. "Better you than me. Lots of danger and low pay. But come in when you can afford to lose a dollar or two."

"I may do that."

☙

The hanging had been perfunctory. One of them was already dead, and the one who did the shooting was soon dead at the end of a rope.

Looking up, Ty saw Judge Parker staring down. *I wonder what a man thinks that's killed forty men with a rope. Not for me.* He made his way back to the courthouse and found another man he had not seen before.

He was a small man, a careless dresser, with intense blue eyes and light brown hair. "Howdy," he said. "What can I do for you?"

"I'd like to see the judge if I can. I'd like to get on as one of his marshals."

"I don't think you'll have much luck right now. The judge always gets behind on hangin' days. Come back though about maybe three o'clock in the afternoon, and you can see him."

"My name's Ty Kincaid."

"Heck Thomas. Glad to know you, Kincaid. You just get into town?"

"Yes, sure did."

"You ever done any law work?"

"A little bit. I soldiered some. I was a deputy in Texas. Can't say I was the best they had, but I did my job."

Thomas grinned and sent a stream of tobacco juice to the floor. "Wal, that's all a mule can do, ain't it?"

"Guess that's right."

"Well, come on back around three o'clock."

Having nothing to do for the rest of the day, Ty Kincaid went into the Lucky Star. He had enough for one beer, and he nursed it along.

The bartender wiped in front of him and said, "Have one of them sandwiches."

"Thanks. I believe I will."

The sandwich was good, and Ty ate two of them. He was finishing the second one when a woman came over.

"Hello, I'm Marie."

"Sorry, Marie, I'm broke."

"Well, that's too bad."

At that instant a big, rough-looking man came over and took Marie's arm. She cried out.

Ty could never stand to see a woman mistreated. He put the stein of beer down and turned to face the big man. "Turn loose of her arm and be on your way."

Somebody said, "You better look out. That's Hal Carson."

"I don't care who he is," Ty said lightly. He stood with his feet slightly apart, ready for anything Carson might offer.

He looked like a drunk and had been drinking, but he had a neck as thick as any that Ty had ever seen. He sneered at Ty and squeezed the woman's arm.

Ty reached out and struck him in the throat.

Carson backed up coughing and gagging, but he came back ready for a fight.

Ty didn't need any more bruises or cuts. He pulled his gun with a lightning draw and hit Carson over the head.

When the man went down, his head split. Finally he crawled to his feet, blood running down both sides of his nose.

Ty said, "You can either leave or I'll shoot your knee off and you can crawl around for the rest of your life."

Sid Driver had come over at that moment. "You better move on, Hal. Maybe you can come back later."

Carson wiped the blood off his face, smearing it and making a worse mess. "You won't always have that gun," he gasped.

"I'll always have the gun, Hal. I sleep with it."

As Carson walked away, Sid said, "You better watch out. He's a pretty mean fellow. He'll try again."

"He'd better not."

Marie had not moved. She was rubbing her arm and said, "Thanks. I'll buy you a drink."

"Drinks on the house for you two." Sid smiled.

Ty refused the offered drink as it was almost time to meet the judge.

Sid walked back to his table, and Ty heard him say to his bouncer, "Pretty fast, isn't he, Jack?"

Jack shook his head. "I ain't seen a draw that fast since Slinger Dunn went down. He could have stopped Carson's clock real easy."

Ty grinned as he left the Lucky Star to go meet with the judge. He was back at the courthouse by three o'clock as Heck Thomas had suggested.

Heck immediately motioned for Ty to follow him. Heck led Ty up to Parker's office on the second floor and without knocking opened the door.

Ty could see from the door that the judge looked tired. It was well known that he took his cases seriously, and after a hanging he was always in bad spirits.

"A fellow wants to see you, Judge," Heck began.

"I'm too tired. What does he want?"

"Wants to be a marshal."

Judge Isaac Parker was a tall man, well built, with an aristocratic face. He had served as a lawyer and as a judge. He was now in Indian Territory as appointed by the government, and his rule was law. He had lost many men. It was a rough and dangerous world he sent them out into. "Well, what does he look like?"

"Well, he roughed up Hal Carson. That ought to count for somethin'."

Ty was surprised Heck had already heard about his confrontation in the Lucky Star. He was also embarrassed by the chief marshal's praise.

"Send him in, Heck."

Heck motioned for Ty to enter. "Come on. The judge will see you."

Ty walked through the door with Parker's name on it.

Judge Parker said at once, "I understand you want to apply for a job as a marshal."

"My name's Ty Kincaid, Judge Parker. I guess that's right."

"Well, you realize it ain't like sellin' peanuts at a circus."

The judge's rough attempt at humor amused Ty. "I never thought it was. I know you lose men."

"Tell me why I should hire you."

"Well, I served as a peace officer in Fort Worth, Texas, quite some time ago. I reckon the sheriff there would give me a recommendation if you wrote him a letter."

"So you've done some law work."

"Yes, a little."

"What else?"

"Well, to be honest, I should tell you that I worked for a time in Mexico and was arrested falsely for being a revolutionist. I escaped with the help of a friend and ended up in Louisiana, where I was taken to jail by a sheriff who recognized me from a Wanted poster. I escaped from there, too, and made my way here. I know you can have me put in jail right now, but I really want to serve as a marshal. I promise to uphold the law the best I can."

The judge stroked his chin. "I thought I recognized your name. I heard a wanted man was on the loose named Ty Kincaid. Well, I can take care of that if I decide to hire you." Parker remained silent as he sat thinking. "All right. I'm gonna take you on tentatively until I hear from the sheriff you worked for and check into that Mexico business. What's his name?"

"Bud Zeller."

"Why, I know Bud. If he'll recommend you, that's all I need. I hate to write letters. You give me your word that this is the truth?"

"No need to lie, Judge."

Heck had come in and picked up on the last of this. "I expect you're broke. I've got a spare bed at my place. You can bunk there until you get a payday."

"Thanks, Judge. And I'll take you up on that, Heck."

He followed Heck out the door, and they went down the street and turned the corner. Heck paused in front of a small house and said, "I'll expect you to help with the expenses when you get paid." He unlocked the door and walked inside. "There are two bedrooms. You can take the one over there. It's got a stove. Can you cook?"

"Ham and eggs."

"That's about my speed, too. I get most of my meals from the Chinese. They're the best cooks." He turned and stared at Ty carefully. He was obviously accustomed to judging men in his line of work. "You ever kilt a man, Kincaid?"

"Yes."

"How'd it feel?"

"Not good."

Heck grinned and shook his head. "You get used to it riding for the judge. Here. I'm giving you twenty dollars out of my pocket. You can give it back when you get paid. Go buy some better clothes. You look like a bum."

"I'll do that."

Ty was leaving when he ran into two more marshals. One of them introduced himself as Larry Dolby. He was a tall man in his midthirties with blond hair and faded blue eyes. He introduced his companion as Gale Young. He was ironically a younger man in his early twenties.

"We're happy to know you. Didn't get your name."

"Ty Kincaid."

"Well, I'm glad you're here," Young said.

"Why's that?"

Young grinned. "Now I ain't the newest man around here. You are."

"You better watch out for this fellow," Dolby said and winked at Ty. "He's a bad man around women."

"I'll keep an eye on him."

Young said, "He's teasin' me, but that's the truth. I ain't no good with women."

"That's probably a good thing," Ty replied. "Well, I have to go buy some clothes. Marshals ought to be dressed right."

Young grinned and said, "Don't know about that. Ain't none of us won prizes in the fine clothes contest. Look at what I'm wearing." Indeed, the marshal was wearing a pair of pants with patches and a shirt that was much too large for him.

"Why don't you buy some nicer ones?"

Larry sniffed. " 'Cause he lost his money playing poker 'fore he could get to the general store. Maybe you better lend him enough to buy something nice."

"Wish I could, but I don't have much. And I'll be as ragged as you are, Gale, before long."

"We'll be a matched set then. See you later, Ty."

Ty left the two marshals behind as he headed out to buy some new clothes. He was thrilled to be counted as one of Judge Parker's marshals and determined to be one of the best in the territory.

CHAPTER 10

The sun was peering over the western mountain range, casting a pink tint along the lower edge of the sky. Overhead, clouds were beginning to form, and there was a feeling of colder weather in the air.

"I don't know why we have to get up so quick."

A group was gathered around the campfire, watching as Joshua Hayes flipped a pancake in the air and caught it in his pan. Hayes was a small man with faded blue eyes. He was worn by what appeared to be hard labor, and now he said, "Come and get it. I've got one for each of you. I learned to cook with three pans when I was no more than fifteen years old."

Aaron Jordan, a big man with black hair and brown eyes, came over and picked the pancake out of one of the pans. "It looks good, Joshua."

"Bless the Lord for good pancakes."

Aaron Jordan grinned. "I believe you'd bless the Lord if you broke your leg."

"As a matter of fact I did, Mr. Jordan. Broke my leg in two places, and all I could do was thank the Lord for it."

"I don't believe all your stories." Leoma Jordan, Aaron's daughter, had come up and removed a pancake and poured syrup over it. She took a bite and chewed. "I think you make up all these stories about how God takes care of you."

"No, I don't make up nothin' about that. Now I do get a little bit wild with my huntin' stories." He poured batter into Leoma's frying pan and watched as it spread out into a perfect circle.

Lottie, Aaron's wife, was a blond woman still pretty despite her forty-three years. "I been thinking about what Oscar Manning told us about this ranch we bought. He made it sound—I don't know—dangerous."

Aaron chewed thoughtfully on his pancake, swallowed, and shook his head. "No," he said, "there're seven of us. We can defend ourselves. I know this is Oklahoma Territory, but we've got enough gun power here to keep the bandits off."

"I don't care. I don't think he told us the truth about this. He sold out too cheap."

Leoma spoke up. "Manning was pretty tired of the ranch. He seemed like a hard man. I wouldn't think he would give up that easily."

"Well, he was a hard man," Ash said, "but he didn't have no family like we've got." Ash was the older son of Aaron and Lottie. He was one inch over six feet tall with black hair and dark eyes. He gulped his breakfast down and said, "How about another pancake, Joshua?"

"Just one minute, boy." He flipped it in the air and caught it and said, "When it bubbles on top it's ready to turn over."

"Pa, I think you ought to go ahead and see what's up ahead of us here. We don't really know where this ranch is for sure."

"Well, I think it's true," Aaron said, "that he had no family to help him. Just sorry drunks he couldn't depend on."

Ash poured more molasses over his pancake and cut it up with a knife at his side. He speared a large chunk, stuck it in his mouth, and chewed it, saying, "I figure we can handle a bunch of drunk Indians and these so-called outlaws that make their home in the Indian Nation." He gave Mingan a sly grin. "Reckon we'll have any trouble with your kinfolk, Mingan?"

Mingan had made another fire and was cooking his own pancakes. He was a tall man, lean but strong. He had jet-black hair, obsidian eyes, and a coppery complexion. His Indian blood showed, but only slightly. "If there are any Comanches come to get our scalps, I'll let you take care of them, Ash."

"You think they're pretty tough?" Ash demanded.

Mingan stirred up the fire, added another few sticks, and put the pan on. "I was working for old man Henderson who was taking a herd across Texas up north. One morning we woke up and found three men dead. They all had their throats cut. We never heard a sound."

"What'd you do?" Leoma asked, her eyes wide with shock.

"Old man Henderson turned the herd around, and we scooted back where we came from. Scared him to death, the old man."

"You a Comanche, Mingan?" Ash said.

"Not really. Just a quarter." He got up and turned to stare off into the distance. Finally he said, "You can cook the rest of these pancakes, Nelson."

Nelson Fox, called Nelly for short, was the smallest man, with brown hair and brown eyes. He was the best man with cattle. Good with horses, too.

"I'd hate to meet up with any of those Comanches." Harry Littleton stood beside him. He was only five-eight with tow hair and blue eyes. He wasn't as tough as the other men, but he was a faithful hand.

"I don't think Mingan's so tough," Ash said.

"He's the best shot we've got with a rifle, a handgun, or a knife," Benny said. He was the younger of the Jordan boys at only nineteen.

The talk ran around the campfire, and when they were through, Aaron said, "Let's get this herd started. We've got to get up to Fort Smith before dark."

Leoma saddled her mare and came to ride beside Benny, who was her favorite. "Don't pay any attention to Ash, Benny. He just likes to brag."

"I wish I was as tough as he is."

She leaned over and slapped him on the arm. "You're sweeter than he is. I'll tell you what. I'll find you a nice girl to fall in love with."

"Good." Benny grinned at her. He had a good grin. He was a pleasant-looking young man. "And I'll find you a marshal who's rich and handsome."

"You do that, Benny." Leoma smiled. "Find one who can write love poems and sing me romantic songs. That's what I'm looking for."

"Somehow I don't think these marshals are too romantic," Benny said, growing more sober. "They're a pretty tough bunch from what I hear. Well, let's get this herd moving."

Soon the air was full of dust made by the herd of cattle. With the hands and Aaron and his two sons, they had no trouble heading them. They crossed a small stream once and let the cattle and their horses water.

Aaron shook his head. "We ought to be getting close to Fort Smith pretty soon."

Mingan was riding by. "Sir, it's right over there. Don't you see that smoke?"

All of them turned, but none of them saw anything.

Ash scowled. "I don't think you see anything. You just like to brag on having good eyes like most Indians."

Mingan said nothing but shrugged and spurred his horse away.

Heck exited the jail and stopped. He looked down the street. "Looky there, Judge."

Parker was right behind him, and he stopped behind him. "Looks like a herd coming in. By the way, how's that new man going to work out?"

"I think he's gonna be a good one. He arrested Big Henry and put him in jail."

"Did Henry go easy? He's a pretty rough cob."

"Ty had to slap him on the head with the barrel of his six-gun."

"Good." He looked down the street and said, "They can't bring those cattle through the middle of town. Go head 'em off, Heck. Tell 'em to go around town. Wait outside."

Heck nodded quickly and mounted his sorrel and rode toward where the herd was approaching town.

Aaron Jordan saw a man approaching. "Howdy. What can we do for you?"

"Hello. I'm Chief Marshal Heck Thomas."

"I'm Aaron Jordan. These are my two sons, Ash and Benny. This is my wife, Lottie, and my daughter, Leoma."

"Well, we're glad to see you, Mr. Jordan, but it'd be better if you didn't go down the middle of town. These cattle make a real mess."

The two stood talking while the men got the cattle turned so they would circle the town. Aaron studied Heck, who was the first of the marshals they had seen, and Heck was rather unimpressive to him. Jordan said, "I bought Oscar Manning's ranch."

"Yeah, I heard Oscar sold out."

"Can you tell me how to get to his place? I've got a map, but I can't make much sense out of it."

"Oh, I can do better than that," Heck said. "I'll send one of my men to take you there."

Aaron shook his head. "You don't have to go to that trouble. We can take care of ourselves."

Heck took off his hat, scratched his head, then put his hat back on and pulled out a corncob pipe. It had tobacco in it evidently, for he struck a match on the seat of his pants and got it to draw. "Well, there's kind of a problem."

"A problem? What kind of a problem?"

"Well, Oscar had been leavin' the ranch all by itself, and a couple of pretty tough hairpins. . .well, they've moved into it."

"Why, what do they say?"

"They claim they own the place, but they can't prove it. They'll probably be pretty hard to move. I'd better send a man with you in case they prove aggravatin'." He turned and rode back toward town.

Aaron only had to wait a few minutes. Heck soon returned, another man riding along. "This is Ty Kincaid," Heck said as soon as he reined in beside Aaron. "Ty, this is Mr. Jordan and his family. You remember I showed you Oscar Manning's ranch?"

"Sure, I remember, Heck."

"Well, Mr. Jordan bought the place, but Long Tom Slaughter and Fritz Holder have moved in on it and act like they own it. As a matter of fact, they ran some folks off. They're actin' like it's their ranch. You go along with these folks and move them two out."

"Sure will, Marshal."

"They may argue. If they do, just arrest 'em and bring 'em back to jail."

Aaron Jordan shifted uncomfortly. Ty Kincaid looked a little tougher than Heck, but Aaron thought himself capable of resolving any kind of trouble. "I like to handle my own problems, Marshal Thomas."

"You're gonna have a lot to do starting your new ranch," Ty said. "Besides, Mr. Heck Thomas is my boss, so I have to mind him. I'll lead the way."

❧

Leoma Jordan walked over to where her father was talking to the two marshals. She found the one named Ty rather attractive and allowed her eyes to trail over him as she asked, "How far is the ranch?"

"Oh, about ten miles."

Pa asked, "Any water along the way?"

"Sure is, Mr. Jordan. A nice little river. You can water your stock on the way."

"All right. Thank you, Marshal Thomas. I don't think we'll have any trouble with two men, but I appreciate a guide."

"You let Ty here do the fightin'. That's what he gets paid for."

Pa laughed. "I'm not sure about that, but we'll see."

The men got the cattle turned, and Ty rode along the outer end.

Leoma rode her mare, a paint that was a bit lively and suited her just fine. She moved closer to where Ty was riding and said, "So, you're a marshal."

"Brand-new one."

"That right? You haven't been a marshal long?"

"No, only a month."

"How do you get to be a marshal?"

"Well, some say you've got to get kicked in the head until you lose all your brains." Ty smiled. "I don't think there's any training involved, any special training, that is."

Leoma noticed that his eyes constantly moved from side to side as if he were aware of and alert to danger of some form. She had not seen a man like him before except Mingan perhaps. She studied him carefully. "Is it really dangerous?"

"It is. The worst men in the world are in the Oklahoma Territory."

"Why do they come here?"

"They get into trouble. They get run out of other places by posses and marshals. They come here to Indian Territory, and nobody can come after 'em except one of Judge Parker's marshals like me."

"What'd you do before you became a marshal?"

"Soldiered for a while. Was a peace officer in Dallas. Did a little prospecting. Didn't make my mark in any of 'em." His lips tipped into a grin.

Leoma was aware that he was a man of rough and durable parts, like a machine intended for hard usage. There was no fineness or smoothness about him. His long mouth was expressive only when he smiled. He had the blackest of hair lying in long chunks on his head, and his eyes were sharp and gray, well bedded in their sockets. He was, she guessed, at least six feet tall, long of arms and meaty of legs with a chest that had breadth rather than thickness. She was impressed by him, which was unusual, for men usually did not impress her. However, she sensed these marshals were a different breed.

"What about you folks? Where are you from?" Ty asked.

"Lately from Texas. Dad bought a ranch there, but it was getting crowded. He heard there was plenty of room in the Indian Territory."

"Yeah, plenty of reasons why there's plenty of room."

"You mean it will be dangerous to start a ranch here?"

"I wouldn't try it unless I had plenty of guns to back it up."

"What about you?"

"What about me?" he asked curiously.

"Are you going to be a marshal for the rest of your life?"

"Nope. Your family has been ranching a lot, I take it."

"Dad likes to try different things. He owned a factory for a while. Did well at it. Made enough money we went into ranching. Did well at that, too, but as I said, it was getting crowded there."

"Well, plenty of room out here. I noticed when I rode by your ranch that there was a creek running through it, so you shouldn't run short of water. That's always a problem ranching."

Ty smiled at her. She was a beautiful woman, and he was not at all unaware of it. He appreciated the supple lines of her body. She was in that maturity that follows girlhood. Her features were quick to express her thoughts, and there was a fire in her that made her very attractive to him. It brought out the rich and headlong qualities of a spirit otherwise hidden by the cool reserve of her lips.

"What about you? You got a wife somewhere?" she asked abruptly.

"No wife. Probably a good thing."

"Why would you say that? You don't like women?"

"I don't think marshals should have wives. I hate to think about the women who open the door and find Heck Thomas or one of the other marshals looking sad, and they know that their husbands are dead."

Leoma didn't have a response to this. But she realized this man was tougher than even she had thought. *I wonder what type of husband he would make. . . .*

At about three o'clock, Ty rode up to Aaron Jordan and said, "There's your ranch, Mr. Jordan."

"Looks right nice."

Ty nodded. "Yes, it's kind of gone downhill lately, but it will make a fine home."

"We appreciate you bringing us this far. I guess you can go on back now."

"No, I have to mind Mr. Heck Thomas. He's pretty hard on marshals who don't obey him. Well, let's see what it's like." He raised his voice. "You fellows bring the herd in slow until I find out how things sit around here."

He spurred his horse, and Jordan followed closely. He was aware of two men who had come out. He said as Jordan slowed down, "I think they're your uninvited guests."

"They look pretty tough."

"Most everybody is out here. You want me to handle this?"

"I guess so. I'll back you up."

They rode in and drew up in front of the two men, one of whom had a rifle, the other a gun at his hip. "I'm Ty Kincaid, federal marshal. Who are you fellows?"

"My name's Slaughter. This is Fritz Holder. What do you want, Marshal? We ain't breakin' no laws."

"Afraid you are. You're living on Mr. Jordan's property here. You'll have to pull out."

Slaughter laughed. "We're not pullin' out."

As Slaughter spoke, Ty suddenly pulled out a revolver. He was very still and said, "You can go to jail, or we'll bury you here. Which will it be?"

The two men were armed and dangerous, but both of them ostensibly saw that the gun in Ty Kincaid's hand was steady as a rock.

Ty kept his eyes fixed on them in terrible intensity.

"I ain't shootin'," Holder said and pulled his hand away from the gun.

"Take that gun out and put it on the ground, Holder. Slaughter, you put that shotgun down. Do it now."

The two obeyed. Slaughter said, "We ain't breakin' no laws except trespassin'."

"You want to bring charges against them, Mr. Jordan?"

"No, just get 'em out of here."

"You fellows git," Ty said. "You come back and give these folks any trouble, you'll have me and Heck and a dozen rangers on your trail. Get your stuff and get out."

Aaron motioned for his party to come in. The Indian, Mingan, said to Nelly Fox, "Good thing they gave up. Kincaid's a killer."

"How can you tell?"

"How can you not tell? Didn't you see he would have put 'em down in a flash if they had gone for their guns? He's a hard man, but marshals have to be, I guess."

Ty pretended not to hear the praise. He had found it best in these situations.

The two outlaws soon left with packhorses laden down with their stuff.

Ty led Aaron and his family into their house.

Leoma and Lottie shook their heads. Leoma said, "This place is terrible, Pa. Those two men lived like pigs."

"Well, we've got to clean it up. Might as well get started. You fellows get the cattle settled down and come and help us."

"I don't mind helping a little bit myself," Ty offered. "I'm too late to get back to Fort Smith."

Leoma smiled. "Most men won't do women's work."

Ty shrugged. "Work is work," he said. "A man does what he has to do. In this case it will be easier than some other things I've done. What do you need first, Mrs. Jordan?"

They, along with the hands, all cleaned up the house as well as they could for one night's occupancy. There were bedrooms enough for the family, and Ty slept out in the bunkhouse with the hands.

When everyone was settling down, Benny came out. "We got some coffee on the stove, Mr. Kincaid. Come along with the other guys and get some."

"No mister about it. Just Ty's good enough. And thanks for the offer. I'll come with them."

Benny turned to go but paused. He faced Ty again, a serious expression dominating his face. "Would you have shot those two men?"

"If I had to. That's why I carry a gun. Don't like to use it, but better to have one than not have one and get shot."

"I wish you'd show me how to shoot."

"Well, you've got a gun."

"I never had no lessons though," Benny said. "I'm pretty good with a rifle, but I can't shoot straight with a forty-four."

"Just like pointing your finger," Ty said. "Sure. We'll go out and get some target practice early in the morning."

"Thanks. I appreciate it. Glad you came along." The young man walked away quickly.

A terrible thought came to Kincaid. *That young fellow could get killed. He don't realize how bad these men are in the Indian Nation. None of them realize it. I hope they don't find out the hard way.*

CHAPTER 11

Raina tried to make yellow laundry soap foam but had no luck. For a moment she walked over and looked out the dirty window, and she remembered that Mrs. Mullins had told her they needed to be cleaned as soon as possible. The order came back to her, and she recalled how she had been glad to find a place to sleep and something to eat. But now, looking back on the days she had spent working as a combination maid, cook, and whatever other work needed to be done, she felt the weariness drain into her. For a moment she considered sitting down at the table, but now that the meal was over, she knew that the rest of the work would have to be done.

She lingered at the window for a few more minutes, and she saw a yellow tomcat creeping across the yard. A smile touched her lips as she saw the mockingbird that daily administered a thrashing to the big tom. The cat's head was scarred, and he crept along as if he could make himself invisible to the bird, but the mockingbird rose in the air, took a dive, and uttering a series of bird sounds, hit the yellow tom who didn't even run but rolled up in a ball as close as he could.

"Stupid tomcat." Raina shook her head in disgust. "All you have to do is reach out and grab that bird, and your troubles would be over. I wish mine were that simple."

She was weary with asking people if they had seen her father, and although she had had several copies of the picture of him made, nobody seemed to have any memory of him. *Maybe he's not here at all,* she thought. *Maybe he went somewhere else. He could be anywhere. He could be dead.* She turned away from her depressing thoughts and began cleaning up the dishes. She raked off the scraps onto one plate.

Going back to the window, she opened it and threw the leftovers out. The birds came at once since she had made a habit of this. She watched as some sparrows began to fight over the scraps and smiled. *I guess the birds in this town are just as mean-spirited as the people here—and everywhere else I've been.*

Moving wearily, she transferred all the dishes to the kitchen then straightened up with disgust when she heard the bell attached to the door ring. "Another customer," she muttered. "Now I'll have to cook him a meal. I wonder who it is."

She moved out of the kitchen, and her eyes opened with surprise when she saw that Ty Kincaid had entered and was standing in the middle of the room.

Their eyes met, and he said, "Hello, Raina."

"Hello, Ty."

Ty seemed at a loss, but then he said, "I just came in from a job and the restaurants are all shut down. You think you can fix me something to eat?"

"It won't be much, but I got some leftover steak and some potatoes and some greens, and I think there's some biscuits."

"You got any buttermilk?"

"Yes, I think there's a little of that. Sit down and I'll heat the food up for you."

She moved back into the kitchen and busied herself with putting the meal together. Fortunately the stove was still warm, so the vegetables and the steak were not cold. She filled up a plate and then a large glass with buttermilk, and adding a knife and fork, she moved back into the dining room.

Ty was slumped in the chair, fatigue etched across his features. She thought again what a fine-looking man he was and wondered that he had never married. He had said nothing much about his life, and she had not asked. The plate rattled when she set it in front of him, and he straightened up.

He looked up and grinned at her. "That looks mighty good, Raina. I haven't had anything to eat in nearly two days."

Raina did not respond and turned to go away.

He suddenly stopped her and said, "Raina, you look tired."

"I guess I am. I thought it was hard working in that saloon on the border, but this work is just as hard. At least I'm away from my brother-in-law. As bad as some of the men act toward me here, it is nothing like having Millard always after me."

Ty began to cut up the steak and said, "Sit down and talk to me. I've had no company but my horse."

"What were you doing?" She sat down, felt the weariness leave her, and then said, "Did you go out after an outlaw?"

"Well, there was three of us, and we looked for the fellow we thought held up the bank over in Green Springs, but he had an alibi so we couldn't bring him in."

Raina sat there watching him eat and noticed that he did not gobble his food like most men did. She saw he was watching her closely, and finally he said, "You know, you look like you need a week's vacation with somebody to wait on you."

Raina smiled, but there was a touch of bitterness in it. "I don't have anybody like that."

"Well," Ty mused and took a sip of buttermilk. Putting it down, he wiped his upper lip with a handkerchief that had seen better days. "There's an old saying. Sometimes there's just a good time waiting to happen."

"I'm having trouble believing that, Ty."

He took another bite, chewed it thoughtfully, and said, "You know, I think a lot about my grandfather. He made me read the Bible every day, and sometimes he read it to me. I remember a verse he quoted to me over and over and over again. I don't know where it is in the Bible, but he would have known."

"What does it say?"

"It says, 'In every thing give thanks: for this is the will of God in Christ Jesus concerning you.' "

"That doesn't make any sense to me. In *everything* give thanks? How could you be thankful when something bad happens?"

"Well, hard to say, but I think it has some truth in it."

"Tell me about how something bad turned out to be something good."

"The thing that I remember most was I was working on a ranch in Missouri, and the horse piled me up and broke my leg. I didn't have any money. Didn't really have a place to stay." He smiled slightly.

Raina saw the strength of his features and noted, as she usually did, what a strong character dwelled inside him.

"I thought of that verse, but I didn't believe it."

She leaned forward and put one of her elbows on the table and cupped her chin with her open palm. "Did you do what it said, give thanks?"

"Well, I tried, but I felt like a fool thanking God for a broken leg. I couldn't see anything to be happy about."

"So you didn't believe."

"No, I didn't."

"I don't blame you. I couldn't believe it either."

"Well, there's some more to that story. A week later, when I was still laid up, the fellows I had been working with went out to round up some cattle. A bunch of Comanches caught them. Killed every one of them. Staked 'em out and tortured 'em. If I had been with them, Raina, I would have lost my scalp. I'd be dead."

"That's a good story, but it doesn't always turn out like that."

"No, not always. But you remember when we were in that cabin and I was so sick, and you was having to keep the fire going to keep us from freezing to death?"

"I think of it a lot."

"Well, I bet if Grandpa had been there, he would have found something to thank God for. He was a thankful man. I think the last thing I heard him say was, 'Be sure you thank the Lord for every blessing, Ty.' He really meant it. I've never met a man like him before."

The two sat there talking while Ty finished his meal. Then he stood up, stretched, and said, "You got time to go for a walk?"

"No. I've got to wash these dishes, and then I have to wash some bedclothes."

"It'll be plum dark."

Raina wanted to complain, but she smiled and said, "Well, let's just give thanks that I've got all these dirty dishes and all these dirty sheets and pillowcases."

Ty smiled slightly and shook his head. "I know it sounds foolish, but sometimes it works out okay. Just remember those times in that cabin. I do. I think I'd have died if you hadn't been there to take care of me."

She didn't answer but noted that he was studying her carefully. Moving back to the kitchen, she thought about what he said as she worked on the dirty dishes and then started on the sheets and the pillowcases. "That's foolishness," she muttered. "Being thankful for something bad—I don't believe it."

※

Three nights later, one of the boarders, a small fellow named Kayo Flynn, tarried after the others had left. Raina was fairly sure that he was going to ask her to go out with him, but she had made a fixed rule not to date any of the men at the boardinghouse. They never gave up hope, but she knew that it was not a good idea.

She was surprised when he said, "Something came up today I thought you'd be interested in, Raina."

"What's that, Kayo?"

"Well, I was ridin' in, and I met a fellow out over by Juno Canyon. We got to talkin'. I've known him awhile, and I showed him the picture of your pa."

A ray of hope enlightened Raina, and she said, "What did he say?"

"Well, he said he wasn't sure. I'll have the man come by and talk to you."

"Oh, that was thoughtful of you, Kayo. I still have hope of finding my dad."

"I don't even remember my pa. I was an orphan. Grew up in an orphanage, but I do know this. He said the fellow was in jail, but you can go by and visit him and ask him."

For the first time in days, a small ray of hope illuminated Raina's mind. She thought about it as she worked all day, and finally when she got the dishes washed from supper, she left without telling Mrs. Mullins. She knew very well the woman would find something for her to do, but she was disappointed when she got to the jail.

The jailer, a tall, lanky man with deeply sunken cheeks, said, "You have to get Judge Parker's permission to visit people in the jail, lady."

"I'll do that. Thank you." She went at once to the courthouse and found Heck Thomas sitting out in front whittling as usual.

"Do you ever make anything out of those sticks you whittle on, Heck?" She smiled. She had learned to like the man. He had a bad reputation of being hard on criminals, but he was cheerful and said, "No, that gets too tedious. I just like to make shavings." He was whittling on a piece of cedar, and the shavings curled off and fell to the floor around his feet. He kicked them aside and said, "What can I do for you, Miss Raina?"

"I was told that I'd have to get Judge Parker's permission to visit somebody in the jail."

"No, that's usually the way, but we don't have to worry about that. Who is it you want to see?"

"His name is Charlie Dean."

"Sure. I know Charlie. We caught him sellin' liquor to the Indians. Catch quite a few that way."

"Kayo Flynn said that Charlie told him he'd possibly seen my father."

"Well, I hope you're right. Folks get lost out here in this part of the world." Heck looked despondent for a moment. "No matter how many criminals we catch and hang, there's always a new crop comin' on. Some of 'em are even women now."

"You've seen them hang women?"

"Sure have. Judge Parker don't show no favoritism to women. You go tell Frank Dillinger, he's in charge of the jail, that I said that you could see Charlie."

"Thank you, Heck."

Raina left and went back to the jail. She found Frank Dillinger eating some biscuits that looked tough enough to kill an ox. "You must be hungry, Frank, to be eating that stuff."

"Well, it was all there was. What can I do for you, Miss Raina?"

"I talked to Heck, and he said you could let me see Charlie Dean."

"Oh yeah. Come on. We've got a room. You don't need to be goin' down to where those no-good criminals are." He led her to a room that had a rickety table and four chairs, all old and looking rather flimsy. "Wait right here, Miss Raina. I'll get Charlie for you. Don't pay much attention to what he says. He's a world champion liar."

"Thank you, Frank. I appreciate that counsel."

Frank left the room.

She sat down in one of the chairs carefully, lest it collapse. She had not waited more than five minutes when she heard footsteps, and the door opened.

Frank and a small man, badly needing a shave and a bath, stepped in. The prisoner's clothes were filthy.

Frank said, "Well, here he is. Charlie, this lady's got some questions for you. You answer her now, you hear me?"

"Will that let me get out of here sooner?"

"You never know. Be nice now. I'll just be right outside the door."

As soon as Dillinger stepped out, Raina said, "I'm looking for my father, Charlie." She reached into her pocket and pulled out the picture she had in an envelope. She removed it and said, "Kayo Flynn said you thought you may have seen him."

"Yeah, I remember talking to Kayo about that. He had a picture like this one." Dean stared at the picture and said, "But no, this ain't the man. One I met was older."

"Oh, this is an old picture. He'd be close to fifty now. What was the man's name?"

"Well, everybody just called him Eddie. He looked older than fifty though."

"Can you tell me where he is?"

"I can tell you where he was. He's with some sheepherders over near Brice Canyon. Here. If you give me a piece of paper, I can draw you a map, but you don't want to be goin' out there by yourself."

"It's dangerous?"

"You bet your bird it is! There's guys out there that would kill you for a quarter."

Raina found a scrap piece of paper and a stub of a pencil.

Charlie Dean began to draw a map. "This right here is where we are in Fort Smith. You take the Old Military Road out of here for about ten miles. Then it divides, and you take the left fork. You'll get up into the high country there, and somewhere in that area, that's where I seen him."

Raina questioned him as closely as she could and asked everything she could think of. She didn't feel encouraged because Charlie Dean kept insisting that the man didn't really look like the picture. And besides, Frank Dillinger's warning that Charlie was a liar kept flitting through her mind. "Well, I'd like to pay you, Charlie, for your information, but I don't have any extra money." A thought came to her, and she smiled. "I can cook you a pie though."

"Oh, that's good. What kind?"

"How about apple?"

"My favorite! But listen, you have to get Heck or Frank to say I get it. Some of these guys in here would steal it from me."

Raina had a thought. "Could you possibly take me out there to this place? I don't really know the country."

"Well, I'd be glad to, but I expect I'll be in this jail for at least two or three months or maybe longer."

"Well, I'll get that pie to you very soon, Charlie. Thank you for your help."

"Sure hope you find your pa. A woman needs menfolk to look out for her."

Raina left the jail and started back toward the boardinghouse. She thought constantly about the man called Eddie whom Charlie Dean had described. He had not been very optimistic, but she realized that the picture she had was made when her father was a young man no more than twenty-three or twenty-four years old, and living a hard life could have made it very difficult for anybody to recognize a picture.

She worked steadily trying to think of a way to get to the man. She thought about asking Ty or one of the other marshals, but she held back. She told herself they were too busy with their jobs and probably wouldn't want to help her find her father anyway. She tried to pray but discovered that she had no confidence in that.

The next morning after breakfast, one of the boarders, Sam Terhune, came in late. "Could I have another one of them pancakes, Miss Raina?"

"Sure you can, Sam, and some more bacon, too." She brought in the bacon and the pancakes.

He said, "I hear tell you been tryin' to get someone to take you over to Brice Canyon lookin' for your pa."

"Yes, I have, Sam. Could you do that?"

"Well, I might could." He grinned at her. He was a homely man, but she recognized the lust in his eyes, for she had seen it often enough in other men. "I would expect a little affection for my trouble."

Raina expected no more out of the man. He had a reputation as a womanizer. "Thanks a lot, but I'll find another way." She became depressed after that and went about her work without a smile, but then, Mrs. Mullins did not require smiles, only hard work.

❧

The sun was high in the sky when Ty rode in. He held the lines to a second horse on which a tall man covered in dust was mounted.

"All right, Horace, you can get down now."

Horace Moore had his hands tied behind his back. He had tried to escape once, but Ty had roped him and jerked him off his horse. To make sure he didn't run away again, he had put him back in the saddle and threatened to shoot him if he tried to get away again. With Ty holding the lines, they had come into town, and when they reached the courthouse, Ty found Heck Thomas just emerging.

"Well, you got Horace this time, did you?" Heck said. He had a disgusted look on his face. "What's the charge this time, Ty?"

"He shot Leonard Hoskins's cow. Not a very daring sort of outlaw, is he? You're not Jesse James, are you, Horace?"

Horace gave him a rough look but refused to say anything. "I want a lawyer," he finally grunted.

"Well, we'll put you in the jail for a month or so, and then if you're a good boy, I'll see about getting you a lawyer. Hey Larry, take this bad criminal in and lock him up."

Larry Dolby shrugged and gave Horace a violent jerk on his arms. "Come on. I want to get you in there before you shoot somebody." He dragged the prisoner to the jail.

"Did he give you any trouble, Ty?" Heck asked.

"No, he just smells pretty bad. That's his worst crime, I think."

"Well, you were gone two days. Did you have trouble catchin' up with him?"

"He was hiding out over in the badlands. I was able to track him though. What's going on here in town?"

"Well, I know you're interested in Miss Vernay, ain't that so?"

Instantly Ty looked up. "Yes, she's a friend of mine. What's the matter?"

"Well, the thing is she's got a lead on where her old man might be, over north of where those new folks moved in."

"You mean the Jordans?"

"That's the one. Probably nothin' to it, but she's been tryin' to get somebody to take her out there."

"Well, she's had a rough time. If you give me a couple days off, I'll take her and see if there's anything to it."

"Oh, the judge won't mind. You just go ahead."

"I'll need to get a horse from the remuda to take her with me. Can't ride double."

"Oh, that's fine. Pick a gentle mare. I don't know how much ridin' she's done."

On second thought, Ty said, "You know, I don't think we ought to keep anything back from the judge. He has a way of finding out things. I'd rather him say no up front than to get back and find him in one of his mad spells."

"He's upstairs starin' at the docket. Go ahead and ask him. He won't care."

"Thanks, Heck, for telling me." Ty ascended the stairs, knocked on the judge's office door.

When he heard someone say, "Come in," he entered. He saw that the judge was sitting in his chair, but he had one foot without a sock or boot propped up on the desk. He was trimming his toenails with a pair of large tin snips, it looked like.

"You better be careful, Judge. You might cut your toe off."

"I'll take care of my own toes, thank you, Kincaid. What do you want?"

"I just heard that Miss Vernay's got a lead on her pa. I thought if it'd be all right with you, I'd take her out to the last place he was seen."

"What's your connection with that young woman? You got anything bad on your mind for her?"

Ty shook his head. "No, Judge, she did me a good turn before we came out here. I owe her something."

"All right, you can go. Get back as soon as you can. We got some fierce criminals roaming around. You ain't got time to romance any young women."

"I'll need a horse. Be all right if I take one of the spares?"

"Yeah, pick her out one. Take care of that young lady and behave yourself, or I'll put you where the dogs won't bite you."

Ty smiled. "I'll be careful, Judge. I know your reputation."

Raina looked up to see Ty coming in. He was dusty as if he had been out on a long ride.

"You look like you need a bath," she said.

"I sure do, but I hear you need some help looking for some man out to the north."

Raina straightened up. "Yes, I heard about a man named Eddie. One of the men in jail thinks he might be my pa, but he's not sure."

"Well, can you get off from work?"

"I'll have to. Why don't you go get cleaned up and I'll meet you?"

"You just wait here. I'll come by and pick you up. I'll have to get you a horse. You can ride, can't you?"

"Of course I can ride."

"All right." He smiled. "You better put some grub up, too. How far is this, you say?"

"Well, maybe forty miles. The man wasn't sure. I've got this map." She took the slip of paper out of her pocket and showed it to him.

"Yeah, that's a lot of territory to cover. We'll have to camp out one night. Maybe two. We'd better get enough grub off of Mrs. Mullins."

"She's not much for giving out grub, but I've saved some leftovers."

"I'll pick up some more stuff at the store. You better bring your blankets, too."

As soon as Ty left, she started thinking how she would tell Mrs. Mullins. Finally she decided there was no easy way, so she simply went and said, "Mrs. Mullins, I think I may have found my pa. I've got to be gone for maybe two days to find out."

"Well, I can't do without you that long." Mrs. Mullins was frowning and in a bad mood. "If you can't stay and do your job, I'll have to get somebody else."

For a moment Raina thought about not going, but then the stubbornness that played a part in her character emerged. "I've got to go, Mrs. Mullins. I'll get back as soon as I can."

"Never you mind. I've got a young woman who can do your work. Just have your room cleared out."

"All right. Thanks for the help you've given me."

"You're not very grateful."

"Come on now, Mrs. Mullins. If you hadn't had your pa around, but suddenly you might be able to find him, wouldn't you go?"

Emma Mullins was a hard woman. Running a boardinghouse for rough men did not bring out the gentleness in any female. She stared at Raina and said, "You can come back, but if anyone comes wantin' a job, I'm gonna put 'em to work. I'll take the best, her or you."

"I'll try my best to get back. I'm gonna have to sleep out. Can I borrow a couple of your blankets?"

"You be sure and bring 'em back, and make sure you wash 'em, too."

"Yes ma'am, I'll do that."

Quickly Raina pulled out some groceries that she had saved in case she did make the trip, put them in a meal sack, and got the two blankets off her bed. She packed a few of her warmer clothes and then looked around. "I'll have to come back for the rest of my things if Mrs. Mullins hires someone else." Quickly she exited the house and sat down in a home-built wooden chair.

Half an hour later, Ty came riding in, mounted on his buckskin and pulling a smaller horse. "Got you a good horse, Raina. Real gentle. Here, let me tie them blankets and that grub down."

"I don't know if I'll have a job when I get back."

Ty was busy folding the blankets. He tied them on with some rawhide thongs and then tied the grub on top of that. "Well, this is more important than a job."

"I don't know what I'll do, Ty."

"You'll find something." He looked at her and said, "You ready?"

"Yes, I am."

"I'm surprised you trust me."

Raina shook her head. She was feeling apprehensive. "I don't have any choice, Ty."

Ty came over and took her by the arm and led her over to the horse. "Here. I see you got that riding skirt on that you made on your way out here. That's good. Let's go." He helped her onto the mare, handed her the lines, and then he stopped long enough to say, "Raina, don't be afraid. I owe you, and I always pay my debt. Now, let's get as much daylight as we can between us and this town." He swung into the saddle, nodded, and then moved off into a slow walk.

As soon as they were out of town, he said, "Let's speed it up." He touched the buckskin and started out at a lope. He saw that Raina was a good rider and was keeping her seat well.

"Ty," Raina said, "I was feeling pretty bad, but I feel better now. Thank you for coming, for helping me."

"Why, it's nothing, Miss Raina. Let's go find that man and see if he's the one you're looking for."

"I—I really appreciate your help, Ty."

"Glad to do it, Raina, and if we don't find him on this trip, we'll go looking until we do. He's got to be somewhere, hasn't he?"

"Yes, but I've been discouraged, Ty."

"Natural you might be, but there's two of us looking now, and there's over a hundred federal marshals. I'll talk all of them into keeping their eyes open."

Ty's words encouraged Raina, and she felt a lift in her spirit. *I was wrong about Ty. He's a good man—just like I first thought he would be.*

CHAPTER 12

"How far do you think we've come, Ty?"

Turning sideways in the saddle, Ty looked back. "You getting tired?"

"I guess I've lost a little bit of my horsemanship doing nothing but washing dirty dishes and bedsheets. Back on the trail I thought I did pretty well."

"You did, but you lose it easy, too. Oh, I expect we've come around fifteen miles."

"How much farther is it to the river?"

"See that low-lying ridge over there? Just on the other side of that there's a canyon. There's a nice camping spot, too. I've stayed there once already. Can you last until then?"

Raina flashed him a smile. She was weary, but the more she had thought about it, the more she was grateful to Ty. She knew he was tired and had come in from a difficult hunt, although he made little of it. "I'm hungry," she said. "As soon as we get a place, we'll eat supper."

"That would go down right good."

The two rode steadily until the land began to lift. The ridge was not over seventy-five or a hundred feet high, but Ty's horse was tired, for he had come a long way. Ty said, "You know this is a tough horse. He's a stayer."

"He's not much to look at."

"Why, most horses and men aren't much to look at. Then you take ladies, they're the ones with the looks. Take you, for instance."

She suddenly laughed. "Never mind that. You're just along to shoot any outlaws that bother us."

"I doubt if we'll see anybody out here. I think I'll—" In a quick movement, he drew his gun from his side and extended it. The shot broke the silence of the badland.

"Did you hit anything?" she asked.

"Jackrabbit. We'll see if he's got enough meat on his bones to make it worth skinning him for."

They stopped fifty yards later, and he said, "This is a nice plump mama jackrabbit. I guess that makes her a doe rabbit. She'll make a good stew. There's the river along that line of trees. Come on." He stepped in the saddle again and led her down the hill, and when he came to the river, which was no more than twenty feet across, he said, "It doesn't look like much, but the water's good and clear. Spring fed, I think. Let's tie these horses out, and we'll make us a house for the night. I wish I had brought that tent I used to have."

"We'll make out."

"If it doesn't rain."

She followed him down, stepped off her horse, and tied the lines to a sapling. Ty came over and pulled their blankets and the food from behind the saddle and said, "I brought some hobbles. The grass isn't too bad here. They'll need to eat, too."

She watched as he put the hobbles on the front feet of the horses. They made no attempt to run away but bent over and began chomping at the grass, which was thin and a sort of brown color. Evidently they found something that they liked.

He said, "I brought some grain. We'll give 'em some first thing in the morning. Let them eat what they can here."

"I'll tell you what," Raina said, "if you'll build up a fire, I'll skin this rabbit. We'll make us a fresh rabbit stew."

"Well, I brought some meat, but it's not much. I'd like to have something fresh."

"You build that fire, and I'll show you how to cook jackrabbit."

As the sun was setting, Raina finished cooking the jackrabbit stew. She dipped out some of the meat into a deep dish and gave it to Ty. "Dinner's served, such as it is."

Ty had sat down and was poking at the fire, adding a branch from time to time. He took the dish she offered. "I bet I've had worse."

"So have I. Smells good. I wish I had some pepper."

"Oh, I got some in my saddlebag and some salt. Let me get it." He went to where his saddle was on the other side of the fire, rummaged through it, and came back. "Got several different things here. Got some spices. I like to try different things."

The two sat eating, and he said finally, "I'm glad you thought to bring that bread. It'd be hard to make biscuits out here in the open."

They finished eating and slowly drank the water from the river. "This is good, cold water," she said.

"See those mountains? I guess the stream that feeds this river comes from there."

When all the food was gone, he said, "I'll wash the dishes."

"No, I'll do it. You just sit back and relax. I know you've had a hard day."

"About usual." He watched her work for a while. "You ever miss your home?" he asked.

"You mean the saloon in La Tete. I guess I never really considered that home."

"But you lived there with your mother at one time, right?"

"I lost my mother. And my sister and I weren't very close. I've been all my life looking for somebody and don't even know if they exist. Hope I can find my pa."

He was quiet for a moment, then looked up and said, "Look at those stars. Aren't they pretty?"

"Yes, they are."

He turned to look at her. "You know, your pa might not want to be found."

"I know. But it's my only chance at a family."

"That's not so. You could marry and have a husband and some kids."

"I don't think about that much. Most married couples I've seen don't seem to care for each other."

Kincaid stretched his legs out and studied the sky thoughtfully. "I guess we're alike. I've been alone, in one way or another, all my life, just like you. You know, I saw an older couple once in San Antonio. They were walking down the street. Both of them had silver hair. Must have been in their sixties at least, and you know what? They were holding hands." He sighed and shook his head. "I've never forgotten that. I almost ran after them and asked, 'What's your secret? How do you keep love alive?' "

"Did you do it?"

"No. I wish I had. I've wondered about it ever since."

The two sat there talking for a time. He told her about the Jordans and their ranch. He planned for them to stop there before they continued on. They fell quiet and soon the weariness of the ride caught up with them.

Ty said, "Let's wrap up in these blankets. I'll keep the fire going. It's cold." He grinned. "You stay on that side now and don't bother me."

"Don't worry about that. You stay on your own side."

"Well, I think we'll get to the ranch tomorrow. That map shows a lot, but it's a big country."

"I think we'll find him, but what if we don't? I told Mrs. Mullins I'd be back in two days."

"I told Judge Parker the same thing, but if we get hot on the trail, we'll just follow it out. Okay?"

"All right. Good night." She spread the blankets on the ground and drew them up around her, fully dressed. She could hear the sound of his breathing as he lay down, and for a moment she thought, *What if he tries something?*

The thought troubled her, but she knew at once that she was safe with him.

❧

Dawn came, and they both rose and cooked bacon and some old biscuits. They fried the biscuits in the bacon grease and again drank the river water.

After they finished eating, Ty said, "I guess we'd better get on the way. I'll saddle the horses and take the hobbles off. You pull everything together."

"All right, Ty."

The two made their preparations quickly, and in ten minutes they were loping out. Ty had fed the horses some of the grain, and they had a spirited attitude. "These horses like to run," Ty said. "That's good sometimes."

"You like horses, don't you?"

"Most of 'em. I had one—a pinto—she'd be good for two months just to get a chance to kick me." He laughed and cast a sly glance at her. "Like some females I've known."

"I'll bet you have."

They rode steadily until Ty said, "Somebody's coming."

Raina had been looking down at the ground, but now she lifted her gaze. Still a good distance away there were three riders. "Do you think they're outlaws?"

"Could be. There are plenty of 'em out here. We need to stop for a bit." He pulled his horse up.

Raina did the same. She was surprised to see him pull his rifle out.

He waited until they were in shouting distance, then hollered, "Turn around and go the other way!"

The leader of the band yelled, pulled out his gun, and shot. Ty at once lifted the rifle, took careful aim, and with one shot dropped the man's horse. He chambered another shell and began peppering the three.

"I think they're running," she said. She watched as the man, who now had no horse, got on behind the other. They then headed off in another direction. "Why did you do that?"

"You didn't see the man in back. He pulled his gun out as soon as he saw us. I don't trust anybody in this territory—not when they come at us with a gun."

Raina did not comment on that, but she was thinking what a dangerous life Ty had chosen for himself. She finally asked him about it. "There must be other jobs you could do that pay more and aren't quite so dangerous."

"I guess there are, but this is where I've landed, and this is where I'll stay for a while."

"You know, sometimes I wonder what it's like to have a family, a place. I never felt secure when I was growing up. We moved a lot, and my sister's husband was a cruel man. Made life miserable for me, and for lots of other people, too. I was always surprised somebody didn't shoot him."

"Why didn't you?"

"Why, I couldn't shoot anybody."

"No, I guess you couldn't. But if we run into him, maybe I can make a gentleman out of him."

"That's not likely. We won't be seeing them anymore."

⁂

By noon they started seeing cattle.

"Look at that brand."

"What brand, Ty?"

"There on that cow. See, it's a running J."

She saw that the brand was indeed a *J* with a tail on it that looked like a running river.

"You know that brand?"

"Yes, it's that family I told you about who came in not long ago. Remember, their name's Jordan? We'll stop here. You can meet them, and I'm sure they will help us with some more supplies. Maybe they even heard something about your pa."

They rode into the ranch, and as they approached the house, what appeared to be a man, his wife, and his daughter came out.

"Why, hello there, Mr. Kincaid," the man said. "Good to see you."

"Good to see you, Mr. Jordan. I'd like for you to meet a friend of mine. This is Miss Raina Vernay."

"Glad to know you, Miss Vernay. I'm Aaron, this is my wife, Lottie, and this is my daughter, Leoma."

"You didn't come out just to see the scenery, did you?" Leoma smiled. She was looking carefully at Raina. "You're not eloping, are you?"

"No, she'd have to be crazier than she is to take a galoot like me." Ty Kincaid grinned. "No, she's looking for her pa. As a matter of fact, we came out here together."

"What's his name?"

"His name is Ed Vernay."

"Don't know the name, but then, we've only been here a few weeks."

Lottie Jordan said, "We're just about to sit down and eat. Be glad to have you take a bite with us."

"Well, I'm in favor of that," Ty said.

"What about you, Miss Vernay?"

"That would be an imposition."

"No, it wouldn't," Leoma said. She smiled then at Ty and said, "Come on in. We'll see if your appetite is as good as the rest of your skills."

Thirty minutes later they were all seated around the table. The women had fixed steak, boiled potatoes, and some canned vegetables. There was also fresh-baked bread.

Ty said, "This is as good a baked bread as I've ever had, Mrs. Jordan. You're a fine cook."

"Why, of course she is. I wouldn't marry a sorry cook," Aaron said. He reached over and pinched his wife on the shoulder. "No, I would have married her if she couldn't cook a bit."

"You're looking for your father, Ed Vernay?" Leoma asked.

"Yes, I am, Miss Jordan. He left my family a long time ago. Wasn't entirely his fault. As a matter of fact, he tried to take me with him, but my mother wouldn't let me go."

"How long ago was that?"

"I was just a little girl."

Leoma seemed to sense Raina's discomfort with discussing her family, and she changed the subject. "How did you and Ty meet up?"

For a moment Raina was embarrassed, but then she began to tell a few of the details.

"You're not telling it right," Ty said. He was dipping into a dish of blackberry preserves and said, "I got sick, and she had to take care of me. Nearly died. We nearly froze, too, didn't we, Raina?"

"It was a hard time."

"Well, it's fortunate you met up with a good nurse," Leoma said.

"You can say that again," Ty said cheerfully.

The talk went on for some time. Aaron finally shook his head. "Well, as far as I can tell, there's nothing in that direction for the next hundred miles but some Basque sheepherders."

"What's Basque?" Ty asked.

"They are some kind of foreigners. I think they came from Spain a long time ago. We had some trouble with them back in Texas once."

"What sort of trouble?" Raina asked.

"Well, miss, you see, cattle and sheep don't go well together."

"Why not?"

"When the cattle eat grass, they leave some sticking up. The sheep will go right down past the dirt and eat the root, just about ruining the grazing ground, so we had some trouble over boundary lines. Well, it wasn't the most pleasant time in my life." He sighed and shook his head. "I hated to see those Basque herders."

"Are they violent men?"

"Not at all," Lottie said. "Most of them are very gentle, but of course that doesn't mean anything to people who are losing their land."

"Well, I guess we can go ask them if they've seen Raina's pa."

Aaron Jordan was still thinking about the situation. "I can't help you much in direction, but if you just head east of here, you'll probably run into them."

"Well, I guess we'll move on. That was a fine meal, ladies," Ty said, smiling at them.

"Yes, it was. I'll stay and help wash dishes," Raina said.

"No, there's no point in that. We have plenty of help around here," Lottie said.

Ty and Raina rode out shortly after that. She said, "They seem like nice people."

"Yeah, one of the boys is a little bit rambunctious. His name is

Ash. He's the oldest boy. They've got another one named Benny."

"Mr. Jordan seems to think that there'd be trouble with the sheepherders."

"Nearly always is. He was right about one thing. Sheep can tear up rangeland. You need a lot of acreage to carry sheep."

"Why do they raise sheep instead of cattle?"

"More money in it, I hear. You get the wool until the sheep get old, and then you sell the meat."

The two fell silent after a while, and the silence was broken only by a few observations by Kincaid. Finally he said, "Look."

Raina turned and said, "What is it?"

"It's a herd of sheep. See how white they look."

"They just run wild out here?"

"No, there'll be some sheepherders, and they'll have some dogs."

"They use dogs to herd the sheep?"

"They sure do. Smart dogs, too. These folks just seem to know how to get the best out of 'em."

They slowed down when Ty saw a man coming toward them on foot. He had a long staff in his hand with a crook on the end. "Looks like a welcoming committee," Ty said. He greeted the man and said, "Hello, neighbor."

"Hello to you." The man had a large-brimmed hat that shaded his face, but he was obviously a white man. He walked slower and finally came to a full stop. He was staring at Raina, and finally she got a complete shock when he said, "I'll bet your name is Raina, ain't it, miss?"

Raina's eyes flew open, and she covered her mouth to keep the exclamation. "Is that you, Pa?"

"It ain't nobody else. Get down off that horse and let me see." He waited until she had come up to stand before him, and he said, "Well, ain't you a pretty one now. I always knew you would be though. How'd you find me way out here?"

"Well, I got tired of living without seeing you," she said, "so I heard that you were here in this country."

"Is this your husband here?"

"Oh no. It's a long story. This is Ty Kincaid. He got us here all right. It was a pretty hard trip."

"Well, I tell you what." He came forward and stuck his hand out, and when Ty took it he felt the steely grip. Eddie, as he was called, was a strong man in his midfifties. "Appreciate you takin' care of my girl."

"Well, wasn't exactly like that," Ty said. "I got sick, and she had to take care of me."

"Is that so? But you both made it out here."

"Yes, we did, but I wouldn't want to go through it again. Would you, Raina?"

"It wasn't so bad."

"Well, come on. I want to introduce you to the hands. The cook has killed a sheep. You like mutton?"

"I don't think I've ever eaten any," Raina said.

"Well, our cook is a good man. His name is Yosu. Very religious fellow. Come along now."

They moved toward the camp leading the horses, and when they got there, several of the sheepherders came to watch them.

"This is Benat," Pa said. "Benat is the strongest man we've got. He's my right hand. Benat, this is my daughter, Raina, and this here is Ty Kincaid."

Benat did not speak. His muscles swelled his shirt out, and when he smiled there was a gentleness about him.

"This here's Danelle. He's little but he's tough. This is Mikel. He's one-quarter Chocktaw and a fast runner. And this is our cook, Yosu. Yosu, what do you say to these people?"

Yosu grinned. He was slowly turning the whole carcass of a sheep over a fire pit. "Are you Jesus people?"

"I'm afraid I'm not. Are you?" Raina asked.

"Yes. Born again. What about you, young man—you in the kingdom of God?"

Ty obviously felt embarrassed at the suddenness of the question, but Pa laughed. "He asks that of everyone. Now, let's eat. That sheep ought to be good enough."

Yosu at once began cutting slabs of meat off and putting them in tin plates. He also had some kind of stew and bread baked in an oven.

"This is good," Ty said. "You're a good cook, Yosu."

"Not as good as the bread that came down from heaven and fed Moses and the children of Israel."

"I read about that," Ty said. "My grandfather told me about it. Bread falling from heaven. That's a good way to get it."

"Yes, and the Lord Jesus is now our bread," Yosu replied. "He said, 'I am the bread from heaven.' You'll have to find that out one day."

The visit lasted quite awhile. Ty finally said, "We'd better get back."

"Not me," Raina said. "I'm going to stay out here. My pa says I can stay with him. He has a house built over the hill there. We can get to know each other now."

"Why, that's fine." Ty nodded with enthusiasm. "You'll find she's a good woman, Eddie."

"Yes, I can tell you I appreciate your looking out for her all the way on that long trip out here. Will you be coming back?"

"Oh, sure. I'm one of Judge Parker's marshals, so I'll be in and out. Do you ever go into town?"

"Once in a while to buy things. Supplies, you know." He looked over to where Raina sat. "It's good for you to be here, Raina. I have missed you all these years." He grinned. "It sure is something, an old ugly codger like me havin' a beautiful daughter like you."

"She is that," Ty said.

Raina blushed at their praise.

When Ty finished getting ready to go, he came back to stand before Raina and said, "Well, we did it, didn't we? You like the idea of staying here?"

"Yes, for a while."

"I'll be coming back to check on you. Anytime somebody goes to town, you go with 'em. I might be gone, but I'll try to keep in touch."

"I'll need to go soon to get the rest of my things. Would you mind packing them up for me? There isn't much. Oh, and please tell Mrs. Mullins what has happened. I'll go by to see her when I make it in."

"I'll take care of it." He put his hand out.

She clasped it in hers as she stared into his eyes. "Thank you for bringing me, Ty."

"No problem." Kincaid cleared his throat as if to break the spell. He then stepped into his saddle, waved at the group, and kicked the stallion into a fast lope.

"That is one good man," Pa said. "You were lucky to find him. You going to marry with him maybe?"

She said quietly, "I don't think so, Pa."

"Well, there'll be plenty of men wanting to marry a beautiful girl like you. Now, let's go to the house. I've got a room that you'll like, and you can fix it up however you want. . . ."

⁂

"Well, you're back again, Ty." Aaron Jordan, along with his wife, came out of their home.

Kincaid stepped off his buckskin and took off his hat. "Howdy, Aaron. Yeah, I'm back."

"Did you find the young woman's father?"

"You know, we did. It's really amazing. He was the only white man there. The rest of them were the Basques."

"The young woman. She didn't come with you?"

"No, she wanted to stay and enjoy her dad. I guess I would, too, if I hadn't had a dad all my life."

"Hope we don't have trouble with them."

Ty looked up suddenly. "Why would you?"

"Well, you know how it is. You've worked with cattle. You know what sheep can do."

"They're a long way from here though, Aaron. I doubt if your paths will ever cross."

"As long as they keep to their ground, I'll keep to mine. But there's been lots of wars fought with the woolies against the cattle."

"Yes, we saw some good land ruined by sheep," Lottie said. "You look tired. Come on in and spend the night."

"Well, I really shouldn't. Judge Parker let me go for two days."

Leoma had joined them as Ty spoke. "You can catch another criminal. We probably got some working here. Come on in. I want to hear some more about this marshaling business." She stepped forward and took Ty's arm. "Come on in. You can watch me make a stew."

"Nothing better than watching a good-looking woman make stew."

The two went inside, and Leoma began pulling ingredients together for a stew. "I've got everything here I need to make you something good. Why don't you tell me about yourself—all that's fit for me to know."

"You sound like you think I've got a lot to hide."

"All men have a lot to hide."

Ty grinned and asked, "You speaking from personal experience?"

"Pretty much. What's the worst thing you ever did?"

"Oh, I guess it was kissing Martha Fleming when she didn't want me to, but then, I always thought she really liked me."

"Nobody is that pure, Ty."

"No, I guess not. How long before that stew is ready?"

"I think your heart is in your stomach, Ty Kincaid. I've seen you eat, remember?"

"Man has to know his strengths." Ty grinned.

"Oh you, go on into the dining room, and I'll bring the food in a minute."

Ty went into the large room and took a seat at the oak table. While he waited, his mind wandered back to Eddie Vernay's land. Of course he could not see Eddie, the sheep, or the herders, but he thought about Raina and wondered how she would make out with her new life.

CHAPTER 13

After Ty ate what Leoma prepared for him, the Jordans persuaded Ty to spend the night with them. "We've got plenty of room here." Aaron Jordan shrugged. "Have your own bed in the bunkhouse. You'd be in the middle of the night getting back to Fort Smith. Just make yourself at home."

Ty was actually happy to stay. It was much better than riding all night or sleeping on the ground. And there were worse things than spending time with Leoma Jordan.

She led him to the parlor. "Let's sit down before the fire and get warm. It's getting colder out there."

"Sounds good to me."

They made their way to the large living area, and she stirred up the fire and put more wood on. The sparks rose upward like myriads of tiny worlds of their own.

When she sat down, he asked, "Are you happy here in this place, Leoma?"

"I hope to be. We needed to find a new life. We cut all of our ties at the old one." She looked over at him. The flickering of the fire on the walls made grotesque shadows and reflections around her. "You think the outlaws will be a problem?"

"They're always a danger. They're wild men, not just naughty but killers. You must be very careful, Leoma, about going out alone. Always carry a gun and take one of the men with you."

"You make it sound so bad."

"Well, it is bad. This is outlaw territory full of killers."

"You think there might be trouble with the sheepherders?"

"It might be troublesome, but I think Ed Vernay is a sensible man. The funny thing is, he's not really interested in sheep much. He's got a plan."

"What sort of a plan?"

"Well, he wants to preach the Gospel. Of course he's not an ordained minister, but he likes to talk to people about the Lord."

"Did he talk with you, Ty?"

"Sure did. Put it right up to me. And he's got a cook who's even more pointed."

The two sat there for a long time, and finally Leoma said, "This is a nice room. It's an old house, I think."

"Yes, it is." Ty watched the fire, and the sparks continued to rise with ebullience. "You never know what's happened in a room like this."

"What do you mean, what's happened? People lived here."

He smiled at her. "I guess I've got too much imagination."

"Have you? What do you think about this room?"

"Well, Leoma, just think about what might have happened right here where we're sitting. A man and a woman might have come in through different doorways, and their eyes could have met, and both of them knew right then that they were destined to love each other and spend all their lives together. They could have decided to raise their children here."

"You *do* have an imagination."

"Well, it could have happened. Or maybe something bad happened."

"Like what?"

"Well, maybe a murder took place here."

"A murder? What an awful thought!"

"Well, murders do take place. On the other hand, maybe a man or a woman found God right in this very room."

"Have you ever found God?"

"No, I guess I'm just a runner. Trying to get away from God takes some of my time."

"Are you an atheist?"

"No, of course not! Do you take me for a fool? Let's go outside. I'm getting too warm in here."

They both rose, went outside, and stood for a while on the porch. "I always liked the night." He looked over at the trees and said, "Look at those trees, Leoma. They look like soldiers in a line, kind of in disorganized ranks. Kind of like a regiment at ease."

"Do you have thoughts like this a lot?"

"I had one friend who told me I had too much imagination. But look at those tall trees there shouldering the moon out of its way before it's gone."

Suddenly both of them looked up, for a star had increased its light, streaked across the darkness, and then disappeared.

"Did you make a wish?" Ty asked.

"Yes."

"What was it?"

She laughed at him then and touched his arm. "I'm not telling. It'll never come true if you tell."

"All right. You keep it. Look at that moon, just a crescent of silver. Argent is what some people call it."

"Argent means silver?"

"Yes, it does."

"How do you know that?"

"Some of my aimless reading, I guess."

They stood on the porch, and she said, "Let's walk a bit."

They walked around the yard, and there were the usual night sounds, a coyote howling mournfully, the cry of some sort of bird.

She stopped and said, "You're a curious man. What do you think about men and women?"

"Well, I don't know much about women. I'm no expert."

"But what do you think?"

"Well, I think when a man and a woman really love each other, it's wonderful. I've seen it a few times. As a matter of fact, I read a poem once. It was so sad I never could get it out of my mind."

"What is it?"

"I don't know the name of it. Don't even remember who wrote it now."

"You remember any of it?"

"Yes. It goes like this:

"So we go no more a-roving
So late into the night,
Though the heart be still as lovely,
And the moon be still as bright.

"For the sword outwears its sheath,
And the soul wears out the breast,
And the heart must pause to breathe,
And love itself have rest.

"Though the night was made for loving,
And the day returns too soon,
Yet we'll go no more a-roving
By the light of the moon."

"What does it mean?"

"It made me sad the first time I read it. I thought about it a lot. It seems to say we'll grow old and die."

"But everybody knows that."

"I guess they do." He went silent.

The two walked along the fence that kept the pasture for the rest of the horses. Some of them were stirring now. One of them came over and stuck his head over the fence.

Leoma reached out and stroked it. "This is a good horse."

"You love horses?"

"Yes, I do."

"So do I. Something we have in common."

They made the circle of the house and came back, and he said, "I guess I need to get to bed. You must be tired, too."

Suddenly she turned to face him. "I think that woman Raina might be in love with you."

"No, not really. We're good friends."

Leoma shook her head. She was a woman of firm convictions, and he could see it in her face. He had told the truth. A breeze ruffled the edges of her hair, and a smile made its small break along her lips. Ty watched the slight changes of her face, the quickening, the loosening, the small expressions coming and going.

Suddenly he reached out, and the old hungers that he usually kept under firm control seemed to intensify. He saw a change go over her face as he pulled her closer. Her lips were heavier, and a warmth began to illuminate her eyes. He kissed her then. Her lips made a softly pursed line, and he felt the sweetness and the humor in the embrace and in her kiss.

When he lifted his head, her face was as purely expressive at that moment as he had ever seen it, graphically registering the light and the shadows of her feelings. She was, he suddenly realized, a woman who was lonely and could not understand why. She seemed to have everything. She wasn't smiling then, but the thought of a smile was a hint at the corners of her mouth and in the tilt of her head.

"You did that very well. You've had lots of practice."

"Not really, Leoma. I had one woman that I thought loved me—but she didn't."

"I'm sorry."

"Well, it was a long time ago."

Suddenly she said, "There's a dance in Fort Smith the day after tomorrow."

"You save me a dance."

"I'll do that. Be sure you come to claim it."

Ty was getting ready for the dance. He was sitting in a straight chair.

Larry Dolby, who claimed to be a barber, was cutting his hair.

"Be sure you make me pretty, Larry."

"Don't ask impossible stuff," Dolby said. He laughed. "I just cut a hunk out that's gonna look like you been hit with a stick."

"Just do the best you can."

"Well, it's free anyhow. You're going to that dance, are you?"

"Sure am," Ty answered. "Haven't been to a dance in a long time. Are you going?"

"No. I'm pretty down on women right now. I got jilted."

"Well, I did, too. But it was a long time ago."

A few of the other marshals gathered around, and Heck Thomas shook his head. "Next time let me cut your hair, Ty. Larry just thinks he's a barber. I believe he really worked for an undertaker."

"I didn't say whose hair I cut," Larry said indignantly.

"You mean you've never cut a live man's hair?" Ty's eyes flew open. "Why didn't you tell me that?"

"You didn't ask."

"Well, I'm going to the dance."

"Here. Try some of this." Heck handed him a bottle and grinned. "It smells good. Straight from France."

"I don't think I want any perfume," Ty said.

"This ain't perfume. It's lotion. All the men wear it."

"Well, I'm going to the dance."

Heck frowned. "You don't look very dressed up."

"This is the best I've got."

Leaving the marshals' quarters, Ty moved on to where he could hear the music playing. He made his way through the crowd that was growing and watched the dance. He saw Leoma. The music stopped, and a slower tune came. Ty moved quickly and said, "Leoma, you look good."

"You think so? This is just an old dress."

"Hello there, Kincaid."

The couple turned to see Judge Parker and his wife.

"Hello, Judge," Ty said. "This is Leoma Jordan. Her family bought the Manning ranch."

"Hello, Miss Jordan. It is nice to meet you. And this is my wife, Mary," Parker said. "She is the woman who keeps me safe. Well, she won't let me dance with any pretty women," Parker said and winked at Leoma.

"Why, Judge, I will so. You go right ahead."

"No, I'm claiming you, my dear. Let's go. By the way, how's the ranch going?"

"Very good. Very good indeed. We appreciate your interest."

"No trouble with the sheepherders?"

"No, not a bit."

"I met some of them, Judge," Ty said. "Real serious men. Good men, I think."

"Let's keep it that way."

"Good to meet you, Miss Jordan," Mrs. Parker said. Judge Parker led his wife onto the dance floor.

Ty turned to Leoma. "Now, how about a dance? I'm not very good."

She grinned. "I'm very good, so you just let me lead."

Ty laughed. "You women always want to lead. All right, that suits me."

They had two more dances, and then Leoma was chosen by several other men for dances.

Ty was getting refreshments when he heard a man cursing. He saw the man had a gun. He had left his own at home. When the man raised the gun, Ty could see he was totally drunk. "Leoma, get down!" Ty cried. He threw himself forward and pushed her to the floor, but at the same time he felt that someone had slapped him on the back, and he thought, *Who would be hitting me on the back?* Then he realized it was a bullet and not a hand that had struck the blow.

There were several marshals, and they grabbed the drunk and hustled him out of the room.

Aaron Jordan came over at once. "Are you all right, Leoma?"

"I am, but Ty took the bullet. Put himself right in the way of it between me and that drunk."

"Well, we are in your debt, Ty. We are indeed."

Judge Parker came over and said, "Well, they got him corralled. What about you?"

Ty grimaced. "Well, I got a bullet hole, but I'll live."

"We're going to get you to the doctor, and then you need to come home with us to recover," Aaron Jordan said. "We've got plenty of room and two good nurses, Leoma here and my wife."

"Why, there's no call for that. I'll be all right," Ty protested.

"No," Parker said. "You just go along with Mr. Jordan here. This will take more out of you than you now realize. Don't let him come back until he's fit, Mr. Jordan."

"I'll see to that. Now, come along. We're going to get you in a wagon."

Ty went protesting, but he was outvoted. As a matter of fact, he did feel somewhat weak, and the wound was becoming very painful. He knew the shock was wearing off. He felt himself slip into unconsciousness as the wagon hurried through the streets of Fort Smith.

☙

Ty awoke confused, then realized he was in the Jordans' wagon and they were on their way to their home. He felt the bandages covering his wound and winced as he tried to sit up.

Leoma sat beside him and kept him from rising. "You need to stay put now. We don't want that wound to start bleeding again. How are you feeling?"

"All right, I guess. It's really not all that much. I've been shot before worse than this."

"Well, we'll get you home and put you to bed so you can rest."

"Sounds like I'm nothing but a burden."

"That other woman. She had to take care of you, too, when you were sick."

"Well, I like being taken care of. Haven't had much experience, but you just pamper me all you want."

☙

Raina and her father got along fine. She discovered that the dream of his heart was to build a church somewhere in the territory.

"There's plenty of folks need the Lord," he said. "Maybe you can help me."

Raina had found that she had a real affection for her father.

After being there a couple of days, she knew she needed to go to town for her things. She told her pa, "I'm going to town to get my things and to get some supplies."

"Take your gun with you," her father said.

"I'll go along to be sure she's all right," Mikel said. Mikel was a nice-looking man somewhere in his early thirties. She questioned him a great deal as they rode along. She had hoped to find out more about him, but he said little about his own life.

"Look, there's the Jordan ranch," she said. "Let's stop there and see if they need anything from town."

"I may not be welcome. They don't like sheepherders."

"They may be a little bit nervous, but we'll just stop for a moment."

As they approached the porch of the house, she saw to her shock Ty Kincaid sitting in a rocker with an arm in a sling. Leoma Jordan sat beside him.

"Hello, Leoma." She stepped off her horse. "Ty, what happened to you?"

"Oh, a little accident. Hello, Mikel."

Raina looked at Leoma. "Do forgive my rudeness. This is Mikel. He works for my pa."

Mikel nodded at Ty and Leoma.

Raina then spoke plainly. "Now, tell me what happened to you, Ty Kincaid."

"He took a bullet for me," Leoma said, and she told of the incident at the dance. "Might've hit me in the heart." She smiled. "So I'm taking care of him." She laughed aloud then, and there was humor in her face. "Ty, it looks like you make a big thing of letting women take care of you."

"I like it that way. That's what women are for, to take care of us helpless men."

"I'm going into town. Can I bring you anything back, Leoma?"

"No, my father has gone there."

"Well, I'll stop back on the way and see how you're doing, Ty."

"How are you making it with your father?" he asked.

"Oh, I like him very much."

Leoma frowned. "I hope he's going to keep the woolies off of our ranch."

"I heard he brought all the sheepherders together and told them plainly to stay off Running J Ranch. I don't think you have anything to worry about. He's a strict man, and he'll work with you."

"That sounds good," Leoma said. "Come back in time for a meal."

"I'll probably be in a hurry, but thanks for the offer."

As they rode out, Raina said to Mikel, "That could have been serious. That bullet could have hit him in the head or in the heart."

"Not according to your father. He said everything happens according to a plan."

"Yes, I know. Do you believe that?"

"I don't know what I believe."

"I guess I don't either, but I'm not giving up hope."

PART THREE

PART THREE

CHAPTER 14

The main street of Fort Smith was practically empty. It was not a day for hangings, and the afternoon had fallen with the sun coming down in the west like a huge yellow ball. A mustard-colored dog ambled out of the Lucky Star Saloon, walked a few feet, and then plopped down and began to scratch his ears with a lazy motion.

"Look at that dog, Ty." Heck Thomas was sitting in his usual position with a straight-backed chair leaning back against the wall. There was no trouble, so there was no call for Heck's law-keeping abilities, and as usual when he had nothing else to do, he whittled on a piece of cedar. At his feet lay a pile of shavings as evidence that he had been at this task for quite a while.

"You look about as tired as I feel, Heck." Ty was sitting beside Heck, his hat pulled down over his eyes to keep out the rays of the dying sun. He had been back in Fort Smith for a couple of days after his recovery time with the Jordans. He was still on light duty as his shoulder was pretty stiff and could affect his shooting

801

ability. "I wish I didn't have any more worries than that critter."

Heck grinned and shot a glance at Ty. "He does have an easy life, don't he? Just a bit of food, a place to sleep. Wish I had it that easy."

"No you don't, Heck. You'd go crazy with nothing to do."

"I reckon you're right, Ty. I tried it once. I had some money saved up, tried just being a bum, but I couldn't make it. I have to have my hand in something. As a matter of fact, I'm surprised we haven't had more action from these so-called outlaws."

Ty looked over at Heck with surprise. "Why do you call them 'so-called'?"

"Aw, the writers of them westerns that's comin' out like popcorn now, they always make the outlaws seem like heroes. You take all them stories about Wild Bill Hickok. He wasn't nothin' but a two-bit crook! They made him out to be a hero who kept the law, but he broke it. His favorite way was to sneak up behind somebody and shoot 'em in the back of the head. That's the kind of *hero* he was."

"Yeah, I tried to read one of those once. It didn't seem like it was very lifelike."

"Lifelike! There ain't nothin' lifelike about 'em. You take these fellows we've been chasin'. . . ."

"What fellows is that, Heck?" Ty asked lazily. His eyes scanned the streets, but there was no trouble, and if there had been, there was a sheriff to take care of the town trouble. The marshals all spent their time in Indian Territory.

"Why, you heard of Jesse James."

"Sure. Everybody's heard of the James boys."

"Yep. Frank and Jesse. They've written a dozen of them little novels about 'em, all makin' heroes out of 'em, and you know they even came here and served as marshals for a while."

This information caused Ty to open his eyes. "I didn't know that, Heck. Why did Judge Parker hire them?"

"They didn't have no reputation back then, but they could ride and they could shoot."

"Were they good marshals?"

"Not worth spit! They went out and broke the very laws they were supposed to enforce. One Indian wouldn't buy any of their rotgut whiskey, so Jesse just pulled his gun out and shot him right in the head. Killed him dead. They didn't last long. Judge Parker found out they were worthless and ran 'em off."

"Well, that's not the way the stories make them out. They call him the Robin Hood of the West. Robbing rich people and giving it to the poor."

"Huh! I'd say that's about as big a lie as you could tell." Heck grunted. He carefully peeled off another long sliver of the cedar, sniffed the stick he had left, and said, "Cedar smells better than anything, don't it?"

"Pretty good, I guess."

Heck peeled off several slivers, watching them curl and fall to his feet. He had a nice pile there, and he would gather them all up and put them in his bed to make it smell good. It was a peculiarity of the famous marshal, Heck Thomas, that few people knew about. "And then there's those Dalton brothers. You heard of them, I guess."

"Sure. They were bank robbers mostly, weren't they?"

"Yeah, there's Grat and Bob, his brother. They made most of the trouble. They were marshals for a while. You know it's a funny thing, they could have been great marshals. Grat was smart, and Bob was good with a gun. They did pretty well for a while here as marshals. Brought in some wanted men, but they didn't last either. Now they're out there stealin' and shootin' and killin'. We got orders to bring 'em in dead or alive."

"I guess they might be a little bit hard to take."

"I could take both of them with one hand." Heck suddenly grinned and turned to face Kincaid. "I sound like one of them boasters down at the saloon, don't I?"

"Well, you're not that."

The two sat silently, soaking up the last rays of the sun. Heck folded his knife and stuck it in his pocket. Then he carefully gathered up the shavings and put them into a small cotton sack he carried for that purpose. He leaned back in his chair and said, "You know, I've been watchin' you, Ty."

"I figured you would be. You keep an eye on all your marshals."

"Well, you know what? I don't think you're happy bein' a marshal."

Surprised by Heck's astute analysis of his mind-set, Ty Kincaid looked at the marshal and asked, "What makes you think that?"

"Well," Heck said slowly, "bein' a marshal ain't for everybody. It's a one-way street. We've lost fifty men, killed, and what have they got to show for it?"

"Nothing, I guess, except they were trying to do their job."

"Some were and some weren't. It's a sorry enough job, Ty. It's a wonder we're able to get any men a-workin' at it. The pay is practically nothing. It's dangerous. You can get killed just walkin' around in the Indian Territory."

"Well, I've got to admit I was glad to get the job. I was pretty low down and felt pretty useless. At least this way I feel like I'm doing a job that needs doing."

"Oh, I guess that's what some of the fellows do, but for others it's just a job. They get out there and get infected by all the criminals on every hand. The Indians cheatin' each other. Of course they got the Indian police to take care of 'em, but there's enough white gunmen out there to keep Judge Parker's court busy."

"Different kinds of men, I guess."

"That's what I'm tryin' to tell you, Ty." Heck Thomas was not a handsome man. He was hard and smart and knew how to handle men, and now he turned to face Ty and said, "You know, Kincaid, you're not fitted for this job. Oh, I know you can *do* it, but it ain't good for you. You need to find a better way to live."

Ty Kincaid did not speak, for he had been thinking exactly the same thing. Finally he sighed and said, "Well, I did what I had to do, Heck. I guess I'll stay at it for a while."

"I wish you wouldn't. You're too good a man to waste, but you're a good marshal. I need all that kind of man I can get."

❧

Raina brought a piece of apple pie on a small cracked plate and set it down before her father. "There, Pa, see how you like that pie."

He looked down at the pie, and then he grinned. "Well, what a nice surprise."

"Taste it. See if it's any good."

He took the fork, cut off the end of the wedge, and stuck it in his mouth. He chewed thoughtfully, and then his eyes opened wide. "Why, this is as good a pie as I ever ate in my life."

"Oh, you eat anything. You throw it back in your mouth, and

you don't chew. I'm surprised you taste anything."

"That ain't so, daughter. Since you've been here cookin' for me, I must have gained five pounds."

Raina sat down and for a while just listened to her father as he talked about the sheep and the job.

Finally he turned and gave her an intent look. "I've been wondering about you, daughter."

"What about me?"

"Well, I've been wondering what you really want." Pa shrugged, ate the last bite of pie, and then swallowed it. "You want more than just chasin' around after a bunch of sheep."

"Well, if it's good enough for you, it's good enough for me."

Pa shook his head. "No, that ain't so. What do you really want if you could have anything you ask for?"

"Well, I'd like a place and a family. I guess every woman wants that. What do you want, Pa?"

"To serve God."

"Why, you're a Christian now."

"I know, but that ain't enough." He put the fork down, then picked the plate up and licked it until it was clean. "Now you don't have to wash it." He grinned at her. "Well, I tell you, daughter, what I really want to do. These poor Indians out here, they worship them heathen idols of theirs. Ain't got no more religion than a stick. They think they do, but they ain't. I want to start a church, a real church, that will hold up the Lord Jesus Christ as the Way for all men to follow."

"Do you think the Indians would come?"

Pa's eyes brightened, and he nodded vehemently. "Yeah, they would come. Where the Gospel is preached, they will come. So I want to start a church. Not a town church where you wear a white shirt and a fancy tie and a black suit. I want to start a church where these Indians, who don't have much anyhow, can have hope of a life after this one."

"I don't know if they would come to a church."

"Jesus said, 'If I be lifted up, I'll draw all men unto me,' " he said firmly. "The Indians would come, and some of these outlaws would come. Just down-and-outers, all of them losers."

Raina was quiet for a while, and then she leaned forward, picked up her father's hand, and held it as she prayed and asked the Lord to come into her heart. She looked up and felt a lightness in her heart. She told her father what she had just done.

He looked at her with surprise and then with a happy light. "Praise the Lord!" He hugged her for several minutes. "It's so good to have you here, daughter. I just want to see you have a good life."

"Well, God's given me a father. That's what I came here for. Now I want to give God whatever I can."

"Well, praise the Lord! We'll do it, daughter," he exclaimed. "We'll start this church, me and you. You do the singin', and I'll do the preachin'."

Raina knew that the Lord now dwelled in her heart. She had found her father, she had found a place, and now she was determined to serve God. "All right, Pa. We'll do it, you and me."

❧

The five men sat around a rickety table in a filthy room. It was a room devoid of any woman's care. Dirty dishes were piled on a table close to a pump. The food had hardened in them, and the men's method was to scrape them off with a knife before they filled them up again. There had once been wallpaper in the room, but it was peeling off now and revealed the bare boards of the house.

The men themselves were as slovenly dressed as the room was adorned, except for one man. Johnny Taylor was only seventeen, but through some miracle he had developed a sense of pride in his appearance. His clothes were clean and fairly new, his hair was cut, and the men in his brother's band often called him Dandy Johnny.

Johnny was only of medium height. He had tow-colored hair, neatly trimmed, and pale blue eyes. He was by far the youngest man, for at the table was Grat Dalton and his brother, Bob, both hardened outlaws.

Mexican Jack had black hair and eyes and a mustache. Fritz Holder was the biggest man there, six-two. He had a scarred face, had lost most of his hair, and had a deadly look about him. The other man was Long Tom Slaughter, very tall with yellow hair. He was a killer to the core.

The men were cursing and playing poker, and Slaughter, who was the best poker player, had won most of their money.

"I think you're cheatin'," Grat Dalton said. He was short and tough, lantern jawed with hazel eyes.

He glared across at Slaughter, who merely laughed at him, saying, "It's all skill, Grat."

"No it ain't. It's just luck."

"All skill." Slaughter grinned. "Well, let's play another hand."

Johnny threw down his cards. He had lost all of his money, and he said, "I'm bored out of my skull. We need to get out of here and do something."

"We can't do nothin' until Garth comes back." Grat Dalton grunted. He spoke of Johnny's brother, the leader of the band, who was tall, strong, and fast with a gun. He had pale hazel eyes and ruled his band of outlaws with a firm hand.

Johnny got up and walked around the room. He picked up a whiskey bottle, poured himself a tumbler half full, and drank it down. "Garth might not come back for another week or two. We need to be doin' something."

"We're not doin' anything until Garth gets back. He's the boss," Long Tom Slaughter said. "We'll wait on Garth."

Johnny shot him a hard look, but though he tried to appear tough like the rest of the outlaws, he had been kept from all sorts of danger by his brother. The bond between the two men was obvious. Garth was old enough to be a big brother, which he was. If Garth Taylor cared about anything, it was his brother, Johnny. He protected him, and well he did, for the other men would have beat him to a pulp for his dandy ways.

Johnny finally threw himself into a chair and said suddenly and abruptly, "Garth might not come back for a month. You know how he is, but I know how we can pick up some easy money."

Fritz Holder grinned. "Where are you proposin' we get all this easy money, Johnny?"

"Why, it's that ranch that new fellow started. The name is Jordan. He's got more cattle than he can even count. We can go down there, take some of them, and go sell 'em across the border to Lowell Gearson. He'll take all the stolen cattle he can get."

Bob Dalton laughed. "So you want us to become cattle rustlers."

"Sure," Johnny said eagerly. He sat up straight, and his eyes were gleaming. "We could just go down there and take a hundred of those cattle and sell 'em, and by the time Garth gets back we'll have plenty of money."

All of the outlaws shook their heads, and it was Mexican Jack who said, "You know Garth. He's just liable to shoot us if we left without him."

"He wouldn't shoot me." Johnny swaggered. "Especially if we make a lot of money. We'll give him part of it."

"Well," Fritz Holder said, "I'm bored like you are, but you know how your brother is. We'll have to wait until he gets back."

"Yeah, your idea sounds good." Bob Dalton nodded. "But Garth will have to say."

Suddenly Johnny's eyes blinked as an idea struck him. "Why, he's already said."

"What are you talkin' about?" Grat Dalton said. "Said what?"

"He told me the day he left that if he didn't come back in a week we could go get some of that cattle."

"He didn't say anything to me about it," Grat said.

"He was on his way out. We just got to talkin' about it. He said it would be the easiest money we ever got."

"Well, I didn't know Garth said that," Grat Dalton said. "He usually tells me what he's got planned."

"Why, he said it'd be so easy we could get as many cattle as we need."

"Well, there's bound to be somebody guardin' those steers," Mexican Jack said. "They're not just runnin' wild."

"Aw, they just got a couple of hands. They won't be no trouble," Johnny said.

The idea caught on, and Johnny kept it going. Finally Grat

Dalton, who was, more or less, the first lieutenant of Garth Taylor, said, "Well, all right. If Garth says it's okay, we'll do it."

"I don't know," his brother, Bob, said, scratching his chin. "We'd better wait for Garth."

But in the end, Johnny convinced them, and they all agreed. They were bored and broke except for Long Tom Slaughter, who had won their money.

When they rode out, Johnny was excited. He said once to Bob, "Now I'm going to show my brother what I can do."

The grass close to the home ranch had been pretty well eaten down by the grazing steers, and only Harry Littleton and Nelly Fox were keeping them. It was really too big a herd for two men, and they were scattered pretty wildly. Many of them were gathered down by the small stream, drinking their fill. Both men looked up when they saw Ash driving his horse at a fast run as he loved to do.

"He's going to kill that horse," Nelly said.

"Well, he's killed others," Harry said. Harry was a small man with tow hair and blue eyes. He wasn't at all a hardened man, but he was good with cattle.

Ash pulled his horse up, and the two men saw that it was lathered. "You're going to ruin that horse."

"It's my horse, not yours," Ash said. "I come out to tell you to try to keep these steers close together, Pa said."

Nelly Fox lifted his head. His hearing was acute. Some said he could hear a cricket chirp a mile away. "Sounds like horses coming."

Ash looked over in the direction that Harry was pointing. "Strangers, ain't they."

Nelly said, "They may be coming to get the cattle. Paul said there would be cattle thieves around here."

"Okay. Scatter out here. If you see 'em take any cattle, shoot 'em down."

"Wait a minute. We're not supposed to shoot people unless they actually steal something," Harry said.

"You do what I tell you. If they give us any trouble, I'll kill the first one."

❧

The outlaws had made the trip taking care their horses were not exhausted. Suddenly Grat said, "There's the cattle."

"There's a bunch of 'em," Johnny said excitedly. "I don't see nobody guardin' 'em. Spread out. We'll take about a hundred of 'em. Doesn't look like there's going to be any trouble."

The band spread out, but when they got close enough, suddenly they heard a yell, and a shot rang out.

"Watch out," Grat yelled. "There's three men guardin'em!"

The outlaws pulled their guns and began shooting. It was too far for any accurate shooting, and all they succeeded in doing was frightening the cattle so they started milling around while some ran away.

"Let's get out of here," Grat yelled. "We don't know how many there are."

"No," Johnny said. "There's only two or three of 'em." He rode forward, but before his horse could cover ten yards, one of the shots hit him.

Johnny heard somebody yell out, "You got him, Ash!"

Grat said, "Are you hurt bad, Johnny?"

"They shot me," Johnny said, surprised as he looked down at his bloody chest. "I didn't think they'd shoot me."

"We've got to get him back so we can take care of him," Slaughter said. He shook his head and said, "Garth's liable to shoot all of us for getting his kid brother shot."

🐟

Garth Taylor did not look the part of an outlaw. He was a handsome man with light hair and strange hazel-colored eyes. He had come out of the house, and when he saw Johnny being held in the saddle by a man on each side, he cursed and said, "Where have you been?"

Grat said, "Johnny told us you said it'd be all right to steal the cattle."

Even as he spoke, Johnny slumped, and Long Tom Slaughter grabbed him. "Get him into the house."

They carried the wounded man into the house, put him in a bed, and stripped his shirt off. When Garth saw the wound, he knew there was no hope. He glared around. "I ought to kill all of you."

"Wait a minute, Garth. Johnny told us you said it'd be all right," Bob said.

"You know I wouldn't have told you to do a thing like that." He leaned over and saw that the blood was bubbling from the wound in Johnny's chest. He had lost too much blood. Garth knew there was no hope.

Suddenly Johnny opened his eyes. He whispered, "I just wanted to be like you, Garth—tough like you." He did not speak anymore.

Garth was stricken. He looked down at the dead body of his brother and asked harshly, "Who shot him?"

Grat said, "Somebody named Ash. I reckon he's one of the owners of the ranch. And they captured Fritz."

Garth stood up and looked down. He gritted his teeth and said, "It's not gonna be safe for anybody who works for that ranch. What do they call it?"

"The Running J."

Mexican Jack said, "We are gonna hunt down that fella that shot Johnny. Ash is as good as dead already."

Garth straightened up and turned his eye away from his brother. "No, not just him. I'm gonna see him dead, but I'm gonna see the rest of them cowpunchers dead, too."

CHAPTER 15

Leoma Jordan bent over a bolt of material in Max's General Store. She had looked at every selection that existed but finally sighed and said, "Well, I guess I'll just have to make do with this."

Ty Kincaid entered the store. When he heard Leoma muttering to herself, he sauntered over. "So, you're talking to yourself."

"I suppose so, Ty. I guess the next step is the insane asylum."

"Oh, it's not that bad. That's a pretty piece of cloth there. You thinking about making me a shirt out of it?"

"Well, it would look better on you than it would me. It's not my color."

The two talked, and finally Ty asked her, "How long you been in town?"

"Oh, I've been here three days. I get so bored out on the ranch. Somebody had to come in and buy some supplies."

"Is all this yours?" He waved at the stack of groceries and supplies that she shoved to one part of the counter.

"Yes, it is."

815

"Well, I'll hang around and help you take it to your wagon."

"I'm ready to go now." She called Max Thornton over and said, "I want to take all this with me, Mr. Thornton."

"Sure thing, Miss Jordan. Let me add it up for you." After a few minutes he said, "That'll be twenty-seven dollars and fifty cents, Miss Leoma."

Leoma shook her head. "Things are sure high these days." She paid the bill, and Thornton put the material in cardboard boxes.

Ty carried them out and stacked them in the wagon. "Have you eaten?" he asked.

"Not much."

"Well, let me buy you a bowl of soup or something."

"That would be nice."

The two of them started down the street, but Leoma stopped abruptly. "Look," she said, "there's my father and my mother. What are they doing in town?"

"Looks like somebody ran into trouble," Ty said.

He saw that the men looked angry, and they pulled their horses up sharply.

Ty and Leoma went out to meet them. She asked, "What's wrong, Pa?"

"We had some trouble. Ty, a bunch of outlaws tried to run our cattle off."

"Any of our men hurt?" Leoma asked quickly.

"No, but we got two of them. That's one of them tied on the horse. You'll recognize him, Ty. He was one of the men you faced down at our ranch when we first arrived. The other one was able to ride off."

Ty walked down and pulled the head of the man on the horse up and looked at him. "Yeah, that's Fritz Holder."

Heck Thomas had approached and said, "Let me take a look." He pulled the head up and said, "Well, Holder, you got caught this time." He turned to Ty and Aaron. "He runs with Garth Taylor's bunch. What about the other one you saw, Mr. Jordan?"

"I wasn't there. You saw it, Ash. Tell him."

"There was a pretty big bunch of 'em and only three of us. When they started to run the cattle off, we opened up on 'em, and I guess they didn't know how many of us there was, so they took off runnin'. I hit one of 'em I think pretty bad, but they managed to get away with him."

Aaron said, "Can you arrest that bunch, Marshal?"

"Well, I don't know, Mr. Jordan. Can you identify any of them?"

"No, we couldn't see that well. It was dusty, and they was a pretty long way away," Ash said. "But I know one of them got hit that didn't fall to the ground."

"Well, you said this was part of a wild bunch, didn't you?"

"Yes, but those fellows move around, Mr. Jordan. They don't stay with one band long. When there's a big job going, they swap members, but I'll send a man out." He glanced at Ty and said, "Kincaid, you go out with Mr. Jordan. See what you can find."

"Sure will, Marshal."

"I might as well go back to the ranch with you, Pa," Leoma said. "I've got all the supplies."

"All right. We'll have to go slow. These horses are pretty tired."

Ty got his horse, tied him to the back of the wagon, and sat down on the seat to drive.

Leoma said, "I hate to hear about things like this. Men getting killed over cattle."

"Well, I've seen men killed over less than that, like a two-dollar bet on a poker game." Ty sighed. "That's the way men are. I think it's gonna be dark by the time we get in. I hope we don't run into that bunch."

"I don't see how you ever catch anybody in such a big space. The range is big," Leoma noted.

"Yes, it is. It's hard to catch 'em. They're pretty slick."

"Do you like being a marshal, Ty?"

"Not all that much."

"Why do you do it then?"

"I have to make a living some way, Leoma. I've done worse."

"I wish you could find a better way."

"So do I. I'd take it in a minute if I could find it."

By the time they reached the ranch, they were all tired. The sun had gone down, and the stars were coming out. "Look, there's just one star in the sky," Leoma said.

"Yes, that's Hesperus. People call it Venus. The evening star."

"It looks lonely up there."

He laughed and said, "I don't know if stars get lonely or not, but I know I do."

"Do you, Ty? You've never been married."

"No, haven't had that good fortune."

"Well, you will have."

"Maybe. Never know about things like that."

The two pulled up at the house, and Ty and the men unloaded the groceries. As Ty took the last bag in, Aaron came over to him and said, "Do you really think you can find something?"

"Well, tomorrow morning early I'd like one of the men that was there to take me out where the shooting took place. You never can tell. Might find some kind of clue that'd lead us to one of them, and then we could get the others."

When the supplies were in, Leoma said, "Come in. I'm sure Ma is fixing something to eat."

"Sounds pretty good." Ty followed Leoma into the parlor.

"We'll relax in here until the food is ready."

They sat for a while in silence until Leoma turned and said, "Why are you looking at me?"

Ty smiled. "I always like to look at good-looking women."

"Don't you try to get next to me, Ty. I know you men," she said playfully.

"Well, some men are pretty bad, but I was always good myself. When I was a kid I went to church every Sunday and helped old ladies cross the street."

"I'll just bet. You were a good-looking young man, and I'll bet women hid their daughters when you came around."

"No, nothing like that." He stretched and said, "I don't know where I'm going really, Leoma. Sometimes I feel like a man who's in the middle of a bridge and I've forgotten both ends of it. I'm just standing there looking down at a river not knowing which way to go."

"That's sad. Have you felt like that long?"

"Long enough. You know, Leoma, a woman should be better than a man."

"I don't know why you'd say that."

"Well, men are squirming around. They just fight and do most every ungodly thing that comes into their minds. Well, a woman should be better than that. Something a man could look up to."

"You've got high standards for women. Maybe women have them for men, too."

"I just don't know. I wonder sometimes if there's any sense to life, but I look around and I see God made everything that works, and there has to be more to it than just men and women wandering around."

They talked for a while, and he said, "You know, we're just like a married couple talking over things."

"I guess we are."

"Well, I'm looking forward to that supper."

"Could I go with you tomorrow?"

"No, it's liable to be dangerous, Leoma. I wouldn't want anything to happen to you."

When Lottie called everyone to supper, all the men came in, and everyone wanted to talk about the raid.

"It's those sheepherders, that's who it is," Ash said.

"I doubt that," Ty said.

Ash looked at Ty. "Why would you doubt it? They killed our cattle."

"Well, for one thing, they were all on horseback. Sheepherders don't have horses."

"How do they get around?" Leoma asked.

"They just walk. You know, one sheepherder can keep up with as many as two thousand sheep. Think how many riders it would take to do that," Ty said.

"I don't have any idea," Aaron said. "But that's the only enemy we've got around here. You've got some funny thoughts there, Ty," Aaron said.

"Yeah, I guess I do. Wish I could turn my head off and stop thinking sometimes."

"Well, you want the rest of us to go with you tomorrow morning?" Aaron asked.

"No, just somebody to tell me how to get there."

"I'll do that," Ash said.

"Okay. I want to leave early."

After the meal was over, Ty went out to the corral and leaned on the top rail. There were a few horses in, and they made snuffling noises. One of them came and stuck his head up to be fed.

"Got nothing for you, boy," Ty said. He stroked the horse's silky nose, but it snorted and walked away.

"Did you get enough to eat, Ty?"

Kincaid turned to see that Leoma had come to stand beside him. "It was a fine meal," he said.

"Do you think you'll find anything out there?"

"I'll be surprised. It sounds like a raid, but that could be anybody. There's a dozen outfits that would like to steal cattle like these fellows did. We don't know if they have anything to do with the sheep."

"What will you look for?"

"Oh, look for tracks, which way they'd go, how many were there. Some of the tracks will have particular appearances. I'd know them anywhere."

She put her arms over the top rail, and the silver moon put its lambent light upon her, lighting up her face. "If you find them, they'll fight, won't they?"

"Most outlaws do."

"You won't go by yourself surely."

"I don't know. It depends on how it falls out."

"I wish you wouldn't go, or I wish you'd promise me if you do find anything you'd come and get help."

"Well, I'll probably do that if they're with a big bunch."

She asked, "Have you seen Raina Vernay lately?"

"Yes, she was in town not long ago. Seems to be doing fine."

"It was strange how you met her."

"Well, it was something you wouldn't read in a book. There I was about to die. She didn't know hardly anything about me. Took care of me while I was sick, fed me, and then she made it possible for us to get out here. I owe her a lot."

"She's a beautiful woman, don't you think?"

He turned and said, "She looks very well. I admire her."

"Why?"

"Because she has grit," Ty said. He shook his head. "A lot of men wouldn't have the nerve to do what she did. She ran off and left everything she knew because she couldn't stand to do things that she didn't like. Not many men could do that."

"I suppose not. I hate it we have this trouble over the sheep."

"I think there's more to it than that. I've met Raina's pa. He's a good man. Starting a church out in the badlands for the Indians and outlaws, I guess."

"Well, I don't think he'll have many converts. The Indians have their own gods."

"That's what I told him, but he's bound and determined to do it."

The two stood talking, and finally she walked away, saying, "Good night, Ty."

"Good night, Leoma."

As he had expected, Ty found no evidence except a great many hoofprints. They could have been the hoofprints of the raiders' horses, but they could just as easily have been from a party crossing on the way to town.

He went back to Fort Smith and gave his report to the judge. "I couldn't find a thing, Judge. I guess if I had been there, I might have seen something."

Judge Parker shook his head. "Well, we've had more trouble. Mr. Jordan came in and said there have been more sheep on his range and more cattle killed. Eddie Vernay says the same thing. Some of his sheep have been killed. I don't understand it. Those sheep have been there for a long time and never gave anybody any trouble."

"The former owner, did he get along all right with the man that owned the ranch?"

"Fine. Eddie Vernay always kept his sheep on his own land. That's what I can't understand, why a man would change like that."

"You want me to go back and see what I can find out?"

"Well, we're going to have to have some kind of a hearing. Both men are complaining, Vernay that Jordan killed his sheep and Jordan that Vernay killed his cattle. Something's beyond this. It's gonna take a smart man to find it."

"Well, you better send somebody else. I never hired myself out as a smart man."

"We'll see how it turns out. I sure get tired of things like this. It's almost as bad as hanging people."

"You feel bad about that, Judge?"

Judge Isaac Parker gave Kincaid a disgusted look. "Of course I feel bad about it. You think I enjoy hangings?"

"No, I wouldn't think so. Why do you do it?"

"I was appointed to keep order in this Indian Territory. We're gonna do it, me and Heck and marshals like you."

"I haven't been much help yet."

"You just stay on the job. We've got to find out what's going on here, Ty."

Kincaid was silent for a time, and then he said, "Do you ever get the feeling that all that goes on here is wasted?"

"What does that mean? We catch killers, and most of the time we hang them. That's something."

"But isn't it true that no matter how many you hang, there's always a new crop you have to find and hang?"

"I can't think like that. It's my duty to do all I can to bring law and order to this territory, and I'm bound to do it."

"Judge, don't you ever get discouraged?"

"Of course I do, Kincaid, but a man can't quit because everything doesn't go right. I look at it like a sacred duty. I think God put me in this job, and I do the best I can. Can't you see that?"

Ty shrugged, and for a moment stood silently regarding the judge. He had immense admiration for Parker but not much faith in the processes of law. Finally he said, "I think you're an honorable man, Judge, and you do what you see as God's work. But it seems like an impossible task."

"Don't you think I've asked myself many times if I'm doing the right thing? No man can sit in my court handing out sentences of death without giving in to some doubts. I may have hanged some innocent men. The system isn't perfect, but it's all we have. Can you imagine what this territory would be like if we didn't do our jobs?"

"It would be bad," Ty admitted. "And I know your job is the hardest. None of us have to wonder about what we do—but I know you are a man of conscience, so you have to have had thoughts of what your life means."

Judge Isaac Parker whispered as if to himself, "I think a lot about that, Ty—more than people think."

CHAPTER 16

Raina looked up at her father and thought how wonderful it was that she had a family, at least a father who loved her. She thought of how he had asked her once, "What do you really want, daughter?" And she had replied, "A place and a family." She had asked him then what he wanted, and he had simply said, "To serve God and to start a church."

Raina brought her mare, Daisy, out past the porch, and she heard her father call out, "Where you going, daughter?"

"Oh, just going to visit the herders and see that no more sheep have been killed."

"Well, you be careful. There's some bad men around here."

"I'm always careful, Pa. You know that." She waved at him and then kicked Daisy in the side. The mare started up at once at a slow trot. She was a good horse, obedient to command, and Raina had become quite attached to her.

Thirty minutes later she drew up to Benat. She talked to him for a while and then asked, "Where's Mikel and Yosu?"

"They're over there to the west, but you be careful."

"Everybody warns me to be careful. I will be."

She rode away with no real goal in mind except simply getting out. For the next hour she rode aimlessly, seeing nothing but coyotes and far off to the left a group of buzzards circling. *Something died*, she thought and had no desire to see what it was.

She turned Daisy around, and as she did something caught her eye over to the right. "Whoa, Daisy." She fixed her eyes on where she thought she had seen the movement and saw another. "What could that be?" she muttered and rode in that direction at a slow walk.

Suddenly she stopped, for she saw that it was a man. He was on foot, but even as he walked, he stumbled and went down. *That man looks hurt*, she thought and immediately kicked Daisy into a gallop. She got to the man and saw that his face was sunburned and his lips were roughly burned also.

She stepped off Daisy, tied her to a bush, and went to him, carrying a canteen. *He's dressed oddly*, she thought, *not like a cowboy or a sheepherder at all*. His skin was so fair that he had burned terribly. She could see that he had blond hair. She could also see that he was practically dying. She removed the cap from the canteen, lifted his head, and put it to his lips.

At first he didn't move, but then he began eagerly gulping.

"Just a little bit at a time," she said and removed the canteen. His eyes opened, and she saw that they were an azure blue, a color she had rarely seen. She wanted to ask him questions about what he was doing out here without a horse or anything, but she knew he would not be able to answer. She sat beside him and from time to time propped him up.

Finally after half an hour and many short sips of water, he gasped, "Thanks, miss."

"What are you doing way out here without a horse?"

The man licked his lips and asked for another drink. When he got it, he sat up feebly. "Well, I was out just taking a ride, and I was robbed and set afoot by two men."

Instantly Raina noticed that he had an accent that she did not recognize. It wasn't Spanish—she would have known that. "You can't stay out here. You're already burned. If I help you, can you get on my horse?"

"I'll try."

"She's very gentle." She helped him up.

He staggered over, holding on to her, and got to where Daisy was. Raina had to put his foot in the stirrup and then shove him until he could throw the other leg over. She removed his foot, mounted behind him, and said, "Okay, Daisy, let's go home."

It took a long time for them to make the trip, but by giving him small sips of water, she found out more about him. "What's your name?" she asked.

"George Fairfax."

"You're not from around here, are you?"

"No, not at all. I'm a stranger in this part of the world."

"You've got an odd accent. Where are you from?"

"England. Could I have some more of that water?"

She pulled off her handkerchief, wet it down, and said, "Keep this on your face, but take a little water first."

It was all the man could do to stay in the saddle, and Raina was relieved when she saw the house in the distance. "We're almost home, Mr. Fairfax."

He nodded but did not speak.

As she rode up to the house, her father came out. "What have you found, daughter?"

"This man was out without a horse. He's been robbed."

"Well, I expect we'd better get him in the house. He looks like he's got sunstroke. What's your name, mister?"

"George Fairfax."

Pa helped the man down, and Fairfax clung to him and to Raina as they helped him up the steps, led him through the door, and got him to a bedroom. He plopped down on the bed and said in a cracked voice, "Thanks."

"How in the world did you get afoot in the desert?"

"Well, I wanted to see the country, so I bought a horse and rode through it."

"Well, that was a bad idea," Pa said. "You could have gotten killed. There are men who do that."

"Well, they took everything I had. What's your name, sir?"

"Eddie Vernay. This is my daughter, Raina."

Fairfax smiled with some difficulty. "Well, you two saved my life, so according to an old Irish folktale, I belong to you."

Raina thought that was odd. "It's not like that. We don't belong to each other. Are you hungry?"

"I think I am."

"Pa, you give him some small sips of this water. Nothing big. I'll go fix something light."

Pa stayed with him until Raina came back. She had a bowl and said, "Can you sit up to eat this?"

"Oh yes. I think so." Fairfax pushed himself up to a sitting position.

She sat down beside him and handed him the bowl. "Can you feed yourself?"

"Yes, I think I can. I haven't had anything to eat in two days now."

"Well, this is just some light chicken broth. You take in little bits, and later on you'll be able to take on something more steady."

He ate the bowl of broth, and she took it, saying, "That's enough now. Is there anybody we can get in touch with and tell them you're not dead?"

"No, I don't think so."

"You're kind of a miracle, Mr. Fairfax. You could have died out there. Been killed by outlaws or Indians or even got snake bit," Pa said.

"Yes sir, I see that now."

"Do you know the Lord, Mr. Fairfax?"

Fairfax smiled slowly and nodded slightly. "Yes, in a way."

Raina was intrigued by the man. He was tall and lanky, with a handsome face and fair hair, and she knew that when the skin peeled he would have a smooth complexion. She asked, "Why did you come here, Mr. Fairfax? Not many people come to the Indian Territory."

"Oh, I inherited some money, and I was pretty tired of England, so I traveled. I went to Africa for a while and then to Australia. While I was in Australia, I read about this place and I thought I might find some adventure here."

"Well, you did that." Pa laughed. "You nearly found too much."

"Could I have some more of that soup?"

She got him a little more. After he finished his second bowl, he fell asleep.

Raina looked at her dad. "It's strange, isn't it, that a man would strike out in a place like this by himself."

"I guess it's not much like England."

∾

For two days Fairfax rested up, and finally he said, "I believe if you had a buggy of some sort, I could go to town and get myself pulled together."

"We've got a buggy. Raina, you drive him in, will you?"

"I will, Pa."

Raina saw that the Englishman moved much more easily, but his face was peeling, so she insisted he keep out of the sun and furnished him with a broad-brimmed hat that someone had left at the house.

"What do you need to do when we get to Fort Smith?"

"Well," Fairfax said, "my skin's tight, and it feels like it's going to fall off. But anyway I need to go to the bank and get some funds."

"You have an account there?"

"Yes, I had a rather large sum of money transferred to the bank there."

They arrived at Fort Smith and went at once to the bank.

Mr. Jenson, the banker, was surprised. "Why, Mr. Fairfax, I didn't expect to see you in this shape."

"I know. I look pretty bad. I got robbed and laid out in the desert. This lady found me, or I would have been dead."

"Well, here's the money. Of course you have a large balance here, as much as you need, but I wouldn't carry large sums if I were you. Not in Fort Smith."

"I believe you're right, sir. Come along, Miss Raina. I need to buy some decent clothes."

They left the bank, and Raina said, "Oh, there's one of the marshals. Ty, would you come here, please?"

Kincaid had been walking the other way, but hearing her call, he changed direction and hurried to her. He ran his eyes up and down the tall man with her.

She said, "This is George Fairfax. Mr. Fairfax, this is one of Judge Parker's marshals, Tyler Kincaid. A good friend of mine."

"You look the worse for wear, Mr. Fairfax."

"I really am. I would have been dead by this time if this young lady hadn't found me."

"What happened?" Ty listened as the man told about how he was robbed. "Can you describe the men who did it?"

"Well, not too well, but they took what I had and knocked me over the head and left me to die."

Ty said, "Well, there's any number of men that'll do that for you in this territory. Give me the description you got."

Ty listened as George gave very brief descriptions and shook his head. "There's not much chance of getting your horse and your money back."

"Well, that doesn't matter," Fairfax said. "I'll just be more careful how I hang on to things." He turned and said, "Miss Raina, would you have a meal with me after I get some decent clothes?"

"Yes, I'll even go shopping with you."

"I never had a lady pick out my clothes—except my mother when I was young."

"Come around and meet the judge when you get presentable," Ty said. "He'll want to hear about this."

"Yes, I'll do that."

For the next hour they picked what clothes Fairfax approved of, which weren't many. "I really will have to order some clothes from somewhere else."

"I don't think you can get anything better in this part of the country," Raina said.

"Well, let's get something to eat. Where's the best restaurant?"

Raina said, "The hotel's nice."

As the two walked along the street, she was aware that Fairfax attracted glances. He had bought an unusual hat, more like a derby than anything else, and with his height and sunburned face, she saw that he was the object of everyone's attention.

They had a good supper, and afterward she said, "You'd better find you a room and lie down."

"Well, I've got to find a barbershop first. I need a bath."

"You can get that at the hotel. They'll bring your hot water up, I'm sure."

"Miss Raina"—Fairfax turned and reached out, taking her hand and holding it with both of his—"I've never had to thank anybody for saving my life before, so I'm not very good at it, but I thank you."

"You're welcome, Mr. Fairfax."

"Oh please, just George if you don't mind."

"And I'm Raina."

"Beautiful name. Will I see you again?"

"Yes. I'll come by later and see how you're getting along."

"I'll look forward to that." Fairfax smiled.

Raina went to get a room in Mrs. Mullins's boardinghouse for the night. She was surprised as she could not stop thinking about the enigmatic Mr. George Fairfax.

CHAPTER 17

Judge Parker was on his way from his house to the courthouse when he met Fairfax and Ty Kincaid with him. They talked for a moment, and after Ty explained the predicament that Fairfax had gotten into, Parker stared at the Englishman. "What are you going to do here in this country?"

"You know, I have a law degree from Oxford. It's possible I might be able to use that here in this country."

"I should think so. A law degree from Oxford, that's better than what most of our lawyers have around here."

"I'd really like to know more about American court procedure."

"Well, come along to the hearing."

"I'll just do that."

Fairfax and Ty went in and found seats. It was crowded there, and as they waited for the judge to appear, Fairfax told Ty how Raina had saved his life.

"Well, we have something in common." Ty grinned. "She saved my life, too. You know, she could make a career out of saving fellows like us."

They sat talking quietly until finally the judge appeared. He was not wearing a robe but his usual black suit. He listened to Ed Vernay, and then he listened to Aaron Jordan. It was a long-drawn-out affair, with Jordan getting angry.

Finally the judge said, "There are no witnesses to this, so my ruling is that you, Mr. Jordan, will pay Mr. Vernay for the sheep that were killed, and you, Mr. Vernay, will pay Mr. Jordan for the cattle that were killed."

This was acceptable enough to Vernay. He said, "I know I'm innocent, Judge, but I'll obey your ruling."

"But it's not fair! I didn't kill any sheep," Aaron Jordan complained.

"That's my ruling, and you'll pay right now before you leave this courtroom." He waited until the men had put up the money and then said, "Now, there'll be no more of this nonsense."

Ty left the courtroom, but Fairfax remained behind as he wanted to see more of the court in action.

Ty met Raina, who said, "Fairfax is pretty well recovered. You know, he said he'd like to see a sheep operation."

"Why would he want to do that?"

"He told me he might want to become a sheepherder."

"Now there's a thought. I might resign from Judge Parker's marshals and become one myself."

"No, it'll be a little bit rough for your taste, I think. You can tell me about your misspent childhood, and George can tell me about England and Africa."

❧

"You know, Judge, I think we need to send somebody to keep an eye on that situation out there about the sheep and the cattle."

"You may be right, Heck. All it takes is one more ambush of sheep on Jordan's ranch and he'll blow his top."

"We'd better see a man out. If they see a marshal hanging around, that might stop them."

"Who will you send?"

"Let's send Kincaid. He's familiar with the people there and with the lay of the land."

"One may not be enough."

"Well, I can send more if the war heats up."

Heck left and found Kincaid coming out of the general store. "The judge wants to send a man out to keep an eye on this trouble between the Jordans and Vernay."

"He thinks there'll be some more of this?"

"Those sheep didn't just wander onto Jordan's land. Sheep don't wander like that."

"Well, what then?"

"That's what we're sending you for."

"All right, Heck. I don't know what good I'll do, but I'll see what I can turn up."

❧

Leoma rose from the porch where she had been sitting and stepped down to meet Ty as he got off his horse. "Come in for some lemonade. It's warm but it's wet."

Ty noticed she looked as beautiful as ever. "Sounds good to me." He followed her inside, and when she had sat down, he asked, "Where are all the men?"

"They're all out looking for a sheep under every bush. I think it's foolishness." She gave him a big glass of the lemonade and asked, "What are you doing now, Ty?"

He tasted the lemonade. "Well, the judge sent me out to see if we could find out what's causing the trouble."

"Well, we know that, don't we?"

"You mean Ed Vernay?"

"Yes, his are the only sheep around here."

"I don't know much about sheep, but I don't think they wander much. Vernay's sheep camp is miles from here."

"Well, how else could they get here?"

"They may have been driven, Leoma."

"By Vernay?"

"That's not likely. Something strange about this. From what I hear, Vernay never lets his sheep stray. He always keeps them on his own land."

She studied him carefully. "Are you going to talk to Pa?"

"Oh yes, and everybody else."

"Vernay, too?"

"Sure."

Leoma seemed troubled, and he asked what was bothering her. She said rather hesitantly, "You and Raina Vernay were pretty close at one time, weren't you?"

"At one time."

"I think you would be more likely to listen to her and to believe her."

"No, that's not so. Tell you what. I'll be roaming around, and if I see something that looks strange with either cattle or sheep, I'll look into it."

They talked for a while. He got up and said, "I'll be back to you and your family."

"Are you going to talk to Vernay now?"

"Well, I'm going to look over the ground where all the sheep were killed. Will you show me where you found the slaughtered cattle?"

"I'll take you."

He stood up and said, "I thought about all those cattle and sheep dying." He shook his head and said sadly, "I hate to see anything wasted."

"So do I," Leoma said.

Ty grinned and gave the young woman a wink. "Especially good-looking young women." He laughed at her expression.

She said, "Never mind that!"

"Just making talk."

"Yes, I notice you do that a lot."

"You're such an interesting lady, I can't help it."

Leoma gave him a quick smile then asked, "How many young women have you run after, Ty?"

"Oh, maybe three or four."

"What a liar."

"I expect I am. My life's been pretty dull."

"Mine, too, I guess. Nothing really exciting has ever happened to me. I wish it would."

Ty glanced at her and said, "Like what?"

"Oh, nothing like you have—lots of adventure."

"Most adventures are pretty hard. I can think of a few that I could have done without. But you'd better be happy you haven't had too many of them."

"Better to have an adventure that hurts than be bored to death."

Ty shook his head, not understanding her. "Haven't you had men who wanted you? I expect so."

"Most of them were boring."

"Marry a juggler. He can entertain you if that's what you need. Didn't you love any of the men who wanted you?"

"Not enough to spend the next forty years with them."

Ty laughed aloud. "Well, that's coming right out with it."

The two studied one another, and then Ty said, "Come along. You can tell me more about your love life."

CHAPTER 18

Raina was enjoying George Fairfax's company tremendously. He was the kind of man she had never met before, cultured, handsome, wealthy, and he had insisted that she take him out to look at the sheep.

"Why do you want to look at sheep, George?"

"Well, I just like to know things."

They rode for a time and finally dismounted by a small stream and let the horses drink. As they stood watching, she asked him about his home in England. "Did you ever see the queen?"

"As a matter of fact, I did."

"I've heard a lot about Victoria and her love for Prince Albert."

"Well, everybody's fascinated by that. She was only a young girl when she married him. Somebody asked her what she was going to do as a queen, and you know what she said?"

"No, what?"

"She said, 'I will be good.' "

"What a fine thing for a woman to say." She remained silent

for a minute, gathering courage to ask her next question. "Have you ever been in love?"

"Well, yes." Fairfax took off his hat and ran his hand over his blond hair. "I know something about love. I loved my wife greatly. Even though she's gone now, I still think about her every day."

"Do you, George?"

"I suppose I always will. I think when you have the right kind of marriage, husband and wife become one. Death may take one or the other, but there will be something still in you." He turned suddenly and took her hand. "You remind me of her in a way, Raina."

"Me? Like a member of the British aristocracy?"

"Yes, you do. You're honest like she was. Beautiful as she was." He suddenly raised her hand and kissed it.

For a moment Raina was unable to speak. Then she felt him release her hand.

"Tell me about this desire of your father's to bring God to the Indians."

"Not just the Indians, George. He wants to bring the Gospel to some of these outlaws."

"Well, that would indeed be a miracle. I'd like to go to your father's church."

"All right. There's a service starting soon. We can go now."

Ty had been spending a great deal of time out on the range, primarily looking over the slaughtered cattle. After looking around for a while, he decided to go to the sheep camp. When he arrived at Vernay's place, he saw Mikel working outside. "Hello, Mikel."

"Hello, Kincaid. What are you doing out here?"

"Just looking around. What about you?"

Mikel stared steadily at Kincaid. "You're not out here just for the ride."

Kincaid arched his back to relieve the tension, then shoved his hat back from his forehead. "I wanted to look over the ground, at least Judge Parker wanted me to. What do you make of it, Mikel?"

Mikel was silent. He was not a man to speak a lot, for that was part of his Indian blood. He studied Kincaid and said finally, "Sheep aren't likely to wander as far as they were. As long as they've got grass and water, they pretty well stay put."

"Well, maybe you can show me where they're supposed to wander from."

Mikel shrugged. "You'd better get the boss to agree with that."

"Sure. Where will I find him, Mikel?"

"In church." Mikel grinned at Ty's expression. "But maybe you're not a church man."

His words troubled Ty. "Well, I'm not, but I need to be."

"The boss has been trying to get a church started. Only Indians come to the meeting."

"How do I get there?"

Mikel turned to point. "He's using an empty barn about a mile from the house." He gave Ty directions.

Ty said, "Aren't you going, Mikel?"

"No. I gave up on God a long time ago." Then he seemed to think better of his words. "But I've been listening to the boss's preaching, and it's got me hooked. Maybe I'll get converted and become a preacher."

Ty laughed. "I'd like to see that. I'd come and hear you." He turned his horse and rode toward the "church."

As Ty rode up to the old, unpainted barn, he saw there were a great many horses and a few wagons outside. He dismounted and heard his name called.

Turning, he saw Raina, who walked over to him. "I'm so glad you came. Did you plan to sing in the choir?"

"No, but I'd like to hear a sermon."

Raina smiled.

Eddie Vernay approached, accompanied by Fairfax. The preacher said, "You're a long way from Judge Parker's court, Kincaid."

"For a fact I am. I came to hear a sermon."

"Well, I suspect you didn't come this far just to hear a sermon."

Ty saw that the older man was good at reading what was in a man's heart. "You're right. The judge wants me to keep a close eye on things."

"Have you found anything?" Vernay asked.

"Not much."

"Well, you will. I'm not much of a preacher, but come in if you like."

"I'll do that."

They all went inside, and Kincaid saw that it was a rough church indeed. The benches consisted of boards put across kegs for the most part. A few roughly hewn boards had been made into seats with straight backs. He grinned and thought, *Nobody's going to go to sleep while the preacher's at it. Nobody could sleep on a bench like that.*

Young Indian children were running around. The Indians had adopted the right side of the benches as their territory, and a group of white people sat on the left.

"Pretty good crowd," Vernay said. "I've got the cook killing a sheep, and we'll feed 'em good." He grinned and said, "They kind of like manna. I don't expect any to fall from heaven, but at least it'll give 'em a motive for coming."

"Good idea." Ty nodded.

"Well, let's get going here." Ed Vernay walked to a spot in front where there was no pulpit at all or even a platform. He looked out at the congregation and smiled. There was a kindly look on his face. He said, "We're going to sing some songs. My daughter, Raina, is a good singer. If you know 'em, just chime in. If you don't, just sit and listen till you learn it."

Raina was obviously startled. Her father had not told her this part of his plan, but she at once began to sing "Near the Cross."

Ty and several others joined in. He enjoyed singing and did so with gusto.

Raina led the congregation in two or three more of the old church songs before she took a seat between Ty and George.

Finally Vernay said, "Now it's time for a little preaching. I just want to remind you of one thing. There's nobody in this church this morning that's led a worse life than I did. I'm ashamed to tell you some of the things I've done." He continued to tell of some of the instances he was not proud of when he was a young man, and he said, "For a long time I felt that I was too bad a man for God to save, but then I was reading the Bible one day, and I read about the death of Jesus on the cross. Let me read you that part of the story." He opened the Bible and read about Jesus on the cross between the two thieves. After he read the story, he said, "It's kind of hard to think about this, but here was a man looking at a Savior who was bloody, whose face was marred, who had been beaten almost to death, but this thief said, 'Lord, remember me when you come into your kingdom.' The first time I read that," Vernay said, "I thought, well, Jesus won't have anything to do with him. But then I read the next line, and I'll tell you it knocked me out of the saddle. Some of you know it. When the thief said, 'Remember me when you come into your kingdom,' Jesus said, 'Today shalt thou be with me in paradise.' "

Vernay halted for a moment, and Kincaid could see tears forming in his eyes. He dashed them away and then continued.

"You know that thief couldn't do one thing to make himself attractive to God. He had been a thief, a criminal, probably a murderer. There was no time for him to go out and do anything good that would please God. He was just a poor, helpless, dying sinner, and I'll remember throughout all eternity, I think, how I felt when I read that Jesus welcomed him into His kingdom that very day. Something seemed to just turn over in my heart, and I realized I could be saved. It was something I'd never even thought of, so I made up my mind right then and there to do the same thing that the thief did. I just simply called on the Lord. I don't remember the words," Vernay said simply, "but I do remember telling God that I was a sinner, and I couldn't do anything about that. I don't know how long I prayed, but when the praying was over, I knew that I was a saved man. That thief has been with Jesus for two thousand years, just about, but his life with God began the day he died with Jesus. That's what I want for myself, and that's what every man and woman and young person here in this church needs. Just to be close to Jesus for all eternity."

Ty was intent on the sermon when he felt Raina touch his arm.

She said, "Does that mean anything to you, Ty?"

He turned to her, a struggle raging in him, and he said, "I guess I'm just about where your father was. I thought I was too bad a man." He said no more but just sat while the sermon ended.

When it was over, Ty, Raina, and Fairfax went at once to speak to Vernay.

George shook his hand. "It was a wonderful sermon, sir. You're a mighty preacher."

"I thank you, Mr. Fairfax."

George added, "If I can do anything to help you, I don't know what it would be. If it's money, I can help with that."

"Could always use money to build a better church, but even that's not necessary."

Ty stood by, and as he left, he saw that Raina had gone to stand beside her father and Fairfax, and he wondered what she thought about the man. He, however, was more troubled about his own condition. The sermon had affected him deeply, and all that day as he rode away and got out by himself, he could not get away from the words of the scripture. *"Today shalt thou be with me in paradise."*

For several days, Ty was very quiet. He couldn't quit thinking about his standing with God, and he couldn't get Ed Vernay's sermon out of his mind. He tried to put it aside but was mostly unsuccessful until he and Gale Young were sent to make an arrest.

Gale Young said, "What about this Jeb Cotton? What's he done?"

"Well, the story is he shot an Indian he claimed had stolen a cow from him. He's not known as a violent man, Gale, so it should be an easy arrest."

Gale was a talkative young man at times, and he began speaking of things he planned to do in his life.

Ty was happy Gale was doing most of the talking, because he was still a bit overwhelmed with the conviction he felt for the life he'd led.

"You know what I want to do most of all, Ty?"

"What's that, Gale?"

"I want to buy a small ranch. It doesn't have to be a big one. And I want to marry Ellen Franklin."

"Ellen Franklin? Who's she?"

"Oh, she's my childhood sweetheart. We both grew up in the same little town. Before I left there to come here, I asked her to marry me, and she said she would."

"Most women wouldn't like to be proposed to and then have the prospective bridegroom ride away."

"She didn't like it much. She begged me to stay. As a matter of fact, she even cried when I left."

"I'm surprised you left her, Gale."

"Well, I almost didn't, but I told her I'd just try this for a while, that in all probability it wouldn't last. I just want a small ranch and a wife. She's waitin' for me."

"What do you plan to do then?"

"Well, I've had about enough of being a marshal. I want to go home, marry Ellen, and have some children and raise them. Then when I get older, I'll be a grandpa and have the grandchildren all around my knees. I can tell them stories about what a great marshal I was and that I knew the great Ty Kincaid."

"That wouldn't impress 'em much."

"Well, we don't have anything, but Ellen says we ought to marry, even though we don't have any money."

Suddenly a strange thought crossed Kincaid's mind. "You know, if I had a feeling like that about a woman, I'd do something about it."

"What would you do, Ty?"

"I'd leave marshaling that very minute. I'd ride to her, and I'd get on my knees and beg her to marry me, and then I'd throw that marshal's badge as far away as I could."

Gale was surprised. "I thought you liked being a marshal."

"No, I don't."

"Well, I've got to save some money first."

"You'll never do it on this job."

"I know it." He was silent for a time and said, "Maybe Ellen's right."

"About what?"

"That we ought to marry even if we don't have any money."

"If you really love the woman, Gale, do it."

Gale turned and faced Ty Kincaid. "I think I will. This will be my last job."

"Good for you, Gale. You get back to that woman. Marry her and have those kids. Maybe I'll come and be a godfather to one of them."

"I'd like that a lot." Gale smiled.

Half an hour later the two rode into Jeb Cotton's place. They found him scalding a hog.

Ty said, "Be careful. He's not known to be a shooter, but you never can tell." The two stepped out of their saddles, and Ty said, "Hello, Cotton."

"Hello, Marshal. What you doin' out here?"

"I'm afraid I've got to take you in. You got to stand trial for shooting that Indian, Jeb."

Jeb was a tall, thin individual, almost gaunt. His eyes suddenly blazed with anger. "I was defending my property. That Indian had a gun, and he drew on me."

"Well, that's not the way we heard about it. There was a witness, you know."

"Some witness! He was another Indian. You going to believe him over a white man?"

Ty saw at once that this was not going to be as simple an arrest as he had thought, but he was still determined to do it easily. "Come on, Jeb. If you're innocent, Judge Parker will let you go. Let me have your gun."

Ty fully expected that Jeb would pull his gun from the holster at his side and hand it over. Instead Cotton drew the gun and fired off a shot. It caught Ty off guard when the bullet struck Gale in the chest and knocked him down. Jeb turned the pistol to shoot Ty, but Ty drew his pistol and put one shot into the man's heart. Ty knew Cotton was dead, so he went to Gale and saw that he had been hit bad. He pulled him up and saw that Gale's eyes were open, but he was breathing in a shallow fashion.

"Ty—"

"What is it, Gale?"

"You know what? I'll never—have Ellen—now." He breathed in short, quick puffs, and with his last gasp he said, "Ty, write

Ellen. Tell her—I loved her more than anything."

"I'll do that, Gale."

Gale's eyes fluttered, and he whispered, "Ty, don't die like this. Don't miss out on life." The light went out of Gale's eyes, and his body slumped.

Ty held him as a sense of utter frustration enveloped him. He hugged the man and shook his head. "You missed it all, Gale, and Ellen's missed it, too."

❧

"Look, there comes Ty, and he's got two men tied down on horses." Heck Thomas stood with Judge Parker outside the courthouse.

"That wasn't supposed to be a hard job. I hope that's not Gale. He's a fine young man."

But when the two men approached Ty, he fell off his horse.

Parker said, "What happened, Ty?"

"I didn't expect any trouble, Judge. Jeb's not known to be a killer, but he drew and shot Gale before I could do anything. I got him, but it was too late. They're both dead now."

"What a shame," Heck said. "Gale's one of the finest young men I ever knew. He had a great life."

"Did you know he was going to marry a girl named Ellen?" Ty asked Heck.

"He did mention it one time."

"Well, he'll never do it now." There was bitterness in Ty's voice, and he said, "I promised him I'd write her a letter, but I don't know what I could say."

"No, there's not anything to say at a time like this."

෨

Raina heard about what had happened from one of the marshals who had come by their home. She and her father immediately got ready and left to attend the funeral that would be held two days later.

When they arrived in Fort Smith and spoke to Heck and Ty, her father was asked to preach a sermon at the service. After the funeral, she tried to find Ty, who had stood on the outer ring of the crowd, but he was gone.

Raina was worried about Ty, so she went to the barracks and found him there. "I've been looking for you, Ty."

"I had to be by myself. I don't feel much like talking."

"Come along." It was nearly dusk now, and the town had gone quiet. "Let's go for a walk."

"All right. If you say so."

The two left the barracks, and for a time she simply walked beside him saying nothing.

Finally, when they were on the edge of the town, he looked over and saw that the sun was setting. "Look at that sun going down," he said quietly. Then he added bitterly, "But it will come up tomorrow. Not like Gale."

"I know it's terrible for you, Ty."

He turned to her and whispered, "He missed out on everything, Raina. He had a sweetheart named Ellen. He had decided to leave Fort Smith and go back and marry her, and now he never will."

Raina was shocked. She thought of Ty as one of the toughest men she knew, but she could see his broken will and the tears standing in his eyes. She suddenly reached out, put her arms around him, and said, "He was a Christian, Ty. He told me that. He won't have Ellen, but he'll be safe. He'll be with Jesus forever."

"I know, but it scares me. He wanted Ellen and kids and a family and a home. That's what I've always wanted."

"Have you, Ty?"

"Yes, and it's a lonely life, being without God."

"You don't have to be alone."

He looked at her with surprise, saying, "It's all I know, Raina."

"You've heard the Gospel. All you need is to find Jesus."

"I don't know how to do that. Wish I did."

"Talk to my pa. You trust him, don't you?"

"Sure, but—"

"Just do it." She hesitated then said, "I think it's easier to become a Christian than to be one from day to day."

"I don't understand that, Raina."

"Just think, a man can become a married man in five minutes— but I think it takes years to be a good husband, for most men at least. You can become a Christian in an instant, but sometimes it takes years to be a good one."

Kincaid blinked with surprise then whispered, "It sounds too easy."

"It's easy for us, but it was difficult for Jesus. He had to die to make a way for all of us to be saved."

Ty Kincaid said, "I'm just not sure that you're right about this, but I hope desperately that you are."

CHAPTER 19

Ty received word that Heck Thomas wanted to see him, so he went at once to the man's office. When he stepped inside, he asked, "You wanted to see me?"

"Yeah. Have you heard what's happened at the Jordan ranch?"

"No, I thought all was pretty well quiet out there."

"Well, Aaron Jordan came roarin' in about as mad as a man can get. He claims the sheepherders killed about twenty of his prime head of cattle."

"I was afraid of this. Did he have any proof?"

"No, not any, but he's on the rampage, Ty. I heard him tell Judge Parker if he don't send some marshals in, he'll take care of the trouble himself."

"Well, I don't imagine the judge liked that. What'd he say?"

"Said he would do his best, but he was short of men. Then the judge told me to ask you to look into it. I guess he knows, like everybody else, that you have good relationships with both sides. He said to go on a longtime scout. Find out what's goin' on."

He stood up. He was not an impressive-looking man, this Heck

Thomas, but he had a mind like a razor. "You're a man who can find out things. This situation is bad, and it could get worse."

"I'll get right at it, Heck."

Ty left Thomas's office and immediately made preparations. He drew a packhorse and loaded it with all the supplies the animal could carry, then saddled his favorite horse. He was still preoccupied with his soul when he stepped into the saddle. More than that, he was more confused about this matter of God and his soul than he had told anybody.

He decided to go to the Jordan ranch first. When he arrived, Aaron Jordan was red in the face still with anger. "Come on. I'll show you those dead steers."

"All right, Aaron." Ty saw there was little reasoning with the man, and he went out and looked at the ground. "I don't see any tracks or sheepherders."

"Well, you're the tracker. You must have found something."

"The only thing I found was that one horseman has been through here, and his horse is missing a shoe on the right foreleg."

"Where does that get us?"

"Not very far, I don't guess. If we found a horse like that, we wouldn't have any proof that the man rode him here."

The two rode back to the ranch, and Aaron rode off still muttering threats.

Leoma came outside and asked Ty to come in the house.

"Don't have much time to stay, Leoma. Let's sit outside instead."

The two sat down on the porch, and he was quiet for so long, she said, "I know Gale Young's death hit you hard."

"Very hard. He was a fine young man, had his life before him. He was going to quit being a marshal and go back and marry his childhood sweetheart. A girl named Ellen."

"He told you that?"

"Yes, he did. And I told him it was a good idea. He got to talking on our way out to Cotton's place about what all he had missed in life." Ty turned and looked at her, his expression sad. He ran his hand over his abundant black hair. "He had it all planned out. He was going to marry her even if they had no money."

"They really loved each other then."

"Yes, you could tell that from talking to Gale."

She waited for him to go on, but he was silent for so long, she said, "It really bothers you, doesn't it?"

"Yes. You know why?"

"No. What is it, Ty?"

"It could happen to me. You know, one time I was going through the mountains, and I saw a deer. I got my rifle out to take a shot, but before I could get it out the deer just fell down."

"Somebody else shoot him?"

"No," Ty said. "That was the funny thing. I got to him and there wasn't a mark on him. He hadn't been hit by a bullet. I guess his heart just gave out, but he was dead, and the thing I thought of was this deer didn't know anything about this. When he woke up this morning, he thought he would have as much life as he ever had, but he didn't make it through the day." He shifted his weight in the chair and leaned over and stared down at the floor. "That's the way it was with Gale. It hit me hard."

"Death always does that."

"I guess so, but if a man's eighty years old you don't notice it so much, but he was just a young fellow. He had everything before him. He was even a Christian. He told me that."

"I'm glad to hear that."

"So am I. Well, I've got to go, Leoma."

"Come back after you've done some looking around."

"I'll do that."

For the next four days Kincaid looked over the ground. He stayed out away from the two men having the trouble, and at night he would build up a fire and read his Bible by the light of the flames. Most of the time he thought about Raina, but he couldn't forget Gale's death. He had written a letter to Ellen Franklin, which had been one of the hardest things he had ever done.

He spent a great deal of time trying to think how he could get right with God, and finally he went to the sheep camp. Raina was there, and he found he was a little bit restrained toward her.

It was Sunday, and he went to the church again. This time the sermon Vernay preached was on forgiveness. He read the scripture of the woman who was found in adultery and then brought to Jesus. Ty listened as Vernay read the story from the Bible: " 'The men who brought the woman asked Jesus, Moses in the law commanded us, that such should be stoned: but what sayest thou? But Jesus said nothing.' "

Ty had forgotten this part.

Vernay continued. "But Jesus simply knelt in the dust and began to write. The Bible says one at a time the men left."

I wonder what He wrote. Maybe the sins of those men, Kincaid thought.

Then Vernay read the most telling part. " 'Jesus said, Woman, where are those thine accusers? Hath no man condemned thee? She said, No man, Lord. And Jesus said unto her, Neither do I condemn thee: go, and sin no more.' "

The last words seemed to stick in Kincaid's mind, *"Go and sin no more."* Somehow he knew this was his problem. He had been a sinner all his life, that he well knew, but he had given little thought to changing. But now Jesus' order to "go and sin no more" was glued to his mind.

Raina knew she liked George Fairfax, and as he rode up and dismounted, she was pleased. "I'm glad to see you, George."

He smiled. "I'm delighted to see you, too."

"That's the way you English talk. No man ever told me he was delighted to see me before."

They talked for a time, and finally George heaved a sigh. "I've always been an impulsive man, and I need to tell you something, Raina."

"What is it, George?"

"Well, I've been thinking. I'm not getting any younger."

"None of us are." She smiled at him.

"And what I'd like to know is if you would entertain a proposal?"

"What sort of proposal?"

"I didn't think there was but one kind." Fairfax smiled. "A proposal of marriage."

Raina was caught off guard. She knew she liked Fairfax tremendously. He had qualities that no other man had ever shown to her. "Well, I'm not sure."

"I think I'm going to court you, and I believe we could be very happy."

"I've never thought of marriage for us."

"Well, think of it. We could do anything you like. I have plenty of money. We could buy us a ranch. We could live in the city. We could travel. You could go see England, Ireland, lots of things."

She stood waiting, and as she had expected, he put his arms around her and kissed her. It was a gentle kiss, and she liked that. She was surprised that she didn't draw back, for she usually held off from men. As he kissed her, she thought of Ty's kiss, and she knew she couldn't compare the two men. They were too different.

"I'll have to think about this," she said when he lifted his head. "There are other things in marriages."

"Yes. Some marriages. Well, you think about it." He kissed her again then left.

Raina's mind was in a whirl. Marriage to George Fairfax might be wonderful. She would certainly never want for anything. But was that enough? What about love? She thought about George's proposal, but somehow Ty kept intruding into her thoughts. She wasn't sure she even wanted to know what that meant.

❦

Ty had spent several days riding around and finding mostly nothing. On the fourth day he was awakened in the middle of the night. It was a dark night with few stars in the skies and no moon except a tiny sliver. He suddenly heard the sound of sheep bleating. *Sheep don't move at night.* He got to his feet and picked up his gun. *Who would be moving sheep at this hour?*

"Who's out there?" he called, but several shots cut him off. One of them hit him in the chest. As he fell, Ty thought, *I'm going to die like Gale, not having done anything good in my life.* And then he knew nothing. . . .

PART FOUR

PART FOUR

CHAPTER 20

The ebony darkness was almost palpable. At times a light appeared far in the darkness, but then it would fade away so he could sense it no more. He had been one acquainted with the night, and under the darkness of the blackest evenings there was always a faint flickering of stars or something that told him he was alive, but now he felt nothing except the slow passage of time.

From time to time a sound came to him—a faint voice from somewhere in the past. It seemed that he recognized the voice at times, but then it faded. He was aware that there was something out there, but his mind was buried so deep in unconsciousness he could not know it.

An acrid smell came to him, and for a moment he rose out of the depth of darkness that enveloped him. Underneath his body he felt the roughness of earth, but he could not recognize it.

Time meant nothing. He had no sense of its passage, and he could have been unconscious for as long as it took to build the pyramids, or it could have been only a few moments.

Finally he began to rise out of the darkness, and strange flashes of memory began to touch his mind. They were not fully developed, and he could not identify them. He was only faintly aware that they came from somewhere out of a past that he had left behind.

A figure and a face took shape in front of him. It was from his past, and he struggled to recognize it. Finally he remembered a scene in the woods, but he could not remember where it was. But there was a young boy there, and slowly as the features of the young man came together, he recognized Roy Gibbons, the best friend of his youth. It was an innocent face, youthful, unmarked by time, and yet he remembered it. It was very vivid. He saw himself and his friend as they crossed the field and came to a fence. Roy leaned his rifle against the fence and straddled it to go over, but as he did, he lost his balance and struck out. There was an explosion, and as clearly as he had seen anything, Ty recognized the crimson blood that spurted from his friend's throat. He cried out then as he must have cried out when he was watching this tragedy. "No, Roy!"

But then the terrible dream faded, and he suddenly knew that it was something he'd experienced as a young man. The darkness came again, and gratefully he lay back, glad not to see the awful scene of his friend dying.

Soon, however, another dream came. The face of a young woman took shape in the darkness and seemed to glow. She had an oval-shaped face. At first he did not recognize her, and then suddenly a name came to him. *Evelyn.* He tried to cry out to her, but she looked at him with a sadness that he could not identify. He lay there struggling, trying to shake the dream from his mind, for the young woman brought memories that he had tried to bury years ago. He remembered she had been his first love, the first young woman he had ever known, and then suddenly he saw the scene where she had come to him and said, "Ty, I'm going to have a baby."

The words seemed to be carved in some sort of glass or marble. *"Ty, I'm going to have a baby."* He remembered how he had been only seventeen and did not really love the girl.

He'd saddled his horse, without a word from anyone, and left the farm where he had been born without even leaving a note to his parents. He remembered fleeing over the country, trying to find a forgetfulness that would blot out the face of the young woman, but now as he lay there, suddenly, not for the first time, the queries came floating into his consciousness: *I wonder if she had a boy or a girl. I wonder if she ever found a man to be a father to the child. . .my child.* And he felt a sharp pang of keen regret.

Suddenly Ty felt a sharp sensation in his back. Something was poking at him, and he rolled over and made a harsh, croaking cry. He had the impression of several dark, hideous birds rising up, their wings flapping as their harsh cries etched into the silence of wherever he was. Finally he fell back into unconsciousness and felt a black hole closing in about him. He felt something seizing his legs, dragging him down, and he cried out in a desperate voice, "No, God! Don't let me die!"

And then came nothingness. No sounds. No smells. No touch. Just the blackness that devoured him.

❦

Raina reached up and patted her mare's head. She took the bit well, and Raina smiled. "That's a good girl. Let's you and me go for a ride."

She stepped into the saddle and waved good-bye to her father, who was talking with one of the herdsmen. He waved back and smiled at her, and somehow the smile brought a good feeling of warm pleasure. She had found a father. Found one who was tied to her by blood and by the past, and somehow this meant that she was now a complete person.

It was a fine time of the morning, the part of the day that she loved best. The sun had risen and now was shedding warm beams over the land. She paused once and looked at the land that dropped below her, then lifted her eyes to where it rose to the hills over to the north. The sight of the Yellow River, as it wound its way across the plain and disappeared into the distance, gave her pleasure. The sun brought a sparkling to the water's surface, and she kept a fast pace until finally she reached a high ridge, the beginning of the Indian Territory.

She looked in both directions and saw not a single thing moving, leaned forward, and whispered, "Let's go, girl." The mare moved forward, and Raina rode slowly, enjoying the freshness and the fullness and the goodness of late morning. Finally she spotted a herd of sheep and lifted the mare to a slow gallop.

She pulled up, and Yosu, a small man with a dark complexion and white, shiny teeth, smiled at her. "Hello, miss," he said. "You're out early this morning."

"I brought you some food, Yosu. I baked yesterday. I remembered how you liked the cake, so I brought you part of it."

"Gracias." Yosu reached out eagerly and took the box that she handed him. He opened it at once, broke off a piece, then chewed and swallowed. His grin flashed again, and he said, "Very good. You're going to make some man a fine wife."

"Maybe." She liked Yosu, and they talked for some time, although she did not dismount. He looked up at her, and finally she smiled and said, "Are you still in love with Juanita?" Juanita was the Mexican daughter of one of the men who helped with the business of the camp.

She saw that Yosu said nothing, but finally he looked up and there was a sadness in his eyes as black as obsidian. "I have nothing to give her."

Yosu's answer shocked Raina, and she thought for a moment. It had not occurred to her that the economics of a sheepherder were not at all prosperous. "Well, you have yourself, Yosu."

Yosu's head went back, and he stared at her then shook his head almost violently. "No, a man needs something to bring to a woman." He hesitated, looked to the ground, and then lifted his eyes to her. "Have you ever loved a man, Miss Raina?"

The question troubled Raina, and she bit her lower lip, trying to think of a proper answer. She said, "No, I haven't—but I know Juanita likes you. My father trusts you. He's going to raise you up. He'll make it possible for you to marry."

"There's a man who lives in town that likes her. He has a house. A rich man." Rich might have meant anything, but his idea of riches would be a small frame house and a job.

Raina felt a twinge of sorrow. "Take a chance. Don't let her get away from you, Yosu. I know she likes you."

He suddenly smiled and said, "Maybe I will say so."

"You do that." Raina touched her heels to the sides of her horse and the mare shot off in a trotting gait. She kept her eyes on the plain before her, noting how it dipped into hollows and rose to slight ridges. The grass was green now, but one day would be gray and dead. It always came back though. The thought of resurrection gave her pleasure.

She was thinking, however, of what Yosu had asked her. *"Have you ever loved a man?"* The question troubled her, and she thought about Ty. Their meeting had been like nothing she had ever experienced before, and she had thought about it at length many times. As for Ty himself, there was some sort of connection between them that she did not understand. She knew he seemed to admire her, at least her looks, and their meeting and subsequent lives being twined together somehow troubled her.

Suddenly she thought of George Fairfax, the Englishman, who had dropped into her life. He had settled in Fort Smith for a time, but she was not sure how long he would be there. He admired her, too; she knew that as a woman always knows such things. She had seen warmth in his eyes when he looked at her, but only once had he commented, saying, "You have a beauty that I've never seen in a woman, Raina. It's not only outward—any man could see that—but it's inward." *What did he mean by that?* She pondered this question as she rode along for the next hour.

Buzzards circled up ahead. *It may be a sheep that's lost and dying,* she thought. She coaxed her mare into a gallop, and when she came over a rise, she looked down and saw the birds were descending. She called out, and with a flapping sound they all rose into the air. She was shocked to see a man lying on the ground facedown. As she drew close, she saw that his back was bloody. *He must be dead.*

She pulled up and dropped the reins. Her horse had been trained to stop and wait when the reins were left hanging. She walked over slowly, thinking it was a corpse, but when she got close she saw movement. Suddenly she recognized the side of his face and cried out, "Ty!"

She removed the canteen from the cantle of the saddle and went to him. He groaned as she turned him over, and the sunlight fell on the jagged gash on the side of his head, but she knew the wound in his back was from a bullet. She removed her neckerchief, soaked it with water, and then bathed his face. Carefully she rolled him over and saw that the bullet had struck him high in the back. She was grateful it seemingly had not hit a lung. His horse was gone, and he was lying there alone in the desert. *He's been shot, and somebody left him to die.* Looking around the scene, she saw a half-buried sharp rock, and it was bloody. *He must have hit his head on that rock.* She whispered, "Ty, can you hear me?"

He did not move, and she held the lip of the canteen to his mouth. At first it simply ran down his chin, but then he gulped thirstily, and his eyes fluttered but did not open.

"We've got to get you out of here, Ty. You'll have to help me." She lowered him carefully then moved over to her mare and led her to stand beside him. He was a big man, and she said, "Ty, you've got to help. Hang on to me and try to get up." At first she thought she could not move him, but then his eyes fluttered and opened. He did not seem to see her; his expression was empty. But when she kept encouraging, he heaved himself and nearly caused her to fall. She led him to the mare. "Lift up your foot. You've got to get into the saddle."

He groaned, and then his eyes opened and he focused on her. "Raina?" he whispered in a creaky voice.

"Yes, it's me. You've got to get on the horse. We've got to get you some help." She helped him guide his left foot into the stirrup, and she said, "Now, I'm going to push you, and you help all you can. Pull yourself into the saddle." At first she thought it was impossible. He was large, and she was not. But then he managed to rise up and throw his leg over the saddle, and then he swayed. Quickly she mounted behind him, and he was loose and disjointed as she reached her arms around him. She pulled him back to lean against her and said, "Come on, girl," then turned the mare around and headed back to where she had seen Yosu.

He saw her coming and came at once running, leaving the sheep. "What is it, señorita?"

"It's Ty. He's been shot. Take my horse and go to the house. Bring a wagon and blanket for a bed. Go as quick as you can. He needs help."

"*Sí.* I will be back very soon."

She said, "Before you go, help me get him in the shade of that sapling." The two of them managed to lower Ty, and the shade blocked off most of the sun's rays.

Yosu slipped into the saddle and rode off at a fast gallop.

Raina did not watch him leave but turned her attention to Ty. His lips were baked and parched, and she moistened them with the water in her neckerchief from time to time and occasionally gave him a swallow.

The sun kept up in the sky, and she didn't know what to do for the wound in his back. Finally his shoulders moved, his head rolled, and his eyes came open. "Where am I, Raina?"

"You've been shot, Ty. What happened? Do you remember?"

His words were slow, and his lips were so parched he had to lick them. She gave him another swallow of water, and he said, "I caught somebody moving sheep, but before I could do anything about it, somebody knocked me down."

"You'll be all right. I sent Yosu to get a wagon. We'll take you to the camp. Dad's good with wounds, and we can send for a doctor."

He did not answer, and she saw that he was in a state of semiconsciousness. She wanted to question him but saw that he was not able to answer.

Finally he whispered, "Could I have some more water?"

"Yes. Just a few swallows. You can have all you want, but not all at once."

He swallowed three times, small, tentative swallows of the tepid water, and then looked at her. "That was good. How'd you find me?"

"I was just out visiting one of the sheepherders. I saw buzzards circling."

"I heard them. They would have got me if you hadn't come along."

"Are you in much pain?"

"Head hurts. My back. . ."

"You took a bullet in the back, but it was high up. I don't think it hit a lung or anything like that. You hit your head on a rock when you fell. The bullet will have to come out when we get you to a doctor."

He lay still, and for a time he didn't speak. Then he said, "You know, Raina, I had strange dreams while I was lying there all shot up and out of it." He looked up at her.

She saw sadness in him she had never seen before, even when she had found him in jail back when they had first met. "What sort of dreams?"

"About bad things that I've done."

"We all have things that we regret."

He began to speak and tell her about his best friend who had died.

"You didn't hurt him. It was an accident."

"I've never forgotten it, but the worst dream was about a young woman. Now—" He broke off and took a deep breath as he grimaced.

Raina knew that talking was taking a lot out of him, but she thought it was better he stay awake, so she encouraged him to go on. "What was her name?"

"Evelyn. She was the first girl I ever courted. No more than a girl really."

"Did you love her, Ty?"

"I thought I did, but I found out different."

"Found out how?"

He shut his eyes, and she saw a quiver go through his whole body. "She told me she was going to have a baby. It scared me. I wasn't ready for that. I ran away and left her, Raina. Been years ago, but I still remember her. I wonder what happened to her. If she had a boy or a girl, and if she found a man to take care of her and the child or gave the child to another family. I think about it almost every day. Never gotten away from it."

"Did you ever think about going back and looking for her?"

"By the time I reached the point I was ready to do that, it was too late. It was three years after I had left, and I knew whatever she had decided to do, it was done."

The wind began to whistle, blowing the loose, sandy soil across the plains. She looked up and saw far off a herd of pronghorn in their beautiful run, bounding into the air seemingly effortlessly. Then she looked back and said, "I'm sorry, Ty, but you can't live forever with a mistake you made."

"After I dreamed about Evelyn, I began thinking about what your pa said in his sermon. He said, 'God made every man and every woman for a purpose,' and that scares me."

"Why should it scare you, Ty?"

"Because I don't have any purpose, Raina. I'm just like a tumbleweed blowing wherever the wind takes it. I'm no good to anybody."

"Did you dream anything else?"

"No, but every time I'd come to, I'd think about God, and I was afraid I was going to die." He moved, turning his face away from the sun. "I've never been afraid of much of anything. Didn't have sense enough, I guess, but I was afraid of dying."

"I think most of us are when we think about it."

"I've been in some tight spots. Nearly died a couple times. You know that better than most. But this was different. It was like I was standing on a precipice. Below there was a horrible blackness. I was about to step off into it. I remembered a friend of mine who died at nineteen. When he died, he cried out, 'I never done anything. I never had a wife or a family. Now I never will.' That scared me, Raina."

Raina kept him talking even though his head nodded from time to time. Finally she saw Yosu coming with a wagon and one of the other sheepherders.

Yosu pulled the team up and said, "I came as quick as I could."

"Help me get him into the wagon."

"We have made a bed. I told your dad. He's going to try to get a doctor there, but if he can't, we'll take him to Fort Smith."

Carefully the two men picked up Ty with some struggle and put him into the wagon. She got on her horse, and the two men mounted the wagon.

She said, "Drive slow and avoid the worst of the ruts if you can, Yosu."

He nodded and said, "Get up!" and the team moved forward.

❧

Leoma had learned about Ty's being shot from one of the hands. She immediately set out toward Vernay's place to see him. She had not traveled far when she looked up and saw George Fairfax coming toward her driving a buggy. She said at once, "Did you hear about Ty?"

George was wearing a fine suit as usual, but when he stopped, surprise washed across his face. "What about him?"

"He was shot."

"Shot? Is he all right?"

"I think he is now. He would have died, but Raina found him out lying on the plains. She and the sheepherders got him back to the camp, and her father evidently knows something about bullet wounds. He got the bullet out. They brought a doctor out to check on him, and he said it wasn't too serious. He was just dehydrated. However, he also said that Ty would have died if Raina hadn't found him. I'm going out to see him now."

"Let me take you."

"Well, that would be good. I'll tie my horse to the buggy and ride her back."

"Yes, certainly tie your horse to the buggy, but I will be happy to take you back home. You really shouldn't be riding around by yourself anyway."

"My father warned me about that, too, but I was too worried to wait on someone to ride along with me."

As they made their way toward the Vernay place, Leoma found herself interested in the Englishman. She said, "It must not be a very pleasant experience for you out here. I've always heard how beautiful England is. This is about as wild and woolly a place as you can find, George."

He was driving the team rather inexpertly and turned and gave her a quick smile. "Well, England is beautiful in a lot of ways. In the summer the grass is so green it almost hurts your eyes. You know, this land has a beauty of its own. It's stark, strange, and a little bit brutal. The other day I was out riding, and I saw a coyote pull down a young doe. She didn't have a chance. He tore her to pieces. That kind of reminds me what this land is like. It's cruel."

"Yes, it is."

"Do you like it here?"

"I haven't known much of any other kind of life."

He was silent, and finally he said, "You know, maybe sometime you could come and visit England. I could show you some beautiful things there."

She smiled and said, "We'd have to take a chaperone."

"Oh, you can always hire one of those," he said briefly. He smiled at her, and she saw goodness in his face that she didn't find in many men, and she finally said, "It was kind of you to ask me though. Your family might get upset, your dragging a wild woman home with you."

"I don't know. They've done nothing but nag me to get married for the last five years."

"Why do they want you to marry?"

"Oh, you know how it is."

"No, I don't."

"Well, the land is entailed. It goes to the oldest son of each family, so I need a son to pass the land on to."

She laughed. "Why don't you put an ad in the paper. Wanted: Young woman to bear son for titled Englishman."

"Oh, there'd be a line of them. There was one already. That's one reason why I left England. Every woman I met was after me, and I know it wasn't because of my good looks. It was because of the money and the title."

Leoma found this fascinating. "What about younger sons?"

"Well, I only have one younger brother. If I died, he'd be the earl. I've got him enrolled in Oxford. He's training to be an educator."

They talked steadily, and the trip seemed very short to Leoma. They pulled up in front of the sheep camp, and Raina came out to meet them along with her father. "We've come out to see how Ty's doing," Leoma said.

Eddie Vernay said, "Get down and come in. You're bound to be thirsty after that hot trip."

"How's Ty?" Leoma asked Raina as they headed toward the house.

"He's much better now. He was in pretty bad shape when I found him."

"A fortunate thing for him," George said, "that you were out there."

"I think it was the will of the Lord." Vernay smiled.

Raina said, "Let me take you in to see him. He's still in bed. He was dehydrated and just about dead from exposure." She entered the house and led them down a hall, where she opened a door. "Visitors, Ty."

They entered the room, and Ty looked up from the bed where he was sitting up with a pillow behind his back. "Well, hello. Good to see you."

"Good to see you, Ty. How do you feel?" Leoma asked.

"A lot better than I did awhile ago. If Raina there hadn't come across me, I'd be buzzard bait by now. How are you, George?"

"I'm fine. Just glad to see you're doing so well. I heard from Leoma that you got shot."

"The bullet took him real high in his shoulder up above the bone. Made a bad flesh wound," Raina said, "but Pa got the bullet out."

They talked for a while, but soon Leoma saw that Ty's eyes were drooping. "You're tired," she said. "We just wanted to find out how you are."

"Nice of you to come," Ty said.

The two left, and George looked to the west at the sun going down. George stared at it for a moment and said, "That looks like a big egg yolk going down."

Leoma laughed and said, "Well, you'll never be a poet. There should be a better way to describe a beautiful sunset like that than it looks like an egg yolk."

"What would you say?"

"Oh, I don't know. I'm not a poet either, George. I don't even read poetry much because I don't understand it."

"You know, I've tried to read some modern poetry, and it seems to me those fellows' worst fear is that someone will understand what they've written." He laughed and shook his head. "As a matter of fact, I've heard some politicians and preachers who did the same thing. They want to sound deep and profound, but if anybody understands them, that means they've been shallow."

The hooves of the team made a clopping sound as they plodded along, sending up a faint cloud of dust. George and Leoma said little for quite some time.

Leoma finally said, "What's it like to live in England?"

"Well, that depends."

"On what?"

"On whether you have money or not. If you have money, you can live in a fine house with fine furniture, have servants to wait on you, and be recognized by the aristocracy, or at least by the leaders in society."

"Well, not everyone lives like that, I'm sure."

"No, as a matter of fact there's that other side of England. Children working in mills when they are only ten years old, putting in twelve-hour days."

"That's frightful."

"The same thing's happening here in the United States in some of the woolen mills in New England and some of the big factories in New York and Chicago."

Leoma turned her head and studied George's profile. Instant charm and perfect diction were things that she had never encountered before, so she was interested in him. His comment on poetry caught at her attention, and she wondered what he was really like. He was of average height but looked taller because he was slender, and he moved with unusual grace. She guessed that he would make a fine dancer at the waltz and other dances at balls in England. She knew he was well educated in the classics, that he had a patrician face with a rather large, aquiline nose, and that his fair hair waved a trifle extravagantly. She found out that he had a quickness of intelligence, lines of wit and laughter around his mouth, and a hint of temper. At times, the space between his brows revealed his emotions. He had the face of a man of unusual charm, and more than that, one who had never had to suffer from any hard times. "What about you, George?"

"What do you mean, what about me?"

"What will you be doing? You won't stay in Fort Smith forever. It must seem pretty wild and woolly to you."

George's mouth twisted in a strange, sardonic manner, and he gave her a quick look and shook his head. "Well, I'll have to marry and produce an heir, a male heir."

Leoma suddenly laughed. "That's pretty much like a stud horse. I suppose you'll marry a duchess or someone like that."

"Oh, not necessarily. The upper class in England is pretty well bred down. Be much more likely to find a good sturdy woman who's not of the aristocracy."

A moment of humor came to Leoma then, and she turned and put her hand on his arm. "Well, how about me, George?"

Fairfax was obviously caught off guard by her direct question. The wind ruffled the edges of her hair, and a smile made a small break along her lips. Some private and ridiculous thought amused her, for he saw the effect of it dancing in her eyes.

"Do you think I might make a good wife for you?"

"Well, that's coming right out with it. I'll tell you what. I'll make me out a list of what the woman I marry will have to do to qualify. You know, beautiful, witty, strong-willed. . ."

"But what if she doesn't meet all your standards?"

Once again he smiled and said, "Well, I'll just cross that item off my list."

They talked nonstop practically until they got to her ranch, and she said, "Too dark to drive into Fort Smith. Come on in. We've got a spare bedroom. As a matter of fact, we've got three of them."

"Well, you don't have to ask anybody's permission?"

"Oh, it's about supper time. You can talk to my pa and my brothers about raising cattle."

"That'll be a one-sided conversation." George smiled. "I hardly know one end from another."

"You know horses though."

"We ride a lot in England. Ride to the hounds."

"What does that mean?"

"Oh, all the rich, titled people get together on horseback and wear funny-looking clothes as they chase a fox."

She stared at him. "I've heard about that. What do you do when you catch one? You don't eat him, do you?"

"Oh bless you, no, we don't eat them. If anybody's made an especially good ride, we give him the brush, that is, the tail."

"That's a funny way to spend an afternoon."

"Well, we English are funny people."

She said no more but was looking forward to his spending the night with them. She had not been entertained by a man so thoroughly in a long time. She knew most of it was the difference between the two of them, and she looked forward to finding out more about his requirements for a wife.

CHAPTER 21

"Sit down, Garth. You're going to wear the floor out," Honey Clagg said.

Garth Taylor had been pacing back and forth, running his hand through his hair in a nervous mannerism. He was a man who had to be in action of some sort or other most of the time, and since the death of his brother, he had been even more nervous. He turned quickly and faced Honey Clagg.

Honey was the biggest man in his gang. He had a neck as wide as his jaw, and his muscles were spectacular. He had whipped many men and kicked one to death, but Garth Taylor kept him on for this very reason.

"Don't tell me what to do, Honey."

"We need to get out on a job. Everybody's gettin' sour just sittin' around here. All we do is argue, and I'm gettin' tired of it."

Garth stared at him. "I can't stop thinking about Johnny. He was the only living relative I had that I know of, except for one uncle somewhere back East who wouldn't claim me. He was a good kid."

Honey Clagg answered, "You might as well forget him. Let's go out and make some money."

"I'll decide when we leave," Garth said stiffly and continued his walking.

The rest of the gang was engaged at the other end of the room in a lackadaisical poker game. They were playing for penny ante stakes, and nobody really cared.

Honey said, "Those Daltons are gonna bust loose if we don't give 'em somethin' to do, Garth."

"We'll get along without 'em."

"They're pretty handy. All we'd have left is Mexican Jack and Long Tom, of course."

"That's all we need." He suddenly sat down in front of Clagg and said, "I've been waiting for the right time to get my revenge, but I can't get that cowman who killed my brother out of my mind. I can't let it pass."

"Well, what you need to do is just go shoot him and forget about it. Get it out of your system."

Garth sat with a dark look on his face. He was staring down at his strong hands, clasping them nervously together. He didn't speak for a long time. Finally Garth muttered, "I'd love nothing better, but I don't want to go to hang for it. I want to be free to enjoy my revenge. In fact, I'd give a big pile of money to any man who'd risk killing Ash Jordan for me." He got up and returned to his pacing.

Honey smiled. "In that case, I just might take care of that little chore myself." Clagg obviously took the statement as a challenge.

"Shouldn't be too hard to do," he said. "He's out riding the range, chasing those cattle half the time. Shouldn't be too hard to catch him off by himself."

Garth stopped his pacing again. "You'd have to bring somethin' in to prove to me that you shot and killed him."

Honey smiled again, but this time it looked like pure evil. "That won't be a problem either."

⤜⤛

Leoma had always been partial to her younger brother, Benny. He was the youngest child and had a sunny disposition in contrast to Ash, who had a hair-trigger temper and could be hard to be around. "What are you going to do with yourself, Benny?"

Benny was five-ten, a well-built young man. He had a trace of the same auburn hair as she did, but his eyes were a warm brown. When he smiled, his whole face grew warm. Now he stared at her with a question in his face. "What do you mean, what am I going to do?"

"Well, are you gonna be a cowpuncher all your life?"

"Never thought about doing anything else."

"Why, you could be something if you wanted to. Why don't you become a doctor or something like that?"

"Not smart enough for that."

"Not all doctors are smart. Some of them are absolute terrors. I wouldn't want 'em doctoring on me."

"No, I guess I'll just stay on the ranch here."

The two were out leaning against the corral, watching Ash as he broke a buckskin. Ash was a fine rider, and he rode the big steed to a halt finally.

Benny called out, "That's good, Ash. He's gonna make a fine

mount." He turned then to Leoma and said, "Why'd you ask me what I was gonna do?"

"Well, you're getting old enough to make some kind of a career for yourself."

Benny smiled at her. "Maybe I could get me a fancy vest and some hair oil and become a gambler on a Mississippi riverboat."

"You're a terrible gambler. You'd go broke overnight."

"I guess you're right, sis." He turned and stared at her. "You've been goin' over to see Ty Kincaid a couple of times."

"I have. I like him."

Benny turned his head to one side. "You mean you like him like a woman likes a man?"

Leoma picked a sliver of wood off the top of the corral, held it up, looked at it, and then threw it away. "I might, but it's hard to tell."

"What's hard to tell, sis? Who's the right man for you?"

"A woman has to make that decision."

"Well, a man does, too."

"It's harder for women though."

Benny shrugged. "I think it'd be pretty easy."

Leoma turned and laughed at him. "You thought you were in love with Joanne Riggs when you were fifteen."

"I'm surprised you'd bring that up. I was just a kid. Anyway, you interested in marrying this Ty Kincaid?"

"I'm thinking about marriage. Not necessarily with him, but with somebody."

Ash called out, "Come and give me a hand with this critter, Benny."

Benny turned at once and left, as he always obeyed Ash's orders.

Leoma watched him go and then slowly walked up to the porch.

Her mother was sitting there in a rocking chair. She asked, "You went over to see Kincaid yesterday?"

"Yes, I did."

"How is he?"

"Oh, he's getting along fine. He's out of bed now. Walking around. Gonna have a scar on his head where he hit that rock."

The two talked about Ty, and Leoma suddenly turned and said, "Benny just asked me if I was interested in Ty."

"Well, you must be. You've gone over there two or three times."

"Well, a woman has to know a man."

"Just think about all the men you turned down. There was Arlie Hicks. He had money and wasn't bad looking. Why'd you turn him down?"

"He was boring."

"You want to marry a clown to perform for you?" She named off several other men back in their older home whom Leoma had refused. Finally she said, "Leoma, what about this George Fairfax? He's a fine-looking man. A little different from most of the men around here."

"He's altogether different from most of the men around here."

"You think he might be interested in you?"

Leoma was nervous. She got up and walked back and forth. "He'll marry an Englishwoman who has a pile of money." She turned toward the door. "I'm going in and set the table."

❦

The supper had been good, but they had a fine cook. Everyone left the table except for Leoma and her father. He stared at her and said, "I'm going to hire some more men to guard the stock."

"Why don't you just let the marshal take care of it?"

"You know why," Pa said shortly. "He doesn't have enough marshals to handle the territory, much less ride herd on my cattle." He turned to her and studied her carefully. "What are you worried about? You've got everything you want."

"Nobody ever has everything they want, Pa."

"Well, I guess that's right enough."

"What do *you* want?" Leoma asked.

"I guess I want a big ranch. Make some money. See you and Benny and Ash grow up and make it in this world."

"That's pretty ambitious."

"Well, I suppose it is." He stirred in his chair and said, "I heard you went over to Vernay's sheep camp."

"Yes, I went to see if Ty Kincaid was all right."

Instantly, suspicion swept across her father's face. "You don't need that kind of man. You need a man with money."

"I've watched people with money. They're no happier than people without it. They're just more comfortable."

"That's crazy talk, girl. These marshals come and go. You know over fifty of them have been killed carrying out Judge Parker's orders."

She did not answer right away, but the thought took root in her mind. Finally she said, "Don't worry about it, Pa. I don't know what's in his heart, or what's in my own for that matter."

❧

Judge Parker looked up, and his eyes opened wide. "Well, hello, Ty. Good to see you up and going."

Ty stood before the judge's desk. "Good to be up, sir."

Parker stared at his face. "That's a bad cut you've got there. You're going to have a scar."

"Well, a man needs a scar now and then to teach him what life is like."

"How's that bullet wound?"

"Oh, it's a little stiff. Didn't hit a bone, so it's all right. Anyway, I'm about ready to go back to work."

Parker leaned back in his chair. "What's bothering you, Ty?"

"Didn't say anything was."

"Well, I've got eyes, haven't I? Somethin's eatin' on ya."

Ty said, "Well, to tell the truth, when I was lying out there shot and dying, at least so I thought, I got scared."

"Scared of dying?"

"Not so much scared of dying," Ty said slowly, "but scared of what comes afterward."

"I didn't take you for a religious man."

"Well, I haven't been. Maybe that's my trouble."

Ty knew that Parker himself was a thoroughgoing Christian. He and his family attended church every Sunday. He never used the vile language he heard from many of the rougher men he had to deal with. "I guess I'm just a coward, sir."

"No, you're not a coward, Ty. A man's a fool not to be afraid of what happens after this life if he has any mind at all."

"You know, Judge, there are too many bad people in this place. I'm thinking of moving to Omaha."

The judge laughed then. "No bad people in Omaha, Ty?"

Kincaid stared back at the judge. "Some, but most of 'em don't kill each other."

"You start back on Wednesday. Until then you take it easy."

"Sure, Judge. See you Wednesday morning." Ty walked outside and sat down in a chair, tilting it back against the wall of the courthouse. His eyes were half shut as he watched men, women, and young people pass by. It was a habit he had, to watch people carefully, cautiously.

"Hello, Ty."

Kincaid looked up and saw Fairfax. "Sit down, George."

"You're looking pretty good except for that scar on your head. The doctor said you'd probably keep that."

"Won't hurt my manly beauty any."

"You know, I was talking with somebody once who wanted to know what I was going to do with my life."

"What did you tell 'em, George?"

"I told 'em back home everybody was jumping up and down with ambition trying to get me married off."

"Why didn't you marry somebody? There must be plenty of women in England who would want to find a rich man with a title."

"That's what I told them. But I hadn't found anybody yet who satisfied me."

"Why does everybody want you to get married?"

"Why, I have a title you know, and it's an entailed property."

"What does that mean?"

"It means the place can't be sold. A male heir will inherit it."

"I'm sure there are plenty of women looking for a rich husband. There's more to it than that, isn't there?"

"I always thought so."

The two men were quiet for a while; then abruptly George Fairfax turned and said, "I've been thinking about Raina Vernay."

The words caught at Ty's attention. He turned at once and said, "You courting her?"

"A little," he said casually.

"You think she'd fit in the English world?" Ty asked.

"She could if she tried." Fairfax stirred restlessly and got to his feet. "Or I might come and live here. It's a different world for me, but I could learn to like it."

"Look at that street," Ty said with a sweeping gesture. "It has people in it, good and bad, but so does London I expect. I don't know if a man can change his world."

George Fairfax was silent. "I could buy a ranch. Become a rancher."

"You don't know anything about cattle."

Fairfax smiled. "I could hire you to run it for me."

Ty laughed at that. "There are better men than I am at cattle. You'd better think this over, George. Marriage is for a long time."

"I'm doing that. It gives me a headache. I'm not used to deep thoughts. I'll see you later, Ty."

Kincaid watched as Fairfax moved down the street, taking in the fine clothes and wondering if he was serious about Raina Vernay. The thought troubled him, for he had felt a vested interest in Raina ever since the two had been thrown together in La Tete. He got up and began walking the streets of Fort Smith. As he thought about his future, he decided the best place for him to be was at church. Since he had a few days off, he saddled his horse and headed out to the Vernay place.

On Sunday, Ty entered the barn-church, which was fuller than the last time he had come, and saw Eddie Vernay. He walked up to him and shook his hand.

"Good to see you, Ty. You can get one of those good five-dollar seats."

"No, too close to you for my benefit."

"How have you been, Ty? How's that head wound?"

"Oh, I've had worse getting kicked by a stubborn mule."

"Come to hear the sermon? Well, I wish we had a better preacher."

"You're good enough for me." Ty smiled. He liked Eddie Vernay as much as he had liked any man. He envied him, for there was a stillness and a contentment in the older man's face that attracted him. It was the sort of thing he longed for, but he had not found it.

Vernay was staring at him. "You're troubled, Ty."

"Sure am."

"What's wrong?"

"Don't know, Eddie. Just don't feel right. I feel like I'm chasing my tail."

"That's what I did when God first got ahold of me. My sermon today on the prodigal son touches on that."

Ty Kincaid smiled slightly. "That sounds like it will fit me."

"That boy ran away from home, but he couldn't get away from himself."

"You been reading my mail, Eddie?"

"Not hard to tell when God's after a man. You sit there and listen to this sermon. It'll do you some good. Then you come and stay the night with us."

"All right. That would be fine."

He saw Raina near the front, but he slipped into a seat nearer the back. He wanted nothing to distract him from taking in every word.

❧

The sermon was indeed about the prodigal son. Vernay had a way of bringing in other scriptures and other stories and personal references to his own life that moved Ty Kincaid greatly. He had heard of people speak of being under conviction, but he had never known what that meant.

Once he had asked Eddie Vernay what that signified, and he had shaken his head. "You'll be absolutely miserable."

"Well, what good does that do?"

"A man gets miserable enough, Ty, he'll do something about it. God's after you, and He's going to get you."

After the service, he went to the house and had dinner with Eddie and Raina. Later in the evening, he and Raina went outside and sat on the front porch. They were quiet, simply enjoying the cool evening breeze. Ty's mind kept going back over the sermon.

Raina finally asked, "What's the matter, Ty? You haven't said ten words."

Ty turned to her and said, "Well, something you probably won't know anything about. I want to serve God, and I don't know how."

Raina suddenly had the experience she heard her father speak of. A scripture came to her mind, and she quoted it for Ty. " 'I have set before thee an open door.' "

"A door set before me? I don't see anything like that."

"You have to wait on God, and He's ready now, Ty, but when

you get ready, that's when things will happen."

Her direct gaze made him nervous, and he said, "Maybe that's meant for you. George Fairfax seems to find you attractive. Maybe he's a door for you."

"Oh, he's a nice fellow."

"He'd make you a good husband. Give you an easier life."

"That's not what I'm looking for, Ty."

"That's what most women want. A good, steady husband with a comfortable income."

"There's more than that."

The two sat talking for a time.

Finally Raina stood. "Just look how the moon casts its lucent rays on the land." She sighed and turned to Ty. "I don't know how to find God's will sometimes, Ty. I wish there were an easier way, but I don't think there is. I remember a scripture where God says, 'Ye shall seek me, and find me, when ye shall search for me with all your heart.' I've never really done that."

"Neither have I. I'll bet your pa has though."

"Yes, he has, but I'm not as close to God as he is." She was silent for a time, then said, "I've just thought of a scripture about a man who sought God like that. Let's go in the house and I'll read it to you."

"I'd like to hear it."

They went into the house and sat down in the living area. Raina looked through the Bible and found what she sought. "Here it is. Daniel is one of the very few individuals in the Bible who seems to have been absolutely devoted to God. Most of the men and women have a black mark against them, even David, who was a man after God's own heart."

"Didn't know that was said about anyone in the Bible."

"This scripture is in the ninth chapter of the book of Daniel. It begins with verse three. The first two verses tell how Daniel wanted to know what the future held for his people, the Israelites. Verse three begins with Daniel setting out to find the answer:

" 'And I set my face unto the Lord God, to seek by prayer and supplications, with fasting, and sackcloth, and ashes.' "

"What does he mean, sackcloth?" Ty asked.

"In those days whenever people were in trouble or suffering, they put on garments made of sackcloth, the cheapest kind of material."

"Do we have to do that?"

"I don't think so." Raina shook her head. "It was a Jewish custom. The important thing is Daniel set out to find God's will, and he made it the most important thing in his life. Listen to what he did to find God. It begins with verse four:

" 'And I prayed unto the Lord my God, and made my confession, and said, O Lord, the great and dreadful God, keeping the covenant and mercy to them that love him, and to them that keep his commandments.' "

"Well, Raina, that lets me out," Ty said. "I haven't done any of that."

"Just listen to the next verse, Ty: 'We have sinned, and have committed iniquity, and have done wickedly, and have rebelled, even by departing from thy precepts and from thy judgments.' You see, Ty, Daniel did what we all have to do, confess to God that he was a sinner."

"But I thought Daniel was a godly man."

"So he was, but even the best of men and women have sinned

against God. Daniel was humble, and we all have to admit that we've sinned."

"Some worse than others, I'd think."

"Yes, all of us have sinned, but not all of us have sinned alike."

Ty said nothing for a moment, then added, "So even the best man or woman in the world has to confess his or her sin to God?"

"Exactly!"

"Well, I can see that."

"This prayer goes on for many verses, but I think this was not a 'one-time' prayer. I think Daniel may have prayed for many days or even weeks like this. Even Jesus prayed for forty days and nights at the beginning of His ministry."

"But Jesus never sinned, did He?"

"No, but God seeks us out so that we can know Him. That's what we need, Ty, to know the Lord."

"That's what I want, Raina, but I'm not a good man like Daniel. I may have to pray for months."

"Not necessarily, Ty. Sometimes God answers a sinner's prayer instantly. Remember the thief on the cross? He prayed one prayer, for Jesus to make him fit for heaven, and you remember that Jesus answered his prayer at once. He said, 'Today shalt thou be with me in paradise.' "

Ty bowed his head and was silent, and Raina wondered if she had disturbed him. Finally he looked up, and his eyes were bright. "I'm going to do it, Raina! I'm going to find Jesus if it takes me the rest of my life."

Tears gathered in Raina's eyes, and she took his hand and whispered, "That's exactly what you need, Ty. And Dad and I will be praying right with you."

CHAPTER 22

Ty arched himself into a sitting position, moving cautiously, and was pleased to find that though the movement was somewhat painful, it was less than it had been. Turning, he walked over to the chair by the window, sat down, and picked up a Bible.

The morning sun was casting golden bars on the worn carpet. As always, he was fascinated by the multitude of tiny motes that danced in the yellow light almost quicker than a man could see. He looked out and saw that the street was busy with people and wondered how he had been rescued from what could have been his death.

He put the Bible on his lap and moved his hand back and forth over the surface. *I've ignored this Bible for years,* he thought. *I should have known better, and I can't do that anymore.* The thought sobered him, and his lips tightened. This had happened often during his time of recovery, and he knew that his days of ignoring God and letting himself do anything he chose were over.

Slowly he opened the Bible to the page where he had placed

a red ribbon for a marker. He read slowly, beginning with the first verse from the ninth chapter of the book of Acts. *"And Saul, yet breathing out threatenings and slaughter against the disciples of the Lord, went unto the high priest, and desired of him letters to Damascus to the synagogues, that if he found any of this way, whether they were men or women, he might bring them bound unto Jerusalem."* The bluntness of the words and the cruelty that Paul had let come into his life were not new to Ty. He had heard this story before and had been affected by it.

He paused and looked out the window and was silent for a moment and absolutely still. Finally he muttered, "Lord, I need to know what to do with my life, but I'm helpless. You'll have to show me the way."

He continued reading the rest of Saul's story, and when he read the verses that spoke of Saul's being knocked to the earth and spoken to by Jesus Himself, his eyes fell on another verse. *"And he trembling and astonished said, Lord, what wilt thou have me to do?"* Again he paused and prayed, *That's what I need, Lord. I need You to speak to me and tell me what to do. You know I'm helpless. I don't know enough about You. I don't even know myself, but I ask You to guide me.* He ran his hand over the paper and slowly shook his head and whispered, "I wish God would just knock me flat like He did Saul and tell me what to do."

Nothing but silence and the sound of traffic on the street came to him. He heaved a sigh, got up, and plucked his gun belt from a peg driven into the wall. As he strapped it on, he paused abruptly, drew the gun, and stared at it. He was remembering something that Jesus said somewhere in the Bible. *"They that take the sword shall perish with the sword."* *I guess, Lord, if You let those that live by the gun perish by the gun, that about describes me.* The thought disturbed him. He slid the gun back into the holster, grabbed his hat from a peg, and left the room.

The sun was warm, and as he made his way toward the courthouse to pick up his duties, he greeted several men who spoke to him. He passed by two small boys playing marbles in the dirt of the street. The smaller one had a freckled face, and as Ty was passing by, the boy asked, "Are you a marshal?"

Ty paused and smiled. "Sure am."

"I'm gonna be a marshal when I get big."

Ty studied the boy and said, "You know, I played marbles when I was about your age. I was pretty good, too."

"Aw, I can beat you."

A notion took Ty. He knelt down, picked up a marble, shot, and sent it spinning toward the marbles in the circle. He missed and grinned. "I guess I've lost my touch."

The larger of the two boys asked, "Did you ever shoot anyone with that gun?"

"I don't like to think about that."

He walked away, but he heard the smaller boy say, "He ain't never shot no outlaws. He'd have said so if he had."

The scene troubled him as he continued his passage along the street. He thought back and realized that when he was the age of these boys he had been reading James Fenimore Cooper books glorifying Hawkeye. He realized that he had changed, and he muttered, "That seems like a thousand years ago, back when I was playing marbles. . . ." He reached headquarters and stepped up on the porch of the courthouse.

As usual, Heck Thomas was whittling on a cedar stick. He

looked up and studied Ty for a moment, then said, "Things are pretty quiet, Ty. Too quiet, I think. I get too itchy when it gets too quiet."

"Not me. I like it quiet." Ty smiled. "Is the judge in his office?"

Before he answered, Heck shaved another curling wisp-like piece of cedar and watched it fall on the mound at his feet. "Yep. There'll be a hangin' in two hours. He'll be at the window lookin' at it." He shaved two more slivers and shook his head. "I'd like to know what he thinks when he sees a man dangle that he's sentenced his own self."

Ty found no answer for that. "I guess I'll go see him." He entered the courtroom, took the stairs, and knocked on the judge's door.

When he heard, "Come in," he went in and found Judge Parker sitting at the desk with a Bible open before him. "Hello, Ty."

"Hello, Judge. Reckon I'd better go back to work."

"Are you sure?"

"Yes, I'm all right. Head's just a little scratched. The bullet wound doesn't amount to anything—but I'm pretty mixed up."

"Mixed up about what?"

Ty hesitated then said, "Well, I've been thinking about God a lot since that day, trying to figure it all out."

Parker ran his hand over his hair, and his lips tightened. "It's hard to be a marshal, and I guess it's hard to be a judge, too. It costs you something. You know, it cost Heck his family."

"How was that?"

"Well, he's the best man I have, but his wife didn't like his work. He was usually gone, and she was afraid he'd get killed, so she gave him his choice. She said, 'Either quit or I'm quitting you.'

Well, he's still here alone, so you can imagine what happened."

"Judge, I don't know what to do. I've been thinking about God ever since I nearly cashed in my chips out there in the territory."

The noise from the street floated in from the open window, and the judge walked over and looked down. "I hate the sight of that gallows."

"It bothers you to find men guilty knowing they're going to hang?"

"Of course it does. Why wouldn't it?"

"Well, maybe you need to quit, Judge."

"No, I'm doin' what God wants me to do, but it's hard."

Ty motioned at the Bible open on the judge's desk. "Do you think a man can find out what he ought to do with his life by reading that Bible?"

"Yes, I do. I think God speaks to us through His Word, but I'd hate to lose you, Ty."

"Plenty can do what I'm doin'."

"No, that's not right, but you do what you have to do. I always like to see a man get right with God."

"I'll take another day off, if that's all right. Read the Bible some more. I admire those fellows that God speaks to directly, like He did to Moses at the burning bush and to Saul on the road to Damascus."

"Doesn't usually happen like that. Usually takes two or three days, or sometimes months."

"Maybe another day will do me." Ty turned and left, and he passed Heck, who was coming up the stairs.

"You comin' back to work, Ty?"

"No, I'm going to take another day off." He shook his head. "Sure am in a messed-up situation, Heck."

Heck watched him go down the stairs, then mounted to the second floor and went in to see the judge. "You let him take some more time off?"

"Yep."

"He's pretty mixed up, Judge. You know, I got an idea he thinks God wants him to be a preacher."

"He tell you that?"

"No, he didn't tell me that, but a lot of fellows get confused like that. They want to do something to make God happy, and that seems to be what some of them do."

"Well, I don't know about that, but he's going to have to choose. I don't see how a man can be a marshal in Indian Territory and a preacher at the same time."

"Reckon you better tell him that, Judge."

"No man can really tell another what to do in a situation like he's in. Give him a few days. Maybe he'll find his way."

Ty had started over to the café to get a late breakfast when he ran into George Fairfax.

"Where you headed, Ty?"

"Going to get some breakfast."

"Well, let me buy for you. I'm hungry myself."

"Sounds good."

The two men made their way to the restaurant and went inside.

George said to the waiter, "Just bring us some of the best breakfast you can round up back there."

"Yes, sir. I'll do that. It'll be good, too."

George leaned back, and for a while they talked about unimportant things until the meal came.

Both men pitched in, and when they had finished their meal and were drinking their third cups of coffee, Ty fastened his gaze on Fairfax. "You look troubled, George."

"Yes, I guess I am."

"I don't see how you could have any problems. You're rich."

"That doesn't solve everything, you know," George said. He shifted in his chair and made an involuntary nervous gesture, pulling his hand across his face. "You know what? I've been having some strong feelings about Raina. In fact, I've asked her to marry me." At the look on Ty's face, George rushed on. "I should have told you sooner, Ty, but, well, this is sort of personal. Before you say anything, she hasn't given me an answer yet. You know her better than I do. Do you think she'd have me as a husband?"

He said simply, "I really don't know, George. All she can do is say no or yes."

"I know you're right." He drank the last of his coffee, put the cup down, and then stared at Kincaid. "I thought you and Raina were pretty close at one time."

"She pulled me out of a real hard time, and I guess that kind of thing never leaves a man. Maybe a woman neither." Kincaid turned the coffee cup around in a circular motion and stared down at the circles it left on the table.

"You have any thoughts about marriage, Ty?"

"I guess every man's got some thoughts about that."

"Well, what do you think?"

"I can't think about marriage now. To tell the truth, George, I don't know where I'm going, so I can't ask a woman to follow me."

"Why, you'll continue to be a marshal, won't you?"

"Not sure about that. I had some odd dreams when I was out there dying. One of them I haven't told anybody about. Maybe I could tell you. I keep thinking of it."

"What kind of a dream?"

"I dreamed I was in some place with a tall table in front of me and I was preaching. That's all I can remember. I don't even remember what I said, but I remember there were people there, and I was preaching to them." He laughed and shook his head. "Nothing further from my mind these last few years than preaching, and I couldn't ask a woman to go into that."

"I want Raina to go back to England with me."

"I don't think Raina would be interested in that. She just found her father and is enjoying being with him right now."

"I keep trying to wonder what would happen if I tried to take her back to England. She'd probably be out of place in my world back home."

"Maybe you could live here."

"No, I'm a misfit."

Ty studied George Fairfax and thought with a strong humor, *He's got some problem. Money and everything, and he's worried about whether he can find a wife or not.*

"I guess I'll head on down the way. Let me know what Raina answers."

"I wouldn't be cutting in on you, would I, Ty?"

"No, nothing like that. I wish you well, whatever happens." Ty did his best to put a lot of sincerity in his words, but he couldn't help but feel like he had lost something special.

꧁

George watched the tall man walk away and sat for a while staring down at the table.

Finally the waiter came and said, "Anything else, Mr. Fairfax?"

"No. Here you go." He put money on the table, including a large tip, and left the café. All morning he wandered around, not knowing what to do with himself, thinking mostly about what he'd said to Ty Kincaid. Finally he threw up his hands and muttered, "I might as well go find out."

He went to the livery stable and had the hostler saddle his buckskin. He mounted up and rode out of town at a fast gait. As he left town and headed toward the sheep camp, he was worried about his way. *She probably never thought of me as a man she might marry. Why should she?*

As he rode along, he studied the land and thought about how different it was from England. There he had been used to grass so green it hurt the eyes in the summer, but here it was summer and the grass was still not greened out. The hills were rough, and rocky buttes broke against the morning sky. It was tough, hard-edged territory, and he was well aware that some of the men and the Indians who inhabited this place were as rough as the land itself.

George finally arrived at the sheep camp early the next morning. He saw Eddie Vernay trimming the wool from a sheep. "Hello, Eddie."

"Hello, Mr. Fairfax."

"That looks like a lot of work."

"It ain't bad. It's when you have to do a hundred of them in a day that it gets tough. Everything gets bad when you have to do a lot of it. What can I do for you?"

"Is Raina here?"

"No, she's gone out to look at the sheep."

George Fairfax stood uncertainly.

Finally Vernay said, "You got somethin' on your mind, Mr. Fairfax?"

"Well, I do, but I'm not sure I need to say it."

"Let it be said. Can't be too bad."

Fairfax hesitated then blurted out, "You know, in my country if a man's serious about a woman, he goes to her father to ask if he can make an offer to his daughter."

Eddie Vernay threw the pile of wool on the ground, then tossed the shears down and let the sheep go. "What kind of an offer?"

"Well, I'm sorry I didn't do this the right way by coming to you first, but I asked Raina to marry me some time ago. She hasn't given me an answer yet."

Vernay took off his hat and scratched his head. "Well, I do wish you had come to me first. But I haven't really been a father to her for long, so I will leave it up to her. However, if you want my two cents' worth, I'm not sure it'd work."

"Why not? You don't like me?"

"No, it ain't that, but you know this ain't England, Mr. Fairfax."

"I know. I thought about that. But if she married me, we could go back to England. I've even got a castle there. It's not the biggest one, but she could have anything she wanted. Anyway, I came to see if I could get an answer from her. I think it's been long enough."

Eddie Vernay stared at the tall Englishman. "You're welcome to go find her."

"Which way do I go?"

"See them two peaks over there? I've got a herd of sheep there. You ride straight for it. When you see sheep, Raina will be close."

"Thank you, Mr. Vernay."

"Good luck, son."

As Fairfax rode away, he felt like a fool. "I could have said that a little bit better. I'm surprised he didn't run me off."

He kept the horse at a fast gait, and finally he saw the sheep. Five minutes later he saw Raina.

She was talking to one of the herders, and they both turned to see him. When he stopped the horse, she cried out, "Hello, George. Get down."

George dismounted, tied his horse to one of the saplings, and said, "What are you doing?"

"Trying to learn about sheep."

"There's a lot to learn, I suppose."

"Yes, there is. There's different kinds, and you have to know a lot to keep them from running away." The sheepherder was Mikel.

"You like sheep, Mikel?"

"No."

His brief answer amused Fairfax. "Well, why do you do it then?"

"A man has to do somethin'. Beats other things I've done."

"Come on, George. Let's go get in the shade. I've got some cool water over there, or it was when I left the house."

He walked over with her, and for the next thirty minutes they stood in the shade and Raina talked about sheep. As she spoke,

George tried to think of some way to say something.

Finally she asked him, "George, have you decided what you're going to do?"

"You mean about where I'm going to live?"

"Yes. You didn't seem too sure the last time we talked about it."

"Well, I've been thinking about one thing. I guess there are better ways to say this, but I've been thinking about you, Raina." He hesitated then said, "Have you thought any more about me as a man you might marry?"

She was staring at him strangely and said quietly, "Yes, I have, George."

When she said nothing more, George nervously said, "I don't know how to court an American woman. And I don't know enough about sheep to talk about that."

"Marriage is more than sheep, isn't it, George?"

"Well, of course it is, but I don't know how you feel about me."

"I'm interested in you. You're an interesting fellow." She did not seem disturbed by his talk of marriage, and he bent to catch a better view of her face. He was not sure what her expression meant, and he had a great dread of making a mistake with this girl.

For a moment he watched her; he saw no anger, and without saying anything else, he reached out and pulled her to him. He saw that she was smiling, and he kissed her. When he lifted his lips, he found that the kiss had disturbed him more than her. She had combed her hair so that it lay soft and neat against her head and there were lights dancing in her eyes.

He said, "I don't know what to think of you. You're not like any woman I ever met."

"I'm just a woman, George."

"You haven't answered my question."

"No, I haven't, but I can tell you this. It's going to take a little bit more courting than you've shown me so far. You've hardly been around since you asked me. I know you've been giving me time to decide, but I need to see you a bit more to really decide a thing as important as this."

"Can't you tell me what you think of me?"

"Well, George, I can tell you one thing," Raina said. "I don't feel about you like I would a man I want to spend the rest of my life with. At least not yet."

George was disappointed, but he determined to see this thing through, believing she could come to love him. "Well, tell me how to go about this."

"That's for you to find out. I'm not even sure I want to get married now to anybody, so you've got to change my mind about that."

"All right. I'll come courting. I guess that's what you mean."

"Yes. Can you play a guitar? I'll have you bring a guitar and sing love songs outside my window."

"I'm sorry about that. I've got no musical talent at all, but I can quote some poetry for you."

"Well, we can make do with that. Come along. I'll show you some more sheep."

CHAPTER 23

Ever since George had spoken to her again about getting married, Raina had been disturbed. She knew many women would jump at the chance to marry a man with his qualities. Not only was he wealthy and entertaining, but she could tell he was a good man, which was to her a most important factor.

The next morning, she got up, helped make breakfast for the herders, and then cleaned up the kitchen. Finally she went out on the porch of the small house and sat down on a chair that her father had built.

The sun was well up, and she could hear the plaintive cries of the sheep, a sound that had almost become second nature to the land where she now lived. She had come to the sheep ranch with prejudice about the woolly animals, but during the months she had been here, she had become aware of their helplessness and how they needed the almost constant watch care of the shepherds. They were foolish in a way, but somehow she found this made them more endearing.

From far off she heard the sound of a coyote, always a lonesome, plaintive cry to her. They were nocturnal creatures, and one was rarely seen or heard during the daylight hours. They also could be destructive, and the shepherds always had to be on constant guard so they would not lose their sheep to a pack of them.

She turned her eyes down toward the corral, where she watched one of the herders, Benat, a huge man, and by far the strongest of the shepherds, break in a horse. He was a good rider, and his heavy weight prevented the small mustang from throwing him off. She watched as the big man pulled himself into the saddle and the horse bucked, but Benat simply sat there until the animal quieted. He stepped off and led the animal away.

Raina got up and walked across the yard, noting that since she had come she had insisted on cleaning it up. The men had been careless with tin cans and papers and other trash that littered the place. Now it was clean, and one of the men was assigned each day to make sure it stayed that way. They had objected at first, but they had become accustomed to it.

She went inside, poured herself a cup of coffee from the pot that sat on the wood-burning stove, and then walked outside again. She could not understand her restlessness, but she knew it had something to do with trying to make up her mind about her future life. She was aware that there was some relationship between her and Ty, but then George had proposed marriage to her, and she found herself unable to think very clearly about it.

For a while she sipped the coffee, and as she was draining the cup, she saw a rider coming. When he came closer, she recognized Ty.

He rode in, dismounted, tied his horse up, and came over to the porch.

"Good morning, Ty. How about some coffee?"

"That sounds good."

"Have you eaten?"

"Just a little."

"I've got some biscuits left and some preserves. I can fry you up some bacon."

"Oh, don't bother. Just coffee will be fine."

Raina went inside and quickly returned with a steaming cup of coffee. She put the cup down on the table beside the chair Ty had sat in. As she took the chair beside his, she said, "How are you feeling?"

"Oh, I'm fine. I've been hurt worse. I came pretty close to cashing in, but now I'm getting better every day."

"Have you gone back to your job yet?"

"I'm actually on the job now. Judge Parker sent me out here to check on things. I think he just wanted to give me an easy assignment as I get back to work." He hesitated. "I guess he sees something in me that I can't hide."

Raina was curious. "What would that be, Ty?"

"I'm just restless. I don't know what to do with myself. And all those dreams I had when I was dying out on the plains, they keep coming back to me." He paused then said, "One of them I haven't told you about."

"What was it?"

Ty hesitated then shook his head. "It sounds meaningless to me. Most of my dreams are, but in this dream I found myself speaking to a group of people. It was like I was a preacher. They were listening and I was speaking. I don't remember a word I said, but that's what it was."

Raina leaned closer to him. "You think God might be leading you to become a preacher?"

"I don't know, Raina. That would have been the last thought in my mind, but now it keeps coming back, and I can even see the faces of the people I was speaking to."

Raina put her hand on his arm and felt the muscular structure. He was a strong man. She studied his face. She found herself wondering what it would be like to be married to a man like this. He had definitely established jaws, and his eyes were sharp and restless. He had high cheekbones and minute weather lines slanting out from his eyes across a smooth and bronzed skin.

"I don't know what to think," he murmured.

Raina instantly was filled with compassion for him. A strong man who did not know what was happening to him. "I'm sure if God wants you for something, He'll let you know what it is."

"Maybe so."

Raina was aware that trouble had painted its shadows on Ty's eyes and weighted silence on his tongue. It had touched his solid face with a brand of loneliness, and he was looking at her with some sort of question that she could not quite understand. She simply sat beside him, noting he was a limber man with gray eyes half hidden. There was a looseness about him, and all of his features were solid. But his expression held a dark preoccupation, and she knew he was in misery.

Finally the silence grew between them until it was almost palpable, and then Ty said, "Did George come out and speak to you?"

Raina was surprised. "Yes, he did. How did you know?"

"He told me he was probably going to do it, that in fact he

already had asked you to marry him, and he just wanted to see if you had an answer for him." He smiled slightly. "I think he was asking me for my permission."

"And what did you tell him?"

"I told him it was your decision."

"Well, he did ask for my answer."

"What did you say? You see him as a husband?"

"No—at least I don't think so."

He said, "It would be an easy life for you."

"I'm not looking for an easy life."

"I'm surprised."

"That I wouldn't marry George?"

"Most women would jump at the chance."

"Well, I'm not most women." She saw a strange expression on his face. "What are you thinking, Ty? I can't read you."

Ty shook his head slightly and then said evenly, "I love you, Raina. I have for a long time. I just couldn't understand it, but we couldn't ever marry."

"Why not, Ty?"

"Well, if this dream means anything, I may wind up being a preacher, but I'd never be a city preacher in a big church. I'd be like your pa. That's what I see about Jesus. He went to the poor and the outcasts. Maybe preaching here in the territory to the bad men and the Indians that are sullen and resentful wouldn't be a happy experience. I don't know much, but I do know that would be too much to ask of a woman."

In a sudden, desperate move, he reached out, took Raina in his arms, and kissed her. She could not speak, and there were tears in her eyes.

"I'm not asking you for anything, Raina, but a woman should know when a man loves her, and that's all I have to offer."

She started to speak, but he shook his head. "Don't say anything, Raina. Maybe God will tell you what to do, but He hasn't told me." He turned, went to his horse, mounted, and rode off quickly.

Raina went inside and found her father sitting at the table doing his book work. "Ty's just left."

"What did he come for?"

"I think he came to ask me to marry him, but he didn't."

Pa leaned back and studied her. "I don't know what to say, daughter. Do you love this man?"

"I'm confused, Pa," Raina said. She bit her lower lip and shook her head with confusion in her eyes. "George asked me to marry him—and now there's Ty, both good men. How am I going to choose between them?"

Pa studied her thoughtfully, and with wisdom in his eyes and certainty in his voice, he said, "You'd better let God make your decision, daughter."

She turned and left the house, knowing she was as uncertain as she had ever been in her life. As she got on her horse and rode out, she thought about nothing but the two men who had sought her as a wife.

☙

Clark Simmons had been hired by Aaron Jordan to handle the excess of cattle that he had accumulated. He was not a good hand, but Jordan couldn't afford to be picky. What he didn't know was that Simmons had been hired by Honey Clagg to keep track of

Ash Jordan. His instructions had been, "I want you to isolate Ash Jordan for me. When he goes out sometime by himself, I want you to get word to me."

"How much is this worth to you, Clagg?"

"A hundred dollars."

"That'll do it. You gonna shoot him?"

"That's none of your business. You just get me word."

Simmons kept his ears opened, and it was late in the afternoon when Aaron Jordan told Ash, "You take the wagon tomorrow and go to town and get some supplies. Here's the list."

"I may stay over for a while."

"No, you come right back. I need you here."

"All right, Pa."

Simmons left at once. It was a hard ride to the outlaws' hideout, but he found it. He got Clagg off to one side and said, "Ash is going to leave to go to town tomorrow."

"Will he be alone?"

"I reckon so. He didn't say anything about takin' anybody. He's takin' a wagon in to get some supplies."

"All right. You did your job."

"How about that hundred dollars."

Clagg dug into his pocket and came out with it and said, "How will he get to town?"

"Same road he always takes. There won't be no witnesses."

"Okay. You forget about this. Just keep your mouth shut. . .if you know what's good for you."

Clagg's evil grin told Simmons all he needed to know to be sure he would never tell a soul about this.

As Ash crawled into the wagon, suddenly Benny came to say, "Reckon I'll come to town with you."

"What for? Pa wants you to stay here and work."

"Aw, all he thinks about is work." Benny climbed up and sat down. "I need a break every now and then."

The trip was boring for most of the time, but when they got to a pass between two hills, suddenly all that changed.

Benny saw a man step out into the open. "You need some help, mister?" he asked. From the look on the man's face, Benny felt a prickle of fear run down his back.

The man said, "Okay, Ash, you killed Johnny Taylor, Garth Taylor's brother, so that's it for you." Without warning he raised his rifle and got off a shot.

Benny was caught off guard, but when Ash slumped over, he pulled his pistol and emptied it. He saw that one of the shots grazed the gunman.

The man rode off, yelling, "We're going to wipe out your whole ranch!"

Benny turned and said, "Are you all right, Ash?"

But Ash had been hit in the chest, and blood stained his shirt.

Benny was so shook up, he didn't know what to do at first. But he quickly came to himself and put his brother in the back and whipped the horses up. "I'll get you to a doctor, Ash. I'll get you there as soon as I can."

The horses broke into a dead run, and dust traced his flight across the range. He feared that Ash was dying and thought of how his pa would take it. He was afraid that his father's answer would be to spill blood all over the territory until those responsible lay dead. . .or Aaron Jordan himself did.

☙

Heck was in his office when Larry Dolby came in, saying with excitement, "Heck, it's some trouble I hear. You'd better come."

Heck was used to trouble coming, and he came up out of his chair and hurried outside. He saw the buggy pulling up and walked over quickly. "What's the matter, Benny?"

"It's Ash. He's been shot. We've got to get Dr. Stapleton."

"Let's take him down to his office. How'd it happen?"

"Let's get Ash there and then I'll tell you."

The doctor's office was only a few doors down. They brought Ash in.

Dr. Stapleton immediately began stripping Ash's clothes off. "He's got a pretty bad gunshot wound here. That bullet's got to come out," he said grimly.

"Is he gonna make it, Doc?" Benny asked, anxiety scoring his face.

"Can't say, but I'll do the best I can."

"How'd this happen, Benny?" Heck said. He listened as Benny told him the story of how they had been ambushed. Heck shook his head. "Had to be the sheepherders."

"No, it wasn't," Benny said. "I saw who it was, and it wasn't one of Vernay's men. In fact, he said something about shooting Ash because he had killed Johnny Taylor, Garth Taylor's brother."

"He must be one of Garth Taylor's band. Johnny must have been the one that Ash shot when that gang tried to run some of your cattle awhile back. You know, when they captured Holder."

"I bet you're right. I think he was gonna shoot me, too, because he threatened that they would be coming to get all of my family. But I got my gun out and emptied it at him. It was a long shot for a pistol, but I grazed him, I think. At least he turned and rode away."

Heck shook his head. "Your father will go after the sheepherders. He'll think it's them."

Ty had come in and was standing beside Heck. "It couldn't have been them. I was at their camp all morning."

"That won't stop Jordan, not if his son may be dead."

Benny said, "I know it's Taylor's gang."

Heck said stolidly, "Everybody knows Garth Taylor is a low-down outlaw."

Ty said, "We'd better get Garth and that bunch. It's the only thing to keep Aaron Jordan from killing every sheepherder in the territory."

"We'll have to get him word. He'll want to be with his boy."

"Now, what are we going to do about Garth's gang?" Ty asked.

"We're gonna have to go after 'em."

"He's got at least seven or eight men in that band of his," Ty said. "At least that's what I hear."

"Well," Heck said, "we've got me and Larry Dolby and you."

Ty said, "That's not enough to handle Garth's bunch."

Heck Thomas thought for a moment then said, "We've got to go after him. Maybe we can get a few more men."

Benny said at once, "I'm going, too."

"Well, that's four of us," Ty said.

"That's still not enough. I reckon Garth will know we're comin'," Heck said. "But it's maybe the best chance we'll have."

❧

Ty was surprised to see Aaron Jordan ride in, his horse lathered, and step off at Dr. Stapleton's office. He came inside, and when the doctor turned, he said, "How's my boy?"

Stapleton nodded. "He's going to make it, Aaron."

"I'll kill every sheepherder in the country!"

"It wasn't the sheepherders that shot Ash," Ty said.

"How do you know that?"

"Benny was with him, and he heard the shooter claim to be part of Garth Taylor's band. They want revenge for Ash killing Johnny Taylor. We figure he was the other one shot when that gang came after some of your cattle awhile back. He also threatened the rest of your family, Aaron."

"How did you find out about Ash so quickly, Jordan?" Heck asked.

"I was actually coming to town as I forgot to tell Ash to get a couple of items we really needed. When I arrived, Larry Dolby told me what happened. Now that I know Ash is going to be all right, I've got to get back to the ranch. I don't know Garth, but I bet he's headed there."

"It sounds like the kind of thing Garth would do. He'll come in and kill everything at your ranch, kill off the cattle, and burn the house. And you're not going alone. Ty, Larry, and me are coming with you," Heck said. "Your boy Benny insists he's comin', too."

"We still need more men," Aaron said. "We've got two more hands at the house."

"That may make it enough," Heck said. "We'll go nail the whole bunch. I've been looking for an excuse to cut down on

Garth Taylor. He's caused enough trouble in this territory."

Garth stood staring at Clagg and listening as the big man told him what he had done.

"So you shot Ash Jordan, but you're not positive he's dead?" Garth stared at Clagg, cursed, and then said, "I should have just done it myself. You've let everyone know someone's after Ash. They'll eventually figure out it's me."

Clagg was taken aback. "Sorry, Garth, but I didn't know his brother would be with him."

Garth's thirst for revenge was still burning, and he said, "We're going to Jordan's ranch as soon as we can get ready. We've got to move now since they know someone is after them. We're going to burn the ranch to the ground and kill as many cattle as we can. Get the men together."

Long Tom Slaughter said, "Maybe we better hold off on this. It'll bring every marshal from Parker's court down on us. We don't want that."

"We're going—and that means all of you. We're going to wipe out the Running J!"

CHAPTER 24

Heck, Ty, Aaron Jordan, Dolby, and Benny rode out of town. The five of them swung toward the north and soon arrived in the Aspen Hills.

Ty cast a glance at Heck and saw his hardness. He was as tough a man as Ty had ever seen, and he knew that Judge Parker trusted him completely.

He turned his glance toward Larry Dolby. He was a good enough marshal, but Ty wished they had half a dozen more with them. As for Benny, he was too young for this but had insisted on coming. Even his father had not been able to dissuade him.

They rode steadily until the sun was half down in the sky. The summer grass made a great yellow-green carpet all the way into the distance that lay before them, and heat gathered as they angled toward the height of the Aspen Hills. They passed through Little Bear Creek, followed it into a trail, and passed the first line of timber.

As they passed the pines, Heck shook his head. "I wish we

had half a dozen marshals with us."

"We'll do all right," Ty said.

"I don't know. I tell myself that every time I go out to take a man, but this is different. Garth's a tough enough man. Tough as I'd ever want to meet, and he's got the Daltons with him. I don't know how many more."

"More than we've got, I expect," Ty said. He was leaning sideways in the saddle, a peculiar way of riding, but it was one he always followed. "I still think we should have waited until we got some more men."

"That wouldn't do," Aaron said. "According to what that shooter said, they'll be comin' to burn our ranch out. We've got to be there to stop 'em."

No one spoke to that, and finally they crossed a creek and followed a parallel trail. The trees made a close stand, free of underbrush, and the five men were sweating freely. Ty saw Heck's face drenched in perspiration, and he wiped his own face. "It's going to be a tough thing, but if we get there first, we'll be all right."

They rode steadily, and finally they came to the high points of the hills where the ranch was located. The sun burned dark red and was sinking as they rode in.

They were met by Lottie and Leoma, who walked out of the house. "What is it?" Lottie asked.

"We've got to get you women out of here," Heck said. "Garth Taylor's comin' with his bunch to raid the ranch."

Leoma stared at her father then said, "I'll take Ma into town."

As Leoma and Lottie stepped inside the house to get ready to leave, Aaron said, "I can go get Mingan and Nelly Fox. That'll make seven of us."

"Better make it quick, Aaron," Ty said instantly. "They're going to be here soon enough."

"I'll get them here quick if I have to break this horse down!" He wheeled his horse around and sped off toward the low-lying hills where Mingan and Nelly were working with the herd.

Leoma came out of the house, accompanied by her mother. Lottie was pale, but she had a steely look on her face.

Leoma looked at the men and said, "We're leaving now. Send us word about what happens as soon as you can."

"We'll do that," Ty said. "Don't linger anywhere." He suddenly remembered that Leoma and Lottie had no idea that Ash had been shot. In a sparse voice, he said, "Sorry to have to tell you this, but Ash was shot earlier today."

"Is he all right?" Lottie asked quickly, fear now in her eyes.

Heck said, "Dr. Stapleton says he's gonna make it. Would be a good thing if you'd go on now, ladies."

Heck waited until the two women got into the buggy, then said, "Ty, you go get in that barn over there. Take your rifle with you. When they ride in, we'll wait until they're all inside and you knock Garth out of the saddle. That'll be the sign for the rest of us to start shootin'."

"You gonna kill him without warning?" Benny said with surprise.

"You don't warn rattlesnakes, Benny. They warn you. We know well and good," Heck said, "what they'll be comin' for."

Benny swallowed hard then nodded. "Where do you want me, Marshal?"

"Go into the house and poke your rifle out the window. You'll have cover there. Larry, you join him in the house. They'll be after that first thing. When the shootin' starts, get as many as you can."

"Where will you be, Heck?" Ty asked.

"I'm gonna get over behind that feeding station. Remember, there's gonna be more of them than there are of us. All of them are wanted men. Any of them that live through this will be tried and hanged. Keep a sharp lookout. As soon as we see them comin', we'll go to our places. Be sure you've got plenty of ammunition."

Ty asked, "You mean what you said about knocking them out of the saddle?"

"This is war, Ty. You know that. Those men are all killers. This bunch has been raisin' trouble in the territory long enough!"

The men were all fairly jumpy and everybody was looking into the direction where they expected the outlaws to come. Mingan and Nelly Fox returned with Aaron, and Heck nodded. "That'll give us some more firepower." He then assigned them to places close by.

Half an hour later, Benny said, "I see some dust out there."

"Where?" Heck demanded.

"Right over there to the east."

"You've got good eyes there, boy. Everybody get to their places. Remember, Ty, let 'em all get in the yard. Knock Garth out of the saddle if you can. The rest of us will open up as soon as we hear your shot."

❧

Garth raised his hand and stopped the men. He looked over and saw that there were seven of them. "We ride in, and anybody gives us any trouble, shoot 'em down."

"There's women in there," Long Tom Slaughter said. "At least they're usually there. That's Jordan's wife and his daughter."

"Well, don't shoot them if you can help it, but everybody else goes. You all ready?" A murmur of assent came to him, and he said, "We go in hard and fast. We take everybody out, fire the house, then run off as many of the cattle as we can."

"You sure you want to do this, Garth?" Long Tom Slaughter said. "It'll stir the marshals up. They'll be after us heavy."

"We'll be out of this country by the time they hear about it. Let's go." He spurred his stallion forward, and the horse broke into a hard run. He glanced to see that all the men were with him, and they swept into the yard. "I don't see anybody," Mexican Jack said. "Why ain't they here?"

Even as they spoke, a rifle shot broke the silence, and Garth Taylor fell off his horse. Even before he hit the ground, other shots were raking the yard. Garth Taylor knew he was done for. He just hoped his men exacted revenge on the Jordans before he died.

"They're all hid," Slaughter hollered. "We can't take this."

"Let's get out of here!" Grat Dalton yelled. "We ain't got a chance!"

They all tried to calm their horses, but some men came into the open. The outlaws emptied their guns.

Mexican Jack emptied his Colt and saw one of the men drop. "I got him!" he yelled, but then a bullet struck him in the heart, and Garth could tell he was dead when he hit the ground.

"Let's get out of here, Bob!" Grat Dalton yelled. "We ain't got a chance!" The two of them fled, but the Dalton brothers left Mexican Jack dead and Clagg, Slaughter, and Garth bleeding their lives out in the dust.

Raina was in town with her father. She had been struggling to figure out the decision she knew she would have to make. Which man? The aristocratic English lord or the hard-bitten marshal? Both men were strong, but she knew that was not enough.

Judge Parker stopped beside her and her father and said, "Some word came in that Tom Rawlings just rode in from a shootout at the Jordan ranch. Let him tell us." He hollered, "Tom, come over here."

A short, well-built man came over, his face drenched with sweat. "Yes, Judge."

"You saw the thing?"

"I was just riding by and heard gunfire. I didn't know what was going on, so I come to get help. Before I left I could see it was quite a slaughter. All of the outlaws went down except two. I didn't know who it was, but they got away."

"Were any of my men hurt?" Parker said.

"I saw one of them go down. I think he's dead. At least he looked like it. I didn't take time to stay around. The two outlaws left were comin' toward me."

"Do you know which one of my men it was?"

"I think it was Kincaid."

At those words, Raina knew that she had lost something that she would mourn for the rest of her life. She turned and walked away, her face frozen and immobile, and she could not speak. Her heart was clutched in an icy grasp.

George came rushing up to say, "I just heard what happened."

"Did you hear that Ty got killed?"

George stared at her. "No, I didn't hear that."

"I might as well tell you, George. I can't marry you."

George studied her face and said, "It's Ty you love."

"I didn't know it before, but it is."

"I'm sorry. Will you be all right?"

"No, I don't think I'll ever be all right."

"Well, I'll be around if I can do anything."

Two hours later, Raina was in the general store. She had wept over Ty and knew she would never cease to regret his death.

She heard a man call, "Here comes the group from the Jordan place."

She walked outside, expecting to see a body draped over a horse. Instead she saw Ty Kincaid, and Raina suddenly did not breathe. Tears began to flow, and she ran out crying, "Ty—Ty!"

Ty had stepped out of the saddle, and when she struck him running full speed, he reached out and held her. "What is it, Raina?"

"I heard you were dead!"

"No, I just stumbled and fell. None of us got hit."

She held on to him, her face against his chest. He smelled of dust and sweat, but she was crying so hard she did not even care.

"What is it, Raina?"

"When I heard you were dead, Ty, it was like the sun went out."

Ty stared at her then said, "I had to stay alive—long enough to do whatever it is that God wants me to do."

She came to him, and as he held her, she suddenly knew what

she wanted. She waited for Ty to speak, to tell her that he loved her, but he only held her tightly.

Thirty yards away, George Fairfax was watching the scene. Leoma Jordan came up, and he turned to look at her. "Well, I asked her about marrying me."

"What did she say?"

"Nothing much, but it would have been no. She loves Kincaid."

"You know what you need, George? You need a cause."

"What kind of a cause?" he said.

"Me." Leoma smiled. "I'll be your cause. You can come courting me."

George suddenly smiled. He liked this girl. She had a vividness and a life about her that he had rarely seen. "I've got a broken heart," he said, but he was smiling.

"I'll fix it," Leoma said. "Come along. We'll talk about how I like to be courted."

"Well, I need something," George said. "Maybe it's you."

"We'll find out about that, won't we?"

CHAPTER 25

Word of the demise of Garth Taylor's bunch of outlaws spread like wildfire through the territory. People talked about nothing else, and most of the decent men of Fort Smith, and the ranchers who were scattered throughout the Indian lands, were glad, for Garth Taylor was a man who could do great harm.

The only fly in the ointment was the escape of the Dalton brothers, but the word was out that they had fled to the east and would not be any problem for Judge Parker or for his marshals.

Heck Thomas sat in the early afternoon sunlight. As usual he had taken station in his cane-bottom chair and tilted it back against the face of the courthouse and the jail. The sun was warm, but Heck could take hot weather. It was the cold weather that troubled him. Now, as usual, he was whittling on a piece of cedar and looking down at the pile of curled shavings, wondering why he had such an impulse to do this. Of course he saved all the shavings and made cushions out of them that made his room smell better, but it seemed like a foolish thing for a grown man and the head of more than a hundred marshals to do.

The people of the town, men and women, youngsters and adolescents, all paraded by, and many of them stopped to congratulate Heck on his action against Garth Taylor's bunch. Heck was aware that he had not done this single-handedly, but he was the one who got the congratulations.

The town drunk, Pete Barton, came down the sidewalk. Heck had learned to gauge Pete's condition by the way he walked. Now he stood straight and kept in the middle of the sidewalk, so he wasn't drunk yet. His drunken progress was a weaving back and forth, sometimes falling down, running into people, mumbling to himself, but Pete showed none of these signs yet.

He stopped in front of Heck and said, "Well, Marshal, it looks like you got yourself a reputation."

"I've had a reputation, Pete, for a long time. I'm not sure I need any more." He studied Pete, who was wearing leftover clothes that he had evidently found. Nothing matched and nothing fit. The hat he had on was far too small and was perched on top of his head like a cap on a small boy. "Where are you headed, Pete?" Heck asked.

Pete took his hat off, scratched his thatch of graying hair, and thought for a moment. Finally he said, "Well, Marshal, I'm going to get drunk, and do I dread it!"

It was an enigmatic answer, and Heck thought for a moment that he had misheard him, but finally he saw that Pete was totally serious. "If you dread it, why do you do it?"

"I don't know why I do it. You know, once, Marshal, I was a respected lawyer back East."

"I've heard that."

"Made lots of money, married a good woman, and had three children. Had everything going for me."

"Well, what happened?"

"I never had a drink until one day at a celebration someone gave me a glass of whiskey. I drank it, and that was the last of my sobriety."

"I can't understand that. If you saw it was ruining you, why did you do it?"

"Can't tell you that. Someone asked me how I lost my honor, and I got me a stock answer. You like to hear it, Marshal?"

"Let her rip, Pete."

"Well, you don't lose your honor in one bad moment."

"What does that mean?"

"I didn't wake up one morning and say, 'I've been a good man, a good husband, a good father, but I've decided I'm going to become a worthless, drunken bum and throw everything away.' It didn't happen like that."

"How did it happen then?"

"Well, it come on slow. I took one little drink, and the next day I took another one. Just them two drinks, but by that time I guess I was a drunk even though I still went on with my work and did my job. But it was like little mice coming in taking away cheese. They didn't take the whole chunk of cheese; they just took a little nibble at it. So whiskey nibbled at me, and I woke up one day and looked around and saw that I had become a drunk, my wife and kids had left me, I didn't have any money, and I wasn't welcome anyplace in the town where I'd practiced. I'd lost my license. So I came out here."

"Is it any better here?"

"It is in one way, Marshal. Nobody cares if you're drunk here."

Heck Thomas felt a sudden sympathy for Pete Barton. He had watched him for years, and the man lived in total misery, and he could not understand why a man would do a thing like that.

"Well, I guess you've gotten enough good advice, so I won't give you any."

"Wouldn't do any good, Marshal." He looked around and said, "What do you think is going to happen to Fort Smith?"

"What do you mean?"

"Well, I mean towns change. Some of them become big cities. Some of them just dry up and blow away."

"You know, I've thought about that, Pete. Right now this is a wild place with Indians and outlaws and Judge Parker hangin' those he can get convicted. But it'll calm down sooner or later. I was at Dodge City when it was at its height. They had a man killed every morning before breakfast, but now it's just a nice little town, not very big, nothing much going on. That'll happen to Fort Smith one of these days."

"Well, you'll be out of a job."

"No, not really. There'll still be crooks and outlaws. They'll need men like me."

"I'm ruined, Marshal. I hope you don't ever fall like I did. Well, I'll be going now."

Heck watched as Pete Barton walked off. He thought about Judge Parker, and suddenly the question came to his mind. *What'll happen to Judge Parker when he can't serve as a judge anymore?* He heard rumors already that there were people in Washington concerned with the severity and the strictness with which Parker ran his court and that there were moves under way to replace him.

Heck got up, stretched, and shook the thought out of his mind. He knew that if Parker left, he would be fired, too. *I wonder if I could go back to Emily. She never has married again, and the kids are grown up. Maybe we could make something out of it.*

He was interrupted when Dave Ennis, the banker at the Cattleman's Bank, stopped in front of him. "That was a good job, Marshal." Ennis beamed. He reached out and shook Heck's hand. "Good to be rid of that bunch of snakes."

"Well, it is. I've been after them for a long time, Dave, but there's plenty more where they came from."

"Well, you'll get them all." Ennis nodded.

"I don't think so. There'll always be bad men."

"Just takes a little time, don't it?"

"Takes time and men willing to die to make the peace. I don't like to think about the young fellows that I've lost. Over fifty of them dead and buried in a cemetery out there."

"Well, this bunch you won't have to hang 'em. They're already dead except for the Dalton brothers."

"I'd just as soon we'd taken them alive and put 'em through the court. The Daltons are gone, but someone will take their place."

"The whole territory is proud of you."

"I didn't do it by myself, you know."

"No, I hear you had some good help. Maybe things are looking up."

"Maybe so, but not this week. Still got work to do."

Ennis moved on, and Heck grew tired of hearing people comment on his ability as a lawman when he knew well that it was not his achievement alone. Heck took a small feed sack out of his pocket, filled it with the cedar shavings, folded his knife, and went inside. He mounted the stairs and went right to Judge Parker's office. He knocked on the door, and when Judge Parker said, "Come in," he opened it.

He found the judge sitting at his desk, staring out into space. "What is it, Heck?"

"I'm tired of sitting out there being told how wonderful I am."

Parker did not laugh often, but he found this amusing. "I don't suppose many men find out they're wonderful when they're as young as you. I wish I could."

"Oh, Judge, everybody knows you're a great man."

"No, they don't."

Heck looked down at his hand and said, "I've shook more hands than a politician running for office."

Parker shook his head. "Soak it up."

"Never was one to do a lot of that."

"Just wait," Parker said. "The first time some more bad men shoot a citizen up, those same folks that have been shaking your hand will be yelling at you to get off your duff and do your job."

"That what they tell you?"

"No, they're afraid of me, but I think most of them would like to bawl me out. But that wouldn't be smart, so they pretty well keep quiet."

"Well, they don't mind tellin' me when things go wrong."

"You did do a good job."

"I guess. At least you didn't have to fool around with a trial, Judge."

"I'm sorry the Daltons got away. They deserved the rope."

"I heard they left the territory."

"Yes, I heard that, too." Judge Parker rubbed his chin and

shook his head. "Good riddance, but they'll not change. That kind never does."

"Well, I think I'll be headin' out. Got a few chores to do. See you later, Judge."

Heck left the judge's office. As he stepped out into the street, he saw Aaron Jordan and his wife. "Hello, Aaron. Mrs. Jordan. How is Ash doing?"

She answered for the pair. "Good morning, Marshal. We just came from seeing him. The doctor says he can come home with us tomorrow. We are so thankful."

"You're looking fine, Mrs. Jordan."

"Thank you." She smiled. "I feel better."

"So do I." Aaron Jordan beamed. "I feel like a new man with those outlaws on the run. We owe you a lot, Marshal."

"Just doing my job."

Aaron said, "I can sleep better at night now that Garth Taylor and his bunch are dead."

Heck Thomas was a plainspoken man, often rough in his speech. He stared at Aaron Jordan and said, "You were ready to go after Ed Vernay with your gun, Mr. Jordan. How do you feel about that now?"

The blunt words seemed to strike against Jordan, and he said, "Well, I was wrong about him, Marshal."

"Yes, you were. Real wrong. About as wrong as a man can be. Have you told him you were wrong?"

"No, he hasn't, Marshal," Lottie Jordan spoke up. "My husband isn't very good at admitting he's wrong."

"It's about time he learns how then. I'd hate to have seen you dangling on the judge's gallows for shooting a man who hadn't done you any harm."

Aaron Jordan dropped his head and stared at his feet. He gnawed on his lower lip; then he raised his head and nodded. "You're both right. I'll go see Ed and tell him I was wrong."

"It'll do you good." Lottie smiled. "You're a good man, Aaron, not nearly as bad as you used to be."

"Great Scot," Jordan said. "That's the nicest thing you ever said about me."

Heck suddenly found that amusing. "You go make it right. Ed Vernay is a good man, and you two can be good neighbors for a long time."

"Well, I'll take my medicine. We'll go by his place soon, Lottie," Jordan said. "You may have to help me apologize."

The two left, and Heck watched them go. He found it amusing that Jordan was ready to change his mind when he had been so adamantly sure that Ed Vernay had been his enemy. He would, no doubt, have shot him if he could, but now he had found out differently. Heck knew there would be no danger of that.

He turned and moved on down the street, thinking of the next outlaws he would have to run down.

CHAPTER 26

Raina and her father had made a trip into town and were in the general store. Pa went at once to look at some farm equipment that he had heard about, and Raina wandered through the store. The odors of coffee, pickles, and fresh meat filled the store. She wandered around alone.

Her father joined her soon and said, "You know, I've been thinking. You need to buy some new clothes. There's a dress over there I seen when we came in."

"I don't need a new dress."

He grinned, took her by the arm, and led her over to where a dress was laid out on a table. "That would suit you."

Raina reached out and stroked the material. "It is fine," she said. "Too fine for me."

"Daughter, nothing's too fine for you. I want to buy it for you."

"I don't have anywhere to wear fancy clothes to."

"Well, we'll find a place. Why don't you go try it on?"

Raina stroked the material again, trying to make up her mind, when suddenly Aaron and Lottie Jordan entered. She braced herself, for Jordan had been outspoken in his rage against her father. She saw that he was wearing a gun as most men did, and this troubled her.

Aaron stopped and said, "I want to talk to you, Vernay."

"Well, you're talking." Pa was staring and keeping his eyes fixed on Aaron Jordan.

"I got something to say all right, and it's mighty hard for me." Aaron shrugged, moved his feet around, and twisted his neck.

Suddenly his wife said, "Go on, Aaron, say what you need to say."

"Well, all right, Lottie." Aaron swallowed hard and said, "I want to tell you that I've been wrong about you, Ed. I acted like an idiot, and I'm sorry. I hope you'll overlook it."

At once Pa smiled. "Of course, Aaron. Since we're going to be neighbors, let's be good ones."

Lottie went over to stand beside Raina. "Are you thinking of buying this dress?" she said while the men continued to talk.

"Pa wants me to have it, but it's too fancy for me."

"Oh, I don't think so. A woman needs fancy clothes once in a while." She hesitated and then said, "I hear you had a bad time during the raid."

"I did. I really did."

"Was it when you heard that Ty was killed?"

"Yes, it was a hard time for me."

Lottie hesitated then said, "You two were pretty close, weren't you?"

"Very close. We went through some hard times together. You know, I think that makes a bond that's not easily broken."

"I think that's right. I hear it's true of soldiers who go through

935

battle together. They never forget it. Well, what are you going to do about Ty?"

Raina stared at Mrs. Jordan. "I don't think I'll do anything."

The men joined them then, effectively ending their conversation.

Aaron said, "I heard about this barbed wire that some stockmen use."

"Yeah, I've heard about that. We don't need that, Aaron. You know how to handle cattle and keep 'em in place, and sheep don't wander all that much."

"Well, we'll work on it. You ready to go, Lottie?"

"Yes, I am."

The two left, and Raina turned to her father and said, "Let's buy our supplies and go home."

"Well, why don't you just go for a walk. I'll take care of the supplies. I've got the list you gave me."

"No, I'll help."

The two went through the store, and Max Thornton put their purchases into boxes and helped load them up. They were about to get into the wagon when Raina heard her name called.

She turned to see Ty, who came up and stood before them. He removed his hat and said, "It's good to see you. Come down for supplies?"

"Yes, and I wanted to see you."

"Well, here I stand."

"I want you to come out for the service Sunday."

"I'll sure do that. I was planning to anyway if I wasn't out on assignment."

"Come to the house early. We'll have a meal cooked after the service," Raina said. "You can come and join us."

"I've never turned a good meal down yet, Raina."

They said their good-byes.

Raina looked back and saw him standing there, and there was something pitiful about him, for he was a confused man.

"You know, Pa, we've talked about God chasing a man. I never was comfortable with that. I thought we had to chase after God."

"I think it works both ways. He chases us first, and when we find out about it, we set out to catch Him. I think God found Ty out there on the prairie when he was dying, but Ty's not sure yet. But we'll just keep praying that he will be."

Leoma Jordan stopped abruptly. She had come into town with her parents but had separated from them when they went after the needed supplies. She had other plans and headed out to find George Fairfax.

She was walking down her third street when she saw George headed toward her. He was not looking up but seemed to be in deep thought.

"Hello, George," Leoma said. She saw him look up, and there was an uncertainty about him that she was not accustomed to.

"Good to see you, Leoma," he said.

"I'm just going down to get a cup of tea. You Englishmen like tea. Come and go with me."

"I'll be glad to. I'm tired of my own company."

The two walked down the boardwalk until they got to the restaurant. They went in and soon were drinking their tea.

"You seem troubled, George."

"I guess all of us have some worries."

"It's not like you to let it show like that. What's the matter?"

Fairfax took a sip of the tea, put it down, and then picked the cup back up and turned it around nervously between his hands. He seemed reluctant to speak, but finally he said, "Well, I got some news from home."

"It must be bad news if it troubles you like this."

"It is. My brother died. He was younger than I am."

"Oh, I'm sorry to hear that, George. Were you close?"

"Not as close as we could have been."

"Will you go to the funeral?"

"No, it takes too long. He's already been buried."

"Will you go back to England now and take over?"

"I don't know. I've never been so confused. What my family wants me to do is to marry and produce more male heirs."

Leoma did not really understand this system, but she felt compassion for the man. "I'm sorry, George. I wish I could help."

"Well, I wish somebody could. I don't want to marry a woman I don't love. You made a joke once," he said, "about our getting married. Or was it a joke?"

Leoma remembered the remark. It had been made as part of a joke, but she saw he was serious. "You need to marry an Englishwoman who is used to nobility and things like that."

Fairfax kept his eyes fixed on Leoma. Suddenly he said, "I don't want to marry a woman just to be sure a legal requirement is met. Were you serious about marriage when we talked?"

"George, I'm serious now, but I'd hate for you to make a mistake. Don't you see if you made a mistake, the woman you would marry would have made a mistake, too?"

"I guess I can see that. I've made my share of mistakes. Marriage is for a lifetime."

Leoma hesitated then said, "I have an idea. Why don't you come back to the ranch with me? It's quiet out there. We can take long rides. Have long talks. You can think about your future."

Fairfax straightened up, and some of the heaviness lifted from his face. "Yes, I'd be glad to do that. When shall we go?"

"I'm ready now. We can follow my parents. They should be finished getting what they needed." Leoma took his arm and led him toward the store.

❧

Ty entered and came to stand before Heck Thomas. "Mason said you wanted me."

"Got a job for you. Doesn't amount to much. Somebody's got to go out and arrest Chester Swan."

"Who's he?"

"Oh, he's sort of a small rancher, got a few cattle, raises some grain. But he's had a feud over land boundaries with a half-breed named Charlie Ten Deer. They never have gotten along. I got word that Swan took a shot at Ten Deer."

"You want me to arrest him?"

"Well, I don't know, Ty. The man's never been in trouble. He's kind of sullen, but he's a good man. Don't really arrest him, but I need for him to think you might. Just bring him in."

"So, it's sort of an arrest then?"

"Yes. His hot temper might give you some trouble. I can scare some sense into him, I'm pretty sure."

"I'll go right away, Heck." Ty picked up some supplies, went to his horse, and saddled him. As he rode out, his mind was on his own troubles. He looked up at the sky and saw the clouds like huge bunches of cotton slowly drifting across an azure sky and tried to pray, but the words wouldn't come. "I wonder if everybody has as much trouble trying to pray as I do," he muttered. Then he continued his journey. He rode for an hour and then came into an Indian trading post. He found White Eagle, who ran the trading post. They had become friends over the last few months.

"Hello, Ty." White Eagle was coppery-skinned and trimmed down so that there was not an ounce of fat on him. "What are you out for today?"

"Oh, got a little job to do."

"Are you married yet?"

The two had a joke about marriage. Both were single, and they all but made a bet about which one of them would marry first.

"No, not yet. How about you?"

"No, but I can give you some advice."

"What's that, White Eagle?"

"Don't marry a woman that's taller than you are."

"Well, that's not likely. Is that the only advice to the lovelorn you can give?" He liked the Indian very much. "I got to go pick up Chester Swan."

"Well, he's a grumpy cuss. Got a good Indian wife though. Two kids. What'd he do?"

"Nothing much. He's having a fuss over some boundary with Ten Deer."

"Well, he's always having a fuss with somebody. You be careful."

"I'll do that. Pick up some more advice for the lovelorn."

Ty left the trading post and rode for another hour. He had

been watching the clouds roll, and from time to time he saw a band of pronghorn and once a dark-colored wolf that was unlike anything he had ever seen. The wolf had a rabbit between his jaws, and he took one look at Ty and wheeled and ran away. "I don't want your dinner," Ty said.

For some reason at that moment he thought about Gale Young's death, and the thought grieved him as it always did. *I'd give anything if I could have saved Gale. His life was all planned out. He never got to do any of it. Could happen to me.* The thought sobered him, and by the time he reached Swan's property, he was depressed.

He rode up, and Swan got to his feet and came out of the house. His wife was with him, holding on to his arm. Ty heard her say, "Don't go out there. You're drunk."

Then Ty saw that she had two small children hanging on to her skirt, but Swan shook her off. "Leave me alone, Dawn."

"Leave that gun here."

It was then that Ty noticed that Swan had a rifle in his hand.

"I've got to keep this gun. That stealin' Ten Deer might creep up and shoot me."

"He's not going to shoot you."

"What do you want, Marshal?"

Ty stepped out of the saddle and said, "I just came to talk a little bit, Swan."

"I ain't talkin' to no marshal. Get off my land."

Then something happened that caught Ty completely off guard. Swan, without a word of warning, lifted the rifle and fired. The bullet knocked his hat off, and he pulled his gun quickly and aimed it right in the middle of Swan's chest. He didn't fire, for he saw Swan pull the trigger, but the rifle wouldn't fire.

"Please don't kill him!" The woman got in front of Swan, standing between him and Ty. The children were hanging on to her, and both of them were big-eyed with fear.

Ty holstered his gun and came up with disgust. He reached out and took the rifle from Swan. "You're a sorry excuse for a man, Chester Swan," he said with disgust. "I could have killed you."

Swan sobered up when he saw that Ty had his gun, and he knew he had come close to being shot.

"I'm going to tell you what I'm going to do with you, Chester. Heck Thomas sent me out here to bring you in, but you've got a good wife here, and people say you are a good man when you're not drunk. You sober up and you go in by yourself. The judge will like that. It'll show you've got a little sense. You tell the judge you were wrong to pull a gun on Ten Deer. Don't tell him about trying to shoot me. Tell him you'll make it right with Ten Deer, and he'll give you a chance to do it. It's the only way out for you, Chester. Otherwise you're going to go down."

"Listen to him," Dawn begged.

Swan dropped his head as he was still swaying. "Okay, Marshal, I'll do as you say."

"Do it then," Ty said. "You make sure of it, Mrs. Swan."

"Yes," Dawn said. "He will do it. I promise you."

Ty got into his saddle and rode away. He was headed back to town, but something came to him, and he headed toward the sheep camp. He suddenly stopped his horse, removed his hat, and began to pray. *Lord, I don't know how to pray. I'm not eloquent. Never was. I'm asking You to do something to me. Tell me what to do.*

He got off his horse and walked slowly, continually asking

God to help him. When the night came, he still had no peace.

By the time morning came, he had stayed up most of the night begging God to help him. And as the sun came up over the eastern hills, he knew suddenly what to do.

He stepped into the saddle and spurred the horse forward. When he got to the sheep camp, he saw Raina hanging clothes on a line.

She saw him and came at once to where he was. "What are you doing out here, Ty?"

"Came on a job, but that's not my news." He took her by the arms and said, "I've been praying all night, and I've given my heart to the Lord."

Raina was excited. Her eyes glowed, and she said, "I'm so glad, Ty. What are you going to do now?"

"I also heard from the Lord about what He wants me to do, and I'm sure now that God wants me to be a preacher."

"My dad and I both thought that would be your decision."

"But what I came to tell you is, Raina, that I love you." He pulled her close and kissed her, and for the moment they were the only two people on the planet. When he lifted his head, he saw the joy in her face and knew he had done the right thing. "The only thing is, we can't marry for a long time."

"Why not, Ty?"

"I've got to save money. I've got to go get some training somewhere. Either go to some preacher who will help me or go to some Bible school. Either one would take money."

She reached up, pulled his head down, and kissed him again. "I love you, Ty, and God has brought you this far. He'll take us the rest of the way."

CHAPTER 27

Judge Isaac Parker sat back in his chair and studied the man in front of him. "Well, Ty, I think I saw this coming. I just wish I had a hundred more like you." He smiled and shook his head. "Are you absolutely sure about this?"

"Yes, Judge, it's got to be." Ty took the badge off his vest pocket and handed it to Judge Parker. "I appreciate you giving me the work, but I've got to move on."

Parker studied the badge in the palm of his hand. "Well, I hate to lose a good man, but I think you're making the right choice. What are you going to do specifically?"

"I'm planning to be a preacher." Ty grinned. "Judge, you have no idea how ignorant I am about so many things. I've got to learn the Bible. I've got to learn how to work with people. I've got to change my whole way of life. So I think I've got to go get some training at a college somewhere."

"Good for you, Ty," Parker said. "I wish all my marshals ended up with lives like you're after, but they won't. Are you going to marry that young woman?"

"No, Judge, at least not right away. Not until I have something to offer her."

"Well, you probably got as much to offer her as I had to offer my wife."

"I doubt that, Judge. You had a good education, and you knew where you were going. I'm setting to sea in a sieve it seems like."

"Don't be an idiot, Kincaid. That young woman loves you. She'll be right with you every step of the way."

"Well, good-bye, Judge. I'll let you know how this story turns out."

"Be sure and do that. My wife and I have grown interested in your life. We'll be praying for you."

"Good-bye, Judge." Ty left the office, went at once to the stable, got his horse, and rode out of Fort Smith.

All the way out to the sheep camp, he was thinking about what would happen to him. He had always had very little planning in his life, but now he had a whole new world of decisions to make, and it troubled him. He knew he was embarking on a voyage that held mystery and wonder, and more than once he prayed, *Well, God, You've got to help me with this. I can't do it by myself. . . .*

"Well, I did it, Raina."

Raina had seen Ty coming. She took him inside the small house. "What have you done?"

"Handed my badge in to the judge. He was real nice about it. I know he hates to lose a man, but he said some nice things."

"Well, you had to do it," Raina said. "Now what?"

"Well, that's the problem," Ty said. He sat at the kitchen table drinking a cup of black, bitter coffee. He sipped it and said, "Kind of funny to be drinking hot coffee on a hot day like this."

"Tell me what you're going to do."

"Well, I'm out of work."

"You'll find something. What are you going to do next?"

"Why, Raina, I'm studying new ways to tell you how I love you."

She laughed suddenly, reached over, and took his hand in both of hers. "Good. I like that. I want you to tell me every day that we're married that you love me. Will you do that?"

"Sure I will."

"I'm going to have it put in the marriage vows when Pa marries us."

"Well, to tell the truth, getting married is kind of a problem."

"Don't you have the money for a wedding license?" She smiled.

"Well, it's not that, but as much as I love you, Raina, I can't ask you to lead the kind of life that I'm gonna probably have. You know how it is. Preachers never get rich that I know of. Sometimes they're the poorest men in town, and I keep thinking that you could have married George and had everything."

"No, I wouldn't. I wouldn't have had you." She smiled and squeezed his hand.

"We'll wait on marrying until I can get enough money to go to school and learn how to be a preacher."

"I'm disappointed."

"Well, so am I. I'd like to get married right now, but that wouldn't be right for me to put you in that kind of a situation."

She rose from her chair, came over, and stood behind him. She reached around, pulled his head back, and kissed him. "Maybe

God will do a miracle."

He reached up and put his hands on her arms and said, "That's about what it's gonna take. A miracle!"

❧

Raina's pa had been watching her very carefully. "What's wrong with you, Raina?"

"Nothing, Pa."

"Well, you don't look happy. You're gonna be a bride, ain't you?"

"No, not anytime soon."

Vernay blinked with surprise. "What's stopping you? Both of you want to get married."

"Well, Ty says he's got to get ready to be a minister, and it's going to take time and money. We've got the time but no money."

"What does he want to do with money?"

"He wants to go to school and at least learn the fundamentals of Bible study. He thinks that's the key to being a good preacher and knowing the Bible."

Pa did not speak for some time, but then he said, "Well, you go get that young man. I've got something that's been jolting around in my head."

"What is it, Pa?"

"I need to tell both of you together."

"All right. I'll get him."

❧

It was that evening before Ty and Raina sat down with Eddie. He smiled at them, saying, "Well, I didn't get to keep you long, daughter, but you got a good man."

"Not as good as she deserves, Eddie, but I promise you she'll never know meanness from me."

"I know that, but I've got to tell you two something. Ty, Raina already told me about your plan to be a preacher. I think that's great, and I know what you mean. I just started out preaching and no tellin' how many ways I blundered, so I kept asking God, 'How can I serve You?' I'm not getting any younger, you know."

"Why, you're as strong as two men, Pa," Raina said.

"We all have our time, and I want to use it the best I can. But I can only have so many years left, and this church is on my heart, so I made a decision. I'm going to keep on with the sheep business now that I made up with Aaron. There won't be no shooting each other, but I've decided what to do with the money."

"You mean earnings off the sheep?" Raina asked.

"It's going really well. So what I'm going to do is this. I'll stay here and preach at the church and try to build it up, and then when the new preacher comes, he can take over."

Ty spoke. "You got a preacher in mind, Eddie?"

"More than that. I know him. It's you, Ty. I'm gonna pay your expenses to go to school, and in a couple of years you come back. I'll be even weaker than I am now, I guess, but you'll be the pastor. Maybe I can be your helper."

"I couldn't take your money," Ty said.

"That's pride," Eddie said.

Raina said, "It certainly is. I made a hard decision about who to marry, and now you've got to make one." When Ty hesitated, she said, "It's your pride, Ty."

"I guess it is."

Raina faced him squarely. "Well, I've got pride, too, but I'm ready to be the wife of a preacher. We'll honeymoon at the school you go to. We both will have a lot to learn."

"You'll take me up on my offer then?" Eddie asked.

Raina laughed and said, "Yes, he does."

"You're getting mighty bossy! Have I got this to put up with for a lifetime, Raina?"

"We both have a lot to learn," she said.

❧

The sanctuary was full of people for the wedding at the Baptist church in Fort Smith.

George and Leoma were in the front row, and they watched as Raina came down the aisle dressed in white. As Ed Vernay stood to perform the ceremony, Leoma turned and whispered, "Well, George, was your heart broken when you lost your prospective bride?"

He turned and smiled at her. They had spent a great deal of time together for the past month. "Well, just sort of bent out of shape, I'd say."

She squeezed his arm. "I can fix that," she said.

They sat listening and were aware of the shining countenances of both Raina and Ty. Ed Vernay was a rough-hewn preacher, but as he tied the knot, he practically shouted, "I now pronounce you man and wife. Now kiss the bride, son!"

❧

Eddie Vernay had been at the session along with Judge Parker to see the newly married couple off on their honeymoon.

Now Ty and Raina waved as the figures receded and the train

pulled out of Fort Smith. Raina turned to Ty and said, "Are you afraid of what lies before us?"

"Maybe a little. I guess that's what men are afraid of, something that they don't know. I don't have any idea of how to be a pastor."

"I do. You love your sheep."

He laughed and pulled her forward and kissed her.

The conductor was passing, and he stopped and grinned. "You got your kissing permit in order?"

"The ink's still wet on the marriage license," Ty said.

They left the conductor and went to their seats. Raina said, "Well, we're man and wife now. Feel any different?"

"I feel happier than I've ever been."

A tall man was sitting across the aisle and said, "You two just get hitched?"

Ty grinned. "Yep. Just got married."

"Well, I'm your man if you need advice. I've worn out three wives. I know all about it."

"Well, I've got my plan already made to keep this one happy."

"What's that, son?"

"I'm gonna give her everything she wants, when she wants it. The Bible says in one place that when a couple gets married the new bridegroom stays at home for a year."

"What does he do all that time, brother?"

"He makes his wife happy."

"Why, you won't last six months with a plan like that."

"Yes, we'll last," Raina said. She reached up and placed her hand on Ty's cheek. "We're in this thing for the long run."

The whistle broke the silence, and Ty felt as if he and his new bride were moving out of one life and into another.

ABOUT THE AUTHOR

Award-winning, bestselling author Gilbert Morris is well known for penning numerous Christian novels for adults and children since 1984 with 6.5 million books in print. He is probably best known for the forty-book House of Winslow series, and his *Edge of Honor* was a 2001 Christy Award winner. He lives with his wife in Gulf Shores, Alabama.

Other books by Gilbert Morris...